Mosses from an Old Manse

Nathaniel Hawthorne

Mosses
from an
Old Manse

Introduction by Mary Oliver

Notes by Gretchen Kay Short

THE MODERN LIBRARY

NEW YORK

2003 Modern Library Paperback Edition

Biographical note copyright © 1993 by Random House, Inc.
Introduction copyright © 2003 by Mary Oliver
Note on the text and notes © 2003 by Random House, Inc.

LIBRARY OF CONGRESS CATALOGING-IN-PUBLICATION DATA
Hawthorne, Nathaniel, 1804–1864.
Mosses from an old manse / Nathaniel Hawthorne ;
introduction by Mary Oliver ; notes by Gretchen Kay Short.
p. cm.
ISBN 0-8129-6605-8
1. United States—Social life and customs—19th century—
Fiction. I. Short, Gretchen Kay. II. Title.
PS1863 .A1 2003
813'.3—dc21   2002026418

Modern Library website address: www.modernlibrary.com

Printed in the United States of America

2 4 6 8 9 7 5 3 1

NATHANIEL HAWTHORNE

Nathaniel Hawthorne was born on July 4, 1804, in Salem, Massachusetts, where his ancestors had been prominent since the sixteen hundreds. His father, a ship captain, died in Surinam when Hawthorne was just four; afterward he was raised with his maternal relatives, the Mannings. Realizing that the boy had special storytelling gifts (he would retell children's stories to his two sisters embellished with his own wild variations), the family sent him to private school and later to Bowdoin College in Maine, where his classmates included Franklin Pierce and Henry Wadsworth Longfellow.

Upon graduation in 1825, Hawthorne returned to Salem to his "chamber under the eaves" in the Manning house and became a virtual recluse; for the next twelve years the family supported him through his literary apprenticeship. These years of self-imprisonment in Salem were the central fact in Hawthorne's career. During this period he became a voracious reader and borrowed from the Salem Athenaeum everything that might shed light on New England's prerevolutionary identity. He also kept a series of notebooks and carried on inner monologues that helped him dream out his stories. Yet Hawthorne ended by burning much of what he wrote during these years—including *Fanshawe* (1828), his anonymously published first novel—not because of the public's indifference but because he had come to think the works unworthy.

"By some witchcraft or other ... I have been carried apart from the main current of life," Hawthorne wrote to Longfellow while in Salem. "I have made a captive of myself ... and now I cannot find the key to let myself out—and if the door were open, I should be almost afraid to come out." However, in 1836, for a salary of $500, he went to Boston and edited *The American Magazine of Useful and Entertaining Knowledge.* Finally, the publication in 1837 of *Twice-Told Tales,* the collection of stories that Edgar Allan Poe acclaimed as belonging "to the highest region of Art," forever liberated Hawthorne from a long stint as a nameless hack writer for New England magazines and Christmas annuals.

Slowly he began to emerge from his long period of solitude and "to open an intercourse with the world." In 1839 he began a two-year political appointment as an officer in the Boston Custom House; at the same time he became engaged to Sophia Peabody. Following their marriage in 1842, the couple settled in the Old Manse in Concord, Massachusetts; there Hawthorne came to know Emerson, Thoreau, and other Transcendentalist thinkers and wrote the tales that were gathered in *Mosses from an Old Manse* (1846). Between 1846 and 1849 he accepted a second government position, as surveyor of the Salem Custom House, in order to provide his family with a regular income. When he was dismissed from that post by the new Whig administration, Hawthorne at once began work on the novel in which he brought into full play all the fictional techniques he had perfected over a period of two decades.

The success of *The Scarlet Letter* (1850) instantly consolidated Hawthorne's reputation. Although it sold no more than 7,800 copies during his lifetime and netted him only $1,500, the book was applauded from the start as a literary classic. "The publication of *The Scarlet Letter* was in the United States a literary event of the first importance," wrote Henry James. "The book was the finest piece of imaginative writing yet put forth in the country. There was a consciousness of this in the welcome that was given it—a satisfaction in the idea of America having produced a novel that belonged to literature, and to the forefront of it. ... The best of it was that the thing was absolutely American; it belonged to the soil, to the air; it came out of the very heart of New England."

The years immediately following the publication of *The Scarlet Letter* were probably the happiest in Hawthorne's life. Recognized as

America's foremost author, he soon produced two more novels—*The House of the Seven Gables* (1851) and *The Blithedale Romance* (1852)—as well as a third collection of stories, *The Snow-Image* (1851). During this time he also published several children's books and wrote the *Life of Franklin Pierce* (1852), a campaign biography of his college classmate who was running for president. When Pierce was elected to the White House, Hawthorne was named United States Consul to Liverpool, England, a position he held from 1853 to 1857. After resigning the consulship, Hawthorne journeyed to Italy with his wife and three children, where he remained until 1859. There he became friends with the poet Robert Browning and began writing his final novel, *The Marble Faun* (1860).

Following an absence of seven years, Hawthorne returned to the United States on June 27, 1860, and settled once more in Concord. In his final years, illness and possibly some failure of literary faith prevented him from completing three novels that he had already outlined. While on a journey to the White Mountains to restore his health, Nathaniel Hawthorne died in Plymouth, New Hampshire, on May 19, 1864. He was buried on May 23, 1864, in Sleepy Hollow Cemetery in Concord.

CONTENTS

MOSSES FROM AN OLD MANSE

VOLUME I

VOLUME II

INTRODUCTION

Mary Oliver

When Nathaniel Hawthorne began gathering his stories and sketches for *Mosses from an Old Manse,* he was living in Concord, Massachusetts, and in just such a house as he describes at the outset of the book. It was a sturdy house, built by Ralph Waldo Emerson's grandfather, the Reverend William Emerson. Some years earlier it had been lived in by Emerson himself, and here—very likely in the same room that Hawthorne describes*—Emerson completed his first book, *Nature.* One would have to look a long time—possibly forever—to find a house, or a chamber, that could claim an equal quantity of splendor.

Hawthorne lived in Reverend Emerson's house from the summer of 1842 into the fall of 1845. In "The Old Manse" he tells us of the pleasure it brought him, and this is no small matter for a man who has left such an impression of his solemnity, who as a neighbor was remembered mostly for his silence, and who as a writer is known best for his aptitude in describing the darker portions of the soul. But clearly, in the writing chamber he was to use, made fresh and comfortable by his wife, Sophia, he was charmed:

---

* Emerson says the room where he wrote was on the second floor, facing northwest. Hawthorne also speaks of a northwest room, that looked "down into the orchard."

When I first saw the room its walls were blackened with the smoke of unnumbered years and made still blacker by the grim prints of Puritan ministers that hung around. These worthies looked strangely like bad angels, or at least like men who had wrestled so continually and so sternly with the devil that somewhat of his sooty fierceness had been imparted to their own visages. They had all vanished now; a cheerful coat of paint and golden-tinted paper hangings lighted up the small apartment; while the shadow of a willow tree that swept against the overhanging eaves attempered the cheery western sunshine.

—"The Old Manse"

Hawthorne tells us that "The Old Manse" came slowly, and only with great difficulty. The rest of the tales and sketches were arranged; publication waited for these delicate and sweet-tempered paragraphs, this welcome into the man's residence, and with that welcome a kind of opening of the heart. The sketch is long; it is not profound, nor mystical, nor does it hold any single theme; yet it is the revelatory piece in the book. In it we meet a Hawthorne rarely otherwise disclosed. Think of *The Scarlet Letter* and *The House of the Seven Gables:* the shadows, the sins, the moral retributions, the gravity, the import. The somber intentions of those books would never allow us to imagine Hawthorne's capacity for gladness and for idling, the cordiality and the enthusiasm he felt toward the surrounding natural world, toward friendship, even toward the ghosts of the old manse, one of whom he describes with both probity and humor:

Houses of any antiquity in New England are so invariably possessed with spirits that the matter seems hardly worth alluding to. Our ghost used to heave deep sighs in a particular corner of the parlor, and sometimes rustled paper, as if he were turning over a sermon in the long upper entry—where nevertheless he was invisible, in spite of the bright moonshine that fell through the eastern window. Not improbably he wished me to edit and publish a selection from a chest full of manuscript discourses that stood in the garret.

—"The Old Manse"

*   *   *

Hawthorne was born on July 4, 1804, in the old port town of Salem, Massachusetts. He and two sisters were the children of Elizabeth

Clarke Manning and Nathaniel Hathorne,* a ship captain. The children were still young when Captain Hathorne perished, in a distant part of the world, of an unnamed fever; the family was left poor, and none of them, certainly not Nathaniel's mother, owned the gift of disarming such loss. Religious devotion and spiritual gloom need not necessarily cling together, but in the Hathorne household, from all we can discover, they were inseparable.

Nathaniel grew up physically active and strikingly handsome; he was also, for good reason, shy, and probably lonely. In 1825 he graduated from Bowdoin College in Maine, then returned to Salem. Residents of the town frequently saw him, in the late afternoons, roaming along the streets and the shore: a solitary wanderer. One may with confidence record that he was steadfast; for a decade he continued to live in his mother's house, where he worked at his writing, finishing stories he later burned and one novel that made not the slightest noise in the literary world. Then he met the Peabody sisters of Salem, and with one of them, Sophia, he fell in love. Five years later, in 1842, they married. They were, Hawthorne wrote to a friend, close to "ridiculous" in their happiness.

* * *

Such happiness, however, neither writes nor sells stories. After the publication of the novels for which he is most widely known, his financial situation would improve—somewhat. Still, as we know, he held the position of surveyor at the Salem Custom House and the finer appointment of American Consul in England even later, for no other reason, at either opportunity, than his need for financial security. One can imagine, then, the difficulty of supporting his family, which soon contained three children, in the early years. He was publishing stories, but the "fame" of being an author was not golden enough, nor silver either. Payment was meager, and in Hawthorne's case, as we learn from his correspondence, often it was no more than visionary.

For this reason, which is neither glorious nor inglorious but very real, his collecting of stories for *Mosses* was not the gathering of a man secure enough, in this world, to pick and choose, or to wait. The invitation to publish the book had come, in 1845, and he intended to fulfill it. Hawthorne had written much and well in the writing chamber in

---

* The *w* in "Hawthorne" was added to the original spelling by Nathaniel the writer.

the old manse, and the major part of *Mosses* represents work produced during that time. Except for the opening piece, he wrote nothing new. He used what existed—not all of it, certainly, but his intent was to fill the pages. The result is a book with an extraordinary breadth of styles; here are dark, brooding tales, arch and humorous sketches, and stories of a curiously intense allegorical slant; here also are writings that have their genesis in Hawthorne's own experiences, or ideas, or reminiscences. Among the most striking of his stories—I am thinking of "The Birthmark," "Young Goodman Brown," "Rappaccini's Daughter," and "The Artist of the Beautiful" in particular—these sketches are interspersed, composed in the flute note of rapture or the little triangle clatter of praise: "Passages from a Relinquished Work," "Sketches from Memory," "Buds and Bird Voices," "The Old Apple Dealer," and also the robust meditation "Fire Worship." One may look at such a collection of writings either way—one may say: but no invisible magnet, or idea, holds these choice particles; how can it then be a book, which is surely more than a simple gathering of accomplishments? Or, just as easily—if one is not staked to the rules—one may say: what variety, what richness!

*   *   *

Hawthorne is one of the great imaginers of evil and also of its henchmen: lassitude, doubt, despair, unmitigated ambition—all varieties of human weakness and vanity that wreck the work of conscience. It is his primary theme, the instructing of the malicious toward its various appearances. Hawthorne's heritage was pure Salem, and not just his mother's house—it was his own great-great-grandfather William Hathorne who ordered the whipping of Anne Coleman and four other Friends through the streets of Salem; and it was his great-grandfather John Hathorne who sat as magistrate at the trial of the accused witches of Salem. The shadow of this history could not fail to reach into the nineteenth century to darken Nathaniel Hawthorne. The Puritan strain was his—not to live by, as his forebearers did, but to brood upon, to examine, to explore.

From it came the novels *The Scarlet Letter* and *The House of the Seven Gables*. Also from the dreadful pall of this history came the turbulent "Young Goodman Brown," very likely his most widely known story. It casts into that old shadow in an attempt to find, I think, the point—the exact point—at which the soul is captured, and how, and why. Young

Goodman Brown simply sets off into the forest on an unnamed errand. We have no notion what sort of journey this is, yet we feel his own wretched uneasiness as the appearances of things, and people, previously reliable, begin to be proven—or believed—false. It is vitally unnerving. "Young Goodman Brown" is not really a story about the perturbation of the actual—the "witches" that sweep across the air, the walking stick that writhes like a serpent; it is about the human heart that, imagining awful things, is responsive to them, and so falls into a pollution and dismay of the mind. The "satanic" theatrics may even be conceived as the leitmotif, compared with the horror of Goodman Brown's spiritual failing. Nor does Hawthorne expend any measure of words of pity for Goodman Brown's fate. The story stands, simply, as an adjudication for spiritual strength.

In "The Birthmark," the malevolent force develops from something admirable gone awry—the desire for knowledge and its attendant power, unsoftened by human warmth; the same force appears equally if not more sinister in "Rappaccini's Daughter." In "Roger Malvin's Burial," a decent man is brought to a life of distress by a moment of deceit, in which he does not tell the truth but rather fabricates an action he wished to but did not accomplish; the retribution is without mercy. Such stories are Hawthorne's finest, and they are Puritan in this sense: they are harsh, unrelenting, and fearful in their certainty. But they are also something else, for the origin of Hawthorne's certainty is not that of the Puritan within his religious confines, but that of the humanist who sees the moral actions of the conscience as the creator of good or evil. In this grand alteration of his inheritance, Hawthorne is timelessly alive, compassionate, elastic, and modern.

Still, a reader may desire relief from such seriousness, and be glad therefore that in another tone altogether Hawthorne plays with fantasy, creating the airy landscapes of a half dozen stories in which the sky is literally the limit: one may walk upon the pale clouds into fantastic marble halls, or vast, improbable castles, or ride in a celestial train to the very edge of heaven. These stories are serious but not somber. They are parables perhaps, but they flow forward in so likable a manner they are able to review the weaknesses and absurdities of humankind without hurt, or the weight we feel with pedantic judgment. Perhaps, of this type of story, the beautiful "Monsieur du Miroir" is the most successful, in which, with sparkling good humor, Hawthorne describes that other man who follows him everywhere there is a water or a mirror surface.

> One of this singular person's most remarkable peculiarities is his fondness for water, wherein he excels any temperance man whatever. . . . When no cleaner bathing-place happened to be at hand, I have seen the foolish fellow in a horse pond. Sometimes he refreshes himself in the trough of a town pump, without caring what the people think about him. Often, while carefully picking my way along the street after a heavy shower, I have been scandalized to see Monsieur du Miroir, in full dress, paddling from one mud puddle to another, and plunging into the filthy depths of each. Seldom have I peeped into a well, without discerning this ridiculous gentleman at the bottom, whence he gazes up, as through a long telescopic tube, and probably makes discoveries among the stars by daylight. Wandering along lonesome paths or in pathless forests, when I have come to virgin fountains, of which it would have been pleasant to deem myself the first discoverer, I have started to find Monsieur du Miroir there before me. The solitude seemed lonelier for his presence.
>
> —"MONSIEUR DU MIROIR"

Of that light and lovely tone, in order to understand Hawthorne, we must speak more. For it is greatly from his unfailing capacity to write the sweetest prose—and to create with it a virtual atmosphere— that his stories take breath, and live. Often enough the forward action is slight, or obvious, and the characters but scantily drawn. But the surround, the detail, is deep and luxurious. Henry James wrote of Hawthorne, "He thought nothing too trivial to be suggestive."* Such a style is not unique to Hawthorne, nor to the nineteenth century; some of Poe's work is equally shaded and embellished by scenery and setting, and it carries as much of the weight of the story as the action. "The Tell-Tale Heart" is one, "The Black Cat" another; "The Pit and the Pendulum" leaps to the list. Hemingway's "Big Two-Hearted River," in which a man simply goes fishing, is another story in which every leaf and ripple of the atmosphere adds to its import, its weight and

---

* From *English Men of Letters,* edited by John Morley (Harper & Brothers, New York, 1887). The long chapter on Hawthorne was written by Henry James, Jr., as he was known at that time.

pressure—its reality. Our own era more commonly offers a brisker prose, with a more complex plot, or plots, threading along, and much of the surround left to the imagination. The difference is neither plus nor minus, of course, but simply one of the alternations which readers must allow as they begin to climb the delectable mountains of old books.

*   *   *

Hawthorne began his consulship in England in 1853; when it was over, he spent two years traveling on the continent and lived for a while in Italy. He and Sophia and the children returned to New England in 1860 and immediately took up residence in another Concord house, known as the Wayside Inn. He was by then the author of four novels and a number of collections of stories. His fame was established, his readers were many, and his literary peers acknowledged him among the foremost writers of his time. He had laid out ideas for and had begun work on two new novels.

But fate had other ideas. Sturdy and vigorous and seemingly full of shining health he had always been; now he began to show signs of decline. No one has given a name to what was wrong, but all saw it; his hair turned white, his energy flagged, his spirit struggled. In his sixtieth year he died while on a trip in New Hampshire, where he had gone hoping to recruit his old health once again. He was brought to Sleepy Hollow, Concord's green and lush burial ground. There, already, were more than a few men he had known, Thoreau among them. Julian, Hawthorne's son, remembers riding with his mother through the Sleepy Hollow gates after the burial ceremony. "There, on each side of the way, stood men with gray heads and lowered eyes...."* The men, standing there to pay homage, were Longfellow, Holmes, Emerson, Franklin Pierce,** Whittier, and Lowell.

*   *   *

Probably the years spent in Concord were Hawthorne's happiest. He worked well there, and for all his taciturnity he liked being part of Concord's select and neighborly society. One friend was Ellery Chan-

---

* *The Memoirs of Julian Hawthorne,* ed. by Edith Garrigues Hawthorne (New York: Macmillan, 1938), pp. 158–59.

** Hawthorne and Franklin Pierce (president from 1853 to 1857) began a lifelong friendship while both were at Bowdoin College.

ning; on any day Channing might arrive at the old manse, and the two friends would go off together:

> Strange and happy times were those when we cast aside all irksome forms and straitlaced habitudes and delivered ourselves up to the free air, to live like the Indians or any less conventional race during one bright semicircle of the sun. Rowing our boat against the current, between wide meadows, we turned aside into the Assabeth. A more lovely stream than this, for a mile above its junction with the Concord, has never flowed on earth—nowhere, indeed, except to lave the interior regions of a poet's imagination.

—"THE OLD MANSE"

No writer is capable of a more tender expressiveness than Hawthorne. In his craft he has the thoughtful charm that is the lighter element of intellect. He has also that gravity which is the pace of moral purpose. In his steadfastness he is another Owen Warland, who, in "The Artist of the Beautiful," feels alive only when striving not to demystify beauty but to commit himself to its spiritual requirements.

In no other book of his, I think, does Hawthorne pass on to us such a sense of the thoughtful, cheerful, easy-hearted atmosphere of his life. Here only, along with his probing tales of evil, we are given stories full of wit and sunshine, which are, though Hawthorne lacked the poet's cadence, created throughout with a poet's skill.

———

MARY OLIVER is the author of eleven books of poetry, including *American Primitive,* for which she was awarded the Pulitzer Prize; *New and Selected Poems,* which won the National Book Award; and *House of Light,* which won the Christopher Award and the L. L. Winship/PEN New England Award. She lives in Provincetown, Massachusetts.

A Note on the Text

With the exception of "The Old Manse," all of the stories included in *Mosses from an Old Manse* were first published either in *The Token*, a gift annual, or in periodicals. Hawthorne marked corrections on the clippings of the pieces from their original publications for the printer's copy of the first 1846 edition of *Mosses*, except for "Roger Malvin's Burial," which was set from a *United States Magazine and Democratic Review* reprint of the original publication in *The Token*. A second edition of *Mosses* was published in 1854; the setting copy for it was the 1846 edition, which Hawthorne marked up. He also added three new pieces: "Passages from a Relinquished Work," "Sketches from Memory," and "Feathertop." The Modern Library Paperback Classics edition of *Mosses from an Old Manse* has been set from the second 1854 edition. In consultation with the Centenary edition of *Mosses from an Old Manse*, the following typographical errors have been corrected:

"Bass-relief" has been replaced with "bas-relief" on page 31, line 5.
A comma has been inserted after "country" on page 73, line 1.
A comma has been inserted after "person" on page 73, line 9.
"Unviersity" has been replaced with "university" on page 77, line 10.
An "a" has been inserted after "her" on page 103, line 23.
"Whereabout" has been replaced with "whereabouts" on page 137, line 12.

"In" has been inserted before "spite" on page 145, line 19.

"Mild" has been replaced with "mile" on page 175, line 11.

"flabs" has been replaced with "flaps" on page 176, line 1.

"Rgiby" has been replaced with "Rigby" on page 177, line 2.

"Department" has been replaced with "deportment" on page 186, line 2.

A period has been inserted after "him" on page 214, line 12.

"Crums" has been replaced with "crumbs" on page 240, line 21.

"Musket" has been replaced with "muskets" on page 280, line 23.

"But" has been replaced with "butt" on page 285, line 20.

A comma has been inserted after "brighter" on page 300, line 4.

"Bran" has been replaced with "brand" on page 303, line 34.

"Puest" has been replaced with "quest" on page 310, line 25.

"Reigning" has been replaced with "reining" on page 335, line 19.

A double open quotation mark has been inserted before "any" on page 363, line 24.

VOLUME I

THE OLD MANSE[1]

The Author makes the Reader acquainted with his Abode.

Between two tall gateposts of roughhewn stone (the gate itself having fallen from its hinges at some unknown epoch) we beheld the gray front of the old parsonage, terminating the vista of an avenue of black ash trees. It was now a twelvemonth since the funeral procession of the venerable clergyman,[2] its last inhabitant, had turned from that gateway towards the village burying ground. The wheel track leading to the door, as well as the whole breadth of the avenue, was almost overgrown with grass, affording dainty mouthfuls to two or three vagrant cows and an old white horse who had his own living to pick up along the roadside. The glimmering shadows that lay half asleep between the door of the house and the public highway were a kind of spiritual medium, seen through which the edifice had not quite the aspect of belonging to the material world. Certainly it had little in common with those ordinary abodes which stand so imminent upon the road that every passer by can thrust his head, as it were, into the domestic circle. From these quiet windows the figures of passing travellers looked too remote and dim to disturb the sense of privacy. In its near retirement and accessible seclusion it was the very spot for the residence of a clergyman—a man not estranged from human life, yet enveloped, in the midst of it, with a veil woven of intermingled gloom and brightness. It was worthy to have been one of the time-honored parsonages of England, in which, through many generations, a succession of holy occupants pass from youth to age, and bequeath each an inheritance of sanctity to pervade the house and hover over it as with an atmosphere.

Nor, in truth, had the Old Manse ever been profaned by a lay occupant until that memorable summer afternoon when I entered it as my home. A priest had built it; a priest had succeeded to it; other priestly men from time to time had dwelt in it; and children born in its chambers had grown up to assume the priestly character. It was awful to reflect how many sermons must have been written there. The latest inhabitant alone—he by whose translation to paradise the dwelling was left vacant—had penned nearly three thousand discourses, besides the better, if not the greater, number that gushed living from his lips. How often, no doubt, had he paced to and fro along the avenue, attuning his meditations to the sighs and gentle murmurs and deep and solemn peals of the wind among the lofty tops of the trees! In that variety of natural utterances he could find something accordant with every passage of his sermon, were it of tenderness or reverential fear. The boughs over my head seemed shadowy with solemn thoughts as well as with rustling leaves. I took shame to myself for having been so long a writer of idle stories, and ventured to hope that wisdom would descend upon me with the falling leaves of the avenue, and that I should light upon an intellectual treasure in the Old Manse well worth those hoards of long-hidden gold which people seek for in mossgrown houses. Profound treatises of morality; a layman's unprofessional, and therefore unprejudiced, views of religion; histories (such as Bancroft[3] might have written had he taken up his abode here as he once purposed) bright with picture, gleaming over a depth of philosophic thought,— these were the works that might fitly have flowed from such a retirement. In the humblest event, I resolved at least to achieve a novel that should evolve some deep lesson and should possess physical substance enough to stand alone.

In furtherance of my design, and as if to leave me no pretext for not fulfilling it, there was in the rear of the house the most delightful little nook of a study that ever afforded its snug seclusion to a scholar. It was here that Emerson wrote Nature;[4] for he was then an inhabitant of the Manse, and used to watch the Assyrian dawn and Paphian sunset and moonrise[5] from the summit of our eastern hill. When I first saw the room its walls were blackened with the smoke of unnumbered years and made still blacker by the grim prints of Puritan ministers that hung around. These worthies looked strangely like bad angels, or at least like men who had wrestled so continually and so sternly with the devil that somewhat of his sooty fierceness had been imparted to their own visages. They had all vanished now; a cheerful coat of paint and golden-tinted paper hangings lighted up the small apartment; while the shadow of a willow tree that swept against the overhanging eaves attempered the cheery western sunshine. In place of the grim prints there was the sweet and lovely head of one of Raphael's Madonnas[6] and two pleasant little pictures of the Lake of Como.[7] The only other decorations were a purple vase of flowers, always fresh, and a bronze one containing graceful ferns. My books (few, and by no means choice; for they were chiefly such waifs as chance had thrown in my way) stood in order about the room, seldom to be disturbed.

The study had three windows, set with little, old-fashioned panes of glass, each with a crack across it. The two on the western side looked, or rather peeped, between the willow branches, down into the orchard, with glimpses of the river through the trees. The third, facing north-ward, commanded a broader view of the river, at a spot where its hith-erto obscure waters gleam forth into the light of history. It was at this window that the clergyman who then dwelt in the Manse stood watch-ing the outbreak of a long and deadly struggle between two nations:[8] he saw the irregular array of his parishioners on the farther side of the river and the glittering line of the British on the hither bank. He awaited, in an agony of suspense, the rattle of the musketry. It came; and there needed but a gentle wind to sweep the battle smoke around this quiet house.

Perhaps the reader, whom I cannot help considering as my guest in the Old Manse and entitled to all courtesy in the way of sightshowing,— perhaps he will choose to take a nearer view of the memorable spot. We stand now on the river's brink. It may well be called the Concord[9]— the river of peace and quietness; for it is certainly the most unexcita-ble and sluggish stream that ever loitered imperceptibly towards its eternity—the sea. Positively I had lived three weeks beside it before it grew quite clear to my perception which way the current flowed. It never has a vivacious aspect except when a north-western breeze is vexing its surface on a sunshiny day. From the incurable indolence of its nature, the stream is happily incapable of becoming the slave of human ingenuity, as is the fate of so many a wild, free mountain torrent. While all things else are compelled to subserve some useful purpose, it idles its sluggish life away in lazy liberty, without turning a solitary spindle[10] or affording even water power enough to grind the corn that grows upon its banks. The torpor of its movement allows it nowhere a bright, pebbly shore, nor so much as a narrow strip of glistening sand, in any part of its course. It slumbers between broad prairies, kissing the long meadow grass, and bathes the overhanging boughs of elder bushes and willows or the roots of elms and ash trees and clumps of maples. Flags and rushes grow along its plashy shore; the yellow water lily spreads its broad, flat leaves on the margin; and the fragrant white pond lily abounds, generally selecting a position just so far from the river's brink that it cannot be grasped save at the hazard of plunging in.

It is a marvel whence this perfect flower derives its loveliness and perfume, springing as it does from the black mud over which the river sleeps, and where lurk the slimy eel, and speckled frog, and the mud turtle, whom continual washing cannot cleanse. It is the very same black mud out of which the yellow lily sucks its obscene life and noisome odor. Thus we see, too, in the world that some persons assimilate only what is ugly and evil from the same moral circumstances which supply good and beautiful results—the fragrance of celestial flowers— to the daily life of others.

The reader must not, from any testimony of mine, contract a dislike towards our slumberous stream. In the light of a calm and golden sunset it becomes lovely beyond expression; the more lovely for the quietude that so well accords with the hour, when even the wind, after blustering all day long, usually hushes itself to rest. Each tree and rock and every blade of grass is distinctly imaged, and, however unsightly in reality, assumes ideal beauty in the reflection. The minutest things of earth and the broad aspect of the firmament are pictured equally without effort and with the same felicity of success. All the sky glows downward at our feet; the rich clouds float through the unruffled bosom of the stream like heavenly thoughts through a peaceful heart. We will not, then, malign our river as gross and impure while it can glorify itself with so adequate a picture of the heaven that broods above it; or, if we remember its tawny hue and the muddiness of its bed, let it be a symbol that the earthliest human soul has an infinite spiritual capacity and may contain the better world within its depths.

But, indeed, the same lesson might be drawn out of any mud puddle in the streets of a city; and, being taught us every where, it must be true.

Come, we have pursued a somewhat devious track in our walk to the battle ground. Here we are, at the point where the river was crossed by the old bridge, the possession of which was the immediate object of the contest. On the hither side grow two or three elms, throwing a wide circumference of shade, but which must have been planted at some period within the threescore years and ten that have passed since the battle day. On the farther shore, overhung by a clump of elder bushes, we discern the stone abutment of the bridge. Looking down into the river, I once discovered some heavy fragments of the timbers, all green with half a century's growth of water moss; for during that length of time the tramp of horses and human footsteps have ceased along this ancient highway. The stream has here about the breadth of twenty strokes of a swimmer's arm—a space not too wide when the bullets were whistling across. Old people who dwell here-abouts will point out the very spots on the western bank where our countrymen fell down and died; and on this side of the river an obelisk of granite has grown up from the soil that was fertilized with British blood. The monument,[11] not more than twenty feet in height, is such as it befitted the inhabitants of a village to erect in illustration of a matter of local interest rather than what was suitable to commemorate an epoch of national history. Still, by the fathers of the village this famous deed was done; and their descendants might rightfully claim the privilege of building a memorial.

A humbler token of the fight, yet a more interesting one than the granite obelisk, may be seen close under the stone wall which separates the battle ground from the precincts of the parsonage. It is the grave,—marked by a small, mossgrown fragment of stone at the head and another at the foot,—the grave of two British soldiers who were slain in the skirmish, and have ever since slept peacefully where Zechariah Brown and Thomas Davis[12] buried them. Soon was their warfare ended; a weary night march from Boston, a rattling volley of musketry across the river and then these many years of rest. In the long procession of slain invaders who passed into eternity from the battle fields of the revolution, these two nameless soldiers led the way.

Lowell,[13] the poet, as we were once standing over this grave, told me a tradition[14] in reference to one of the inhabitants below. The story has something deeply impressive, though its circumstances cannot altogether be reconciled with probability. A youth in the service of the clergyman happened to be chopping wood, that April morning, at the back door of the Manse; and when the noise of battle rang from side to side of the bridge he hastened across the intervening field to see what might be going forward. It is rather strange, by the way, that this lad should have been so diligently at work when the whole population of town and country were startled out of their customary business by the advance of the British troops. Be that as it might, the tradition says that the lad now left his task and hurried to the battle field with the axe still in his hand. The British had by this time retreated; the Americans were in pursuit; and the late scene of strife was thus deserted by both parties. Two soldiers lay on the ground—one was a corpse; but, as the young New Englander drew nigh, the other Briton raised himself painfully upon his hands and knees and gave a ghastly stare into his face. The boy,—it must have been a nervous impulse, without purpose, without thought, and betokening a sensitive and impressible nature rather than a hardened one,—the boy uplifted his axe and dealt the wounded soldier a fierce and fatal blow upon the head.

I could wish that the grave might be opened; for I would fain know whether either of the skeleton soldiers has the mark of an axe in his skull. The story comes home to me like truth. Oftentimes, as an intellectual and moral exercise, I have sought to follow that poor youth through his subsequent career and observe how his soul was tortured by the blood stain, contracted as it had been before the long custom of war had robbed human life of its sanctity and while it still seemed murderous to slay a brother man. This one circumstance has borne more fruit for me than all that history tells us of the fight.

Many strangers come in the summer time to view the battle ground. For my own part, I have never found my imagination much excited by this or any other scene of historic celebrity; nor would the placid margin of the river have lost any of its charm for me had men never fought and died there. There is a wilder interest in the tract of land—perhaps a hundred yards in breadth—which extends between the battle field and the northern face of our Old Manse, with its contiguous avenue and orchard. Here, in some unknown age, before the white man came, stood an Indian village, convenient to the river, whence its inhabitants must have drawn so large a part of their substance. The site is identified by the spear and arrowheads, the chisels, and other implements of war, labor, and the chase, which the plough turns up from the soil. You see a splinter of stone, half hidden beneath a sod; it looks like nothing worthy of note; but, if you have faith enough to pick it up, behold a relic! Thoreau,[15] who has a strange faculty of finding what the Indians have left behind them, first set me on the search; and I afterwards enriched myself with some very perfect specimens, so rudely wrought that it seemed almost as if chance had fashioned them. Their great charm consists in this rudeness and in the individuality of each article, so different from the productions of civilized machinery, which shapes every thing on one pattern. There is exquisite delight, too, in picking up for one's self an arrowhead that was dropped centuries ago and has never been handled since, and which we thus receive directly from the hand of the red hunter, who purposed to shoot it at his game or at an enemy. Such an incident builds up again the Indian village and its encircling forest, and recalls to life the painted chiefs and warriors, the squaws at their household toil, and the children sporting among the wigwams, while the little wind rocked pappoose swings from the branch of a tree. It can hardly be told whether it is a joy or a pain, after such a momentary vision, to gaze around in the broad daylight of reality and see stone fences, white houses, potato fields, and men doggedly hoeing in their shirt sleeves and homespun pantaloons.[16] But this is nonsense. The Old Manse is better than a thousand wigwams.

The Old Manse! We had almost forgotten it, but will return thither through the orchard. This was set out by the last clergyman, in the decline of his life, when the neighbors laughed at the hoary-headed man for planting trees from which he could have no prospect of gathering fruit. Even had that been the case, there was only so much the better motive for planting them, in the pure and unselfish hope of benefiting his successors—an end so seldom achieved by more ambitious efforts. But the old minister, before reaching his patriarchal age of ninety, ate the apples from this orchard during many years, and added silver and gold to his annual stipend by disposing of the superfluity. It is pleasant to think of him walking among the trees in the quiet afternoons of early autumn and picking up here and there a windfall, while he observes how heavily the branches are weighed down, and computes the number of empty flour barrels that will be filled by their burden. He loved each tree, doubtless, as if it had been his own child. An orchard has a relation to mankind, and readily connects itself with matters of the heart. The trees possess a domestic character; they have lost the wild nature of their forest kindred, and have grown humanized by receiving the care of man as well as by contributing to his wants. There is so much individuality of character, too, among apple trees that it gives them an additional claim to be the objects of human interest. One is harsh and crabbed in its manifestations; another gives us fruit as mild as charity. One is churlish and illiberal, evidently grudging the few apples that it bears; another exhausts itself in freehearted benevolence. The variety of grotesque shapes into which apple trees contort themselves has its effect on those who get acquainted with them: they stretch out their crooked branches, and take such hold of the imagination that we remember them as humorists and odd fellows. And what is more melancholy than the old apple trees that linger about the spot where once stood a homestead, but where there is now only a ruined chimney rising out of a grassy and weedgrown cellar? They offer their fruit to every wayfarer—apples that are bitter sweet with the moral of Time's vicissitude.

I have met with no other such pleasant trouble in the world as that of finding myself, with only the two or three mouths which it was my privilege to feed, the sole inheritor of the old clergyman's wealth of fruits. Throughout the summer there were cherries and currants; and then came autumn, with his immense burden of apples, dropping them continually from his overladen shoulders as he trudged along. In the stillest afternoon, if I listened, the thump of a great apple was audible, falling without a breath of wind, from the mere necessity of perfect ripeness. And, besides, there were pear trees, that flung down bushels upon bushels of heavy pears; and peach trees, which, in a good year, tormented me with peaches, neither to be eaten nor kept, nor, without labor and perplexity, to be given away. The idea of an infinite generosity and exhaustless bounty on the part of our Mother Nature was well worth obtaining through such cares as these. That feeling can be enjoyed in perfection only by the natives of summer islands where the bread fruit, the cocoa, the palm and the orange grow spontaneously and hold forth the ever-ready meal; but likewise almost as well by a man long habituated to city life, who plunges into such a solitude as that of the Old Manse, where he plucks the fruit of trees that he did not plant, and which therefore, to my heterodox taste, bear the closest resemblance to those that grew in Eden. It has been an apothegm these five thousand years, that toil sweetens the bread it earns. For my part, (speaking from hard experience, acquired while belaboring the rugged furrows of Brook Farm,)[17] I relish best the free gifts of Providence.

Not that it can be disputed that the light toil requisite to cultivate a moderately-sized garden imparts such zest to kitchen vegetables as is never found in those of the market gardener. Childless men, if they would know something of the bliss of paternity, should plant a seed,—be it squash, bean, Indian corn,[18] or perhaps a mere flower or worthless weed,—should plant it with their own hands, and nurse it from infancy to maturity altogether by their own care. If there be not too many of them, each individual plant becomes an object of separate interest. My garden, that skirted the avenue of the Manse, was of precisely the right extent. An hour or two of morning labor was all that it required. But I used to visit and revisit it a dozen times a day, and stand in deep contemplation over my vegetable progeny with a love that nobody could share or conceive of who had never taken part in the process of creation. It was one of the most bewitching sights in the world to observe a hill of beans thrusting aside the soil, or a row of early peas just peeping forth sufficiently to trace a line of delicate green. Later in the season the humming birds were attracted by the blossoms of a peculiar variety of bean; and they were a joy to me, those little spiritual visitants, for deigning to sip airy food out of my nectar cups. Multitudes of bees used to bury themselves in the yellow blossoms of the summer squashes. This, too, was a deep satisfaction; although, when they had laden themselves with sweets, they flew away to some unknown hive, which would give back nothing in requital of what my garden had contributed. But I was glad thus to fling a benefaction upon the passing breeze with the certainty that somebody must profit by it and that there would be a little more honey in the world to allay the sourness and bitterness which mankind is always complaining of. Yes, indeed; my life was the sweeter for that honey.

Speaking of summer squashes, I must say a word of their beautiful and varied forms. They presented an endless diversity of urns and vases, shallow or deep, scalloped or plain, moulded in patterns which a sculptor would do well to copy, since Art has never invented any thing more graceful. A hundred squashes in the garden were worthy, in my eyes at least, of being rendered indestructible in marble. If ever Providence (but I know it never will) should assign me a superfluity of gold, part of it shall be expended for a service of plate, or most delicate porcelain, to be wrought into the shapes of summer squashes gathered from vines which I will plant with my own hands. As dishes for containing vegetables, they would be peculiarly appropriate.

But not merely the squeamish love of the beautiful was gratified by my toil in the kitchen garden. There was a hearty enjoyment, likewise, in observing the growth of the crook-necked winter squashes, from the first little bulb, with the withered blossom adhering to it, until they lay strewn upon the soil, big, round fellows, hiding their heads beneath the leaves, but turning up their great yellow rotundities to the noontide sun. Gazing at them, I felt that by my agency something worth living for had been done. A new substance was born into the world. They were real and tangible existences, which the mind could seize hold of and rejoice in. A cabbage, too,—especially the early Dutch cabbage,[19] which swells to a monstrous circumference, until its ambitious heart often bursts asunder,—is a matter to be proud of when we can claim a share with the earth and sky in producing it. But, after all, the hugest pleasure is reserved until these vegetable children of ours are smoking on the table, and we, like Saturn,[20] make a meal of them.

What with the river, the battle field, the orchard, and the garden, the reader begins to despair of finding his way back into the Old Manse. But, in agreeable weather, it is the truest hospitality to keep him out of doors. I never grew quite acquainted with my habitation till a long spell of sulky rain had confined me beneath its roof. There could not be a more sombre aspect of external Nature than as then seen from the windows of my study. The great willow tree had caught and retained among its leaves a whole cataract of water, to be shaken down at intervals by the frequent gusts of wind. All day long, and for a week together, the rain was drip-drip-dripping and splash-splash-splashing from the eaves and bubbling and foaming into the tubs beneath the spouts. The old, unpainted shingles of the house and out buildings were black with moisture; and the mosses of ancient growth upon the walls looked green and fresh, as if they were the newest things and afterthought of Time. The usually mirrored surface of the river was blurred by an infinity of raindrops; the whole landscape had a completely water-soaked appearance, conveying the impression that the earth was wet through like a sponge; while the summit of a wooded hill, about a mile distant, was enveloped in a dense mist, where the demon of the tempest seemed to have his abiding-place and to be plotting still direr inclemencies.

Nature has no kindness, no hospitality, during a rain. In the fiercest heat of sunny days she retains a secret mercy, and welcomes the way-farer to shady nooks of the woods whither the sun cannot penetrate; but she provides no shelter against her storms. It makes us shiver to think of those deep, umbrageous[21] recesses, those overshadowing banks, where we found such enjoyment during the sultry afternoons. Not a twig of foliage there but would dash a little shower into our faces. Looking reproachfully towards the impenetrable sky,—if sky there be above that dismal uniformity of cloud,—we are apt to murmur against the whole system of the universe, since it involves the extinction of so many summer days in so short a life by the hissing and spluttering rain. In such spells of weather—and it is to be supposed such weather came—Eve's bower in paradise must have been but a cheerless and aguish[22] kind of shelter, nowise comparable to the old parsonage, which had resources of its own to beguile the week's imprisonment. The idea of sleeping on a couch of wet roses!

Happy the man who in a rainy day can betake himself to a huge gar-ret, stored, like that of the Manse, with lumber[23] that each generation has left behind it from a period before the revolution. Our garret was an arched hall, dimly illuminated through small and dusty windows; it was but a twilight at the best; and there were nooks, or rather caverns, of deep obscurity, the secrets of which I never learned, being too rev-erent of their dust and cobwebs. The beams and rafters, roughly hewn and with strips of bark still on them, and the rude masonry of the chimneys, made the garret look wild and uncivilized—an aspect un-like what was seen elsewhere in the quiet and decorous old house. But on one side there was a little whitewashed apartment, which bore the traditionary title of the Saint's Chamber, because holy men in their youth had slept, and studied, and prayed there. With its elevated re-tirement, its one window, its small fireplace, and its closet convenient for an oratory,[24] it was the very spot where a young man might inspire himself with solemn enthusiasm and cherish saintly dreams. The oc-cupants, at various epochs, had left brief records and ejaculations in-scribed upon the walls. There, too, hung a tattered and shrivelled roll of canvas, which on inspection proved to be the forcibly wrought picture of a clergyman, in wig, band,[25] and gown, holding a Bible in his hand. As I turned his face towards the light he eyed me with an air of authority such as men of his profession seldom assume in our days. The original had been pastor of the parish more than a century ago, a friend of Whitefield,[26] and almost his equal in fervid eloquence. I bowed before the effigy of the dignified divine, and felt as if I had now met face to face with the ghost by whom, as there was reason to apprehend, the Manse was haunted.

Houses of any antiquity in New England are so invariably possessed with spirits that the matter seems hardly worth alluding to. Our ghost used to heave deep sighs in a particular corner of the parlor, and sometimes rustled paper, as if he were turning over a sermon in the long upper entry—where nevertheless he was invisible, in spite of the bright moonshine that fell through the eastern window. Not improbably he wished me to edit and publish a selection from a chest full of manuscript discourses that stood in the garret. Once, while Hillard[27] and other friends sat talking with us in the twilight, there came a rustling noise as of a minister's silk gown, sweeping through the very midst of the company, so closely as almost to brush against the chairs. Still there was nothing visible. A yet stranger business was that of a ghostly servant maid, who used to be heard in the kitchen at deepest midnight, grinding coffee, cooking, ironing,—performing, in short, all kinds of domestic labor,—although no traces of any thing accomplished could be detected the next morning. Some neglected duty of her servitude—some ill-starched ministerial band—disturbed the poor damsel in her grave and kept her at work without any wages.

But to return from this digression. A part of my predecessor's library was stored in the garret—no unfit receptacle indeed for such dreary trash as comprised the greater number of volumes. The old books would have been worth nothing at an auction. In this venerable garret, however, they possessed an interest, quite apart from their literary value, as heirlooms, many of which had been transmitted down through a series of consecrated hands from the days of the mighty Puritan divines. Autographs of famous names were to be seen in faded ink on some of their flyleaves; and there were marginal observations or interpolated pages closely covered with manuscript in illegible shorthand, perhaps concealing matter of profound truth and wisdom. The world will never be the better for it. A few of the books were Latin folios, written by Catholic authors; others demolished Papistry,[28] as with a sledge hammer, in plain English. A dissertation on the book of Job[29]—which only Job himself could have had patience to read—filled at least a score of small, thickset quartos, at the rate of two or three volumes to a chapter. Then there was a vast folio body of divinity—too corpulent a body, it might be feared, to comprehend the spiritual element of religion. Volumes of this form dated back two hundred years or more, and were generally bound in black leather, exhibiting precisely such an appearance as we should attribute to books of enchantment. Others equally antique were of a size proper to be carried in the large waistcoat pockets of old times—diminutive, but as black as their bulkier brethren, and abundantly interfused with Greek and Latin quotations. These little old volumes impressed me as if they had been intended for very large ones, but had been unfortunately blighted at an early stage of their growth.

The rain pattered upon the roof and the sky gloomed through the dusty garret windows while I burrowed among these venerable books in search of any living thought which should burn like a coal of fire or glow like an inextinguishable gem beneath the dead trumpery that had long hidden it. But I found no such treasure; all was dead alike; and I could not but muse deeply and wonderingly upon the humiliating fact that the works of man's intellect decay like those of his hands. Thought grows mouldy. What was good and nourishing food for the spirits of one generation affords no sustenance for the next. Books of religion, however, cannot be considered a fair test of the enduring and vivacious properties of human thought, because such books so seldom really touch upon their ostensible subject, and have, therefore, so little business to be written at all. So long as an unlettered soul can attain to saving grace there would seem to be no deadly error in holding theological libraries to be accumulations of, for the most part, stupendous impertinence.

Many of the books had accrued in the latter years of the last clergyman's lifetime. These threatened to be of even less interest than the elder works a century hence to any curious inquirer who should then rummage them as I was doing now. Volumes of the Liberal Preacher[30] and Christian Examiner,[31] occasional sermons, controversial pamphlets, tracts, and other productions of a like fugitive nature took the place of the thick and heavy volumes of past time. In a physical point of view, there was much the same difference as between a feather and a lump of lead; but, intellectually regarded, the specific gravity of old and new was about upon a par. Both also were alike frigid. The elder books nevertheless seemed to have been earnestly written, and might be conceived to have possessed warmth at some former period; although, with the lapse of time, the heated masses had cooled down even to the freezing point. The frigidity of the modern productions, on the other hand, was characteristic and inherent, and evidently had little to do with the writer's qualities of mind and heart. In fine, of this whole dusty heap of literature I tossed aside all the sacred part, and felt myself none the less a Christian for eschewing it. There appeared no hope of either mounting to the better world on a Gothic staircase of ancient folios or of flying thither on the wings of a modern tract.

Nothing, strange to say, retained any sap except what had been written for the passing day and year without the remotest pretension or idea of permanence. There were a few old newspapers, and still older almanacs, which reproduced to my mental eye the epochs when they had issued from the press with a distinctness that was altogether unaccountable. It was as if I had found bits of magic looking glass among the books with the images of a vanished century in them. I turned my eyes towards the tattered picture above mentioned, and asked of the austere divine wherefore it was that he and his brethren, after the most painful rummaging and groping into their minds, had been able to produce nothing half so real as these newspaper scribblers and almanac makers had thrown off in the effervescence of a moment. The portrait responded not; so I sought an answer for myself. It is the age itself that writes newspapers and almanacs, which therefore have a distinct purpose and meaning at the time, and a kind of intelligible truth for all times; whereas most other works—being written by men who, in the very act, set themselves apart from their age—are likely to possess little significance when new, and none at all when old. Genius, indeed, melts many ages into one, and thus effects something permanent, yet still with a similarity of office to that of the more ephemeral writer. A work of genius is but the newspaper of a century, or perchance of a hundred centuries.

Lightly as I have spoken of these old books, there yet lingers with me a superstitious reverence for literature of all kinds. A bound volume has a charm in my eyes similar to what scraps of manuscript possess for the good Mussulman.[32] He imagines that those wind-wafted records are perhaps hallowed by some sacred verse; and I, that every new book or antique one may contain the "open sesame"[33]—the spell to disclose treasures hidden in some unsuspected cave of Truth. Thus it was not without sadness that I turned away from the library of the Old Manse.

Blessed was the sunshine when it came again at the close of another stormy day, beaming from the edge of the western horizon; while the massive firmament of clouds threw down all the gloom it could, but served only to kindle the golden light into a more brilliant glow by the strongly contrasted shadows. Heaven smiled at the earth, so long unseen, from beneath its heavy eyelid. To-morrow for the hill tops and the woodpaths.

Or it might be that Ellery Channing[34] came up the avenue to join me in a fishing excursion on the river. Strange and happy times were those when we cast aside all irksome forms and straitlaced habitudes and delivered ourselves up to the free air, to live like the Indians or any less conventional race during one bright semicircle of the sun. Rowing our boat against the current, between wide meadows, we turned aside into the Assabeth.[35] A more lovely stream than this, for a mile above its junction with the Concord, has never flowed on earth—nowhere, indeed, except to lave the interior regions of a poet's imagination. It is sheltered from the breeze by woods and a hillside; so that elsewhere there might be a hurricane, and here scarcely a ripple across the shaded water. The current lingers along so gently that the mere force of the boatman's will seems sufficient to propel his craft against it. It comes flowing softly through the midmost privacy and deepest heart of a wood which whispers it to be quiet; while the stream whispers back again from its sedgy borders, as if river and wood were hushing one another to sleep. Yes; the river sleeps along its course and dreams of the sky and of the clustering foliage, amid which fall showers of broken sunlight, imparting specks of vivid cheerfulness, in contrast with the quiet depth of the prevailing tint. Of all this scene, the slumbering river has a dream picture in its bosom. Which, after all, was the most real—the picture, or the original?—the objects palpable to our grosser senses, or their apotheosis in the stream beneath? Surely the disembodied images stand in closer relation to the soul. But both the original and the reflection had here an ideal charm; and, had it been a thought more wild, I could have fancied that this river had strayed forth out of the rich scenery of my companion's inner world; only the vegetation along its banks should then have had an Oriental character.

Gentle and unobtrusive as the river is, yet the tranquil woods seem hardly satisfied to allow it passage. The trees are rooted on the very verge of the water, and dip their pendent branches into it. At one spot there is a lofty bank, on the slope of which grow some hemlocks, declining across the stream with outstretched arms, as if resolute to take the plunge. In other places the banks are almost on a level with the water; so that the quiet congregation of trees set their feet in the flood, and are fringed with foliage down to the surface. Cardinal flowers kindle their spiral flames and illuminate the dark nooks among the shrubbery. The pond lily grows abundantly along the margin—that delicious flower, which, as Thoreau tells me, opens its virgin bosom to the first sunlight and perfects its being through the magic of that genial kiss. He has beheld beds of them unfolding in due succession as the sunrise stole gradually from flower to flower—a sight not to be hoped for unless when a poet adjusts his inward eye to a proper focus with the outward organ. Grape vines here and there twine themselves around shrub and tree and hang their clusters over the water within reach of the boatman's hand. Oftentimes they unite two trees of alien race in an inextricable twine, marrying the hemlock and the maple against their will and enriching them with a purple offspring of which neither is the parent. One of these ambitious parasites has climbed into the upper branches of a tall, white pine, and is still ascending from bough to bough, unsatisfied till it shall crown the tree's airy summit with a wreath of its broad foliage and a cluster of its grapes.

The winding course of the stream continually shut out the scene behind us and revealed as calm and lovely a one before. We glided from depth to depth, and breathed new seclusion at every turn. The shy kingfisher flew from the withered branch close at hand to another at a distance, uttering a shrill cry of anger or alarm. Ducks that had been floating there since the preceding eve were startled at our approach and skimmed along the glassy river, breaking its dark surface with a bright streak. The pickerel leaped from among the lilypads. The turtle, sunning itself upon a rock or at the root of a tree, slid suddenly into the water with a plunge. The painted Indian who paddled his canoe along the Assabeth three hundred years ago could hardly have seen a wilder gentleness displayed upon its banks and reflected in its bosom than we did. Nor could the same Indian have prepared his noontide meal with more simplicity. We drew up our skiff at some point where the overarching shade formed a natural bower, and there kindled a fire with the pine cones and decayed branches that lay strewn plentifully around. Soon the smoke ascended among the trees, impregnated with a savory incense, not heavy, dull, and surfeiting, like the steam of cookery within doors, but sprightly and piquant. The smell of our feast was akin to the woodland odors with which it mingled: there was no sacrilege committed by our intrusion there: the sacred solitude was hospitable, and granted us free leave to cook and eat in the recess that was at once our kitchen and banqueting hall. It is strange what humble offices may be performed in a beautiful scene without destroying its poetry. Our fire, red gleaming among the trees, and we beside it, busied with culinary rites and spreading out our meal on a mossgrown log, all seemed in unison with the river gliding by and the foliage rustling over us. And, what was strangest, neither did our mirth seem to disturb the propriety of the solemn woods; although the hobgoblins of the old wilderness and the will-of-the-wisps that glimmered in the marshy places might have come trooping to share our table talk and have added their shrill laughter to our merriment. It was the very spot in which to utter the extremest nonsense or the profoundest wisdom, or that ethereal product of the mind which partakes of both, and may become one or the other, in correspondence with the faith and insight of the auditor.

So, amid sunshine and shadow, rustling leaves and sighing waters, up gushed our talk like the babble of a fountain. The evanescent spray was Ellery's; and his, too, the lumps of golden thought that lay glimmering in the fountain's bed and brightened both our faces by the reflection. Could he have drawn out that virgin gold, and stamped it with the mint mark that alone gives currency, the world might have had the profit, and he the fame. My mind was the richer merely by the knowledge that it was there. But the chief profit of those wild days, to him and me, lay, not in any definite idea, not in any angular or rounded truth, which we dug out of the shapeless mass of problematical stuff, but in the freedom which we thereby won from all custom and conventionalism and fettering influences of man on man. We were so free to-day that it was impossible to be slaves again to-morrow. When we crossed the threshold of the house or trod the thronged pavements of a city, still the leaves of the trees that overhang the Assabeth were whispering to us, "Be free! be free!" Therefore along that shady river bank there are spots, marked with a heap of ashes and half-consumed brands, only less sacred in my remembrance than the hearth of a household fire.

And yet how sweet, as we floated homeward adown the golden river at sunset,—how sweet was it to return within the system of human society, not as to a dungeon and a chain, but as to a stately edifice, whence we could go forth at will into statelier simplicity! How gently, too, did the sight of the Old Manse, best seen from the river, overshadowed with its willow and all environed about with the foliage of its orchard and avenue,—how gently did its gray, homely aspect rebuke the speculative extravagances of the day! It had grown sacred in connection with the artificial life against which we inveighed; it had been a home for many years in spite of all; it was my home too; and, with these thoughts, it seemed to me that all the artifice and conventionalism of life was but an impalpable thinness upon its surface, and that the depth below was none the worse for it. Once, as we turned our boat to the bank, there was a cloud, in the shape of an immensely gigantic figure of a hound, couched[36] above the house, as if keeping guard over it. Gazing at this symbol, I prayed that the upper influences might long protect the institutions that had grown out of the heart of mankind.

If ever my readers should decide to give up civilized life, cities, houses, and whatever moral or material enormities in addition to these the perverted ingenuity of our race has contrived let it be in the early autumn. Then Nature will love him better than at any other season, and will take him to her bosom with a more motherly tenderness. I could scarcely endure the roof of the old house above me in those first autumnal days. How early in the summer, too, the prophecy of autumn comes! Earlier in some years than in others; sometimes even in the first weeks of July. There is no other feeling like what is caused by this faint, doubtful, yet real perception—if it be not rather a foreboding—of the year's decay, so blessedly sweet and sad in the same breath.

Did I say that there was no feeling like it? Ah, but there is a half-acknowledged melancholy like to this when we stand in the perfected vigor of our life and feel that Time has now given us all his flowers, and that the next work of his never idle fingers must be to steal them one by one away.

I have forgotten whether the song of the cricket be not as early a token of autumn's approach as any other—that song which may be called an audible stillness; for though very loud and heard afar, yet the mind does not take note of it as a sound, so completely is its individual existence merged among the accompanying characteristics of the season. Alas for the pleasant summer time! In August the grass is still verdant on the hills and in the valleys; the foliage of the trees is as dense as ever and as green; the flowers gleam forth in richer abundance along the margin of the river and by the stone walls and deep among the woods; the days, too, are as fervid now as they were a month ago; and yet in every breath of wind and in every beam of sunshine we hear the whispered farewell and behold the parting smile of a dear friend. There is a coolness amid all the heat, a mildness in the blazing noon. Not a breeze can stir but it thrills us with the breath of autumn. A pensive glory is seen in the far, golden gleams, among the shadows of the trees. The flowers—even the brightest of them, and they are the most gorgeous of the year—have this gentle sadness wedded to their pomp, and typify the character of the delicious time each within itself. The brilliant cardinal flower has never seemed gay to me.

Still later in the season Nature's tenderness waxes stronger. It is impossible not to be fond of our mother now; for she is so fond of us! At other periods she does not make this impression on me, or only at rare intervals; but in those genial days of autumn, when she has perfected her harvests and accomplished every needful thing that was given her to do, then she overflows with a blessed superfluity of love. She has leisure to caress her children now. It is good to be alive and at such times. Thank Heaven for breath—yes, for mere breath—when it is made up of a heavenly breeze like this! It comes with a real kiss upon our cheeks; it would linger fondly around us if it might; but, since it must be gone, it embraces us with its whole kindly heart and passes onward to embrace likewise the next thing that it meets. A blessing is flung abroad and scattered far and wide over the earth, to be gathered up by all who choose. I recline upon the still unwithered grass and whisper to myself, "O perfect day! O beautiful world! O beneficent God!" And it is the promise of a blessed eternity; for our Creator would never have made such lovely days and have given us the deep hearts to enjoy them, above and beyond all thought, unless we were meant to be immortal. This sunshine is the golden pledge thereof. It beams through the gates of paradise and shows us glimpses far inward.

By and by, in a little time, the outward world puts on a drear austerity. On some October morning there is a heavy hoarfrost on the grass and along the tops of the fences; and at sunrise the leaves fall from the trees of our avenue without a breath of wind, quietly descending by their own weight. All summer long they have murmured like the noise of waters; they have roared loudly while the branches were wrestling with the thunder gust; they have made music both glad and solemn; they have attuned my thoughts by their quiet sound as I paced to and fro beneath the arch of intermingling boughs. Now they can only rustle under my feet. Henceforth the gray parsonage begins to assume a larger importance, and draws to its fireside,—for the abomination of the airtight stove is reserved till wintry weather,—draws closer and closer to its fireside the vagrant impulses that had gone wandering about through the summer.

When summer was dead and buried the Old Manse became as lonely as a hermitage. Not that ever—in my time at least—it had been thronged with company; but, at no rare intervals, we welcomed some friend out of the dusty glare and tumult of the world, and rejoiced to share with him the transparent obscurity that was floating over us. In one respect our precincts were like the Enchanted Ground through which the pilgrim travelled on his way to the Celestial City.[37] The guests, each and all, felt a slumberous influence upon them; they fell asleep in chairs, or took a more deliberate siesta on the sofa, or were seen stretched among the shadows of the orchard, looking up dreamily through the boughs. They could not have paid a more acceptable compliment to my abode nor to my own qualities as a host. I held it as a proof that they left their cares behind them as they passed between the stone gateposts at the entrance of our avenue, and that the so powerful opiate was the abundance of peace and quiet within and all around us. Others could give them pleasure and amusement or instruction— these could be picked up any where; but it was for me to give them rest—rest in a life of trouble. What better could be done for those weary and worldworn spirits?—for him whose career of perpetual action[38] was impeded and harassed by the rarest of his powers and the richest of his acquirements?—for another who had thrown his ardent heart[39] from earliest youth into the strife of politics, and now, perchance, began to suspect that one lifetime is too brief for the accomplishment of any lofty aim?—for her on whose feminine nature had been imposed[40] the heavy gift of intellectual power, such as a strong man might have staggered under, and with it the necessity to act upon the world?—in a word, not to multiply instances, what better could be done for any body who came within our magic circle than to throw the spell of a tranquil spirit over him? And when it had wrought its full effect, then we dismissed him, with but misty reminiscences, as if he had been dreaming of us.

Were I to adopt a pet idea as so many people do, and fondle it in my embraces to the exclusion of all others, it would be, that the great want which mankind labors under at this present period is sleep. The world should recline its vast head on the first convenient pillow and take an agelong nap. It has gone distracted through a morbid activity, and, while preternaturally wide awake, is nevertheless tormented by visions that seem real to it now, but would assume their true aspect and character were all things once set right by an interval of sound repose. This is the only method of getting rid of old delusions and avoiding new ones; of regenerating our race, so that it might in due time awake as an infant out of dewy slumber; of restoring to us the simple perception of what is right and the single-hearted desire to achieve it, both of which have long been lost in consequence of this weary activity of brain and torpor or passion of the heart that now afflict the universe. Stimulants, the only mode of treatment hitherto attempted, cannot quell the disease; they do but heighten the delirium.

Let not the above paragraph ever be quoted against the author; for, though tinctured with its modicum of truth, it is the result and expression of what he knew, while he was writing, to be but a distorted survey of the state and prospects of mankind. There were circumstances around me which made it difficult to view the world precisely as it exists; for, severe and sober as was the Old Manse, it was necessary to go but a little way beyond its threshold before meeting with stranger moral shapes of men than might have been encountered elsewhere in a circuit of a thousand miles.

These hobgoblins of flesh and blood were attracted thither by the widespreading influence of a great original thinker, who had his earthly abode at the opposite extremity of our village. His mind acted upon other minds of a certain constitution with wonderful magnetism, and drew many men upon long pilgrimages to speak with him face to face. Young visionaries—to whom just so much of insight had been imparted as to make life all a labyrinth around them—came to seek the clew that should guide them out of their self-involved bewilderment. Grayheaded theorists—whose systems, at first air, had finally imprisoned them in an iron framework—travelled painfully to his door, not to ask deliverance, but to invite the free spirit into their own thraldom. People that had lighted on a new thought or a thought that they fancied new came to Emerson,[41] as the finder of a glittering gem hastens to a lapidary,[42] to ascertain its quality and value. Uncertain, troubled, earnest wanderers through the midnight of the moral world beheld his intellectual fire as a beacon burning on a hill top, and, climbing the difficult ascent, looked forth into the surrounding obscurity more hopefully than hitherto. The light revealed objects unseen before— mountains, gleaming lakes, glimpses of a creation among the chaos; but also, as was unavoidable, it attracted bats and owls and the whole host of night birds, which flapped their dusky wings against the gazer's eyes, and sometimes were mistaken for fowls of angelic feather. Such delusions always hover nigh whenever a beacon fire of truth is kindled.

For myself, there had been epochs of my life when I, too, might have asked of this prophet the master word that should solve me the riddle of the universe; but now, being happy, I felt as if there were no question to be put, and therefore admired Emerson as a poet of deep beauty and austere tenderness, but sought nothing from him as a philosopher. It was good, nevertheless, to meet him in the woodpaths, or sometimes in our avenue, with that pure, intellectual gleam diffused about his presence like the garment of a shining one; and he, so quiet, so simple, so without pretension, encountering each man alive as if expecting to receive more than he could impart. And, in truth, the heart of many an ordinary man had, perchance, inscriptions which he could not read. But it was impossible to dwell in his vicinity without inhaling more or less the mountain atmosphere of his lofty thought, which, in the brains of some people, wrought a singular giddiness—new truth being as heady as new wine. Never was a poor little country village infested with such a variety of queer, strangely-dressed, oddly-behaved mortals, most of whom took upon themselves to be important agents of the world's destiny, yet were simply bores of a very intense water.

Such, I imagine, is the invariable character of persons who crowd so closely about an original thinker as to draw in his unuttered breath and thus become imbued with a false originality. This triteness of novelty is enough to make any man of common sense blaspheme at all ideas of less than a century's standing, and pray that the world may be petrified and rendered immovable in precisely the worst moral and physical state that it ever yet arrived at, rather than be benefited by such schemes of such philosophers.

And now I begin to feel—and perhaps should have sooner felt—that we have talked enough of the Old Manse. Mine honored reader, it may be, will vilify the poor author as an egotist for babbling through so many pages about a mossgrown country parsonage, and his life within its walls, and on the river, and in the woods, and the influences that wrought upon him from all these sources. My conscience, however, does not reproach me with betraying any thing too sacredly individual to be revealed by a human spirit to its brother or sister spirit. How narrow—how shallow and scanty too—is the stream of thought that has been flowing from my pen, compared with the broad tide of dim emotions, ideas, and associations which swell around me from that portion of my existence! How little have I told! and of that little, how almost nothing is even tinctured with any quality that makes it exclusively my own! Has the reader gone wandering, hand in hand with me, through the inner passages of my being? and have we groped together into all its chambers and examined their treasures or their rubbish? Not so. We have been standing on the greensward, but just within the cavern's mouth, where the common sunshine is free to penetrate, and where every footstep is therefore free to come. I have appealed to no sentiment or sensibilities save such as are diffused among us all. So far as I am a man of really individual attributes I veil my face; nor am I, nor have I ever been, one of those supremely hospitable people who serve up their own hearts, delicately fried, with brain sauce, as a tidbit for their beloved public.

Glancing back over what I have written, it seems but the scattered reminiscences of a single summer. In fairyland there is no measurement of time; and, in a spot so sheltered from the turmoil of life's ocean, three years hastened away with a noiseless flight, as the breezy sunshine chases the cloud shadows across the depths of a still valley. Now came hints, growing more and more distinct, that the owner of the old house was pining for his native air. Carpenters next appeared, making a tremendous racket among the out buildings, strewing the green grass with pine shavings and chips of chestnut joists and vexing the whole antiquity of the place with their discordant renovations. Soon, moreover, they divested our abode of the veil of woodbine which had crept over a large portion of its southern face. All the aged mosses were cleared unsparingly away; and there were horrible whispers about brushing up the external walls with a coat of paint—a purpose as little to my taste as might be that of rouging the venerable cheeks of one's grandmother. But the hand that renovates is always more sacrilegious than that which destroys. In fine, we gathered up our household goods, drank a farewell cup of tea in our pleasant little breakfast room,—delicately fragrant tea, an unpurchasable luxury, one of the many angel gifts that had fallen like dew upon us,—and passed forth between the tall stone gateposts as uncertain as the wandering Arabs where our tent might next be pitched. Providence took me by the hand, and—an oddity of dispensation which, I trust, there is no irreverence in smiling at—has led me, as the newspapers announce while I am writing, from the Old Manse into a custom house.[43] As a story teller, I have often contrived strange vicissitudes for my imaginary personages, but none like this.

The treasure of intellectual gold which I hoped to find in our secluded dwelling had never come to light. No profound treatise of ethics, no philosophic history, no novel even, that could stand unsupported on its edges. All that I had to show, as a man of letters, were these few tales and essays, which had blossomed out like flowers in the calm summer of my heart and mind. Save editing (an easy task) the journal of my friend of many years, the African Cruiser,[44] I had done nothing else. With these idle weeds and withering blossoms I have intermixed some that were produced long ago,[45]—old, faded things, reminding me of flowers pressed between the leaves of a book,—and now offer the bouquet, such as it is, to any whom it may please. These fitful sketches, with so little of external life about them, yet claiming no profundity of purpose,—so reserved, even while they sometimes seem so frank,—often but half in earnest, and never, even when most so, expressing satisfactorily the thoughts which they profess to image,—such trifles, I truly feel, afford no solid basis for a literary reputation. Nevertheless, the public—if my limited number of readers, whom I venture to regard rather as a circle of friends, may be termed a public—will receive them the more kindly, as the last offering, the last collection, of this nature which it is my purpose ever to put forth. Unless I could do better, I have done enough in this kind. For myself the book will always retain one charm—as reminding me of the river, with its delightful solitudes, and of the avenue, the garden, and the orchard, and especially the dear Old Manse, with the little study on its western side, and the sunshine glimmering through the willow branches while I wrote.

Let the reader, if he will do me so much honor, imagine himself my guest, and that, having seen whatever may be worthy of notice within and about the Old Manse, he has finally been ushered into my study. There, after seating him in an antique elbow chair, an heirloom of the house, I take forth a roll of manuscript and entreat his attention to the following tales—an act of personal inhospitality, however, which I never was guilty of, nor ever will be, even to my worst enemy.

THE BIRTHMARK

In the latter part of the last century there lived a man of science, an eminent proficient in every branch of natural philosophy, who not long before our story opens had made experience of a spiritual affinity more attractive than any chemical one. He had left his laboratory to the care of an assistant, cleared his fine countenance from the furnace smoke, washed the stain of acids from his fingers, and persuaded a beautiful woman to become his wife. In those days, when the comparatively recent discovery of electricity and other kindred mysteries of Nature seemed to open paths into the region of miracle, it was not unusual for the love of science to rival the love of woman in its depth and absorbing energy. The higher intellect, the imagination, the spirit, and even the heart might all find their congenial ailment[1] in pursuits which, as some of their ardent votaries believed, would ascend from one step of powerful intelligence to another, until the philosopher should lay his hand on the secret of creative force and perhaps make new worlds for himself. We know not whether Aylmer possessed this degree of faith in man's ultimate control over Nature. He had devoted himself, however, too unreservedly to scientific studies ever to be weaned from them by any second passion. His love for his young wife might prove the stronger of the two; but it could only be by intertwining itself with his love of science and uniting the strength of the latter to his own.

Such a union accordingly took place, and was attended with truly remarkable consequences and a deeply impressive moral. One day, very soon after their marriage, Aylmer sat gazing at his wife with a trouble in his countenance that grew stronger until he spoke.

"Georgiana," said he, "has it never occurred to you that the mark upon your cheek might be removed?"

"No, indeed," said she, smiling; but, perceiving the seriousness of his manner, she blushed deeply. "To tell you the truth, it has been so often called a charm that I was simple enough to imagine it might be so."

"Ah, upon another face perhaps it might," replied her husband; "but never on yours. No, dearest Georgiana, you came so nearly perfect from the hand of Nature that this slightest possible defect, which we hesitate whether to term a defect or a beauty, shocks me, as being the visible mark of earthly imperfection."

"Shocks you, my husband!" cried Georgiana, deeply hurt; at first reddening with momentary anger, but then bursting into tears. "Then why did you take me from my mother's side? You cannot love what shocks you!"

To explain this conversation, it must be mentioned that in the centre of Georgiana's left cheek there was a singular mark, deeply interwoven, as it were, with the texture and substance of her face. In the usual state of her complexion—a healthy though delicate bloom—the mark wore a tint of deeper crimson, which imperfectly defined its shape amid the surrounding rosiness. When she blushed it gradually became more indistinct, and finally vanished amid the triumphant rush of blood that bathed the whole cheek with its brilliant glow. But if any shifting motion caused her to turn pale there was the mark again, a crimson stain upon the snow, in what Aylmer sometimes deemed an almost fearful distinctness. Its shape bore not a little similarity to the human hand, though of the smallest pygmy size. Georgiana's lovers were wont to say that some fairy at her birth hour had laid her tiny hand upon the infant's cheek, and left this impress there in token of the magic endowments that were to give her such sway over all hearts. Many a desperate swain would have risked life for the privilege of pressing his lips to the mysterious hand. It must not be concealed, however, that the impression wrought by this fairy sign manual varied exceedingly according to the difference of temperament in the beholders. Some fastidious persons—but they were exclusively of her own sex—affirmed that the bloody hand, as they chose to call it, quite destroyed the effect of Georgiana's beauty and rendered her countenance even hideous. But it would be as reasonable to say that one of those small blue stains which sometimes occur in the purest statuary marble would convert the Eve of Powers[2] to a monster. Masculine observers, if the birthmark did not heighten their admiration, contented themselves with wishing it away, that the world might possess one living specimen of ideal loveliness without the semblance of a flaw. After his marriage,—for he thought little or nothing of the matter before,—Aylmer discovered that this was the case with himself.

Had she been less beautiful,—if Envy's self could have found aught else to sneer at,—he might have felt his affection heightened by the prettiness of this mimic hand, now vaguely portrayed, now lost, now stealing forth again and glimmering to and fro with every pulse of emotion that throbbed within her heart; but, seeing her otherwise so perfect, he found this one defect grow more and more intolerable with every moment of their united lives. It was the fatal flaw of humanity which Nature, in one shape or another, stamps ineffaceably on all her productions, either to imply that they are temporary and finite, or that their perfection must be wrought by toil and pain. The crimson hand expressed the ineludible gripe[3] in which mortality clutches the highest and purest of earthly mould, degrading them into kindred with the lowest, and even with the very brutes, like whom their visible frames return to dust. In this manner, selecting it as the symbol of his wife's liability to sin, sorrow, decay, and death, Aylmer's sombre imagination was not long in rendering the birthmark a frightful object, causing him more trouble and horror than ever Georgiana's beauty, whether of soul or sense, had given him delight.

At all the seasons which should have been their happiest he invariably, and without intending it, nay, in spite of a purpose to the contrary, reverted to this one disastrous topic. Trifling as it at first appeared, it so connected itself with innumerable trains of thought and modes of feeling that it became the central point of all. With the morning twilight Aylmer opened his eyes upon his wife's face and recognized the symbol of imperfection; and when they sat together at the evening hearth his eyes wandered stealthily to her cheek, and beheld, flickering with the blaze of the wood fire, the spectral hand that wrote mortality where he would fain have worshipped. Georgiana soon learned to shudder at his gaze. It needed but a glance with the peculiar expression that his face often wore to change the roses of her cheek into a death-like paleness, amid which the crimson hand was brought strongly out, like a bas-relief of ruby[4] on the whitest marble.

Late one night, when the lights were growing dim so as hardly to betray the stain on the poor wife's cheek, she herself, for the first time, voluntarily took up the subject.

"Do you remember, my dear Aylmer," said she, with a feeble attempt at a smile, "have you any recollection, of a dream last night about this odious hand?"

"None! none whatever!" replied Aylmer, starting; but then he added, in a dry, cold tone, affected for the sake of concealing the real depth of his emotion, "I might well dream of it; for, before I fell asleep, it had taken a pretty firm hold of my fancy."

"And you did dream of it?" continued Georgiana, hastily; for she dreaded lest a gush of tears should interrupt what she had to say. "A terrible dream! I wonder that you can forget it. Is it possible to forget this one expression?—'It is in her heart now; we must have it out!' Reflect, my husband; for by all means I would have you recall that dream."

The mind is in a sad state when Sleep, the all-involving, cannot confine her spectres within the dim region of her sway, but suffers them to break forth, affrighting this actual life with secrets that perchance belong to a deeper one. Aylmer now remembered his dream. He had fancied himself with his servant Aminadab, attempting an operation for the removal of the birthmark; but the deeper went the knife, the deeper sank the hand, until at length its tiny grasp appeared to have caught hold of Georgiana's heart; whence, however, her husband was inexorably resolved to cut or wrench it away.

When the dream had shaped itself perfectly in his memory Aylmer sat in his wife's presence with a guilty feeling. Truth often finds its way to the mind close muffled in robes of sleep, and then speaks with uncompromising directness of matters in regard to which we practise an unconscious self-deception during our waking moments. Until now he had not been aware of the tyrannizing influence acquired by one idea over his mind, and of the lengths which he might find in his heart to go for the sake of giving himself peace.

"Aylmer," resumed Georgiana, solemnly, "I know not what may be the cost to both of us to rid me of this fatal birthmark. Perhaps its removal may cause cureless deformity; or it may be the stain goes as deep as life itself. Again: do we know that there is a possibility, on any terms, of unclasping the firm gripe of this little hand which was laid upon me before I came into the world?"

"Dearest Georgiana, I have spent much thought upon the subject," hastily interrupted Aylmer. "I am convinced of the perfect practicability of its removal."

"If there be the remotest possibility of it," continued Georgiana, "let the attempt be made, at whatever risk. Danger is nothing to me; for life, while this hateful mark makes me the object of your horror and disgust,—life is a burden which I would fling down with joy. Either remove this dreadful hand, or take my wretched life! You have deep science. All the world bears witness of it. You have achieved great wonders. Cannot you remove this little, little mark, which I cover with the tips of two small fingers? Is this beyond your power, for the sake of your own peace, and to save your poor wife from madness?"

"Noblest, dearest, tenderest wife," cried Aylmer, rapturously, "doubt not my power. I have already given this matter the deepest thought— thought which might almost have enlightened me to create a being less perfect than yourself. Georgiana, you have led me deeper than ever into the heart of science. I feel myself fully competent to render this dear cheek as faultless as its fellow; and then, most beloved, what will be my triumph when I shall have corrected what Nature left imperfect in her fairest work! Even Pygmalion,[5] when his sculptured woman assumed life, felt not greater ecstasy than mine will be."

"It is resolved, then," said Georgiana, faintly smiling. "And, Aylmer, spare me not, though you should find the birthmark take refuge in my heart at last."

Her husband tenderly kissed her cheek—her right cheek—not that which bore the impress of the crimson hand.

The next day Aylmer apprised his wife of a plan that he had formed whereby he might have opportunity for the intense thought and constant watchfulness which the proposed operation would require; while Georgiana, likewise, would enjoy the perfect repose essential to its success. They were to seclude themselves in the extensive apartments occupied by Aylmer as a laboratory, and where, during his toilsome youth, he had made discoveries in the elemental powers of Nature that had roused the admiration of all the learned societies in Europe. Seated calmly in this laboratory, the pale philosopher had investigated the secrets of the highest cloud region and of the profoundest mines; he had satisfied himself of the causes that kindled and kept alive the fires of the volcano; and had explained the mystery of fountains, and how it is that they gush forth, some so bright and pure, and others with such rich medicinal virtues, from the dark bosom of the earth. Here, too, at an earlier period, he had studied the wonders of the human frame, and attempted to fathom the very process by which Nature assimilates all her precious influences from earth and air, and from the spiritual world, to create and foster man, her masterpiece. The latter pursuit, however, Aylmer had long laid aside in unwilling recognition of the truth—against which all seekers sooner or later stumble—that our great creative Mother, while she amuses us with apparently working in the broadest sunshine, is yet severely careful to keep her own secrets, and, in spite of her pretended openness, shows us nothing but results. She permits us, indeed, to mar, but seldom to mend, and, like a jealous patentee, on no account to make. Now, however, Aylmer resumed these half-forgotten investigations; not, of course, with such hopes or wishes as first suggested them; but because they involved much physiological truth and lay in the path of his proposed scheme for the treatment of Georgiana.

As he led her over the threshold of the laboratory, Georgiana was cold and tremulous. Aylmer looked cheerfully into her face, with intent to reassure her, but was so startled with the intense glow of the birthmark upon the whiteness of her cheek that he could not restrain a strong convulsive shudder. His wife fainted.

"Aminadab! Aminadab!" shouted Aylmer, stamping violently on the floor.

Forthwith there issued from an inner apartment a man of low stature, but bulky frame, with shaggy hair hanging about his visage, which was grimed with the vapors of the furnace. This personage had been Aylmer's underworker during his whole scientific career, and was admirably fitted for that office by his great mechanical readiness, and the skill with which, while incapable of comprehending a single principle, he executed all the details of his master's experiments. With his vast strength, his shaggy hair, his smoky aspect, and the indescribable earthiness that incrusted him, he seemed to represent man's physical nature; while Aylmer's slender figure, and pale, intellectual face, were no less apt a type of the spiritual element.

"Throw open the door of the boudoir, Aminadab," said Aylmer, "and burn a pastil."[6]

"Yes, master," answered Aminadab, looking intently at the lifeless form of Georgiana; and then he muttered to himself, "If she were my wife, I'd never part with that birthmark."

When Georgiana recovered consciousness she found herself breathing an atmosphere of penetrating fragrance, the gentle potency of which had recalled her from her deathlike faintness. The scene around her looked like enchantment. Aylmer had converted those smoky, dingy, sombre rooms, where he had spent his brightest years in recondite pursuits, into a series of beautiful apartments not unfit to be the secluded abode of a lovely woman. The walls were hung with gorgeous curtains, which imparted the combination of grandeur and grace that no other species of adornment can achieve; and, as they fell from the ceiling to the floor, their rich and ponderous folds, concealing all angles and straight lines, appeared to shut in the scene from infinite space. For aught Georgiana knew, it might be a pavilion among the clouds. And Aylmer, excluding the sunshine, which would have interfered with his chemical processes, had supplied its place with perfumed lamps, emitting flames of various hue, but all uniting in a soft, impurpled radiance. He now knelt by his wife's side, watching her earnestly, but without alarm; for he was confident in his science, and felt that he could draw a magic circle round her within which no evil might intrude.

"Where am I? Ah, I remember," said Georgiana, faintly; and she placed her hand over her cheek to hide the terrible mark from her husband's eyes.

"Fear not, dearest!" exclaimed he. "Do not shrink from me! Believe me, Georgiana, I even rejoice in this single imperfection, since it will be such a rapture to remove it."

"O, spare me!" sadly replied his wife. "Pray do not look at it again. I never can forget that convulsive shudder."

In order to soothe Georgiana, and, as it were, to release her mind from the burden of actual things, Aylmer now put in practice some of the light and playful secrets which science had taught him among its profounder lore. Airy figures, absolutely bodiless ideas, and forms of unsubstantial beauty came and danced before her, imprinting their momentary footsteps on beams of light. Though she had some indistinct idea of the method of these optical phenomena, still the illusion was almost perfect enough to warrant the belief that her husband possessed sway over the spiritual world. Then again, when she felt a wish to look forth from her seclusion, immediately, as if her thoughts were answered, the procession of external existence flitted across a screen. The scenery and the figures of actual life were perfectly represented, but with that bewitching yet indescribable difference which always makes a picture, an image, or a shadow so much more attractive than the original. When wearied of this, Aylmer bade her cast her eyes upon a vessel containing a quantity of earth. She did so, with little interest at first; but was soon startled to perceive the germ of a plant shooting upward from the soil. Then came the slender stalk; the leaves gradually unfolded themselves; and amid them was a perfect and lovely flower.

"It is magical!" cried Georgiana. "I dare not touch it."

"Nay, pluck it," answered Aylmer,—"pluck it, and inhale its brief perfume while you may. The flower will wither in a few moments and leave nothing save its brown seed vessels; but thence may be perpetuated a race as ephemeral as itself."

But Georgiana had no sooner touched the flower than the whole plant suffered a blight, its leaves turning coal-black as if by the agency of fire.

"There was too powerful a stimulus," said Aylmer, thoughtfully.

To make up for this abortive experiment, he proposed to take her portrait by a scientific process of his own invention. It was to be effected by rays of light striking upon a polished plate of metal. Georgiana assented; but, on looking at the result, was affrighted to find the features of the portrait blurred and indefinable; while the minute figure of a hand appeared where the cheek should have been. Aylmer snatched the metallic plate and threw it into a jar of corrosive acid.

Soon, however, he forgot these mortifying failures. In the intervals of study and chemical experiment he came to her flushed and exhausted, but seemed invigorated by her presence, and spoke in glowing language of the resources of his art. He gave a history of the long dynasty of the alchemists, who spent so many ages in quest of the universal solvent[7] by which the golden principle might be elicited from all things vile and base. Aylmer appeared to believe that, by the plainest scientific logic, it was altogether within the limits of possibility to discover this long-sought medium; "but," he added, "a philosopher who should go deep enough to acquire the power would attain too lofty a wisdom to stoop to the exercise of it." Not less singular were his opinions in regard to the elixir vitæ.[8] He more than intimated that it was at his option to concoct a liquid that should prolong life for years, perhaps interminably; but that it would produce a discord in Nature which all the world, and chiefly the quaffer of the immortal nostrum,[9] would find cause to curse.

"Aylmer, are you in earnest?" asked Georgiana, looking at him with amazement and fear. "It is terrible to possess such power, or even to dream of possessing it."

"O, do not tremble, my love," said her husband. "I would not wrong either you or myself by working such inharmonious effects upon our lives; but I would have you consider how trifling, in comparison, is the skill requisite to remove this little hand."

At the mention of the birthmark, Georgiana, as usual, shrank as if a redhot iron had touched her cheek.

Again Aylmer applied himself to his labors. She could hear his voice in the distant furnace room giving directions to Aminadab, whose harsh, uncouth, misshapen tones were audible in response, more like the grunt or growl of a brute than human speech. After hours of absence, Aylmer reappeared and proposed that she should now examine his cabinet of chemical products and natural treasures of the earth. Among the former he showed her a small vial, in which, he remarked, was contained a gently yet most powerful fragrance, capable of impregnating all the breezes that blow across a kingdom. They were of inestimable value, the contents of that little vial; and, as he said so, he threw some of the perfume into the air and filled the room with piercing and invigorating delight.

"And what is this?" asked Georgiana, pointing to a small crystal globe containing a gold-colored liquid. "It is so beautiful to the eye that I could imagine it the elixir of life."

"In one sense it is," replied Aylmer; "or rather, the elixir of immortality. It is the most precious poison that ever was concocted in this world. By its aid I could apportion the lifetime of any mortal at whom you might point your finger. The strength of the dose would determine whether he were to linger out years, or drop dead in the midst of a breath. No king on his guarded throne could keep his life if I, in my private station, should deem that the welfare of millions justified me in depriving him of it."

"Why do you keep such a terrific drug?" inquired Georgiana in horror.

"Do not mistrust me, dearest," said her husband, smiling; "its virtuous potency is yet greater than its harmful one. But see! here is a powerful cosmetic. With a few drops of this in a vase of water, freckles may be washed away as easily as the hands are cleansed. A stronger infusion would take the blood out of the cheek, and leave the rosiest beauty a pale ghost."

"Is it with this lotion that you intend to bathe my cheek?" asked Georgiana, anxiously.

"O, no," hastily replied her husband; "this is merely superficial. Your case demands a remedy that shall go deeper."

In his interviews with Georgiana, Aylmer generally made minute inquiries as to her sensations, and whether the confinement of the rooms and the temperature of the atmosphere agreed with her. These questions had such a particular drift that Georgiana began to conjecture that she was already subjected to certain physical influences, either breathed in with the fragrant air or taken with her food. She fancied likewise, but it might be altogether fancy, that there was a stirring up of her system—a strange, indefinite sensation creeping through her veins, and tingling, half painfully, half pleasurably, at her heart. Still, whenever she dared to look into the mirror, there she beheld herself pale as a white rose and with the crimson birthmark stamped upon her cheek. Not even Aylmer now hated it so much as she.

To dispel the tedium of the hours which her husband found it necessary to devote to the processes of combination and analysis, Georgiana turned over the volumes of his scientific library. In many dark old tomes she met with chapters full of romance and poetry. They were the works of the philosophers of the middle ages, such as Albertus Magnus, Cornelius Agrippa, Paracelsus, and the famous friar who created the prophetic Brazen Head.[10] All these antique naturalists stood in advance of their centuries, yet were imbued with some of their credulity, and therefore were believed, and perhaps imagined themselves to have acquired from the investigation of Nature a power above Nature, and from physics a sway over the spiritual world. Hardly less curious and imaginative were the early volumes of the Transactions of the Royal Society,[11] in which the members, knowing little of the limits of natural possibility, were continually recording wonders or proposing methods whereby wonders might be wrought.

But, to Georgiana, the most engrossing volume was a large folio from her husband's own hand, in which he had recorded every experiment of his scientific career, its original aim, the methods adopted for its development, and its final success or failure, with the circumstances to which either event was attributable. The book, in truth, was both the history and emblem of his ardent, ambitious, imaginative, yet practical and laborious life. He handled physical details as if there were nothing beyond them; yet spiritualized them all and redeemed himself from materialism by his strong and eager aspiration towards the infinite. In his grasp the veriest clod of earth assumed a soul. Georgiana, as she read, reverenced Aylmer and loved him more profoundly than ever, but with a less entire dependence on his judgment than heretofore. Much as he had accomplished, she could not but observe that his most splendid successes were almost invariably failures, if compared with the ideal at which he aimed. His brightest diamonds were the merest pebbles, and felt to be so by himself, in comparison with the inestimable gems which lay hidden beyond his reach. The volume, rich with achievements that had won renown for its author, was yet as melancholy a record as ever mortal hand had penned. It was the sad confession and continual exemplification of the shortcomings of the composite man, the spirit burdened with clay and working in matter, and of the despair that assails the higher nature at finding itself so miserably thwarted by the earthly part. Perhaps every man of genius, in whatever sphere, might recognize the image of his own experience in Aylmer's journal.

So deeply did these reflections affect Georgiana that she laid her face upon the open volume and burst into tears. In this situation she was found by her husband.

"It is dangerous to read in a sorcerer's books," said he with a smile, though his countenance was uneasy and displeased. "Georgiana, there are pages in that volume which I can scarcely glance over and keep my senses. Take heed lest it prove as detrimental to you."

"It has made me worship you more than ever," said she.

"Ah, wait for this one success," rejoined he, "then worship me if you will. I shall deem myself hardly unworthy of it. But come, I have sought you for the luxury of your voice. Sing to me, dearest."

So she poured out the liquid music of her voice to quench the thirst of his spirit. He then took his leave with a boyish exuberance of gayety, assuring her that her seclusion would endure but a little longer, and that the result was already certain. Scarcely had he departed when Georgiana felt irresistibly impelled to follow him. She had forgotten to inform Aylmer of a symptom which for two or three hours past had begun to excite her attention. It was a sensation in the fatal birthmark, not painful, but which induced a restlessness throughout her system. Hastening after her husband, she intruded for the first time into the laboratory.

The first thing that struck her eye was the furnace, that hot and feverish worker, with the intense glow of its fire, which by the quantities of soot clustered above it seemed to have been burning for ages. There was a distilling apparatus in full operation. Around the room were retorts, tubes, cylinders, crucibles, and other apparatus of chemical research. An electrical machine stood ready for immediate use. The atmosphere felt oppressively close, and was tainted with gaseous odors which had been tormented forth by the processes of science. The severe and homely simplicity of the apartment, with its naked walls and brick pavement, looked strange, accustomed as Georgiana had become to the fantastic elegance of her boudoir. But what chiefly, indeed almost solely, drew her attention, was the aspect of Aylmer himself.

He was pale as death, anxious and absorbed, and hung over the furnace as if it depended upon his utmost watchfulness whether the liquid which it was distilling should be the draught of immortal happiness or misery. How different from the sanguine and joyous mien that he had assumed for Georgiana's encouragement!

"Carefully now, Aminadab; carefully, thou human machine; carefully, thou man of clay," muttered Aylmer, more to himself than his assistant. "Now, if there be a thought too much or too little, it is all over."

"Ho! ho!" mumbled Aminadab. "Look, master! look!"

Aylmer raised his eyes hastily, and at first reddened, then grew paler than ever, on beholding Georgiana. He rushed towards her and seized her arm with a gripe that left the print of his fingers upon it.

"Why do you come hither? Have you no trust in your husband?" cried he, impetuously. "Would you throw the blight of that fatal birthmark over my labors? It is not well done. Go, prying woman! go!"

"Nay, Aylmer," said Georgiana with the firmness of which she possessed no stinted endowment, "it is not you that have a right to complain. You mistrust your wife; you have concealed the anxiety with which you watch the development of this experiment. Think not so unworthily of me, my husband. Tell me all the risk we run, and fear not that I shall shrink; for my share in it is far less than your own."

"No, no, Georgiana!" said Aylmer, impatiently; "it must not be."

"I submit," replied she, calmly. "And, Aylmer, I shall quaff whatever draught you bring me; but it will be on the same principle that would induce me to take a dose of poison if offered by your hand."

"My noble wife," said Aylmer, deeply moved, "I knew not the height and depth of your nature until now. Nothing shall be concealed. Know, then, that this crimson hand, superficial as it seems, has clutched its grasp into your being with a strength of which I had no previous conception. I have already administered agents powerful enough to do aught except to change your entire physical system. Only one thing remains to be tried. If that fail us we are ruined."

"Why did you hesitate to tell me this?" asked she.

"Because, Georgiana," said Aylmer, in a low voice, "there is danger."

"Danger? There is but one danger—that this horrible stigma shall be left upon my cheek!" cried Georgiana. "Remove it, remove it, whatever be the cost, or we shall both go mad!"

"Heaven knows your words are too true," said Aylmer, sadly. "And now, dearest, return to your boudoir. In a little while all will be tested."

He conducted her back and took leave of her with a solemn tenderness which spoke far more than his words how much was now at stake. After his departure Georgiana became rapt in musings. She considered the character of Aylmer and did it completer justice than at any previous moment. Her heart exulted, while it trembled, at his honorable love—so pure and lofty that it would accept nothing less than perfection nor miserably make itself contented with an earthlier nature than he had dreamed of. She felt how much more precious was such a sentiment than that meaner kind which would have borne with the imperfection for her sake, and have been guilty of treason to holy love by degrading its perfect idea to the level of the actual; and with her whole spirit she prayed that, for a single moment, she might satisfy his highest and deepest conception. Longer than one moment she well knew it could not be; for his spirit was ever on the march, ever ascending, and each instant required something that was beyond the scope of the instant before.

The sound of her husband's footsteps aroused her. He bore a crystal goblet containing a liquor colorless as water, but bright enough to be the draught of immortality. Aylmer was pale; but it seemed rather the consequence of a highly-wrought state of mind and tension of spirit than of fear or doubt.

"The concoction of the draught has been perfect," said he, in answer to Georgiana's look. "Unless all my science have deceived me, it cannot fail."

"Save on your account, my dearest Aylmer," observed his wife, "I might wish to put off this birthmark of mortality by relinquishing mortality itself in preference to any other mode. Life is but a sad possession to those who have attained precisely the degree of moral advancement at which I stand. Were I weaker and blinder, it might be happiness. Were I stronger, it might be endured hopefully. But, being what I find myself, methinks I am of all mortals the most fit to die."

"You are fit for heaven without tasting death!" replied her husband. "But why do we speak of dying? The draught cannot fail. Behold its effect upon this plant."

On the window seat there stood a geranium diseased with yellow blotches which had overspread all its leaves. Aylmer poured a small quantity of the liquid upon the soil in which it grew. In a little time, when the roots of the plant had taken up the moisture, the unsightly blotches began to be extinguished in a living verdure.

"There needed no proof," said Georgiana, quietly. "Give me the goblet. I joyfully stake all upon your word."

"Drink, then, thou lofty creature!" exclaimed Aylmer, with fervid admiration. "There is no taint of imperfection on thy spirit. Thy sensible frame, too, shall soon be all perfect."

She quaffed the liquid and returned the goblet to his hand.

"It is grateful," said she, with a placid smile. "Methinks it is like water from a heavenly fountain; for it contains I know not what of unobtrusive fragrance and deliciousness. It allays a feverish thirst that had parched me for many days. Now, dearest, let me sleep. My earthly senses are closing over my spirit like the leaves around the heart of a rose at sunset."

She spoke the last words with a gentle reluctance, as if it required almost more energy than she could command to pronounce the faint and lingering syllables. Scarcely had they loitered through her lips ere she was lost in slumber. Aylmer sat by her side, watching her aspect with the emotions proper to a man the whole value of whose existence was involved in the process now to be tested. Mingled with this mood, however, was the philosophic investigation characteristic of the man of science. Not the minutest symptom escaped him. A heightened flush of the cheek, a slight irregularity of breath, a quiver of the eye-lid, a hardly perceptible tremor through the frame,—such were the details which, as the moments passed, he wrote down in his folio volume. Intense thought had set its stamp upon every previous page of that volume; but the thoughts of years were all concentrated upon the last.

While thus employed, he failed not to gaze often at the fatal hand, and not without a shudder. Yet once, by a strange and unaccountable impulse, he pressed it with his lips. His spirit recoiled, however, in the very act; and Georgiana, out of the midst of her deep sleep, moved uneasily and murmured as if in remonstrance. Again Aylmer resumed his watch. Nor was it without avail. The crimson hand, which at first had been strongly visible upon the marble paleness of Georgiana's cheek, now grew more faintly outlined. She remained not less pale than ever; but the birthmark, with every breath that came and went, lost somewhat of its former distinctness. Its presence had been awful; its departure was more awful still. Watch the stain of the rainbow fading out of the sky, and you will know how that mysterious symbol passed away.

"By Heaven! it is well nigh gone!" said Aylmer to himself, in almost irrepressible ecstasy. "I can scarcely trace it now. Success! success! And now it is like the faintest rose color. The lightest flush of blood across her cheek would overcome it. But she is so pale!"

He drew aside the window curtain and suffered the light of natural day to fall into the room and rest upon her cheek. At the same time he heard a gross, hoarse chuckle, which he had long known as his servant Aminadab's expression of delight.

"Ah, clod! ah, earthly mass!" cried Aylmer, laughing in a sort of frenzy, "you have served me well! Matter and spirit—earth and heaven—have both done their part in this! Laugh, thing of the senses! You have earned the right to laugh."

These exclamations broke Georgiana's sleep. She slowly unclosed her eyes and gazed into the mirror which her husband had arranged for that purpose. A faint smile flitted over her lips when she recognized how barely perceptible was now that crimson hand which had once blazed forth with such disastrous brilliancy as to scare away all their happiness. But then her eyes sought Aylmer's face with a trouble and anxiety that he could by no means account for.

"My poor Aylmer!" murmured she.

"Poor? Nay, richest, happiest, most favored!" exclaimed he. "My peerless bride, it is successful! You are perfect!"

"My poor Aylmer," she repeated, with a more than human tenderness, "you have aimed loftily; you have done nobly. Do not repent that, with so high and pure a feeling, you have rejected the best the earth could offer. Aylmer, dearest Aylmer, I am dying!"

Alas! it was too true! The fatal hand had grappled with the mystery of life, and was the bond by which an angelic spirit kept itself in union with a mortal frame. As the last crimson tint of the birthmark—that sole token of human imperfection—faded from her cheek, the parting breath of the now perfect woman passed into the atmosphere, and her soul, lingering a moment near her husband, took its heavenward flight. Then a hoarse, chuckling laugh was heard again! Thus ever does the gross fatality of earth exult in its invariable triumph over the immortal essence which, in this dim sphere of half development, demands the completeness of a higher state. Yet, had Aylmer reached a profounder wisdom, he need not thus have flung away the happiness which would have woven his mortal life of the selfsame texture with the celestial. The momentary circumstance was too strong for him; he failed to look beyond the shadowy scope of time, and, living once for all in eternity, to find the perfect future in the present.

A SELECT PARTY

A Man of Fancy made an entertainment at one of his castles in the air, and invited a select number of distinguished personages to favor him with their presence. The mansion, though less splendid than many that have been situated in the same region, was nevertheless of a magnificence such as is seldom witnessed by those acquainted only with terrestrial architecture. Its strong foundations and massive walls were quarried out of a ledge of heavy and sombre clouds which had hung brooding over the earth, apparently as dense and ponderous as its own granite, throughout a whole autumnal day. Perceiving that the general effect was gloomy,—so that the airy castle looked like a feudal fortress, or a monastery of the middle ages, or a state prison of our own times, rather than the home of pleasure and repose which he intended it to be,—the owner, regardless of expense, resolved to gild the exterior from top to bottom. Fortunately, there was just then a flood of evening sunshine in the air. This being gathered up and poured abundantly upon the roof and walls, imbued them with a kind of solemn cheerfulness; while the cupolas and pinnacles were made to glitter with the purest gold, and all the hundred windows gleamed with a glad light, as if the edifice itself were rejoicing in its heart. And now, if the people of the lower world chanced to be looking upward out of the turmoil of their petty perplexities, they probably mistook the castle in the air for a heap of sunset clouds, to which the magic of light and shade had imparted the aspect of a fantastically constructed mansion. To such beholders it was unreal, because they lacked the imaginative faith. Had they been worthy to pass within its portal, they would have recognized the truth, that the dominions which the spirit conquers for itself among unrealities become a thousand times more real than the earth whereon they stamp their feet, saying, "This is solid and substantial; this may be called a fact."

At the appointed hour, the host stood in his great saloon to receive the company. It was a vast and noble room, the vaulted ceiling of which was supported by double rows of gigantic pillars that had been hewn entire out of masses of variegated clouds. So brilliantly were they polished, and so exquisitely wrought by the sculptor's skill, as to resemble the finest specimens of emerald, porphyry,[1] opal, and chrysolite,[2] thus producing a delicate richness of effect which their immense size rendered not incompatible with grandeur. To each of these pillars a meteor was suspended. Thousands of these ethereal lustres are continually wandering about the firmament, burning out to waste, yet capable of imparting a useful radiance to any person who has the art of converting them to domestic purposes. As managed in the saloon, they are far more economical than ordinary lamplight. Such, however, was the intensity of their blaze that it had been found expedient to cover each meteor with a globe of evening mist, thereby muffling the too potent glow and soothing it into a mild and comfortable splendor. It was like the brilliancy of a powerful yet chastened imagination—a light which seemed to hide whatever was unworthy to be noticed and give effect to every beautiful and noble attribute. The guests, therefore, as they advanced up the centre of the saloon, appeared to better advantage than ever before in their lives.

The first that entered, with old-fashioned punctuality, was a venerable figure in the costume of by-gone days, with his white hair flowing down over his shoulders and a reverend beard upon his breast. He leaned upon a staff, the tremulous stroke of which, as he set it carefully upon the floor, reëchoed through the saloon at every footstep. Recognizing at once this celebrated personage, whom it had cost him a vast deal of trouble and research to discover, the host advanced nearly three fourths of the distance down between the pillars to meet and welcome him.

"Venerable sir," said the Man of Fancy, bending to the floor, "the honor of this visit would never be forgotten were my term of existence to be as happily prolonged as your own."

The old gentleman received the compliment with gracious condescension. He then thrust up his spectacles over his forehead and appeared to take a critical survey of the saloon.

"Never within my recollection," observed he, "have I entered a more spacious and noble hall. But are you sure that it is built of solid materials and that the structure will be permanent?"

"O, never fear, my venerable friend," replied the host. "In reference to a lifetime like your own, it is true, my castle may well be called a temporary edifice. But it will endure long enough to answer all the purposes for which it was erected."

But we forget that the reader has not yet been made acquainted with the guest. It was no other than that universally accredited character so constantly referred to in all seasons of intense cold or heat; he that remembers the hot Sunday and the cold Friday; the witness of a past age, whose negative reminiscences find their way into every newspaper, yet whose antiquated and dusky abode is so overshadowed by accumulated years and crowded back by modern edifices that none but the Man of Fancy could have discovered it; it was, in short, that twin brother of Time, and great-grandsire of mankind, and hand-and-glove associate of all forgotten men and things—the Oldest Inhabitant. The host would willingly have drawn him into conversation, but succeeded only in eliciting a few remarks as to the oppressive atmosphere of this present summer evening compared with one which the guest had experienced about fourscore years ago. The old gentleman, in fact, was a good deal overcome by his journey among the clouds, which, to a frame so earth-incrusted by long continuance in a lower region, was unavoidably more fatiguing than to younger spirits. He was therefore conducted to an easy chair, well cushioned and stuffed with vaporous softness, and left to take a little repose.

The Man of Fancy now discerned another guest, who stood so quietly in the shadow of one of the pillars that he might easily have been overlooked.

"My dear sir," exclaimed the host, grasping him warmly by the hand, "allow me to greet you as the hero of the evening. Pray do not take it as an empty compliment; for, if there were not another guest in my castle, it would be entirely pervaded with your presence."

"I thank you," answered the unpretending stranger; "but, though you happened to overlook me, I have not just arrived. I came very early; and, with your permission, shall remain after the rest of the company have retired."

And who does the reader imagine was this unobtrusive guest? It was the famous performer of acknowledged impossibilities—a character of superhuman capacity and virtue, and, if his enemies are to be credited, of no less remarkable weaknesses and defects. With a generosity with which he alone sets us an example, we will glance merely at his nobler attributes. He it is, then, who prefers the interests of others to his own and a humble station to an exalted one. Careless of fashion, custom, the opinions of men, and the influence of the press, he assimilates his life to the standard of ideal rectitude, and thus proves himself the one independent citizen of our free country. In point of ability, many people declare him to be the only mathematician capable of squaring the circle; the only mechanic acquainted with the principle of perpetual motion; the only scientific philosopher who can compel water to run up hill; the only writer of the age whose genius is equal to the production of an epic poem; and finally, so various are his accomplishments, the only professor of gymnastics who has succeeded in jumping down his own throat. With all these talents, however, he is so far from being considered a member of good society that it is the severest censure of any fashionable assemblage to affirm that this re markable individual was present. Public orators, lecturers, and theatrical performers particularly eschew his company. For especial reasons, we are not at liberty to disclose his name, and shall mention only one other trait,—a most singular phenomenon in natural philosophy,— that, when he happens to cast his eyes upon a looking glass, he beholds Nobody reflected there!

Several other guests now made their appearance; and among them, chattering with immense volubility, a brisk little gentleman of universal vogue in private society, and not unknown in the public journals under the title of Monsieur On-Dit.[3] The name would seem to indicate a Frenchman; but, whatever be his country, he is thoroughly versed in all the languages of the day, and can express himself quite as much to the purpose in English as in any other tongue. No sooner were the ceremonies of salutation over than this talkative little person put his mouth to the host's ear and whispered three secrets of state, an important piece of commercial intelligence, and a rich item of fashionable scandal. He then assured the Man of Fancy that he would not fail to circulate in the society of the lower world a minute description of this magnificent castle in the air and of the festivities at which he had the honor to be a guest. So saying, Monsieur On-Dit made his bow and hurried from one to another of the company, with all of whom he seemed to be acquainted and to possess some topic of interest or amusement for every individual. Coming at last to the Oldest Inhabitant, who was slumbering comfortably in the easy chair, he applied his mouth to that venerable ear.

"What do you say?" cried the old gentleman, starting from his nap and putting up his hand to serve the purpose of an ear trumpet.

Monsieur On-Dit bent forward again and repeated his communication.

"Never within my memory," exclaimed the Oldest Inhabitant, lifting his hands in astonishment, "has so remarkable an incident been heard of."

Now came in the Clerk of the Weather, who had been invited out of deference to his official station, although the host was well aware that his conversation was likely to contribute but little to the general enjoyment. He soon, indeed, got into a corner with his acquaintance of long ago, the Oldest Inhabitant, and began to compare notes with him in reference to the great storms, gales of wind, and other atmospherical facts that had occurred during a century past. It rejoiced the Man of Fancy that his venerable and much-respected guest had met with so congenial an associate. Entreating them both to make themselves perfectly at home, he now turned to receive the Wandering Jew.[4] This personage, however, had latterly grown so common, by mingling in all sorts of society and appearing at the beck of every entertainer, that he could hardly be deemed a proper guest in a very exclusive circle. Besides, being covered with dust from his continual wanderings along the highways of the world, he really looked out of place in a dress party; so that the host felt relieved of an incommodity when the restless individual in question, after a brief stay, took his departure on a ramble towards Oregon.

The portal was now thronged by a crowd of shadowy people with whom the man of fancy had been acquainted in his visionary youth.

He had invited them hither for the sake of observing how they would compare, whether advantageously or otherwise, with the real characters to whom his maturer life had introduced him. They were beings of crude imagination, such as glide before a young man's eye and pretend to be actual inhabitants of the earth; the wise and witty with whom he would hereafter hold intercourse; the generous and heroic friends whose devotion would be requited with his own; the beautiful dream woman who would become the helpmate of his human toils and sorrows and at once the source and partaker of his happiness. Alas! it is not good for the fullgrown man to look too closely at these old acquaintances, but rather to reverence them at a distance through the medium of years that have gathered duskily between. There was something laughably untrue in their pompous stride and exaggerated sentiment; they were neither human nor tolerable likenesses of humanity, but fantastic maskers, rendering heroism and nature alike ridiculous by the grave absurdity of their pretensions to such attributes; and as for the peerless dream lady, behold! there advanced up the saloon, with a movement like a jointed doll, a sort of wax figure of an angel, a creature as cold as moonshine, an artifice in petticoats, with an intellect of pretty phrases and only the semblance of a heart, yet in all these particulars the true type of a young man's imaginary mistress. Hardly could the host's punctilious courtesy restrain a smile as he paid his respects to this unreality and met the sentimental glance with which the Dream sought to remind him of their former love passages.

"No, no, fair lady," murmured he betwixt sighing and smiling; "my taste is changed; I have learned to love what Nature makes better than my own creations in the guise of womanhood."

"Ah, false one," shrieked the dream lady, pretending to faint, but dissolving into thin air, out of which came the deplorable murmur of her voice, "your inconstancy has annihilated me."

"So be it," said the cruel Man of Fancy to himself; "and a good riddance too."

Together with these shadows, and from the same region, there came an uninvited multitude of shapes which at any time during his life had tormented the Man of Fancy in his moods of morbid melancholy or had haunted him in the delirium of fever. The walls of his castle in the air were not dense enough to keep them out, nor would the strongest of earthly architecture have availed to their exclusion. Here were those forms of dim terror which had beset him at the entrance of life, waging warfare with his hopes; here were strange uglinesses of earlier date, such as haunt children in the nighttime. He was particularly startled by the vision of a deformed old black woman whom he imagined as lurking in the garret of his native home, and who, when he was an infant, had once come to his bedside and grinned at him in the crisis of a scarlet fever. This same black shadow, with others almost as hideous, now glided among the pillars of the magnificent saloon, grinning recognition, until the man shuddered anew at the forgotten terrors of his childhood. It amused him, however, to observe the black woman, with the mischievous caprice peculiar to such beings, steal up to the chair of the Oldest Inhabitant and peep into his half-dreamy mind.

"Never within my memory," muttered that venerable personage, aghast, "did I see such a face."

Almost immediately after the unrealities just described, arrived a number of guests whom incredulous readers may be inclined to rank equally among creatures of imagination. The most noteworthy were an incorruptible Patriot; a Scholar without pedantry; a Priest without worldly ambition; and a Beautiful Woman without pride or coquetry; a Married Pair whose life had never been disturbed by incongruity of feeling; a Reformer untrammelled by his theory; and a Poet who felt no jealousy towards other votaries of the lyre. In truth, however, the host was not one of the cynics who consider these patterns of excellence, without the fatal flaw, such rarities in the world; and he had invited them to his select party chiefly out of humble deference to the judgment of society, which pronounces them almost impossible to be met with.

"In my younger days," observed the Oldest Inhabitant, "such characters might be seen at the corner of every street."

Be that as it might, these specimens of perfection proved to be not half so entertaining companions as people with the ordinary allowance of faults.

But now appeared a stranger, whom the host had no sooner recognized than, with an abundance of courtesy unlavished on any other, he hastened down the whole length of the saloon in order to pay him emphatic honor. Yet he was a young man in poor attire, with no insignia of rank or acknowledged eminence, nor any thing to distinguish him among the crowd except a high, white forehead, beneath which a pair of deepset eyes were glowing with warm light. It was such a light as never illuminates the earth save when a great heart burns as the household fire of a grand intellect. And who was he?—who but the Master Genius for whom our country is looking anxiously into the mist of Time, as destined to fulfil the great mission of creating an American literature, hewing it, as it were, out of the unwrought granite of our intellectual quarries? From him, whether moulded in the form of an epic poem or assuming a guise altogether new as the spirit itself may determine, we are to receive our first great original work, which shall do all that remains to be achieved for our glory among the nations. How this child of a mighty destiny had been discovered by the Man of Fancy it is of little consequence to mention. Suffice it that he dwells as yet unhonored among men, unrecognized by those who have known him from his cradle; the noble countenance which should be distinguished by a halo diffused around it passes daily amid the throng of people toiling and troubling themselves about the trifles of a moment, and none pay reverence to the worker of immortality. Nor does it matter much to him, in his triumph over all the ages, though a generation or two of his own times shall do themselves the wrong to disregard him.

By this time Monsieur On-Dit had caught up the stranger's name and destiny and was busily whispering the intelligence among the other guests.

"Pshaw!" said one. "There can never be an American genius."

"Pish!" cried another. "We have already as good poets as any in the world. For my part, I desire to see no better."

And the Oldest Inhabitant, when it was proposed to introduce him to the Master Genius, begged to be excused, observing that a man who had been honored with the acquaintance of Dwight, and Freneau, and Joel Barlow,[5] might be allowed a little austerity of taste.

The saloon was now fast filling up by the arrival of other remarkable characters, among whom were noticed Davy Jones,[6] the distinguished nautical personage, and a rude, carelessly-dressed, harum-scarum sort of elderly fellow, known by the nickname of Old Harry.[7] The latter, however, after being shown to a dressing room, reappeared with his gray hair nicely combed, his clothes brushed, a clean dicky on his neck, and altogether so changed in aspect as to merit the more respectful appellation of Venerable Henry. Joel Doe and Richard Roe came arm in arm, accompanied by a Man of Straw, a fictitious indorser, and several persons who had no existence except as voters in closely-contested elections. The celebrated Seatsfield,[8] who now entered, was at first supposed to belong to the same brotherhood, until he made it apparent that he was a real man of flesh and blood and had his earthly domicile in Germany. Among the latest comers, as might reasonably be expected, arrived a guest from the far future.

"Do you know him? do you know him?" whispered Monsieur On-Dit, who seemed to be acquainted with every body. "He is the representative of Posterity—the man of an age to come."

"And how came he here?" asked a figure who was evidently the prototype of the fashion plate in a magazine, and might be taken to represent the vanities of the passing moment. "The fellow infringes upon our rights by coming before his time."

"But you forget where we are," answered the Man of Fancy, who overheard the remark. "The lower earth, it is true, will be forbidden ground to him for many long years hence; but a castle in the air is a sort of no man's land, where Posterity may make acquaintance with us on equal terms."

No sooner was his identity known than a throng of guests gathered about Posterity, all expressing the most generous interest in his welfare, and many boasting of the sacrifices which they had made, or were willing to make, in his behalf. Some, with as much secrecy as possible, desired his judgment upon certain copies of verses or great manuscript rolls of prose; others accosted him with the familiarity of old friends, taking it for granted that he was perfectly cognizant of their names and characters. At length, finding himself thus beset, Posterity was put quite beside his patience.

"Gentlemen, my good friends," cried he, breaking loose from a misty poet who strove to hold him by the button, "I pray you to attend to your own business, and leave me to take care of mine! I expect to owe you nothing, unless it be certain national debts, and other encumbrances and impediments, physical and moral, which I shall find it troublesome enough to remove from my path. As to your verses, pray read them to your contemporaries. Your names are as strange to me as your faces; and even were it otherwise,—let me whisper you a secret,—the cold, icy memory which one generation may retain of another is but a poor recompense to barter life for. Yet, if your heart is set on being known to me, the surest, the only, method is, to live truly and wisely for your own age, whereby, if the native force be in you, you may likewise live for posterity."

"It is nonsense," murmured the Oldest Inhabitant, who, as a man of the past, felt jealous that all notice should be withdrawn from himself to be lavished on the future, "sheer nonsense, to waste so much thought on what only is to be."

To divert the minds of his guests, who were considerably abashed by this little incident, the Man of Fancy led them through several apartments of the castle, receiving their compliments upon the taste and varied magnificence that were displayed in each. One of these rooms was filled with moonlight, which did not enter through the window, but was the aggregate of all the moonshine that is scattered around the earth on a summer night while no eyes are awake to enjoy its beauty. Airy spirits had gathered it up, wherever they found it gleaming on the broad bosom of a lake, or silvering the meanders of a stream, or glimmering among the wind-stirred boughs of a wood, and had garnered it in this one spacious hall. Along the walls, illuminated by the mild intensity of the moonshine, stood a multitude of ideal statues, the original conceptions of the great works of ancient or modern art, which the sculptors did but imperfectly succeed in putting into marble; for it is not to be supposed that the pure idea of an immortal creation ceases to exist; it is only necessary to know where they are deposited in order to obtain possession of them. In the alcoves of another vast apartment was arranged a splendid library, the volumes of which were inestimable, because they consisted, not of actual performances, but of the works which the authors only planned, without ever finding the happy season to achieve them. To take familiar instances, here were the untold tales of Chaucer's Canterbury Pilgrims; the unwritten cantos of the Fairy Queen; the conclusion of Coleridge's Christabel; and the whole of Dryden's projected epic on the subject of King Arthur.[9] The shelves were crowded; for it would not be too much to affirm that every author has imagined and shaped out in his thought more and far better works than those which actually proceeded from his pen. And here, likewise, were the unrealized conceptions of youthful poets who died of the very strength of their own genius before the world had caught one inspired murmur from their lips.

When the peculiarities of the library and statue gallery were explained to the Oldest Inhabitant he appeared infinitely perplexed, and exclaimed, with more energy than usual, that he had never heard of such a thing within his memory, and, moreover, did not at all understand how it could be.

"But my brain, I think," said the good old gentleman, "is getting not so clear as it used to be. You young folks, I suppose, can see your way through these strange matters. For my part, I give it up."

"And so do I," muttered the Old Harry. "It is enough to puzzle the——Ahem!"

Making as little reply as possible to these observations, the Man of Fancy preceded the company to another noble saloon, the pillars of which were solid golden sunbeams taken out of the sky in the first hour in the morning. Thus, as they retained all their living lustre, the room was filled with the most cheerful radiance imaginable, yet not too dazzling to be borne with comfort and delight. The windows were beautifully adorned with curtains made of the many-colored clouds of sunrise, all imbued with virgin light and hanging in magnificent festoons from the ceiling to the floor. Moreover, there were fragments of rainbows scattered through the room; so that the guests, astonished at one another, reciprocally saw their heads made glorious by the seven primary hues; or, if they chose,—as who would not?—they could grasp a rainbow in the air and convert it to their own apparel and adornment. But the morning light and scattered rainbows were only a type and symbol of the real wonders of the apartment. By an influence akin to magic, yet perfectly natural, whatever means and opportunities of joy are neglected in the lower world had been carefully gathered up and deposited in the saloon of morning sunshine. As may well be conceived, therefore, there was material enough to supply, not merely a joyous evening, but also a happy lifetime, to more than as many people as that spacious apartment could contain. The company seemed to renew their youth; while that pattern and proverbial standard of innocence, the Child Unborn, frolicked to and fro among them, communicating his own unwrinkled gayety to all who had the good fortune to witness his gambols.

"My honored friends," said the Man of Fancy, after they had enjoyed themselves a while, "I am now to request your presence in the banqueting hall, where a slight collation[10] is awaiting you."

"Ah, well said!" ejaculated a cadaverous figure, who had been invited for no other reason than that he was pretty constantly in the habit of dining with Duke Humphrey.[11] "I was beginning to wonder whether a castle in the air were provided with a kitchen."

It was curious, in truth, to see how instantaneously the guests were diverted from the high moral enjoyments which they had been tasting with so much apparent zest by a suggestion of the more solid as well as liquid delights of the festive board. They thronged eagerly in the rear of the host, who now ushered them into a lofty and extensive hall, from end to end of which was arranged a table, glittering all over with innumerable dishes and drinking vessels of gold. It is an uncertain point whether these rich articles of plate were made for the occasion out of molten sunbeams, or recovered from the wrecks of Spanish galleons that had lain for ages at the bottom of the sea. The upper end of the table was overshadowed by a canopy, beneath which was placed a chair of elaborate magnificence, which the host himself declined to occupy, and besought his guests to assign it to the worthiest among them. As a suitable homage to his incalculable antiquity and eminent distinction, the post of honor was at first tendered to the Oldest Inhabitant. He, however, eschewed it, and requested the favor of a bowl of gruel at a side table, where he could refresh himself with a quiet nap. There was some little hesitation as to the next candidate, until Posterity took the Master Genius of our country by the hand and led him to the chair of state beneath the princely canopy. When once they beheld him in his true place, the company acknowledged the justice of the selection by a long thunder roll of vehement applause.

Then was served up a banquet, combining, if not all the delicacies of the season, yet all the rarities which careful purveyors had met with in the flesh, fish, and vegetable markets of the land of Nowhere. The bill of fare being unfortunately lost, we can only mention a phœnix, roasted in its own flames, cold potted birds of paradise, ice creams from the Milky Way, and whip syllabubs and flummery[12] from the Paradise of Fools, whereof there was a very great consumption. As for drinkables, the temperance people contented themselves with water as usual; but it was the water of the Fountain of Youth; the ladies sipped

Nepenthe;[13] the lovelorn, the careworn, and the sorrow-stricken were supplied with brimming goblets of Lethe;[14] and it was shrewdly conjectured that a certain golden vase, from which only the more distinguished guests were invited to partake, contained nectar that had been mellowing ever since the days of classical mythology. The cloth being removed, the company, as usual, grew eloquent over their liquor and delivered themselves of a succession of brilliant speeches—the task of reporting which we resign to the more adequate ability of Counsellor Gill,[15] whose indispensable coöperation the Man of Fancy had taken the precaution to secure.

When the festivity of the banquet was at its most ethereal point, the Clerk of the Weather was observed to steal from the table and thrust his head between the purple and golden curtains of one of the windows.

"My fellow-guests," he remarked aloud, after carefully noting the signs of the night, "I advise such of you as live at a distance to be going as soon as possible; for a thunder storm is certainly at hand."

"Mercy on me!" cried Mother Carey, who had left her brood of chickens[16] and come hither in gossamer drapery, with pink silk stockings. "How shall I ever get home?"

All now was confusion and hasty departure, with but little superfluous leavetaking. The Oldest Inhabitant, however, true to the rule of those long past days in which his courtesy had been studied, paused on the threshold of the meteor-lighted hall to express his vast satisfaction at the entertainment.

"Never, within my memory," observed the gracious old gentleman, "has it been my good fortune to spend a pleasanter evening or in more select society."

The wind here took his breath away, whirled his three-cornered hat into infinite space, and drowned what further compliments it had been his purpose to bestow. Many of the company had bespoken will-o'-the-wisps to convey them home; and the host, in his general beneficence, had engaged the Man in the Moon, with an immense horn lantern,[17] to be the guide of such desolate spinsters as could do no better for themselves. But a blast of the rising tempest blew out all their lights in the twinkling of an eye. How, in the darkness that ensued, the guests contrived to get back to earth, or whether the greater part of them contrived to get back at all, or are still wandering among clouds, mists, and puffs of tempestuous wind, bruised by the beams and rafters of the overthrown castle in the air, and deluded by all sorts of unrealities, are points that concern themselves much more than the writer or the public. People should think of these matters before they trust themselves on a pleasure party into the realm of Nowhere.

Young Goodman Brown

Young Goodman Brown came forth at sunset into the street of Salem village;[1] but put his head back, after crossing the threshold, to exchange a parting kiss with his young wife. And Faith, as the wife was aptly named, thrust her own pretty head into the street, letting the wind play with the pink ribbons of her cap while she called to Goodman Brown.

"Dearest heart," whispered she, softly and rather sadly, when her lips were close to his ear, "prithee put off your journey until sunrise and sleep in your own bed to-night. A lone woman is troubled with such dreams and such thoughts that she's afeard of herself sometimes. Pray tarry with me this night, dear husband, of all nights in the year."

"My love and my Faith," replied young Goodman Brown, "of all nights in the year, this one night must I tarry away from thee. My journey, as thou callest it, forth and back again, must needs be done 'twixt now and sunrise. What, my sweet, pretty wife, dost thou doubt me already, and we but three months married?"

"Then God bless you!" said Faith, with the pink ribbons; "and may you find all well when you come back."

"Amen!" cried Goodman Brown. "Say thy prayers, dear Faith, and go to bed at dusk, and no harm will come to thee."

So they parted; and the young man pursued his way until, being about to turn the corner by the meeting house, he looked back and saw the head of Faith still peeping after him with a melancholy air, in spite of her pink ribbons.

"Poor little Faith!" thought he, for his heart smote him. "What a wretch am I to leave her on such an errand! She talks of dreams, too. Methought as she spoke there was trouble in her face, as if a dream had warned her what work is to be done to-night. But no, no; 'twould kill her to think it. Well, she's a blessed angel on earth; and after this one night I'll cling to her skirts and follow her to heaven."

With this excellent resolve for the future, Goodman Brown felt himself justified in making more haste on his present evil purpose. He had taken a dreary road, darkened by all the gloomiest trees of the forest, which barely stood aside to let the narrow path creep through, and closed immediately behind. It was all as lonely as could be; and there is this peculiarity in such a solitude, that the traveller knows not who may be concealed by the innumerable trunks and the thick boughs overhead; so that with lonely footsteps he may yet be passing through an unseen multitude.

"There may be a devilish Indian behind every tree," said Goodman Brown to himself; and he glanced fearfully behind him as he added, "What if the devil himself should be at my very elbow!"

His head being turned back, he passed a crook of the road, and, looking forward again, beheld the figure of a man, in grave and decent attire, seated at the foot of an old tree. He arose at Goodman Brown's approach and walked onward side by side with him.

"You are late, Goodman Brown," said he. "The clock of the Old South[2] was striking as I came through Boston; and that is full fifteen minutes agone."

"Faith kept me back a while," replied the young man, with a tremor in his voice, caused by the sudden appearance of his companion, though not wholly unexpected.

It was now deep dusk in the forest, and deepest in that part of it where these two were journeying. As nearly as could be discerned, the second traveller was about fifty years old, apparently in the same rank of life as Goodman Brown, and bearing a considerable resemblance to him, though perhaps more in expression than features. Still they might have been taken for father and son. And yet, though the elder person was as simply clad as the younger and as simple in manner too, he had an indescribable air of one who knew the world, and who would not have felt abashed at the governor's dinner table or in King William's court,[3] were it possible that his affairs should call him thither. But the only thing about him that could be fixed upon as remarkable was his staff, which bore the likeness of a great black snake, so curiously wrought that it might almost be seen to twist and wriggle itself like a living serpent. This, of course, must have been an ocular deception, assisted by the uncertain light.

"Come, Goodman Brown," cried his fellow-traveller, "this is a dull pace for the beginning of a journey. Take my staff, if you are so soon weary."

"Friend," said the other, exchanging his slow pace for a full stop, "having kept covenant by meeting thee here, it is my purpose now to return whence I came. I have scruples touching the matter thou wot'st[4] of."

"Sayest thou so?" replied he of the serpent, smiling apart. "Let us walk on, nevertheless, reasoning as we go; and if I convince thee not thou shalt turn back. We are but a little way in the forest yet."

"Too far! too far!" exclaimed the goodman, unconsciously resuming his walk. "My father never went into the woods on such an errand, nor his father before him. We have been a race of honest men and good Christians since the days of the martyrs;[5] and shall I be the first of the name of Brown that ever took this path and kept——"

"Such company, thou wouldst say," observed the elder person, interpreting his pause. "Well said, Goodman Brown! I have been as well acquainted with your family as with ever a one among the Puritans; and that's no trifle to say. I helped your grandfather, the constable, when he lashed the Quaker woman so smartly through the streets of Salem; and it was I that brought your father a pitch-pine knot, kindled at my own hearth, to set fire to an Indian village, in King Philip's war.[6] They were my good friends, both; and many a pleasant walk have we had along this path, and returned merrily after midnight. I would fain be friends with you for their sake."

"If it be as thou sayest," replied Goodman Brown, "I marvel they never spoke of these matters; or, verily, I marvel not, seeing that the least rumor of the sort would have driven them from New England. We are a people of prayer, and good works to boot, and abide no such wickedness."

"Wickedness or not," said the traveller with the twisted staff, "I have a very general acquaintance here in New England. The deacons of many a church have drunk the communion wine with me; the selectmen of divers towns make me their chairman; and a majority of the Great and General Court[7] are firm supporters of my interest. The governor and I, too—— But these are state secrets."

"Can this be so?" cried Goodman Brown, with a stare of amazement at his undisturbed companion. "Howbeit, I have nothing to do with the governor and council; they have their own ways, and are no rule for a simple husbandman like me. But, were I to go on with thee, how should I meet the eye of that good old man, our minister, at Salem village? O, his voice would make me tremble both Sabbath day and lecture day."[8]

Thus far the elder traveller had listened with due gravity; but now burst into a fit of irrepressible mirth, shaking himself so violently that his snakelike staff actually seemed to wriggle in sympathy.

"Ha! ha! ha!" shouted he again and again; then composing himself. "Well, go on, Goodman Brown, go on; but, prithee, don't kill me with laughing."

"Well, then, to end the matter at once," said Goodman Brown, considerably nettled, "there is my wife, Faith. It would break her dear little heart; and I'd rather break my own."

"Nay, if that be the case," answered the other, "e'en go thy ways, Goodman Brown. I would not for twenty old women like the one hobbling before us that Faith should come to any harm."

As he spoke, he pointed his staff at a female figure on the path, in whom Goodman Brown recognized a very pious and exemplary dame, who had taught him his catechism in youth, and was still his moral and spiritual adviser, jointly with the minister and Deacon Gookin.

"A marvel, truly, that Goody Cloyse should be so far in the wilderness at nightfall," said he. "But, with your leave, friend, I shall take a cut through the woods until we have left this Christian woman behind. Being a stranger to you, she might ask whom I was consorting with and whither I was going."

"Be it so," said his fellow-traveller. "Betake you to the woods, and let me keep the path."

Accordingly the young man turned aside, but took care to watch his companion, who advanced softly along the road until he had come within a staff's length of the old dame. She, meanwhile, was making the best of her way, with singular speed for so aged a woman, and mumbling some indistinct words—a prayer, doubtless—as she went. The traveller put forth his staff and touched her withered neck with what seemed the serpent's tail.

"The devil!" screamed the pious old lady.

"Then Goody Cloyse knows her old friend?" observed the traveller, confronting her and leaning on his writhing stick.

"Ah, forsooth, and is it your worship indeed?" cried the good dame. "Yea, truly is it, and in the very image of my old gossip, Goodman Brown, the grandfather of the silly fellow that now is. But—would your worship believe it?—my broomstick hath strangely disappeared, stolen, as I suspect, by that unhanged witch, Goody Cory, and that, too, when I was all anointed with the juice of smallage, and cinquefoil, and wolf's bane[9]——"

"Mingled with fine wheat and the fat of a new-born babe," said the shape of old Goodman Brown.

"Ah, your worship knows the recipe," cried the old lady, cackling aloud. "So, as I was saying, being all ready for the meeting, and no horse to ride on, I made up my mind to foot it; for they tell me there is a nice young man to be taken into communion to-night. But now your good worship will lend me your arm, and we shall be there in a twinkling."

"That can hardly be," answered her friend. "I may not spare you my arm, Goody Cloyse; but here is my staff, if you will."

So saying, he threw it down at her feet, where, perhaps, it assumed life, being one of the rods which its owner had formerly lent to the Egyptian magi.[10] Of this fact, however, Goodman Brown could not take cognizance. He had cast up his eyes in astonishment, and, looking down again, beheld neither Goody Cloyse nor the serpentine staff, but his fellow-traveller alone, who waited for him as calmly as if nothing had happened.

"That old woman taught me my catechism," said the young man; and there was a world of meaning in this simple comment.

They continued to walk onward, while the elder traveller exhorted his companion to make good speed and persevere in the path, discoursing so aptly that his arguments seemed rather to spring up in the bosom of his auditor than to be suggested by himself. As they went, he plucked a branch of maple to serve for a walking stick, and began to strip it of the twigs and little boughs, which were wet with evening dew. The moment his fingers touched them they became strangely withered and dried up as with a week's sunshine. Thus the pair proceeded, at a good free pace, until suddenly, in a gloomy hollow of the road, Goodman Brown sat himself down on the stump of a tree and refused to go any farther.

"Friend," said he, stubbornly, "my mind is made up. Not another step will I budge on this errand. What if a wretched old woman do choose to go to the devil when I thought she was going to heaven: is that any reason why I should quit my dear Faith and go after her?"

"You will think better of this by and by," said his acquaintance, composedly. "Sit here and rest yourself a while; and when you feel like moving again, there is my staff to help you along."

Without more words, he threw his companion the maple stick, and was as speedily out of sight as if he had vanished into the deepening gloom. The young man sat a few moments by the roadside, applauding himself greatly, and thinking with how clear a conscience he should meet the minister in his morning walk, nor shrink from the eye of good old Deacon Gookin. And what calm sleep would be his that very night, which was to have been spent so wickedly, but so purely and sweetly now, in the arms of Faith! Amidst these pleasant and praiseworthy meditations, Goodman Brown heard the tramp of horses along the road, and deemed it advisable to conceal himself within the verge of the forest, conscious of the guilty purpose that had brought him thither, though now so happily turned from it.

On came the hoof tramps and the voices of the riders, two grave old voices, conversing soberly as they drew near. These mingled sounds appeared to pass along the road, within a few yards of the young man's hiding-place; but, owing doubtless to the depth of the gloom at that particular spot, neither the travellers nor their steeds were visible. Though their figures brushed the small boughs by the wayside, it could not be seen that they intercepted, even for a moment, the faint gleam from the strip of bright sky athwart which they must have passed. Goodman Brown alternately crouched and stood on tiptoe, pulling aside the branches and thrusting forth his head as far as he durst without discerning so much as a shadow. It vexed him the more, because he could have sworn, were such a thing possible, that he recognized the voices of the minister and Deacon Gookin, jogging along quietly, as they were wont to do, when bound to some ordination or ecclesiastical council. While yet within hearing, one of the riders stopped to pluck a switch.

"Of the two, reverend sir," said the voice like the deacon's, "I had rather miss an ordination dinner than to-night's meeting. They tell me that some of our community are to be here from Falmouth[11] and beyond, and others from Connecticut and Rhode Island, besides several of the Indian powwows,[12] who, after their fashion, know almost as much deviltry as the best of us. Moreover, there is a goodly young woman to be taken into communion."

"Mighty well, Deacon Gookin!" replied the solemn old tones of the minister. "Spur up, or we shall be late. Nothing can be done, you know, until I get on the ground."

The hoofs clattered again; and the voices, talking so strangely in the empty air, passed on through the forest, where no church had ever been gathered or solitary Christian prayed. Whither, then, could these holy men be journeying so deep into the heathen wilderness? Young Goodman Brown caught hold of a tree for support, being ready to sink down on the ground, faint and overburdened with the heavy sickness of his heart. He looked up to the sky, doubting whether there really was a heaven above him. Yet there was the blue arch, and the stars brightening in it.

"With heaven above and Faith below, I will yet stand firm against the devil!" cried Goodman Brown.

While he still gazed upward into the deep arch of the firmament and had lifted his hands to pray, a cloud, though no wind was stirring, hurried across the zenith and hid the brightening stars. The blue sky was still visible except directly overhead, where this black mass of cloud was sweeping swiftly northward. Aloft in the air, as if from the depths of the cloud, came a confused and doubtful sound of voices. Once the listener fancied that he could distinguish the accents of townspeople of his own, men and women, both pious and ungodly, many of whom he had met at the communion table, and had seen others rioting at the tavern. The next moment, so indistinct were the sounds, he doubted whether he had heard aught but the murmur of the old forest, whispering without a wind. Then came a stronger swell of those familiar tones, heard daily in the sunshine at Salem village, but never until now from a cloud of night. There was one voice, of a young woman, uttering lamentations, yet with an uncertain sorrow, and entreating for some favor, which, perhaps, it would grieve her to obtain; and all the unseen multitude, both saints and sinners, seemed to encourage her onward.

"Faith!" shouted Goodman Brown, in a voice of agony and desperation; and the echoes of the forest mocked him, crying, "Faith! Faith!" as if bewildered wretches were seeking her all through the wilderness.

The cry of grief, rage, and terror was yet piercing the night, when the unhappy husband held his breath for a response. There was a scream, drowned immediately in a louder murmur of voices, fading into far-off laughter, as the dark cloud swept away, leaving the clear and silent sky above Goodman Brown. But something fluttered lightly down through the air and caught on the branch of a tree. The young man seized it, and beheld a pink ribbon.

"My Faith is gone!" cried he, after one stupefied moment. "There is no good on earth; and sin is but a name. Come, devil; for to thee is this world given."

And, maddened with despair, so that he laughed loud and long, did Goodman Brown grasp his staff and set forth again, at such a rate that he seemed to fly along the forest path rather than to walk or run. The road grew wilder and drearier and more faintly traced, and vanished at length, leaving him in the heart of the dark wilderness, still rushing onward with the instinct that guides mortal man to evil. The whole forest was peopled with frightful sounds—the creaking of the trees, the howling of wild beasts, and the yell of Indians; while sometimes the wind tolled like a distant church bell, and sometimes gave a broad roar around the traveller, as if all Nature were laughing him to scorn. But he was himself the chief horror of the scene, and shrank not from its other horrors.

"Ha! ha! ha!" roared Goodman Brown when the wind laughed at him. "Let us hear which will laugh loudest. Think not to frighten me with your deviltry. Come witch, come wizard, come Indian powwow, come devil himself, and here comes Goodman Brown. You may as well fear him as he fear you."

In truth, all through the haunted forest there could be nothing more frightful than the figure of Goodman Brown. On he flew among the black pines, brandishing his staff with frenzied gestures, now giving vent to an inspiration of horrid blasphemy, and now shouting forth such laughter as set all the echoes of the forest laughing like demons around him. The fiend in his own shape is less hideous than when he rages in the breast of man. Thus sped the demoniac[13] on his course, until, quivering among the trees, he saw a red light before him, as when the felled trunks and branches of a clearing have been set on fire, and throw up their lurid blaze against the sky, at the hour of midnight. He paused, in a lull of the tempest that had driven him onward, and heard the swell of what seemed a hymn, rolling solemnly from a distance with the weight of many voices. He knew the tune; it was a familiar one in the choir of the village meeting house. The verse died heavily away, and was lengthened by a chorus, not of human voices, but of all the sounds of the benighted wilderness pealing in awful harmony together. Goodman Brown cried out; and his cry was lost to his own ear by its unison with the cry of the desert.

In the interval of silence he stole forward until the light glared full upon his eyes. At one extremity of an open space, hemmed in by the dark wall of the forest, arose a rock, bearing some rude, natural resemblance either to an altar or a pulpit, and surrounded by four blazing pines, their tops aflame, their stems untouched, like candles at an evening meeting. The mass of foliage that had overgrown the summit of the rock was all on fire, blazing high into the night and fitfully illuminating the whole field. Each pendent twig and leafy festoon was in a blaze. As the red light arose and fell, a numerous congregation alternately shone forth, then disappeared in shadow, and again grew, as it were, out of the darkness, peopling the heart of the solitary woods at once.

"A grave and dark-clad company," quoth Goodman Brown.

In truth they were such. Among them, quivering to and fro between gloom and splendor, appeared faces that would be seen next day at the council board of the province, and others which, Sabbath after Sabbath, looked devoutly heavenward, and benignantly over the crowded pews, from the holiest pulpits in the land. Some affirm that the lady of the governor was there. At least there were high dames well known to her, and wives of honored husbands, and widows, a great multitude, and ancient maidens, all of excellent repute, and fair young girls, who trembled lest their mothers should espy them. Either the sudden gleams of light flashing over the obscure field bedazzled Goodman Brown, or he recognized a score of the church members of Salem village famous for their especial sanctity. Good old Deacon Gookin had arrived, and waited at the skirts of that venerable saint, his revered pastor. But, irreverently consorting with these grave, reputable, and pious people, these elders of the church, these chaste dames and dewy virgins, there were men of dissolute lives and women of spotted fame, wretches given over to all mean and filthy vice, and suspected even of horrid crimes. It was strange to see that the good shrank not from the wicked, nor were the sinners abashed by the saints. Scattered also among their palefaced enemies were the Indian priests, or powwows, who had often scared their native forest with more hideous incantations than any known to English witchcraft.

"But where is Faith?" thought Goodman Brown, and, as hope came into his heart, he trembled.

Another verse of the hymn arose, a slow and mournful strain, such as the pious love, but joined to words which expressed all that our nature can conceive of sin, and darkly hinted at far more. Unfathomable to mere mortals is the lore of fiends. Verse after verse was sung; and still the chorus of the desert swelled between like the deepest tone of a mighty organ; and with the final peal of that dreadful anthem there came a sound, as if the roaring wind, the rushing streams, the howling beasts, and every other voice of the unconverted wilderness were mingling and according with the voice of guilty man in homage to the prince of all. The four blazing pines threw up a loftier flame, and obscurely discovered shapes and visages of horror on the smoke wreaths above the impious assembly. At the same moment the fire on the rock shot redly forth and formed a glowing arch above its base, where now appeared a figure. With reverence be it spoken, the figure bore no slight similitude, both in garb and manner, to some grave divine of the New England churches.

"Bring forth the converts!" cried a voice that echoed through the field and rolled into the forest.

At the word, Goodman Brown stepped forth from the shadow of the trees and approached the congregation, with whom he felt a loathful brotherhood by the sympathy of all that was wicked in his heart. He could have well nigh sworn that the shape of his own dead father beckoned him to advance, looking downward from a smoke wreath, while a woman, with dim features of despair, threw out her hand to warn him back. Was it his mother? But he had no power to retreat one step, nor to resist, even in thought, when the minister and good old Deacon Gookin seized his arms and led him to the blazing rock. Thither came also the slender form of a veiled female, led between Goody Cloyse, that pious teacher of the catechism, and Martha Carrier,[14] who had received the devil's promise to be queen of hell. A rampant hag was she. And there stood the proselytes beneath the canopy of fire.

"Welcome, my children," said the dark figure, "to the communion of your race. Ye have found thus young your nature and your destiny. My children, look behind you!"

They turned; and flashing forth, as it were, in a sheet of flame, the fiend worshippers were seen; the smile of welcome gleamed darkly on every visage.

"There," resumed the sable form, "are all whom ye have reverenced from youth. Ye deemed them holier than yourselves, and shrank from your own sin, contrasting it with their lives of righteousness and prayerful aspirations heavenward. Yet here are they all in my worshipping assembly. This night it shall be granted you to know their secret deeds; how hoary-bearded elders of the church have whispered wanton words to the young maids of their households; how many a woman, eager for widows' weeds, has given her husband a drink at bedtime and let him sleep his last sleep in her bosom; how beardless youths have made haste to inherit their fathers' wealth; and how fair damsels—blush not, sweet ones—have dug little graves in the garden, and bidden me, the sole guest, to an infant's funeral. By the sympathy of your human hearts for sin ye shall scent out all the places—whether in church, bed chamber, street, field, or forest—where crime has been committed, and shall exult to behold the whole earth one stain of guilt, one mighty blood spot. Far more than this. It shall be yours to penetrate, in every bosom, the deep mystery of sin, the fountain of all wicked arts, and which inexhaustibly supplies more evil impulses than human power—than my power at its utmost—can make manifest in deeds. And now, my children, look upon each other."

They did so; and, by the blaze of the hell-kindled torches, the wretched man beheld his Faith, and the wife her husband, trembling before that unhallowed altar.

"Lo, there ye stand, my children," said the figure, in a deep and solemn tone, almost sad with its despairing awfulness, as if his once angelic nature[15] could yet mourn for our miserable race. "Depending upon one another's hearts, ye had still hoped that virtue were not all a dream. Now are ye undeceived. Evil is the nature of mankind. Evil must be your only happiness. Welcome again, my children, to the communion of your race."

"Welcome," repeated the fiend worshippers, in one cry of despair and triumph.

And there they stood, the only pair, as it seemed, who were yet hesitating on the verge of wickedness in this dark world. A basin was hollowed, naturally, in the rock. Did it contain water, reddened by the lurid light? or was it blood? or, perchance, a liquid flame? Herein did the shape of evil dip his hand and prepare to lay the mark of baptism upon their foreheads, that they might be partakers of the mystery of sin, more conscious of the secret guilt of others, both in deed and thought, than they could now be of their own. The husband cast one look at his pale wife, and Faith at him. What polluted wretches would the next glance show them to each other, shuddering alike at what they disclosed and what they saw!

"Faith! Faith!" cried the husband, "look up to heaven, and resist the wicked one."

Whether Faith obeyed, he knew not. Hardly had he spoken when he found himself amid calm night and solitude, listening to a roar of the wind which died heavily away through the forest. He staggered against the rock, and felt it chill and damp; while a hanging twig, that had been all on fire, besprinkled his cheek with the coldest dew.

The next morning young Goodman Brown came slowly into the street of Salem village, staring around him like a bewildered man. The good old minister was taking a walk along the graveyard to get an appetite for breakfast and meditate his sermon, and bestowed a blessing, as he passed, on Goodman Brown. He shrank from the venerable saint as if to avoid an anathema. Old Deacon Gookin was at domestic worship, and the holy words of his prayer were heard through the open window. "What God doth the wizard pray to?" quoth Goodman Brown. Goody Cloyse, that excellent old Christian, stood in the early sunshine at her own lattice, catechizing a little girl who had brought her a pint of morning's milk. Goodman Brown snatched away the child as from the grasp of the fiend himself. Turning the corner by the meeting house, he spied the head of Faith, with the pink ribbons, gazing anxiously forth, and bursting into such joy at sight of him that she skipped along the street and almost kissed her husband before the whole village. But Goodman Brown looked sternly and sadly into her face, and passed on without a greeting.

Had Goodman Brown fallen asleep in the forest and only dreamed a wild dream of a witch meeting?

Be it so, if you will; but, alas! it was a dream of evil omen for young Goodman Brown. A stern, a sad, a darkly meditative, a distrustful, if not a desperate, man did he become from the night of that fearful dream. On the Sabbath day, when the congregation were singing a holy psalm, he could not listen, because an anthem of sin rushed loudly upon his ear and drowned all the blessed strain. When the minister spoke from the pulpit, with power and fervid eloquence and with his hand on the open Bible, of the sacred truths of our religion, and of saintlike lives and triumphant deaths, and of future bliss or misery unutterable, then did Goodman Brown turn pale, dreading lest the roof should thunder down upon the gray blasphemer and his hearers. Often, awaking suddenly at midnight, he shrank from the bosom of Faith; and at morning or eventide, when the family knelt down at prayer, he scowled, and muttered to himself, and gazed sternly at his wife, and turned away. And when he had lived long, and was borne to his grave, a hoary corpse, followed by Faith, an aged woman, and children and grandchildren, a goodly procession, besides neighbors not a few, they carved no hopeful verse upon his tombstone; for his dying hour was gloom.

RAPPACCINI'S DAUGHTER

[From the writings of Aubépine.[1]]

We do not remember to have seen any translated specimens of the productions of M. de l'Aubépine—a fact the less to be wondered at, as his very name is unknown to many of his own countrymen as well as to the student of foreign literature. As a writer, he seems to occupy an unfortunate position between the Transcendentalists[2] (who, under one name or another, have their share in all the current literature of the world) and the great body of pen-and-ink men who address the intellect and sympathies of the multitude. If not too refined, at all events too remote, too shadowy, and unsubstantial in his modes of development to suit the taste of the latter class, and yet too popular to satisfy the spiritual or metaphysical requisitions of the former, he must necessarily find himself without an audience, except here and there an individual or possibly an isolated clique. His writings, to do them justice, are not altogether destitute of fancy and originality; they might have won him greater reputation but for an inveterate love of allegory, which is apt to invest his plots and characters with the aspect of scenery and people in the clouds and to steal away the human warmth out of his conceptions. His fictions are sometimes historical, sometimes of the present day, and sometimes, so far as can be discovered, have little or no reference either to time or space. In any case, he generally contents himself with a very slight embroidery of outward manners,—the faintest possible counterfeit of real life,—and endeavors to create an interest by some less obvious peculiarity of the subject. Occasionally a breath of Nature, a raindrop of pathos and tenderness, or a gleam of humor will find its way into the midst of his fantastic imagery, and make us feel as if, after all, we were yet within the limits of our native earth. We will only add to this very cursory notice that M. de l'Aubépine's productions, if the reader chance to take them in precisely the proper point of view, may amuse a leisure hour as well as those of a brighter man; if otherwise, they can hardly fail to look excessively like nonsense.

Our author is voluminous; he continues to write and publish with as much praiseworthy and indefatigable prolixity as if his efforts were crowned with the brilliant success that so justly attends those of Eugene Sue.[3] His first appearance was by a collection of stories in a long series of volumes entitled *Contes deux fois racontées.*[4] The titles of some of his more recent works (we quote from memory) are as follows: *Le Voyage Céleste à Chemin de Fer,* 3 tom.,[5] 1838. *Le nouveau Père Adam et la nouvelle Mère Eve,*[6] 2 tom., 1839. *Roderic; ou le Serpent à l'estomac,*[7] 2 tom., 1840. *Le Culte du Feu,*[8] a folio volume of ponderous research into the religion and ritual of the old Persian Ghebers,[9] published in 1841. *La Soirée du Chateau en Espagne,*[10] 1 tom. 8vo.,[11] 1842; and *L'Artiste du Beau; ou le Papillon Mécanique,*[12] 5 tom. 4to.,[13] 1843. Our somewhat wearisome perusal of this startling catalogue of volumes has left behind it a certain personal affection and sympathy, though by no means admiration, for M. de l'Aubépine; and we would fain do the little in our power towards introducing him favorably to the American public. The ensuing tale is a translation of his *Beatrice; ou la Belle Empoisonneuse,*[14] recently published in *La Revue Anti-Aristocratique.*[15] This journal, edited by the Comte de Bearhaven,[16] has for some years past led the defence of liberal principles and popular rights with a faithfulness and ability worthy of all praise.

———

A young man, named Giovanni Guasconti, came, very long ago, from the more southern region of Italy, to pursue his studies at the University of Padua.[17] Giovanni, who had but a scanty supply of gold ducats in his pocket, took lodgings in a high and gloomy chamber of an old edifice which looked not unworthy to have been the palace of a Paduan noble, and which, in fact, exhibited over its entrance the armorial bearings of a family long since extinct. The young stranger, who was

not unstudied in the great poem of his country, recollected that one of
the ancestors of this family, and perhaps an occupant of this very mansion, had been pictured by Dante as a partaker of the immortal agonies
of his Inferno.[18] These reminiscences and associations, together with
the tendency to heartbreak natural to a young man for the first time
out of his native sphere, caused Giovanni to sigh heavily as he looked
around the desolate and ill-furnished apartment.

"Holy Virgin, signor!" cried old Dame Lisabetta, who, won by the
youth's remarkable beauty of person, was kindly endeavoring to give
the chamber a habitable air, "what a sigh was that to come out of a
young man's heart! Do you find this old mansion gloomy? For the love
of Heaven, then, put your head out of the window, and you will see as
bright sunshine as you have left in Naples."

Guasconti mechanically did as the old woman advised, but could
not quite agree with her that the Paduan sunshine was as cheerful as
that of southern Italy. Such as it was, however, it fell upon a garden beneath the window and expended its fostering influences on a variety of
plants, which seemed to have been cultivated with exceeding care.

"Does this garden belong to the house?" asked Giovanni.

"Heaven forbid, signor, unless it were fruitful of better pot herbs
than any that grow there now," answered old Lisabetta. "No; that garden is cultivated by the own hands of Signor Giacomo Rappaccini, the
famous doctor, who, I warrant him, has been heard of as far as Naples.
It is said that he distils these plants into medicines that are as potent as
a charm. Oftentimes you may see the signor doctor at work, and perchance the signora, his daughter, too, gathering the strange flowers that
grow in the garden."

The old woman had now done what she could for the aspect of the
chamber; and, commending the young man to the protection of
the saints, took her departure.

Giovanni still found no better occupation than to look down into
the garden beneath his window. From its appearance, he judged it to be
one of those botanic gardens which were of earlier date in Padua than
elsewhere in Italy or in the world. Or, not improbably, it might once
have been the pleasure-place of an opulent family; for there was the
ruin of a marble fountain in the centre, sculptured with rare art, but so
wofully shattered that it was impossible to trace the original design
from the chaos of remaining fragments. The water, however, contin-

ued to gush and sparkle into the sunbeams as cheerfully as ever. A little gurgling sound ascended to the young man's window and made
him feel as if the fountain were an immortal spirit, that sung its song
unceasingly and without heeding the vicissitudes around it, while one
century imbodied it in marble and another scattered the perishable
garniture[19] on the soil. All about the pool into which the water subsided grew various plants, that seemed to require a plentiful supply of
moisture for the nourishment of gigantic leaves, and, in some instances, flowers gorgeously magnificent. There was one shrub in particular, set in a marble vase in the midst of the pool, that bore a
profusion of purple blossoms, each of which had the lustre and richness of a gem; and the whole together made a show so resplendent that
it seemed enough to illuminate the garden, even had there been no
sunshine. Every portion of the soil was peopled with plants and herbs,
which, if less beautiful, still bore tokens of assiduous care, as if all had
their individual virtues, known to the scientific mind that fostered
them. Some were placed in urns, rich with old carving, and others in
common garden pots; some crept serpent-like along the ground or
climbed on high, using whatever means of ascent was offered them.
One plant had wreathed itself round a statue of Vertumnus,[20] which
was thus quite veiled and shrouded in a drapery of hanging foliage, so
happily arranged that it might have served a sculptor for a study.

While Giovanni stood at the window he heard a rustling behind a
screen of leaves, and became aware that a person was at work in the
garden. His figure soon emerged into view, and showed itself to be that
of no common laborer, but a tall, emaciated, sallow, and sickly-looking
man, dressed in a scholar's garb of black. He was beyond the middle
term of life, with gray hair, a thin, gray beard, and a face singularly
marked with intellect and cultivation, but which could never, even in
his more youthful days, have expressed much warmth of heart.

Nothing could exceed the intentness with which this scientific gardener examined every shrub which grew in his path: it seemed as if he
was looking into their inmost nature, making observations in regard to
their creative essence, and discovering why one leaf grew in this shape
and another in that, and wherefore such and such flowers differed
among themselves in hue and perfume. Nevertheless, in spite of this
deep intelligence on his part, there was no approach to intimacy between himself and these vegetable existences. On the contrary, he

avoided their actual touch or the direct inhaling of their odors with a caution that impressed Giovanni most disagreeably; for the man's demeanor was that of one walking among malignant influences, such as savage beasts, or deadly snakes, or evil spirits, which, should he allow them one moment of license, would wreak upon him some terrible fatality. It was strangely frightful to the young man's imagination to see this air of insecurity in a person cultivating a garden, that most simple and innocent of human toils, and which had been alike the joy and labor of the unfallen parents of the race. Was this garden, then, the Eden of the present world? And this man, with such a perception of harm in what his own hands caused to grow,—was he the Adam?

The distrustful gardener, while plucking away the dead leaves or pruning the too luxuriant growth of the shrubs, defended his hands with a pair of thick gloves. Nor were these his only armor. When, in his walk through the garden, he came to the magnificent plant that hung its purple gems beside the marble fountain, he placed a kind of mask over his mouth and nostrils, as if all this beauty did but conceal a deadlier malice; but, finding his task still too dangerous, he drew back, removed the mask, and called loudly, but in the infirm voice of a person affected with inward disease,—

"Beatrice! Beatrice!"

"Here am I, my father. What would you?" cried a rich and youthful voice from the window of the opposite house—a voice as rich as a tropical sunset, and which made Giovanni, though he knew not why, think of deep hues of purple or crimson and of perfumes heavily delectable. "Are you in the garden?"

"Yes, Beatrice," answered the gardener; "and I need your help."

Soon there emerged from under a sculptured portal the figure of a young girl, arrayed with as much richness of taste as the most splendid of the flowers, beautiful as the day, and with a bloom so deep and vivid that one shade more would have been too much. She looked redundant with life, health, and energy; all of which attributes were bound down and compressed, as it were, and girdled tensely, in their luxuriance, by her virgin zone.[21] Yet Giovanni's fancy must have grown morbid while he looked down into the garden; for the impression which the fair stranger made upon him was as if here were another flower, the human sister of those vegetable ones, as beautiful as they, more beautiful than the richest of them, but still to be touched only with a glove, nor to be approached without a mask. As Beatrice came down the garden path, it was observable that she handled and inhaled the odor of several of the plants which her father had most sedulously avoided.

"Here, Beatrice," said the latter, "see how many needful offices require to be done to our chief treasure. Yet, shattered as I am, my life might pay the penalty of approaching it so closely as circumstances demand. Henceforth, I fear, this plant must be consigned to your sole charge."

"And gladly will I undertake it," cried again the rich tones of the young lady, as she bent towards the magnificent plant and opened her arms as if to embrace it. "Yes, my sister, my splendor, it shall be Beatrice's task to nurse and serve thee; and thou shalt reward her with thy kisses and perfumed breath, which to her is as the breath of life."

Then, with all the tenderness in her manner that was so strikingly expressed in her words, she busied herself with such attentions as the plant seemed to require; and Giovanni, at his lofty window, rubbed his eyes, and almost doubted whether it were a girl tending her favorite flower, or one sister performing the duties of affection to another. The scene soon terminated. Whether Dr. Rappaccini had finished his labors in the garden, or that his watchful eye had caught the stranger's face, he now took his daughter's arm and retired. Night was already closing in; oppressive exhalations seemed to proceed from the plants and steal upward past the open window; and Giovanni, closing the lattice, went to his couch and dreamed of a rich flower and beautiful girl. Flower and maiden were different, and yet the same, and fraught with some strange peril in either shape.

But there is an influence in the light of morning that tends to rectify whatever errors of fancy, or even of judgment, we may have incurred during the sun's decline, or among the shadows of the night, or in the less wholesome glow of moonshine. Giovanni's first movement, on starting from sleep, was to throw open the window and gaze down into the garden which his dreams had made so fertile of mysteries. He was surprised, and a little ashamed, to find how real and matter-of-fact an affair it proved to be, in the first rays of the sun which gilded the dewdrops that hung upon leaf and blossom, and, while giving a brighter beauty to each rare flower, brought every thing within the limits of ordinary experience. The young man rejoiced that, in the heart of the barren city, he had the privilege of overlooking this spot of lovely and luxuriant vegetation. It would serve, he said to himself, as a symbolic language to keep him in communion with Nature. Neither the sickly and thoughtworn Dr. Giacomo Rappaccini, it is true, nor his brilliant daughter, were now visible; so that Giovanni could not determine how much of the singularity which he attributed to both was due to their own qualities and how much to his wonder-working fancy; but he was inclined to take a most rational view of the whole matter.

In the course of the day he paid his respects to Signor Pietro Baglioni, professor of medicine in the university, a physician of eminent repute, to whom Giovanni had brought a letter of introduction. The professor was an elderly personage, apparently of genial nature and habits that might almost be called jovial. He kept the young man to dinner, and made himself very agreeable by the freedom and liveliness of his conversation, especially when warmed by a flask or two of Tuscan wine. Giovanni, conceiving that men of science, inhabitants of the same city, must needs be on familiar terms with one another, took an opportunity to mention the name of Dr. Rappaccini. But the professor did not respond with so much cordiality as he had anticipated.

"Ill would it become a teacher of the divine art of medicine," said Professor Pietro Baglioni, in answer to a question of Giovanni, "to withhold due and well-considered praise of a physician so eminently skilled as Rappaccini; but, on the other hand, I should answer it but scantily to my conscience were I to permit a worthy youth like yourself, Signor Giovanni, the son of an ancient friend, to imbibe erroneous ideas respecting a man who might hereafter chance to hold your life and death in his hands. The truth is, our worshipful Dr. Rappaccini has as much science as any member of the faculty—with perhaps one single exception—in Padua, or all Italy; but there are certain grave objections to his professional character."

"And what are they?" asked the young man.

"Has my friend Giovanni any disease of body or heart, that he is so inquisitive about physicians?" said the professor, with a smile. "But as for Rappaccini, it is said of him—and I, who know the man well, can answer for its truth—that he cares infinitely more for science than for mankind. His patients are interesting to him only as subjects for some new experiment. He would sacrifice human life, his own among the rest, or whatever else was dearest to him, for the sake of adding so much as a grain of mustard seed to the great heap of his accumulated knowledge."

"Methinks he is an awful man indeed," remarked Guasconti, mentally recalling the cold and purely intellectual aspect of Rappaccini. "And yet, worshipful professor, is it not a noble spirit? Are there many men capable of so spiritual a love of science?"

"God forbid," answered the professor, somewhat testily; "at least, unless they take sounder views of the healing art than those adopted by Rappaccini. It is his theory that all medicinal virtues are comprised within those substances which we term vegetable poisons. These he cultivates with his own hands, and is said even to have produced new varieties of poison, more horribly deleterious than Nature, without the assistance of this learned person, would ever have plagued the world withal. That the signor doctor does less mischief than might be expected with such dangerous substances, is undeniable. Now and then, it must be owned, he has effected, or seemed to effect, a marvellous cure; but, to tell you my private mind, Signor Giovanni, he should receive little credit for such instances of success,—they being probably the work of chance,—but should be held strictly accountable for his failures, which may justly be considered his own work."

The youth might have taken Baglioni's opinions with many grains of allowance had he known that there was a professional warfare of long continuance between him and Dr. Rappaccini, in which the latter was generally thought to have gained the advantage. If the reader be inclined to judge for himself, we refer him to certain black-letter[22] tracts on both sides, preserved in the medical department of the University of Padua.

"I know not, most learned professor," returned Giovanni, after musing on what had been said of Rappaccini's exclusive zeal for science,— "I know not how dearly this physician may love his art; but surely there is one object more dear to him. He has a daughter."

"Aha!" cried the professor, with a laugh. "So now our friend Giovanni's secret is out. You have heard of this daughter, whom all the young men in Padua are wild about, though not half a dozen have ever had the good hap to see her face. I know little of the Signora Beatrice save that Rappaccini is said to have instructed her deeply in his science, and that, young and beautiful as fame reports her, she is already qualified to fill a professor's chair. Perchance her father destines her for mine! Other absurd rumors there be, not worth talking about or listening to. So now, Signor Giovanni, drink off your glass of lachryma."[23]

Guasconti returned to his lodgings somewhat heated with the wine he had quaffed, and which caused his brain to swim with strange fantasies in reference to Dr. Rappaccini and the beautiful Beatrice. On his way, happening to pass by a florist's, he bought a fresh bouquet of flowers.

Ascending to his chamber, he seated himself near the window, but within the shadow thrown by the depth of the wall, so that he could look down into the garden with little risk of being discovered. All beneath his eye was a solitude. The strange plants were basking in the sunshine, and now and then nodding gently to one another, as if in acknowledgment of sympathy and kindred. In the midst, by the shattered fountain, grew the magnificent shrub, with its purple gems clustering all over it; they glowed in the air, and gleamed back again out of the depths of the pool, which thus seemed to overflow with colored radiance from the rich reflection that was steeped in it. At first, as we have said, the garden was a solitude. Soon, however,—as Giovanni had half hoped, half feared, would be the case,—a figure appeared beneath the antique sculptured portal, and came down between the rows of plants, inhaling their various perfumes as if she were one of those beings of old classic fable that lived upon sweet odors. On again beholding Beatrice, the young man was even startled to perceive how much her beauty exceeded his recollection of it; so brilliant, so vivid, was its character, that she glowed amid the sunlight, and, as Giovanni whispered to himself, positively illuminated the more shadowy intervals of the garden path. Her face being now more revealed than on the former occasion, he was struck by its expression of simplicity and sweetness— qualities that had not entered into his idea of her character, and which made him ask anew what manner of mortal she might be. Nor did he fail again to observe, or imagine, an analogy between the beautiful girl and the gorgeous shrub that hung its gemlike flowers over the fountain—a resemblance which Beatrice seemed to have indulged a fantastic humor in heightening, both by the arrangement of her dress and the selection of its hues.

Approaching the shrub, she threw open her arms, as with a passionate ardor, and drew its branches into an intimate embrace—so intimate that her features were hidden in its leafy bosom and her glistening ringlets all intermingled with the flowers.

"Give me thy breath, my sister," exclaimed Beatrice; "for I am faint with common air. And give me this flower of thine, which I separate with gentlest fingers from the stem and place it close beside my heart."

With these words the beautiful daughter of Rappaccini plucked one of the richest blossoms of the shrub, and was about to fasten it in her bosom. But now, unless Giovanni's draughts of wine had bewildered his senses, a singular incident occurred. A small orange-colored reptile, of the lizard or chameleon species, chanced to be creeping along the path, just at the feet of Beatrice. It appeared to Giovanni,—but, at the distance from which he gazed, he could scarcely have seen any thing so minute,—it appeared to him, however, that a drop or two of moisture from the broken stem of the flower descended upon the lizard's head. For an instant the reptile contorted itself violently, and then lay motionless in the sunshine. Beatrice observed this remarkable phenomenon, and crossed herself, sadly, but without surprise; nor did she therefore hesitate to arrange the fatal flower in her bosom. There it blushed, and almost glimmered with the dazzling effect of a precious stone, adding to her dress and aspect the one appropriate charm which nothing else in the world could have supplied. But Giovanni, out of the shadow of his window, bent forward and shrank back, and murmured and trembled.

"Am I awake? Have I my senses?" said he to himself. "What is this being? Beautiful shall I call her, or inexpressibly terrible?"

Beatrice now strayed carelessly through the garden, approaching closer beneath Giovanni's window, so that he was compelled to thrust his head quite out of its concealment in order to gratify the intense and painful curiosity which she excited. At this moment there came a beautiful insect over the garden wall: it had, perhaps, wandered through the city, and found no flowers or verdure among those antique haunts of men until the heavy perfumes of Dr. Rappaccini's shrubs had lured it from afar. Without alighting on the flowers, this winged brightness seemed to be attracted by Beatrice, and lingered in the air and fluttered about her head. Now, here it could not be but that Giovanni Guasconti's eyes deceived him. Be that as it might, he fancied that, while Beatrice was gazing at the insect with childish delight, it grew faint and fell at her feet; its bright wings shivered; it was dead—from no cause that he could discern, unless it were the atmosphere of her breath. Again Beatrice crossed herself and sighed heavily as she bent over the dead insect.

An impulsive movement of Giovanni drew her eyes to the window. There she beheld the beautiful head of the young man—rather a Grecian than an Italian head, with fair, regular features, and a glistening of gold among his ringlets—gazing down upon her like a being that hovered in mid air. Scarcely knowing what he did, Giovanni threw down the bouquet which he had hitherto held in his hand.

"Signora," said he, "there are pure and healthful flowers. Wear them for the sake of Giovanni Guasconti."

"Thanks, signor," replied Beatrice, with her rich voice, that came forth as it were like a gush of music, and with a mirthful expression half childish and half womanlike. "I accept your gift, and would fain recompense it with this precious purple flower; but, if I toss it into the air, it will not reach you. So Signor Guasconti must even content himself with my thanks."

She lifted the bouquet from the ground, and then, as if inwardly ashamed at having stepped aside from her maidenly reserve to respond to a stranger's greeting, passed swiftly homeward through the garden. But, few as the moments were, it seemed to Giovanni, when she was on the point of vanishing beneath the sculptured portal, that his beautiful bouquet was already beginning to wither in her grasp. It was an idle thought; there could be no possibility of distinguishing a faded flower from a fresh one at so great a distance.

For many days after this incident the young man avoided the window that looked into Dr. Rappaccini's garden, as if something ugly and monstrous would have blasted his eyesight had he been betrayed into a glance. He felt conscious of having put himself, to a certain extent, within the influence of an unintelligible power by the communication which he had opened with Beatrice. The wisest course would have been, if his heart were in any real danger, to quit his lodgings and Padua itself at once; the next wiser, to have accustomed himself, as far as possible, to the familiar and daylight view of Beatrice—thus bringing her rigidly and systematically within the limits of ordinary experience. Least of all, while avoiding her sight, ought Giovanni to have remained so near this extraordinary being that the proximity and possibility even of intercourse should give a kind of substance and reality to the wild vagaries which his imagination ran riot continually in producing. Guasconti had not a deep heart—or, at all events, its depths were not sounded now; but he had a quick fancy, and an ardent southern temperament, which rose every instant to a higher fever pitch. Whether or no Beatrice possessed those terrible attributes, that fatal breath, the affinity with those so beautiful and deadly flowers which were indicated by what Giovanni had witnessed, she had at least instilled a fierce and subtle poison into his system. It was not love, although her rich beauty was a madness to him; nor horror, even while he fancied her spirit to be imbued with the same baneful essence that seemed to pervade her physical frame; but a wild offspring of both love and horror that had each parent in it, and burned like one and shivered like the other. Giovanni knew not what to dread; still less did he know what to hope; yet hope and dread kept a continual warfare in his breast, alternately vanquishing one another and starting up afresh to renew the contest. Blessed are all simple emotions, be they dark or bright! It is the lurid intermixture of the two that produces the illuminating blaze of the infernal regions.

Sometimes he endeavored to assuage the fever of his spirit by a rapid walk through the streets of Padua or beyond its gates: his footsteps kept time with the throbbings of his brain, so that the walk was apt to accelerate itself to a race. One day he found himself arrested; his arm was seized by a portly personage, who had turned back on recognizing the young man and expended much breath in overtaking him.

"Signor Giovanni! Stay, my young friend!" cried he. "Have you forgotten me? That might well be the case if I were as much altered as yourself."

It was Baglioni, whom Giovanni had avoided ever since their first meeting, from a doubt that the professor's sagacity would look too deeply into his secrets. Endeavoring to recover himself, he stared forth wildly from his inner world into the outer one and spoke like a man in a dream.

"Yes; I am Giovanni Guasconti. You are Professor Pietro Baglioni. Now let me pass!"

"Not yet, not yet, Signor Giovanni Guasconti," said the professor, smiling, but at the same time scrutinizing the youth with an earnest glance. "What! did I grow up side by side with your father? and shall his son pass me like a stranger in these old streets of Padua? Stand still, Signor Giovanni; for we must have a word or two before we part."

"Speedily, then, most worshipful professor, speedily," said Giovanni, with feverish impatience. "Does not your worship see that I am in haste?"

Now, while he was speaking there came a man in black along the street, stooping and moving feebly like a person in inferior health. His face was all overspread with a most sickly and sallow hue, but yet so pervaded with an expression of piercing and active intellect that an observer might easily have overlooked the merely physical attributes and have seen only this wonderful energy. As he passed, this person exchanged a cold and distant salutation with Baglioni, but fixed his eyes upon Giovanni with an intentness that seemed to bring out whatever was within him worthy of notice. Nevertheless, there was a peculiar quietness in the look, as if taking merely a speculative, not a human, interest in the young man.

"It is Dr. Rappaccini!" whispered the professor when the stranger had passed. "Has he ever seen your face before?"

"Not that I know," answered Giovanni, starting at the name.

"He *has* seen you! he must have seen you!" said Baglioni, hastily. "For some purpose or other, this man of science is making a study of you. I know that look of his! It is the same that coldly illuminates his face as he bends over a bird, a mouse, or a butterfly; which, in pursuance of some experiment, he has killed by the perfume of a flower; a look as deep as Nature itself, but without Nature's warmth of love. Signor Giovanni, I will stake my life upon it, you are the subject of one of Rappaccini's experiments!"

"Will you make a fool of me?" cried Giovanni, passionately. "*That,* signor professor, were an untoward experiment."

"Patience! patience!" replied the imperturbable professor. "I tell thee, my poor Giovanni, that Rappaccini has a scientific interest in thee. Thou hast fallen into fearful hands! And the Signora Beatrice,—what part does she act in this mystery?"

But Guasconti, finding Baglioni's pertinacity intolerable, here broke away, and was gone before the professor could again seize his arm. He looked after the young man intently and shook his head.

"This must not be," said Baglioni to himself. "The youth is the son of my old friend, and shall not come to any harm from which the arcana[24] of medical science can preserve him. Besides, it is too insufferable an impertinence in Rappaccini thus to snatch the lad out of my own hands, as I may say, and make use of him for his infernal experiments. This daughter of his! It shall be looked to. Perchance, most learned Rappaccini, I may foil you where you little dream of it!"

Meanwhile Giovanni had pursued a circuitous route, and at length found himself at the door of his lodgings. As he crossed the threshold he was met by old Lisabetta, who smirked and smiled, and was evidently desirous to attract his attention; vainly, however, as the ebullition of his feelings had momentarily subsided into a cold and dull vacuity. He turned his eyes full upon the withered face that was puckering itself into a smile, but seemed to behold it not. The old dame, therefore, laid her grasp upon his cloak.

"Signor! signor!" whispered she, still with a smile over the whole breadth of her visage, so that it looked not unlike a grotesque carving in wood, darkened by centuries. "Listen, signor! There is a private entrance into the garden!"

"What do you say?" exclaimed Giovanni, turning quickly about, as if an inanimate thing should start into feverish life. "A private entrance into Dr. Rappaccini's garden?"

"Hush! hush! not so loud!" whispered Lisabetta, putting her hand over his mouth. "Yes; into the worshipful doctor's garden, where you may see all his fine shrubbery. Many a young man in Padua would give gold to be admitted among those flowers."

Giovanni put a piece of gold into her hand.

"Show me the way," said he.

A surmise, probably excited by his conversation with Baglioni, crossed his mind, that this interposition of old Lisabetta might perchance be connected with the intrigue, whatever were its nature, in which the professor seemed to suppose that Dr. Rappaccini was involving him. But such a suspicion, though it disturbed Giovanni, was inadequate to restrain him. The instant that he was aware of the possibility of approaching Beatrice, it seemed an absolute necessity of his existence to do so. It mattered not whether she were angel or demon; he was irrevocably within her sphere, and must obey the law that whirled him onward, in ever-lessening circles, towards a result which he did not attempt to foreshadow; and yet, strange to say, there came across him a sudden doubt whether this intense interest on his part were not delusory; whether it were really of so deep and positive a nature as to justify him in now thrusting himself into an incalculable position; whether it were not merely the fantasy of a young man's brain, only slightly or not at all connected with his heart.

He paused, hesitated, turned half about, but again went on. His withered guide led him along several obscure passages, and finally undid a door, through which, as it was opened, there came the sight and sound of rustling leaves, with the broken sunshine glimmering among them. Giovanni stepped forth, and, forcing himself through the entanglement of a shrub that wreathed its tendrils over the hidden entrance, stood beneath his own window in the open area of Dr. Rappaccini's garden.

How often is it the case that, when impossibilities have come to pass and dreams have condensed their misty substance into tangible realities, we find ourselves calm, and even coldly self-possessed, amid circumstances which it would have been a delirium of joy or agony to anticipate! Fate delights to thwart us thus. Passion will choose his own time to rush upon the scene, and lingers sluggishly behind when an appropriate adjustment of events would seem to summon his appearance. So was it now with Giovanni. Day after day his pulses had throbbed with feverish blood at the improbable idea of an interview with Beatrice, and of standing with her, face to face, in this very garden, basking in the Oriental sunshine of her beauty, and snatching from her full gaze the mystery which he deemed the riddle of his own existence. But now there was a singular and untimely equanimity within his breast. He threw a glance around the garden to discover if Beatrice or her father were present, and, perceiving that he was alone, began a critical observation of the plants.

The aspect of one and all of them dissatisfied him; their gorgeousness seemed fierce, passionate, and even unnatural. There was hardly an individual shrub which a wanderer, straying by himself through a forest, would not have been startled to find growing wild, as if an unearthly face had glared at him out of the thicket. Several also would have shocked a delicate instinct by an appearance of artificialness indicating that there had been such commixture, and, as it were, adultery of various vegetable species, that the production was no longer of God's making, but the monstrous offspring of man's depraved fancy, glowing with only an evil mockery of beauty. They were probably the result of experiment, which in one or two cases had succeeded in mingling plants individually lovely into a compound possessing the questionable and ominous character that distinguished the whole growth of the garden. In fine, Giovanni recognized but two or three plants in the collection, and those of a kind that he well knew to be poisonous. While busy with these contemplations he heard the rustling of a silken garment, and, turning, beheld Beatrice emerging from beneath the sculptured portal.

Giovanni had not considered with himself what should be his deportment; whether he should apologize for his intrusion into the garden, or assume that he was there with the privity[25] at least, if not by the desire, of Dr. Rappaccini or his daughter; but Beatrice's manner placed him at his ease, though leaving him still in doubt by what agency he had gained admittance. She came lightly along the path and met him near the broken fountain. There was surprise in her face, but brightened by a simple and kind expression of pleasure.

"You are a connoisseur in flowers, signor," said Beatrice, with a smile, alluding to the bouquet which he had flung her from the window. "It is no marvel, therefore, if the sight of my father's rare collection has tempted you to take a nearer view. If he were here, he could tell you many strange and interesting facts as to the nature and habits of these shrubs; for he has spent a lifetime in such studies, and this garden is his world."

"And yourself, lady," observed Giovanni, "if fame says true,—you likewise are deeply skilled in the virtues indicated by these rich blossoms and these spicy perfumes. Would you deign to be my instructress, I should prove an apter scholar than if taught by Signor Rappaccini himself."

"Are there such idle rumors?" asked Beatrice, with the music of a pleasant laugh. "Do people say that I am skilled in my father's science of plants? What a jest is there! No; though I have grown up among these flowers, I know no more of them than their hues and perfume; and sometimes methinks I would fain rid myself of even that small knowledge. There are many flowers here, and those not the least brilliant, that shock and offend me when they meet my eye. But pray, signor, do not believe these stories about my science. Believe nothing of me save what you see with your own eyes."

"And must I believe all that I have seen with my own eyes?" asked Giovanni, pointedly, while the recollection of former scenes made him shrink. "No, signora; you demand too little of me. Bid me believe nothing save what comes from your own lips."

It would appear that Beatrice understood him. There came a deep flush to her cheek; but she looked full into Giovanni's eyes, and responded to his gaze of uneasy suspicion with a queenlike haughtiness.

"I do so bid you, signor," she replied. "Forget whatever you may have fancied in regard to me. If true to the outward senses, still it may be false in its essence; but the words of Beatrice Rappaccini's lips are true from the depths of the heart outward. Those you may believe."

A fervor glowed in her whole aspect and beamed upon Giovanni's consciousness like the light of truth itself; but while she spoke there was a fragrance in the atmosphere around her, rich and delightful, though evanescent, yet which the young man, from an indefinable reluctance, scarcely dared to draw into his lungs. It might be the odor of the flowers. Could it be Beatrice's breath which thus embalmed her words with a strange richness, as if by steeping them in her heart? A faintness passed like a shadow over Giovanni and flitted away; he seemed to gaze through the beautiful girl's eyes into her transparent soul, and felt no more doubt or fear.

The tinge of passion that had colored Beatrice's manner vanished; she became gay, and appeared to derive a pure delight from her communion with the youth not unlike what the maiden of a lonely island might have felt conversing with a voyager from the civilized world. Evidently her experience of life had been confined within the limits of that garden. She talked now about matters as simple as the daylight or summer clouds, and now asked questions in reference to the city, or Giovanni's distant home, his friends, his mother, and his sisters—questions indicating such seclusion, and such lack of familiarity with modes and forms, that Giovanni responded as if to an infant. Her spirit gushed out before him like a fresh rill that was just catching its first glimpse of the sunlight and wondering at the reflections of earth and sky which were flung into its bosom. There came thoughts, too, from a deep source, and fantasies of a gemlike brilliancy, as if diamonds and rubies sparkled upward among the bubbles of the fountain. Ever and anon there gleamed across the young man's mind a sense of wonder that he should be walking side by side with the being who had so wrought upon his imagination, whom he had idealized in such hues of terror, in whom he had positively witnessed such manifestations of dreadful attributes—that he should be conversing with Beatrice like a brother, and should find her so human and so maidenlike. But such reflections were only momentary; the effect of her character was too real not to make itself familiar at once.

In this free intercourse they had strayed through the garden, and now, after many turns among its avenues, were come to the shattered fountain, beside which grew the magnificent shrub, with its treasury of glowing blossoms. A fragrance was diffused from it which Giovanni recognized as identical with that which he had attributed to Beatrice's breath, but incomparably more powerful. As her eyes fell upon it, Giovanni beheld her press her hand to her bosom as if her heart were throbbing suddenly and painfully.

"For the first time in my life," murmured she, addressing the shrub, "I had forgotten thee."

"I remember, signora," said Giovanni, "that you once promised to reward me with one of these living gems for the bouquet which I had the happy boldness to fling at your feet. Permit me now to pluck it as a memorial of this interview."

He made a step towards the shrub with extended hand; but Beatrice darted forward, uttering a shriek that went through his heart like a dagger. She caught his hand and drew it back with the whole force of her slender figure. Giovanni felt her touch thrilling through his fibres.

"Touch it not!" exclaimed she, in a voice of agony. "Not for thy life! It is fatal!"

Then, hiding her face, she fled from him and vanished beneath the sculptured portal. As Giovanni followed her with his eyes, he beheld the emaciated figure and pale intelligence of Dr. Rappaccini, who had been watching the scene, he knew not how long, within the shadow of the entrance.

No sooner was Guasconti alone in his chamber than the image of Beatrice came back to his passionate musings, invested with all the witchery that had been gathering around it ever since his first glimpse of her, and now likewise imbued with a tender warmth of girlish womanhood. She was human; her nature was endowed with all gentle and feminine qualities; she was worthiest to be worshipped; she was capable, surely, on her part, of the height and heroism of love. Those

tokens which he had hitherto considered as proofs of a frightful peculiarity in her physical and moral system were now either forgotten or
by the subtle sophistry of passion transmitted into a golden crown of
enchantment, rendering Beatrice the more admirable by so much as
she was the more unique. Whatever had looked ugly was now beautiful; or, if incapable of such a change, it stole away and hid itself among
those shapeless half ideas which throng the dim region beyond the
daylight of our perfect consciousness. Thus did he spend the night,
nor fell asleep until the dawn had begun to awake the slumbering flowers in Dr. Rappaccini's garden, whither Giovanni's dreams doubtless
led him. Up rose the sun in his due season, and, flinging his beams
upon the young man's eyelids, awoke him to a sense of pain. When
thoroughly aroused, he became sensible of a burning and tingling agony
in his hand—in his right hand—the very hand which Beatrice had
grasped in her own when he was on the point of plucking one of the
gemlike flowers. On the back of that hand there was now a purple print
like that of four small fingers, and the likeness of a slender thumb upon
his wrist.

O, how stubbornly does love,—or even that cunning semblance of
love which flourishes in the imagination, but strikes no depth of root
into the heart,—how stubbornly does it hold its faith until the moment
comes when it is doomed to vanish into thin mist! Giovanni wrapped a
handkerchief about his hand and wondered what evil thing had stung
him, and soon forgot his pain in a revery of Beatrice.

After the first interview, a second was in the inevitable course of
what we call fate. A third; a fourth; and a meeting with Beatrice in the
garden was no longer an incident in Giovanni's daily life, but the whole
space in which he might be said to live; for the anticipation and memory
of that ecstatic hour made up the remainder. Nor was it otherwise with
the daughter of Rappaccini. She watched for the youth's appearance
and flew to his side with confidence as unreserved as if they had been
playmates from early infancy—as if they were such playmates still. If,
by any unwonted chance, he failed to come at the appointed moment,
she stood beneath the window and sent up the rich sweetness of her
tones to float around him in his chamber and echo and reverberate
throughout his heart: "Giovanni! Giovanni! Why tarriest thou? Come
down!" And down he hastened into that Eden of poisonous flowers.

But, with all this intimate familiarity, there was still a reserve in

Beatrice's demeanor, so rigidly and invariably sustained that the idea of infringing it scarcely occurred to his imagination. By all appreciable signs, they loved; they had looked love with eyes that conveyed the holy secret from the depths of one soul into the depths of the other, as if it were too sacred to be whispered by the way; they had even spoken love in those gushes of passion when their spirits darted forth in articulated breath like tongues of long hidden flame; and yet there had been no seal of lips, no clasp of hands, nor any slightest caress such as love claims and hallows. He had never touched one of the gleaming ringlets of her hair; her garment—so marked was the physical barrier between them—had never been waved against him by a breeze. On the few occasions when Giovanni had seemed tempted to overstep the limit, Beatrice grew so sad, so stern, and withal wore such a look of desolate separation, shuddering at itself, that not a spoken word was requisite to repel him. At such times he was startled at the horrible suspicions that rose, monsterlike, out of the caverns of his heart and stared him in the face; his love grew thin and faint as the morning mist; his doubts alone had substance. But, when Beatrice's face brightened again after the momentary shadow, she was transformed at once from the mysterious, questionable being whom he had watched with so much awe and horror; she was now the beautiful and unsophisticated girl whom he felt that his spirit knew with a certainty beyond all other knowledge.

A considerable time had now passed since Giovanni's last meeting with Baglioni. One morning, however, he was disagreeably surprised by a visit from the professor, whom he had scarcely thought of for whole weeks, and would willingly have forgotten still longer. Given up as he had long been to a pervading excitement, he could tolerate no companions except upon condition of their perfect sympathy with his present state of feeling. Such sympathy was not to be expected from Professor Baglioni.

The visitor chatted carelessly for a few moments about the gossip of the city and the university, and then took up another topic.

"I have been reading an old classic author lately," said he, "and met with a story that strangely interested me. Possibly you may remember it. It is of an Indian prince, who sent a beautiful woman as a present to Alexander the Great.[26] She was as lovely as the dawn and gorgeous as the sunset; but what especially distinguished her was a certain rich perfume in her breath—richer than a garden of Persian roses. Alexander, as was natural to a youthful conqueror, fell in love at first sight with this magnificent stranger; but a certain sage physician, happening to be present, discovered a terrible secret in regard to her."

"And what was that?" asked Giovanni, turning his eyes downward to avoid those of the professor.

"That this lovely woman," continued Baglioni, with emphasis, "had been nourished with poisons from her birth upward, until her whole nature was so imbued with them that she herself had become the deadliest poison in existence. Poison was her element of life. With that rich perfume of her breath she blasted the very air. Her love would have been poison—her embrace death. Is not this a marvellous tale?"

"A childish fable," answered Giovanni, nervously starting from his chair. "I marvel how your worship finds time to read such nonsense among your graver studies."

"By the by," said the professor, looking uneasily about him, "what singular fragrance is this in your apartment? Is it the perfume of your gloves? It is faint, but delicious; and yet, after all, by no means agreeable. Were I to breathe it long, methinks it would make me ill. It is like the breath of a flower; but I see no flowers in the chamber."

"Nor are there any," replied Giovanni, who had turned pale as the professor spoke; "nor, I think, is there any fragrance except in your worship's imagination. Odors, being a sort of element combined of the sensual and the spiritual, are apt to deceive us in this manner. The recollection of a perfume, the bare idea of it, may easily be mistaken for a present reality."

"Ay; but my sober imagination does not often play such tricks," said Baglioni; "and, were I to fancy any kind of odor, it would be that of some vile apothecary drug, wherewith my fingers are likely enough to be imbued. Our worshipful friend Rappaccini, as I have heard, tinctures his medicaments with odors richer than those of Araby.[27] Doubtless, likewise, the fair and learned Signora Beatrice would minister to her patients with draughts as sweet as a maiden's breath; but woe to him that sips them!"

Giovanni's face evinced many contending emotions. The tone in which the professor alluded to the pure and lovely daughter of Rappaccini was a torture to his soul; and yet the intimation of a view of her character, opposite to his own, gave instantaneous distinctness to a thousand dim suspicions, which now grinned at him like so many demons. But he strove hard to quell them and to respond to Baglioni with a true lover's perfect faith.

"Signor professor," said he, "you were my father's friend; perchance, too, it is your purpose to act a friendly part towards his son. I would fain feel nothing towards you save respect and deference; but I pray you to observe, signor, that there is one subject on which we must not speak. You know not the Signora Beatrice. You cannot, therefore, estimate the wrong—the blasphemy, I may even say—that is offered to her character by a light or injurious word."

"Giovanni! my poor Giovanni!" answered the professor, with a calm expression of pity, "I know this wretched girl far better than yourself. You shall hear the truth in respect to the poisoner Rappaccini and his poisonous daughter; yes, poisonous as she is beautiful. Listen; for, even should you do violence to my gray hairs, it shall not silence me. That old fable of the Indian woman has become a truth by the deep and deadly science of Rappaccini and in the person of the lovely Beatrice."

Giovanni groaned and hid his face.

"Her father," continued Baglioni, "was not restrained by natural affection from offering up his child in this horrible manner as the victim of his insane zeal for science; for, let us do him justice, he is as true a man of science as ever distilled his own heart in an alembic.[28] What, then, will be your fate? Beyond a doubt you are selected as the material of some new experiment. Perhaps the result is to be death; perhaps a fate more awful still. Rappaccini, with what he calls the interest of science before his eyes, will hesitate at nothing."

"It is a dream," muttered Giovanni to himself; "surely it is a dream."

"But," resumed the professor, "be of good cheer, son of my friend. It is not yet too late for the rescue. Possibly we may even succeed in bringing back this miserable child within the limits of ordinary nature, from which her father's madness has estranged her. Behold this little silver vase! It was wrought by the hands of the renowned Benvenuto Cellini,[29] and is well worthy to be a love gift to the fairest dame in Italy. But its contents are invaluable. One little sip of this antidote would have rendered the most virulent poisons of the Borgias[30] innocuous. Doubt not that it will be as efficacious against those of Rappaccini. Bestow the vase, and the precious liquid within it, on your Beatrice, and hopefully await the result."

Baglioni laid a small, exquisitely wrought silver vial on the table and withdrew, leaving what he had said to produce its effect upon the young man's mind.

"We will thwart Rappaccini yet," thought he, chuckling to himself, as he descended the stairs; "but, let us confess the truth of him, he is a wonderful man—a wonderful man indeed; a vile empiric,[31] however, in his practice, and therefore not to be tolerated by those who respect the good old rules of the medical profession."

Throughout Giovanni's whole acquaintance with Beatrice, he had occasionally, as we have said, been haunted by dark surmises as to her character; yet so thoroughly had she made herself felt by him as a simple, natural, most affectionate, and guileless creature, that the image now held up by Professor Baglioni looked as strange and incredible as if it were not in accordance with his own original conception. True, there were ugly recollections connected with his first glimpses of the beautiful girl; he could not quite forget the bouquet that withered in her grasp, and the insect that perished amid the sunny air, by no ostensible agency save the fragrance of her breath. These incidents, however, dissolving in the pure light of her character, had no longer the efficacy of facts, but were acknowledged as mistaken fantasies, by whatever testimony of the senses they might appear to be substantiated. There is something truer and more real than what we can see with the eyes and touch with the finger. On such better evidence had Giovanni founded his confidence in Beatrice, though rather by the necessary force of her high attributes than by any deep and generous faith on his part. But now his spirit was incapable of sustaining itself at the height to which the early enthusiasm of passion had exalted it; he fell down, grovelling among earthly doubts, and defiled therewith the pure whiteness of Beatrice's image. Not that he gave her up; he did but distrust. He resolved to institute some decisive test that should satisfy him, once for all, whether there were those dreadful peculiarities in her physical nature which could not be supposed to exist without some corresponding monstrosity of soul. His eyes, gazing down afar, might have deceived him as to the lizard, the insect, and the flowers; but if he could witness, at the distance of a few paces, the sudden blight of one fresh and healthful flower in Beatrice's hand, there would be room for no further question. With this idea he hastened to the florist's and purchased a bouquet that was still gemmed with the morning dewdrops.

It was now the customary hour of his daily interview with Beatrice. Before descending into the garden, Giovanni failed not to look at his figure in the mirror—a vanity to be expected in a beautiful young man, yet, as displaying itself at that troubled and feverish moment, the token of a certain shallowness of feeling and insincerity of character. He did gaze, however, and said to himself that his features had never before possessed so rich a grace, nor his eyes such vivacity, nor his cheeks so warm a hue of superabundant life.

"At least," thought he, "her poison has not yet insinuated itself into my system. I am no flower to perish in her grasp."

With that thought he turned his eyes on the bouquet, which he had never once laid aside from his hand. A thrill of indefinable horror shot through his frame on perceiving that those dewy flowers were already beginning to droop; they wore the aspect of things that had been fresh and lovely yesterday. Giovanni grew white as marble, and stood motionless before the mirror, staring at his own reflection there as at the likeness of something frightful. He remembered Baglioni's remark about the fragrance that seemed to pervade the chamber. It must have been the poison in his breath! Then he shuddered—shuddered at himself. Recovering from his stupor, he began to watch with curious eye a spider that was busily at work hanging its web from the antique cornice of the apartment, crossing and recrossing the artful system of interwoven lines—as vigorous and active a spider as ever dangled from an old ceiling. Giovanni bent towards the insect, and emitted a deep, long breath. The spider suddenly ceased its toil; the web vibrated with a tremor originating in the body of the small artisan. Again Giovanni sent forth a breath, deeper, longer, and imbued with a venomous feeling out of his heart: he knew not whether he were wicked, or only desperate. The spider made a convulsive gripe with his limbs and hung dead across the window.

"Accursed! accursed!" muttered Giovanni, addressing himself. "Hast thou grown so poisonous that this deadly insect perishes by thy breath?"

At that moment a rich, sweet voice came floating up from the garden.

"Giovanni! Giovanni! It is past the hour! Why tarriest thou? Come down!"

"Yes," muttered Giovanni again. "She is the only being whom my breath may not slay! Would that it might!"

He rushed down, and in an instant was standing before the bright and loving eyes of Beatrice. A moment ago his wrath and despair had been so fierce that he could have desired nothing so much as to wither her by a glance; but with her actual presence there came influences which had too real an existence to be at once shaken off; recollections of the delicate and benign power of her feminine nature, which had so often enveloped him in a religious calm; recollections of many a holy and passionate outgush of her heart, when the pure fountain had been unsealed from its depths and made visible in its transparency to his mental eye; recollections which, had Giovanni known how to estimate them, would have assured him that all this ugly mystery was but an earthly illusion, and that, whatever mist of evil might seem to have gathered over her, the real Beatrice was a heavenly angel. Incapable as he was of such high faith, still her presence had not utterly lost its magic. Giovanni's rage was quelled into an aspect of sullen insensibility. Beatrice, with a quick spiritual sense, immediately felt that there was a gulf of blackness between them which neither he nor she could pass. They walked on together, sad and silent, and came thus to the marble fountain and to its pool of water on the ground, in the midst of which grew the shrub that bore gemlike blossoms. Giovanni was affrighted at the eager enjoyment—the appetite, as it were—with which he found himself inhaling the fragrance of the flowers.

"Beatrice," asked he, abruptly, "whence came this shrub?"

"My father created it," answered she, with simplicity.

"Created it! created it!" repeated Giovanni. "What mean you, Beatrice?"

"He is a man fearfully acquainted with the secrets of Nature," replied Beatrice; "and, at the hour when I first drew breath, this plant sprang from the soil, the offspring of his science, of his intellect, while I was but his earthly child. Approach it not!" continued she, observing with terror that Giovanni was drawing nearer to the shrub. "It has qualities that you little dream of. But I, dearest Giovanni,—I grew up and blossomed with the plant and was nourished with its breath. It was my sister, and I loved it with a human affection; for, alas!—hast thou not suspected it?—there was an awful doom."

Here Giovanni frowned so darkly upon her that Beatrice paused and trembled. But her faith in his tenderness reassured her, and made her blush that she had doubted for an instant.

"There was an awful doom," she continued, "the effect of my father's fatal love of science, which estranged me from all society of my kind. Until Heaven sent thee, dearest Giovanni, O, how lonely was thy poor Beatrice!"

"Was it a hard doom?" asked Giovanni, fixing his eyes upon her.

"Only of late have I known how hard it was," answered she, tenderly. "O, yes; but my heart was torpid, and therefore quiet."

Giovanni's rage broke forth from his sullen gloom like a lightning flash out of a dark cloud.

"Accursed one!" cried he, with venomous scorn and anger. "And, finding thy solitude wearisome, thou hast severed me likewise from all the warmth of life and enticed me into thy region of unspeakable horror!"

"Giovanni!" exclaimed Beatrice, turning her large bright eyes upon his face. The force of his words had not found its way into her mind; she was merely thunderstruck.

"Yes, poisonous thing!" repeated Giovanni, beside himself with passion. "Thou hast done it! Thou hast blasted me! Thou hast filled my veins with poison! Thou hast made me as hateful, as ugly, as loathsome and deadly a creature as thyself—a world's wonder of hideous monstrosity! Now, if our breath be happily as fatal to ourselves as to all others, let us join our lips in one kiss of unutterable hatred, and so die!"

"What has befallen me?" murmured Beatrice, with a low moan out of her heart. "Holy Virgin, pity me, a poor heart-broken child!"

"Thou,—dost thou pray?" cried Giovanni, still with the same fiendish scorn. "Thy very prayers, as they come from thy lips, taint the atmosphere with death. Yes, yes; let us pray! Let us to church and dip our fingers in the holy water at the portal! They that come after us will perish as by a pestilence! Let us sign crosses in the air! It will be scattering curses abroad in the likeness of holy symbols!"

"Giovanni," said Beatrice, calmly, for her grief was beyond passion, "why dost thou join thyself with me thus in those terrible words? I, it is true, am the horrible thing thou namest me. But thou,—what hast thou to do, save with one other shudder at my hideous misery to go forth out of the garden and mingle with thy race, and forget that there ever crawled on earth such a monster as poor Beatrice?"

"Dost thou pretend ignorance?" asked Giovanni, scowling upon her.

"Behold! this power have I gained from the pure daughter of Rappaccini."

There was a swarm of summer insects flitting through the air in search of the food promised by the flower odors of the fatal garden. They circled round Giovanni's head, and were evidently attracted towards him by the same influence which had drawn them for an instant within the sphere of several of the shrubs. He sent forth a breath among them, and smiled bitterly at Beatrice as at least a score of the insects fell dead upon the ground.

"I see it! I see it!" shrieked Beatrice. "It is my father's fatal science! No, no, Giovanni; it was not I! Never! never! I dreamed only to love thee and be with thee a little time, and so to let thee pass away, leaving but thine image in mine heart; for, Giovanni, believe it, though my body be nourished with poison, my spirit is God's creature, and craves love as its daily food. But my father,—he has united us in this fearful sympathy. Yes; spurn me, tread upon me, kill me! O, what is death after such words as thine? But it was not I. Not for a world of bliss would I have done it."

Giovanni's passion had exhausted itself in its outburst from his lips. There now came across him a sense, mournful, and not without tenderness, of the intimate and peculiar relationship between Beatrice and himself. They stood, as it were, in an utter solitude, which would be made none the less solitary by the densest throng of human life. Ought not, then, the desert of humanity around them to press this insulated pair closer together? If they should be cruel to one another, who was there to be kind to them? Besides, thought Giovanni, might there not still be a hope of his returning within the limits of ordinary nature, and leading Beatrice, the redeemed Beatrice, by the hand? O, weak, and selfish, and unworthy spirit, that could dream of an earthly union and earthly happiness as possible, after such deep love had been so bitterly wronged as was Beatrice's love by Giovanni's blighting words! No, no; there could be no such hope. She must pass heavily, with that broken heart, across the borders of Time—she must bathe her hurts in some fount of paradise, and forget her grief in the light of immortality, and *there* be well.

But Giovanni did not know it.

"Dear Beatrice," said he, approaching her, while she shrank away as always at his approach, but now with a different impulse, "dearest Beatrice, our fate is not yet so desperate. Behold! there is a medicine, potent, as a wise physician has assured me, and almost divine in its efficacy. It is composed of ingredients the most opposite to those by which thy awful father has brought this calamity upon thee and me. It is distilled of blessed herbs. Shall we not quaff it together, and thus be purified from evil?"

"Give it me!" said Beatrice, extending her hand to receive the little silver vial which Giovanni took from his bosom. She added, with a peculiar emphasis, "I will drink; but do thou await the result."

She put Baglioni's antidote to her lips; and, at the same moment, the figure of Rappaccini emerged from the portal and came slowly towards the marble fountain. As he drew near, the pale man of science seemed to gaze with a triumphant expression at the beautiful youth and maiden, as might an artist who should spend his life in achieving a picture or a group of statuary and finally be satisfied with his success. He paused; his bent form grew erect with conscious power; he spread out his hands over them in the attitude of a father imploring a blessing upon his children; but those were the same hands that had thrown poison into the stream of their lives. Giovanni trembled. Beatrice shuddered nervously, and pressed her hand upon her heart.

"My daughter," said Rappaccini, "thou art no longer lonely in the world. Pluck one of those precious gems from thy sister shrub and bid thy bridegroom wear it in his bosom. It will not harm him now. My science and the sympathy between thee and him have so wrought within his system that he now stands apart from common men, as thou dost, daughter of my pride and triumph, from ordinary women. Pass on, then, through the world, most dear to one another and dreadful to all besides!"

"My father," said Beatrice, feebly,—and still as she spoke she kept her hand upon her heart,—"wherefore didst thou inflict this miserable doom upon thy child?"

"Miserable!" exclaimed Rappaccini. "What mean you, foolish girl? Dost thou deem it misery to be endowed with marvellous gifts against which no power nor strength could avail an enemy—misery, to be able to quell the mightiest with a breath—misery, to be as terrible as thou art beautiful? Wouldst thou, then, have preferred the condition of a weak woman, exposed to all evil and capable of none?"

"I would fain have been loved, not feared," murmured Beatrice, sinking down upon the ground. "But now it matters not. I am going, father, where the evil which thou hast striven to mingle with my being will pass away like a dream—like the fragrance of these poisonous flowers, which will no longer taint my breath among the flowers of Eden. Farewell, Giovanni! Thy words of hatred are like lead within my heart; but they, too, will fall away as I ascend. O, was there not, from the first, more poison in thy nature than in mine?"

To Beatrice,—so radically had her earthly part been wrought upon by Rappaccini's skill,—as poison had been life, so the powerful antidote was death; and thus the poor victim of man's ingenuity and of thwarted nature, and of the fatality that attends all such efforts of perverted wisdom, perished there, at the feet of her father and Giovanni. Just at that moment Professor Pietro Baglioni looked forth from the window, and called loudly, in a tone of triumph mixed with horror, to the thunderstricken man of science,—

"Rappaccini! Rappaccini! and is *this* the upshot of your experiment?"

MRS. BULLFROG

It makes me melancholy to see how like fools some very sensible people act in the matter of choosing wives. They perplex their judgments by a most undue attention to little niceties of personal appearance, habits, disposition, and other trifles which concern nobody but the lady herself. An unhappy gentleman, resolving to wed nothing short of perfection, keeps his heart and hand till both get so old and withered that no tolerable woman will accept them. Now, this is the very height of absurdity. A kind Providence has so skillfully adapted sex to sex and the mass of individuals to each other, that, with certain obvious exceptions, any male and female may be moderately happy in the married state. The true rule is, to ascertain that the match is fundamentally a good one, and then to take it for granted that all minor objections, should there be such, will vanish, if you let them alone. Only put yourself beyond hazard as to the real basis of matrimonial bliss, and it is scarcely to be imagined what miracles, in the way of recognizing smaller incongruities, connubial love will effect.

For my own part, I freely confess that, in my bachelorship, I was precisely such an over-curious simpleton as I now advise the reader not to be. My early habits had gifted me with a feminine sensibility and too exquisite refinement. I was the accomplished graduate of a dry goods store, where, by dint of ministering to the whims of fine ladies, and suiting silken hose to delicate limbs, and handling satins, ribbons, chintzes, calicoes, tapes, gauze, and cambric needles, I grew up a very ladylike sort of a gentleman. It is not assuming too much to affirm that the ladies themselves were hardly so ladylike as Thomas Bullfrog. So painfully acute was my sense of female imperfection, and such varied excellence did I require in the woman whom I could love, that there was an awful risk of my getting no wife at all, or of being driven to perpetrate matrimony with my own image in the looking glass. Besides the fundamental principle already hinted at, I demanded the fresh bloom of youth, pearly teeth, glossy ringlets, and the whole list of lovely items, with the utmost delicacy of habits and sentiments, a silken texture of mind, and, above all, a virgin heart. In a word, if a young angel just from paradise, yet dressed in earthly fashion, had come and offered me her hand, it is by no means certain that I should have taken it. There was every chance of my becoming a most miserable old bachelor, when, by the best luck in the world, I made a journey into another state, and was smitten by, and smote again, and wooed, won, and married, the present Mrs. Bullfrog, all in the space of a fortnight. Owing to these extempore measures, I not only gave my bride credit for certain perfections which have not as yet come to light, but also overlooked a few trifling defects, which, however, glimmered on my perception long before the close of the honeymoon. Yet, as there was no mistake about the fundamental principle aforesaid, I soon learned, as will be seen, to estimate Mrs. Bullfrog's deficiencies and superfluities at exactly their proper value.

The same morning that Mrs. Bullfrog and I came together as a unit, we took two seats in the stage coach and began our journey towards my place of business. There being no other passengers, we were as much alone and as free to give vent to our raptures as if I had hired a hack for the matrimonial jaunt. My bride looked charmingly in a green silk calash[1] and riding habit of pelisse cloth;[2] and, whenever her red lips parted with a smile, each tooth appeared like an inestimable pearl. Such was my passionate warmth that—we had rattled out of the village, gentle reader, and were lonely as Adam and Eve in paradise—I plead guilty to no less freedom than a kiss. The gentle eye of Mrs. Bullfrog scarcely rebuked me for the profanation. Emboldened by her indulgence, I threw back the calash from her polished brow, and suffered my fingers, white and delicate as her own, to stray among those dark and glossy curls which realized my daydreams of rich hair.

"My love," said Mrs. Bullfrog, tenderly, "you will disarrange my curls."

"O, no, my sweet Laura!" replied I, still playing with the glossy ringlet. "Even your fair hand could not manage a curl more delicately than mine. I propose myself the pleasure of doing up your hair in papers every evening at the same time with my own."

"Mr. Bullfrog," repeated she, "you must not disarrange my curls."

This was spoken in a more decided tone than I had happened to hear, until then, from my gentlest of all gentle brides. At the same time she put up her hand and took mine prisoner; but merely drew it away from the forbidden ringlet, and then immediately released it. Now, I am a fidgety little man, and always love to have something in my fingers; so that, being debarred from my wife's curls, I looked about me for any other plaything. On the front seat of the coach there was one of those small baskets in which travelling ladies who are too delicate to appear at a public table generally carry a supply of gingerbread, biscuits and cheese, cold ham, and other light refreshments, merely to sustain nature to the journey's end. Such airy diet will sometimes keep them in pretty good flesh for a week together. Laying hold of this same little basket, I thrust my hand under the newspaper with which it was carefully covered.

"What's this, my dear?" cried I; for the black neck of a bottle had popped out of the basket.

"A bottle of Kalydor,[3] Mr. Bullfrog," said my wife, coolly taking the basket from my hands and replacing it on the front seat.

There was no possibility of doubting my wife's word; but I never knew genuine Kalydor, such as I use for my own complexion, to smell so much like cherry brandy. I was about to express my fears that the lotion would injure her skin, when an accident occurred which threatened more than a skin-deep injury. Our Jehu[4] had carelessly driven over a heap of gravel and fairly capsized the coach, with the wheels in the air and our heels where our heads should have been. What became of my wits I cannot imagine; they have always had a perverse trick of deserting me just when they were most needed; but so it chanced, that in the confusion of our overthrow I quite forgot that there was a Mrs. Bullfrog in the world. Like many men's wives, the good lady served her husband as a stepping stone. I had scrambled out of the coach and was instinctively settling my cravat, when somebody brushed roughly by me, and I heard a smart thwack upon the coachman's ear.

"Take that, you villain!" cried a strange, hoarse voice. "You have ruined me, you blackguard! I shall never be the woman I have been!"

And then came a second thwack, aimed at the driver's other ear; but which missed it, and hit him on the nose, causing a terrible effusion of blood. Now, who or what fearful apparition was inflicting this punishment on the poor fellow remained an impenetrable mystery to me. The blows were given by a person of grisly aspect, with a head almost bald, and sunken cheeks, apparently of the feminine gender, though hardly to be classed in the gentler sex. There being no teeth to modulate the voice, it had a mumbled fierceness, not passionate, but stern, which absolutely made me quiver like calf's-foot jelly. Who could the phantom be? The most awful circumstance of the affair is yet to be told; for this ogre, or whatever it was, had a riding habit like Mrs. Bullfrog's, and also a green silk calash dangling down her back by the strings. In my terror and turmoil of mind I could imagine nothing less than that the Old Nick,[5] at the moment of our overturn, had annihilated my wife and jumped into her petticoats. This idea seemed the more probable, since I could nowhere perceive Mrs. Bullfrog alive, nor, though I looked very sharply about the coach, could I detect any traces of that beloved woman's dead body. There would have been a comfort in giving her a Christian burial.

"Come, sir, bestir yourself! Help this rascal to set up the coach," said the hobgoblin to me; then, with a terrific screech to three countrymen at a distance, "Here, you fellows, ain't you ashamed to stand off when a poor woman is in distress?"

The countrymen, instead of fleeing for their lives, came running at full speed, and laid hold of the topsy-turvy coach. I, also, though a small-sized man, went to work like a son of Anak.[6] The coachman, too, with the blood still streaming from his nose, tugged and toiled most manfully, dreading, doubtless, that the next blow might break his head. And yet, bemauled as the poor fellow had been, he seemed to glance at me with an eye of pity, as if my case were more deplorable than his. But I cherished a hope that all would turn out a dream, and seized the opportunity, as we raised the coach, to jam two of my fingers under the wheel, trusting that the pain would awaken me.

"Why, here we are, all to rights again!" exclaimed a sweet voice behind. "Thank you for your assistance, gentlemen. My dear Mr. Bullfrog, how you perspire! Do let me wipe your face. Don't take this little accident too much to heart, good driver. We ought to be thankful that none of our necks are broken."

"We might have spared one neck out of the three," muttered the driver, rubbing his ear and pulling his nose, to ascertain whether he had been cuffed or not. "Why, the woman's a witch!"

I fear that the reader will not believe, yet it is positively a fact, that there stood Mrs. Bullfrog, with her glossy ringlets curling on her brow, and two rows of orient pearls gleaming between her parted lips, which wore a most angelic smile. She had regained her riding habit and calash from the grisly phantom, and was, in all respects, the lovely woman who had been sitting by my side at the instant of our overturn. How she had happened to disappear, and who had supplied her place, and whence she did now return, were problems too knotty for me to solve. There stood my wife. That was the one thing certain among a heap of mysteries. Nothing remained but to help her into the coach, and plod on, through the journey of the day and the journey of life, as comfortably as we could. As the driver closed the door upon us, I heard him whisper to the three countrymen,—

"How do you suppose a fellow feels shut up in the cage with a she tiger?"

Of course this query could have no reference to my situation. Yet, unreasonable as it may appear, I confess that my feelings were not altogether so ecstatic as when I first called Mrs. Bullfrog mine. True, she was a sweet woman and an angel of a wife; but what if a Gorgon[7] should return, amid the transports of our connubial bliss, and take the angel's place. I recollected the tale of a fairy, who half the time was a beautiful woman and half the time a hideous monster. Had I taken that very fairy to be the wife of my bosom? While such whims and chimeras were flitting across my fancy I began to look askance at Mrs. Bullfrog, almost expecting that the transformation would be wrought before my eyes.

To divert my mind, I took up the newspaper which had covered the little basket of refreshments, and which now lay at the bottom of the coach, blushing with a deep-red stain and emitting a potent spirituous fume from the contents of the broken bottle of Kalydor. The paper was two or three years old, but contained an article of several columns, in which I soon grew wonderfully interested. It was the report of a trial for breach of promise of marriage, giving the testimony in full, with fervid extracts from both the gentleman's and lady's amatory[8] correspondence. The deserted damsel had personally appeared in court, and had borne energetic evidence to her lover's perfidy and the strength of her blighted affections. On the defendant's part there had been an attempt, though insufficiently sustained, to blast the plaintiff's character, and a plea, in mitigation of damages, on account of her unamiable temper. A horrible idea was suggested by the lady's name.

"Madam," said I, holding the newspaper before Mrs. Bullfrog's eyes,—and, though a small, delicate, and thin-visaged man, I feel assured that I looked very terrific,—"madam," repeated I, through my shut teeth, "were you the plaintiff in this cause?"

"O, my dear Mr. Bullfrog," replied my wife, sweetly, "I thought all the world knew that!"

"Horror! horror!" exclaimed I, sinking back on the seat.

Covering my face with both hands, I emitted a deep and deathlike groan, as if my tormented soul were rending me asunder—I, the most exquisitely fastidious of men, and whose wife was to have been the most delicate and refined of women, with all the fresh dewdrops glittering on her virgin rosebud of a heart!

I thought of the glossy ringlets and pearly teeth; I thought of the Kalydor; I thought of the coachman's bruised ear and bloody nose; I thought of the tender love secrets which she had whispered to the judge and jury and a thousand tittering auditors,—and gave another groan!

"Mr. Bullfrog," said my wife.

As I made no reply, she gently took my hands within her own, removed them from my face, and fixed her eyes steadfastly on mine.

"Mr. Bullfrog," said she, not unkindly, yet with all the decision of her strong character, "let me advise you to overcome this foolish weakness, and prove yourself, to the best of your ability, as good a husband as I will be a wife. You have discovered, perhaps, some little imperfections in your bride. Well, what did you expect? Women are not angels. If they were, they would go to heaven for husbands; or, at least, be more difficult in their choice on earth."

"But why conceal those imperfections?" interposed I, tremulously.

"Now, my love, are not you a most unreasonable little man?" said Mrs. Bullfrog, patting me on the cheek. "Ought a woman to disclose her frailties earlier than the wedding day? Few husbands, I assure you, make the discovery in such good season, and still fewer complain that these trifles are concealed too long. Well, what a strange man you are! Poh! you are joking."

"But the suit for breach of promise!" groaned I.

"Ah, and is that the rub?" exclaimed my wife. "Is it possible that you view that affair in an objectionable light? Mr. Bullfrog, I never could have dreamed it! Is it an objection that I have triumphantly defended myself against slander and vindicated my purity in a court of justice? Or do you complain because your wife has shown the proper spirit of a woman, and punished the villain who trifled with her affections?"

"But," persisted I, shrinking into a corner of the coach, however; for I did not know precisely how much contradiction the proper spirit of a woman would endure,—"but, my love, would it not have been more dignified to treat the villain with the silent contempt he merited?"

"That is all very well, Mr. Bullfrog," said my wife, slyly; "but, in that case, where would have been the five thousand dollars which are to stock your dry goods store?"

"Mrs. Bullfrog, upon your honor," demanded I, as if my life hung upon her words, "is there no mistake about those five thousand dollars?"

"Upon my word and honor there is none," replied she. "The jury gave me every cent the rascal had; and I have kept it all for my dear Bullfrog."

"Then, thou dear woman," cried I, with an overwhelming gush of tenderness, "let me fold thee to my heart. The basis of matrimonial bliss is secure, and all thy little defects and frailties are forgiven. Nay, since the result has been so fortunate, I rejoice at the wrongs which drove thee to this blessed lawsuit. Happy Bullfrog that I am!"

Fire Worship

It is a great revolution in social and domestic life, and no less so in the life of a secluded student, this almost universal exchange of the open fireplace for the cheerless and ungenial stove. On such a morning as now lowers around our old gray parsonage I miss the bright face of my ancient friend, who was wont to dance upon the hearth and play the part of more familiar sunshine. It is sad to turn from the cloudy sky and sombre landscape; from yonder hill, with its crown of rusty, black pines, the foliage of which is so dismal in the absence of the sun; that bleak pasture land, and the broken surface of the potato field, with the brown clods partly concealed by the snow fall of last night; the swollen and sluggish river, with ice-incrusted borders, dragging its bluish-gray stream along the verge of our orchard like a snake half torpid with the cold,—it is sad to turn from an outward scene of so little comfort and find the same sullen influences brooding within the precincts of my study. Where is that brilliant guest, that quick and subtle spirit, whom Prometheus[1] lured from heaven to civilize mankind and cheer them in their wintry desolation—that comfortable inmate, whose smile, during eight months of the year, was our sufficient consolation for summer's lingering advance and early flight? Alas! blindly inhospitable, grudging the food that kept him cheery and mercurial, we have thrust him into an iron prison, and compel him to smoulder away his life on a daily pittance which once would have been too scanty for his breakfast. Without a metaphor, we now make our fire in an airtight stove, and supply it with some half a dozen sticks of wood between dawn and nightfall.

I never shall be reconciled to this enormity. Truly may it be said that the world looks darker for it. In one way or another, here and there and all around us, the inventions of mankind are fast blotting the picturesque, the poetic, and the beautiful out of human life. The domestic fire was a type of all these attributes, and seemed to bring might and majesty, and wild Nature and a spiritual essence, into our inmost home, and yet to dwell with us in such friendliness that its mysteries and marvels excited no dismay. The same mild companion that smiled so placidly in our faces was he that comes roaring out of Ætna[2] and rushes madly up the sky like a fiend breaking loose from torment and fighting for a place among the upper angels. He it is, too, that leaps from cloud to cloud amid the crashing thunder storm. It was he whom the Gheber[3] worshipped with no unnatural idolatry; and it was he who devoured London and Moscow and many another famous city, and who loves to riot through our own dark forests and sweep across our prairies, and to whose ravenous maw, it is said, the universe shall one day be given as a final feast. Meanwhile he is the great artisan and laborer by whose aid men are enabled to build a world within a world, or, at least, to smooth down the rough creation which Nature flung to us. He forges the mighty anchor and every lesser instrument; he drives the steamboat and drags the rail car; and it was he—this creature of terrible might, and so many-sided utility and all-comprehensive destructiveness—that used to be the cheerful, homely friend of our wintry days, and whom we have made the prisoner of this iron cage.

How kindly he was! and, though the tremendous agent of change, yet bearing himself with such gentleness, so rendering himself a part of all lifelong and age-coeval associations, that it seemed as if he were the great conservative of Nature. While a man was true to the fireside, so long would he be true to country and law, to the God whom his fathers worshipped, to the wife of his youth, and to all things else which instinct or religion has taught us to consider sacred. With how sweet humility did this elemental spirit perform all needful offices for the household in which he was domesticated! He was equal to the concoction of a grand dinner, yet scorned not to roast a potato or toast a bit of cheese. How humanely did he cherish the schoolboy's icy fingers, and thaw the old man's joints with a genial warmth which almost equalled the glow of youth! And how carefully did he dry the cowhide boots that had trudged through mud and snow, and the shaggy outside garment stiff with frozen sleet! taking heed, likewise, to the comfort of the faithful dog who had followed his master through the storm. When did he refuse a coal to light a pipe, or even a part of his own substance to kindle a neighbor's fire? And then, at twilight, when laborer, or scholar, or mortal of whatever age, sex, or degree, drew a chair beside him and looked into his glowing face, how acute, how profound, how comprehensive was his sympathy with the mood of each and all! He pictured forth their very thoughts. To the youthful he showed the scenes of the adventurous life before them; to the aged the shadows of departed love and hope; and, if all earthly things had grown distasteful, he could gladden the fireside muser with golden glimpses of a better world. And, amid this varied communion with the human soul, how busily would the sympathizer, the deep moralist, the painter of magic pictures be causing the teakettle to boil!

Nor did it lessen the charm of his soft, familiar courtesy and helpfulness that the mighty spirit, were opportunity offered him, would run riot through the peaceful house, wrap its inmates in his terrible embrace, and leave nothing of them save their whitened bones. This possibility of mad destruction only made his domestic kindness the more beautiful and touching. It was so sweet of him, being endowed with such power, to dwell day after day, and one long lonesome night after another, on the dusky hearth, only now and then betraying his wild nature by thrusting his red tongue out of the chimney top! True, he had done much mischief in the world, and was pretty certain to do more; but his warm heart atoned for all. He was kindly to the race of man; and they pardoned his characteristic imperfections.

The good old clergyman, my predecessor in this mansion, was well acquainted with the comforts of the fireside. His yearly allowance of wood, according to the terms of his settlement, was no less than sixty cords. Almost an annual forest was converted from sound oak logs into ashes, in the kitchen, the parlor, and this little study, where now an unworthy successor, not in the pastoral office, but merely in his earthly abode, sits scribbling beside an airtight stove. I love to fancy one of those fireside days while the good man, a contemporary of the revolution,[4] was in his early prime, some five and sixty years ago. Before sunrise, doubtless, the blaze hovered upon the gray skirts of night and dissolved the frostwork that had gathered like a curtain over the small window panes. There is something peculiar in the aspect of the morning fireside; a fresher, brisker glare; the absence of that mellowness which can be produced only by half-consumed logs, and shapeless brands with the white ashes on them, and mighty coals, the remnant of tree trunks that the hungry elements have gnawed for hours. The morning hearth, too, is newly swept, and the brazen andirons well brightened, so that the cheerful fire may see its face in them. Surely it was happiness, when the pastor, fortified with a substantial breakfast, sat down in his arm chair and slippers and opened the Whole Body of Divinity, or the Commentary on Job, or whichever of his old folios or quartos might fall within the range of his weekly sermons. It must have been his own fault if the warmth and glow of this abundant hearth did not permeate the discourse and keep his audience comfortable in spite of the bitterest northern blast that ever wrestled with the church steeple. He reads while the heat warps the stiff covers of the volume; he writes without numbness either in his heart or fingers; and, with unstinted hand, he throws fresh sticks of wood upon the fire.

A parishioner comes in. With what warmth of benevolence—how should he be otherwise than warm in any of his attributes?—does the minister bid him welcome, and set a chair for him in so close proximity to the hearth that soon the guest finds it needful to rub his scorched shins with his great red hands! The melted snow drips from his steaming boots and bubbles upon the hearth. His puckered forehead unravels its entanglement of crisscross wrinkles. We lose much of the enjoyment of fireside heat without such an opportunity of marking its genial effect upon those who have been looking the inclement weather in the face. In the course of the day our clergyman himself strides forth, perchance to pay a round of pastoral visits;⁵ or, it may be, to visit his mountain of a wood pile and cleave the monstrous logs into billets suitable for the fire. He returns with fresher life to his beloved hearth. During the short afternoon the western sunshine comes into the study and strives to stare the ruddy blaze out of countenance, but with only a brief triumph, soon to be succeeded by brighter glories of its rival. Beautiful it is to see the strengthening gleam, the deepening light, that gradually casts distinct shadows of the human figure, the table, and the highbacked chairs upon the opposite wall, and at length, as twilight comes on, replenishes the room with living radiance and makes life all rose color. Afar the wayfarer discerns the flickering flame as it dances upon the windows, and hails it as a beacon light of humanity, reminding him, in his cold and lonely path, that the world is not all snow, and solitude, and desolation. At eventide, probably, the study was peopled with the clergyman's wife and family, and children tumbled themselves upon the hearth rug, and grave puss sat with her back to the fire, or gazed, with a semblance of human meditation, into its fervid depths. Seasonably the plenteous ashes of the day were raked over the mouldering brands, and from the heap came jets of flame, and an incense of nightlong smoke creeping quietly up the chimney.

Heaven forgive the old clergyman! In his later life, when for almost ninety winters he had been gladdened by the firelight,—when it had gleamed upon him from infancy to extreme age, and never without brightening his spirits as well as his visage, and perhaps keeping him alive so long,—he had the heart to brick up his chimney-place and bid farewell to the face of his old friend forever, why did he not take an eternal leave of the sunshine too? His sixty cords of wood had probably dwindled to a far less ample supply in modern times; and it is certain that the parsonage had grown crazy with time and tempest and pervious to the cold; but still it was one of the saddest tokens of the decline and fall of open fireplaces that the gray patriarch should have deigned to warm himself at an airtight stove.

And I, likewise,—who have found a home in this ancient owl's nest since its former occupant took his heavenward flight,—I, to my shame, have put up stoves in kitchen, and parlor, and chamber. Wander where you will about the house, not a glimpse of the earth-born, heaven-aspiring fiend of Ætna,—him that sports in the thunder storm, the idol of the Ghebers, the devourer of cities, the forest rioter and prairie sweeper, the future destroyer of our earth, the old chimney-corner companion who mingled himself so sociably with household joys and sorrows,—not a glimpse of this mighty and kindly one will greet your eyes. He is now an invisible presence. There is his iron cage. Touch it, and he scorches your fingers. He delights to singe a garment or perpetrate any other little unworthy mischief; for his temper is ruined by the ingratitude of mankind, for whom he cherished such warmth of feeling, and to whom he taught all their arts, even that of making his own prison house. In his fits of rage he puffs volumes of smoke and noisome gas through the crevices of the door, and shakes the iron walls of his dungeon so as to overthrow the ornamental urn upon its summit. We tremble lest he should break forth amongst us. Much of his time is spent in sighs, burdened with unutterable grief, and long drawn through the funnel. He amuses himself, too, with repeating all the whispers, the moans, and the louder utterances or tempestuous howls of the wind; so that the stove becomes a microcosm of the aerial world. Occasionally there are strange combinations of sounds,—voices talking almost articulately within the hollow chest of iron,—insomuch that fancy beguiles me with the idea that my firewood must have grown in that infernal forest of lamentable trees which breathed their complaints to Dante.[6] When the listener is half asleep he may readily take these voices for the conversation of spirits and assign them an intelligible meaning. Anon there is a pattering noise,—drip, drip, drip,—as if a summer shower were falling within the narrow circumference of the stove.

These barren and tedious eccentricities are all that the airtight stove can bestow in exchange for the invaluable moral influences which we have lost by our desertion of the open fireplace. Alas! is this world so very bright that we can afford to choke up such a domestic fountain of gladsomeness, and sit down by its darkened source without being conscious of a gloom?

It is my belief that social intercourse cannot long continue what it has been, now that we have subtracted from it so important and vivifying an element as firelight. The effects will be more perceptible on our children and the generations that shall succeed them than on ourselves, the mechanism of whose life may remain unchanged, though its spirit be far other than it was. The sacred trust of the household fire has been transmitted in unbroken succession from the earliest ages and faithfully cherished in spite of every discouragement such as the curfew law of the Norman conquerors,[7] until in these evil days physical science has nearly succeeded in extinguishing it. But we at least have our youthful recollections tinged with the glow of the hearth and our lifelong habits and associations arranged on the principle of a mutual bond in the domestic fire. Therefore, though the sociable friend be forever departed, yet in a degree he will be spiritually present with us; and still more will the empty forms which were once full of his rejoicing presence continue to rule our manners. We shall draw our chairs together as we and our forefathers have been wont for thousands of years back, and sit around some blank and empty corner of the room, babbling with unreal cheerfulness of topics suitable to the homely fireside. A warmth from the past—from the ashes of by-gone years and the raked-up embers of long ago—will sometimes thaw the ice about our hearts; but it must be otherwise with our successors. On the most favorable supposition, they will be acquainted with the fireside in no better shape than that of the sullen stove; and more probably they will have grown up amid furnace heat in houses which might be fancied to have their foundation over the infernal pit, whence sulphurous steams and unbreathable exhalations ascend through the apertures of the floor. There will be nothing to attract these poor children to one centre. They will never behold one another through that peculiar medium of vision—the ruddy gleam of blazing wood or bituminous[8] coal—which gives the human spirit so deep an insight into its fellows and melts all humanity into one cordial heart of hearts. Domestic life, if it may still be termed domestic, will seek its separate corners, and never gather itself into groups. The easy gossip; the merry yet unambitious jest; the lifelike, practical discussion of real matters in a casual way; the soul of truth which is so often incarnated in a simple fireside word,—will disappear from earth. Conversation will contract the air of debate and all mortal intercourse be chilled with a fatal frost.

In classic times, the exhortation to fight "pro aris et focis,"[9] for the altars and the hearths, was considered the strongest appeal that could be made to patriotism. And it seemed an immortal utterance; for all subsequent ages and people have acknowledged its force and responded to it with the full portion of manhood that Nature had assigned to each. Wisely were the altar and the hearth conjoined in one mighty sentence; for the hearth, too, had its kindred sanctity. Religion sat down beside it, not in the priestly robes which decorated and perhaps disguised her at the altar, but arrayed in a simple matron's garb, and uttering her lessons with the tenderness of a mother's voice and heart. The holy hearth! If any earthly and material thing, or rather a divine idea imbodied in brick and mortar, might be supposed to possess the permanence of moral truth, it was this. All revered it. The man who did not put off his shoes upon this holy ground would have deemed it pastime to trample upon the altar. It has been our task to uproot the hearth. What further reform is left for our children to achieve, unless they overthrow the altar too? And by what appeal hereafter, when the breath of hostile armies may mingle with the pure, cold breezes of our country, shall we attempt to rouse up native valor? Fight for your hearths? There will be none throughout the land. FIGHT FOR YOUR STOVES! Not I, in faith. If in such a cause I strike a blow, it shall be on the invader's part; and Heaven grant that it may shatter the abomination all to pieces!

BUDS AND BIRD VOICES

Balmy Spring—weeks later than we expected and months later than we longed for her—comes at last to revive the moss on the roof and walls of our old mansion. She peeps brightly into my study window, inviting me to throw it open and create a summer atmosphere by the intermixture of her genial breath with the black and cheerless comfort of the stove. As the casement ascends, forth into infinite space fly the innumerable forms of thought or fancy that have kept me company in the retirement of this little chamber during the sluggish lapse of wintry weather; visions, gay, grotesque, and sad; pictures of real life, tinted with Nature's homely gray and russet; scenes in dreamland, bedizened with rainbow hues which faded before they were well laid on,—all these may vanish now, and leave me to mould a fresh existence out of sunshine. Brooding Meditation may flap her dusky wings and take her owllike flight, blinking amid the cheerfulness of noontide. Such companions befit the season of frosted window panes and crackling fires, when the blast howls through the black ash trees of our avenue and the drifting snow storm chokes up the woodpaths and fills the highway from stone wall to stone wall. In the spring and summer time all sombre thoughts should follow the winter northward with the sombre and thoughtful crows. The old paradisiacal economy of life is again in force; we live, not to think or to labor, but for the simple end of being happy. Nothing for the present hour is worthy of man's infinite capacity save to imbibe the warm smile of heaven and sympathize with the reviving earth.

The present Spring comes onward with fleeter footsteps, because Winter lingered so unconscionably long that with her best diligence she can hardly retrieve half the allotted period of her reign. It is but a fortnight since I stood on the brink of our swollen river and beheld the accumulated ice of four frozen months go down the stream. Except in streaks here and there upon the hillsides, the whole visible universe was then covered with deep snow, the nethermost layer of which had been deposited by an early December storm. It was a sight to make the beholder torpid, in the impossibility of imagining how this vast white napkin was to be removed from the face of the corpselike world in less time than had been required to spread it there. But who can estimate the power of gentle influences, whether amid material desolation or the moral winter of man's heart? There have been no tempestuous rains, even no sultry days, but a constant breath of southern winds, with now a day of kindly sunshine and now a no less kindly mist or a soft descent of showers, in which a smile and a blessing seemed to have been steeped. The snow has vanished as if by magic; whatever heaps may be hidden in the woods and deep gorges of the hills, only two solitary specks remain in the landscape; and those I shall almost regret to miss when to-morrow I look for them in vain. Never before, methinks, has spring pressed so closely on the footsteps of retreating winter. Along the roadside the green blades of grass have sprouted on the very edge of the snow drifts. The pastures and mowing fields have not yet assumed a general aspect of verdure; but neither have they the cheerless brown tint which they wear in latter autumn when vegetation has entirely ceased; there is now a faint shadow of life, gradually brightening into the warm reality. Some tracts in a happy exposure,—as, for instance, yonder south-western slope of an orchard, in front of that old red farm house beyond the river,—such patches of land already wear a beautiful and tender green, to which no future luxuriance can add a charm. It looks unreal; a prophecy, a hope, a transitory effect of some peculiar light, which will vanish with the slightest motion of the eye. But beauty is never a delusion; not these verdant tracts, but the dark and barren landscape all around them, is a shadow and a dream. Each moment wins some portion of the earth from death to life; a sudden gleam of verdure brightens along the sunny slope of a bank which an instant ago was brown and bare. You look again, and behold an apparition of green grass!

The trees in our orchard and elsewhere are as yet naked, but already appear full of life and vegetable blood. It seems as if by one magic touch they might instantaneously burst into full foliage, and that the wind which now sighs through their naked branches might make sudden music amid innumerable leaves. The mossgrown willow tree which for forty years past has overshadowed these western windows will be among the first to put on its green attire. There are some objections to the willow; it is not a dry and cleanly tree, and impresses the beholder with an association of sliminess. No trees, I think, are perfectly agreeable as companions unless they have glossy leaves, dry bark, and a firm and hard texture of trunk and branches. But the willow is almost the earliest to gladden us with the promise and reality of beauty in its graceful and delicate foliage, and the last to scatter its yellow yet scarcely withered leaves upon the ground. All through the winter, too, its yellow twigs give it a sunny aspect, which is not without a cheering influence, even in the grayest and gloomiest day. Beneath a clouded sky it faithfully remembers the sunshine. Our old house would lose a charm were the willow to be cut down, with its golden crown over the snow-covered roof and its heap of summer verdure.

The lilac shrubs under my study windows are likewise almost in leaf: in two or three days more I may put forth my hand and pluck the topmost bough in its freshest green. These lilacs are very aged, and have lost the luxuriant foliage of their prime. The heart, or the judgment, or the moral sense, or the taste is dissatisfied with their present aspect. Old age is not venerable when it imbodies itself in lilacs, rose bushes, or any other ornamental shrub; it seems as if such plants, as they grow only for beauty, ought to flourish always in immortal youth, or, at least, to die before their sad decrepitude. Trees of beauty are trees of paradise, and therefore not subject to decay by their original nature, though they have lost that precious birthright by being transplanted to an earthly soil. There is a kind of ludicrous unfitness in the idea of a timestricken and grandfatherly lilac bush. The analogy holds good in human life. Persons who can only be graceful and ornamental—who can give the world nothing but flowers—should die young, and never be seen with gray hair and wrinkles, any more than the flower shrubs with mossy bark and blighted foliage, like the lilacs under my window.

Not that beauty is worthy of less than immortality; no, the beautiful should live forever—and thence, perhaps, the sense of impropriety when we see it triumphed over by time. Apple trees, on the other hand, grow old without reproach. Let them live as long as they may, and contort themselves into whatever perversity of shape they please, and deck their withered limbs with a spring-time gaudiness of pink blossoms; still they are respectable, even if they afford us only an apple or two in a season. Those few apples—or, at all events, the remembrance of apples in by-gone years—are the atonement which utilitarianism inexorably demands for the privilege of lengthened life. Human flower shrubs, if they will grow old on earth, should, besides their lovely blossoms, bear some kind of fruit that will satisfy earthly appetites, else neither man nor the decorum of Nature will deem it fit that the moss should gather on them.

One of the first things that strikes the attention when the white sheet of winter is withdrawn is the neglect and disarray that lay hidden beneath it. Nature is not cleanly, according to our prejudices. The beauty of preceding years, now transformed to brown and blighted deformity, obstructs the brightening loveliness of the present hour. Our avenue is strewn with the whole crop of autumn's withered leaves. There are quantities of decayed branches which one tempest after another has flung down, black and rotten, and one or two with the ruin of a bird's nest clinging to them. In the garden are the dried bean vines, the brown stalks of the asparagus bed, and melancholy old cabbages which were frozen into the soil before their unthrifty cultivator could find time to gather them. How invariably, throughout all the forms of life, do we find these intermingled memorials of death! On the soil of thought and in the garden of the heart, as well as in the sensual world, lie withered leaves—the ideas and feelings that we have done with. There is no wind strong enough to sweep them away; infinite space will not garner them from our sight. What mean they? Why may we not be permitted to live and enjoy, as if this were the first life and our own the primal enjoyment, instead of treading always on these dry bones and mouldering relics, from the aged accumulation of which springs all that now appears so young and new? Sweet must have been the spring time of Eden, when no earlier year had strewn its decay upon the virgin turf and no former experience had ripened into summer and faded into autumn in the hearts of its inhabitants! That was a world worth living in. O thou murmurer, it is out of the very wantonness of such a life that thou feignest these idle lamentations. There is no decay. Each human soul is the first-created inhabitant of its own Eden. We dwell in an old moss-covered mansion, and tread in the worn footprints of the past, and have a gray clergyman's ghost for our daily and nightly inmate; yet all these outward circumstances are made less than visionary by the renewing power of the spirit. Should the spirit ever lose this power,—should the withered leaves, and the rotten branches, and the moss-covered house, and the ghost of the gray past ever become its realities, and the verdure and the freshness merely its faint dream,—then let it pray to be released from earth. It will need the air of heaven to revive its pristine energies.

What an unlooked-for flight was this from our shadowy avenue of black ash and balm of Gilead[1] trees into the infinite! Now we have our feet again upon the turf. Nowhere does the grass spring up so industriously as in this homely yard, along the base of the stone wall, and in the sheltered nooks of the buildings, and especially around the southern doorstep—a locality which seems particularly favorable to its growth, for it is already tall enough to bend over and wave in the wind. I observe that several weeds—and most frequently a plant that stains the fingers with its yellow juice—have survived and retained their freshness and sap throughout the winter. One knows not how they have deserved such an exception from the common lot of their race. They are now the patriarchs of the departed year, and may preach mortality to the present generation of flowers and weeds.

Among the delights of spring, how is it possible to forget the birds? Even the crows were welcome as the sable harbingers of a brighter and livelier race. They visited us before the snow was off, but seem mostly to have betaken themselves to remote depths of the woods, which they haunt all summer long. Many a time shall I disturb them there, and feel as if I had intruded among a company of silent worshippers, as they sit in Sabbath stillness among the tree tops. Their voices, when they speak, are in admirable accordance with the tranquil solitude of a summer afternoon; and, resounding so far above the head, their loud clamor increases the religious quiet of the scene instead of breaking it. A crow, however, has no real pretensions to religion, in spite of his gravity of mien and black attire; he is certainly a thief, and probably an infidel. The gulls are far more respectable, in a moral point of view.

These denizens of sea-beaten rocks and haunters of the lonely beach come up our inland river at this season, and soar high overhead, flapping their broad wings in the upper sunshine. They are among the most picturesque of birds, because they so float and rest upon the air as to become almost stationary parts of the landscape. The imagination has time to grow acquainted with them; they have not flitted away in a moment. You go up among the clouds and greet these lofty-flighted gulls, and repose confidently with them upon the sustaining atmosphere. Ducks have their haunts along the solitary places of the river, and alight in flocks upon the broad bosom of the overflowed meadows. Their flight is too rapid and determined for the eye to catch enjoyment from it, although it never fails to stir up the heart with the sportsman's ineradicable instinct. They have now gone farther northward, but will visit us again in autumn.

The smaller birds,—the little songsters of the woods, and those that haunt man's dwellings and claim human friendship by building their nests under the sheltering caves or among the orchard trees,—these require a touch more delicate and a gentler heart than mine to do them justice. Their outburst of melody is like a brook let loose from wintry chains. We need not deem it a too high and solemn word to call it a hymn of praise to the Creator; since Nature, who pictures the reviving year in so many sights of beauty, has expressed the sentiment of renewed life in no other sound save the notes of these blessed birds. Their music, however, just now, seems to be incidental, and not the result of a set purpose. They are discussing the economy of life and love and the site and architecture of their summer residences, and have no time to sit on a twig and pour forth solemn hymns, or overtures, operas, symphonies, and waltzes. Anxious questions are asked; grave subjects are settled in quick and animated debate; and only by occasional accident, as from pure ecstasy, does a rich warble roll its tiny waves of golden sound through the atmosphere. Their little bodies are as busy as their voices; they are in a constant flutter and restlessness. Even when two or three retreat to a tree top to hold council, they wag their tails and heads all the time with the irrepressible activity of their nature, which perhaps renders their brief span of life in reality as long as the patriarchal age of sluggish man. The blackbirds, three species of which consort together, are the noisiest of all our feathered citizens. Great companies of them—more than the famous "four and twenty" whom Mother Goose has immortalized[2]—congregate in contiguous tree tops and vociferate with all the clamor and confusion of a turbulent political meeting. Politics, certainly, must be the occasion of such tumultuous debates; but still, unlike all other politicians, they instil melody into their individual utterances and produce harmony as a general effect. Of all bird voices, none are more sweet and cheerful to my ear than those of swallows, in the dim, sun-streaked interior of a lofty barn; they address the heart with even a closer sympathy than robin redbreast. But, indeed, all these winged people, that dwell in the vicinity of homesteads, seem to partake of human nature, and possess the germ, if not the development, of immortal souls. We hear them saying their melodious prayers at morning's blush and eventide. A little while ago, in the deep of night, there came the lively thrill of a bird's note from a neighboring tree—a real song, such as greets the purple dawn or mingles with the yellow sunshine. What could the little bird mean by pouring it forth at midnight? Probably the music gushed out of the midst of a dream in which he fancied himself in paradise with his mate, but suddenly awoke on a cold, leafless bough, with a New England mist penetrating through his feathers. That was a sad exchange of imagination for reality.

Insects are among the earliest births of spring. Multitudes of I know not what species appeared long ago on the surface of the snow. Clouds of them, almost too minute for sight, hover in a beam of sunshine, and vanish, as if annihilated, when they pass into the shade. A mosquito has already been heard to sound the small horror of his bugle horn. Wasps infest the sunny windows of the house. A bee entered one of the chambers with a prophecy of flowers. Rare butterflies came before the snow was off, flaunting in the chill breeze, and looking forlorn and all astray, in spite of the magnificence of their dark, velvet cloaks, with golden borders.

The fields and woodpaths have as yet few charms to entice the wanderer. In a walk, the other day, I found no violets, nor anemones, nor any thing in the likeness of a flower. It was worth while, however, to ascend our opposite hill for the sake of gaining a general idea of the advance of spring, which I had hitherto been studying in its minute developments. The river lay around me in a semicircle, overflowing all the meadows which give it its Indian name,[3] and offering a noble breadth to sparkle in the sunbeams. Along the hither shore a row of trees stood up to their knees in water; and afar off, on the surface of the stream, tufts of bushes thrust up their heads, as it were, to breathe. The most striking objects were great solitary trees here and there, with a mile wide waste of water all around them. The curtailment of the trunk, by its immersion in the river, quite destroys the fair proportions of the tree, and thus makes us sensible of a regularity and propriety in the usual forms of Nature. The flood of the present season—though it never amounts to a freshet on our quiet stream—has encroached far-ther upon the land than any previous one for at least a score of years. It has overflowed stone fences, and even rendered a portion of the highway navigable for boats. The waters, however, are now gradually subsiding; islands become annexed to the main land; and other islands emerge, like new creations, from the watery waste. The scene supplies an admirable image of the receding of the Nile,[4] except that there is no deposit of black slime; or of Noah's flood, only that there is a fresh-ness and novelty in these recovered portions of the continent which give the impression of a world just made rather than of one so polluted that a deluge had been requisite to purify it. These upspringing islands are the greenest spots in the landscape; the first gleam of sunlight suf-fices to cover them with verdure.

Thank Providence for spring! The earth—and man himself, by sympathy with his birthplace—would be far other than we find them if life toiled wearily onward without this periodical infusion of the pri-mal spirit. Will the world ever be so decayed that spring may not renew its greenness? Can man be so dismally agestricken that no faintest sunshine of his youth may revisit him once a year? It is impos-sible. The moss on our timeworn mansion brightens into beauty; the good old pastor who once dwelt here renewed his prime, regained his boyhood, in the genial breezes of his ninetieth spring. Alas for the worn and heavy soul if, whether in youth or age, it have outlived its privilege of spring-time sprightliness! From such a soul the world must hope no reformation of its evil, no sympathy with the lofty faith and gallant struggles of those who contend in its behalf. Summer works in the present, and thinks not of the future; autumn is a rich conservative; winter has utterly lost its faith, and clings tremulously to the remembrance of what has been; but spring, with its outgushing life, is the true type of the movement.

MONSIEUR DU MIROIR

Than the gentleman above named, there is nobody, in the whole circle of my acquaintance, whom I have more attentively studied, yet of whom I have less real knowledge, beneath the surface which it pleases him to present. Being anxious to discover who and what he really is, and how connected with me, and what are to be the results to him and to myself of the joint interest which, without any choice on my part, seems to be permanently established between us,—and incited, further-more, by the propensities of a student of human nature, though doubt-ful whether Monsieur du Miroir have aught of humanity but the figure,—I have determined to place a few of his remarkable points be-fore the public, hoping to be favored with some clew[1] to the explana-tion of his character. Nor let the reader condemn any part of the narrative as frivolous, since a subject of such grave reflection diffuses its importance through the minutest particulars; and there is no judg-ing beforehand what odd little circumstance may do the office of a blind man's dog among the perplexities of this dark investigation; and however extraordinary, marvellous, preternatural, and utterly incredi-ble some of the meditated disclosures may appear, I pledge my honor to maintain as sacred a regard to fact as if my testimony were given on oath and involved the dearest interests of the personage in question. Not that there is matter for a criminal accusation against Monsieur du Miroir, nor am I the man to bring it forward if there were. The chief that I complain of is his impenetrable mystery, which is no better than nonsense if it conceal any thing good, and much worse in the contrary case.

But, if undue partialities could be supposed to influence me, Monsieur du Miroir might hope to profit rather than to suffer by them, for in the whole of our long intercourse we have seldom had the slightest disagreement; and, moreover, there are reasons for supposing him a near relative of mine, and consequently entitled to the best word that I can give him. He bears indisputably a strong personal resemblance to myself, and generally puts on mourning at the funerals of the family. On the other hand, his name would indicate a French descent; in which case, infinitely preferring that my blood should flow from a bold British and pure Puritan[2] source, I beg leave to disclaim all kindred with Monsieur du Miroir. Some genealogists trace his origin to Spain, and dub him a knight of the order of the CABALLEROS DE LOS ESPEJOZ, one of whom was overthrown by Don Quixote.[3] But what says Monsieur du Miroir himself of his paternity and his fatherland? Not a word did he ever say about the matter; and herein, perhaps, lies one of his most especial reasons for maintaining such a vexatious mystery, that he lacks the faculty of speech to expound it. His lips are sometimes seen to move; his eyes and countenance are alive with shifting expression, as if corresponding by visible hieroglyphics to his modulated breath; and anon he will seem to pause with as satisfied an air as if he had been talking excellent sense. Good sense or bad, Monsieur du Miroir is the sole judge of his own conversational powers, never having whispered so much as a syllable that reached the ears of any other auditor. Is he really dumb? or is all the world deaf? or is it merely a piece of my friend's waggery, meant for nothing but to make fools of us? If so, he has the joke all to himself.

This dumb devil which possesses Monsieur du Miroir is, I am persuaded, the sole reason that he does not make me the most flattering protestations of friendship. In many particulars—indeed, as to all his cognizable and not preternatural points, except that, once in a great while, I speak a word or two—there exists the greatest apparent sympathy between us. Such is his confidence in my taste that he goes astray from the general fashion and copies all his dresses after mine. I never try on a new garment without expecting to meet Monsieur du Miroir in one of the same pattern. He has duplicates of all my waistcoats and cravats, shirt bosoms of precisely a similar plait, and an old coat for private wear, manufactured, I suspect, by a Chinese tailor, in exact imitation of a beloved old coat of mine, with a facsimile, stitch by stitch, of a patch upon the elbow. In truth, the singular and minute coincidences that occur, both in the accidents of the passing day and the serious events of our lives, remind me of those doubtful legends of lovers, or twin children, twins of fate, who have lived, enjoyed, suffered, and died in unison, each faithfully repeating the last tremor of the other's breath, though separated by vast tracts of sea and land. Strange to say, my incommodities belong equally to my companion, though the burden is nowise alleviated by his participation. The other morning, after a night of torment from the toothache, I met Monsieur du Miroir with such a swollen anguish in his cheek that my own pangs were redoubled, as were also his, if I might judge by a fresh contortion of his visage. All the inequalities of my spirits are communicated to him, causing the unfortunate Monsieur du Miroir to mope and scowl through a whole summer's day, or to laugh as long, for no better reason than the gay or gloomy crotchets of my brain. Once we were joint sufferers of a three months' sickness, and met like mutual ghosts in the first days of convalescence. Whenever I have been in love, Monsieur du Miroir has looked passionate and tender; and never did my mistress discard me but this too susceptible gentleman grew lackadaisical. His temper, also, rises to blood heat, fever heat, or boiling water heat, according to the measure of any wrong which might seem to have fallen entirely on myself. I have sometimes been calmed down by the sight of my own inordinate wrath depicted on his frowning brow. Yet, however prompt in taking up my quarrels, I cannot call to mind that he ever struck a downright blow in my behalf; nor, in fact, do I perceive that any real and tangible good has resulted from his constant interference in my affairs; so that, in my distrustful moods, I am apt to suspect Monsieur du Miroir's sympathy to be mere outward show, not a whit better nor worse than other people's sympathy. Nevertheless, as mortal man must have something in the guise of sympathy,—and whether the true metal, or merely copperwashed,[4] is of less moment,—I choose rather to content myself with Monsieur du Miroir's, such as it is, than to seek the sterling coin, and perhaps miss even the counterfeit.

In my age of vanities I have often seen him in the ball room, and might again were I to seek him there. We have encountered each other at the Tremont Theatre,[5] where, however, he took his seat neither in the dress circle, pit, nor upper regions, nor threw a single glance at the stage, though the brightest star, even Fanny Kemble[6] herself, might be culminating there. No; this whimsical friend of mine chose to linger in the saloon, near one of the large looking glasses which throw back their pictures of the illuminated room. He is so full of these unaccountable eccentricities that I never like to notice Monsieur du Miroir, nor to acknowledge the slightest connection with him, in places of public resort. He, however, has no scruple about claiming my acquaintance, even when his common sense, if he had any, might teach him that I would as willingly exchange a nod with the Old Nick.[7] It was but the other day that he got into a large brass kettle at the entrance of a hardware store, and thrust his head, the moment afterwards, into a bright, new warming pan,[8] whence he gave me a most merciless look of recognition. He smiled, and so did I; but these childish tricks make decent people rather shy of Monsieur du Miroir, and subject him to more dead cuts than any other gentleman in town.

One of this singular person's most remarkable peculiarities is his fondness for water, wherein he excels any temperance man whatever. His pleasure, it must be owned, is not so much to drink it (in which respect a very moderate quantity will answer his occasions) as to souse himself over head and ears wherever he may meet with it. Perhaps he is a merman, or born of a mermaid's marriage with a mortal, and thus amphibious by hereditary right, like the children which the old river deities, or nymphs of fountains,[9] gave to earthly love. When no cleaner bathing-place happened to be at hand, I have seen the foolish fellow in a horse pond. Sometimes he refreshes himself in the trough of a town pump, without caring what the people think about him. Often, while carefully picking my way along the street after a heavy shower, I have been scandalized to see Monsieur du Miroir, in full dress, paddling from one mud puddle to another, and plunging into the filthy depths of each. Seldom have I peeped into a well without discerning this ridiculous gentleman at the bottom, whence he gazes up, as through a long telescopic tube, and probably makes discoveries among the stars by daylight. Wandering along lonesome paths or in pathless forests, when I have come to virgin fountains, of which it would have been pleasant to deem myself the first discoverer, I have started to find Monsieur du Miroir there before me. The solitude seemed lonelier for his presence. I have leaned from a precipice that frowns over Lake George, which the French call Nature's font of sacramental water,[10] and used it in their log churches here and their cathedrals beyond the sea, and seen him far below in that pure element. At Niagara,[11] too, where I would gladly have forgotten both myself and him, I could not help observing my companion in the smooth water on the very verge of the cataract just above the Table Rock.[12] Were I to reach the sources of the Nile,[13] I should expect to meet him there. Unless he be another Ladurlad,[14] whose garments the depths of ocean could not moisten, it is difficult to conceive how he keeps himself in any decent pickle; though I am bound to confess that his clothes seem always as dry and comfortable as my own. But, as a friend, I could wish that he would not so often expose himself in liquor.

All that I have hitherto related may be classed among those little personal oddities which agreeably diversify the surface of society, and, though they may sometimes annoy us, yet keep our daily intercourse fresher and livelier than if they were done away. By an occasional hint, however, I have endeavored to pave the way for stranger things to come, which, had they been disclosed at once, Monsieur du Miroir might have been deemed a shadow, and myself a person of no veracity, and this truthful history a fabulous legend. But, now that the reader knows me worthy of his confidence, I will begin to make him stare.

To speak frankly, then, I could bring the most astounding proofs that Monsieur du Miroir is at least a conjurer, if not one of that unearthly tribe with whom conjurers deal. He has inscrutable methods of conveying himself from place to place with the rapidity of the swiftest steamboat or rail car. Brick walls, and oaken doors, and iron bolts are no impediment to his passage. Here in my chamber, for instance, as the evening deepens into night, I sit alone—the key turned and withdrawn from the lock, the keyhole stuffed with paper to keep out a peevish little blast of wind. Yet, lonely as I seem, were I to lift one of the lamps and step five paces eastward, Monsieur du Miroir would be sure to meet me with a lamp also in his hand; and were I to take the stage coach to-morrow, without giving him the least hint of my design, and post onward till the week's end, at whatever hotel I might find myself I should expect to share my private apartment with this inevitable Monsieur du Miroir. Or, out of a mere wayward fantasy, were I to go, by moonlight, and stand beside the stone font of the Shaker Spring at

Canterbury,[15] Monsieur du Miroir would set forth on the same fool's errand, and would not fail to meet me there. Shall I heighten the reader's wonder? While writing these latter sentences, I happened to glance towards the large, round globe of one of the brass andirons, and lo! a miniature apparition of Monsieur du Miroir, with his face widened and grotesquely contorted, as if he were making fun of my amazement! But he has played so many of these jokes that they begin to lose their effect. Once, presumptuous that he was, he stole into the heaven of a young lady's eyes; so that, while I gazed and was dreaming only of herself, I found him also in my dream. Years have so changed him since that he need never hope to enter those heavenly orbs again.

From these veritable statements it will be readily concluded that, had Monsieur du Miroir played such pranks in old witch times, matters might have gone hard with him; at least, if the constable and posse comitatus[16] could have executed a warrant, or the jailer had been cunning enough to keep him. But it has often occurred to me as a very singular circumstance, and as betokening either a temperament morbidly suspicious or some weighty cause of apprehension, that he never trusts himself within the grasp even of his most intimate friend. If you step forward to meet him, he readily advances; if you offer him your hand, he extends his own with an air of the utmost frankness; but, though you calculate upon a hearty shake, you do not get hold of his little finger. Ah, this Monsieur du Miroir is a slippery fellow!

These truly are matters of special admiration. After vainly endeavoring, by the strenuous exertion of my own wits, to gain a satisfactory insight into the character of Monsieur du Miroir, I had recourse to certain wise men, and also to books of abstruse philosophy, seeking who it was that haunted me, and why. I heard long lectures and read huge volumes with little profit beyond the knowledge that many former instances are recorded, in successive ages, of similar connections between ordinary mortals and beings possessing the attributes of Monsieur du Miroir. Some now alive, perhaps, besides myself have such attendants. Would that Monsieur du Miroir could be persuaded to transfer his attachment to one of those, and allow some other of his race to assume the situation that he now holds in regard to me! If I must needs have so intrusive an intimate, who stares me in the face in my closest privacy and follows me even to my bed chamber, I should prefer—scandal apart—the laughing bloom of a young girl to the dark and bearded gravity of my present companion. But such desires are never to be gratified. Though the members of Monsieur du Miroir's family have been accused, perhaps justly, of visiting their friends often in splendid halls, and seldom in darksome dungeons, yet they exhibit a rare constancy to the objects of their first attachment, however unlovely in person or unamiable in disposition—however unfortunate, or even infamous, and deserted by all the world besides. So will it be with my associate. Our fates appear inseparably blended. It is my belief, as I find him mingling with my earliest recollections, that we came into existence together, as my shadow follows me into the sunshine, and that hereafter, as heretofore, the brightness or gloom of my fortunes will shine upon, or darken, the face of Monsieur du Miroir. As we have been young together, and as it is now near the summer noon with both of us, so, if long life be granted, shall each count his own wrinkles on the other's brow and his white hairs on the other's head. And when the coffin lid shall have closed over me and that face and form, which, more truly than the lover swears it to his beloved, are the sole light of his existence,—when they shall be laid in that dark chamber, whither his swift and secret footsteps cannot bring him,—then what is to become of poor Monsieur du Miroir? Will he have the fortitude, with my other friends, to take a last look at my pale countenance? Will he walk foremost in the funeral train? Will he come often and haunt around my grave, and weed away the nettles, and plant flowers amid the verdure, and scrape the moss out of the letters of my burial stone? Will he linger where I have lived, to remind the neglectful world of one who staked much to win a name, but will not then care whether he lost or won?

Not thus will he prove his deep fidelity. O, what terror, if this friend of mine, after our last farewell, should step into the crowded street, or roam along our old frequented path by the still waters, or sit down in the domestic circle where our faces are most familiar and beloved! No; but when the rays of heaven shall bless me no more, nor the thoughtful lamplight gleam upon my studies, nor the cheerful fireside gladden the meditative man, then, his task fulfilled, shall this mysterious being vanish from the earth forever. He will pass to the dark realm of nothingness, but will not find me there.

There is something fearful in bearing such a relation to a creature so imperfectly known, and in the idea that, to a certain extent, all which concerns myself will be reflected in its consequences upon him. When we feel that another is to share the selfsame fortune with ourselves we judge more severely of our prospects, and withhold our confidence from that delusive magic which appears to shed an infallibility of happiness over our own pathway. Of late years, indeed, there has been much to sadden my intercourse with Monsieur du Miroir. Had not our union been a necessary condition of our life, we must have been estranged ere now. In early youth, when my affections were warm and free, I loved him well, and could always spend a pleasant hour in his society, chiefly because it gave me an excellent opinion of myself. Speechless as he was, Monsieur du Miroir had then a most agreeable way of calling me a handsome fellow; and I, of course, returned the compliment; so that, the more we kept each other's company, the greater coxcombs[17] we mutually grew. But neither of us need apprehend any such misfortune now. When we chance to meet,—for it is chance oftener than design,—each glances sadly at the other's forehead, dreading wrinkles there; and at our temples, whence the hair is thinning away too early; and at the sunken eyes, which no longer shed a gladsome light over the whole face. I involuntarily peruse him as a record of my heavy youth, which has been wasted in sluggishness for lack of hope and impulse, or equally thrown away in toil that had no wise motive and has accomplished no good end. I perceive that the tranquil gloom of a disappointed soul has darkened through his countenance, where the blackness of the future seems to mingle with the shadows of the past, giving him the aspect of a fated man. Is it too wild a thought that my fate may have assumed this image of myself, and therefore haunts me with such inevitable pertinacity, originating every act which it appears to imitate, while it deludes me by pretending to share the events of which it is merely the emblem and the prophecy? I must banish this idea, or it will throw too deep an awe round my companion. At our next meeting, especially if it be at midnight or in solitude, I fear that I shall glance aside and shudder; in which case, as Monsieur du Miroir is extremely sensitive to ill treatment, he also will avert his eyes and express horror or disgust.

But no; this is unworthy of me. As of old I sought his society for the bewitching dreams of woman's love which he inspired and because I fancied a bright fortune in his aspect, so now will I hold daily and long communion with him for the sake of the stern lessons that he will teach my manhood. With folded arms we will sit face to face, and lengthen out our silent converse till a wiser cheerfulness shall have been wrought from the very texture of despondency. He will say, perhaps indignantly, that it befits only him to mourn for the decay of outward grace, which, while he possessed it, was his all. But have not you, he will ask, a treasure in reserve, to which every year may add far more value than age or death itself can snatch from that miserable clay? He will tell me that though the bloom of life has been nipped with a frost, yet the soul must not sit shivering in its cell, but bestir itself manfully, and kindle a genial warmth from its own exercise against the autumnal and the wintry atmosphere. And I, in return, will bid him be of good cheer, nor take it amiss that I must blanch his locks and wrinkle him up like a wilted apple, since it shall be my endeavor so to beautify his face with intellect and mild benevolence that he shall profit immensely by the change. But here a smile will glimmer somewhat sadly over Monsieur du Miroir's visage.

When this subject shall have been sufficiently discussed we may take up others as important. Reflecting upon his power of following me to the remotest regions and into the deepest privacy, I will compare the attempt to escape him to the hopeless race that men sometimes run with memory, or their own hearts, or their moral selves, which, though burdened with cares enough to crush an elephant, will never be one step behind. I will be self-contemplative, as Nature bids me, and make him the picture or visible type of what I muse upon, that my mind may not wander so vaguely as heretofore, chasing its own shadow through a chaos and catching only the monsters that abide there. Then will we turn our thoughts to the spiritual world, of the reality of which my companions shall furnish me an illustration, if not an argument; for, as we have only the testimony of the eye to Monsieur du Miroir's existence, while all the other senses would fail to inform us that such a figure stands within arm's length, wherefore should there not be beings innumerable close beside us, and filling heaven and earth with their multitude, yet of whom no corporeal perception can take cognizance? A blind man might as reasonably deny that Monsieur du Miroir exists as we, because the Creator has hitherto withheld the spiritual perception, can therefore contend that there are no spirits. O, there are! And, at this moment, when the subject of which I write has grown strong within me and surrounded itself with those solemn and awful associations which might have seemed most alien to it, I could fancy that Monsieur du Miroir himself is a wanderer from the spiritual world, with nothing human except his delusive garment of visibility. Methinks I should tremble now were his wizard power of gliding through all impediments in search of me to place him suddenly before my eyes.

Ha! What is yonder? Shape of mystery, did the tremor of my heartstrings vibrate to thine own, and call thee from thy home among the dancers of the northern lights, and shadows flung from departed sunshine, and giant spectres that appear on clouds at daybreak and affright the climber of the Alps? In truth it startled me, as I threw a wary glance eastward across the chamber, to discern an unbidden guest with his eyes bent on mine. The identical MONSIEUR DU MIROIR! Still there he sits and returns my gaze with as much of awe and curiosity as if he, too, had spent a solitary evening in fantastic musings and made me his theme. So inimitably does he counterfeit that I could almost doubt which of us is the visionary form, or whether each be not the other's mystery, and both twin brethren of one fate, in mutually reflected spheres. O friend, canst thou not hear and answer me? Break down the barrier between us! Grasp my hand! Speak! Listen! A few words, perhaps, might satisfy the feverish yearning of my soul for some master thought that should guide me through this labyrinth of life, teaching wherefore I was born, and how to do my task on earth, and what is death. Alas! Even that unreal image should forget to ape me and smile at these vain questions. Thus do mortals deify, as it were, a mere shadow of themselves, a spectre of human reason, and ask of that to unveil the mysteries which Divine Intelligence has revealed so far as needful to our guidance, and hid the rest.

Farewell, Monsieur du Miroir. Of you, perhaps, as of many men, it may be doubted whether you are the wiser, though your whole business is REFLECTION.

THE HALL OF FANTASY

It has happened to me, on various occasions, to find myself in a certain edifice which would appear to have some of the characteristics of a public exchange. Its interior is a spacious hall, with a pavement of white marble. Overhead is a lofty dome, supported by long rows of pillars of fantastic architecture, the idea of which was probably taken from the Moorish ruins of the Alhambra,[1] or perhaps from some enchanted edifice in the Arabian tales.[2] The windows of this hall have a breadth and grandeur of design and an elaborateness of workmanship that have nowhere been equalled except in the Gothic cathedrals of the old world. Like their prototypes, too, they admit the light of heaven only through stained and pictured glass, thus filling the hall with many-colored radiance and painting its marble floor with beautiful or grotesque designs; so that its inmates breathe, as it were, a visionary atmosphere, and tread upon the fantasies of poetic minds. These peculiarities, combining a wilder mixture of styles than even an American architect usually recognizes as allowable,—Grecian, Gothic, Oriental, and nondescript,—cause the whole edifice to give the impression of a dream, which might be dissipated and shattered to fragments by merely stamping the foot upon the pavement. Yet, with such modifications and repairs as successive ages demand, the Hall of Fantasy is likely to endure longer than the most substantial structure that ever cumbered the earth.

It is not at all times that one can gain admittance into this edifice, although most persons enter it at some period or other of their lives; if not in their waking moments, then by the universal passport of a dream. At my last visit I wandered thither unawares while my mind was busy with an idle tale, and was startled by the throng of people who seemed suddenly to rise up around me.

"Bless me! Where am I?" cried I, with but a dim recognition of the place.

"You are in a spot," said a friend who chanced to be near at hand, "which occupies in the world of fancy the same position which the Bourse, the Rialto, and the Exchange[3] do in the commercial world. All who have affairs in that mystic region, which lies above, below, or beyond the actual, may here meet and talk over the business of their dreams."

"It is a noble hall," observed I.

"Yes," he replied. "Yet we see but a small portion of the edifice. In its upper stories are said to be apartments where the inhabitants of earth may hold converse with those of the moon; and beneath our feet are gloomy cells, which communicate with the infernal regions, and where monsters and chimeras are kept in confinement and fed with all unwholesomeness."

In niches and on pedestals around about the hall stood the statues or busts of men who in every age have been rulers and demigods in the realms of imagination and its kindred regions. The grand old countenance of Homer;[4] the shrunken and decrepit form but vivid face of Æsop;[5] the dark presence of Dante;[6] the wild Ariosto;[7] Rabelais' smile[8] of deep-wrought mirth; the profound, pathetic humor of Cervantes;[9] the all-glorious Shakspeare;[10] Spenser,[11] meet guest for an allegoric structure; the severe divinity of Milton;[12] and Bunyan,[13] moulded of homeliest clay, but instinct with celestial fire,—were those that chiefly attracted my eye. Fielding, Richardson, and Scott[14] occupied conspicuous pedestals. In an obscure and shadowy niche was deposited the bust of our countryman, the author of Arthur Mervyn.[15]

"Besides these indestructible memorials of real genius," remarked my companion, "each century has erected statues of its own ephemeral favorites in wood."

"I observe a few crumbling relics of such," said I. "But ever and anon, I suppose, Oblivion comes with her huge broom and sweeps them all from the marble floor. But such will never be the fate of this fine statue of Goethe."[16]

"Nor of that next to it—Emanuel Swedenborg,"[17] said he. "Were ever two men of transcendent imagination more unlike?"

In the centre of the hall springs an ornamental fountain, the water of which continually throws itself into new shapes and snatches the most diversified hues from the stained atmosphere around. It is impossible to conceive what a strange vivacity is imparted to the scene by the magic dance of this fountain, with its endless transformations, in which the imaginative beholder may discern what form he will. The water is supposed by some to flow from the same source as the Castalian spring,[18] and is extolled by others as uniting the virtues of the Fountain of Youth with those of many other enchanted wells long celebrated in tale and song. Having never tasted it, I can bear no testimony to its quality.

"Did you ever drink this water?" I inquired of my friend.

"A few sips now and then," answered he. "But there are men here who make it their constant beverage—or, at least, have the credit of doing so. In some instances it is known to have intoxicating qualities."

"Pray let us look at these water drinkers," said I.

So we passed among the fantastic pillars till we came to a spot where a number of persons were clustered together in the light of one of the great stained windows, which seemed to glorify the whole group as well as the marble that they trod on. Most of them were men of broad foreheads, meditative countenances, and thoughtful, inward eyes; yet it required but a trifle to summon up mirth, peeping out from the very midst of grave and lofty musings. Some strode about, or leaned against the pillars of the hall, alone and in silence; their faces wore a rapt expression, as if sweet music were in the air around them or as if their inmost souls were about to float away in song. One or two, perhaps, stole a glance at the bystanders, to watch if their poetic absorption were observed. Others stood talking in groups, with a liveliness of expression, a ready smile, and a light, intellectual laughter, which showed how rapidly the shafts of wit were glancing to and fro among them.

A few held higher converse, which caused their calm and melancholy souls to beam moonlight from their eyes. As I lingered near them,—for I felt an inward attraction towards these men, as if the sympathy of feeling, if not of genius, had united me to their order,—my friend mentioned several of their names. The world has likewise heard those names; with some it has been familiar for years; and others are daily making their way deeper into the universal heart.

"Thank Heaven," observed I to my companion, as we passed to another part of the hall, "we have done with this techy,[19] wayward, shy, proud, unreasonable set of laurel gatherers. I love them in their works, but have little desire to meet them elsewhere."

"You have adopted an old prejudice, I see," replied my friend, who was familiar with most of these worthies, being himself a student of poetry, and not without the poetic flame. "But, so far as my experience goes, men of genius are fairly gifted with the social qualities; and in this age there appears to be a fellow-feeling among them which had not heretofore been developed. As men, they ask nothing better than to be on equal terms with their fellow-men; and as authors, they have thrown aside their proverbial jealousy, and acknowledge a generous brotherhood."

"The world does not think so," answered I. "An author is received in general society pretty much as we honest citizens are in the Hall of Fantasy. We gaze at him as if he had no business among us, and question whether he is fit for any of our pursuits."

"Then it is a very foolish question," said he. "Now, here are a class of men whom we may daily meet on 'Change.[20] Yet what poet in the hall is more a fool of fancy than the sagest of them?"

He pointed to a number of persons, who, manifest as the fact was, would have deemed it an insult to be told that they stood in the Hall of Fantasy. Their visages were traced into wrinkles and furrows, each of which seemed the record of some actual experience in life. Their eyes had the shrewd, calculating glance which detects so quickly and so surely all that it concerns a man of business to know about the characters and purposes of his fellow-men. Judging them as they stood, they might be honored and trusted members of the Chamber of Commerce, who had found the genuine secret of wealth and whose sagacity gave them the command of fortune. There was a character of detail and matter of fact in their talk which concealed the extravagance of its purport, insomuch that the wildest schemes had the aspect of everyday realities. Thus the listener was not startled at the idea of cities to be built, as if by magic, in the heart of pathless forests; and of streets to be laid out where now the sea was tossing; and of mighty rivers to be stayed in their courses in order to turn the machinery of a cotton mill. It was only by an effort, and scarcely then, that the mind convinced itself that such speculations were as much matter of fantasy as the old dream of Eldorado,[21] or as Mammon's Cave,[22] or any other vision of gold ever conjured up by the imagination of needy poet or romantic adventurer.

"Upon my word," said I, "it is dangerous to listen to such dreamers as these. Their madness is contagious."

"Yes," said my friend, "because they mistake the Hall of Fantasy for actual brick and mortar and its purple atmosphere for unsophisticated sunshine. But the poet knows his whereabouts, and therefore is less likely to make a fool of himself in real life."

"Here again," observed I, as we advanced a little farther, "we see another order of dreamers, peculiarly characteristic, too, of the genius of our country."

These were the inventors of fantastic machines. Models of their contrivances were placed against some of the pillars of the hall, and afforded good emblems of the result generally to be anticipated from an attempt to reduce daydreams to practice. The analogy may hold in morals as well as physics; for instance, here was the model of a railroad through the air and a tunnel under the sea. Here was a machine— stolen, I believe—for the distillation of heat from moonshine; and another for the condensation of morning mist into square blocks of granite, wherewith it was proposed to rebuild the entire Hall of Fantasy. One man exhibited a sort of lens whereby he had succeeded in making sunshine out of a lady's smile; and it was his purpose wholly to irradiate the earth by means of this wonderful invention.

"It is nothing new," said I; "for most of our sunshine comes from woman's smile already."

"True," answered the inventor; "but my machine will secure a constant supply for domestic use; whereas hitherto it has been very precarious."

Another person had a scheme for fixing the reflections of objects in a pool of water, and thus taking the most lifelike portraits imaginable; and the same gentleman demonstrated the practicability of giving a permanent dye to ladies' dresses, in the gorgeous clouds of sunset. There were at least fifty kinds of perpetual motion, one of which was applicable to the wits of newspaper editors and writers of every description. Professor Espy[23] was here, with a tremendous storm in a gum-elastic[24] bag. I could enumerate many more of these Utopian inventions; but, after all, a more imaginative collection is to be found in the patent office at Washington.

Turning from the inventors we took a more general survey of the inmates of the hall. Many persons were present whose right of entrance appeared to consist in some crotchet of the brain, which, so long as it might operate, produced a change in their relation to the actual world. It is singular how very few there are who do not occasionally gain admittance on such a score, either in abstracted musings, or momentary thoughts, or bright anticipations, or vivid remembrances; for even the actual becomes ideal, whether in hope or memory, and beguiles the dreamer into the Hall of Fantasy. Some unfortunates make their whole abode and business here, and contract habits which unfit them for all the real employments of life. Others—but these are few— possess the faculty, in their occasional visits, of discovering a purer truth than the world can impart among the lights and shadows of these pictured windows.

And with all its dangerous influences, we have reason to thank God that there is such a place of refuge from the gloom and chillness of actual life. Hither may come the prisoner, escaping from his dark and narrow cell and cankerous chain, to breathe free air in this enchanted atmosphere. The sick man leaves his weary pillow, and finds strength to wander hither, though his wasted limbs might not support him even to the threshold of his chamber. The exile passes through the Hall of Fantasy to revisit his native soil. The burden of years rolls down from the old man's shoulders the moment that the door uncloses. Mourners leave their heavy sorrows at the entrance, and here rejoin the lost ones whose faces would else be seen no more, until thought shall have become the only fact. It may be said, in truth, that there is but half a life—the meaner and earthlier half—for those who never find their way into the hall. Nor must I fail to mention that in the observatory of the edifice is kept that wonderful perspective glass, through which the shepherds of the Delectable Mountains[25] showed Christian the far-off gleam of the Celestial City. The eye of Faith still loves to gaze through it.

"I observe some men here," said I to my friend, "who might set up a strong claim to be reckoned among the most real personages of the day."

"Certainly," he replied. "If a man be in advance of his age, he must be content to make his abode in this hall until the lingering generations of his fellow-men come up with him. He can find no other shelter in the universe. But the fantasies of one day are the deepest realities of a future one."

"It is difficult to distinguish them apart amid the gorgeous and bewildering light of this hall," rejoined I. "The white sunshine of actual life is necessary in order to test them. I am rather apt to doubt both men and their reasonings till I meet them in that truthful medium."

"Perhaps your faith in the ideal is deeper than you are aware," said my friend. "You are at least a democrat; and methinks no scanty share of such faith is essential to the adoption of that creed."

Among the characters who had elicited these remarks were most of the noted reformers of the day, whether in physics, politics, morals, or religion. There is no surer method of arriving at the Hall of Fantasy than to throw one's self into the current of a theory; for, whatever landmarks of fact may be set up along the stream, there is a law of nature that impels it thither. And let it be so; for here the wise head and capacious heart may do their work; and what is good and true becomes gradually hardened into fact, while error melts away and vanishes among the shadows of the hall. Therefore may none who believe and rejoice in the progress of mankind be angry with me because I recognized their apostles and leaders amid the fantastic radiance of those pictured windows. I love and honor such men as well as they.

It would be endless to describe the herd of real or self-styled reformers that peopled this place of refuge. They were the representatives of an unquiet period, when mankind is seeking to cast off the whole tissue of ancient custom like a tattered garment. Many of them had got possession of some crystal fragment of truth, the brightness of which so dazzled them that they could see nothing else in the wide universe. Here were men whose faith had imbodied itself in the form of a potato; and others whose long beards had a deep spiritual significance. Here was the abolitionist, brandishing his one idea like an iron flail. In a word, there were a thousand shapes of good and evil, faith and infidelity, wisdom and nonsense—a most incongruous throng.

Yet, withal, the heart of the stanchest conservative, unless he abjured his fellowship with man, could hardly have helped throbbing in sympathy with the spirit that pervaded these innumerable theorists. It was good for the man of unquickened heart to listen even to their folly. Far down beyond the fathom of the intellect the soul acknowledged that all these varying and conflicting developments of humanity were united in one sentiment. Be the individual theory as wild as fancy could make it, still the wiser spirit would recognize the struggle of the race after a better and purer life than had yet been realized on earth. My faith revived even while I rejected all their schemes. It could not be that the world should continue forever what it has been; a soil where Happiness is so rare a flower and Virtue so often a blighted fruit; a battle field where the good principle, with its shield flung above its head, can hardly save itself amid the rush of adverse influences. In the enthusiasm of such thoughts I gazed through one of the pictured windows, and, behold! the whole external world was tinged with the dimly glorious aspect that is peculiar to the Hall of Fantasy, insomuch that it seemed practicable at that very instant to realize some plan for the perfection of mankind. But, alas! if reformers would understand the sphere in which their lot is cast they must cease to look through pictured windows. Yet they not only use this medium, but mistake it for the whitest sunshine.

"Come," said I to my friend, starting from a deep revery, "let us hasten hence or I shall be tempted to make a theory, after which there is little hope of any man."

"Come hither, then," answered he. "Here is one theory that swallows up and annihilates all others."

He led me to a distant part of the hall where a crowd of deeply attentive auditors were assembled round an elderly man of plain, honest, trustworthy aspect. With an earnestness that betokened the sincerest faith in his own doctrine, he announced that the destruction of the world was close at hand.

"It is Father Miller[26] himself!" exclaimed I.

"No less a man," said my friend; "and observe how picturesque a contrast between his dogma and those of the reformers whom we have just glanced at. They look for the earthly perfection of mankind and are forming schemes which imply that the immortal spirit will be connected with a physical nature for innumerable ages of futurity. On the other hand, here comes good Father Miller, and with one puff of his relentless theory scatters all their dreams like so many withered leaves upon the blast."

"It is, perhaps, the only method of getting mankind out of the various perplexities into which they have fallen," I replied. "Yet I could wish that the world might be permitted to endure until some great moral shall have been evolved. A riddle is propounded. Where is the solution? The sphinx did not slay herself until her riddle had been guessed. Will it not be so with the world? Now, if it should be burned to-morrow morning, I am at a loss to know what purpose will have been accomplished, or how the universe will be wiser or better for our existence and destruction."

"We cannot tell what mighty truths may have been imbodied in act through the existence of the globe and its inhabitants," rejoined my companion. "Perhaps it may be revealed to us after the fall of the curtain over our catastrophe; or not impossibly, the whole drama, in which we are involuntary actors, may have been performed for the instruction of another set of spectators. I cannot perceive that our own comprehension of it is at all essential to the matter. At any rate, while our view is so ridiculously narrow and superficial it would be absurd to argue the continuance of the world from the fact that it seems to have existed hitherto in vain."

"The poor old earth," murmured I. "She has faults enough, in all conscience, but I cannot bear to have her perish."

"It is no great matter," said my friend. "The happiest of us has been weary of her many a time and oft."

"I doubt it," answered I, pertinaciously; "the root of human nature strikes down deep into this earthly soil, and it is but reluctantly that we submit to be transplanted, even for a higher cultivation in heaven. I query whether the destruction of the earth would gratify any one individual, except perhaps some embarrassed man of business whose notes fall due a day after the day of doom."

Then methought I heard the expostulating cry of a multitude against the consummation prophesied by Father Miller. The lover wrestled with Providence for his foreshadowed bliss. Parents entreated that the earth's span of endurance might be prolonged by some seventy years, so that their new-born infant should not be defrauded of his lifetime. A youthful poet murmured because there would be no posterity to recognize the inspiration of his song. The reformers, one and all, demanded a few thousand years to test their theories, after which the universe might go to wreck. A mechanician, who was busied with an improvement of the steam engine, asked merely time to perfect his model. A miser insisted that the world's destruction would be a personal wrong to himself, unless he should first be permitted to add a specified sum to his enormous heap of gold. A little boy made dolorous inquiry whether the last day would come before Christmas, and thus deprive him of his anticipated dainties. In short, nobody seemed satisfied that this mortal scene of things should have its close just now. Yet, it must be confessed, the motives of the crowd for desiring its continuance were mostly so absurd that unless infinite Wisdom had been aware of much better reasons, the solid earth must have melted away at once.

For my own part, not to speak of a few private and personal ends, I really desired our old mother's prolonged existence for her own dear sake.

"The poor old earth!" I repeated. "What I should chiefly regret in her destruction would be that very earthliness which no other sphere or state of existence can renew or compensate. The fragrance of flowers and of new-mown hay; the genial warmth of sunshine, and the beauty of a sunset among clouds; the comfort and cheerful glow of the fireside; the deliciousness of fruits and of all good cheer; the magnificence of mountains, and seas, and cataracts, and the softer charm of rural scenery; even the fast falling snow, and the gray atmosphere through which it descends—all these and innumerable other enjoyable things of earth must perish with her. Then the country frolics; the homely humor; the broad, open-mouthed roar of laughter, in which body and soul conjoin so heartily! I fear that no other world can show us any thing just like this. As for purely moral enjoyments, the good will find them in every state of being. But where the material and the moral exist together, what is to happen then? And then our mute four-footed friends and the winged songsters of our woods! Might it not be lawful to regret them, even in the hallowed groves of paradise?"

"You speak like the very spirit of earth, imbued with a scent of freshly turned soil," exclaimed my friend.

"It is not that I so much object to giving up these enjoyments on my own account," continued I, "but I hate to think that they will have been eternally annihilated from the list of joys."

"Nor need they be," he replied. "I see no real force in what you say. Standing in this Hall of Fantasy, we perceive what even the earth-clogged intellect of man can do in creating circumstances which, though we call them shadowy and visionary, are scarcely more so than those that surround us in actual life. Doubt not then that man's disimbodied spirit may recreate time and the world for itself, with all their peculiar enjoyments, should there still be human yearnings amid life eternal and infinite. But I doubt whether we shall be inclined to play such a poor scene over again."

"O, you are ungrateful to our mother earth!" rejoined I. "Come what may, I never will forget her! Neither will it satisfy me to have her exist merely in idea. I want her great, round, solid self to endure interminably, and still be peopled with the kindly race of man, whom I uphold to be much better than he thinks himself. Nevertheless, I confide the whole matter to Providence, and shall endeavor so to live that the world may come to an end at any moment without leaving me at a loss to find foothold somewhere else."

"It is an excellent resolve," said my companion, looking at his watch. "But come; it is the dinner hour. Will you partake of my vegetable diet?"

A thing so matter-of-fact as an invitation to dinner, even when the fare was to be nothing more substantial than vegetables and fruit, compelled us forthwith to remove from the Hall of Fantasy. As we passed out of the portal we met the spirits of several persons who had been sent thither in magnetic sleep. I looked back among the sculptured pillars and at the transformations of the gleaming fountain, and almost desired that the whole of life might be spent in that visionary scene where the actual world, with its hard angles, should never rub against me, and only be viewed through the medium of pictured windows. But for those who waste all their days in the Hall of Fantasy good Father Miller's prophecy is already accomplished, and the solid earth has come to an untimely end. Let us be content, therefore, with merely an occasional visit, for the sake of spiritualizing the grossness of this actual life, and prefiguring to ourselves a state in which the Idea shall be all in all.

The Celestial Railroad

Not a great while ago, passing through the gate of dreams, I visited
that region of the earth in which lies the famous City of Destruction.[1]
It interested me much to learn that by the public spirit of some of the
inhabitants a railroad has recently been established between this popu-
lous and flourishing town and the Celestial City. Having a little time
upon my hands, I resolved to gratify a liberal curiosity by making a
trip thither. Accordingly, one fine morning after paying my bill at the
hotel and directing the porter to stow my luggage behind a coach, I
took my seat in the vehicle and set out for the station house. It was my
good fortune to enjoy the company of a gentleman—one Mr. Smooth-
it-away—who, though he had never actually visited the Celestial City,
yet seemed as well acquainted with its laws, customs, policy, and sta-
tistics as with those of the City of Destruction, of which he was a native townsman. Being moreover a director of the railroad corporation
and one of its largest stockholders, he had it in his power to give me all
desirable information respecting that praiseworthy enterprise.

Our coach rattled out of the city, and at a short distance from its
outskirts passed over a bridge of elegant construction, but somewhat
too slight, as I imagined, to sustain any considerable weight. On both
sides lay an extensive quagmire, which could not have been more disagreeable, either to sight or smell, had all the kennels[2] of the earth
emptied their pollution there.

"This," remarked Mr. Smooth-it-away, "is the famous Slough of Despond[3]—a disgrace to all the neighborhood; and the greater, that it might so easily be converted into firm ground."

"I have understood," said I, "that efforts have been made for that purpose from time immemorial. Bunyan mentions that above twenty thousand cartloads of wholesome instructions had been thrown in here without effect."

"Very probably! And what effect could be anticipated from such unsubstantial stuff?" cried Mr. Smooth-it-away. "You observe this convenient bridge. We obtained a sufficient foundation for it by throwing into the slough some editions of books of morality; volumes of French philosophy and German rationalism; tracts, sermons, and essays of modern clergymen; extracts from Plato,[4] Confucius,[5] and various Hindoo sages, together with a few ingenious commentaries upon texts of Scripture,—all of which, by some scientific process, have been converted into a mass like granite. The whole bog might be filled up with similar matter."

It really seemed to me, however, that the bridge vibrated and heaved up and down in a very formidable manner, and, in spite of Mr. Smooth-it-away's testimony to the solidity of its foundation, I should be loath to cross it in a crowded omnibus, especially if each passenger were encumbered with as heavy luggage as that gentleman and myself. Nevertheless we got over without accident, and soon found ourselves at the station house. This very neat and spacious edifice is erected on the site of the little wicket gate,[6] which formerly, as all old pilgrims will recollect, stood directly across the highway, and, by its inconvenient narrowness, was a great obstruction to the traveller of liberal mind and expansive stomach. The reader of John Bunyan will be glad to know that Christian's old friend Evangelist,[7] who was accustomed to supply each pilgrim with a mystic roll, now presides at the ticket office. Some malicious persons it is true deny the identity of this reputable character with the Evangelist of old times, and even pretend to bring competent evidence of an imposture. Without involving myself in a dispute I shall merely observe that, so far as my experience goes, the square pieces of pasteboard now delivered to passengers are much more convenient and useful along the road than the antique roll of parchment. Whether they will be as readily received at the gate of the Celestial City I decline giving an opinion.

A large number of passengers were already at the station house awaiting the departure of the cars. By the aspect and demeanor of these persons it was easy to judge that the feelings of the community had undergone a very favorable change in reference to the celestial pilgrimage. It would have done Bunyan's heart good to see it. Instead of a lonely and ragged man, with a huge burden on his back, plodding along sorrowfully on foot while the whole city hooted after him, here were parties of the first gentry and most respectable people in the neighborhood setting forth towards the Celestial City as cheerfully as if the pilgrimage were merely a summer tour. Among the gentlemen were characters of deserved eminence—magistrates, politicians, and men of wealth, by whose example religion could not but be greatly recommended to their meaner brethren. In the ladies' apartment, too, I rejoiced to distinguish some of those flowers of fashionable society who are so well fitted to adorn the most elevated circles of the Celestial City. There was much pleasant conversation about the news of the day, topics of business, and politics, or the lighter matters of amusement; while religion, though indubitably the main thing at heart, was thrown tastefully into the background. Even an infidel would have heard little or nothing to shock his sensibility.

One great convenience of the new method of going on pilgrimage I must not forget to mention. Our enormous burdens,[8] instead of being carried on our shoulders as had been the custom of old, were all snugly deposited in the baggage car, and, as I was assured, would be delivered to their respective owners at the journey's end. Another thing, likewise, the benevolent reader will be delighted to understand. It may be remembered that there was an ancient feud between Prince Beelzebub and the keeper of the wicket gate,[9] and that the adherents of the former distinguished personage were accustomed to shoot deadly arrows at honest pilgrims while knocking at the door. This dispute, much to the credit as well of the illustrious potentate above mentioned as of the worthy and enlightened directors of the railroad, has been pacifically arranged on the principle of mutual compromise. The prince's subjects are now pretty numerously employed about the station house, some in taking care of the baggage, others in collecting fuel, feeding the engines, and such congenial occupations; and I can conscientiously affirm that persons more attentive to their business, more willing to accommodate, or more generally agreeable to the passengers, are not to be found on any railroad. Every good heart must surely exult at so satisfactory an arrangement of an immemorial difficulty.

"Where is Mr. Greatheart?"[10] inquired I. "Beyond a doubt the directors have engaged that famous old champion to be chief conductor on the railroad?"

"Why, no," said Mr. Smooth-it-away, with a dry cough. "He was offered the situation of brakeman; but, to tell you the truth, our friend Greatheart has grown preposterously stiff and narrow in his old age. He has so often guided pilgrims over the road on foot that he considers it a sin to travel in any other fashion. Besides, the old fellow had entered so heartily into the ancient feud with Prince Beelzebub that he would have been perpetually at blows or ill language with some of the prince's subjects, and thus have embroiled us anew. So, on the whole, we were not sorry when honest Greatheart went off to the Celestial City in a huff and left us at liberty to choose a more suitable and accommodating man. Yonder comes the engineer of the train. You will probably recognize him at once."

The engine at this moment took its station in advance of the cars, looking, I must confess, much more like a sort of mechanical demon that would hurry us to the infernal regions than a laudable contrivance for smoothing our way to the Celestial City. On its top sat a personage almost enveloped in smoke and flame, which, not to startle the reader, appeared to gush from his own mouth and stomach as well as from the engine's brazen abdomen.

"Do my eyes deceive me?" cried I. "What on earth is this! A living creature? If so, he is own brother to the engine he rides upon!"

"Poh, poh, you are obtuse!" said Mr. Smooth-it-away, with a hearty laugh. "Don't you know Apollyon,[11] Christian's old enemy, with whom he fought so fierce a battle in the Valley of Humiliation? He was the very fellow to manage the engine; and so we have reconciled him to the custom of going on pilgrimage, and engaged him as chief engineer."

"Bravo, bravo!" exclaimed I, with irrepressible enthusiasm; "this shows the liberality of the age; this proves, if any thing can, that all musty prejudices are in a fair way to be obliterated. And how will

Christian rejoice to hear of this happy transformation of his old antagonist! I promise myself great pleasure in informing him of it when we reach the Celestial City."

The passengers being all comfortably seated, we now rattled away merrily, accomplishing a greater distance in ten minutes than Christian probably trudged over in a day. It was laughable, while we glanced along, as it were, at the tail of a thunderbolt, to observe two dusty foot travellers in the old pilgrim guise, with cockle shell and staff,[12] their mystic rolls of parchment in their hands and their intolerable burdens on their backs. The preposterous obstinacy of these honest people in persisting to groan and stumble along the difficult pathway rather than take advantage of modern improvements, excited great mirth among our wiser brotherhood. We greeted the two pilgrims with many pleasant gibes and a roar of laughter; whereupon they gazed at us with such woful and absurdly compassionate visages that our merriment grew tenfold more obstreperous. Apollyon also entered heartily into the fun, and contrived to flirt the smoke and flame of the engine, or of his own breath, into their faces, and envelop them in an atmosphere of scalding steam. These little practical jokes amused us mightily, and doubtless afforded the pilgrims the gratification of considering themselves martyrs.

At some distance from the railroad Mr. Smooth-it-away pointed to a large, antique edifice, which, he observed, was a tavern of long standing, and had formerly been a noted stopping-place for pilgrims. In Bunyan's road book it is mentioned as the Interpreter's House.[13]

"I have long had a curiosity to visit that old mansion," remarked I.

"It is not one of our stations, as you perceive," said my companion. "The keeper was violently opposed to the railroad; and well he might be, as the track left his house of entertainment on one side, and thus was pretty certain to deprive him of all his reputable customers. But the footpath still passes his door; and the old gentleman now and then receives a call from some simple traveller, and entertains him with fare as old fashioned as himself."

Before our talk on this subject came to a conclusion we were rushing by the place where Christian's burden fell from his shoulders at the sight of the Cross. This served as a theme for Mr. Smooth-it-away, Mr. Live-for-the-world, Mr. Hide-sin-in-the-heart, Mr. Scaly-conscience, and a knot of gentlemen from the town of Shun-repentance, to descant upon the inestimable advantages resulting from the safety of our baggage. Myself, and all the passengers indeed, joined with great unanimity in this view of the matter; for our burdens were rich in many things esteemed precious throughout the world; and, especially, we each of us possessed a great variety of favorite Habits, which we trusted would not be out of fashion even in the polite circles of the Celestial City. It would have been a sad spectacle to see such an assortment of valuable articles tumbling into the sepulchre. Thus pleasantly conversing on the favorable circumstances of our position as compared with those of past pilgrims and of narrow minded ones at the present day, we soon found ourselves at the foot of the Hill Difficulty.[14] Through the very heart of this rocky mountain a tunnel has been constructed of most admirable architecture, with a lofty arch and a spacious double track; so that, unless the earth and rocks should chance to crumble down, it will remain an eternal monument of the builder's skill and enterprise. It is a great though incidental advantage that the materials from the heart of the Hill Difficulty have been employed in filling up the Valley of Humiliation, thus obviating the necessity of descending into that disagreeable and unwholesome hollow.

"This is a wonderful improvement, indeed," said I. "Yet I should have been glad of an opportunity to visit the Palace Beautiful[15] and be introduced to the charming young ladies—Miss Prudence, Miss Piety, Miss Charity, and the rest—who have the kindness to entertain pilgrims there."

"Young ladies!" cried Mr. Smooth-it-away, as soon as he could speak for laughing. "And charming young ladies! Why, my dear fellow, they are old maids, every soul of them—prim, starched, dry, and angular; and not one of them, I will venture to say, has altered so much as the fashion of her gown since the days of Christian's pilgrimage."

"Ah, well," said I, much comforted, "then I can very readily dispense with their acquaintance."

The respectable Apollyon was now putting on the steam at a prodigious rate, anxious, perhaps, to get rid of the unpleasant reminiscences connected with the spot where he had so disastrously encountered Christian. Consulting Mr. Bunyan's road book, I perceived that we must now be within a few miles of the Valley of the Shadow of Death,[16] into which doleful region, at our present speed, we should plunge much sooner than seemed at all desirable. In truth, I expected nothing better than to find myself in the ditch on one side or the quag on the other; but on communicating my apprehensions to Mr. Smooth-it-away, he assured me that the difficulties of this passage, even in its worst condition, had been vastly exaggerated, and that, in its present state of improvement, I might consider myself as safe as on any rail-road in Christendom.

Even while we were speaking the train shot into the entrance of this dreaded Valley. Though I plead guilty to some foolish palpitations of the heart during our headlong rush over the causeway here constructed, yet it were unjust to withhold the highest encomiums on the boldness of its original conception and the ingenuity of those who executed it. It was gratifying, likewise, to observe how much care had been taken to dispel the everlasting gloom and supply the defect of cheerful sunshine, not a ray of which has ever penetrated among these awful shadows. For this purpose, the inflammable gas which exudes plentifully from the soil is collected by means of pipes, and thence communicated to a quadruple row of lamps along the whole extent of the passage. Thus a radiance has been created even out of the fiery and sulphurous curse that rests forever upon the valley—a radiance hurtful, however, to the eyes, and somewhat bewildering, as I discovered by the changes which it wrought in the visages of my companions. In this respect, as compared with natural daylight, there is the same difference as between truth and falsehood; but if the reader have ever travelled through the dark Valley, he will have learned to be thankful for any light that he could get—if not from the sky above, then from the blasted soil beneath. Such was the red brilliancy of these lamps that they appeared to build walls of fire on both sides of the track, between which we held our course at lightning speed, while a reverberating thunder filled the Valley with its echoes. Had the engine run off the track,—a catastrophe, it is whispered, by no means unprecedented,— the bottomless pit, if there be any such place, would undoubtedly have received us. Just as some dismal fooleries of this nature had made my heart quake there came a tremendous shriek, careering along the valley as if a thousand devils had burst their lungs to utter it, but which proved to be merely the whistle of the engine on arriving at a stopping-place.

The spot where we had now paused is the same that our friend

Bunyan—a truthful man, but infected with many fantastic notions—
has designated, in terms plainer than I like to repeat, as the mouth of
the infernal region. This, however, must be a mistake, inasmuch as Mr.
Smooth-it-away, while we remained in the smoky and lurid cavern,
took occasion to prove that Tophet[17] has not even a metaphorical existence. The place, he assured us, is no other than the crater of a half-
extinct volcano, in which the directors had caused forges to be set up
for the manufacture of railroad iron. Hence, also, is obtained a plentiful supply of fuel for the use of the engines. Whoever had gazed into
the dismal obscurity of the broad cavern mouth, whence ever and
anon darted huge tongues of dusky flame, and had seen the strange,
half-shaped monsters, and visions of faces horribly grotesque, into
which the smoke seemed to wreathe itself, and had heard the awful
murmurs, and shrieks, and deep, shuddering whispers of the blast,
sometimes forming themselves into words almost articulate, would
have seized upon Mr. Smooth-it-away's comfortable explanation as
greedily as we did. The inhabitants of the cavern, moreover, were
unlovely personages, dark, smoke-begrimed, generally deformed, with
misshapen feet, and a glow of dusky redness in their eyes as if their
hearts had caught fire and were blazing out of the upper windows. It
struck me as a peculiarity that the laborers at the forge and those who
brought fuel to the engine, when they began to draw short breath,
positively emitted smoke from their mouth and nostrils.

Among the idlers about the train, most of whom were puffing cigars
which they had lighted at the flame of the crater, I was perplexed to
notice several who, to my certain knowledge, had heretofore set forth
by railroad for the Celestial City. They looked dark, wild, and smoky,
with a singular resemblance, indeed, to the native inhabitants, like
whom, also, they had a disagreeable propensity to ill-natured gibes and
sneers, the habit of which had wrought a settled contortion of their
visages. Having been on speaking terms with one of these persons,—
an indolent, good-for-nothing fellow, who went by the name of Take-
it-easy,—I called him, and inquired what was his business there.

"Did you not start," said I, "for the Celestial City?"

"That's a fact," said Mr. Take-it-easy, carelessly puffing some smoke
into my eyes. "But I heard such bad accounts that I never took pains to
climb the hill on which the city stands. No business doing, no fun

going on, nothing to drink, and no smoking allowed, and a thrumming of church music from morning till night. I would not stay in such a place if they offered me house room and living free."

"But, my good Mr. Take-it-easy," cried I, "why take up your residence here, of all places in the world?"

"O," said the loafer, with a grin, "it is very warm hereabouts, and I meet with plenty of old acquaintances, and altogether the place suits me. I hope to see you back again some day soon. A pleasant journey to you."

While he was speaking the bell of the engine rang, and we dashed away, after dropping a few passengers, but receiving no new ones. Rattling onward through the Valley, we were dazzled with the fiercely gleaming gas lamps, as before. But sometimes, in the dark of intense brightness, grim faces, that bore the aspect and expression of individual sins, or evil passions, seemed to thrust themselves through the veil of light, glaring upon us, and stretching forth a great, dusky hand, as if to impede our progress. I almost thought that they were my own sins that appalled me there. These were freaks of imagination—nothing more, certainly—mere delusions, which I ought to be heartily ashamed of; but all through the Dark Valley I was tormented, and pestered, and dolefully bewildered with the same kind of waking dreams. The mephitic[18] gases of that region intoxicate the brain. As the light of natural day, however, began to struggle with the glow of the lanterns, these vain imaginations lost their vividness, and finally vanished with the first ray of sunshine that greeted our escape from the Valley of the Shadow of Death. Ere we had gone a mile beyond it I could well nigh have taken my oath that this whole gloomy passage was a dream.

At the end of the valley, as John Bunyan mentions, is a cavern, where, in his days, dwelt two cruel giants, Pope and Pagan,[19] who had strown the ground about their residence with the bones of slaughtered pilgrims. These vile old troglodytes[20] are no longer there; but into their deserted cave another terrible giant has thrust himself, and makes it his business to seize upon honest travellers and fatten them for his table with plentiful meals of smoke, mist, moonshine, raw potatoes, and sawdust. He is a German by birth, and is called Giant Transcendentalist;[21] but as to his form, his features, his substance, and his nature generally, it is the chief peculiarity of this huge miscreant that neither he for himself, nor any body for him, has ever been able to describe them. As we rushed by the cavern's mouth we caught a hasty glimpse of him, looking somewhat like an ill-proportioned figure, but considerably more like a heap of fog and duskiness. He shouted after us, but in so strange a phraseology that we knew not what he meant, nor whether to be encouraged or affrighted.

It was late in the day when the train thundered into the ancient city of Vanity, where Vanity Fair[22] is still at the height of prosperity, and exhibits an epitome of whatever is brilliant, gay, and fascinating beneath the sun. As I purposed to make a considerable stay here, it gratified me to learn that there is no longer the want of harmony between the town's people and pilgrims, which impelled the former to such lamentably mistaken measures as the persecution of Christian and the fiery martyrdom of Faithful.[23] On the contrary, as the new railroad brings with it great trade and a constant influx of strangers, the lord of Vanity Fair is its chief patron, and the capitalists of the city are among the largest stockholders. Many passengers stop to take their pleasure or make their profit in the Fair, instead of going onward to the Celestial City. Indeed, such are the charms of the place that people often affirm it to be the true and only heaven; stoutly contending that there is no other, that those who seek further are mere dreamers, and that, if the fabled brightness of the Celestial City lay but a bare mile beyond the gates of Vanity, they would not be fools enough to go thither. Without subscribing to these perhaps exaggerated encomiums, I can truly say that my abode in the city was mainly agreeable, and my intercourse with the inhabitants productive of much amusement and instruction.

Being naturally of a serious turn, my attention was directed to the solid advantages derivable from a residence here, rather than to the effervescent pleasures which are the grand object with too many visitants. The Christian reader, if he have had no accounts of the city later than Bunyan's time, will be surprised to hear that almost every street has its church, and that the reverend clergy are nowhere held in higher respect than at Vanity Fair. And well do they deserve such honorable estimation; for the maxims of wisdom and virtue which fall from their lips come from as deep a spiritual source, and tend to as lofty a religious aim, as those of the sagest philosophers of old. In justification of this high praise I need only mention the names of the Rev. Mr. Shallow-deep, the Rev. Mr. Stumble-at-truth, that fine old clerical character the

Rev. Mr. This-to-day, who expects shortly to resign his pulpit to the Rev. Mr. That-to-morrow; together with the Rev. Mr. Bewilderment, the Rev. Mr. Clog-the-spirit, and, last and greatest, the Rev. Dr. Wind-of-doctrine. The labors of these eminent divines are aided by those of innumerable lecturers, who diffuse such a various profundity, in all subjects of human or celestial science, that any man may acquire an omnigenous erudition without the trouble of even learning to read. Thus literature is etherealized by assuming for its medium the human voice; and knowledge, depositing all its heavier particles, except, doubtless, its gold, becomes exhaled into a sound, which forthwith steals into the ever-open ear of the community. These ingenious methods constitute a sort of machinery, by which thought and study are done to every person's hand without his putting himself to the slightest inconvenience in the matter. There is another species of machine for the wholesale manufacture of individual morality. This excellent result is effected by societies for all manner of virtuous purposes, with which a man has merely to connect himself, throwing, as it were, his quota of virtue into the common stock, and the president and directors will take care that the aggregate amount be well applied. All these, and other wonderful improvements in ethics, religion, and literature, being made plain to my comprehension by the ingenious Mr. Smooth-it-away, inspired me with a vast admiration of Vanity Fair.

It would fill a volume, in an age of pamphlets, were I to record all my observations in this great capital of human business and pleasure. There was an unlimited range of society—the powerful, the wise, the witty, and the famous in every walk of life; princes, presidents, poets, generals, artists, actors, and philanthropists,—all making their own market at the fair, and deeming no price too exorbitant for such commodities as hit their fancy. It was well worth one's while, even if he had no idea of buying or selling, to loiter through the bazaars and observe the various sorts of traffic that were going forward.

Some of the purchasers, I thought, made very foolish bargains. For instance, a young man having inherited a splendid fortune, laid out a considerable portion of it in the purchase of diseases, and finally spent all the rest for a heavy lot of repentance and a suit of rags. A very pretty girl bartered a heart as clear as crystal, and which seemed her most valuable possession, for another jewel of the same kind, but so worn and defaced as to be utterly worthless. In one shop there were a

great many crowns of laurel and myrtle, which soldiers, authors, statesmen, and various other people pressed eagerly to buy; some purchased
these paltry wreaths with their lives, others by a toilsome servitude of
years, and many sacrificed whatever was most valuable, yet finally
slunk away without the crown. There was a sort of stock or scrip, called
Conscience, which seemed to be in great demand, and would purchase
almost any thing. Indeed, few rich commodities were to be obtained
without paying a heavy sum in this particular stock, and a man's business was seldom very lucrative unless he knew precisely when and
how to throw his hoard of conscience into the market. Yet, as this stock
was the only thing of permanent value, whoever parted with it was
sure to find himself a loser in the long run. Several of the speculations
were of a questionable character. Occasionally a member of Congress
recruited his pocket by the sale of his constituents; and I was assured
that public officers have often sold their country at very moderate
prices. Thousands sold their happiness for a whim. Gilded chains were
in great demand, and purchased with almost any sacrifice. In truth,
those who desired, according to the old adage, to sell any thing valuable for a song, might find customers all over the Fair; and there were
innumerable messes of pottage,[24] piping hot, for such as chose to buy
them with their birthrights. A few articles, however, could not be
found genuine at Vanity Fair. If a customer wished to renew his stock
of youth the dealers offered him a set of false teeth and an auburn wig;
if he demanded peace of mind, they recommended opium or a brandy
bottle.

Tracts of land and golden mansions, situate in the Celestial City,
were often exchanged, at very disadvantageous rates, for a few years'
lease of small, dismal, inconvenient tenements in Vanity Fair. Prince
Beelzebub himself took great interest in this sort of traffic, and sometimes condescended to meddle with smaller matters. I once had the
pleasure to see him bargaining with a miser for his soul, which, after
much ingenious skirmishing on both sides, his highness succeeded in
obtaining at about the value of sixpence. The prince remarked, with a
smile, that he was a loser by the transaction.

Day after day, as I walked the streets of Vanity, my manners and deportment became more and more like those of the inhabitants. The
place began to seem like home; the idea of pursuing my travels to the
Celestial City was almost obliterated from my mind. I was reminded of

it, however, by the sight of the same pair of simple pilgrims at whom we had laughed so heartily when Apollyon puffed smoke and steam into their faces at the commencement of our journey. There they stood, amid the densest bustle of Vanity; the dealers offering them their purple and fine linen and jewels, the men of wit and humor gibing at them, a pair of buxom ladies ogling them askance, while the benevolent Mr. Smooth-it-away whispered some of his wisdom at their elbows, and pointed to a newly-erected temple; but there were these worthy simpletons, making the scene look wild and monstrous, merely by their sturdy repudiation of all part in its business or pleasures.

One of them—his name was Stick-to-the-right—perceived in my face, I suppose, a species of sympathy and almost admiration, which, to my own great surprise, I could not help feeling for this pragmatic couple. It prompted him to address me.

"Sir," inquired he, with a sad, yet mild and kindly voice, "do you call yourself a pilgrim?"

"Yes," I replied, "my right to that appellation is indubitable. I am merely a sojourner here in Vanity Fair, being bound to the Celestial City by the new railroad."

"Alas, friend," rejoined Mr. Stick-to-the-right, "I do assure you, and beseech you to receive the truth of my words, that that whole concern is a bubble. You may travel on it all your lifetime, were you to live thousands of years, and yet never get beyond the limits of Vanity Fair. Yea, though you should deem yourself entering the gates of the blessed city, it will be nothing but a miserable delusion."

"The Lord of the Celestial City," began the other pilgrim, whose name was Mr. Foot-it-to-heaven, "has refused, and will ever refuse, to grant an act of incorporation for this railroad; and, unless that be obtained, no passenger can ever hope to enter his dominions. Wherefore every man who buys a ticket must lay his account with losing the purchase money, which is the value of his own soul."

"Poh, nonsense!" said Mr. Smooth-it-away, taking my arm and leading me off, "these fellows ought to be indicted for a libel. If the law stood as it once did in Vanity Fair we should see them grinning through the iron bars of the prison window."

This incident made a considerable impression on my mind, and contributed with other circumstances to indispose me to a permanent residence in the city of Vanity; although, of course, I was not simple

enough to give up my original plan of gliding along easily and commodiously by railroad. Still, I grew anxious to be gone. There was one
strange thing that troubled me. Amid the occupations or amusements
of the Fair, nothing was more common than for a person—whether at
feast, theatre, or church, or trafficking for wealth and honors, or whatever he might be doing, and however unseasonable the interruption—
suddenly to vanish like a soap bubble, and be never more seen of his
fellows; and so accustomed were the latter to such little accidents that
they went on with their business as quietly as if nothing had happened.
But it was otherwise with me.

Finally, after a pretty long residence at the Fair, I resumed my journey towards the Celestial City, still with Mr. Smooth-it-away at my
side. At a short distance beyond the suburbs of Vanity we passed the
ancient silver mine, of which Demas[25] was the first discoverer, and
which is now wrought to great advantage, supplying nearly all the
coined currency of the world. A little further onward was the spot
where Lot's wife had stood for ages under the semblance of a pillar of
salt.[26] Curious travellers have long since carried it away piecemeal.
Had all regrets been punished as rigorously as this poor dame's were,
my yearning for the relinquished delights of Vanity Fair might have
produced a similar change in my own corporeal substance, and left me
a warning to future pilgrims.

The next remarkable object was a large edifice, constructed of
mossgrown stone, but in a modern and airy style of architecture. The
engine came to a pause in its vicinity, with the usual tremendous
shriek.

"This was formerly the castle of the redoubted giant Despair,"[27] observed Mr. Smooth-it-away; "but since his death Mr. Flimsy-faith has
repaired it, and keeps an excellent house of entertainment here. It is
one of our stopping-places."

"It seems but slightly put together," remarked I, looking at the frail
yet ponderous walls. "I do not envy Mr. Flimsy-faith his habitation.
Some day it will thunder down upon the heads of the occupants."

"We shall escape, at all events," said Mr. Smooth-it-away, "for Apollyon is putting on the steam again."

The road now plunged into a gorge of the Delectable Mountains,
and traversed the field where in former ages the blind men wandered[28]
and stumbled among the tombs. One of these ancient tombstones had

been thrust across the track by some malicious person, and gave the train of cars a terrible jolt. Far up the rugged side of a mountain I perceived a rusty iron door, half overgrown with bushes and creeping plants, but with smoke issuing from its crevices.

"Is that," inquired I, "the very door in the hillside which the shepherds assured Christian was a byway to hell?"[29]

"That was a joke on the part of the shepherds," said Mr. Smooth-it-away, with a smile. "It is neither more nor less than the door of a cavern which they use as a smoke house for the preparation of mutton hams."

My recollections of the journey are now, for a little space, dim and confused, inasmuch as a singular drowsiness here overcame me, owing to the fact that we were passing over the enchanted ground, the air of which encourages a disposition to sleep. I awoke, however, as soon as we crossed the borders of the pleasant land of Beulah.[30] All the passengers were rubbing their eyes, comparing watches, and congratulating one another on the prospect of arriving so seasonably at the journey's end. The sweet breezes of this happy clime came refreshingly to our nostrils; we beheld the glimmering gush of silver fountains, overhung by trees of beautiful foliage and delicious fruit, which were propagated by grafts from the celestial gardens. Once, as we dashed onward like a hurricane, there was a flutter of wings and the bright appearance of an angel in the air, speeding forth on some heavenly mission. The engine now announced the close vicinity of the final station house by one last and horrible scream, in which there seemed to be distinguishable every kind of wailing and woe, and bitter fierceness of wrath, all mixed up with the wild laughter of a devil or a madman. Throughout our journey, at every stopping-place, Apollyon had exercised his ingenuity in screwing the most abominable sounds out of the whistle of the steam engine; but in this closing effort he outdid himself, and created an infernal uproar, which, besides disturbing the peaceful inhabitants of Beulah, must have sent its discord even through the celestial gates.

While the horrid clamor was still ringing in our ears, we heard an exulting strain, as if a thousand instruments of music, with height, and depth, and sweetness in their tones, at once tender and triumphant, were struck in unison, to greet the approach of some illustrious hero, who had fought the good fight and won a glorious victory, and was come to lay aside his battered arms forever. Looking to ascertain what might be the occasion of this glad harmony, I perceived, on alighting from the cars, that a multitude of shining ones had assembled on the other side of the river,[31] to welcome two poor pilgrims, who were just emerging from its depths. They were the same whom Apollyon and ourselves had persecuted with taunts, and gibes, and scalding steam, at the commencement of our journey—the same whose unworldly aspect and impressive words had stirred my conscience amid the wild revellers of Vanity Fair.

"How amazingly well those men have got on," cried I to Mr. Smooth-it-away. "I wish we were secure of as good a reception."

"Never fear, never fear!" answered my friend. "Come, make haste; the ferry boat will be off directly, and in three minutes you will be on the other side of the river. No doubt you will find coaches to carry you up to the city gates."

A steam ferry boat, the last improvement on this important route, lay at the river side, puffing, snorting, and emitting all those other disagreeable utterances which betoken the departure to be immediate. I hurried on board with the rest of the passengers, most of whom were in great perturbation; some bawling out for their baggage; some tearing their hair and exclaiming that the boat would explode or sink; some already pale with the heaving of the stream; some gazing affrighted at the ugly aspect of the steersman; and some still dizzy with the slumberous influences of the Enchanted Ground. Looking back to the shore, I was amazed to discern Mr. Smooth-it-away waving his hand in token of farewell.

"Don't you go over to the Celestial City?" exclaimed I.

"O, no!" answered he with a queer smile, and that same disagreeable contortion of visage which I had remarked in the inhabitants of the Dark Valley. "O, no! I have come thus far only for the sake of your pleasant company. Good by! We shall meet again."

And then did my excellent friend Mr. Smooth-it-away laugh outright, in the midst of which cachinnation a smoke-wreath issued from his mouth and nostrils, while a twinkle of lurid flame darted out of either eye, proving indubitably that his heart was all of a red blaze. The impudent fiend! To deny the existence of Tophet, when he felt its fiery tortures raging within his breast. I rushed to the side of the boat, intending to fling myself on shore; but the wheels, as they began their revolutions, threw a dash of spray over me so cold—so deadly cold, with the chill that will never leave those waters until Death be drowned in his own river—that, with a shiver and a heartquake I awoke. Thank heaven it was a Dream!

The Procession of Life

Life figures itself to me as a festal or funereal procession. All of us have our places, and are to move onward under the direction of the Chief Marshal. The grand difficulty results from the invariably mistaken principles on which the deputy marshals seek to arrange this immense concourse of people, so much more numerous than those that train their interminable length through streets and highways in times of political excitement. Their scheme is ancient, far beyond the memory of man or even the record of history, and has hitherto been very little modified by the innate sense of something wrong, and the dim perception of better methods, that have disquieted all the ages through which the procession has taken its march. Its members are classified by the merest external circumstances, and thus are more certain to be thrown out of their true positions than if no principle of arrangement were attempted. In one part of the procession we see men of landed estate or moneyed capital gravely keeping each other company, for the preposterous reason that they chance to have a similar standing in the tax gatherer's book. Trades and professions march together with scarcely a more real bond of union. In this manner, it cannot be denied, people are disentangled from the mass and separated into various classes according to certain apparent relations; all have some artificial badge which the world, and themselves among the first, learn to consider as a genuine characteristic. Fixing our attention on such outside shows of similarity or difference, we lose sight of those realities by which nature, fortune, fate, or Providence has constituted for every man a brotherhood, wherein it is one great office of human wisdom to classify him. When the mind has once accustomed itself to a proper arrangement of the Procession of Life, or a true classification of society, even though merely speculative, there is thenceforth a satisfaction which pretty well suffices for itself without the aid of any actual reformation in the order of march.

For instance, assuming to myself the power of marshalling the aforesaid procession, I direct a trumpeter to send forth a blast loud enough to be heard from hence to China; and a herald, with world-pervading voice, to make proclamation for a certain class of mortals to take their places. What shall be their principle of union? After all, an external one, in comparison with many that might be found, yet far more real than those which the world has selected for a similar purpose. Let all who are afflicted with like physical diseases form themselves into ranks.

Our first attempt at classification is not very successful. It may gratify the pride of aristocracy to reflect, that disease, more than any other circumstance of human life, pays due observance to the distinctions which rank and wealth, and poverty and lowliness, have established among mankind. Some maladies are rich and precious, and only to be acquired by the right of inheritance or purchased with gold. Of this kind is the gout,[1] which serves as a bond of brotherhood to the purple-visaged gentry, who obey the herald's voice, and painfully hobble from all civilized regions of the globe to take their post in the grand procession. In mercy to their toes, let us hope that the march may not be long. The Dyspeptics,[2] too, are people of good standing in the world. For them the earliest salmon is caught in our eastern rivers, and the shy woodcock stains the dry leaves with his blood in his remotest haunts, and the turtle comes from the far Pacific Islands to be gobbled up in soup. They can afford to flavor all their dishes with indolence, which, in spite of the general opinion, is a sauce more exquisitely piquant than appetite won by exercise. Apoplexy[3] is another highly respectable disease. We will rank together all who have the symptom of dizziness in the brain, and as fast as any drop by the way supply their places with new members of the board of aldermen.

On the other hand, here come whole tribes of people, whose physical lives are but a deteriorated variety of life, and themselves a meaner species of mankind; so sad an effect has been wrought by the tainted breath of cities, scanty and unwholesome food, destructive modes of labor, and the lack of those moral supports that might partially have counteracted such bad influences. Behold here a train of house painters, all afflicted with a peculiar sort of colic. Next in place we will marshal those workmen in cutlery, who have breathed a fatal disorder into their lungs with the impalpable dust of steel. Tailors and shoe-makers, being sedentary men, will chiefly congregate into one part of the procession, and march under similar banners of disease; but among them we may observe here and there a sickly student, who has left his health between the leaves of classic volumes; and clerks, likewise, who have caught their deaths on high official stools; and men of genius too, who have written sheet after sheet with pens dipped in their heart's blood. These are a wretched, quaking, short-breathed set. But what is this cloud of pale-cheeked, slender girls, who disturb the ear with the multiplicity of their short, dry coughs? They are seamstresses, who have plied the daily and nightly needle in the service of master tailors and close-fisted contractors, until now it is almost time for each to hem the borders of her own shroud. Consumption[4] points their place in the procession. With their sad sisterhood are intermingled many youthful maidens who have sickened in aristocratic mansions, and for whose aid science has unavailingly searched its volumes, and whom breathless love has watched. In our ranks the rich maiden and the poor seamstress may walk arm in arm. We might find innumerable other instances, where the bond of mutual disease—not to speak of nation-sweeping pestilence—embraces high and low, and makes the king a brother of the clown. But it is not hard to own that disease is the natural aristo-crat. Let him keep his state, and have his established orders of rank, and wear his royal mantle of the color of a fever flush; and let the noble and wealthy boast their own physical infirmities, and display their symptoms as the badges of high station. All things considered, these are as proper subjects of human pride as any relations of human rank that men can fix upon.

Sound again, thou deep-breathed trumpeter! and herald, with thy voice of might, shout forth another summons that shall reach the old baronial castles of Europe, and the rudest cabin of our western wilder-ness! What class is next to take its place in the procession of mortal life? Let it be those whom the gifts of intellect have united in a noble brotherhood.

Ay, this is a reality, before which the conventional distinctions of society melt away like a vapor when we would grasp it with the hand. Were Byron[5] now alive, and Burns,[6] the first would come from his ancestral abbey, flinging aside, although unwillingly, the inherited honors of a thousand years, to take the arm of the mighty peasant who grew immortal while he stooped behind his plough. These are gone; but the hall, the farmer's fireside, the hut, perhaps the palace, the counting room, the workshop, the village, the city, life's high places and low ones, may all produce their poets, whom a common temperament pervades like an electric sympathy. Peer or ploughman, we will muster them pair by pair and shoulder to shoulder. Even society, in its most artificial state, consents to this arrangement. These factory girls from Lowell[7] shall mate themselves with the pride of drawing rooms and literary circles, the bluebells in fashion's nosegay, the Sapphos, and Montagues, and Nortons[8] of the age. Other modes of intellect bring together as strange companies. Silk-gowned professor of languages, give your arm to this sturdy blacksmith, and deem yourself honored by the conjunction, though you behold him grimy from the anvil. All varieties of human speech are like his mother tongue to this rare man. Indiscriminately, let those take their places, of whatever rank they come, who possess the kingly gifts to lead armies or to sway a people— Nature's generals, her lawgivers, her kings, and with them also the deep philosophers who think the thought in one generation that is to revolutionize society in the next. With the hereditary legislator in whom eloquence is a far-descended attainment—a rich echo repeated by powerful voices from Cicero[9] downward—we will match some wondrous backwoodsman, who has caught a wild power of language from the breeze among his native forest boughs. But we may safely leave these brethren and sisterhood to settle their own congenialities. Our ordinary distinctions become so trifling, so impalpable, so ridiculously visionary, in comparison with a classification founded on truth, that all talk about the matter is immediately a common place.

Yet the longer I reflect the less am I satisfied with the idea of forming a separate class of mankind on the basis of high intellectual power. At best it is but a higher development of innate gifts common to all. Perhaps, moreover, he whose genius appears deepest and truest excels his fellows in nothing save the knack of expression; he throws out occasionally a lucky hint at truths of which every human soul is profoundly, though unutterably, conscious. Therefore, though we suffer the brotherhood of intellect to march onward together, it may be doubted whether their peculiar relation will not begin to vanish as soon as the procession shall have passed beyond the circle of this present world. But we do not classify for eternity.

And next, let the trumpet pour forth a funereal wail, and the herald's voice give breath in one vast cry to all the groans and grievous utterances that are audible throughout the earth. We appeal now to the sacred bond of sorrow, and summon the great multitude who labor under similar afflictions to take their places in the march.

How many a heart that would have been insensible to any other call has responded to the doleful accents of that voice! It has gone far and wide, and high and low, and left scarcely a mortal roof unvisited. Indeed, the principle is only too universal for our purpose, and unless we limit it will quite break up our classification of mankind, and convert the whole procession into a funeral train. We will therefore be at some pains to discriminate. Here comes a lonely rich man; he has built a noble fabric for his dwelling house, with a front of stately architecture and marble floors and doors of precious woods; the whole structure is as beautiful as a dream and as substantial as the native rock. But the visionary shapes of a long posterity, for whose home this mansion was intended, have faded into nothingness since the death of the founder's only son. The rich man gives a glance at his sable garb in one of the splendid mirrors of his drawing room, and descending a flight of lofty steps instinctively offers his arm to yonder poverty stricken widow in the rusty black bonnet, and with a check apron over her patched gown. The sailor boy, who was her sole earthly stay, was washed overboard in a late tempest. This couple from the palace and the almshouse are but the types of thousands more who represent the dark tragedy of life, and seldom quarrel for the upper parts. Grief is such a leveller, with its own dignity and its own humility, that the noble and the peasant, the beggar and the monarch, will waive their pretensions to external rank without the officiousness of interference on our part. If pride—the influence of the world's false distinctions—remain in the heart, then sorrow lacks the earnestness which makes it holy and reverend. It loses its reality and becomes a miserable shadow. On this ground we have an opportunity to assign over multitudes who would willingly claim places here to other parts of the procession. If the mourner have any thing dearer than his grief he must seek his true position elsewhere. There are so many unsubstantial sorrows which the necessity of our mortal state begets on idleness, that an observer, casting aside sentiment, is sometimes led to question whether there be any real woe, except absolute physical suffering and the loss of closest friends. A crowd who exhibit what they deem to be broken hearts—and among them many lovelorn maids and bachelors, and men of disappointed ambition in arts or politics, and the poor who were once rich, or who have sought to be rich in vain—the great majority of these may ask admittance into some other fraternity. There is no room here. Perhaps we may institute a separate class where such unfortunates will naturally fall into the procession. Meanwhile let them stand aside and patiently await their time.

If our trumpeter can borrow a note from the doomsday trumpet blast, let him sound it now. The dread alarum should make the earth quake to its centre, for the herald is about to address mankind with a summons to which even the purest mortal may be sensible of some faint responding echo in his breast. In many bosoms it will awaken a still small voice more terrible than its own reverberating uproar.

The hideous appeal has swept around the globe. Come, all ye guilty ones, and rank yourselves in accordance with the brotherhood of crime. This, indeed, is an awful summons. I almost tremble to look at the strange partnerships that begin to be formed, reluctantly, but by the invincible necessity of like to like in this part of the procession. A forger from the state prison seizes the arm of a distinguished financier. How indignantly does the latter plead his fair reputation upon 'Change,[10] and insist that his operations, by their magnificence of scope, were removed into quite another sphere of morality than those of his pitiful companion! But let him cut the connection if he can. Here comes a murderer with his clanking chains, and pairs himself—horrible to tell—with as pure and upright a man, in all observable respects, as ever partook of the consecrated bread and wine. He is one of those, perchance the most hopeless of all sinners, who practise such an exemplary system of outward duties, that even a deadly crime may be hidden from their own sight and remembrance, under this unreal frostwork. Yet he now finds his place. Why do that pair of flaunting girls, with the pert, affected laugh and the sly leer at the bystanders, intrude themselves into the same rank with yonder decorous matron, and that somewhat prudish maiden? Surely these poor creatures, born to vice as their sole and natural inheritance, can be no fit associates for women who have been guarded round about by all the proprieties of domestic life, and who could not err unless they first created the opportunity. O, no; it must be merely the impertinence of those unblushing hussies; and we can only wonder how such respectable ladies should have responded to a summons that was not meant for them.

We shall make short work of this miserable class; each member of which is entitled to grasp any other member's hand, by that vile degradation wherein guilty error has buried all alike. The foul fiend to whom it properly belongs must relieve us of our loathsome task. Let the bond servants of sin pass on. But neither man nor woman, in whom good predominates, will smile or sneer, nor bid the Rogues' March[11] be played, in derision of their array. Feeling within their breasts a shuddering sympathy, which at least gives token of the sin that might have been, they will thank God for any place in the grand procession of human existence, save among those most wretched ones. Many, however, will be astonished at the fatal impulse that drags them thitherward. Nothing is more remarkable than the various deceptions by which guilt conceals itself from the perpetrator's conscience, and oftenest, perhaps, by the splendor of its garments. Statesmen, rulers, generals, and all men who act over an extensive sphere, are most liable to be deluded in this way; they commit wrong, devastation, and murder, on so grand a scale, that it impresses them as speculative rather than actual; but in our procession we find them linked in detestable conjunction with the meanest criminals whose deeds have the vulgarity of petty details. Here the effect of circumstance and accident is done away, and a man finds his rank according to the spirit of his crime, in whatever shape it may have been developed.

We have called the Evil; now let us call the Good. The trumpet's brazen throat should pour heavenly music over the earth, and the herald's voice go forth with the sweetness of an angel's accents, as if to summon each upright man to his reward. But how is this? Does none answer to the call? Not one: for the just, the pure, the true, and all who might most worthily obey it, shrink sadly back, as most conscious of error and imperfection. Then let the summons be to those whose pervading principle is Love. This classification will embrace all the truly good, and none in whose souls there exists not something that may expand itself into a heaven, both of well-doing and felicity.

The first that presents himself is a man of wealth, who has bequeathed the bulk of his property to a hospital; his ghost, methinks, would have a better right here than his living body. But here they come, the genuine benefactors of their race. Some have wandered about the earth with pictures of bliss in their imagination, and with hearts that shrank sensitively from the idea of pain and woe, yet have studied all varieties of misery that human nature can endure. The prison, the insane asylum, the squalid chamber of the almshouse, the manufactory where the demon of machinery annihilates the human soul, and the cotton field where God's image becomes a beast of burden; to these and every other scene where man wrongs or neglects his brother, the apostles of humanity have penetrated. This missionary, black with India's burning sunshine, shall give his arm to a pale-faced brother who has made himself familiar with the infected alleys and loathsome haunts of vice in one of our own cities. The generous founder of a college shall be the partner of a maiden lady of narrow substance, one of whose good deeds it has been to gather a little school of orphan children. If the mighty merchant whose benefactions are reckoned by thousands of dollars, deem himself worthy, let him join the procession with her whose love has proved itself by watchings at the sick bed and all those lowly offices which bring her into actual contact with disease and wretchedness. And with those whose impulses have guided them to benevolent actions, we will rank others to whom Providence has assigned a different tendency and different powers. Men who have spent their lives in generous and holy contemplation for the human race; those who, by a certain heavenliness of spirit, have purified the atmosphere around them, and thus supplied a medium in which good and high things may be projected and performed—give to these a lofty place among the benefactors of mankind, although no deed, such as the world calls deeds, may be recorded of them. There are some individuals of whom we cannot conceive it proper that they should apply their hands to any earthly instrument, or work out any definite act; and others, perhaps not less high, to whom it is an essential attribute to labor in body as well as spirit, for the welfare of their brethren. Thus, if we find a spiritual sage whose unseen, inestimable influence has exalted the moral standard of mankind, we will choose for his companion some poor laborer who has wrought for love in the potato field of a neighbor poorer than himself.

We have summoned this various multitude—and, to the credit of our nature, it is a large one—on the principle of Love. It is singular, nevertheless, to remark the shyness that exists among many members of the present class, all of whom we might expect to recognize one another by the freemasonry of mutual goodness, and to embrace like brethren, giving God thanks for such various specimens of human excellence. But it is far otherwise. Each sect surrounds its own righteousness with a hedge of thorns. It is difficult for the good Christian to acknowledge the good Pagan; almost impossible for the good Orthodox to grasp the hand of the good Unitarian, leaving to their Creator to settle the matters in dispute, and giving their mutual efforts strongly and trustingly to whatever right thing is too evident to be mistaken. Then again, though the heart be large, yet the mind is often of such moderate dimensions as to be exclusively filled up with one idea. When a good man has long devoted himself to a particular kind of beneficence—to one species of reform—he is apt to become narrowed into the limits of the path wherein he treads, and to fancy that there is no other good to be done on earth but that selfsame good to which he has put his hand, and in the very mode that best suits his own conceptions. All else is worthless. His scheme must be wrought out by the united strength of the whole world's stock of love, or the world is no longer worthy of a position in the universe. Moreover, powerful Truth, being the rich grape juice expressed from the vineyard of the ages, has an intoxicating quality, when imbibed by any save a powerful intellect, and often, as it were, impels the quaffer to quarrel in his cups. For such reasons, strange to say, it is harder to contrive a friendly arrangement of these brethren of love and righteousness, in the procession of life, than to unite even the wicked, who, indeed, are chained together by their crimes. The fact is too preposterous for tears, too lugubrious for laughter.

But, let good men push and elbow one another as they may during their earthly march, all will be peace among them when the honorable array of their procession shall tread on heavenly ground. There they will doubtless find that they have been working each for the other's cause, and that every well-delivered stroke, which, with an honest purpose, any mortal struck, even for a narrow object, was indeed stricken for the universal cause of good. Their own view may be bounded by country, creed, profession, the diversities of individual character—but above them all is the breadth of Providence. How many, who have deemed themselves antagonists, will smile hereafter, when they look back upon the world's wide harvest field, and perceive that, in unconscious brotherhood, they were helping to bind the selfsame sheaf!

But, come! The sun is hastening westward, while the march of human life, that never paused before, is delayed by our attempt to rearrange its order. It is desirable to find some comprehensive principle, that shall render our task easier by bringing thousands into the ranks where hitherto we have brought one. Therefore let the trumpet, if possible, split its brazen throat with a louder note than ever, and the herald summon all mortals who, from whatever cause, have lost, or never found, their proper places in the world.

Obedient to this call, a great multitude come together, most of them with a listless gait, betokening weariness of soul, yet with a gleam of satisfaction in their faces, at a prospect of at length reaching those positions which, hitherto, they have vainly sought. But here will be another disappointment; for we can attempt no more than merely to associate, in one fraternity, all who are afflicted with the same vague trouble. Some great mistake in life is the chief condition of admittance into this class. Here are members of the learned professions, whom Providence endowed with special gifts for the plough, the forge, and the wheelbarrow, or for the routine of unintellectual business. We will assign to them, as partners in the march, those lowly laborers and handicraftsmen, who have pined, as with a dying thirst, after the unattainable fountains of knowledge. The latter have lost less than their companions; yet more, because they deem it infinite. Perchance the two species of unfortunates may comfort one another. Here are Quakers[12] with the instinct of battle in them; and men of war who should have worn the broad brim. Authors shall be ranked here, whom some freak of Nature, making game of her poor children, had imbued with the confidence of genius, and strong desire of fame, but has favored with no corresponding power; and others, whose lofty gifts were unaccompanied with the faculty of expression, or any of that earthly machinery, by which ethereal endowments must be manifested to mankind. All these, therefore, are melancholy laughing-stocks. Next, here are honest and well-intentioned persons, who by a want of tact—by inaccurate perceptions—by a distorting imagination—have been kept continually at cross purposes with the world, and bewildered upon the path of life. Let us see if they can confine themselves within the line of our procession. In this class, likewise, we must assign places to those who have encountered that worst of ill success, a higher fortune than their abilities could vindicate; writers, actors, painters, the pets of a day, but whose laurels wither unrenewed amid their hoary hair; politicians, whom some malicious contingency of affairs has thrust into conspicuous station, where, while the world stands gazing at them, the dreary consciousness of imbecility makes them curse their birth hour. To such men, we give for a companion him whose rare talents, which perhaps require a Revolution for their exercise, are buried in the tomb of sluggish circumstances.

Not far from these, we must find room for one whose success has been of the wrong kind; the man who should have lingered in the cloisters of a university, digging new treasures out of the Herculaneum[13] of antique lore, diffusing depth and accuracy of literature throughout his country, and thus making for himself a great and quiet fame. But the outward tendencies around him have proved too powerful for his inward nature, and have drawn him into the arena of political tumult, there to contend at disadvantage, whether front to front, or side by side, with the brawny giants of actual life. He becomes, it may be, a name for brawling parties to bandy to and fro, a legislator of the Union; a governor of his native State; an ambassador to the courts of kings or queens; and the world may deem him a man of happy stars. But not so the wise; and not so himself, when he looks through his experience, and sighs to miss that fitness, the one invaluable touch which makes all things true and real. So much achieved, yet how abortive is his life! Whom shall we choose for his companion? Some weak framed blacksmith, perhaps, whose delicacy of muscle might have suited a tailor's shopboard better than the anvil.

Shall we bid the trumpet sound again? It is hardly worth the while. There remain a few idle men of fortune, tavern and grog-shop loungers, lazzaroni,[14] old bachelors, decaying maidens, and people of crooked intellect or temper, all of whom may find their like, or some tolerable approach to it, in the plentiful diversity of our latter class. There too, as his ultimate destiny, must we rank the dreamer, who, all his life long, has cherished the idea that he was peculiarly apt for something, but never could determine what it was; and there the most unfortunate of men, whose purpose it has been to enjoy life's pleasures, but to avoid a manful struggle with its toil and sorrow. The remainder, if any, may connect themselves with whatever rank of the procession they shall find best adapted to their tastes and consciences. The worst possible fate would be to remain behind, shivering in the solitude of time, while all the world is on the move towards eternity. Our attempt to classify society is now complete. The result may be any thing but perfect; yet better—to give it the very lowest praise—than the antique rule of the herald's office, or the modern one of the tax gatherer, whereby the accidents and superficial attributes, with which the real nature of individuals has least to do, are acted upon as the deepest characteristics of mankind. Our task is done! Now let the grand procession move!

Yet pause a while! We had forgotten the Chief Marshal.

Hark! That world-wide swell of solemn music, with the clang of a mighty bell breaking forth through its regulated uproar, announces his approach. He comes; a severe, sedate, immovable, dark rider, waving his truncheon of universal sway, as he passes along the lengthened line, on the pale horse of the Revelation.[15] It is Death! Who else could assume the guidance of a procession that comprehends all humanity? And if some, among these many millions, should deem themselves classed amiss, yet let them take to their hearts the comfortable truth, that Death levels us all into one great brotherhood, and that another state of being will surely rectify the wrong of this. Then breathe thy wail upon the earth's wailing wind, thou band of melancholy music, made up of every sigh that the human heart, unsatisfied, has uttered! There is yet triumph in thy tones. And now we move! Beggars in their rags, and Kings trailing the regal purple in the dust; the Warrior's gleaming helmet; the Priest in his sable robe; the hoary Grandsire, who has run life's circle and come back to childhood; the ruddy Schoolboy with his golden curls, frisking along the march; the Artisan's stuff jacket; the Noble's star-decorated coat;—the whole presenting a motley spectacle, yet with a dusky grandeur brooding over it. Onward, onward, into that dimness where the lights of Time, which have blazed along the procession, are flickering in their sockets! And whither! We know not; and Death, hitherto our leader, deserts us by the wayside, as the tramp of our innumerable footsteps echoes beyond his sphere. He knows not, more than we, our destined goal. But God, who made us, knows, and will not leave us on our toilsome and doubtful march, either to wander in infinite uncertainty, or perish by the way!

FEATHERTOP; A MORALIZED LEGEND

"Dickon,"[1] cried Mother Rigby, "a coal for my pipe!"

The pipe was in the old dame's mouth when she said these words. She had thrust it there after filling it with tobacco, but without stooping to light it at the hearth, where indeed there was no appearance of a fire having been kindled that morning. Forthwith, however, as soon as the order was given, there was an intense red glow out of the bowl of the pipe, and a whiff of smoke from Mother Rigby's lips. Whence the coal came, and how brought thither by an invisible hand, I have never been able to discover.

"Good!" quoth Mother Rigby, with a nod of her head. "Thank ye, Dickon! And now for making this scarecrow. Be within call, Dickon, in case I need you again."

The good woman had risen thus early, (for as yet it was scarcely sunrise,) in order to set about making a scarecrow, which she intended to put in the middle of her cornpatch. It was now the latter week of May, and the crows and blackbirds had already discovered the little, green, rolled-up leaf of the Indian corn just peeping out of the soil. She was determined, therefore, to contrive as lifelike a scarecrow as ever was seen, and to finish it immediately, from top to toe, so that it should begin its sentinel's duty that very morning. Now Mother Rigby, (as every body must have heard,) was one of the most cunning and potent witches in New England, and might, with very little trouble, have made a scarecrow ugly enough to frighten the minister himself. But on this occasion, as she had awakened in an uncommonly pleasant humor, and was further dulcified by her pipe of tobacco, she resolved to produce something fine, beautiful, and splendid, rather than hideous and horrible.

"I don't want to set up a hobgoblin in my own corn patch, and almost at my own doorstep," said Mother Rigby to herself, puffing out a whiff of smoke; "I could do it if I pleased, but I'm tired of doing marvellous things, and so I'll keep within the bounds of everyday business, just for variety's sake. Besides, there is no use in scaring the little children for a mile roundabout, though 'tis true I'm a witch."

It was settled, therefore, in her own mind, that the scarecrow should represent a fine gentleman of the period, so far as the materials at hand would allow. Perhaps it may be as well to enumerate the chief of the articles that went to the composition of this figure.

The most important item of all, probably, although it made so little show, was a certain broomstick, on which Mother Rigby had taken many an airy gallop at midnight, and which now served the scarecrow by way of a spinal column, or, as the unlearned phrase it, a backbone. One of its arms was a disabled flail which used to be wielded by Goodman Rigby, before his spouse worried him out of this troublesome world; the other, if I mistake not, was composed of the pudding stick and a broken rung of a chair, tied loosely together at the elbow. As for its legs, the right was a hoe handle, and the left an undistinguished and miscellaneous stick from the woodpile. Its lungs, stomach, and other affairs of that kind were nothing better than a meal bag stuffed with straw. Thus we have made out the skeleton and entire corporcity[2] of the scarecrow, with the exception of its head; and this was admirably supplied by a somewhat withered and shrivelled pumpkin, in which Mother Rigby cut two holes for the eyes, and a slit for the mouth, leaving a bluish-colored knob in the middle to pass for a nose. It was really quite a respectable face.

"I've seen worse ones on human shoulders, at any rate," said Mother Rigby. "And many a fine gentleman has a pumpkin head, as well as my scarecrow."

But the clothes, in this case, were to be the making of the man. So the good old woman took down from a peg an ancient plum-colored coat of London make, and with relics of embroidery on its seams, cuffs, pocket flaps, and button holes, but lamentably worn and faded, patched at the elbows, tattered at the skirts, and threadbare all over. On the left breast was a round hole, whence either a star of nobility had been rent away, or else the hot heart of some former wearer had scorched it through and through. The neighbors said that this rich garment belonged to the Black Man's[3] wardrobe, and that he kept it at Mother Rigby's cottage for the convenience of slipping it on whenever he wished to make a grand appearance at the governor's table. To match the coat there was a velvet waistcoat of very ample size and formerly embroidered with foliage that had been as brightly golden as the maple leaves in October, but which had now quite vanished out of the substance of the velvet. Next came a pair of scarlet breeches, once worn by the French governor of Louisbourg,[4] and the knees of which had touched the lower step of the throne of Louis le Grand.[5] The Frenchman had given these smallclothes[6] to an Indian powwow,[7] who parted with them to the old witch for a gill[8] of strong waters, at one of their dances in the forest. Furthermore, Mother Rigby produced a pair of silk stockings and put them on the figure's legs, where they showed as unsubstantial as a dream, with the wooden reality of the two sticks making itself miserably apparent through the holes. Lastly, she put her dead husband's wig on the bare scalp of the pumpkin, and surmounted the whole with a dusty three-cornered hat, in which was stuck the longest tail feather of a rooster.

Then the old dame stood the figure up in a corner of her cottage and chuckled to behold its yellow semblance of a visage, with its nobby little nose thrust into the air. It had a strangely self-satisfied aspect, and seemed to say, "Come look at me!"

"And you are well worth looking at, that's a fact!" quoth Mother Rigby, in admiration at her own handiwork. "I've made many a puppet since I've been a witch; but methinks this is the finest of them all. 'Tis almost too good for a scarecrow. And, by the by, I'll just fill a fresh pipe of tobacco, and then take him out to the corn patch."

While filling her pipe, the old woman continued to gaze with almost motherly affection at the figure in the corner. To say the truth, whether it were chance, or skill, or downright witchcraft, there was something wonderfully human in this ridiculous shape, bedizened with its tattered finery; and as for the countenance, it appeared to shrivel its yellow surface into a grin—a funny kind of expression betwixt scorn and merriment, as if it understood itself to be a jest at mankind. The more Mother Rigby looked the better she was pleased.

"Dickon," cried she sharply, "another coal for my pipe!"

Hardly had she spoken, than, just as before, there was a red-glowing coal on the top of the tobacco. She drew in a long whiff and puffed it forth again into the bar of morning sunshine which struggled through the one dusty pane of her cottage window. Mother Rigby always liked to flavor her pipe with a coal of fire from the particular chimney corner whence this had been brought. But where that chimney corner might be, or who brought the coal from it—further than that the invisible messenger seemed to respond to the name of Dickon—I cannot tell.

"That puppet yonder," thought Mother Rigby, still with her eyes fixed on the scarecrow, "is too good a piece of work to stand all summer in a corn patch, frightening away the crows and blackbirds. He's capable of better things. Why, I've danced with a worse one, when partners happened to be scarce, at our witch meetings in the forest! What if I should let him take his chance among the other men of straw and empty fellows who go bustling about the world?"

The old witch took three or four more whiffs of her pipe and smiled.

"He'll meet plenty of his brethren at every street corner!" continued she. "Well, I didn't mean to dabble in witchcraft to-day, further than the lighting of my pipe; but a witch I am, and a witch I'm likely to be, and there's no use trying to shirk it. I'll make a man of my scarecrow, were it only for the joke's sake!"

While muttering these words Mother Rigby took the pipe from her own mouth and thrust it into the crevice which represented the same feature in the pumpkin visage of the scarecrow.

"Puff, darling, puff!" said she. "Puff away, my fine fellow! your life depends on it!"

This was a strange exhortation, undoubtedly, to be addressed to a mere thing of sticks, straw, and old clothes, with nothing better than a shrivelled pumpkin for a head; as we know to have been the scarecrow's case. Nevertheless, as we must carefully hold in remembrance, Mother Rigby was a witch of singular power and dexterity; and, keeping this fact duly before our minds, we shall see nothing beyond credibility in the remarkable incidents of our story. Indeed, the great difficulty will be at once got over, if we can only bring ourselves to believe that, as soon as the old dame bade him puff, there came a whiff of smoke from the scarecrow's mouth. It was the very feeblest of whiffs, to be sure; but it was followed by another and another, each more decided than the preceding one.

"Puff away, my pet! puff away, my pretty one!" Mother Rigby kept repeating, with her pleasantest smile. "It is the breath of life to ye; and that you may take my word for."

Beyond all question the pipe was bewitched. There must have been a spell either in the tobacco or in the fiercely-glowing coal that so mysteriously burned on top of it, or in the pungently-aromatic smoke which exhaled from the kindled weed. The figure, after a few doubtful attempts, at length blew forth a volley of smoke extending all the way from the obscure corner into the bar of sunshine. There it eddied and melted away among the motes of dust. It seemed a convulsive effort; for the two or three next whiffs were fainter, although the coal still glowed and threw a gleam over the scarecrow's visage. The old witch clapped her skinny hands together, and smiled encouragingly upon her handiwork. She saw that the charm worked well. The shrivelled, yellow face, which heretofore had been no face at all, had already a thin, fantastic haze, as it were, of human likeness, shifting to and fro across it; sometimes vanishing entirely, but growing more perceptible than ever with the next whiff from the pipe. The whole figure, in like manner, assumed a show of life, such as we impart to ill-defined shapes among the clouds, and half deceive ourselves with the pastime of our own fancy.

If we must needs pry closely into the matter, it may be doubted whether there was any real change, after all, in the sordid, wornout, worthless, and ill-jointed substance of the scarecrow; but merely a spectral illusion, and a cunning effect of light and shade so colored and contrived as to delude the eyes of most men. The miracles of witchcraft seem always to have had a very shallow subtlety; and, at least, if the above explanation do not hit the truth of the process, I can suggest no better.

"Well puffed, my pretty lad!" still cried old Mother Rigby. "Come, another good stout whiff, and let it be with might and main. Puff for thy life, I tell thee! Puff out of the very bottom of thy heart; if any heart thou hast, or any bottom to it! Well done, again! Thou didst suck in that mouthful as if for the pure love of it."

And then the witch beckoned to the scarecrow, throwing so much magnetic potency into her gesture that it seemed as if it must inevitably be obeyed, like the mystic call of the loadstone[9] when it summons the iron.

"Why lurkest thou in the corner, lazy one?" said she. "Step forth! Thou hast the world before thee!"

Upon my word, if the legend were not one which I heard on my grandmother's knee, and which had established its place among things credible before my childish judgment could analyze its probability, I question whether I should have the face to tell it now.

In obedience to Mother Rigby's word, and extending its arm as if to reach her outstretched hand, the figure made a step forward—a kind of hitch and jerk, however, rather than a step—then tottered and almost lost its balance. What could the witch expect? It was nothing, after all, but a scarecrow stuck upon two sticks. But the strong-willed old beldam scowled, and beckoned, and flung the energy of her purpose so forcibly at this poor combination of rotten wood, and musty straw, and ragged garments, that it was compelled to show itself a man, in spite of the reality of things. So it stepped into the bar of sunshine. There it stood—poor devil of a contrivance that it was!—with only the thinnest vesture of human similitude about it, through which was evident the stiff, ricketty, incongruous, faded, tattered, good-for-nothing patchwork of its substance, ready to sink in a heap upon the floor, as conscious of its own unworthiness to be erect. Shall I confess the truth? At its present point of vivification, the scarecrow reminds me of some of the lukewarm and abortive characters, composed of heterogeneous materials, used for the thousandth time, and never worth using, with which romance writers, (and myself, no doubt, among the rest,) have so overpeopled the world of fiction.

But the fierce old hag began to get angry and show a glimpse of her diabolic nature, (like a snake's head, peeping with a hiss out of her bosom,) at this pusillanimous behavior of the thing which she had taken the trouble to put together.

"Puff away, wretch!" cried she, wrathfully. "Puff, puff, puff, thou thing of straw and emptiness! thou rag or two! thou meal bag! thou pumpkin head! thou nothing! Where shall I find a name vile enough to call thee by? Puff, I say, and suck in thy fantastic life along with the smoke; else I snatch the pipe from thy mouth and hurl thee where that red coal came from."

Thus threatened, the unhappy scarecrow had nothing for it but to puff away for dear life. As need was, therefore, it applied itself lustily to the pipe and sent forth such abundant volleys of tobacco smoke that the small cottage kitchen became all vaporous. The one sunbeam struggled mistily through, and could but imperfectly define the image of the cracked and dusty window pane on the opposite wall. Mother Rigby, meanwhile, with one brown arm akimbo and the other stretched towards the figure, loomed grimly amid the obscurity with such port and expression as when she was wont to heave a ponderous nightmare on her victims and stand at the bedside to enjoy their agony. In fear and trembling did this poor scarecrow puff. But its efforts, it must be acknowledged, served an excellent purpose; for, with each successive whiff, the figure lost more and more of its dizzy and perplexing tenuity[10] and seemed to take denser substance. Its very garments, moreover, partook of the magical change, and shone with the gloss of novelty and glistened with the skilfully embroidered gold that had long ago been rent away. And, half revealed among the smoke, a yellow visage bent its lustreless eyes on Mother Rigby.

At last the old witch clinched[11] her fist and shook it at the figure. Not that she was positively angry, but merely acting on the principle— perhaps untrue, or not the only truth, though as high a one as Mother Rigby could be expected to attain—that feeble and torpid natures, being incapable of better inspiration, must be stirred up by fear. But here was the crisis. Should she fail in what she now sought to effect, it was her ruthless purpose to scatter the miserable simulacre[12] into its original elements.

"Thou hast a man's aspect," said she, sternly. "Have also the echo and mockery of a voice! I bid thee speak!"

The scarecrow gasped, struggled, and at length emitted a murmur, which was so incorporated with its smoky breath that you could scarcely tell whether it were indeed a voice or only a whiff of tobacco. Some narrators of this legend hold the opinion that Mother Rigby's conjurations and the fierceness of her will had compelled a familiar spirit into the figure, and that the voice was his.

"Mother," mumbled the poor stifled voice, "be not so awful with me! I would fain speak; but being without wits, what can I say?"

"Thou canst speak, darling, canst thou?" cried Mother Rigby, relaxing her grim countenance into a smile. "And what shalt thou say, quotha! Say, indeed! Art thou of the brotherhood of the empty skull and demandest of me what thou shalt say? Thou shalt say a thousand things, and saying them a thousand times over, thou shalt still have said nothing! Be not afraid, I tell thee! When thou comest into the world, (whither I purpose sending thee forthwith,) thou shalt not lack the wherewithal to talk. Talk! Why, thou shalt babble like a mill stream, if thou wilt. Thou hast brains enough for that, I trow!"[13]

"At your service, mother," responded the figure.

"And that was well said, my pretty one," answered Mother Rigby. "Then thou spakest like thyself, and meant nothing. Thou shalt have a hundred such set phrases, and five hundred to the boot of them.[14] And now, darling, I have taken so much pains with thee, and thou art so beautiful, that, by my troth, I love thee better than any witch's puppet in the world; and I've made them of all sorts—clay, wax, straw, sticks, night fog, morning mist, sea foam, and chimney smoke. But thou art the very best. So give heed to what I say."

"Yes, kind mother," said the figure, "with all my heart!"

"With all thy heart!" cried the old witch, setting her hands to her sides and laughing loudly. "Thou hast such a pretty way of speaking. With all thy heart! And thou didst put thy hand to the left side of thy waistcoat as if thou really hadst one!"

So now, in high good humor with this fantastic contrivance of hers, Mother Rigby told the scarecrow that it must go and play its part in the great world, where not one man in a hundred, she affirmed, was gifted with more real substance than itself. And, that he might hold up his head with the best of them, she endowed him, on the spot, with an unreckonable amount of wealth. It consisted partly of a gold mine in Eldorado,[15] and of ten thousand shares in a broken bubble, and of half a million acres of vineyard at the North Pole, and of a castle in the air, and a chateau in Spain, together with all the rents and income therefrom accruing. She further made over to him the cargo of a certain ship, laden with salt of Cadiz,[16] which she herself, by her necromantic arts, had caused to founder, ten years before, in the deepest part of mid ocean. If the salt were not dissolved, and could be brought to market, it would fetch a pretty penny among the fishermen. That he might not lack ready money, she gave him a copper farthing[17] of Birmingham manufacture, being all the coin she had about her, and likewise a great deal of brass, which she applied to his forehead, thus making it yellower than ever.

"With that brass alone," quoth Mother Rigby, "thou canst pay thy way all over the earth. Kiss me, pretty darling! I have done my best for thee."

Furthermore, that the adventurer might lack no possible advantage towards a fair start in life, this excellent old dame gave him a token by which he was to introduce himself to a certain magistrate, member of the council, merchant, and elder of the church, (the four capacities constituting but one man,) who stood at the head of society in the neighboring metropolis. The token was neither more nor less than a single word, which Mother Rigby whispered to the scarecrow, and which the scarecrow was to whisper to the merchant.

"Gouty[18] as the old fellow is, he'll run thy errands for thee, when once thou hast given him that word in his ear," said the old witch. "Mother Rigby knows the worshipful Justice Gookin, and the worshipful Justice knows Mother Rigby!"

Here the witch thrust her wrinkled face close to the puppet's, chuckling irrepressibly, and fidgeting all through her system, with delight at the idea which she meant to communicate.

"The worshipful Master Gookin," whispered she, "hath a comely maiden to his daughter. And hark ye, my pet! Thou hast a fair outside, and a pretty wit enough of thine own. Yea, a pretty wit enough! Thou wilt think better of it when thou hast seen more of other people's wits. Now, with thy outside and thy inside, thou art the very man to win a young girl's heart. Never doubt it! I tell thee it shall be so. Put but a bold face on the matter, sigh, smile, flourish thy hat, thrust forth thy leg like a dancing master, put thy right hand to the left side of thy waistcoat, and pretty Polly Gookin is thine own!"

All this while the new creature had been sucking in and exhaling the vapory fragrance of his pipe, and seemed now to continue this occupation as much for the enjoyment it afforded as because it was an essential condition of his existence. It was wonderful to see how exceedingly like a human being it behaved. Its eyes, (for it appeared to possess a pair,) were bent on Mother Rigby, and at suitable junctures it nodded or shook its head. Neither did it lack words proper for the occasion: "Really! Indeed! Pray tell me! Is it possible! Upon my word! By no means! O! Ah! Hem!" and other such weighty utterances as imply attention, inquiry, acquiescence, or dissent on the part of the auditor. Even had you stood by and seen the scarecrow made you could scarcely have resisted the conviction that it perfectly understood the cunning counsels which the old witch poured into its counterfeit of an ear. The more earnestly it applied its lips to the pipe the more distinctly was its human likeness stamped among visible realities, the more sagacious grew its expression, the more lifelike its gestures and movements, and the more intelligibly audible its voice. Its garments, too, glistened so much the brighter with an illusory magnificence. The very pipe, in which burned the spell of all this wonderwork, ceased to appear as a smoke-blackened earthen stump, and became a meerschaum,[19] with painted bowl and amber mouthpiece.

It might be apprehended, however, that as the life of the illusion seemed identical with the vapor of the pipe, it would terminate simultaneously with the reduction of the tobacco to ashes. But the beldam foresaw the difficulty.

"Hold thou the pipe, my precious one," said she, "while I fill it for thee again."

It was sorrowful to behold how the fine gentleman began to fade back into a scarecrow while Mother Rigby shook the ashes out of the pipe and proceeded to replenish it from her tobacco box.

"Dickon," cried she, in her high, sharp tone, "another coal for this pipe!"

No sooner said than the intensely red speck of fire was glowing within the pipe bowl; and the scarecrow, without waiting for the witch's bidding, applied the tube to his lips and drew in a few short, convulsive whiffs, which soon, however, became regular and equable.

"Now, mine own heart's darling," quoth Mother Rigby, "whatever may happen to thee, thou must stick to thy pipe. Thy life is in it; and that, at least, thou knowest well, if thou knowest nought besides. Stick to thy pipe, I say! Smoke, puff, blow thy cloud; and tell the people, if any question be made, that it is for thy health, and that so the physician orders thee to do. And, sweet one, when thou shalt find thy pipe getting low, go apart into some corner, and, (first filling thyself with smoke,) cry sharply, 'Dickon, a fresh pipe of tobacco!' and, 'Dickon, another coal for my pipe!' and have it into thy pretty mouth as speedily as may be. Else, instead of a gallant gentleman in a gold-laced coat, thou wilt be but a jumble of sticks and tattered clothes, and a bag of straw, and a withered pumpkin! Now depart, my treasure, and good luck go with thee!"

"Never fear, mother!" said the figure, in a stout voice, and sending forth a courageous whiff of smoke. "I will thrive, if an honest man and a gentleman may!"

"O, thou wilt be the death of me!" cried the old witch, convulsed with laughter. "That was well said. If an honest man and a gentleman may! Thou playest thy part to perfection. Get along with thee for a smart fellow; and I will wager on thy head, as a man of pith and substance, with a brain, and what they call a heart, and all else that a man should have, against any other thing on two legs. I hold myself a better witch than yesterday, for thy sake. Did not I make thee? And I defy any witch in New England to make such another! Here; take my staff along with thee!"

The staff, though it was but a plain oaken stick, immediately took the aspect of a gold-headed cane.

"That gold head has as much sense in it as thine own," said Mother Rigby, "and it will guide thee straight to worshipful Master Gookin's door. Get thee gone, my pretty pet, my darling, my precious one, my treasure; and if any ask thy name, it is Feathertop. For thou hast a feather in thy hat, and I have thrust a handful of feathers into the hollow of thy head, and thy wig too is of the fashion they call Feathertop,—so be Feathertop thy name!"

And, issuing from the cottage, Feathertop strode manfully towards town. Mother Rigby stood at the threshold, well pleased to see how the sunbeams glistened on him, as if all his magnificence were real, and how diligently and lovingly he smoked his pipe, and how handsomely he walked, in spite of a little stiffness of his legs. She watched him until out of sight, and threw a witch benediction after her darling, when a turn of the road snatched him from her view.

Betimes in the forenoon, when the principal street of the neighboring town was just at its acme of life and bustle, a stranger of very distinguished figure was seen on the sidewalk. His port as well as his garments betokened nothing short of nobility. He wore a richly-embroidered plum-colored coat, a waistcoat of costly velvet magnificently adorned with golden foliage, a pair of splendid scarlet breeches, and the finest and glossiest of white silk stockings. His head was covered with a peruke,[20] so daintily powdered and adjusted that it would have been sacrilege to disorder it with a hat; which, therefore, (and it was a gold-laced hat, set off with a snowy feather,) he carried beneath his arm. On the breast of his coat glistened a star. He managed his gold-headed cane with an airy grace peculiar to the fine gentlemen of the period ; and, to give the highest possible finish to his equipment, he had lace ruffles at his wrist, of a most ethereal delicacy, sufficiently avouching how idle and aristocratic must be the hands which they half concealed.

It was a remarkable point in the accoutrement of this brilliant personage, that he held in his left hand a fantastic kind of a pipe, with an exquisitely painted bowl and an amber mouthpiece. This he applied to his lips as often as every five or six paces, and inhaled a deep whiff of smoke, which, after being retained a moment in his lungs, might be seen to eddy gracefully from his mouth and nostrils.

As may well be supposed, the street was all astir to find out the stranger's name.

"It is some great nobleman, beyond question," said one of the townspeople. "Do you see the star at his breast?"

"Nay; it is too bright to be seen," said another. "Yes; he must needs be a nobleman, as you say. But by what conveyance, think you, can his lordship have voyaged or travelled hither? There has been no vessel from the old country for a month past; and if he have arrived overland from the southward, pray where are his attendants and equipage?"[21]

"He needs no equipage to set off his rank," remarked a third. "If he came among us in rags, nobility would shine through a hole in his elbow. I never saw such dignity of aspect. He has the old Norman blood in his veins, I warrant him."

"I rather take him to be a Dutchman, or one of your high Germans," said another citizen. "The men of those countries have always the pipe at their mouths."

"And so has a Turk," answered his companion. "But, in my judgment, this stranger hath been bred at the French court, and hath there learned politeness and grace of manner, which none understand so well as the nobility of France. That gait, now! A vulgar spectator might deem it stiff—he might call it a hitch and jerk—but, to my eye, it hath an unspeakable majesty, and must have been acquired by constant observation of the deportment of the Grand Monarque.[22] The stranger's character and office are evident enough. He is a French ambassador, come to treat with our rulers about the cession of Canada."[23]

"More probably a Spaniard," said another, "and hence his yellow complexion; or, most likely, he is from the Havana, or from some port on the Spanish main,[24] and comes to make investigation about the piracies which our governor is thought to connive at. Those settlers in Peru and Mexico have skins as yellow as the gold which they dig out of their mines."

"Yellow or not," cried a lady, "he is a beautiful man!—so tall, so slender! such a fine, noble face, with so well-shaped a nose, and all that delicacy of expression about the mouth! And, bless me, how bright his star is! It positively shoots out flames!"

"So do your eyes, fair lady," said the stranger, with a bow and a flourish of his pipe; for he was just passing at the instant. "Upon my honor, they have quite dazzled me."

"Was ever so original and exquisite a compliment?" murmured the lady, in an ecstasy of delight.

Amid the general admiration excited by the stranger's appearance, there were only two dissenting voices. One was that of an impertinent cur,[25] which, after snuffing at the heels of the glistening figure, put its tail between its legs and skulked into its master's back yard, vociferating an execrable howl. The other dissentient was a young child, who squalled at the fullest stretch of his lungs, and babbled some unintelligible nonsense about a pumpkin.

Feathertop meanwhile pursued his way along the street. Except for the few complimentary words to the lady, and now and then a slight inclination of the head in requital of the profound reverences of the bystanders, he seemed wholly absorbed in his pipe. There needed no other proof of his rank and consequence than the perfect equanimity with which he comported himself, while the curiosity and admiration of the town swelled almost into clamor around him. With a crowd gathering behind his footsteps, he finally reached the mansion house of the worshipful Justice Gookin, entered the gate, ascended the steps of the front door, and knocked. In the interim, before his summons was answered, the stranger was observed to shake the ashes out of his pipe.

"What did he say in that sharp voice?" inquired one of the spectators.

"Nay, I know not," answered his friend. "But the sun dazzles my eyes strangely. How dim and faded his lordship looks all of a sudden! Bless my wits, what is the matter with me?"

"The wonder is," said the other, "that his pipe, which was out only an instant ago, should be all alight again, and with the reddest coal I ever saw. There is something mysterious about this stranger. What a whiff of smoke was that! Dim and faded did you call him? Why, as he turns about the star on his breast is all ablaze."

"It is, indeed," said his companion; "and it will go near to dazzle pretty Polly Gookin, whom I see peeping at it out of the chamber window."

The door being now opened, Feathertop turned to the crowd, made a stately bend of his body like a great man acknowledging the reverence of the meaner sort, and vanished into the house. There was a mysterious kind of a smile, if it might not better be called a grin or grimace, upon his visage; but, of all the throng that beheld him, not an individual appears to have possessed insight enough to detect the illusive character of the stranger except a little child and a cur dog.

Our legend here loses somewhat of its continuity, and, passing over the preliminary explanation between Feathertop and the merchant, goes in quest of the pretty Polly Gookin. She was a damsel of a soft, round figure, with light hair and blue eyes, and a fair, rosy face, which seemed neither very shrewd nor very simple. This young lady had caught a glimpse of the glistening stranger while standing at the threshold, and had forthwith put on a laced cap, a string of beads, her finest kerchief, and her stiffest damask petticoat, in preparation for the interview. Hurrying from her chamber to the parlor, she had ever since been viewing herself in the large looking glass and practising pretty airs—now a smile, now a ceremonious dignity of aspect, and now a softer smile than the former, kissing her hand likewise, tossing her head, and managing her fan; while within the mirror an unsubstantial little maid repeated every gesture and did all the foolish things that Polly did, but without making her ashamed of them. In short, it was the fault of pretty Polly's ability rather than her will if she failed to be as complete an artifice as the illustrious Feathertop himself; and, when she thus tampered with her own simplicity, the witch's phantom might well hope to win her.

No sooner did Polly hear her father's gouty footsteps approaching the parlor door, accompanied with the stiff clatter of Feathertop's high-heeled shoes, than she seated herself bolt upright and innocently began warbling a song.

"Polly! daughter Polly!" cried the old merchant. "Come hither, child."

Master Gookin's aspect, as he opened the door, was doubtful and troubled.

"This gentleman," continued he, presenting the stranger, "is the Chevalier Feathertop,—nay, I beg his pardon, my Lord Feathertop,—who hath brought me a token of remembrance from an ancient friend of mine. Pay your duty to his lordship, child, and honor him as his quality deserves."

After these few words of introduction the worshipful magistrate immediately quitted the room. But, even in that brief moment, had the fair Polly glanced aside at her father instead of devoting herself wholly to the brilliant guest, she might have taken warning of some mischief nigh at hand. The old man was nervous, fidgety, and very pale. Purposing a smile of courtesy, he had deformed his face with a sort of galvanic[26] grin, which, when Feathertop's back was turned, he exchanged for a scowl, at the same time shaking his fist and stamping his gouty foot—an incivility which brought its retribution along with it. The truth appears to have been, that Mother Rigby's word of introduction, whatever it might be, had operated far more on the rich merchant's fears than on his good will. Moreover, being a man of wonderfully acute observation, he had noticed that the painted figures on the bowl of Feathertop's pipe were in motion. Looking more closely, he became convinced that these figures were a party of little demons, each duly provided with horns and a tail, and dancing hand in hand, with gestures of diabolical merriment, round the circumference of the pipe bowl. As if to confirm his suspicions, while Master Gookin ushered his guest along a dusky passage from his private room to the parlor, the star on Feathertop's breast had scintillated actual flames, and threw a flickering gleam upon the wall, the ceiling, and the floor.

With such sinister prognostics manifesting themselves on all hands, it is not to be marvelled at that the merchant should have felt that he was committing his daughter to a very questionable acquaintance. He cursed, in his secret soul, the insinuating elegance of Feathertop's manners, as this brilliant personage bowed, smiled, put his hand on his heart, inhaled a long whiff from his pipe, and enriched the atmosphere with the smoky vapor of a fragrant and visible sigh. Gladly would poor Master Gookin have thrust his dangerous guest into the street; but there was a constraint and terror within him. This respectable old gentleman, we fear, at an earlier period of life, had given some pledge or other to the evil principle, and perhaps was now to redeem it by the sacrifice of his daughter.

It so happened that the parlor door was partly of glass, shaded by a silken curtain, the folds of which hung a little awry. So strong was the merchant's interest in witnessing what was to ensue between the fair Polly and the gallant Feathertop that after quitting the room he could by no means refrain from peeping through the crevice of the curtain.

But there was nothing very miraculous to be seen; nothing—except the trifles previously noticed—to confirm the idea of a supernatural peril environing the pretty Polly. The stranger, it is true, was evidently a thorough and practised man of the world, systematic and self-possessed, and therefore the sort of a person to whom a parent ought not to confide a simple, young girl without due watchfulness for the result. The worthy magistrate, who had been conversant with all degrees and qualities of mankind, could not but perceive every motion and gesture of the distinguished Feathertop came in its proper place; nothing had been left rude or native in him; a well-digested conventionalism had incorporated itself thoroughly with his substance and transformed him into a work of art. Perhaps it was this peculiarity that invested him with a species of ghastliness and awe. It is the effect of any thing completely and consummately artificial, in human shape, that the person impresses us as an unreality and as having hardly pith enough to cast a shadow upon the floor. As regarded Feathertop, all this resulted in a wild, extravagant, and fantastical impression, as if his life and being were akin to the smoke that curled upward from his pipe.

But pretty Polly Gookin felt not thus. The pair were now promenading the room; Feathertop with his dainty stride and no less dainty grimace; the girl with a native maidenly grace, just touched, not spoiled, by a slightly affected manner, which seemed caught from the perfect artifice of her companion. The longer the interview continued, the more charmed was pretty Polly, until, within the first quarter of an hour, (as the old magistrate noted by his watch,) she was evidently beginning to be in love. Nor need it have been witchcraft that subdued her in such a hurry; the poor child's heart, it may be, was so very fervent that it melted her with its own warmth as reflected from the hollow semblance of a lover. No matter what Feathertop said, his words found depth and reverberation in her ear; no matter what he did, his action was heroic to her eye. And by this time it is to be supposed there was a blush on Polly's cheek, a tender smile about her mouth, and a liquid softness in her glance; while the star kept coruscating on Feathertop's breast, and the little demons careered with more frantic merriment than ever about the circumference of his pipe bowl. O pretty Polly Gookin, why should these imps rejoice so madly that a silly maiden's heart was about to be given to a shadow! Is it so unusual a misfortune, so rare a triumph?

By and by Feathertop paused, and, throwing himself into an imposing attitude, seemed to summon the fair girl to survey his figure and resist him longer if she could. His star, his embroidery, his buckles glowed at that instant with unutterable splendor; the picturesque hues of his attire took a richer depth of coloring; there was a gleam and polish over his whole presence betokening the perfect witchery of well-ordered manners. The maiden raised her eyes and suffered them to linger upon her companion with a bashful and admiring gaze. Then, as if desirous of judging what value her own simple comeliness might have side by side with so much brilliancy, she cast a glance towards the full-length looking glass in front of which they happened to be standing. It was one of the truest plates in the world, and incapable of flattery. No sooner did the images therein reflected meet Polly's eye than she shrieked, shrank from the stranger's side, gazed at him for a moment in the wildest dismay, and sank insensible upon the floor. Feathertop likewise had looked towards the mirror, and there beheld, not the glittering mockery of his outside show, but a picture of the sordid patchwork of his real composition, stripped of all witchcraft.

The wretched simulacrum! We almost pity him. He threw up his arms with an expression of despair that went further than any of his previous manifestations towards vindicating his claims to be reckoned human; for, perchance the only time since this so often empty and deceptive life of mortals began its course, an illusion had seen and fully recognized itself.

Mother Rigby was seated by her kitchen hearth in the twilight of this eventful day, and had just shaken the ashes out of a new pipe, when she heard a hurried tramp along the road. Yet it did not seem so much the tramp of human footsteps as the clatter of sticks or the rattling of dry bones.

"Ha!" thought the old witch, "what step is that? Whose skeleton is out of its grave now, I wonder?"

A figure burst headlong into the cottage door. It was Feathertop! His pipe was still alight; the star still flamed upon his breast; the embroidery still glowed upon his garments; nor had he lost, in any degree or manner that could be estimated, the aspect that assimilated him with our mortal brotherhood. But yet, in some indescribable way, (as is the case with all that has deluded us when once found out,) the poor reality was felt beneath the cunning artifice.

"What has gone wrong?" demanded the witch. "Did yonder sniffling hypocrite thrust my darling from his door? The villain! I'll set twenty fiends to torment him till he offer thee his daughter on his bended knees!"

"No, mother," said Feathertop despondingly; "it was not that."

"Did the girl scorn my precious one?" asked Mother Rigby, her fierce eyes glowing like two coals of Tophet.[27] "I'll cover her face with pimples! Her nose shall be as red as the coal in thy pipe! Her front teeth shall drop out! In a week hence she shall not be worth thy having!"

"Let her alone, mother," answered poor Feathertop; "the girl was half won; and methinks a kiss from her sweet lips might have made me altogether human. But," he added, after a brief pause and then a howl of self-contempt, "I've seen myself, mother! I've seen myself for the wretched, ragged, empty thing I am! I'll exist no longer!"

Snatching the pipe from his mouth, he flung it with all his might against the chimney, and at the same instant sank upon the floor, a medley of straw and tattered garments, with some sticks protruding from the heap, and a shrivelled pumpkin in the midst. The eyeholes were now lustreless; but the rudely-carved gap, that just before had been a mouth, still seemed to twist itself into a despairing grin, and was so far human.

"Poor fellow!" quoth Mother Rigby, with a rueful glance at the relics of her ill-fated contrivance. "My poor, dear, pretty Feathertop! There are thousands upon thousands of coxcombs[28] and charlatans in the world, made up of just such a jumble of wornout, forgotten, and good-for-nothing trash as he was! Yet they live in fair repute, and never see themselves for what they are. And why should my poor puppet be the only one to know himself and perish for it?"

While thus muttering, the witch had filled a fresh pipe of tobacco, and held the stem between her fingers, as doubtful whether to thrust it into her own mouth or Feathertop's.

"Poor Feathertop!" she continued. "I could easily give him another chance and send him forth again to-morrow. But no; his feelings are too tender, his sensibilities too deep. He seems to have too much heart to bustle for his own advantage in such an empty and heartless world. Well! well! I'll make a scarecrow of him after all. 'Tis an innocent and a useful vocation, and will suit my darling well; and, if each of his human brethren had as fit a one, 'twould be the better for mankind; and as for this pipe of tobacco, I need it more than he."

So saying, Mother Rigby put the stem between her lips. "Dickon!" cried she, in her high, sharp tone, "another coal for my pipe!"

VOLUME II

THE NEW ADAM AND EVE

We who are born into the world's artificial system can never adequately know how little in our present state and circumstances is natural, and how much is merely the interpolation of the perverted mind and heart of man. Art has become a second and stronger nature; she is a stepmother, whose crafty tenderness has taught us to despise the bountiful and wholesome ministrations of our true parent. It is only through the medium of the imagination that we can lessen those iron fetters, which we call truth and reality, and make ourselves even partially sensible what prisoners we are. For instance, let us conceive good Father Miller's interpretation[1] of the prophecies to have proved true. The Day of Doom has burst upon the globe and swept away the whole race of men. From cities and fields, seashore and midland mountain region, vast continents, and even the remotest islands of the ocean, each living thing is gone. No breath of a created being disturbs this earthly atmosphere. But the abodes of man, and all that he has accomplished, the footprints of his wanderings and the results of his toil, the visible symbols of his intellectual cultivation and moral progress—in short, every thing physical that can give evidence of his present position—shall remain untouched by the hand of destiny. Then, to inherit and repeople this waste and deserted earth, we will suppose a new Adam and a new Eve to have been created, in the full development of mind and heart, but with no knowledge of their predecessors nor of the diseased circumstances that had become encrusted around them. Such a pair would at once distinguish between art and nature. Their instincts and intuitions would immediately recognize the wisdom and simplicity of the latter; while the former, with its elaborate perversities, would offer them a continual succession of puzzles.

Let us attempt, in a mood half sportive and half thoughtful, to track these imaginary heirs of our mortality through their first day's experience. No longer ago than yesterday the flame of human life was extinguished; there has been a breathless night; and now another morn approaches, expecting to find the earth no less desolate than at eventide.

It is dawn. The east puts on its immemorial blush, although no human eye is gazing at it; for all the phenomena of the natural world renew themselves, in spite of the solitude that now broods around the globe. There is still beauty of earth, sea, and sky, for beauty's sake. But soon there are to be spectators. Just when the earliest sunshine gilds earth's mountain tops, two beings have come into life, not in such an Eden as bloomed to welcome our first parents, but in the heart of a modern city. They find themselves in existence, and gazing into one another's eyes. Their emotion is not astonishment; nor do they perplex themselves with efforts to discover what, and whence, and why they are. Each is satisfied to be, because the other exists likewise; and their first consciousness is of calm and mutual enjoyment, which seems not to have been the birth of that very moment, but prolonged from a past eternity. Thus content with an inner sphere which they inhabit together, it is not immediately that the outward world can obtrude itself upon their notice.

Soon, however, they feel the invincible necessity of this earthly life, and begin to make acquaintance with the objects and circumstances that surround them. Perhaps no other stride so vast remains to be taken as when they first turn from the reality of their mutual glance to the dreams and shadows that perplex them every where else.

"Sweetest Eve, where are we?" exclaims the new Adam; for speech, or some equivalent mode of expression, is born with them, and comes just as natural as breath. "Methinks I do not recognize this place."

"Nor I, dear Adam," replies the new Eve. "And what a strange place, too! Let me come closer to thy side and behold thee only; for all other sights trouble and perplex my spirit."

"Nay, Eve," replies Adam, who appears to have the stronger tendency towards the material world; "it were well that we gain some insight into these matters. We are in an odd situation here. Let us look about us."

Assuredly there are sights enough to throw the new inheritors of earth into a state of hopeless perplexity. The long lines of edifices, their windows glittering in the yellow sunrise, and the narrow street between, with its barren pavement tracked and battered by wheels that have now rattled into an irrevocable past! The signs, with their unintelligible hieroglyphics! The squareness and ugliness, and regular or irregular deformity of every thing that meets the eye! The marks of wear and tear, and unrenewed decay, which distinguish the works of man from the growth of nature! What is there in all this, capable of the slightest significance to minds that know nothing of the artificial system which is implied in every lamp post and each brick of the houses? Moreover, the utter loneliness and silence, in a scene that originally grew out of noise and bustle, must needs impress a feeling of desolation even upon Adam and Eve, unsuspicious as they are of the recent extinction of human existence. In a forest, solitude would be life; in a city, it is death.

The new Eve looks round with a sensation of doubt and distrust, such as a city dame, the daughter of numberless generations of citizens, might experience if suddenly transported to the garden of Eden. At length her downcast eye discovers a small tuft of grass, just beginning to sprout among the stones of the pavement; she eagerly grasps it, and is sensible that this little herb awakens some response within her heart. Nature finds nothing else to offer her. Adam, after staring up and down the street without detecting a single object that his comprehension can lay hold of, finally turns his forehead to the sky. There, indeed, is something which the soul within him recognizes.

"Look up yonder, mine own Eve," he cries; "surely we ought to dwell among those gold-tinged clouds or in the blue depths beyond them. I know not how nor when, but evidently we have strayed away from our home; for I see nothing hereabouts that seems to belong to us."

"Can we not ascend thither," inquires Eve.

"Why not?" answers Adam, hopefully. "But no; something drags us down in spite of our best efforts. Perchance we may find a path hereafter."

In the energy of new life it appears no such impracticable feat to climb into the sky. But they have already received a woful lesson, which may finally go far towards reducing them to the level of the departed race, when they acknowledge the necessity of keeping the beaten track of earth. They now set forth on a ramble through the city, in the hope of making their escape from this uncongenial sphere. Already in the fresh elasticity of their spirits they have found the idea of weariness. We will watch them as they enter some of the shops and public or private edifices; for every door, whether of alderman or beggar, church or hall of state, has been flung wide open by the same agency that swept away the inmates.

It so happens—and not unluckily for an Adam and Eve who are still in the costume that might better have befitted Eden—it so happens that their first visit is to a fashionable dry goods store. No courteous and importunate attendants hasten to receive their orders; no throng of ladies are tossing over the rich Parisian fabrics. All is deserted; trade is at a stand still; and not even an echo of the national watchword, "Go ahead!" disturbs the quiet of the new customers. But specimens of the latest earthly fashions, silks of every shade, and whatever is most delicate or splendid for the decoration of the human form, lie scattered around, profusely as bright autumnal leaves in a forest. Adam looks at a few of the articles, but throws them carelessly aside with whatever exclamation may correspond to "Pish!" or "Pshaw!" in the new vocabulary of nature. Eve, however,—be it said without offence to her native modesty,—examines these treasures of her sex with somewhat livelier interest. A pair of corsets chance to lie upon the counter; she inspects them curiously, but knows not what to make of them. Then she handles a fashionable silk with dim yearnings, thoughts that wander hither and thither, instincts groping in the dark.

"On the whole, I do not like it," she observes, laying the glossy fabric upon the counter. "But, Adam, it is very strange. What can these things mean? Surely I ought to know; yet they put me in a perfect maze."

"Poh! my dear Eve, why trouble thy little head about such nonsense?" cries Adam, in a fit of impatience. "Let us go somewhere else. But stay; how very beautiful! My loveliest Eve, what a charm you have imparted to that robe by merely throwing it over your shoulders!"

For Eve, with the taste that nature moulded into her composition, has taken a remnant of exquisite silver gauze and drawn it around her form, with an effect that gives Adam his first idea of the witchery of dress. He beholds his spouse in a new light and with renewed admiration; yet is hardly reconciled to any other attire than her own golden locks. However, emulating Eve's example, he makes free with a mantle of blue velvet, and puts it on so picturesquely that it might seem to have fallen from heaven upon his stately figure. Thus garbed they go in search of new discoveries.

They next wander into a Church, not to make a display of their fine clothes, but attracted by its spire, pointing upwards to the sky, whither they have already yearned to climb. As they enter the portal, a clock, which it was the last earthly act of the sexton to wind up, repeats the hour in deep reverberating tones; for Time has survived his former progeny, and, with the iron tongue that man gave him, is now speaking to his two grandchildren. They listen, but understand him not. Nature would measure time by the succession of thoughts and acts which constitute real life, and not by hours of emptiness. They pass up the church aisle, and raise their eyes to the ceiling. Had our Adam and Eve become mortal in some European city, and strayed into the vastness and sublimity of an old cathedral, they might have recognized the purpose for which the deep-souled founders reared it. Like the dim awfulness of an ancient forest, its very atmosphere would have incited them to prayer. Within the snug walls of a metropolitan church there can be no such influence.

Yet some odor of religion is still lingering here, the bequest of pious souls, who had grace to enjoy a foretaste of immortal life. Perchance they breathe a prophecy of a better world to their successors, who have become obnoxious to all their own cares and calamities in the present one.

"Eve, something impels me to look upward," says Adam; "but it troubles me to see this roof between us and the sky. Let us go forth, and perhaps we shall discern a Great Face looking down upon us."

"Yes; a Great Face, with a beam of love brightening over it, like sunshine," responds Eve. "Surely, we have seen such a countenance somewhere."

They go out of the church, and kneeling at its threshold give way to the spirit's natural instinct of adoration towards a beneficent Father. But, in truth, their life thus far has been a continual prayer. Purity and simplicity hold converse at every moment with their Creator.

We now observe them entering a Court of Justice. But what remotest conception can they attain of the purposes of such an edifice? How should the idea occur to them that human brethren, of like nature with themselves, and originally included in the same law of love which is their only rule of life, should ever need an outward enforcement of the true voice within their souls? And what, save a woful experience, the dark result of many centuries, could teach them the sad mysteries of crime? O, Judgment Seat, not by the pure in heart wast thou established, nor in the simplicity of nature; but by hard and wrinkled men, and upon the accumulated heap of earthly wrong. Thou art the very symbol of man's perverted state.

On as fruitless an errand our wanderers next visit a Hall of Legislature, where Adam places Eve in the Speaker's chair, unconscious of the moral which he thus exemplifies. Man's intellect, moderated by Woman's tenderness and moral sense! Were such the legislation of the world there would be no need of State Houses, Capitols, Halls of Parliament, nor even of those little assemblages of patriarchs beneath the shadowy trees, by whom freedom was first interpreted to mankind on our native shores.

Whither go they next? A perverse destiny seems to perplex them with one after another of the riddles which mankind put forth to the wandering universe, and left unsolved in their own destruction. They enter an edifice of stern gray stone standing insulated in the midst of others, and gloomy even in the sunshine, which it barely suffers to penetrate through its iron grated windows. It is a prison. The jailer has left his post at the summons of a stronger authority than the sheriff's. But the prisoners? Did the messenger of fate, when he shook open all the doors, respect the magistrate's warrant and the judge's sentence, and leave the inmates of the dungeons to be delivered by due course of earthly law? No; a new trial has been granted in a higher court, which may set judge, jury, and prisoner at its bar all in a row, and perhaps find one no less guilty than another. The jail, like the whole earth, is now a solitude, and has thereby lost something of its dismal gloom. But here are the narrow cells, like tombs, only drearier and deadlier, because in these the immortal spirit was buried with the body. Inscriptions appear on the walls, scribbled with a pencil or scratched with a rusty nail; brief words of agony, perhaps, or guilt's desperate defiance to the world, or merely a record of a date by which the writer strove to keep up with the march of life. There is not a living eye that could now decipher these memorials.

Nor is it while so fresh from their Creator's hand that the new denizens of earth—no, nor their descendants for a thousand years—could discover that this edifice was a hospital for the direst disease which could afflict their predecessors. Its patients bore the outward marks of that leprosy with which all were more or less infected. They were sick—and so were the purest of their brethren—with the plague of sin. A deadly sickness, indeed! Feeling its symptoms within the breast, men concealed it with fear and shame, and were only the more cruel to those unfortunates whose pestiferous sores were flagrant to the common eye. Nothing save a rich garment could ever hide the plague spot. In the course of the world's lifetime, every remedy was tried for its cure and extirpation, except the single one, the flower that grew in Heaven and was sovereign for all the miseries of earth. Man never had attempted to cure sin by LOVE! Had he but once made the effort it might well have happened that there would have been no more need of the dark lazar house[2] into which Adam and Eve have wandered. Hasten forth with your native innocence, lest the damps of these still conscious walls infect you likewise, and thus another fallen race be propagated!

Passing from the interior of the prison into the space within its outward wall, Adam pauses beneath a structure of the simplest contrivance, yet altogether unaccountable to him. It consists merely of two upright posts, supporting a transverse beam, from which dangles a cord.

"Eve, Eve!" cries Adam, shuddering with a nameless horror. "What can this thing be?"

"I know not," answers Eve; "but, Adam, my heart is sick! There seems to be no more sky—no more sunshine!"

Well might Adam shudder and poor Eve be sick at heart; for this mysterious object was the type of mankind's whole system in regard to the great difficulties which God had given to be solved—a system of fear and vengeance, never successful, yet followed to the last. Here, on the morning when the final summons came, a criminal—one criminal, where none were guiltless—had died upon the gallows. Had the world heard the footfall of its own approaching doom, it would have been no inappropriate act thus to close the record of its deeds by one so characteristic.

The two pilgrims now hurry from the prison. Had they known how the former inhabitants of earth were shut up in artificial error and cramped and chained by their perversions, they might have compared the whole moral world to a prison house, and have deemed the removal of the race a general jail delivery.

They next enter, unannounced, but they might have rung at the door in vain, a private mansion, one of the stateliest in Beacon Street.[3] A wild and plaintive strain of music is quivering through the house, now rising like a solemn organ peal, and now dying into the faintest murmur, as if some spirit that had felt an interest in the departed family were bemoaning itself in the solitude of hall and chamber. Perhaps a virgin, the purest of mortal race, has been left behind to perform a requiem for the whole kindred of humanity. Not so. These are the tones of an Æolian harp,[4] through which Nature pours the harmony that lies concealed in her every breath, whether of summer breeze or tempest. Adam and Eve are lost in rapture, unmingled with surprise. The passing wind, that stirred the harp strings, has been hushed, before they can think of examining the splendid furniture, the gorgeous carpets, and the architecture of the rooms. These things amuse their unpractised eyes, but appeal to nothing within their hearts. Even the pictures upon the walls scarcely excite a deeper interest; for there is something radically artificial and deceptive in painting with which minds in the primal simplicity cannot sympathize. The unbidden guests examine a row of family portraits, but are too dull to recognize them as men and women, beneath the disguise of a preposterous garb, and with features and expression debased, because inherited through ages of moral and physical decay.

Chance, however, presents them with pictures of human beauty, fresh from the hand of Nature. As they enter a magnificent apartment they are astonished, but not affrighted, to perceive two figures advancing to meet them. Is it not awful to imagine that any life, save their own, should remain in the wide world?

"How is this?" exclaims Adam. "My beautiful Eve, are you in two places at once?"

"And you, Adam!" answers Eve, doubtful, yet delighted. "Surely that noble and lovely form is yours. Yet here you are by my side. I am content with one—methinks there should not be two."

This miracle is wrought by a tall looking glass, the mystery of which they soon fathom, because Nature creates a mirror for the human face in every pool of water, and for her own great features in waveless lakes. Pleased and satisfied with gazing at themselves, they now discover the marble statue of a child in a corner of the room so exquisitely idealized that it is almost worthy to be the prophetic likeness of their first born. Sculpture, in its highest excellence, is more genuine than painting, and might seem to be evolved from a natural germ, by the same law as a leaf or flower. The statue of the child impresses the solitary pair as if it were a companion; it likewise hints at secrets both of the past and future.

"My husband!" whispers Eve.

"What would you say, dearest Eve?" inquires Adam.

"I wonder if we are alone in the world," she continues, with a sense of something like fear at the thought of other inhabitants. "This lovely little form! Did it ever breathe? Or is it only the shadow of something real, like our pictures in the mirror?"

"It is strange!" replies Adam, pressing his hand to his brow. "There are mysteries all around us. An idea flits continually before me— would that I could seize it! Eve, Eve, are we treading in the footsteps of beings that bore a likeness to ourselves? If so, whither are they gone?— and why is their world so unfit for our dwelling place?"

"Our great Father only knows," answers Eve. "But something tells me that we shall not always be alone. And how sweet if other beings were to visit us in the shape of this fair image!"

Then they wander through the house, and every where find tokens of human life, which now, with the idea recently suggested, excite a deeper curiosity in their bosoms. Woman has here left traces of her delicacy and refinement, and of her gentle labors. Eve ransacks a work basket and instinctively thrusts the rosy tip of her finger into a thimble. She takes up a piece of embroidery, glowing with mimic flowers, in one of which a fair damsel of the departed race has left her needle. Pity that the Day of Doom should have anticipated the completion of such a useful task! Eve feels almost conscious of the skill to finish it. A pianoforte has been left open. She flings her hand carelessly over the keys, and strikes out a sudden melody, no less natural than the strains of the Æolian harp, but joyous with the dance of her yet unburdened life. Passing through a dark entry they find a broom behind the door; and Eve, who comprises the whole nature of womanhood, has a dim idea that it is an instrument proper for her hand. In another apartment they behold a canopied bed, and all the appliances of luxurious repose. A heap of forest leaves would be more to the purpose. They enter the nursery, and are perplexed with the sight of little gowns and caps, tiny shoes, and a cradle, amid the drapery of which is still to be seen the impress of a baby's form. Adam slightly notices these trifles; but Eve becomes involved in a fit of mute reflection from which it is hardly possible to rouse her.

By a most unlucky arrangement there was to have been a grand dinner party in this mansion on the very day when the whole human family, including the invited guests, were summoned to the unknown regions of illimitable space. At the moment of fate, the table was actually spread, and the company on the point of sitting down. Adam and Eve come unbidden to the banquet; it has now been some time cold, but otherwise furnishes them with highly favorable specimens of the gastronomy of their predecessors. But it is difficult to imagine the perplexity of the unperverted couple, in endeavoring to find proper food for their first meal, at a table where the cultivated appetites of a fashionable party were to have been gratified. Will Nature teach them the mystery of a plate of turtle soup? Will she embolden them to attack a haunch of venison? Will she initiate them into the merits of a Parisian pasty, imported by the last steamer that ever crossed the Atlantic? Will she not, rather, bid them turn with disgust from fish, fowl, and flesh, which, to their pure nostrils, steam with a loathsome odor of death and corruption?—Food? The bill of fare contains nothing which they recognize as such.

Fortunately, however, the dessert is ready upon a neighboring table. Adam, whose appetite and animal instincts are quicker than those of Eve, discovers this fitting banquet.

"Here, dearest Eve," he exclaims, "here is food."

"Well," answered she, with the germ of a housewife stirring within her, "we have been so busy to-day, that a picked-up dinner must serve."

So Eve comes to the table and receives a red-cheeked apple from her husband's hand in requital of her predecessor's fatal gift to our common grandfather. She eats it without sin, and, let us hope, with no disastrous consequences to her future progeny. They make a plentiful, yet temperate, meal of fruit, which, though not gathered in paradise, is legitimately derived from the seeds that were planted there. Their primal appetite is satisfied.

"What shall we drink, Eve?" inquires Adam.

Eve peeps among some bottles and decanters, which, as they contain fluids, she naturally conceives must be proper to quench thirst. But never before did claret, hock, and madeira, of rich and rare perfume, excite such disgust as now.

"Pah!" she exclaims, after smelling at various wines. "What stuff is here? The beings who have gone before us could not have possessed the same nature that we do; for neither their hunger nor thirst were like our own."

"Pray hand me yonder bottle," says Adam. "If it be drinkable by any manner of mortal, I must moisten my throat with it."

After some remonstrances, she takes up a champagne bottle, but is frightened by the sudden explosion of the cork, and drops it upon the floor. There the untasted liquor effervesces. Had they quaffed it they would have experienced that brief delirium whereby, whether excited by moral or physical causes, man sought to recompense himself for the calm, lifelong joys which he had lost by his revolt from Nature. At length, in a refrigerator, Eve finds a glass pitcher of water, pure, cold, and bright as ever gushed from a fountain among the hills. Both drink; and such refreshment does it bestow, that they question one another if this precious liquid be not identical with the stream of life within them.

"And now," observes Adam, "we must again try to discover what sort of a world this is, and why we have been sent hither."

"Why? to love one another," cries Eve. "Is not that employment enough?"

"Truly is it," answers Adam, kissing her; "but still—I know not—something tells us there is labor to be done. Perhaps our allotted task is no other than to climb into the sky, which is so much more beautiful than earth."

"Then would we were there now," murmurs Eve, "that no task or duty might come between us!"

They leave the hospitable mansion, and we next see them passing down State Street.[5] The clock on the old State House[6] points to high noon, when the Exchange[7] should be in its glory and present the liveliest emblem of what was the sole business of life, as regarded a multitude of the foregone worldlings. It is over now. The Sabbath of eternity has shed its stillness along the street. Not even a newsboy assails the two solitary passers by with an extra penny paper from the office of the Times or Mail, containing a full account of yesterday's terrible catastrophe. Of all the dull times that merchants and speculators have known, this is the very worst; for, so far as they were concerned, creation itself has taken the benefit of the bankrupt act. After all, it is a pity. Those mighty capitalists who had just attained the wished-for wealth! Those shrewd men of traffic who had devoted so many years to the most intricate and artificial of sciences, and had barely mastered it when the universal bankruptcy was announced by peal of trumpet! Can they have been so incautious as to provide no currency of the country whither they have gone, nor any bills of exchange, or letters of credit from the needy on earth to the cash keepers of heaven?

Adam and Eve enter a Bank. Start not, ye whose funds are treasured there! You will never need them now. Call not for the police. The stones of the street and the coin of the vaults are of equal value to this simple pair. Strange sight! They take up the bright gold in handfuls and throw it sportively into the air for the sake of seeing the glittering worthlessness descend again in a shower. They know not that each of those small yellow circles was once a magic spell, potent to sway men's hearts and mystify their moral sense. Here let them pause in the investigation of the past. They have discovered the mainspring, the life, the very essence of the system that had wrought itself into the vitals of mankind, and choked their original nature in its deadly gripe. Yet how powerless over these young inheritors of earth's hoarded wealth! And here, too, are huge packages of bank notes, those talismanic slips of paper which once had the efficacy to build up enchanted palaces like exhalations, and work all kinds of perilous wonders, yet were themselves but the ghosts of money, the shadows of a shade. How like is this vault to a magician's cave when the all-powerful wand is broken, and the visionary splendor vanished, and the floor strown with fragments of shattered spells, and lifeless shapes, once animated by demons!

"Every where, my dear Eve," observes Adam, "we find heaps of rubbish of one kind or another. Somebody, I am convinced, has taken pains to collect them, but for what purpose? Perhaps, hereafter, we shall be moved to do the like. Can that be our business in the world?"

"O, no, no, Adam!" answers Eve. "It would be better to sit down quietly and look upward to the sky."

They leave the Bank, and in good time; for had they tarried later they would probably have encountered some gouty[8] old goblin of a capitalist, whose soul could not long be any where save in the vault with his treasure.

Next they drop into a jeweller's shop. They are pleased with the glow of gems; and Adam twines a string of beautiful pearls around the head of Eve, and fastens his own mantle with a magnificent diamond brooch. Eve thanks him, and views herself with delight in the nearest looking glass. Shortly afterward, observing a bouquet of roses and other brilliant flowers in a vase of water, she flings away the inestimable pearls, and adorns herself with these lovelier gems of nature. They charm her with sentiment as well as beauty.

"Surely they are living beings," she remarks to Adam.

"I think so," replies Adam, "and they seem to be as little at home in the world as ourselves."

We must not attempt to follow every footstep of these investigators whom their Creator has commissioned to pass unconscious judgment upon the works and ways of the vanished race. By this time, being endowed with quick and accurate perceptions, they begin to understand the purpose of the many things around them. They conjecture, for instance, that the edifices of the city were erected, not by the immediate hand that made the world, but by beings somewhat similar to themselves, for shelter and convenience. But how will they explain the magnificence of one habitation as compared with the squalid misery of another? Through what medium can the idea of servitude enter their minds? When will they comprehend the great and miserable fact—the evidences of which appeal to their senses every where—that one portion of earth's lost inhabitants was rolling in luxury while the multitude was toiling for scanty food? A wretched change, indeed, must be wrought in their own hearts ere they can conceive the primal decree of Love to have been so completely abrogated, that a brother should ever want what his brother had. When their intelligence shall have reached so far, Earth's new progeny will have little reason to exult over her old rejected one.

Their wanderings have now brought them into the suburbs of the city. They stand on a grassy brow of a hill at the foot of a granite obelisk which points its great finger upwards, as if the human family had agreed, by a visible symbol of age-long endurance, to offer some high sacrifice of thanksgiving or supplication. The solemn height of the monument, its deep simplicity, and the absence of any vulgar and practical use, all strengthen its effect upon Adam and Eve, and leave them to interpret it by a purer sentiment than the builders thought of expressing.

"Eve, it is a visible prayer," observed Adam.

"And we will pray too," she replies.

Let us pardon these poor children of neither father nor mother for so absurdly mistaking the purport of the memorial which man founded and woman finished on far-famed Bunker Hill.[9] The idea of war is not native to their souls. Nor have they sympathies for the brave defenders of liberty, since oppression is one of their unconjectured mysteries. Could they guess that the green sward on which they stand so peacefully was once strewn with human corpses and purple with their blood, it would equally amaze them that one generation of men should perpetrate such carnage, and that a subsequent generation should triumphantly commemorate it.

With a sense of delight they now stroll across green fields and along the margin of a quiet river. Not to track them too closely, we next find the wanderers entering a Gothic edifice of gray stone, where the bygone world has left whatever it deemed worthy of record, in the rich library of Harvard University.[10]

No student ever yet enjoyed such solitude and silence as now broods within its deep alcoves. Little do the present visitors understand what opportunities are thrown away upon them. Yet Adam looks anxiously at the long rows of volumes, those storied heights of human lore, ascending one above another from floor to ceiling. He takes up a bulky folio. It opens in his hands as if spontaneously to impart the spirit of its author to the yet unworn and untainted intellect of the fresh-created mortal. He stands poring over the regular columns of mystic characters, seemingly in studious mood; for the unintelligible thought upon the page has a mysterious relation to his mind, and makes itself felt as if it were a burden flung upon him. He is even painfully perplexed, and grasps vainly at he knows not what. O, Adam,

it is too soon, too soon by at least five thousand years, to put on spectacles and bury yourself in the alcoves of a library!

"What can this be?" he murmurs at last. "Eve, methinks nothing is
so desirable as to find out the mystery of this big and heavy object with
its thousand thin divisions. See! it stares me in the face as if it were
about to speak!"

Eve, by a feminine instinct, is dipping into a volume of fashionable
poetry, the production certainly the most fortunate of earthly bards,
since his lay continues in vogue when all the great masters of the lyre
have passed into oblivion. But let not his ghost be too exultant! The
world's one lady tosses the book upon the floor and laughs merrily at
her husband's abstracted mien.

"My dear Adam," cries she, "you look pensive and dismal. Do fling
down that stupid thing; for even if it should speak it would not be
worth attending to. Let us talk with one another, and with the sky, and
the green earth, and its trees and flowers. They will teach us better
knowledge than we can find here."

"Well, Eve, perhaps you are right," replies Adam, with a sort of sigh.
"Still I cannot help thinking that the interpretation of the riddles amid
which we have been wandering all day long might here be discovered."

"It may be better not to seek the interpretation," persists Eve. "For
my part, the air of this place does not suit me. If you love me, come
away!"

She prevails, and rescues him from the mysterious perils of the library. Happy influence of woman! Had he lingered there long enough
to obtain a clue to its treasures,—as was not impossible, his intellect
being of human structure, indeed, but with an untransmitted vigor and
acuteness,—had he then and there become a student, the annalist of
our poor world would soon have recorded the downfall of a second
Adam. The fatal apple of another Tree of Knowledge[11] would have
been eaten. All the perversions, and sophistries, and false wisdom so
aptly mimicking the true—all the narrow truth, so partial that it becomes more deceptive than falsehood—all the wrong principles and
worse practice, the pernicious examples and mistaken rules of life—
all the specious theories which turn earth into cloudland and men into
shadows—all the sad experience which it took mankind so many ages
to accumulate, and from which they never drew a moral for their future guidance,—the whole heap of this disastrous lore would have

tumbled at once upon Adam's head. There would have been nothing left for him but to take up the already abortive experiment of life where we had dropped it, and toil onward with it a little further.

But, blessed in his ignorance, he may still enjoy a new world in our wornout one. Should he fall short of good, even as far as we did, he has at least the freedom—no worthless one—to make errors for himself. And his literature, when the progress of centuries shall create it, will be no interminably repeated echo of our own poetry and reproduction of the images that were moulded by our great fathers of song and fiction, but a melody never yet heard on earth, and intellectual forms unbreathed upon by our conceptions. Therefore let the dust of ages gather upon the volumes of the library, and in due season the roof of the edifice crumble down upon the whole. When the second Adam's descendants shall have collected as much rubbish of their own, it will be time enough to dig into our ruins and compare the literary advancement of two independent races.

But we are looking forward too far. It seems to be the vice of those who have a long past behind them. We will return to the new Adam and Eve, who, having no reminiscences save dim and fleeting visions of a preëxistence, are content to live and be happy in the present.

The day is near its close when these pilgrims, who derive their being from no dead progenitors, reach the cemetery of Mount Auburn.[12] With light hearts—for earth and sky now gladden each other with beauty—they tread along the winding paths, among marble pillars, mimic temples, urns, obelisks, and sarcophagi, sometimes pausing to contemplate these fantasies of human growth, and sometimes to admire the flowers wherewith Nature converts decay to loveliness. Can death, in the midst of his old triumphs, make them sensible that they have taken up the heavy burden of mortality which a whole species had thrown down? Dust kindred to their own has never lain in the grave. Will they then recognize, and so soon, that Time and the elements have an indefeasible claim upon their bodies? Not improbably they may. There must have been shadows enough, even amid the primal sunshine of their existence, to suggest the thought of the soul's incongruity with its circumstances. They have already learned that something is to be thrown aside. The idea of Death is in them, or not far off. But, were they to choose a symbol for him, it would be the butterfly soaring upward, or the bright angel beckoning them aloft, or the child asleep, with soft dreams visible through her transparent purity.

Such a Child, in whitest marble, they have found among the monuments of Mount Auburn.

"Sweetest Eve," observes Adam, while hand in hand they contemplate this beautiful object, "yonder sun has left us, and the whole world is fading from our sight. Let us sleep as this lovely little figure is sleeping. Our Father only knows whether what outward things we have possessed to-day are to be snatched from us forever. But should our earthly life be leaving us with the departing light, we need not doubt that another morn will find us somewhere beneath the smile of God. I feel that he has imparted the boon of existence never to be resumed."

"And no matter where we exist," replies Eve, "for we shall always be together."

Egotism;* or, The Bosom Serpent

From the unpublished "Allegories of the Heart"

"Here he comes!" shouted the boys along the street. "Here comes the man with a snake in his bosom!"

This outcry, saluting Herkimer's ears as he was about to enter the iron gate of the Elliston mansion, made him pause. It was not without a shudder that he found himself on the point of meeting his former acquaintance, whom he had known in the glory of youth, and whom now, after an interval of five years, he was to find the victim either of a diseased fancy or a horrible physical misfortune.

"A snake in his bosom!" repeated the young sculptor to himself. "It must be he. No second man on earth has such a bosom friend. And now, my poor Rosina, Heaven grant me wisdom to discharge my errand aright! Woman's faith must be strong indeed since thine has not yet failed."

Thus musing, he took his stand at the entrance of the gate and waited until the personage so singularly announced should make his appearance. After an instant or two he beheld the figure of a lean man, of unwholesome look, with glittering eyes and long black hair, who seemed to imitate the motion of a snake; for, instead of walking straight forward with open front, he undulated along the pavement in a curved

* The physical fact, to which it is here attempted to give a moral signification, has been known to occur in more than one instance.

line. It may be too fanciful to say that something, either in his moral or material aspect, suggested the idea that a miracle had been wrought by transforming a serpent into a man, but so imperfectly that the snaky nature was yet hidden, and scarcely hidden, under the mere outward guise of humanity. Herkimer remarked that his complexion had a greenish tinge over its sickly white, reminding him of a species of marble out of which he had once wrought a head of Envy, with her snaky locks.

The wretched being approached the gate, but, instead of entering, stopped short and fixed the glitter of his eye full upon the compassionate yet steady countenance of the sculptor.

"It gnaws me! It gnaws me!" he exclaimed.

And then there was an audible hiss, but whether it came from the apparent lunatic's own lips, or was the real hiss of a serpent, might admit of a discussion. At all events, it made Herkimer shudder to his heart's core.

"Do you know me, George Herkimer?" asked the snake-possessed.

Herkimer did know him; but it demanded all the intimate and practical acquaintance with the human face, acquired by modelling actual likenesses in clay, to recognize the features of Roderick Elliston in the visage that now met the sculptor's gaze. Yet it was he. It added nothing to the wonder to reflect that the once brilliant young man had undergone this odious and fearful change during the no more than five brief years of Herkimer's abode at Florence. The possibility of such a transformation being granted, it was as easy to conceive it effected in a moment as in an age. Inexpressibly shocked and startled, it was still the keenest pang when Herkimer remembered that the fate of his cousin Rosina, the ideal of gentle womanhood, was indissolubly interwoven with that of a being whom Providence seemed to have unhumanized.

"Elliston! Roderick!" cried he, "I had heard of this; but my conception came far short of the truth. What has befallen you? Why do I find you thus?"

"O, 'tis a mere nothing! A snake! A snake! The commonest thing in the world. A snake in the bosom—that's all," answered Roderick Elliston. "But how is your own breast?" continued he, looking the sculptor in the eye with the most acute and penetrating glance that it had ever been his fortune to encounter. "All pure and wholesome? No reptile there? By my faith and conscience, and by the devil within me, here is a wonder! A man without a serpent in his bosom!"

"Be calm, Elliston," whispered George Herkimer, laying his hand upon the shoulder of the snake-possessed. "I have crossed the ocean to meet you. Listen! Let us be private. I bring a message from Rosina—from your wife!"

"It gnaws me! It gnaws me!" muttered Roderick.

With this exclamation, the most frequent in his mouth, the unfortunate man clutched both hands upon his breast as if an intolerable sting or torture impelled him to rend it open and let out the living mischief, even should it be intertwined with his own life. He then freed himself from Herkimer's grasp by a subtle motion, and, gliding through the gate, took refuge in his antiquated family residence. The sculptor did not pursue him. He saw that no available intercourse could be expected at such a moment, and was desirous, before another meeting, to inquire closely into the nature of Roderick's disease and the circumstances that had reduced him to so lamentable a condition. He succeeded in obtaining the necessary information from an eminent medical gentleman.

Shortly after Elliston's separation from his wife—now nearly four years ago—his associates had observed a singular gloom spreading over his daily life, like those chill, gray mists that sometimes steal away the sunshine from a summer's morning. The symptoms caused them endless perplexity. They knew not whether ill health were robbing his spirits of elasticity, or whether a canker of the mind was gradually eating, as such cankers do, from his moral system into the physical frame, which is but the shadow of the former. They looked for the root of this trouble in his shattered schemes of domestic bliss,—wilfully shattered by himself,—but could not be satisfied of its existence there. Some thought that their once brilliant friend was in an incipient stage of insanity, of which his passionate impulses had perhaps been the forerunners; others prognosticated a general blight and gradual decline. From Roderick's own lips they could learn nothing. More than once, it is true, he had been heard to say, clutching his hands convulsively upon his breast—"It gnaws me! It gnaws me!"—but, by different auditors, a great diversity of explanation was assigned to this ominous expression. What could it be, that gnawed the breast of Roderick Elliston? Was it sorrow? Was it merely the tooth of physical disease? Or, in his reckless course, often verging upon profligacy, if not plunging into its depths, had he been guilty of some deed, which made his bosom a prey to the deadlier fangs of remorse? There was plausible ground for each of these conjectures; but it must not be concealed that more than one elderly gentleman, the victim of good cheer and slothful habits, magisterially pronounced the secret of the whole matter to be Dyspepsia![1]

Meanwhile, Roderick seemed aware how generally he had become the subject of curiosity and conjecture, and, with a morbid repugnance to such notice, or to any notice whatsoever, estranged himself from all companionship. Not merely the eye of man was a horror to him; not merely the light of a friend's countenance; but even the blessed sunshine, likewise, which, in its universal beneficence typifies the radiance of the Creator's face, expressing his love for all the creatures of his hand. The dusky twilight was now too transparent for Roderick Elliston; the blackest midnight was his chosen hour to steal abroad; and if ever he were seen, it was when the watchman's lantern gleamed upon his figure, gliding along the street, with his hands clutched upon his bosom, still muttering, "It gnaws me! It gnaws me!" What could it be that gnawed him?

After a time, it became known that Elliston was in the habit of resorting to all the noted quacks that infested the city, or whom money would tempt to journey thither from a distance. By one of these persons, in the exultation of a supposed cure, it was proclaimed far and wide, by dint of handbills and little pamphlets on dingy paper, that a distinguished gentleman, Roderick Elliston, Esq., had been relieved of a SNAKE in his stomach! So here was the monstrous secret, ejected from its lurking place into public view, in all its horrible deformity. The mystery was out; but not so the bosom serpent. He, if it were any thing but a delusion, still lay coiled in his living den. The empiric's cure had been a sham, the effect, it was supposed, of some stupefying drug, which more nearly caused the death of the patient than of the odious reptile that possessed him. When Roderick Elliston regained entire sensibility, it was to find his misfortune the town talk—the more than nine days' wonder and horror—while, at his bosom, he felt the sickening motion of a thing alive, and the gnawing of that restless fang, which seemed to gratify at once a physical appetite and a fiendish spite.

He summoned the old black servant, who had been bred up in his father's house, and was a middle-aged man while Roderick lay in his cradle.

"Scipio!"[2] he began; and then paused, with his arms folded over his heart. "What do people say of me, Scipio?"

"Sir! my poor master! that you had a serpent in your bosom," answered the servant, with hesitation.

"And what else?" asked Roderick, with a ghastly look at the man.

"Nothing else, dear master," replied Scipio; "only that the doctor gave you a powder, and that the snake leaped out upon the floor."

"No, no!" muttered Roderick to himself, as he shook his head, and pressed his hands with a more convulsive force upon his breast, "I feel him still. It gnaws me! It gnaws me!"

From this time the miserable sufferer ceased to shun the world, but rather solicited and forced himself upon the notice of acquaintances and strangers. It was partly the result of desperation on finding that the cavern of his own bosom had not proved deep and dark enough to hide the secret, even while it was so secure a fortress for the loathsome fiend that had crept into it. But still more, this craving for notoriety was a symptom of the intense morbidness which now pervaded his nature. All persons, chronically diseased, are egotists, whether the disease be of the mind or body; whether it be sin, sorrow, or merely the more tolerable calamity of some endless pain, or mischief among the cords of mortal life. Such individuals are made acutely conscious of a self, by the torture in which it dwells. Self, therefore, grows to be so prominent an object with them that they cannot but present it to the face of every casual passer by. There is a pleasure—perhaps the greatest of which the sufferer is susceptible—in displaying the wasted or ulcerated limb, or the cancer in the breast; and the fouler the crime, with so much the more difficulty does the perpetrator prevent it from thrusting up its snakelike head to frighten the world; for it is that cancer, or that crime, which constitutes their respective individuality. Roderick Elliston, who, a little while before, had held himself so scornfully above the common lot of men, now paid full allegiance to this humiliating law. The snake in his bosom seemed the symbol of a monstrous egotism to which every thing was referred, and which he pampered, night and day, with a continual and exclusive sacrifice of devil worship.

He soon exhibited what most people considered indubitable tokens of insanity. In some of his moods, strange to say, he prided and gloried himself on being marked out from the ordinary experience of mankind, by the possession of a double nature, and a life within a life. He appeared to imagine that the snake was a divinity—not celestial, it is true, but darkly infernal—and that he thence derived an eminence and a sanctity, horrid, indeed, yet more desirable than whatever ambition aims at. Thus he drew his misery around him like a regal mantle, and looked down triumphantly upon those whose vitals nourished no deadly monster. Oftener, however, his human nature asserted its empire over him in the shape of a yearning for fellowship. It grew to be his custom to spend the whole day in wandering about the streets, aimlessly, unless it might be called an aim to establish a species of brotherhood between himself and the world. With cankered ingenuity, he sought out his own disease in every breast. Whether insane or not, he showed so keen a perception of frailty, error, and vice, that many persons gave him credit for being possessed not merely with a serpent but with an actual fiend, who imparted this evil faculty of recognizing whatever was ugliest in man's heart.

For instance, he met an individual, who, for thirty years, had cherished a hatred against his own brother. Roderick, amidst the throng of the street, laid his hand on this man's chest, and looking full into his forbidding face,—

"How is the snake to-day?" he inquired, with a mock expression of sympathy.

"The snake!" exclaimed the brother hater—"what do you mean?"

"The snake! The snake! Does he gnaw you?" persisted Roderick. "Did you take counsel with him this morning, when you should have been saying your prayers? Did he sting, when you thought of your brother's health, wealth, and good repute? Did he caper for joy, when you remembered the profligacy of his only son? And whether he stung, or whether he frolicked, did you feel his poison throughout your body and soul, converting every thing to sourness and bitterness? That is the way of such serpents. I have learned the whole nature of them from my own!"

"Where is the police?" roared the object of Roderick's persecution, at the same time giving an instinctive clutch to his breast. "Why is this lunatic allowed to go at large?"

"Ha, ha!" chuckled Roderick, releasing his grasp of the man. "His bosom serpent has stung him, then!"

Often it pleased the unfortunate young man to vex people with a lighter satire, yet still characterized by somewhat of snakelike virulence. One day he encountered an ambitious statesman, and gravely inquired after the welfare of his boa constrictor; for of that species, Roderick affirmed, this gentleman's serpent must needs be, since its appetite was enormous enough to devour the whole country and constitution. At another time, he stopped a close-fisted old fellow, of great wealth, but who skulked about the city in the guise of a scarecrow, with a patched blue surtout,[3] brown hat, and mouldy boots, scraping pence together, and picking up rusty nails. Pretending to look earnestly at this respectable person's stomach, Roderick assured him that his snake was a copper-head, and had been generated by the immense quantities of that base metal, with which he daily defiled his fingers. Again, he assaulted a man of rubicund visage, and told him that few bosom serpents had more of the devil in them than those that breed in the vats of a distillery. The next whom Roderick honored with his attention was a distinguished clergyman, who happened just then to be engaged in a theological controversy, where human wrath was more perceptible than divine inspiration.

"You have swallowed a snake in a cup of sacramental wine," quoth he.

"Profane wretch!" exclaimed the divine; but, nevertheless, his hand stole to his breast.

He met a person of sickly sensibility, who, on some early disappointment, had retired from the world, and thereafter held no intercourse with his fellow-men, but brooded sullenly or passionately over the irrevocable past. This man's very heart, if Roderick might be believed, had been changed into a serpent, which would finally torment both him and itself to death. Observing a married couple, whose domestic troubles were matter of notoriety, he condoled with both on having mutually taken a house adder to their bosoms. To an envious author, who depreciated works which he could never equal, he said that his snake was the slimiest and filthiest of all the reptile tribe, but was fortunately without a sting. A man of impure life, and a brazen face, asking Roderick if there were any serpent in his breast, he told him that there was, and of the same species that once tortured Don Rodrigo, the Goth.[4] He took a fair young girl by the hand, and gazing sadly into her eyes, warned her that she cherished a serpent of the deadliest kind within her gentle breast; and the world found the truth of those ominous words, when, a few months afterwards, the poor girl died of love and shame. Two ladies, rivals in fashionable life, who tormented one another with a thousand little stings of womanish spite, were given to understand that each of their hearts was a nest of diminutive snakes, which did quite as much mischief as one great one.

But nothing seemed to please Roderick better than to lay hold of a person infected with jealousy, which he represented as an enormous green reptile, with an ice-cold length of body, and the sharpest sting of any snake save one.

"And what one is that?" asked a bystander, overhearing him.

It was a dark-browed man, who put the question; he had an evasive eye, which, in the course of a dozen years, had looked no mortal directly in the face. There was an ambiguity about this person's character—a stain upon his reputation—yet none could tell precisely of what nature, although the city gossips, male and female, whispered the most atrocious surmises. Until a recent period he had followed the sea, and was, in fact, the very shipmaster whom George Herkimer had encountered, under such singular circumstances, in the Grecian Archipelago.

"What bosom serpent has the sharpest sting?" repeated this man; but he put the question as if by a reluctant necessity, and grew pale while he was uttering it.

"Why need you ask?" replied Roderick, with a look of dark intelligence. "Look into your own breast. Hark! my serpent bestirs himself! He acknowledges the presence of a master fiend!"

And then, as the bystanders afterwards affirmed, a hissing sound was heard, apparently in Roderick Elliston's breast. It was said, too, that an answering hiss came from the vitals of the shipmaster, as if a snake were actually lurking there and had been aroused by the call of its brother reptile. If there were in fact any such sound, it might have been caused by a malicious exercise of ventriloquism on the part of Roderick.

Thus, making his own actual serpent—if a serpent there actually was in his bosom—the type of each man's fatal error, or hoarded sin, or unquiet conscience, and striking his sting so unremorsefully into the sorest spot, we may well imagine that Roderick became the pest of the city. Nobody could elude him—none could withstand him. He grappled with the ugliest truth that he could lay his hand on, and compelled his adversary to do the same. Strange spectacle in human life where it is the instinctive effort of one and all to hide those sad realities, and leave them undisturbed beneath a heap of superficial topics, which constitute the materials of intercourse between man and man! It was not to be tolerated that Roderick Elliston should break through the tacit compact by which the world has done its best to secure repose without relinquishing evil. The victims of his malicious remarks, it is true, had brothers enough to keep them in countenance; for, by Roderick's theory, every mortal bosom harbored either a brood of small serpents or one overgrown monster that had devoured all the rest. Still the city could not bear this new apostle. It was demanded by nearly all, and particularly by the most respectable inhabitants, that Roderick should no longer be permitted to violate the received rules of decorum by obtruding his own bosom serpent to the public gaze, and dragging those of decent people from their lurking places.

Accordingly, his relatives interfered and placed him in a private asylum for the insane. When the news was noised abroad, it was observed that many persons walked the streets with freer countenances and covered their breasts less carefully with their hands.

His confinement, however, although it contributed not a little to the peace of the town, operated unfavorably upon Roderick himself. In solitude his melancholy grew more black and sullen. He spent whole days—indeed, it was his sole occupation—in communing with the serpent. A conversation was sustained, in which, as it seemed, the hidden monster bore a part, though unintelligibly to the listeners, and inaudible except in a hiss. Singular as it may appear, the sufferer had now contracted a sort of affection for his tormentor, mingled, however, with the intensest loathing and horror. Nor were such discordant emotions incompatible. Each, on the contrary, imparted strength and poignancy to its opposite. Horrible love—horrible antipathy—embracing one another in his bosom, and both concentrating themselves upon a being that had crept into his vitals or been engendered there, and which was nourished with his food, and lived upon his life, and was as intimate with him as his own heart, and yet was the foulest of all created things! But not the less was it the true type of a morbid nature.

Sometimes, in his moments of rage and bitter hatred against the snake and himself, Roderick determined to be the death of him, even at the expense of his own life. Once he attempted it by starvation; but, while the wretched man was on the point of famishing, the monster seemed to feed upon his heart, and to thrive and wax gamesome, as if it were his sweetest and most congenial diet. Then he privily took a dose of active poison, imagining that it would not fail to kill either himself or the devil that possessed him, or both together. Another mistake; for if Roderick had not yet been destroyed by his own poisoned heart, nor the snake by gnawing it, they had little to fear from arsenic or corrosive sublimate.[5] Indeed, the venomous pest appeared to operate as an antidote against all other poisons. The physicians tried to suffocate the fiend with tobacco smoke. He breathed it as freely as if it were his native atmosphere. Again, they drugged their patient with opium and drenched him with intoxicating liquors, hoping that the snake might thus be reduced to stupor and perhaps be ejected from the stomach. They succeeded in rendering Roderick insensible; but, placing their hands upon his breast, they were inexpressibly horror stricken to feel the monster wriggling, twining, and darting to and fro within his narrow limits, evidently enlivened by the opium or alcohol, and incited to unusual feats of activity. Thenceforth they gave up all attempts at cure or palliation. The doomed sufferer submitted to his fate, resumed his former loathsome affection for the bosom fiend, and spent whole miserable days before a looking glass, with his mouth wide open, watching, in hope and horror, to catch a glimpse of the snake's head far down within his throat. It is supposed that he succeeded; for the attendants once heard a frenzied shout, and, rushing into the room, found Roderick lifeless upon the floor.

He was kept but little longer under restraint. After minute investigation, the medical directors of the asylum decided that his mental disease did not amount to insanity nor would warrant his confinement, especially as its influence upon his spirits was unfavorable, and might produce the evil which it was meant to remedy. His eccentricities were doubtless great; he had habitually violated many of the customs and prejudices of society; but the world was not, without surer ground, entitled to treat him as a madman. On this decision of such competent authority Roderick was released, and had returned to his native city the very day before his encounter with George Herkimer.

As soon as possible after learning these particulars the sculptor, together with a sad and tremulous companion, sought Elliston at his own house. It was a large, sombre edifice of wood, with pilasters[6] and a balcony, and was divided from one of the principal streets by a terrace of three elevations, which was ascended by successive flights of stone steps. Some immense old elms almost concealed the front of the mansion. This spacious and once magnificent family residence was built by a grandee of the race early in the past century, at which epoch, land being of small comparative value, the garden and other grounds had formed quite an extensive domain. Although a portion of the ancestral heritage had been alienated, there was still a shadowy enclosure in the rear of the mansion where a student, or a dreamer, or a man of stricken heart might lie all day upon the grass, amid the solitude of murmuring boughs, and forget that a city had grown up around him.

Into this retirement the sculptor and his companion were ushered by Scipio, the old black servant, whose wrinkled visage grew almost sunny with intelligence and joy as he paid his humble greetings to one of the two visitors.

"Remain in the arbor," whispered the sculptor to the figure that leaned upon his arm. "You will know whether, and when, to make your appearance."

"God will teach me," was the reply. "May he support me too!"

Roderick was reclining on the margin of a fountain, which gushed into the fleckered sunshine with the same clear sparkle and the same voice of airy quietude as when trees of primeval growth flung their shadows across its bosom. How strange is the life of a fountain!—born at every moment, yet of an age coeval with the rocks, and far surpassing the venerable antiquity of a forest.

"You are come! I have expected you," said Elliston, when he became aware of the sculptor's presence.

His manner was very different from that of the preceding day—quiet, courteous, and, as Herkimer thought, watchful both over his guest and himself. This unnatural restraint was almost the only trait that betokened any thing amiss. He had just thrown a book upon the grass, where it lay half opened, thus disclosing itself to be a natural history of the serpent tribe, illustrated by lifelike plates. Near it lay that bulky volume, the Ductor Dubitantium of Jeremy Taylor,[7] full of cases of conscience, and in which most men, possessed of a conscience, may find something applicable to their purpose.

"You see," observed Elliston, pointing to the book of serpents, while a smile gleamed upon his lips, "I am making an effort to become better acquainted with my bosom friend; but I find nothing satisfactory in this volume. If I mistake not, he will prove to be *sui generis*,[8] and akin to no other reptile in creation."

"Whence came this strange calamity?" inquired the sculptor.

"My sable friend Scipio has a story," replied Roderick, "of a snake that had lurked in this fountain—pure and innocent as it looks—ever since it was known to the first settlers. This insinuating personage once crept into the vitals of my great grandfather and dwelt there many years, tormenting the old gentleman beyond mortal endurance. In short, it is a family peculiarity. But, to tell you the truth, I have no faith in this idea of the snake's being an heirloom. He is my own snake, and no man's else."

"But what was his origin?" demanded Herkimer.

"O, there is poisonous stuff in any man's heart sufficient to generate a brood of serpents," said Elliston, with a hollow laugh. "You should have heard my homilies to the good town's people. Positively, I deem myself fortunate in having bred but a single serpent. You, however, have none in your bosom, and therefore cannot sympathize with the rest of the world. It gnaws me! It gnaws me!"

With this exclamation, Roderick lost his self-control and threw himself upon the grass, testifying his agony by intricate writhings, in which Herkimer could not but fancy a resemblance to the motions of a snake. Then, likewise, was heard that frightful hiss, which often ran through the sufferer's speech, and crept between the words and syllables without interrupting their succession.

"This is awful indeed!" exclaimed the sculptor—"an awful infliction, whether it be actual or imaginary. Tell me, Roderick Elliston, is there any remedy for this loathsome evil?"

"Yes, but an impossible one," muttered Roderick, as he lay wallowing with his face in the grass. "Could I for one instant forget myself, the serpent might not abide within me. It is my diseased self-contemplation that has engendered and nourished him."

"Then forget yourself, my husband," said a gentle voice above him; "forget yourself in the idea of another!"

Rosina had emerged from the arbor, and was bending over him with the shadow of his anguish reflected in her countenance, yet so mingled with hope and unselfish love that all anguish seemed but an earthly shadow and a dream. She touched Roderick with her hand. A tremor shivered through his frame. At that moment, if report be trustworthy, the sculptor beheld a waving motion through the grass, and heard a tinkling sound, as if something had plunged into the fountain. Be the truth as it might, it is certain that Roderick Elliston sat up like a man renewed, restored to his right mind, and rescued from the fiend which had so miserably overcome him in the battle field of his own breast.

"Rosina!" cried he, in broken and passionate tones, but with nothing of the wild wail that had haunted his voice so long, "forgive! forgive!"

Her happy tears bedewed his face.

"The punishment has been severe," observed the sculptor. "Even Justice might now forgive; how much more a woman's tenderness! Roderick Elliston, whether the serpent was a physical reptile, or whether the morbidness of your nature suggested that symbol to your fancy, the moral of the story is not the less true and strong. A tremendous Egotism, manifesting itself in your case in the form of jealousy, is as fearful a fiend as ever stole into the human heart. Can a breast, where it has dwelt so long, be purified?"

"O yes," said Rosina, with a heavenly smile. "The serpent was but a dark fantasy, and what it typified was as shadowy as itself. The past, dismal as it seems, shall fling no gloom upon the future. To give it its due importance we must think of it but as an anecdote in our Eternity."

THE CHRISTMAS BANQUET

From the unpublished "Allegories of the Heart"

"I have here attempted," said Roderick, unfolding a few sheets of manuscript, as he sat with Rosina and the sculptor in the summer house,—"I have attempted to seize hold of a personage who glides past me, occasionally, in my walk through life. My former sad experience, as you know, has gifted me with some degree of insight into the gloomy mysteries of the human heart, through which I have wandered like one astray in a dark cavern, with his torch fast flickering to extinction. But this man, this class of men, is a hopeless puzzle."

"Well, but propound him," said the sculptor. "Let us have an idea of him, to begin with."

"Why, indeed," replied Roderick, "he is such a being as I could conceive you to carve out of marble, and some yet unrealized perfection of human science to endow with an exquisite mockery of intellect; but still there lacks the last inestimable touch of a divine Creator. He looks like a man; and, perchance, like a better specimen of man than you ordinarily meet. You might esteem him wise; he is capable of cultivation and refinement, and has at least an external conscience; but the demands that spirit makes upon spirit are precisely those to which he cannot respond. When at last you come close to him you find him chill and unsubstantial—a mere vapor."

"I believe," said Rosina, "I have a glimmering idea of what you mean."

"Then be thankful," answered her husband, smiling; "but do not anticipate any further illumination from what I am about to read. I have here imagined such a man to be—what, probably, he never is—conscious of the deficiency in his spiritual organization. Methinks the result would be a sense of cold unreality wherewith he would go shivering through the world, longing to exchange his load of ice for any burden of real grief that fate could fling upon a human being."

Contenting himself with this preface, Roderick began to read.

* * *

In a certain old gentleman's last will and testament there appeared a bequest, which, as his final thought and deed, was singularly in keeping with a long life of melancholy eccentricity. He devised a considerable sum for establishing a fund, the interest of which was to be expended, annually forever, in preparing a Christmas Banquet for ten of the most miserable persons that could be found. It seemed not to be the testator's purpose to make these half a score of sad hearts merry, but to provide that the stern or fierce expression of human discontent should not be drowned, even for that one holy and joyful day, amid the acclamations of festal gratitude which all Christendom sends up. And he desired, likewise, to perpetuate his own remonstrance against the earthly course of Providence, and his sad and sour dissent from those systems of religion or philosophy which either find sunshine in the world or draw it down from heaven.

The task of inviting the guests, or of selecting among such as might advance their claims to partake of this dismal hospitality, was confided to the two trustees or stewards of the fund. These gentlemen, like their deceased friend, were sombre humorists, who made it their principal occupation to number the sable threads in the web of human life, and drop all the golden ones out of the reckoning. They performed their present office with integrity and judgment. The aspect of the assembled company, on the day of the first festival, might not, it is true, have satisfied every beholder that these were especially the individuals, chosen forth from all the world, whose griefs were worthy to stand as indicators of the mass of human suffering. Yet, after due consideration, it could not be disputed that here was a variety of hopeless discomfort, which, if it sometimes arose from causes apparently inadequate, was thereby only the shrewder imputation against the nature and mechanism of life.

The arrangements and decorations of the banquet were probably intended to signify that death in life which had been the testator's definition of existence. The hall, illuminated by torches, was hung round with curtains of deep and dusky purple, and adorned with branches of cypress and wreaths of artificial flowers, imitative of such as used to be strown over the dead. A sprig of parsley was laid by every plate. The main reservoir of wine was a sepulchral urn of silver, whence the liquor was distributed around the table in small vases, accurately copied from those that held the tears of ancient mourners. Neither had the stewards—if it were their taste that arranged these details—forgotten the fantasy of the old Egyptians, who seated a skeleton at every festive board,[1] and mocked their own merriment with the imperturbable grin of a death's head. Such a fearful guest, shrouded in a black mantle, sat now at the head of the table. It was whispered, I know not with what truth, that the testator himself had once walked the visible world with the machinery of that same skeleton, and that it was one of the stipulations of his will, that he should thus be permitted to sit, from year to year, at the banquet which he had instituted. If so, it was perhaps covertly implied that he had cherished no hopes of bliss beyond the grave to compensate for the evils which he felt or imagined here. And if, in their bewildered conjectures as to the purpose of earthly existence, the banqueters should throw aside the veil, and cast an inquiring glance at this figure of death, as seeking thence the solution otherwise unattainable, the only reply would be a stare of the vacant eye caverns and a grin of the skeleton jaws. Such was the response that the dead man had fancied himself to receive when he asked of Death to solve the riddle of his life; and it was his desire to repeat it when the guests of his dismal hospitality should find themselves perplexed with the same question.

"What means that wreath?" asked several of the company, while viewing the decorations of the table.

They alluded to a wreath of cypress, which was held on high by a skeleton arm, protruding from within the black mantle.

"It is a crown," said one of the stewards, "not for the worthiest, but for the wofulest, when he shall prove his claim to it."

The guest earliest bidden to the festival was a man of soft and gentle character, who had not energy to struggle against the heavy despondency to which his temperament rendered him liable; and therefore with nothing outwardly to excuse him from happiness, he had spent a life of quiet misery that made his blood torpid, and weighed upon his breath, and sat like a ponderous night fiend upon every throb of his unresisting heart. His wretchedness seemed as deep as his original nature, if not identical with it. It was the misfortune of a second guest to cherish within his bosom a diseased heart, which had become so wretchedly sore that the continual and unavoidable rubs of the world, the blow of an enemy, the careless jostle of a stranger, and even the faithful and loving touch of a friend, alike made ulcers in it. As is the habit of people thus afflicted, he found his chief employment in exhibiting these miserable sores to any who would give themselves the pain of viewing them. A third guest was a hypochondriac, whose imagination wrought necromancy[2] in his outward and inward world, and caused him to see monstrous faces in the household fire, and dragons in the clouds of sunset, and fiends in the guise of beautiful women, and something ugly or wicked beneath all the pleasant surfaces of nature. His neighbor at table was one who, in his early youth, had trusted mankind too much, and hoped too highly in their behalf, and, in meeting with many disappointments, had become desperately soured. For several years back this misanthrope had employed himself in accumulating motives for hating and despising his race—such as murder, lust, treachery, ingratitude, faithlessness of trusted friends, instinctive vices of children, impurity of women, hidden guilt in men of saintlike aspect—and, in short, all manner of black realities that sought to decorate themselves with outward grace or glory. But at every atrocious fact that was added to his catalogue, at every increase of the sad knowledge which he spent his life to collect, the native impulses of the poor man's loving and confiding heart made him groan with anguish. Next, with his heavy brow bent downward, there stole into the hall a man naturally earnest and impassioned, who, from his immemorial infancy, had felt the consciousness of a high message to the world; but, essaying to deliver it, had found either no voice or form of speech, or else no ears to listen. Therefore his whole life was a bitter questioning of himself—"Why have not men acknowledged my mission? Am I not a self-deluding fool? What business have I on earth? Where is my grave?" Throughout the festival, he quaffed frequent draughts from the sepulchral urn of wine, hoping thus to quench the celestial fire that tortured his own breast and could not benefit his race.

Then there entered, having flung away a ticket for a ball, a gay gallant of yesterday, who had found four or five wrinkles in his brow, and more gray hairs than he could well number on his head. Endowed with sense and feeling, he had nevertheless spent his youth in folly, but had reached at last that dreary point in life where Folly quits us of her own accord, leaving us to make friends with Wisdom if we can. Thus, cold and desolate, he had come to seek Wisdom at the banquet, and wondered if the skeleton were she. To eke out the company, the stewards had invited a distressed poet from his home in the almshouse, and a melancholy idiot from the street corner. The latter had just the glimmering of sense that was sufficient to make him conscious of a vacancy, which the poor fellow, all his life long, had mistily sought to fill up with intelligence, wandering up and down the streets, and groaning miserably because his attempts were ineffectual. The only lady in the hall was one who had fallen short of absolute and perfect beauty, merely by the trifling defect of a slight cast in her left eye. But this blemish, minute as it was, so shocked the pure ideal of her soul, rather than her vanity, that she passed her life in solitude, and veiled her countenance even from her own gaze. So the skeleton sat shrouded at one end of the table and this poor lady at the other.

One other guest remains to be described. He was a young man of smooth brow, fair cheek, and fashionable mien. So far as his exterior developed him, he might much more suitably have found a place at some merry Christmas table, than have been numbered among the blighted, fate-stricken, fancy-tortured set of ill-starred banqueters. Murmurs arose among the guests as they noted the glance of general scrutiny which the intruder threw over his companions. What had he to do among them? Why did not the skeleton of the dead founder of the feast unbend its rattling joints, arise, and motion the unwelcome stranger from the board?

"Shameful!" said the morbid man, while a new ulcer broke out in his heart. "He comes to mock us!—we shall be the jest of his tavern friends!—he will make a farce of our miseries, and bring it out upon the stage!"

"O, never mind him!" said the hypochondriac, smiling sourly. "He shall feast from yonder tureen of viper soup; and if there is a fricassee of scorpions on the table, pray let him have his share of it. For the dessert, he shall taste the apples of Sodom.[3] Then, if he like our Christmas fare, let him return again next year!"

"Trouble him not," murmured the melancholy man, with gentleness. "What matters it whether the consciousness of misery come a few years sooner or later? If this youth deem himself happy now, yet let him sit with us for the sake of the wretchedness to come."

The poor idiot approached the young man with that mournful aspect of vacant inquiry which his face continually wore, and which caused people to say that he was always in search of his missing wits. After no little examination he touched the stranger's hand, but immediately drew back his own, shaking his head and shivering.

"Cold, cold, cold!" muttered the idiot.

The young man shivered too, and smiled.

"Gentlemen—and you, madam,"—said one of the stewards of the festival, "do not conceive so ill either of our caution or judgment, as to imagine that we have admitted this young stranger—Gervayse Hastings by name—without a full investigation and thoughtful balance of his claims. Trust me, not a guest at the table is better entitled to his seat."

The steward's guaranty was perforce satisfactory. The company, therefore, took their places, and addressed themselves to the serious business of the feast, but were soon disturbed by the hypochondriac, who thrust back his chair, complaining that a dish of stewed toads and vipers was set before him, and that there was green ditch water in his cup of wine. This mistake being amended, he quietly resumed his seat. The wine, as it flowed freely from the sepulchral urn, seemed to come imbued with all gloomy inspirations; so that its influence was not to cheer, but either to sink the revellers into a deeper melancholy, or elevate their spirits to an enthusiasm of wretchedness. The conversation was various. They told sad stories about people who might have been worthy guests at such a festival as the present. They talked of grisly incidents in human history; of strange crimes, which, if truly considered, were but convulsions of agony; of some lives that had been altogether wretched, and of others, which, wearing a general semblance of happiness, had yet been deformed, sooner or later, by misfortune, as by the intrusion of a grim face at a banquet; of death-bed scenes, and what dark intimations might be gathered from the words of dying men; of suicide, and whether the more eligible mode were by halter, knife, poison, drowning, gradual starvation, or the fumes of charcoal. The majority of the guests, as is the custom with people thoroughly and profoundly sick at heart, were anxious to make their own woes the theme of discussion, and prove themselves most excellent in anguish. The misanthropist went deep into the philosophy of evil, and wandered about in the darkness, with now and then a gleam of discolored light hovering on ghastly shapes and horrid scenery. Many a miserable thought, such as men have stumbled upon from age to age, did he now rake up again, and gloat over it as an inestimable gem, a diamond, a treasure far preferable to those bright, spiritual revelations of a better world, which are like precious stones from heaven's pavement. And then, amid his lore of wretchedness he hid his face and wept.

It was a festival at which the woful man of Uz[4] might suitably have been a guest, together with all, in each succeeding age, who have tasted deepest of the bitterness of life. And be it said, too, that every son or daughter of woman, however favored with happy fortune, might, at one sad moment or another, have claimed the privilege of a stricken heart, to sit down at this table. But, throughout the feast, it was remarked that the young stranger, Gervayse Hastings, was unsuccessful in his attempts to catch its pervading spirit. At any deep, strong thought that found utterance, and which was torn out, as it were, from the saddest recesses of human consciousness, he looked mystified and bewildered; even more than the poor idiot, who seemed to grasp at such things with his earnest heart, and thus occasionally to comprehend them. The young man's conversation was of a colder and lighter kind, often brilliant, but lacking the powerful characteristics of a nature that had been developed by suffering.

"Sir," said the misanthropist, bluntly, in reply to some observation by Gervayse Hastings, "pray do not address me again. We have no right to talk together. Our minds have nothing in common. By what claim you appear at this banquet I cannot guess; but methinks, to a man who could say what you have just now said, my companions and myself must seem no more than shadows flickering on the wall. And precisely such a shadow are you to us."

The young man smiled and bowed, but drawing himself back in his chair, he buttoned his coat over his breast, as if the banqueting hall were growing chill. Again the idiot fixed his melancholy stare upon the youth, and murmured, "Cold! cold! cold!"

The banquet drew to its conclusion, and the guests departed.

Scarcely had they stepped across the threshold of the hall, when the scene that had there passed seemed like the vision of a sick fancy, or an exhalation from a stagnant heart. Now and then, however, during the year that ensued, these melancholy people caught glimpses of one another, transient, indeed, but enough to prove that they walked the earth with the ordinary allotment of reality. Sometimes a pair of them came face to face, while stealing through the evening twilight, enveloped in their sable cloaks. Sometimes they casually met in churchyards. Once, also, it happened that two of the dismal banqueters mutually started at recognizing each other in the noonday sunshine of a crowded street, stalking there like ghosts astray. Doubtless they wondered why the skeleton did not come abroad at noonday too.

But whenever the necessity of their affairs compelled these Christmas guests into the bustling world, they were sure to encounter the young man who had so unaccountably been admitted to the festival. They saw him among the gay and fortunate; they caught the sunny sparkle of his eye; they heard the light and careless tones of his voice, and muttered to themselves with such indignation as only the aristocracy of wretchedness could kindle—"The traitor! The vile impostor! Providence, in its own good time, may give him a right to feast among us!" But the young man's unabashed eye dwelt upon their gloomy figures as they passed him, seeming to say, perchance with somewhat of a sneer, "First, know my secret!—then, measure your claims with mine!"

The step of Time stole onward, and soon brought merry Christmas round again, with glad and solemn worship in the churches, and sports, games, festivals, and every where the bright face of Joy beside the household fire. Again likewise the hall, with its curtains of dusky purple, was illuminated by the death torches gleaming on the sepulchral decorations of the banquet. The veiled skeleton sat in state, lifting the cypress wreath above its head, as the guerdon of some guest illustrious in the qualifications which there claimed precedence. As the stewards deemed the world inexhaustible in misery, and were desirous of recognizing it in all its forms, they had not seen fit to reassemble the company of the former year. New faces now threw their gloom across the table.

There was a man of nice conscience, who bore a blood stain in his heart—the death of a fellow-creature—which, for his more exquisite torture, had chanced with such a peculiarity of circumstances, that he could not absolutely determine whether his will had entered into the deed or not. Therefore, his whole life was spent in the agony of an inward trial for murder, with a continual sifting of the details of his terrible calamity, until his mind had no longer any thought, nor his soul any emotion, disconnected with it. There was a mother, too—a mother once, but a desolation now—who, many years before, had gone out on a pleasure party, and, returning, found her infant smothered in its little bed. And ever since she has been tortured with the fantasy that her buried baby lay smothering in its coffin. Then there was an aged lady, who had lived from time immemorial with a constant tremor quivering through her frame. It was terrible to discern her dark shadow tremulous upon the wall; her lips, likewise, were tremulous; and the expression of her eye seemed to indicate that her soul was trembling too. Owing to the bewilderment and confusion which made almost a chaos of her intellect, it was impossible to discover what dire misfortune had thus shaken her nature to its depths; so that the stewards had admitted her to the table, not from any acquaintance with her history, but on the safe testimony of her miserable aspect. Some surprise was expressed at the presence of a bluff, red-faced gentleman, a certain Mr. Smith, who had evidently the fat of many a rich feast within him, and the habitual twinkle of whose eye betrayed a disposition to break forth into uproarious laughter for little cause or none. It turned out, however, that with the best possible flow of spirits, our poor friend was afflicted with a physical disease of the heart, which threatened instant death on the slightest cachinnatory[5] indulgence, or even that titillation of the bodily frame produced by merry thoughts. In this dilemma he had sought admittance to the banquet, on the ostensible plea of his irksome and miserable state, but, in reality, with the hope of imbibing a life-preserving melancholy.

A married couple had been invited from a motive of bitter humor, it being well understood that they rendered each other unutterably miserable whenever they chanced to meet, and therefore must necessarily be fit associates at the festival. In contrast with these was another couple still unmarried, who had interchanged their hearts in early life, but had been divided by circumstances as impalpable as morning mist, and kept apart so long that their spirits now found it impossible to meet. Therefore, yearning for communion, yet shrinking from one another and choosing none beside, they felt themselves companionless in life, and looked upon eternity as a boundless desert. Next to the skeleton sat a mere son of earth—a hunter of the Exchange[6]—a gatherer of shining dust—a man whose life's record was in his leger, and whose soul's prison house the vaults of the bank where he kept his deposits. This person had been greatly perplexed at his invitation, deeming himself one of the most fortunate men in the city; but the stewards persisted in demanding his presence, assuring him that he had no conception how miserable he was.

And now appeared a figure which we must acknowledge as our acquaintance of the former festival. It was Gervayse Hastings, whose presence had then caused so much question and criticism, and who now took his place with the composure of one whose claims were satisfactory to himself and must needs be allowed by others. Yet his easy and unruffled face betrayed no sorrow. The well-skilled beholders gazed a moment into his eyes and shook their heads, to miss the unuttered sympathy—the countersign, never to be falsified—of those whose hearts are cavern mouths, through which they descend into a region of illimitable woe and recognize other wanderers there.

"Who is this youth?" asked the man with a blood stain on his conscience. "Surely he has never gone down into the depths! I know all the aspects of those who have passed through the dark valley. By what right is he among us?"

"Ah, it is a sinful thing to come hither without a sorrow," murmured the aged lady, in accents that partook of the eternal tremor which pervaded her whole being. "Depart, young man! Your soul has never been shaken, and, therefore, I tremble so much the more to look at you."

"His soul shaken! No; I'll answer for it," said bluff Mr. Smith, pressing his hand upon his heart and making himself as melancholy as he could, for fear of a fatal explosion of laughter. "I know the lad well; he has as fair prospects as any young man about town, and has no more right among us miserable creatures than the child unborn. He never was miserable and probably never will be!"

"Our honored guests," interposed the stewards, "pray have patience with us, and believe, at least, that our deep veneration for the sacredness of this solemnity would preclude any wilful violation of it. Receive this young man to your table. It may not be too much to say, that no guest here would exchange his own heart for the one that beats within that youthful bosom!"

"I'd call it a bargain, and gladly too," muttered Mr. Smith, with a perplexing mixture of sadness and mirthful conceit. "A plague upon their nonsense! My own heart is the only really miserable one in the company; it will certainly be the death of me at last!"

Nevertheless, as on the former occasion, the judgment of the stewards being without appeal, the company sat down. The obnoxious guest made no more attempt to obtrude his conversation on those about him, but appeared to listen to the table talk with peculiar assiduity, as if some inestimable secret, otherwise beyond his reach, might be conveyed in a casual word. And in truth, to those who could understand and value it, there was rich matter in the upgushings and outpourings of these initiated souls to whom sorrow had been a talisman, admitting them into spiritual depths which no other spell can open. Sometimes out of the midst of densest gloom there flashed a momentary radiance, pure as crystal, bright as the flame of stars, and shedding such a glow upon the mysteries of life that the guests were ready to exclaim, "Surely the riddle is on the point of being solved!" At such illuminated intervals the saddest mourners felt it to be revealed that mortal griefs are but shadowy and external; no more than the sable robes voluminously shrouding a certain divine reality, and thus indicating what might otherwise be altogether invisible to mortal eye.

"Just now," remarked the trembling old woman, "I seemed to see beyond the outside. And then my everlasting tremor passed away!"

"Would that I could dwell always in these momentary gleams of light!" said the man of stricken conscience. "Then the blood stain in my heart would be washed clean away."

This strain of conversation appeared so unintelligibly absurd to good Mr. Smith, that he burst into precisely the fit of laughter which his physicians had warned him against, as likely to prove instantaneously fatal. In effect, he fell back in his chair a corpse, with a broad grin upon his face, while his ghost, perchance, remained beside it bewildered at its unpremeditated exit. This catastrophe of course broke up the festival.

"How is this? You do not tremble?" observed the tremulous old woman to Gervayse Hastings, who was gazing at the dead man with singular intentness. "Is it not awful to see him so suddenly vanish out of the midst of life—this man of flesh and blood, whose earthly nature was so warm and strong? There is a never-ending tremor in my soul, but it trembles afresh at this! And you are calm!"

"Would that he could teach me somewhat!" said Gervayse Hastings, drawing a long breath. "Men pass before me like shadows on the wall; their actions, passions, feelings are flickerings of the light, and then they vanish! Neither the corpse, nor yonder skeleton, nor this old woman's everlasting tremor, can give me what I seek."

And then the company departed.

We cannot linger to narrate, in such detail, more circumstances of these singular festivals, which, in accordance with the founder's will, continued to be kept with the regularity of an established institution. In process of time the stewards adopted the custom of inviting, from far and near, those individuals whose misfortunes were prominent above other men's, and whose mental and moral development might, therefore, be supposed to possess a corresponding interest. The exiled noble of the French Revolution, and the broken soldier of the Empire, were alike represented at the table. Fallen monarchs, wandering about the earth, have found places at that forlorn and miserable feast. The statesman, when his party flung him off, might, if he chose it, be once more a great man for the space of a single banquet. Aaron Burr's name[7] appears on the record at a period when his ruin—the profoundest and most striking, with more of moral circumstance in it than that of almost any other man—was complete in his lonely age. Stephen Girard,[8] when his wealth weighed upon him like a mountain, once sought admittance of his own accord. It is not probable, however, that these men had any lesson to teach in the lore of discontent and misery which might not equally well have been studied in the common walks of life. Illustrious unfortunates attract a wider sympathy, not because their griefs are more intense, but because, being set on lofty pedestals, they the better serve mankind as instances and bywords of calamity.

It concerns our present purpose to say that, at each successive festival, Gervayse Hastings showed his face, gradually changing from the smooth beauty of his youth to the thoughtful comeliness of manhood, and thence to the bald, impressive dignity of age. He was the only individual invariably present. Yet on every occasion there were murmurs, both from those who knew his character and position, and from them whose hearts shrank back as denying his companionship in their mystic fraternity.

"Who is this impassive man?" had been asked a hundred times. "Has he suffered? Has he sinned? There are no traces of either. Then wherefore is he here?"

"You must inquire of the stewards or of himself," was the constant reply. "We seem to know him well here in our city, and know nothing of him but what is creditable and fortunate. Yet hither he comes, year after year, to this gloomy banquet, and sits among the guests like a marble statue. Ask yonder skeleton, perhaps that may solve the riddle!"

It was in truth a wonder. The life of Gervayse Hastings was not merely a prosperous, but a brilliant one. Every thing had gone well with him. He was wealthy, far beyond the expenditure that was required by habits of magnificence, a taste of rare purity and cultivation, a love of travel, a scholar's instinct to collect a splendid library, and, moreover, what seemed a magnificent liberality to the distressed. He had sought happiness, and not vainly, if a lovely and tender wife, and children of fair promise, could insure it. He had, besides, ascended above the limit which separates the obscure from the distinguished, and had won a stainless reputation in affairs of the widest public importance. Not that he was a popular character, or had within him the mysterious attributes which are essential to that species of success. To the public he was a cold abstraction, wholly destitute of those rich hues of personality, that living warmth, and the peculiar faculty of stamping his own heart's impression on a multitude of hearts by which the people recognize their favorites. And it must be owned that, after his most intimate associates had done their best to know him thoroughly, and love him warmly, they were startled to find how little hold he had upon their affections. They approved, they admired, but still in those moments when the human spirit most craves reality, they shrank back from Gervayse Hastings, as powerless to give them what they sought. It was the feeling of distrustful regret with which we should draw back the hand after extending it, in an illusive twilight, to grasp the hand of a shadow upon the wall.

As the superficial fervency of youth decayed, this peculiar effect of Gervayse Hastings's character grew more perceptible. His children, when he extended his arms, came coldly to his knees, but never climbed them of their own accord. His wife wept secretly, and almost adjudged herself a criminal because she shivered in the chill of his bosom. He, too, occasionally appeared not unconscious of the chillness of his moral atmosphere, and willing, if it might be so, to warm himself at a kindly fire. But age stole onward and benumbed him more and more. As the hoarfrost began to gather on him his wife went to her grave, and was doubtless warmer there; his children either died or were scattered to different homes of their own; and old Gervayse Hastings, unscathed by grief—alone, but needing no companionship, continued his steady walk through life, and still on every Christmas day attended at the dismal banquet. His privilege as a guest had become prescriptive now. Had he claimed the head of the table, even the skeleton would have been ejected from its seat.

Finally, at the merry Christmas tide, when he had numbered fourscore years complete, this pale, high-browed, marble-featured old man once more entered the long-frequented hall, with the same impassive aspect that had called forth so much dissatisfied remark at his first attendance. Time, except in matters merely external, had done nothing for him, either of good or evil. As he took his place he threw a calm, inquiring glance around the table, as if to ascertain whether any guest had yet appeared, after so many unsuccessful banquets, who might impart to him the mystery—the deep, warm secret—the life within the life—which, whether manifested in joy or sorrow, is what gives substance to a world of shadows.

"My friends," said Gervayse Hastings, assuming a position which his long conversance with the festival caused to appear natural, "you are welcome! I drink to you all in this cup of sepulchral wine."

The guests replied courteously, but still in a manner that proved them unable to receive the old man as a member of their sad fraternity. It may be well to give the reader an idea of the present company at the banquet.

One was formerly a clergyman, enthusiastic in his profession, and apparently of the genuine dynasty of those old puritan divines whose faith in their calling, and stern exercise of it, had placed them among the mighty of the earth. But yielding to the speculative tendency of the age, he had gone astray from the firm foundation of an ancient faith, and wandered into a cloud region, where every thing was misty and deceptive, ever mocking him with a semblance of reality, but still dissolving when he flung himself upon it for support and rest. His instinct and early training demanded something steadfast; but, looking forward, he beheld vapors piled on vapors, and behind him an impassable gulf between the man of yesterday and to-day, on the borders of which he paced to and fro, sometimes wringing his hands in agony, and often making his own woe a theme of scornful merriment. This surely was a miserable man. Next, there was a theorist—one of a numerous tribe, although he deemed himself unique since the creation—a theorist, who had conceived a plan by which all the wretchedness of earth, moral and physical, might be done away, and the bliss of the millennium at once accomplished. But, the incredulity of mankind debarring him from action, he was smitten with as much grief as if the whole mass of woe which he was denied the opportunity to remedy were crowded into his own bosom. A plain old man in black attracted much of the company's notice, on the supposition that he was no other than Father Miller,[9] who, it seemed, had given himself up to despair at the tedious delay of the final conflagration. Then there was a man distinguished for native pride and obstinacy, who, a little while before, had possessed immense wealth, and held the control of a vast moneyed interest which he had wielded in the same spirit as a despotic monarch would wield the power of his empire, carrying on a tremendous moral warfare, the roar and tremor of which was felt at every fireside in the land. At length came a crushing ruin—a total overthrow of fortune, power, and character—the effect of which on his imperious and, in many respects, noble and lofty nature, might have entitled him to a place, not merely at our festival, but among the peers of Pandemonium.[10]

There was a modern philanthropist, who had become so deeply sensible of the calamities of thousands and millions of his fellow-creatures, and of the impracticableness of any general measures for their relief, that he had no heart to do what little good lay immediately within his power, but contented himself with being miserable for sympathy. Near him sat a gentleman in a predicament hitherto unprecedented, but of which the present epoch probably affords numerous examples. Ever since he was of capacity to read a newspaper this person had prided himself on his consistent adherence to one political party, but, in the confusion of these latter days, had got bewildered and knew not whereabouts his party was. This wretched condition, so morally desolate and disheartening to a man who has long accustomed himself to merge his individuality in the mass of a great body, can only be conceived by such as have experienced it. His next companion was a popular orator who had lost his voice, and—as it was pretty much all that he had to lose—had fallen into a state of hopeless melancholy. The table was likewise graced by two of the gentler sex—one, a half-starved, consumptive seamstress, the representative of thousands just as wretched; the other, a woman of unemployed energy, who found herself in the world with nothing to achieve, nothing to enjoy, and nothing even to suffer. She had, therefore, driven herself to the verge of madness by dark broodings over the wrongs of her sex, and its exclusion from a proper field of action. The roll of guests being thus complete, a side table had been set for three or four disappointed office seekers, with hearts as sick as death, whom the stewards had admitted partly because their calamities really entitled them to entrance here, and partly that they were in especial need of a good dinner. There was likewise a homeless dog, with his tail between his legs, licking up the crumbs and gnawing the fragments of the feast—such a melancholy cur[11] as one sometimes sees about the streets without a master, and willing to follow the first that will accept his service.

In their own way, these were as wretched a set of people as ever had assembled at the festival. There they sat, with the veiled skeleton of the founder holding aloft the cypress wreath, at one end of the table, and at the other, wrapped in furs, the withered figure of Gervayse Hastings, stately, calm, and cold, impressing the company with awe, yet so little interesting their sympathy that he might have vanished into thin air without their once exclaiming, "Whither is he gone?"

"Sir," said the philanthropist, addressing the old man, "you have been so long a guest at this annual festival, and have thus been conversant with so many varieties of human affliction, that, not improbably, you have thence derived some great and important lessons. How blessed were your lot could you reveal a secret by which all this mass of woe might be removed!"

"I know of but one misfortune," answered Gervayse Hastings, quietly, "and that is my own."

"Your own!" rejoined the philanthropist. "And, looking back on your serene and prosperous life, how can you claim to be the sole unfortunate of the human race?"

"You will not understand it," replied Gervayse Hastings, feebly, and with a singular inefficiency of pronunciation, and sometimes putting one word for another. "None have understood it—not even those who experience the like. It is a chillness—a want of earnestness—a feeling as if what should be my heart were a thing of vapor—a haunting perception of unreality! Thus seeming to possess all that other men have—all that men aim at—I have really possessed nothing, neither joy nor griefs. All things, all persons—as was truly said to me at this table long and long ago—have been like shadows flickering on the wall. It was so with my wife and children—with those who seemed my friends: it is so with yourselves, whom I see now before me. Neither have I myself any real existence, but am a shadow like the rest."

"And how is it with your views of a future life?" inquired the speculative clergyman.

"Worse than with you," said the old man, in a hollow and feeble tone; "for I cannot conceive it earnestly enough to feel either hope or fear. Mine—mine is the wretchedness! This cold heart—this unreal life! Ah! it grows colder still."

It so chanced that at this juncture the decayed ligaments of the skeleton gave way, and the dry bones fell together in a heap, thus causing the dusty wreath of cypress to drop upon the table. The attention of the company being thus diverted for a single instant from Gervayse Hastings, they perceived, on turning again towards him, that the old man had undergone a change. His shadow had ceased to flicker on the wall.

*   *   *

"Well, Rosina, what is your criticism?" asked Roderick, as he rolled up the manuscript.

"Frankly, your success is by no means complete," replied she. "It is true, I have an idea of the character you endeavor to describe; but it is rather by dint of my own thought than your expression."

"That is unavoidable," observed the sculptor, "because the characteristics are all negative. If Gervayse Hastings could have imbibed one human grief at the gloomy banquet, the task of describing him would have been infinitely easier. Of such persons—and we do meet with these moral monsters now and then—it is difficult to conceive how they came to exist here, or what there is in them capable of existence hereafter. They seem to be on the outside of every thing; and nothing wearies the soul more than an attempt to comprehend them within its grasp."

Drowne's Wooden Image

One sunshiny morning, in the good old times of the town of Boston, a young carver in wood, well known by the name of Drowne, stood contemplating a large oaken log, which it was his purpose to convert into the figure head of a vessel. And while he discussed within his own mind what sort of shape or similitude it were well to bestow upon this excellent piece of timber, there came into Drowne's workshop a certain Captain Hunnewell, owner and commander of the good brig called the Cynosure,[1] which had just returned from her first voyage to Fayal.[2]

"Ah! that will do, Drowne, that will do!" cried the jolly captain, tapping the log with his ratan. "I bespeak this very piece of oak for the figure head of the Cynosure. She has shown herself the sweetest craft that ever floated, and I mean to decorate her prow with the handsomest image that the skill of man can cut out of timber. And, Drowne, you are the fellow to execute it."

"You give me more credit than I deserve, Captain Hunnewell," said the carver, modestly, yet as one conscious of eminence in his art. "But, for the sake of the good brig, I stand ready to do my best. And which of these designs do you prefer? Here"—pointing to a staring, half-length figure, in a white wig and scarlet coat—"here is an excellent model, the likeness of our gracious king. Here is the valiant Admiral Vernon.[3]

Or, if you prefer a female figure, what say you to Britannia[4] with the trident?"

"All very fine, Drowne; all very fine," answered the mariner. "But as nothing like the brig ever swam the ocean, so I am determined she shall have such a figure head as old Neptune[5] never saw in his life. And what is more, as there is a secret in the matter, you must pledge your credit not to betray it."

"Certainly," said Drowne, marvelling, however, what possible mystery there could be in reference to an affair so open, of necessity, to the inspection of all the world as the figure head of a vessel. "You may depend, captain, on my being as secret as the nature of the case will permit."

Captain Hunnewell then took Drowne by the button, and communicated his wishes in so low a tone that it would be unmannerly to repeat what was evidently intended for the carver's private ear. We shall, therefore, take the opportunity to give the reader a few desirable particulars about Drowne himself.

He was the first American who is known to have attempted—in a very humble line, it is true—that art in which we can now reckon so many names already distinguished, or rising to distinction. From his earliest boyhood he had exhibited a knack—for it would be too proud a word to call it genius—a knack, therefore, for the imitation of the human figure in whatever material came most readily to hand. The snows of a New England winter had often supplied him with a species of marble as dazzlingly white, at least, as the Parian or the Carrara,[6] and if less durable, yet sufficiently so to correspond with any claims to permanent existence possessed by the boy's frozen statues. Yet they won admiration from maturer judges than his schoolfellows, and were, indeed, remarkably clever, though destitute of the native warmth that might have made the snow melt beneath his hand. As he advanced in life, the young man adopted pine and oak as eligible materials for the display of his skill, which now began to bring him a return of solid silver as well as the empty praise that had been an apt reward enough for his productions of evanescent snow. He became noted for carving ornamental pump heads, and wooden urns for gate posts, and decorations, more grotesque than fanciful, for mantelpieces. No apothecary would have deemed himself in the way of obtaining custom without setting up a gilded mortar, if not a head of Galen or Hippocrates,[7] from the skilful hand of Drowne.

But the great scope of his business lay in the manufacture of figure heads for vessels. Whether it were the monarch himself, or some famous British admiral or general, or the governor of the province, or perchance the favorite daughter of the ship owner, there the image stood above the prow, decked out in gorgeous colors, magnificently gilded, and staring the whole world out of countenance, as if from an innate consciousness of its own superiority. These specimens of native sculpture had crossed the sea in all directions, and been not ignobly noticed among the crowded shipping of the Thames,[8] and wherever else the hardy mariners of New England had pushed their adventures. It must be confessed that a family likeness pervaded these respectable progeny of Drowne's skill; that the benign countenance of the king resembled those of his subjects, and that Miss Peggy Hobart, the merchant's daughter, bore a remarkable similitude to Britannia, Victory, and other ladies of the allegoric sisterhood; and, finally, that they all had a kind of wooden aspect, which proved an intimate relationship with the unshaped blocks of timber in the carver's workshop. But at least there was no inconsiderable skill of hand, nor a deficiency of any attribute to render them really works of art, except that deep quality, be it of soul or intellect, which bestows life upon the lifeless and warmth upon the cold, and which, had it been present, would have made Drowne's wooden image instinct with spirit.

The captain of the Cynosure had now finished his instructions.

"And Drowne," said he, impressively, "you must lay aside all other business and set about this forthwith. And as to the price, only do the job in first rate style, and you shall settle that point yourself."

"Very well, captain," answered the carver, who looked grave and somewhat perplexed, yet had a sort of smile upon his visage; "depend upon it, I'll do my utmost to satisfy you."

From that moment the men of taste about Long Wharf and the Town Dock who were wont to show their love for the arts by frequent visits to Drowne's workshop, and admiration of his wooden images, began to be sensible of a mystery in the carver's conduct. Often he was absent in the daytime. Sometimes, as might be judged by gleams of light from the shop windows, he was at work until a late hour of the evening; although neither knock nor voice, on such occasions, could gain admittance for a visitor, or elicit any word of response. Nothing remarkable, however, was observed in the shop at those hours when it was thrown open. A fine piece of timber, indeed, which Drowne was known to have reserved for some work of especial dignity, was seen to be gradually assuming shape. What shape it was destined ultimately to take was a problem to his friends and a point on which the carver himself preserved a rigid silence. But day after day, though Drowne was seldom noticed in the act of working upon it, this rude form began to be developed until it became evident to all observers that a female figure was growing into mimic life. At each new visit they beheld a larger pile of wooden chips and a nearer approximation to something beautiful. It seemed as if the hamadryad[9] of the oak had sheltered herself from the unimaginative world within the heart of her native tree, and that it was only necessary to remove the strange shapelessness that had incrusted her, and reveal the grace and loveliness of a divinity. Imperfect as the design, the attitude, the costume, and especially the face of the image still remained, there was already an effect that drew the eye from the wooden cleverness of Drowne's earlier productions and fixed it upon the tantalizing mystery of this new project.

Copley,[10] the celebrated painter, then a young man and a resident of Boston, came one day to visit Drowne; for he had recognized so much of moderate ability in the carver as to induce him, in the dearth of professional sympathy, to cultivate his acquaintance. On entering the shop the artist glanced at the inflexible image of king, commander, dame, and allegory that stood around, on the best of which might have been bestowed the questionable praise that it looked as if a living man had here been changed to wood, and that not only the physical, but the intellectual and spiritual part, partook of the stolid transformation. But in not a single instance did it seem as if the wood were imbibing the ethereal essence of humanity. What a wide distinction is here! and how far would the slightest portion of the latter merit have outvalued the utmost degree of the former!

"My friend Drowne," said Copley, smiling to himself, but alluding to the mechanical and wooden cleverness that so invariably distinguished the images, "you are really a remarkable person! I have seldom met with a man in your line of business that could do so much; for one other touch might make this figure of General Wolfe,[11] for instance, a breathing and intelligent human creature."

"You would have me think that you are praising me highly, Mr. Copley," answered Drowne, turning his back upon Wolfe's image in apparent disgust. "But there has come a light into my mind. I know, what you know as well, that the one touch which you speak of as deficient is the only one that would be truly valuable, and that without it these works of mine are no better than worthless abortions. There is the same difference between them and the works of an inspired artist as between a sign-post daub and one of your best pictures."

"This is strange," cried Copley, looking him in the face, which now, as the painter fancied, had a singular depth of intelligence, though hitherto it had not given him greatly the advantage over his own family of wooden images. "What has come over you? How is it that, possessing the idea which you have now uttered, you should produce only such works as these?"

The carver smiled, but made no reply. Copley turned again to the images, conceiving that the sense of deficiency which Drowne had just expressed, and which is so rare in a merely mechanical character, must surely imply a genius, the tokens of which had heretofore been overlooked. But no; there was not a trace of it. He was about to withdraw when his eyes chanced to fall upon a half-developed figure which lay in a corner of the workshop, surrounded by scattered chips of oak. It arrested him at once.

"What is here? Who has done this?" he broke out, after contemplating it in speechless astonishment for an instant. "Here is the divine, the life-giving touch. What inspired hand is beckoning this wood to arise and live? Whose work is this?"

"No man's work," replied Drowne. "The figure lies within that block of oak, and it is my business to find it."

"Drowne," said the true artist, grasping the carver fervently by the hand, "you are a man of genius!"

As Copley departed, happening to glance backward from the threshold, he beheld Drowne bending over the half-created shape, and stretching forth his arms as if he would have embraced and drawn it to his heart; while, had such a miracle been possible, his countenance expressed passion enough to communicate warmth and sensibility to the lifeless oak.

"Strange enough!" said the artist to himself. "Who would have looked for a modern Pygmalion[12] in the person of a Yankee mechanic!"[13]

As yet, the image was but vague in its outward presentment; so that, as in the cloud shapes around the western sun, the observer rather felt, or was led to imagine, than really saw what was intended by it. Day by day, however, the work assumed greater precision, and settled its irregular and misty outline into distincter grace and beauty. The general design was now obvious to the common eye. It was a female figure, in what appeared to be a foreign dress; the gown being laced over the bosom, and opening in front so as to disclose a skirt or petticoat, the folds and inequalities of which were admirably represented in the oaken substance. She wore a hat of singular gracefulness, and abundantly laden with flowers, such as never grew in the rude soil of New England, but which, with all their fanciful luxuriance, had a natural truth that it seemed impossible for the most fertile imagination to have attained without copying from real prototypes. There were several little appendages to this dress, such as a fan, a pair of earrings, a chain about the neck, a watch in the bosom, and a ring upon the finger, all of which would have been deemed beneath the dignity of sculpture. They were put on, however, with as much taste as a lovely woman might have shown in her attire, and could therefore have shocked none but a judgment spoiled by artistic rules.

The face was still imperfect; but gradually, by a magic touch, intelligence and sensibility brightened through the features, with all the effect of light gleaming forth from within the solid oak. The face became alive. It was a beautiful, though not precisely regular, and somewhat haughty aspect, but with a certain piquancy about the eyes and mouth, which, of all expressions, would have seemed the most impossible to throw over a wooden countenance. And now, so far as carving went, this wonderful production was complete.

"Drowne," said Copley, who had hardly missed a single day in his visits to the carver's workshop, "if this work were in marble it would make you famous at once; nay, I would almost affirm that it would make an era in the art. It is as ideal as an antique statue, and yet as real as any lovely woman whom one meets at a fireside or in the street. But I trust you do not mean to desecrate this exquisite creature with paint, like those staring kings and admirals yonder?"

"Not paint her!" exclaimed Captain Hunnewell, who stood by; "not paint the figure head of the Cynosure! And what sort of a figure should I cut in a foreign port with such an unpainted oaken stick as this over my prow! She must, and she shall, be painted to the life, from the topmost flower in her hat down to the silver spangles on her slippers."

"Mr. Copley," said Drowne, quietly, "I know nothing of marble statuary, and nothing of the sculptor's rules of art; but of this wooden image, this work of my hands, this creature of my heart,"—and here his voice faltered and choked in a very singular manner,—"of this—of her—I may say that I know something. A wellspring of inward wisdom gushed within me as I wrought upon the oak with my whole strength, and soul, and faith. Let others do what they may with marble, and adopt what rules they choose. If I can produce my desired effect by painted wood, those rules are not for me, and I have a right to disregard them."

"The very spirit of genius," muttered Copley to himself. "How otherwise should this carver feel himself entitled to transcend all rules, and make me ashamed of quoting them?"

He looked earnestly at Drowne, and again saw that expression of human love which, in a spiritual sense, as the artist could not help imagining, was the secret of the life that had been breathed into this block of wood.

The carver, still in the same secrecy that marked all his operations upon this mysterious image, proceeded to paint the habiliments in their proper colors, and the countenance with Nature's red and white. When all was finished he threw open his workshop, and admitted the townspeople to behold what he had done. Most persons, at their first entrance, felt impelled to remove their hats, and pay such reverence as was due to the richly-dressed and beautiful young lady who seemed to stand in a corner of the room, with oaken chips and shavings scattered at her feet. Then came a sensation of fear; as if, not being actually human, yet so like humanity, she must therefore be something preternatural. There was, in truth, an indefinable air and expression that might reasonably induce the query, Who and from what sphere this daughter of the oak should be? The strange, rich flowers of Eden on her head; the complexion, so much deeper and more brilliant than those of our native beauties; the foreign, as it seemed, and fantastic garb, yet not too fantastic to be worn decorously in the street; the delicately-wrought embroidery of the skirt; the broad gold chain about her neck; the curious ring upon her finger; the fan, so exquisitely sculptured in open work, and painted to resemble pearl and ebony;—where could Drowne, in his sober walk of life, have beheld the vision here so matchlessly imbodied! And then her face! In the dark eyes and around the voluptuous mouth there played a look made up of pride, coquetry, and a gleam of mirthfulness, which impressed Copley with the idea that the image was secretly enjoying the perplexing admiration of himself and other beholders.

"And will you," said he to the carver, "permit this masterpiece to become the figure head of a vessel? Give the honest captain yonder figure of Britannia—it will answer his purpose far better—and send this fairy queen to England, where, for aught I know, it may bring you a thousand pounds."

"I have not wrought it for money," said Drowne.

"What sort of a fellow is this!" thought Copley. "A Yankee, and throw away the chance of making his fortune! He has gone mad; and thence has come this gleam of genius."

There was still further proof of Drowne's lunacy, if credit were due to the rumor that he had been seen kneeling at the feet of the oaken lady, and gazing with a lover's passionate ardor into the face that his own hands had created. The bigots of the day hinted that it would be no matter of surprise if an evil spirit were allowed to enter this beautiful form, and seduce the carver to destruction.

The fame of the image spread far and wide. The inhabitants visited it so universally, that after a few days of exhibition there was hardly an old man or a child who had not become minutely familiar with its aspect. Even had the story of Drowne's wooden image ended here, its celebrity might have been prolonged for many years by the reminiscences of those who looked upon it in their childhood, and saw nothing else so beautiful in after life. But the town was now astounded by an event the narrative of which has formed itself into one of the most singular legends that are yet to be met with in the traditionary chimney corners of the New England metropolis, where old men and women sit dreaming of the past, and wag their heads at the dreamers of the present and the future.

One fine morning, just before the departure of the Cynosure on her second voyage to Fayal, the commander of that gallant vessel was seen to issue from his residence in Hanover Street. He was stylishly dressed in a blue broadcloth coat, with gold lace at the seams and button holes, an embroidered scarlet waistcoat, a triangular hat, with a loop and broad binding of gold, and wore a silver-hilted hanger[14] at his side. But the good captain might have been arrayed in the robes of a prince or the rags of a beggar, without in either case attracting notice, while obscured by such a companion as now leaned on his arm. The people in the street started, rubbed their eyes, and either leaped aside from their path, or stood as if transfixed to wood or marble in astonishment.

"Do you see it?—do you see it?" cried one, with tremulous eagerness. "It is the very same!"

"The same?" answered another, who had arrived in town only the night before. "Who do you mean? I see only a sea captain in his shore-going clothes, and a young lady in a foreign habit, with a bunch of beautiful flowers in her hat. On my word, she is as fair and bright a damsel as my eyes have looked on this many a day!"

"Yes; the same!—the very same!" repeated the other. "Drowne's wooden image has come to life!"

Here was a miracle indeed! Yet, illuminated by the sunshine, or darkened by the alternate shade of the houses, and with its garments fluttering lightly in the morning breeze, there passed the image along the street. It was exactly and minutely the shape, the garb, and the face which the townspeople had so recently thronged to see and admire. Not a rich flower upon her head, not a single leaf, but had had its prototype in Drowne's wooden workmanship, although now their fragile grace had become flexible, and was shaken by every footstep that the wearer made. The broad gold chain upon the neck was identical with the one represented on the image, and glistened with the motion imparted by the rise and fall of the bosom which it decorated. A real diamond sparkled on her finger. In her right hand she bore a pearl and ebony fan, which she flourished with a fantastic and bewitching coquetry, that was likewise expressed in all her movements as well as in the style of her beauty and the attire that so well harmonized with it. The face, with its brilliant depth of complexion, had the same piquancy of mirthful mischief that was fixed upon the countenance of the image, but which was here varied and continually shifting, yet always essentially the same, like the sunny gleam upon a bubbling fountain. On the whole, there was something so airy and yet so real in the figure, and withal so perfectly did it represent Drowne's image, that people knew not whether to suppose the magic wood etherealized into a spirit or warmed and softened into an actual woman.

"One thing is certain," muttered a Puritan of the old stamp, "Drowne has sold himself to the devil; and doubtless this gay Captain Hunnewell is a party to the bargain."

"And I," said a young man who overheard him, "would almost consent to be the third victim, for the liberty of saluting those lovely lips."

"And so would I," said Copley, the painter, "for the privilege of taking her picture."

The image, or the apparition, whichever it might be, still escorted by the bold captain, proceeded from Hanover Street through some of the cross lanes that make this portion of the town so intricate, to Ann Street, thence into Dock Square, and so downward to Drowne's shop, which stood just on the water's edge. The crowd still followed, gathering volume as it rolled along. Never had a modern miracle occurred in such broad daylight, nor in the presence of such a multitude of witnesses. The airy image, as if conscious that she was the object of the murmurs and disturbance that swelled behind her, appeared slightly vexed and flustered, yet still in a manner consistent with the light vivacity and sportive mischief that were written in her countenance. She was observed to flutter her fan with such vehement rapidity that the elaborate delicacy of its workmanship gave way, and it remained broken in her hand.

Arriving at Drowne's door, while the captain threw it open, the marvellous apparition paused an instant on the threshold, assuming the very attitude of the image, and casting over the crowd that glance of sunny coquetry which all remembered on the face of the oaken lady. She and her cavalier then disappeared.

"Ah!" murmured the crowd, drawing a deep breath, as with one vast pair of lungs.

"The world looks darker now that she has vanished," said some of the young men.

But the aged, whose recollections dated as far back as witch times, shook their heads, and hinted that our forefathers would have thought it a pious deed to burn the daughter of the oak with fire.

"If she be other than a bubble of the elements," exclaimed Copley, "I must look upon her face again."

He accordingly entered the shop; and there, in her usual corner, stood the image, gazing at him, as it might seem, with the very same expression of mirthful mischief that had been the farewell look of the apparition when, but a moment before, she turned her face towards the crowd. The carver stood beside his creation mending the beautiful fan, which by some accident was broken in her hand. But there was no longer any motion in the lifelike image, nor any real woman in the workshop, nor even the witchcraft of a sunny shadow, that might have deluded people's eyes as it flitted along the street. Captain Hunnewell, too, had vanished. His hoarse, sea-breezy tones, however, were audible on the other side of a door that opened upon the water.

"Sit down in the stern sheets, my lady," said the gallant captain. "Come, bear a hand, you lubbers, and set us on board in the turning of a minute glass."

And then was heard the stroke of oars.

"Drowne," said Copley, with a smile of intelligence, "you have been a truly fortunate man. What painter or statuary ever had such a subject! No wonder that she inspired a genius into you, and first created the artist who afterwards created her image."

Drowne looked at him with a visage that bore the traces of tears, but from which the light of imagination and sensibility, so recently illuminating it, had departed. He was again the mechanical carver that he had been known to be all his lifetime.

"I hardly understand what you mean, Mr. Copley," said he, putting his hand to his brow. "This image! Can it have been my work? Well, I have wrought it in a kind of dream; and now that I am broad awake I must set about finishing yonder figure of Admiral Vernon."

And forthwith he employed himself on the stolid countenance of one of his wooden progeny, and completed it in his own mechanical style, from which he was never known afterwards to deviate. He followed his business industriously for many years, acquired a competence, and in the latter part of his life attained to a dignified station in the church, being remembered in records and traditions as Deacon Drowne,[15] the carver. One of his productions, an Indian chief, gilded all over, stood during the better part of a century on the cupola of the Province House,[16] bedazzling the eyes of those who looked upward, like an angel of the sun. Another work of the good deacon's hand—a reduced likeness of his friend Captain Hunnewell, holding a telescope and quadrant—may be seen to this day, at the corner of Broad and

State Streets, serving in the useful capacity of sign to the shop of a nautical instrument maker. We know not how to account for the inferiority of this quaint old figure, as compared with the recorded excellence of the Oaken Lady, unless on the supposition that in every human spirit there is imagination, sensibility, creative power, genius, which, according to circumstances, may either be developed in this world, or shrouded in a mask of dulness until another state of being. To our friend Drowne there came a brief season of excitement, kindled by love. It rendered him a genius for that one occasion, but, quenched in disappointment, left him again the mechanical carver in wood, without the power even of appreciating the work that his own hands had wrought. Yet who can doubt that the very highest state to which a human spirit can attain, in its loftiest aspirations, is its truest and most natural state, and that Drowne was more consistent with himself when he wrought the admirable figure of the mysterious lady, than when he perpetrated a whole progeny of blockheads?

There was a rumor in Boston, about this period, that a young Portuguese lady of rank, on some occasion of political or domestic disquietude, had fled from her home in Fayal and put herself under the protection of Captain Hunnewell, on board of whose vessel, and at whose residence, she was sheltered until a change of affairs. This fair stranger must have been the original of Drowne's Wooden Image.

The Intelligence Office

A grave figure, with a pair of mysterious spectacles on his nose and a pen behind his ear, was seated at a desk in the corner of a metropolitan office. The apartment was fitted up with a counter, and furnished with an oaken cabinet and a chair or two, in simple and business-like style. Around the walls were stuck advertisements of articles lost, or articles wanted, or articles to be disposed of; in one or another of which classes were comprehended nearly all the conveniences, or otherwise, that the imagination of man has contrived. The interior of the room was thrown into shadow, partly by the tall edifices that rose on the opposite side of the street, and partly by the immense show bills of blue and crimson paper that were expanded over each of the three windows. Undisturbed by the tramp of feet, the rattle of wheels, the hum of voices, the shout of the city crier, the scream of the news boys, and other tokens of the multitudinous life that surged along in front of the office, the figure at the desk pored diligently over a folio volume, of legerlike size and aspect. He looked like the spirit of a record—the soul of his own great volume—made visible in mortal shape.

But scarcely an instant elapsed without the appearance at the door of some individual from the busy population whose vicinity was manifested by so much buzz, and clatter, and outcry. Now, it was a thriving mechanic in quest of a tenement that should come within his moderate means of rent; now, a ruddy Irish girl from the banks of Killarney,[1] wandering from kitchen to kitchen of our land, while her heart still hung in the peat smoke of her native cottage; now, a single gentleman looking out for economical board; and now—for this establishment offered an epitome of worldly pursuits—it was a faded beauty inquiring for her lost bloom; or Peter Schlemihl[2] for his lost shadow; or an author of ten years' standing for his vanished reputation; or a moody man for yesterday's sunshine.

At the next lifting of the latch there entered a person with his hat awry upon his head, his clothes perversely ill suited to his form, his eyes staring in directions opposite to their intelligence, and a certain odd unsuitableness pervading his whole figure. Wherever he might chance to be, whether in palace or cottage, church or market, on land or sea, or even at his own fireside, he must have worn the characteristic expression of a man out of his right place.

"This," inquired he, putting his question in the form of an assertion, "this is the Central Intelligence Office?"

"Even so," answered the figure at the desk, turning another leaf of his volume; he then looked the applicant in the face and said briefly, "Your business?"

"I want," said the latter, with tremulous earnestness, "a place!"

"A place! and of what nature?" asked the Intelligencer. "There are many vacant, or soon to be so, some of which will probably suit, since they range from that of a footman up to a seat at the council board, or in the cabinet, or a throne, or a presidential chair."

The stranger stood pondering before the desk with an unquiet, dissatisfied air—a dull, vague pain of heart, expressed by a slight contortion of the brow—an earnestness of glance, that asked and expected, yet continually wavered, as if distrusting. In short, he evidently wanted, not in a physical or intellectual sense, but with an urgent moral necessity that is the hardest of all things to satisfy, since it knows not its own object.

"Ah, you mistake me!" said he at length, with a gesture of nervous impatience. "Either of the places you mention, indeed, might answer my purpose; or, more probably, none of them. I want my place! my own place! my true place in the world! my proper sphere! my thing to do, which nature intended me to perform when she fashioned me thus awry, and which I have vainly sought all my lifetime! Whether it be a footman's duty or a king's is of little consequence, so it be naturally mine. Can you help me here?"

"I will enter your application," answered the Intelligencer, at the same time writing a few lines in his volume. "But to undertake such a business, I tell you frankly, is quite apart from the ground covered by my official duties. Ask for something specific, and it may doubtless be negotiated for you, on your compliance with the conditions. But were I to go further, I should have the whole population of the city upon my shoulders; since far the greater proportion of them are, more or less, in your predicament."

The applicant sank into a fit of despondency, and passed out of the door without again lifting his eyes; and, if he died of the disappointment, he was probably buried in the wrong tomb, inasmuch as the fatality of such people never deserts them, and, whether alive or dead, they are invariably out of place.

Almost immediately another foot was heard on the threshold. A youth entered hastily, and threw a glance around the office to ascertain whether the man of intelligence was alone. He then approached close to the desk, blushed like a maiden, and seemed at a loss how to broach his business.

"You come upon an affair of the heart," said the official personage, looking into him through his mysterious spectacles. "State it in as few words as may be."

"You are right," replied the youth. "I have a heart to dispose of."

"You seek an exchange?" said the Intelligencer. "Foolish youth, why not be contented with your own?"

"Because," exclaimed the young man, losing his embarrassment in a passionate glow, "because my heart burns me with an intolerable fire; it tortures me all day long with yearnings for I know not what, and feverish throbbings, and the pangs of a vague sorrow; and it awakens me in the night time with a quake, when there is nothing to be feared. I cannot endure it any longer. It were wiser to throw away such a heart, even if it brings me nothing in return."

"O, very well," said the man of office, making an entry in his volume. "Your affair will be easily transacted. This species of brokerage makes no inconsiderable part of my business; and there is always a large assortment of the article to select from. Here, if I mistake not, comes a pretty fair sample."

Even as he spoke the door was gently and slowly thrust ajar, affording a glimpse of the slender figure of a young girl, who, as she timidly entered, seemed to bring the light and cheerfulness of the outer atmosphere into the somewhat gloomy apartment. We know not her errand there, nor can we reveal whether the young man gave up his heart into her custody. If so, the arrangement was neither better nor worse than in ninety-nine cases out of a hundred, where the parallel sensibilities of a similar age, importunate affections, and the easy satisfaction of characters not deeply conscious of themselves, supply the place of any profounder sympathy.

Not always, however, was the agency of the passions and affections an office of so little trouble. It happened, rarely, indeed, in proportion to the cases that came under an ordinary rule, but still it did happen— that a heart was occasionally brought hither of such exquisite material, so delicately attempered, and so curiously wrought, that no other heart could be found to match it. It might almost be considered a misfortune, in a worldly point of view, to be the possessor of such a diamond of the purest water; since in any reasonable probability it could only be exchanged for an ordinary pebble, or a bit of cunningly-manufactured glass, or, at least, for a jewel of native richness, but ill set, or with some fatal flaw, or an earthy vein running through its central lustre. To choose another figure, it is sad that hearts which have their wellspring in the infinite, and contain inexhaustible sympathies, should ever be doomed to pour themselves into shallow vessels, and thus lavish their rich affections on the ground. Strange that the finer and deeper nature, whether in man or woman, while possessed of every other delicate instinct, should so often lack that most invaluable one of preserving itself from contamination with what is of a baser kind! Sometimes, it is true, the spiritual fountain is kept pure by a wisdom within itself, and sparkles into the light of heaven without a stain from the earthy strata through which it had gushed upward. And sometimes, even here on earth, the pure mingles with the pure, and the inexhaustible is recompensed with the infinite. But these miracles, though he should claim the credit of them, are far beyond the scope of such a superficial agent in human affairs as the figure in the mysterious spectacles.

Again the door was opened, admitting the bustle of the city with a fresher reverberation into the Intelligence Office. Now entered a man of wo-begone and downcast look; it was such an aspect as if he had lost the very soul out of his body, and had traversed all the world over, searching in the dust of the highways, and along the shady footpaths, and beneath the leaves of the forest, and among the sands of the sea shore in hopes to recover it again. He had bent an anxious glance along the pavement of the street as he came hitherward; he looked also in the angle of the doorstep, and upon the floor of the room; and, finally, coming up to the Man of Intelligence, he gazed through the in-scrutable spectacles which the latter wore, as if the lost treasure might be hidden within his eyes.

"I have lost—" he began; and then he paused.

"Yes," said the Intelligencer, "I see that you have lost—but what?"

"I have lost a precious jewel!" replied the unfortunate person, "the like of which is not to be found among any prince's treasures. While I possessed it, the contemplation of it was my sole and sufficient happi-ness. No price should have purchased it of me; but it has fallen from my bosom where I wore it in my careless wanderings about the city."

After causing the stranger to describe the marks of his lost jewel, the Intelligencer opened a drawer of the oaken cabinet which has been mentioned as forming a part of the furniture of the room. Here were deposited whatever articles had been picked up in the streets, until the right owners should claim them. It was a strange and heterogeneous collection. Not the least remarkable part of it was a great number of wedding rings, each one of which had been riveted upon the finger with holy vows, and all the mystic potency that the most solemn rites could attain, but had, nevertheless, proved too slippery for the wearer's vigilance. The gold of some was worn thin, betokening the attrition of years of wedlock; others, glittering from the jeweller's shop, must have been lost within the honeymoon. There were ivory tablets, the leaves scribbled over with sentiments that had been the deepest truths of the writer's earlier years, but which were now quite obliterated from his memory. So scrupulously were articles preserved in this depository, that not even withered flowers were rejected; white roses, and blush roses, and moss roses, fit emblems of virgin purity and shamefaced-ness, which had been lost or flung away, and trampled into the pollu-tion of the streets; locks of hair—the golden and the glossy dark—the long tresses of woman and the crisp curls of man, signified that lovers were now and then so heedless of the faith entrusted to them as to drop its symbol from the treasure place of the bosom. Many of these things were imbued with perfumes, and perhaps a sweet scent had departed from the lives of their former possessors ever since they had so wilfully or negligently lost them. Here were gold pencil cases, little ruby hearts with golden arrows through them, bosom pins, pieces of coin, and small articles of every description, comprising nearly all that have been lost since a long time ago. Most of them, doubtless, had a history and a meaning, if there were time to search it out and room to tell it. Whoever has missed any thing valuable, whether out of his heart, mind, or pocket, would do well to make inquiry at the Central Intelligence Office.

And in the corner of one of the drawers of the oaken cabinet, after considerable research, was found a great pearl, looking like the soul of celestial purity, congealed and polished.

"There is my jewel! my very pearl!" cried the stranger, almost beside himself with rapture. "It is mine! Give it me, this moment! or I shall perish!"

"I perceive," said the Man of Intelligence, examining it more closely, "that this is the Pearl of Great Price."[3]

"The very same," answered the stranger. "Judge, then, of my misery at losing it out of my bosom! Restore it to me! I must not live without it an instant longer."

"Pardon me," rejoined the Intelligencer, calmly. "You ask what is beyond my duty. This pearl, as you well know, is held upon a peculiar tenure; and having once let it escape from your keeping, you have no greater claim to it—nay, not so great—as any other person. I cannot give it back."

Nor could the entreaties of the miserable man—who saw before his eyes the jewel of his life without the power to reclaim it—soften the heart of this stern being, impassive to human sympathy, though exercising such an apparent influence over human fortunes. Finally the loser of the inestimable pearl clutched his hands among his hair, and ran madly forth into the world, which was affrighted at his desperate looks. There passed him on the doorstep a fashionable young gentleman, whose business was to inquire for a damask rosebud, the gift of his lady love, which he had lost out of his button hole within an hour after receiving it. So various were the errands of those who visited this Central Office, where all human wishes seemed to be made known, and so far as destiny would allow, negotiated to their fulfilment.

The next that entered was a man beyond the middle age, bearing the look of one who knew the world and his own course in it. He had just alighted from a handsome private carriage, which had orders to wait in the street while its owner transacted his business. This person came up to the desk with a quick, determined step, and looked the Intelligencer in the face with a resolute eye; though, at the same time, some secret trouble gleamed from it in red and dusky light.

"I have an estate to dispose of," said he, with a brevity that seemed characteristic.

"Describe it," said the Intelligencer.

The applicant proceeded to give the boundaries of his property, its nature, comprising tillage, pasture, woodland, and pleasure grounds, in ample circuit; together with a mansion house, in the construction of which it had been his object to realize a castle in the air, hardening its shadowy walls into granite, and rendering its visionary splendor perceptible to the awakened eye. Judging from his description, it was beautiful enough to vanish like a dream, yet substantial enough to endure for centuries. He spoke, too, of the gorgeous furniture, the refinements of upholstery, and all the luxurious artifices that combined to render this a residence where life might flow onward in a stream of golden days, undisturbed by the ruggedness which fate loves to fling into it.

"I am a man of strong will," said he, in conclusion; "and at my first setting out in life, as a poor, unfriended youth, I resolved to make myself the possessor of such a mansion and estate as this, together with the abundant revenue necessary to uphold it. I have succeeded to the extent of my utmost wish. And this is the estate which I have now concluded to dispose of."

"And your terms?" asked the Intelligencer, after taking down the particulars with which the stranger had supplied him.

"Easy, abundantly easy!" answered the successful man, smiling, but with a stern and almost frightful contraction of the brow, as if to quell an inward pang. "I have been engaged in various sorts of business—a distiller, a trader to Africa, an East India merchant, a speculator in the stocks—and, in the course of these affairs, have contracted an incumbrance of a certain nature. The purchaser of the estate shall merely be required to assume this burden to himself."

"I understand you," said the Man of Intelligence, putting his pen behind his ear. "I fear that no bargain can be negotiated on these conditions. Very probably the next possessor may acquire the estate with a similar incumbrance, but it will be of his own contracting, and will not lighten your burden in the least."

"And am I to live on," fiercely exclaimed the stranger, "with the dirt of these accursed acres and the granite of this infernal mansion crushing down my soul? How, if I should turn the edifice into an almshouse or a hospital, or tear it down and build a church?"

"You can at least make the experiment," said the Intelligencer; "but the whole matter is one which you must settle for yourself."

The man of deplorable success withdrew, and got into his coach, which rattled off lightly over the wooden pavements, though laden with the weight of much land, a stately house, and ponderous heaps of gold, all compressed into an evil conscience.

There now appeared many applicants for places; among the most noteworthy of whom was a small, smoke-dried figure, who gave himself out to be one of the bad spirits that had waited upon Doctor Faustus[4] in his laboratory. He pretended to show a certificate of character, which, he averred, had been given him by that famous necromancer, and countersigned by several masters whom he had subsequently served.

"I am afraid, my good friend," observed the Intelligencer, "that your chance of getting a service is but poor. Nowadays, men act the evil spirit for themselves and their neighbors, and play the part more effectually than ninety-nine out of a hundred of your fraternity."

But, just as the poor fiend was assuming a vaporous consistency, being about to vanish through the floor in sad disappointment and chagrin, the editor of a political newspaper chanced to enter the office in quest of a scribbler of party paragraphs. The former servant of Doctor Faustus, with some misgivings as to his sufficiency of venom, was allowed to try his hand in this capacity. Next appeared, likewise seeking a service, the mysterious man in Red, who had aided Bonaparte[5] in his ascent to imperial power. He was examined as to his qualifications by an aspiring politician, but finally rejected, as lacking familiarity with the cunning tactics of the present day.

People continued to succeed each other with as much briskness as if every body turned aside, out of the roar and tumult of the city, to record here some want, or superfluity, or desire. Some had goods or possessions, of which they wished to negotiate the sale. A China merchant had lost his health by a long residence in that wasting climate.

He very liberally offered his disease, and his wealth along with it, to any physician who would rid him of both together. A soldier offered his wreath of laurels for as good a leg as that which it had cost him on the battle field. One poor weary wretch desired nothing but to be accommodated with any creditable method of laying down his life; for misfortune and pecuniary troubles had so subdued his spirits that he could no longer conceive the possibility of happiness, nor had the heart to try for it. Nevertheless, happening to overhear some conversation in the Intelligence Office respecting wealth to be rapidly accumulated by a certain mode of speculation, he resolved to live out this one other experiment of better fortune. Many persons desired to exchange their youthful vices for others better suited to the gravity of advancing age; a few, we are glad to say, made earnest efforts to exchange vice for virtue, and, hard as the bargain was, succeeded in effecting it. But it was remarkable that what all were the least willing to give up, even on the most advantageous terms, were the habits, the oddities, the characteristic traits, the little ridiculous indulgences, somewhere between faults and follies, of which nobody but themselves could understand the fascination.

The great folio, in which the Man of Intelligence recorded all these freaks of idle hearts, and aspirations of deep hearts, and desperate longings of miserable hearts, and evil prayers of perverted hearts, would be curious reading were it possible to obtain it for publication. Human character in its individual developments—human nature in the mass—may best be studied in its wishes; and this was the record of them all. There was an endless diversity of mode and circumstance, yet withal such a similarity in the real groundwork, that any one page of the volume—whether written in the days before the Flood,[6] or the yesterday that is just gone by, or to be written on the morrow that is close at hand, or a thousand ages hence—might serve as a specimen of the whole. Not but that there were wild sallies of fantasy that could scarcely occur to more than one man's brain, whether reasonable or lunatic. The strangest wishes—yet most incident to men who had gone deep into scientific pursuits, and attained a high intellectual stage, though not the loftiest—were, to contend with Nature, and wrest from her some secret, or some power, which she had seen fit to withhold from mortal grasp. She loves to delude her aspiring students, and mock them with mysteries that seem but just beyond their utmost reach. To concoct new minerals, to produce new forms of vegetable life, to create an insect, if nothing higher in the living scale, is a sort of wish that has often revelled in the breast of a man of science. An astronomer, who lived far more among the distant worlds of space than in this lower sphere, recorded a wish to behold the opposite side of the moon, which, unless the system of the firmament be reversed, she can never turn towards the earth. On the same page of the volume was written the wish of a little child to have the stars for playthings.

The most ordinary wish, that was written down with wearisome recurrence, was of course, for wealth, wealth, wealth, in sums from a few shillings up to unreckonable thousands. But in reality this often-repeated expression covered as many different desires. Wealth is the golden essence of the outward world, imbodying almost every thing that exists beyond the limits of the soul; and therefore it is the natural yearning for the life in the midst of which we find ourselves, and of which gold is the condition of enjoyment, that men abridge into this general wish. Here and there, it is true, the volume testified to some heart so perverted as to desire gold for its own sake. Many wished for power; a strange desire indeed, since it is but another form of slavery. Old people wished for the delights of youth; a fop, for a fashionable coat; an idle reader, for a new novel; a versifier, for a rhyme to some stubborn word; a painter, for Titian's secret of coloring;[7] a prince, for a cottage; a republican, for a kingdom and a palace; a libertine for his neighbor's wife; a man of palate, for green peas; and a poor man, for a crust of bread. The ambitious desires of public men, elsewhere so craftily concealed, were here expressed openly and boldly, side by side with the unselfish wishes of the philanthropist for the welfare of the race, so beautiful, so comforting, in contrast with the egotism that continually weighed self against the world. Into the darker secrets of the Book of Wishes we will not penetrate.

It would be an instructive employment for a student of mankind, perusing this volume carefully and comparing its records with men's perfected designs, as expressed in their deeds and daily life, to ascertain how far the one accorded with the other. Undoubtedly, in most cases, the correspondence would be found remote. The holy and generous wish, that rises like incense from a pure heart towards heaven, often lavishes its sweet perfume on the blast of evil times. The foul, selfish, murderous wish, that steams forth from a corrupted heart, often passes into the spiritual atmosphere without being concreted into an earthly deed. Yet this volume is probably truer, as a representation of the human heart, than is the living drama of action as it evolves around us. There is more of good and more of evil in it; more redeeming points of the bad and more errors of the virtuous; higher upsoarings, and baser degradation of the soul; in short, a more perplexing amalgamation of vice and virtue than we witness in the outward world. Decency and external conscience often produce a far fairer outside than is warranted by the stains within. And be it owned, on the other hand, that a man seldom repeats to his nearest friend, any more than he realizes in act, the purest wishes, which, at some blessed time or other, have arisen from the depths of his nature and witnessed for him in this volume. Yet there is enough on every leaf to make the good man shudder for his own wild and idle wishes, as well as for the sinner, whose whole life is the incarnation of a wicked desire.

But again the door is opened, and we hear the tumultuous stir of the world—a deep and awful sound, expressing in another form some portion of what is written in the volume that lies before the Man of Intelligence. A grandfatherly personage tottered hastily into the office, with such an earnestness in his infirm alacrity that his white hair floated backward as he hurried up to the desk, while his dim eyes caught a momentary lustre from his vehemence of purpose. This venerable figure explained that he was in search of To-morrow.

"I have spent all my life in pursuit of it," added the sage old gentleman, "being assured that To-morrow has some vast benefit or other in store for me. But I am now getting a little in years, and must make haste; for, unless I overtake To-morrow soon, I begin to be afraid it will finally escape me."

"This fugitive To-morrow, my venerable friend," said the Man of Intelligence, "is a stray child of Time, and is flying from his father into the region of the infinite. Continue your pursuit, and you will doubtless come up with him; but as to the earthly gifts which you expect, he has scattered them all among a throng of Yesterdays."

Obliged to content himself with this enigmatical response, the grandsire hastened forth with a quick clatter of his staff upon the floor; and, as he disappeared, a little boy scampered through the door in chase of a butterfly which had got astray amid the barren sunshine of the city. Had the old gentleman been shrewder, he might have detected To-morrow under the semblance of that gaudy insect. The golden butterfly glistened through the shadowy apartment, and brushed its wings against the Book of Wishes, and fluttered forth again with the child still in pursuit.

A man now entered, in neglected attire, with the aspect of a thinker, but somewhat too roughhewn and brawny for a scholar. His face was full of sturdy vigor, with some finer and keener attribute beneath. Though harsh at first, it was tempered with the glow of a large, warm heart, which had force enough to heat his powerful intellect through and through. He advanced to the Intelligencer and looked at him with a glance of such stern sincerity that perhaps few secrets were beyond its scope.

"I seek for Truth," said he.

"It is precisely the most rare pursuit that has ever come under my cognizance," replied the Intelligencer, as he made the new inscription in his volume. "Most men seek to impose some cunning falsehood upon themselves for truth. But I can lend no help to your researches. You must achieve the miracle for yourself. At some fortunate moment you may find Truth at your side, or perhaps she may be mistily discerned far in advance, or possibly behind you."

"Not behind me," said the seeker; "for I have left nothing on my track without a thorough investigation. She flits before me, passing now through a naked solitude, and now mingling with the throng of a popular assembly, and now writing with the pen of a French philosopher, and now standing at the altar of an old cathedral, in the guise of a Catholic priest, performing the high mass. O weary search! But I must not falter; and surely my heart-deep quest of Truth shall avail at last."

He paused and fixed his eyes upon the Intelligencer with a depth of investigation that seemed to hold commerce with the inner nature of this being, wholly regardless of his external development.

"And what are you?" said he. "It will not satisfy me to point to this fantastic show of an Intelligence Office and this mockery of business. Tell me what is beneath it, and what your real agency in life and your influence upon mankind."

"Yours is a mind," answered the Man of Intelligence, "before which the forms and fantasies that conceal the inner idea from the multitude vanish at once and leave the naked reality beneath. Know, then, the secret. My agency in worldly action, my connection with the press, and tumult, and intermingling, and development of human affairs is merely delusive. The desire of man's heart does for him whatever I seem to do. I am no minister of action, but the Recording Spirit."

What further secrets were then spoken remains a mystery, inasmuch as the roar of the city, the bustle of human business, the outcry of the jostling masses, the rush and tumult of man's life, in its noisy and brief career, arose so high that it drowned the words of these two talkers; and whether they stood talking in the moon, or in Vanity Fair,[8] or in a city of this actual world, is more than I can say.

Roger Malvin's Burial

One of the few incidents of Indian warfare naturally susceptible of the moonlight of romance was that expedition undertaken for the defence of the frontiers in the year 1725, which resulted in the well-remembered "Lovell's Fight."[1] Imagination, by casting certain circumstances judicially into the shade, may see much to admire in the heroism of a little band who gave battle to twice their number in the heart of the enemy's country. The open bravery displayed by both parties was in accordance with civilized ideas of valor; and chivalry itself might not blush to record the deeds of one or two individuals. The battle, though so fatal to those who fought, was not unfortunate in its consequences to the country; for it broke the strength of a tribe and conduced to the peace which subsisted during several ensuing years. History and tradition are unusually minute in their memorials of this affair; and the captain of a scouting party of frontier men has acquired as actual a military renown as many a victorious leader of thousands. Some of the incidents contained in the following pages will be recognized, notwithstanding the substitution of fictitious names, by such as have heard, from old men's lips, the fate of the few combatants who were in a condition to retreat after "Lovell's Fight."

*   *   *

The early sunbeams hovered cheerfully upon the tree tops, beneath which two weary and wounded men had stretched their limbs the night before. Their bed of withered oak leaves was strewn upon the small level space, at the foot of a rock, situated near the summit of one of the gentle swells by which the face of the country is there diversified. The mass of granite, rearing its smooth, flat surface fifteen or twenty feet above their heads, was not unlike a gigantic gravestone, upon which the veins seemed to form an inscription in forgotten characters. On a tract of several acres around this rock, oaks and other hard-wood trees had supplied the place of the pines, which were the usual growth of the land; and a young and vigorous sapling stood close beside the travellers.

The severe wound of the elder man had probably deprived him of sleep; for, so soon as the first ray of sunshine rested on the top of the highest tree, he reared himself painfully from his recumbent posture and sat erect. The deep lines of his countenance and the scattered gray of his hair marked him as past the middle age; but his muscular frame would, but for the effects of his wound, have been as capable of sustaining fatigue as in the early vigor of life. Languor and exhaustion now sat upon his haggard features; and the despairing glance which he sent forward through the depths of the forest proved his own conviction that his pilgrimage was at an end. He next turned his eyes to the companion who reclined by his side. The youth—for he had scarcely attained the years of manhood—lay, with his head upon his arm, in the embrace of an unquiet sleep, which a thrill of pain from his wounds seemed each moment on the point of breaking. His right hand grasped a musket; and, to judge from the violent action of his features, his slumbers were bringing back a vision of the conflict of which he was one of the few survivors. A shout—deep and loud in his dreaming fancy—found its way in an imperfect murmur to his lips; and, starting even at the slight sound of his own voice, he suddenly awoke. The first act of reviving recollection was to make anxious inquiries respecting the condition of his wounded fellow-traveller. The latter shook his head.

"Reuben, my boy," said he, "this rock beneath which we sit will serve for an old hunter's gravestone. There is many and many a long mile of howling wilderness before us yet; nor would it avail me any thing if the smoke of my own chimney were but on the other side of that swell of land. The Indian bullet was deadlier than I thought."

"You are weary with our three days' travel," replied the youth, "and a little longer rest will recruit you. Sit you here while I search the woods for the herbs and roots that must be our sustenance; and, having eaten, you shall lean on me, and we will turn our faces homeward. I doubt not that, with my help, you can attain to some one of the frontier garrisons."

"There is not two days' life in me, Reuben," said the other, calmly, "and I will no longer burden you with my useless body, when you can scarcely support your own. Your wounds are deep and your strength is failing fast; yet, if you hasten onward alone, you may be preserved. For me there is no hope, and I will await death here."

"If it must be so, I will remain and watch by you," said Reuben, resolutely.

"No, my son, no," rejoined his companion. "Let the wish of a dying man have weight with you; give me one grasp of your hand, and get you hence. Think you that my last moments will be eased by the thought that I leave you to die a more lingering death? I have loved you like a father, Reuben; and at a time like this I should have something of a father's authority. I charge you to be gone, that I may die in peace."

"And because you have been a father to me, should I therefore leave you to perish and to lie unburied in the wilderness?" exclaimed the youth. "No; if your end be in truth approaching, I will watch by you and receive your parting words. I will dig a grave here by the rock, in which, if my weakness overcome me, we will rest together; or, if Heaven gives me strength, I will seek my way home."

"In the cities and wherever men dwell," replied the other, "they bury their dead in the earth; they hide them from the sight of the living; but here, where no step may pass perhaps for a hundred years, wherefore should I not rest beneath the open sky, covered only by the oak leaves when the autumn winds shall strew them? And for a monument, here is this gray rock, on which my dying hand shall carve the name of Roger Malvin; and the traveller in days to come will know that here sleeps a hunter and a warrior. Tarry not, then, for a folly like this, but hasten away, if not for your own sake, for hers who will else be desolate."

Malvin spoke the last few words in a faltering voice, and their effect upon his companion was strongly visible. They reminded him that there were other and less questionable duties than that of sharing the fate of a man whom his death could not benefit. Nor can it be affirmed that no selfish feeling strove to enter Reuben's heart, though the consciousness made him more earnestly resist his companion's entreaties.

"How terrible to wait the slow approach of death in this solitude!" exclaimed he. "A brave man does not shrink in the battle; and, when friends stand round the bed, even women may die composedly; but here——"

"I shall not shrink even here, Reuben Bourne," interrupted Malvin. "I am a man of no weak heart; and, if I were, there is a surer support than that of earthly friends. You are young, and life is dear to you. Your last moments will need comfort far more than mine; and when you have laid me in the earth, and are alone, and night is settling on the forest, you will feel all the bitterness of the death that may now be escaped. But I will urge no selfish motive to your generous nature. Leave me for my sake, that, having said a prayer for your safety, I may have space to settle my account undisturbed by worldly sorrows."

"And your daughter,—how shall I dare to meet her eye?" exclaimed Reuben. "She will ask the fate of her father, whose life I vowed to defend with my own. Must I tell her that he travelled three days' march with me from the field of battle, and that then I left him to perish in the wilderness? Were it not better to lie down and die by your side than to return safe and say this to Dorcas?"

"Tell my daughter," said Roger Malvin, "that, though yourself sore wounded, and weak, and weary, you led my tottering footsteps many a mile, and left me only at my earnest entreaty, because I would not have your blood upon my soul. Tell her that through pain and danger you were faithful, and that, if your lifeblood could have saved me, it would have flowed to its last drop; and tell her that you will be something dearer than a father, and that my blessing is with you both, and that my dying eyes can see a long and pleasant path in which you will journey together."

As Malvin spoke he almost raised himself from the ground, and the energy of his concluding words seemed to fill the wild and lonely forest with a vision of happiness; but, when he sank exhausted upon his bed of oak leaves, the light which had kindled in Reuben's eye was quenched. He felt as if it were both sin and folly to think of happiness at such a moment. His companion watched his changing countenance, and sought with generous art to wile him to his own good.

"Perhaps I deceive myself in regard to the time I have to live," he resumed. "It may be that, with speedy assistance, I might recover of my wound. The foremost fugitives must, ere this, have carried tidings of our fatal battle to the frontiers, and parties will be out to succor those in like condition with ourselves. Should you meet one of these and guide them hither, who can tell but that I may sit by my own fire-side again?"

A mournful smile strayed across the features of the dying man as he insinuated that unfounded hope; which, however, was not without its effect on Reuben. No merely selfish motive, nor even the desolate condition of Dorcas, could have induced him to desert his companion at such a moment—but his wishes seized upon the thought that Malvin's life might be preserved, and his sanguine nature heightened almost to certainty the remote possibility of procuring human aid.

"Surely there is reason, weighty reason, to hope that friends are not far distant," he said, half aloud. "There fled one coward, unwounded, in the beginning of the fight, and most probably he made good speed. Every true man on the frontier would shoulder his musket at the news; and, though no party may range so far into the woods as this, I shall perhaps encounter them in one day's march. Counsel me faith-fully," he added, turning to Malvin, in distrust of his own motives. "Were your situation mine, would you desert me while life remained?"

"It is now twenty years," replied Roger Malvin, sighing, however, as he secretly acknowledged the wide dissimilarity between the two cases,—"it is now twenty years since I escaped with one dear friend from Indian captivity near Montreal. We journeyed many days through the woods, till at length, overcome with hunger and weariness, my friend lay down and besought me to leave him; for he knew that, if I remained, we both must perish; and, with but little hope of obtaining succor, I heaped a pillow of dry leaves beneath his head and hastened on."

"And did you return in time to save him?" asked Reuben, hanging on Malvin's words as if they were to be prophetic of his own success.

"I did," answered the other. "I came upon the camp of a hunting party before sunset of the same day. I guided them to the spot where my comrade was expecting death; and he is now a hale and hearty man upon his own farm, far within the frontiers, while I lie wounded here in the depths of the wilderness."

This example, powerful in effecting Reuben's decision, was aided, unconsciously to himself, by the hidden strength of many another motive. Roger Malvin perceived that the victory was nearly won.

"Now, go, my son, and Heaven prosper you!" he said. "Turn not back with your friends when you meet them, lest your wounds and weariness overcome you; but send hitherward two or three, that may be spared, to search for me; and believe me, Reuben, my heart will be lighter with every step you take towards home." Yet there was, perhaps, a change both in his countenance and voice as he spoke thus; for, after all, it was a ghastly fate to be left expiring in the wilderness.

Reuben Bourne, but half convinced that he was acting rightly, at length raised himself from the ground and prepared himself for his departure. And first, though contrary to Malvin's wishes, he collected a stock of roots and herbs, which had been their only food during the last two days. This useless supply he placed within reach of the dying man, for whom, also, he swept together a fresh bed of dry oak leaves. Then climbing to the summit of the rock, which on one side was rough and broken, he bent the oak sapling downward, and bound his handkerchief to the topmost branch. This precaution was not unnecessary to direct any who might come in search of Malvin; for every part of the rock, except its broad, smooth front, was concealed at a little distance by the dense undergrowth of the forest. The handkerchief had been the bandage of a wound upon Reuben's arm; and, as he bound it to the tree, he vowed by the blood that stained it that he would return, either to save his companion's life, or to lay his body in the grave. He then descended, and stood, with downcast eyes, to receive Roger Malvin's parting words.

The experience of the latter suggested much and minute advice respecting the youth's journey through the trackless forest. Upon this subject he spoke with calm earnestness, as if he were sending Reuben to the battle or the chase while he himself remained secure at home, and not as if the human countenance that was about to leave him were the last he would ever behold. But his firmness was shaken before he concluded.

"Carry my blessing to Dorcas, and say that my last prayer shall be for her and you. Bid her to have no hard thoughts because you left me here,"—Reuben's heart smote him,—"for that your life would not have weighed with you if its sacrifice could have done me good. She will marry you after she has mourned a little while for her father; and Heaven grant you long and happy days, and may your children's children stand round your death bed! And, Reuben," added he, as the weakness of mortality made its way at last, "return, when your wounds are healed and your weariness refreshed,—return to this wild rock, and lay my bones in the grave, and say a prayer over them."

An almost superstitious regard, arising perhaps from the customs of the Indians, whose war was with the dead as well as the living, was paid by the frontier inhabitants to the rites of sepulture; and there are many instances of the sacrifice of life in the attempt to bury those who had fallen by the "sword of the wilderness." Reuben, therefore, felt the full importance of the promise which he most solemnly made to return and perform Roger Malvin's obsequies. It was remarkable that the latter, speaking his whole heart in his parting words, no longer endeavored to persuade the youth that even the speediest succor might avail to the preservation of his life. Reuben was internally convinced that he should see Malvin's living face no more. His generous nature would fain have delayed him, at whatever risk, till the dying scene were past; but the desire of existence and the hope of happiness had strengthened in his heart, and he was unable to resist them.

"It is enough," said Roger Malvin, having listened to Reuben's promise. "Go, and God speed you!"

The youth pressed his hand in silence, turned, and was departing. His slow and faltering steps, however, had borne him but a little way before Malvin's voice recalled him.

"Reuben, Reuben," said he, faintly; and Reuben returned and knelt down by the dying man.

"Raise me, and let me lean against the rock," was his last request. "My face will be turned towards home, and I shall see you a moment longer as you pass among the trees."

Reuben, having made the desired alteration in his companion's posture, again began his solitary pilgrimage. He walked more hastily at first than was consistent with his strength; for a sort of guilty feeling, which sometimes torments men in their most justifiable acts, caused him to seek concealment from Malvin's eyes; but after he had trodden far upon the rustling forest leaves he crept back, impelled by a wild and painful curiosity, and, sheltered by the earthy roots of an uptorn tree, gazed earnestly at the desolate man. The morning sun was unclouded, and the trees and shrubs imbibed the sweet air of the month of May; yet there seemed a gloom on Nature's face, as if she sympathized with mortal pain and sorrow. Roger Malvin's hands were uplifted in a fervent prayer, some of the words of which stole through the stillness of the woods and entered Reuben's heart, torturing it with an unutterable pang. They were the broken accents of a petition for his own happiness and that of Dorcas; and, as the youth listened, conscience, or something in its similitude, pleaded strongly with him to return and lie down again by the rock. He felt how hard was the doom of the kind and generous being whom he had deserted in his extremity. Death would come like the slow approach of a corpse, stealing gradually towards him through the forest, and showing its ghastly and motionless features from behind a nearer and yet a nearer tree. But such must have been Reuben's own fate had he tarried another sunset; and who shall impute blame to him if he shrink from so useless a sacrifice? As he gave a parting look, a breeze waved the little banner upon the sapling oak and reminded Reuben of his vow.

*   *   *

Many circumstances contributed to retard the wounded traveller in his way to the frontiers. On the second day the clouds, gathering densely over the sky, precluded the possibility of regulating his course by the position of the sun; and he knew not but that every effort of his almost exhausted strength was removing him farther from the home he sought. His scanty sustenance was supplied by the berries and other spontaneous products of the forest. Herds of deer, it is true, sometimes bounded past him, and partridges frequently whirred up before his footsteps; but his ammunition had been expended in the fight, and he had no means of slaying them. His wounds, irritated by the constant exertion in which lay the only hope of life, wore away his strength and at intervals confused his reason. But, even in the wanderings of intellect, Reuben's young heart clung strongly to existence; and it was only through absolute incapacity of motion that he at last sank down beneath a tree, compelled there to await death.

In this situation he was discovered by a party who, upon the first intelligence of the fight, had been despatched to the relief of the survivors. They conveyed him to the nearest settlement, which chanced to be that of his own residence.

Dorcas, in the simplicity of the olden time, watched by the bedside of her wounded lover and administered all those comforts that are in the sole gift of woman's heart and hand. During several days Reuben's recollection strayed drowsily among the perils and hardships through which he had passed, and he was incapable of returning definite answers to the inquiries with which many were eager to harass him. No authentic particulars of the battle had yet been circulated; nor could mothers, wives, and children tell whether their loved ones were detained by captivity or by the stronger chain of death. Dorcas nourished her apprehensions in silence till one afternoon when Reuben awoke from an unquiet sleep and seemed to recognize her more perfectly than at any previous time. She saw that his intellect had become composed, and she could no longer restrain her filial anxiety.

"My father, Reuben?" she began; but the change in her lover's countenance made her pause.

The youth shrank as if with a bitter pain, and the blood gushed vividly into his wan and hollow cheeks. His first impulse was to cover his face; but, apparently with a desperate effort, he half raised himself and spoke vehemently, defending himself against an imaginary accusation.

"Your father was sore wounded in the battle, Dorcas; and he bade me not burden myself with him, but only to lead him to the lakeside, that he might quench his thirst and die. But I would not desert the old man in his extremity, and, though bleeding myself, I supported him; I gave him half my strength, and led him away with me. For three days we journeyed on together, and your father was sustained beyond my hopes; but, awaking at sunrise on the fourth day, I found him faint and exhausted; he was unable to proceed; his life had ebbed away fast; and——"

"He died!" exclaimed Dorcas, faintly.

Reuben felt it impossible to acknowledge that his selfish love of life had hurried him away before her father's fate was decided. He spoke not; he only bowed his head; and, between shame and exhaustion, sank back and hid his face in the pillow. Dorcas wept when her fears were thus confirmed; but the shock, as it had been long anticipated, was on that account the less violent.

"You dug a grave for my poor father in the wilderness, Reuben?" was the question by which her filial piety manifested itself.

"My hands were weak; but I did what I could," replied the youth in a smothered tone. "There stands a noble tombstone above his head; and I would to Heaven I slept as soundly as he!"

Dorcas, perceiving the wildness of his latter words, inquired no further at the time; but her heart found ease in the thought that Roger Malvin had not lacked such funeral rites as it was possible to bestow. The tale of Reuben's courage and fidelity lost nothing when she communicated it to her friends; and the poor youth, tottering from his sick chamber to breathe the sunny air, experienced from every tongue the miserable and humiliating torture of unmerited praise. All acknowledged that he might worthily demand the hand of the fair maiden to whose father he had been "faithful unto death;" and, as my tale is not of love, it shall suffice to say that in the space of a few months Reuben became the husband of Dorcas Malvin. During the marriage ceremony the bride was covered with blushes; but the bridegroom's face was pale.

There was now in the breast of Reuben Bourne an incommunicable thought—something which he was to conceal most heedfully from her whom he most loved and trusted. He regretted, deeply and bitterly, the moral cowardice that had restrained his words when he was about to disclose the truth to Dorcas; but pride, the fear of losing her affection, the dread of universal scorn forbade him to rectify this falsehood. He felt that for leaving Roger Malvin he deserved no censure. His presence, the gratuitous sacrifice of his own life, would have added only another and a needless agony to the last moments of the dying man; but concealment had imparted to a justifiable act much of the secret effect of guilt; and Reuben, while reason told him that he had done right, experienced in no small degree the mental horrors which punish the perpetrator of undiscovered crime. By a certain association of ideas, he at times almost imagined himself a murderer. For years, also, a thought would occasionally recur, which, though he perceived all its folly and extravagance, he had not power to banish from his mind. It was a haunting and torturing fancy that his father-in-law was yet sitting at the foot of the rock, on the withered forest leaves, alive, and awaiting his pledged assistance. These mental deceptions, however, came and went, nor did he ever mistake them for realities; but in the calmest and clearest moods of his mind he was conscious that he had a deep vow unredeemed, and that an unburied corpse was calling to him out of the wilderness. Yet such was the consequence of his prevarication that he could not obey the call. It was now too late to require the assistance of Roger Malvin's friends in performing his long-deferred sepulture; and superstitious fears, of which none were more susceptible than the people of the outward settlements, forbade Reuben to go alone. Neither did he know where in the pathless and illimitable forest to seek that smooth and lettered rock at the base of which the body lay: his remembrance of every portion of his travel thence was indistinct, and the latter part had left no impression upon his mind. There was, however, a continual impulse, a voice audible only to himself, commanding him to go forth and redeem his vow; and he had a strange impression that, were he to make the trial, he would be led straight to Malvin's bones. But year after year that summons, unheard but felt, was disobeyed. His one secret thought became like a chain binding down his spirit and like a serpent gnawing into his heart; and he was transformed into a sad and downcast yet irritable man.

In the course of a few years after their marriage changes began to be visible in the external prosperity of Reuben and Dorcas. The only riches of the former had been his stout heart and strong arm; but the latter, her father's sole heiress, had made her husband master of a farm, under older cultivation, larger, and better stocked than most of the frontier establishments. Reuben Bourne, however, was a neglectful husbandman; and, while the lands of the other settlers became annually more fruitful, his deteriorated in the same proportion. The discouragements to agriculture were greatly lessened by the cessation of Indian war, during which men held the plough in one hand and the musket in the other, and were fortunate if the products of their dangerous labor were not destroyed, either in the field or in the barn, by the savage enemy. But Reuben did not profit by the altered condition of the country; nor can it be denied that his intervals of industrious attention to his affairs were but scantily rewarded with success. The irritability by which he had recently become distinguished, was another cause of his declining prosperity, as it occasioned frequent quarrels in his unavoidable intercourse with the neighboring settlers. The results of these were innumerable lawsuits; for the people of New England, in the earliest stages and wildest circumstances of the country, adopted, whenever attainable, the legal mode of deciding their differences. To be brief, the world did not go well with Reuben Bourne; and, though not till many years after his marriage, he was finally a ruined man, with but one remaining expedient against the evil fate that had pursued him. He was to throw sunlight into some deep recess of the forest, and seek subsistence from the virgin bosom of the wilderness.

The only child of Reuben and Dorcas was a son, now arrived at the age of fifteen years, beautiful in youth, and giving promise of a glorious manhood. He was peculiarly qualified for, and already began to excel in, the wild accomplishments of frontier life. His foot was fleet, his aim true, his apprehension quick, his heart glad and high; and all who anticipated the return of Indian war spoke of Cyrus Bourne as a future leader in the land. The boy was loved by his father with a deep and silent strength, as if whatever was good and happy in his own nature had been transferred to his child, carrying his affections with it. Even Dorcas, though loving and beloved, was far less dear to him; for Reuben's secret thoughts and insulated emotions had gradually made him a selfish man, and he could no longer love deeply except where he saw or imagined some reflection or likeness of his own mind. In Cyrus he recognized what he had himself been in other days; and at intervals he seemed to partake of the boy's spirit and to be revived with a fresh and happy life. Reuben was accompanied by his son in the expedition, for the purpose of selecting a tract of land and felling and burning the timber, which necessarily preceded the removal of the household gods. Two months of autumn were thus occupied; after which Reuben Bourne and his young hunter returned to spend their last winter in the settlements.

*   *   *

It was early in the month of May that the little family snapped asunder whatever tendrils of affections had clung to inanimate objects, and bade farewell to the few who, in the blight of fortune, called themselves their friends. The sadness of the parting moment had, to each of the pilgrims, its peculiar alleviations. Reuben, a moody man, and misanthropic because unhappy, strode onward with his usual stern brow and downcast eye, feeling few regrets and disdaining to acknowledge any. Dorcas, while she wept abundantly over the broken ties by which her simple and affectionate nature had bound itself to every thing, felt that the inhabitants of her inmost heart moved on with her, and that all else would be supplied wherever she might go. And the boy dashed one teardrop from his eye, and thought of the adventurous pleasures of the untrodden forest.

O, who, in the enthusiasm of a daydream, has not wished that he were a wanderer in a world of summer wilderness, with one fair and gentle being hanging lightly on his arm? In youth his free and exulting step would know no barrier but the rolling ocean or the snow-topped mountains; calmer manhood would choose a home where Nature had strewn a double wealth in the vale of some transparent stream; and when hoary age, after long, long years of that pure life, stole on and found him there, it would find him the father of a race, the patriarch of a people, the founder of a mighty nation yet to be. When death, like the sweet sleep which we welcome after a day of happiness, came over him, his far descendants would mourn over the venerated dust. Enveloped by tradition in mysterious attributes, the men of future generations would call him godlike; and remote posterity would see him standing, dimly glorious, far up the valley of a hundred centuries.

The tangled and gloomy forest through which the personages of my tale were wandering differed widely from the dreamer's land of fantasy; yet there was something in their way of life that Nature asserted as her own, and the gnawing cares which went with them from the world were all that now obstructed their happiness. One stout and shaggy steed, the bearer of all their wealth, did not shrink from the added weight of Dorcas; although her hardy breeding sustained her, during the latter part of each day's journey, by her husband's side. Reuben and his son, their muskets on their shoulders and their axes slung behind them, kept an unwearied pace, each watching with a hunter's eye for the game that supplied their food. When hunger bade, they halted and prepared their meal on the bank of some unpolluted forest brook, which, as they knelt down with thirsty lips to drink, murmured a sweet unwillingness, like a maiden at love's first kiss. They slept beneath a hut of branches, and awoke at peep of light refreshed for the toils of another day. Dorcas and the boy went on joyously, and even Reuben's spirit shone at intervals with an outward gladness; but inwardly there was a cold, cold sorrow, which he compared to the snow drifts lying deep in the glens and hollows of the rivulets while the leaves were brightly green above.

Cyrus Bourne was sufficiently skilled in the travel of the woods to observe that his father did not adhere to the course they had pursued in their expedition of the preceding autumn. They were now keeping farther to the north, striking out more directly from the settlements, and into a region of which savage beasts and savage men were as yet the sole possessors. The boy sometimes hinted his opinions upon the subject, and Reuben listened attentively, and once or twice altered the direction of their march in accordance with his son's counsel; but, having so done, he seemed ill at ease. His quick and wandering glances were sent forward, apparently in search of enemies lurking behind the tree trunks; and, seeing nothing there, he would cast his eyes backwards as if in fear of some pursuer. Cyrus, perceiving that his father gradually resumed the old direction, forbore to interfere; nor, though something began to weigh upon his heart, did his adventurous nature permit him to regret the increased length and the mystery of their way.

On the afternoon of the fifth day they halted, and made their simple encampment nearly an hour before sunset. The face of the country, for the last few miles, had been diversified by swells of land resembling huge waves of a petrified sea; and in one of the corresponding hollows, a wild and romantic spot, had the family reared their hut and kindled their fire. There is something chilling, and yet heart-warming, in the thought of these three, united by strong bands of love and insulated from all that breathe beside. The dark and gloomy pines looked down upon them, and, as the wind swept through their tops, a pitying sound was heard in the forest; or did those old trees groan in fear that men were come to lay the axe to their roots at last? Reuben and his son, while Dorcas made ready their meal, proposed to wander out in search of game, of which that day's march had afforded no supply. The boy, promising not to quit the vicinity of the encampment, bounded off with a step as light and elastic as that of the deer he hoped to slay; while his father, feeling a transient happiness as he gazed after him, was about to pursue an opposite direction. Dorcas, in the meanwhile, had seated herself near their fire of fallen branches, upon the moss-grown and mouldering trunk of a tree uprooted years before. Her employment, diversified by an occasional glance at the pot, now beginning to simmer over the blaze, was the perusal of the current year's Massachusetts Almanac, which, with the exception of an old black-letter[2] Bible, comprised all the literary wealth of the family. None pay a greater regard to arbitrary divisions of time than those who are excluded from society; and Dorcas mentioned, as if the information were of importance, that it was now the twelfth of May. Her husband started.

"The twelfth of May! I should remember it well," muttered he, while many thoughts occasioned a momentary confusion in his mind. "Where am I? Whither am I wandering? Where did I leave him?"

Dorcas, too well accustomed to her husband's wayward moods to note any peculiarity of demeanor, now laid aside the almanac and addressed him in that mournful tone which the tender hearted appropriate to griefs long cold and dead.

"It was near this time of the month, eighteen years ago, that my poor father left this world for a better. He had a kind arm to hold his head and a kind voice to cheer him, Reuben, in his last moments; and the thought of the faithful care you took of him has comforted me many a time since. O, death would have been awful to a solitary man in a wild place like this!"

"Pray Heaven, Dorcas," said Reuben, in a broken voice,—"pray Heaven that neither of us three dies solitary and lies unburied in this howling wilderness!" And he hastened away, leaving her to watch the fire beneath the gloomy pines.

Reuben Bourne's rapid pace gradually slackened as the pang, unintentionally inflicted by the words of Dorcas, became less acute. Many strange reflections, however, thronged upon him; and, straying onward rather like a sleep walker than a hunter, it was attributable to no care of his own that his devious course kept him in the vicinity of the encampment. His steps were imperceptibly led almost in a circle; nor did he observe that he was on the verge of a tract of land heavily timbered, but not with pine trees. The place of the latter was here supplied by oaks and other of the harder woods; and around their roots clustered a dense and bushy undergrowth, leaving, however, barren spaces between the trees, thick strewn with withered leaves. Whenever the rustling of the branches or the creaking of the trunks made a sound, as if the forest were waking from slumber, Reuben instinctively raised the musket that rested on his arm, and cast a quick, sharp glance on every side; but, convinced by a partial observation that no animal was near, he would again give himself up to his thoughts. He was musing on the strange influence that had led him away from his premeditated course and so far into the depths of the wilderness. Unable to penetrate to the secret place of his soul where his motives lay hidden, he believed that a supernatural voice had called him onward and that a supernatural power had obstructed his retreat. He trusted that it was Heaven's intent to afford him an opportunity of expiating his sin; he hoped that he might find the bones so long unburied; and that, having laid the earth over them, peace would throw its sunlight into the sepulchre of his heart. From these thoughts he was aroused by a rustling in the forest at some distance from the spot to which he had wandered. Perceiving the motion of some object behind a thick veil of undergrowth, he fired, with the instinct of a hunter and the aim of a practised marksman. A low moan, which told his success, and by which even animals can express their dying agony, was unheeded by Reuben Bourne. What were the recollections now breaking upon him?

The thicket into which Reuben had fired was near the summit of a swell of land, and was clustered around the base of a rock, which, in the shape and smoothness of one of its surfaces, was not unlike a gigantic gravestone. As if reflected in a mirror, its likeness was in Reuben's memory. He even recognized the veins which seemed to form an inscription in forgotten characters: every thing remained the same, except that a thick covert of bushes shrouded the lower part of the rock, and would have hidden Roger Malvin had he still been sitting there. Yet in the next moment Reuben's eye was caught by another change that time had effected since he last stood where he was now standing again behind the earthy roots of the uptorn tree. The sapling to which he had bound the bloodstained symbol of his vow had increased and strengthened into an oak, far indeed from its maturity, but with no mean spread of shadowy branches. There was one singularity observable in this tree which made Reuben tremble. The middle and lower branches were in luxuriant life, and an excess of vegetation had fringed the trunk almost to the ground; but a blight had apparently stricken the upper part of the oak, and the very topmost bough was withered, sapless, and utterly dead. Reuben remembered how the little banner had fluttered on that topmost bough, when it was green and lovely, eighteen years before. Whose guilt had blasted it?

*   *   *

Dorcas, after the departure of the two hunters, continued her preparations for their evening repast. Her sylvan table was the moss-covered trunk of a large fallen tree, on the broadest part of which she had spread a snow-white cloth and arranged what were left of the bright pewter vessels that had been her pride in the settlements. It had a strange aspect, that one little spot of homely comfort in the desolate heart of Nature. The sunshine yet lingered upon the higher branches of the trees that grew on rising ground; but the shadows of evening had deepened into the hollow where the encampment was made, and the firelight began to redden as it gleamed up the tall trunks of the pines or hovered on the dense and obscure mass of foliage that circled round the spot. The heart of Dorcas was not sad; for she felt that it was better to journey in the wilderness with two whom she loved than to be a lonely woman in a crowd that cared not for her. As she busied herself in arranging seats of mouldering wood, covered with leaves, for Reuben and her son, her voice danced through the gloomy forest in the measure of a song that she had learned in youth. The rude melody, the production of a bard who won no name, was descriptive of a winter evening in a frontier cottage, when, secured from savage inroad by the high-piled snow drifts, the family rejoiced by their own fireside. The whole song possessed the nameless charm peculiar to unborrowed thought; but four continually-recurring lines shone out from the rest like the blaze of the hearth whose joys they celebrated. Into them, working magic with a few simple words, the poet had instilled the very essence of domestic love and household happiness, and they were poetry and picture joined in one. As Dorcas sang, the walls of her forsaken home seemed to encircle her; she no longer saw the gloomy pines, nor heard the wind, which still, as she began each verse, sent a heavy breath through the branches and died away in a hollow moan from the burden of the song. She was aroused by the report of a gun in the vicinity of the encampment; and either the sudden sound or her loneliness by the glowing fire caused her to tremble violently. The next moment she laughed in the pride of a mother's heart.

"My beautiful young hunter! My boy has slain a deer!" she exclaimed, recollecting that in the direction whence the shot proceeded Cyrus had gone to the chase.

She waited a reasonable time to hear her son's light step bounding over the rustling leaves to tell of his success. But he did not immediately appear; and she sent her cheerful voice among the trees in search of him.

"Cyrus! Cyrus!"

His coming was still delayed; and she determined, as the report had apparently been very near, to seek for him in person. Her assistance, also, might be necessary in bringing home the venison which she flattered herself he had obtained. She therefore set forward, directing her steps by the long-past sound, and singing as she went, in order that the boy might be aware of her approach and run to meet her. From behind the trunk of every tree and from every hiding-place in the thick foliage of the undergrowth she hoped to discover the countenance of her son, laughing with the sportive mischief that is born of affection. The sun was now beneath the horizon, and the light that came down among the trees was sufficiently dim to create many illusions in her expecting fancy. Several times she seemed indistinctly to see his face gazing out from among the leaves; and once she imagined that he stood beckoning to her at the base of a craggy rock. Keeping her eyes on this object, however, it proved to be no more than the trunk of an oak, fringed to the very ground with little branches, one of which, thrust out farther than the rest, was shaken by the breeze. Making her way round the foot of the rock, she suddenly found herself close to her husband, who had approached in another direction. Leaning upon the butt of his gun, the muzzle of which rested upon the withered leaves, he was apparently absorbed in the contemplation of some object at his feet.

"How is this, Reuben? Have you slain the deer and fallen asleep over him?" exclaimed Dorcas, laughing cheerfully, on her first slight observation of his posture and appearance.

He stirred not, neither did he turn his eyes towards her; and a cold, shuddering fear, indefinite in its source and object, began to creep into her blood. She now perceived that her husband's face was ghastly pale, and his features were rigid, as if incapable of assuming any other expression than the strong despair which had hardened upon them. He gave not the slightest evidence that he was aware of her approach.

"For the love of Heaven, Reuben, speak to me!" cried Dorcas; and the strange sound of her own voice affrighted her even more than the dead silence.

Her husband started, stared into her face, drew her to the front of the rock, and pointed with his finger.

O, there lay the boy, asleep, but dreamless, upon the fallen forest leaves! His cheek rested upon his arm—his curled locks were thrown back from his brow—his limbs were slightly relaxed. Had a sudden weariness overcome the youthful hunter? Would his mother's voice arouse him? She knew that it was death.

"This broad rock is the gravestone of your near kindred, Dorcas," said her husband. "Your tears will fall at once over your father and your son."

She heard him not. With one wild shriek, that seemed to force its way from the sufferer's inmost soul, she sank insensible by the side of her dead boy. At that moment the withered topmost bough of the oak loosened itself in the stilly air, and fell in soft, light fragments upon the rock, upon the leaves, upon Reuben, upon his wife and child, and upon Roger Malvin's bones. Then Reuben's heart was stricken, and the tears gushed out like water from a rock. The vow that the wounded youth had made the blighted man had come to redeem. His sin was expiated—the curse was gone from him; and in the hour when he had shed blood dearer to him than his own, a prayer, the first for years, went up to Heaven from the lips of Reuben Bourne.

P.'s Correspondence

My unfortunate friend P. has lost the thread of his life by the interposition of long intervals of partially disordered reason. The past and present are jumbled together in his mind in a manner often productive of curious results, and which will be better understood after the perusal of the following letter than from any description that I could give. The poor fellow, without once stirring from the little whitewashed, iron-grated room to which he alludes in his first paragraph, is nevertheless a great traveller, and meets in his wanderings a variety of personages who have long ceased to be visible to any eye save his own. In my opinion, all this is not so much a delusion as a partly wilful and partly involuntary sport of the imagination, to which his disease has imparted such morbid energy that he beholds these spectral scenes and characters with no less distinctness than a play upon the stage, and with somewhat more of illusive credence. Many of his letters are in my possession, some based upon the same vagary as the present one, and others upon hypotheses not a whit short of it in absurdity. The whole form a series of correspondence, which, should fate seasonably remove my poor friend from what is to him a world of moonshine, I promise myself a pious pleasure in editing for the public eye. P. had always a hankering after literary reputation, and has made more than one unsuccessful effort to achieve it. It would not be a little odd if, after missing his object while seeking it by the light of reason, he should prove to have stumbled upon it in his misty excursions beyond the limits of sanity.

LONDON, FEBRUARY 29, 1845.

MY DEAR FRIEND: Old associations cling to the mind with astonishing tenacity. Daily custom grows up about us like a stone wall, and consolidates itself into almost as material an entity as mankind's strongest architecture. It is sometimes a serious question with me whether ideas be not really visible and tangible and endowed with all the other qualities of matter. Sitting as I do at this moment in my hired apartment, writing beside the hearth, over which hangs a print of Queen Victoria,[1] listening to the muffled roar of the world's metropolis, and with a window at but five paces distant, through which, whenever I please, I can gaze out on actual London,—with all this positive certainty as to my whereabouts, what kind of notion, do you think, is just now perplexing my brain? Why,—would you believe it?—that all this time I am still an inhabitant of that wearisome little chamber—that whitewashed little chamber—that little chamber with its one small window, across which, from some inscrutable reason of taste or convenience, my landlord had placed a row of iron bars—that same little chamber, in short, whither your kindness has so often brought you to visit me! Will no length of time or breadth of space enfranchise me from that unlovely abode? I travel; but it seems to be like the snail, with my house upon my head. Ah, well! I am verging, I suppose, on that period of life when present scenes and events make but feeble impressions in comparison with those of yore; so that I must reconcile myself to be more and more the prisoner of Memory, who merely lets me hop about a little with her chain around my leg.

My letters of introduction have been of the utmost service, enabling me to make the acquaintance of several distinguished characters who, until now, have seemed as remote from the sphere of my personal intercourse as the wits of Queen Anne's time[2] or Ben Jonson's compotators at the Mermaid.[3] One of the first of which I availed myself was the letter to Lord Byron.[4] I found his lordship looking much older than I had anticipated, although, considering his former irregularities of life and the various wear and tear of his constitution, not older than a man on the verge of sixty reasonably may look. But I had invested his earthly frame, in my imagination, with the poet's spiritual immortality. He wears a brown wig, very luxuriantly curled, and extending down over his forehead. The expression of his eyes is concealed by spectacles. His early tendency to obesity having increased, Lord Byron is now enormously fat—so fat as to give the impression of a person quite overladen with his own flesh, and without sufficient vigor to diffuse his personal life through the great mass of corporeal substance which weighs upon him so cruelly. You gaze at the mortal heap; and, while it fills your eye with what purports to be Byron, you murmur within yourself, "For Heaven's sake, where is he?" Were I disposed to be caustic, I might consider this mass of earthly matter as the symbol, in a material shape, of those evil habits and carnal vices which unspiritualize man's nature and clog up his avenues of communication with the better life. But this would be too harsh; and, besides, Lord Byron's morals have been improving while his outward man has swollen to such unconscionable circumference. Would that he were leaner; for, though he did me the honor to present his hand, yet it was so puffed out with alien substance that I could not feel as if I had touched the hand that wrote Childe Harold.[5]

On my entrance his lordship apologized for not rising to receive me, on the sufficient plea that the gout[6] for several years past had taken up its constant residence in his right foot, which accordingly was swathed in many rolls of flannel and deposited upon a cushion. The other foot was hidden in the drapery of his chair. Do you recollect whether Byron's right or left foot was the deformed one?[7]

The noble poet's reconciliation with Lady Byron[8] is now, as you are aware, of ten years' standing; nor does it exhibit, I am assured, any symptom of breach or fracture. They are said to be, if not a happy, at least a contented, or at all events a quiet couple, descending the slope of life with that tolerable degree of mutual support which will enable them to come easily and comfortably to the bottom. It is pleasant to reflect how entirely the poet has redeemed his youthful errors in this particular. Her ladyship's influence, it rejoices me to add, has been productive of the happiest results upon Lord Byron in a religious point of view. He now combines the most rigid tenets of Methodism with the ultra doctrines of the Puseyites;[9] the former being perhaps due to the convictions wrought upon his mind by his noble consort, while the latter are the embroidery and picturesque illumination demanded by his imaginative character. Much of whatever expenditure his increasing habits of thrift continue to allow him is bestowed in the reparation or beautifying of places of worship; and this nobleman, whose name was once considered a synonyme of the foul fiend, is now all but canonized as a saint in many pulpits of the metropolis and elsewhere. In politics, Lord Byron is an uncompromising conservative, and loses no opportunity, whether in the House of Lords[10] or in private circles, of denouncing and repudiating the mischievous and anarchical notions of his earlier day. Nor does he fail to visit similar sins in other people with the sincerest vengeance which his somewhat blunted pen is capable of inflicting. Southey[11] and he are on the most intimate terms. You are aware that, some little time before the death of Moore,[12] Byron caused that brilliant but reprehensible man to be ejected from his house. Moore took the insult so much to heart that it is said to have been one great cause of the fit of illness which brought him to the grave. Others pretend that the lyrist died in a very happy state of mind, singing one of his own sacred melodies, and expressing his belief that it would be heard within the gate of paradise, and gain him instant and honorable admittance. I wish he may have found it so.

I failed not, as you may suppose, in the course of conversation with Lord Byron, to pay the meed of homage due to a mighty poet, by allusions to passages in Childe Harold, and Manfred, and Don Juan[13] which have made so large a portion of the music of my life. My words, whether apt or otherwise, were at least warm with the enthusiasm of one worthy to discourse of immortal poesy. It was evident, however, that they did not go precisely to the right spot. I could perceive that there was some mistake or other, and was not a little angry with myself, and ashamed of my abortive attempt to throw back, from my own heart to the gifted author's ear, the echo of those strains that have resounded throughout the world. But by and by the secret peeped quietly out. Byron,—I have the information from his own lips, so that you need not hesitate to repeat it in literary circles,—Byron is preparing a new edition of his complete works, carefully corrected, expurgated, and amended, in accordance with his present creed of taste, morals, politics, and religion. It so happened that the very passages of highest inspiration to which I had alluded were among the condemned and rejected rubbish which it is his purpose to cast into the gulf of oblivion. To whisper you the truth, it appears to me that his passions having burned out, the extinction of their vivid and riotous flame has deprived Lord Byron of the illumination by which he not merely wrote, but was enabled to feel and comprehend what he had written. Positively he no longer understands his own poetry.

This became very apparent on his favoring me so far as to read a few specimens of Don Juan in the moralized version. Whatever is licentious, whatever disrespectful to the sacred mysteries of our faith, whatever morbidly melancholic or splenetically sportive, whatever assails settled constitutions of government or systems of society, whatever could wound the sensibility of any mortal, except a pagan, a republican, or a dissenter, has been unrelentingly blotted out, and its place supplied by unexceptionable verses in his lordship's later style. You may judge how much of the poem remains as hitherto published. The result is not so good as might be wished; in plain terms, it is a very sad affair indeed; for, though the torches kindled in Tophet[14] have been extinguished, they leave an abominably ill odor, and are succeeded by no glimpses of hallowed fire. It is to be hoped, nevertheless, that this attempt on Lord Byron's part to atone for his youthful errors will at length induce the Dean of Westminster, or whatever churchman is concerned, to allow Thorwaldsen's statue of the poet[15] its due niche in the grand old Abbey.[16] His bones, you know, when brought from Greece, were denied sepulture[17] among those of his tuneful brethren there.

What a vile slip of the pen was that! How absurd in me to talk about burying the bones of Byron, whom I have just seen alive, and incased in a big, round bulk of flesh! But, to say the truth, a prodigiously fat man always impresses me as a kind of hobgoblin; in the very extravagance of his mortal system I find something akin to the immateriality of a ghost. And then that ridiculous old story darted into my mind, how that Byron died of fever at Missolonghi,[18] above twenty years ago. More and more I recognize that we dwell in a world of shadows; and, for my part, I hold it hardly worth the trouble to attempt a distinction between shadows in the mind and shadows out of it. If there be any difference, the former are rather the more substantial.

Only think of my good fortune! The venerable Robert Burns[19]— now, if I mistake not, in his eighty-seventh year—happens to be making a visit to London, as if on purpose to afford me an opportunity of grasping him by the hand. For upwards of twenty years past he has hardly left his quiet cottage in Ayrshire[20] for a single night, and has only been drawn hither now by the irresistible persuasions of all the distinguished men in England. They wish to celebrate the patriarch's birthday by a festival. It will be the greatest literary triumph on record. Pray Heaven the little spirit of life within the aged bard's bosom may not be extinguished in the lustre of that hour! I have already had the honor of an introduction to him at the British Museum, where he was examining a collection of his own unpublished letters, interspersed with songs, which have escaped the notice of all his biographers.

Poh! Nonsense! What am I thinking of? How should Burns have been embalmed in biography when he is still a hearty old man?

The figure of the bard is tall and in the highest degree reverend, nor the less so that it is much bent by the burden of time. His white hair floats like a snow drift around his face, in which are seen the furrows of intellect and passion, like the channels of headlong torrents that have foamed themselves away. The old gentleman is in excellent preservation considering his time of life. He has that crickety sort of liveliness—I mean the cricket's humor of chirping for any cause or none—which is perhaps the most favorable mood that can befall extreme old age. Our pride forbids us to desire it for ourselves, although we perceive it to be a beneficence of nature in the case of others. I was surprised to find it in Burns. It seems as if his ardent heart and brilliant imagination had both burned down to the last embers, leaving only a little flickering flame in one corner, which keeps dancing upward and laughing all by itself. He is no longer capable of pathos. At the request of Allan Cunningham,[21] he attempted to sing his own song to Mary in Heaven;[22] but it was evident that the feeling of those verses, so profoundly true and so simply expressed, was entirely beyond the scope of his present sensibilities; and, when a touch of it did partially awaken him, the tears immediately gushed into his eyes and his voice broke into a tremulous cackle. And yet he but indistinctly knew wherefore he was weeping. Ah, he must not think again of Mary in Heaven until he shake off the dull impediment of time and ascend to meet her there.

Burns then began to repeat Tam O'Shanter;[23] but was so tickled with its wit and humor—of which, however, I suspect he had but a traditionary sense—that he soon burst into a fit of chirruping laughter, succeeded by a cough, which brought this not very agreeable exhibition to a close. On the whole, I would rather not have witnessed it. It is a satisfactory idea, however, that the last forty years of the peasant poet's life have been passed in competence and perfect comfort. Having been cured of his bardic improvidence for many a day past, and grown as attentive to the main chance as a canny Scotsman should be, he is now considered to be quite well off as to pecuniary circumstances. This, I suppose, is worth having lived so long for.

I took occasion to inquire of some of the countrymen of Burns in regard to the health of Sir Walter Scott.[24] His condition, I am sorry to say, remains the same as for ten years past; it is that of a hopeless paralytic, palsied not more in body than in those nobler attributes of which the body is the instrument. And thus he vegetates from day to day and from year to year at that splendid fantasy of Abbotsford,[25] which grew out of his brain, and became a symbol of the great romancer's tastes, feelings, studies, prejudices, and modes of intellect. Whether in verse, prose, or architecture, he could achieve but one thing, although that one in infinite variety. There he reclines, on a couch in his library, and is said to spend whole hours of every day in dictating tales to an amanuensis[26]—to an imaginary amanuensis; for it is not deemed worth any one's trouble now to take down what flows from that once brilliant fancy, every image of which was formerly worth gold and capable of being coined. Yet Cunningham, who has lately seen him, assures me that there is now and then a touch of the genius—a striking combination of incident, or a picturesque trait of character, such as no other man alive could have hit off—a glimmer from that ruined mind, as if the sun had suddenly flashed on a half-rusted helmet in the gloom of an ancient hall. But the plots of these romances become inextricably confused; the characters melt into one another; and the tale loses itself like the course of a stream flowing through muddy and marshy ground.

For my part, I can hardly regret that Sir Walter Scott had lost his consciousness of outward things before his works went out of vogue. It was good that he should forget his fame rather than that fame should first have forgotten him. Were he still a writer, and as brilliant a one as ever, he could no longer maintain any thing like the same position in literature. The world, nowadays, requires a more earnest purpose, a deeper moral, and a closer and homelier truth than he was qualified to supply it with. Yet who can be to the present generation even what Scott has been to the past? I had expectations from a young man—one Dickens[27]—who published a few magazine articles, very rich in humor, and not without symptoms of genuine pathos; but the poor fellow died shortly after commencing an odd series of sketches, entitled, I think, the Pickwick Papers.[28] Not impossibly the world has lost more than it dreams of by the untimely death of this Mr. Dickens.

Whom do you think I met in Pall Mall[29] the other day? You would not hit it in ten guesses. Why, no less a man than Napoleon Bonaparte,[30] or all that is now left of him—that is to say, the skin, bones, and corporeal substance, little cocked hat, green coat, white breeches, and small sword, which are still known by his redoubtable name. He was attended only by two policemen, who walked quietly behind the phantasm of the old ex-emperor, appearing to have no duty in regard to him except to see that none of the light-fingered gentry should possess themselves of the star of the Legion of Honor.[31] Nobody save myself so much as turned to look after him; nor, it grieves me to confess, could even I contrive to muster up any tolerable interest, even by all that the warlike spirit, formerly manifested within that now decrepit shape, had wrought upon our globe. There is no surer method of annihilating the magic influence of a great renown than by exhibiting the possessor of it in the decline, the overthrow, the utter degradation of his powers,—buried beneath his own mortality,—and lacking even the qualities of sense that enable the most ordinary men to bear themselves decently in the eye of the world. This is the state to which disease, aggravated by long endurance of a tropical climate, and assisted by old age,—for he is now above seventy,—has reduced Bonaparte. The British government has acted shrewdly in retransporting him from St. Helena[32] to England. They should now restore him to Paris, and there let him once again review the relics of his armies. His eye is dull and rheumy; his nether lip hung down upon his chin. While I was observing him there chanced to be a little extra bustle in the street; and he, the brother of Cæsar and Hannibal,[33]—the great captain who had veiled the world in battle smoke and tracked it round with bloody footsteps,—was seized with a nervous trembling, and claimed the protection of the two policemen by a cracked and dolorous cry. The fellows winked at one another, laughed aside, and, patting Napoleon on the back, took each an arm and led him away.

Death and fury! Ha, villain, how came you hither? Avaunt! or I fling my inkstand at your head. Tush, tush; it is all a mistake. Pray, my dear friend, pardon this little outbreak. The fact is, the mention of those two policemen, and their custody of Bonaparte, had called up the idea of that odious wretch—you remember him well—who was pleased to take such gratuitous and impertinent care of my person before I quitted New England. Forthwith up rose before my mind's eye that same little whitewashed room, with the iron-grated window,—strange that it should have been iron-grated!—where, in too easy compliance with the absurd wishes of my relatives, I have wasted several good years of my life. Positively it seemed to me that I was still sitting there, and that the keeper—not that he ever was my keeper neither, but only a kind of intrusive devil of a body servant—had just peeped in at the door. The rascal! I owe him an old grudge, and will find a time to pay it yet. Fie! fie! The mere thought of him has exceedingly discomposed me. Even now that hateful chamber—the iron-grated window, which blasted the blessed sunshine as it fell through the dusty panes and made it poison to my soul—looks more distinct to my view than does this my comfortable apartment in the heart of London. The reality—that which I know to be such—hangs like remnants of tattered scenery over the intolerably prominent illusion. Let us think of it no more.

You will be anxious to hear of Shelley.[34] I need not say, what is known to all the world, that this celebrated poet has for many years past been reconciled to the church of England. In his more recent works he has applied his fine powers to the vindication of the Christian faith, with an especial view to that particular development. Latterly, as you may not have heard, he has taken orders,[35] and been inducted to a small country living in the gift of the lord chancellor. Just now, luckily for me, he has come to the metropolis to superintend the publication of a volume of discourses treating of the poeticophilosophical proofs of Christianity on the basis of the Thirty-nine Articles.[36] On my first introduction I felt no little embarrassment as to the manner of combining what I had to say to the author of Queen Mab, the Revolt of Islam, and Prometheus Unbound[37] with such acknowledgments as might be acceptable to a Christian minister and zealous upholder of the established church. But Shelley soon placed me at my ease. Standing where he now does, and reviewing all his successive productions from a higher point, he assures me that there is a harmony, an order, a regular procession, which enables him to lay his hand upon any one of the earlier poems and say, "This is my work," with precisely the same complacency of conscience wherewithal he contemplates the volume of discourses above mentioned. They are like the successive steps of a staircase, the lowest of which, in the depth of chaos, is as essential to the support of the whole as the highest and final one resting upon the threshold of the heavens. I felt half inclined to ask him what would have been his fate had he perished on the lower steps of his staircase instead of building his way aloft into the celestial brightness.

How all this may be I neither pretend to understand nor greatly care, so long as Shelley has really climbed, as it seems he has, from a lower region to a loftier one. Without touching upon their religious merits, I consider the productions of his maturity superior, as poems, to those of his youth. They are warmer with human love, which has served as an interpreter between his mind and the multitude. The author has learned to dip his pen oftener into his heart, and has thereby avoided the faults into which a too exclusive use of fancy and intellect are wont to betray him. Formerly his page was often little other than a concrete arrangement of crystallizations, or even of icicles, as cold as they were brilliant. Now you take it to your heart, and are conscious of a heart warmth responsive to your own. In his private character Shelley can hardly have grown more gentle, kind, and affectionate than his friends always represented him to be up to that disastrous night when he was drowned in the Mediterranean. Nonsense, again—sheer nonsense! What am I babbling about? I was thinking of that old figment of his being lost in the Bay of Spezzia,[38] and washed ashore near Via Reggio, and burned to ashes on a funeral pyre, with wine, and spices, and frankincense; while Byron stood on the beach and beheld a flame of marvellous beauty rise heavenward from the dead poet's heart, and that his fire-purified relics were finally buried near his child in Roman earth. If all this happened three and twenty years ago, how could I have met the drowned, and burned, and buried man here in London only yesterday?

Before quitting the subject, I may mention that Dr. Reginald Heber,[39] heretofore Bishop of Calcutta, but recently translated to a see[40] in England, called on Shelley while I was with him. They appeared to be on terms of very cordial intimacy, and are said to have a joint poem in contemplation. What a strange, incongruous dream is the life of man!

Coleridge[41] has at last finished his poem of Christabel.[42] It will be issued entire by old John Murray[43] in the course of the present publishing season. The poet, I hear, is visited with a troublesome affection of the tongue, which has put a period, or some lesser stop, to the life-long discourse that has hitherto been flowing from his lips. He will not survive it above a month unless his accumulation of ideas be sluiced off in some other way. Wordsworth[44] died only a week or two ago. Heaven rest his soul, and grant that he may not have completed The Excursion![45] Methinks I am sick of every thing he wrote except his Laodamia.[46] It is very sad, this inconstancy of the mind to the poets whom it once worshipped. Southey[47] is as hale as ever, and writes with his usual diligence. Old Gifford[48] is still alive, in the extremity of age, and with most pitiable decay of what little sharp and narrow intellect the devil had gifted him withal. One hates to allow such a man the privilege of growing old and infirm. It takes away our speculative license of kicking him.

Keats?[49] No; I have not seen him except across a crowded street, with coaches, drays, horsemen, cabs, omnibuses, foot passengers, and divers other sensual obstructions intervening betwixt his small and slender figure and my eager glance. I would fain have met him on the sea shore, or beneath a natural arch of forest trees, or the Gothic arch of an old cathedral, or among Grecian ruins, or at a glimmering fire-side on the verge of evening, or at the twilight entrance of a cave, into the dreamy depths of which he would have led me by the hand; any where, in short, save at Temple Bar,[50] where his presence was blotted out by the porter-swollen[51] bulks of these gross Englishmen. I stood and watched him fading away, fading away along the pavement, and could hardly tell whether he were an actual man or a thought that had slipped out of my mind and clothed itself in human form and habiliments merely to beguile me. At one moment he put his handkerchief to his lips, and withdrew it, I am almost certain, stained with blood. You never saw any thing so fragile as his person. The truth is, Keats has all his life felt the effects of that terrible bleeding at the lungs[52] caused by the article on his Endymion[53] in the Quarterly Review,[54] and which so nearly brought him to the grave. Ever since he has glided about the world like a ghost, sighing a melancholy tone in the ear of here and there a friend, but never sending forth his voice to greet the multitude. I can hardly think him a great poet. The burden of a mighty genius would never have been imposed upon shoulders so physically frail and a spirit so infirmly sensitive. Great poets should have iron sinews.

Yet Keats, though for so many years he has given nothing to the world, is understood to have devoted himself to the composition of an epic poem. Some passages of it have been communicated to the inner circle of his admirers, and impressed them as the loftiest strains that have been audible on earth since Milton's days.[55] If I can obtain copies of these specimens, I will ask you to present them to James Russell Lowell,[56] who seems to be one of the poet's most fervent and worthiest worshippers. The information took me by surprise. I had supposed that all Keats's poetic incense, without being imbodied in human language, floated up to heaven and mingled with the songs of the immortal choristers, who perhaps were conscious of an unknown voice among them, and thought their melody the sweeter for it. But it is not so; he has positively written a poem on the subject of Paradise Regained,[57] though in another sense than that which presented itself to the mind of Milton. In compliance, it may be imagined, with the dogma of those who pretend that all epic possibilities in the past history of the world are exhausted, Keats has thrown his poem forward into an indefinitely remote futurity. He pictures mankind amid the closing circumstances of the timelong warfare between good and evil. Our race is on the eve of its final triumph. Man is within the last stride of perfection; Woman, redeemed from the thraldom against which our sibyl[58] uplifts so powerful and so sad a remonstrance, stands equal by his side or communes for herself with angels; the Earth, sympathizing with her children's happier state, has clothed herself in such luxuriant and loving beauty as no eye ever witnessed since our first parents saw the sun rise over dewy Eden. Nor then indeed; for this is the fulfilment of what was then but a golden promise. But the picture has its shadows. There remains to mankind another peril—a last encounter with the evil principle. Should the battle go against us, we sink back into the slime and misery of ages. If we triumph—— But it demands a poet's eye to contemplate the splendor of such a consummation and not to be dazzled.

To this great work Keats is said to have brought so deep and tender a spirit of humanity that the poem has all the sweet and warm interest of a village tale no less than the grandeur which befits so high a theme. Such, at least, is the perhaps partial representation of his friends; for I have not read or heard even a single line of the performance in question. Keats, I am told, withholds it from the press, under an idea that the age has not enough of spiritual insight to receive it worthily. I do not like this distrust; it makes me distrust the poet. The universe is waiting to respond to the highest word that the best child of time and immortality can utter. If it refuse to listen, it is because he mumbles and stammers, or discourses things unseasonable and foreign to the purpose.

I visited the House of Lords[59] the other day to hear Canning,[60] who, you know, is now a peer, with I forget what title. He disappointed me. Time blunts both point and edge, and does great mischief to men of his order of intellect. Then I stepped into the lower house and listened to a few words from Cobbett,[61] who looked as earthy as a real clodhopper, or rather as if he had lain a dozen years beneath the clods. The men whom I meet nowadays often impress me thus; probably because my spirits are not very good, and lead me to think much about graves, with the long grass upon them, and weather-worn epitaphs, and dry bones of people who made noise enough in their day, but now can only clatter, clatter, clatter when the sexton's spade disturbs them. Were it only possible to find out who are alive and who dead, it would contribute infinitely to my peace of mind. Every day of my life somebody comes and stares me in the face whom I had quietly blotted out of the tablet of living men, and trusted nevermore to be pestered with the sight or sound of him. For instance, going to Drury Lane Theatre[62] a few evenings since, up rose before me, in the ghost of Hamlet's father, the bodily presence of the elder Kean,[63] who did die, or ought to have died, in some drunken fit or other, so long ago that his fame is scarcely traditionary now. His powers are quite gone; he was rather the ghost of himself than the ghost of the Danish king.

In the stage box sat several elderly and decrepit people, and among them a stately ruin of a woman on a very large scale, with a profile— for I did not see her front face—that stamped itself into my brain as a seal impresses hot wax. By the tragic gesture with which she took a pinch of snuff, I was sure it must be Mrs. Siddons.[64] Her brother, John Kemble,[65] sat behind—a broken-down figure, but still with a kingly majesty about him. In lieu of all former achievements, Nature enables him to look the part of Lear far better than in the meridian of his genius. Charles Matthews[66] was likewise there; but a paralytic affection has distorted his once mobile countenance into a most disagreeable onesidedness, from which he could no more wrench it into proper form than he could rearrange the face of the great globe itself. It looks as if, for the joke's sake, the poor man had twisted his features into an expression at once the most ludicrous and horrible that he could contrive, and at that very moment, as a judgment for making himself so hideous, an avenging Providence had seen fit to petrify him. Since it is out of his own power, I would gladly assist him to change countenance, for his ugly visage haunts me both at noontide and nighttime. Some other players of the past generation were present, but none that greatly interested me. It behooves actors, more than all other men of publicity, to vanish from the scene betimes. Being at best but painted shadows flickering on the wall and empty sounds that echo another's thought, it is a sad disenchantment when the colors begin to fade and the voice to croak with age.

What is there new in the literary way on your side of the water? Nothing of the kind has come under my inspection except a volume of poems published above a year ago by Dr. Channing.[67] I did not before know that this eminent writer is a poet; nor does the volume alluded to exhibit any of the characteristics of the author's mind as displayed in his prose works; although some of the poems have a richness that is not merely of the surface, but glows still the brighter, the deeper and more faithfully you look into them. They seem carelessly wrought, however, like those rings and ornaments of the very purest gold, but of rude, native manufacture, which are found among the gold dust from Africa. I doubt whether the American public will accept them; it looks less to the assay of metal than to the neat and cunning manufacture. How slowly our literature grows up! Most of our writers of promise have come to untimely ends. There was that wild fellow, John Neal,[68] who almost turned my boyish brain with his romances; he surely has long been dead, else he never could keep himself so quiet. Bryant has gone to his last sleep, with the Thanatopsis[69] gleaming over him like a sculptured marble sepulchre by moonlight. Halleck, who used to write queer verses in the newspapers and published a Don Juanic poem called Fanny,[70] is defunct as a poet, though averred to be exemplifying the metempsychosis[71] as a man of business. Somewhat later there was Whittier,[72] a fiery Quaker youth, to whom the muse had perversely assigned a battle trumpet, and who got himself lynched, ten years agone, in South Carolina. I remember, too, a lad just from college, Longfellow[73] by name, who scattered some delicate verses to the winds, and went to Germany, and perished, I think, of intense application, at the University of Gottingen. Willis[74]—what a pity!—was lost, if I recollect rightly, in 1833, on his voyage to Europe, whither he was going to give us sketches of the world's sunny face. If these had lived, they might, one or all of them, have grown to be famous men.

And yet there is no telling; it may be as well that they have died. I was myself a young man of promise. O shattered brain, O broken spirit, where is the fulfilment of that promise? The sad truth is, that, when fate would gently disappoint the world, it takes away the hopefulest mortals in their youth; when it would laugh the world's hopes to scorn, it lets them live. Let me die upon this apothegm, for I shall never make a truer one.

What a strange substance is the human brain! Or rather,—for there is no need of generalizing the remark,—what an odd brain is mine! Would you believe it? Daily and nightly there come scraps of poetry humming in my intellectual ear—some as airy as bird notes, and some as delicately neat as parlor music, and a few as grand as organ peals—

that seem just such verses as those departed poets would have written had not an inexorable destiny snatched them from their inkstands. They visit me in spirit, perhaps desiring to engage my services as the amanuensis of their posthumous productions, and thus secure the endless renown that they have forfeited by going hence too early. But I have my own business to attend to; and besides, a medical gentleman, who interests himself in some little ailments of mine, advises me not to make too free use of pen and ink. There are clerks enough out of employment who would be glad of such a job.

Good by! Are you alive or dead? and what are you about? Still scribbling for the Democratic?[75] And do those infernal compositors and proof readers misprint your unfortunate productions as vilely as ever? It is too bad. Let every man manufacture his own nonsense, say I. Expect me home soon, and—to whisper you a secret—in company with the poet Campbell,[76] who purposes to visit Wyoming and enjoy the shadow of the laurels that he planted there. Campbell is now an old man. He calls himself well, better than ever in his life, but looks strangely pale, and so shadow-like that one might almost poke a finger through his densest material. I tell him, by way of joke, that he is as dim and forlorn as Memory, though as unsubstantial as Hope.

YOUR TRUE FRIEND,
P.

P.S.—Pray present my most respectful regards to our venerable and revered friend Mr. Brockden Brown.[77] It gratifies me to learn that a complete edition of his works, in a double-columned octavo volume, is shortly to issue from the press at Philadelphia. Tell him that no American writer enjoys a more classic reputation on this side of the water. *Is* old Joel Barlow[78] yet alive? Unconscionable man! Why, he must have nearly fulfilled his century. And *does* he meditate an epic on the war between Mexico and Texas[79] with machinery contrived on the principle of the steam engine, as being the nearest to celestial agency that our epoch can boast? How can he expect ever to rise again, if, while just sinking into his grave, he persists in burdening himself with such a ponderosity of leaden verses?

Earth's Holocaust

Once upon a time—but whether in the time past or time to come is a matter of little or no moment—this wide world had become so overburdened with an accumulation of wornout trumpery that the inhabitants determined to rid themselves of it by a general bonfire. The site fixed upon at the representation of the insurance companies, and as being as central a spot as any other on the globe, was one of the broadest prairies of the west, where no human habitation would be endangered by the flames, and where a vast assemblage of spectators might commodiously admire the show. Having a taste for sights of this kind, and imagining, likewise, that the illumination of the bonfire might reveal some profundity of moral truth heretofore hidden in mist or darkness, I made it convenient to journey thither and be present. At my arrival, although the heap of condemned rubbish was as yet comparatively small, the torch had already been applied. Amid that boundless plain, in the dusk of the evening, like a far-off star alone in the firmament, there was merely visible one tremulous gleam, whence none could have anticipated so fierce a blaze as was destined to ensue. With every moment, however, there came foot travellers, women holding up their aprons, men on horseback, wheelbarrows, lumbering baggage wagons, and other vehicles, great and small, and from far and near, laden with articles that were judged fit for nothing but to be burned.

"What materials have been used to kindle the flame?" inquired I of a bystander; for I was desirous of knowing the whole process of the affair from beginning to end.

The person whom I addressed was a grave man, fifty years old or thereabout, who had evidently come thither as a looker on. He struck me immediately as having weighed for himself the true value of life and its circumstances, and therefore as feeling little personal interest in whatever judgment the world might form of them. Before answering my question, he looked me in the face by the kindling light of the fire.

"O, some very dry combustibles," replied he, "and extremely suitable to the purpose—no other, in fact, than yesterday's newspapers, last month's magazines, and last year's withered leaves. Here now comes some antiquated trash that will take fire like a handful of shavings."

As he spoke, some rough-looking men advanced to the verge of the bonfire, and threw in, as it appeared, all the rubbish of the herald's office—the blazonry of coat armor, the crests and devices of illustrious families, pedigrees that extended back, like lines of light, into the mist of the dark ages, together with stars, garters, and embroidered collars, each of which, as paltry a bawble as it might appear to the uninstructed eye, had once possessed vast significance, and was still, in truth, reckoned among the most precious of moral or material facts by the worshippers of the gorgeous past. Mingled with this confused heap, which was tossed into the flames by armfuls at once, were innumerable badges of knighthood, comprising those of all the European sovereignties, and Napoleon's decoration of the Legion of Honor,[1] the ribbons of which were entangled with those of the ancient order of St. Louis.[2] There, too, were the medals of our own Society of Cincinnati,[3] by means of which, as history tells us, an order of hereditary knights came near being constituted out of the king quellers of the revolution. And besides, there were the patents of nobility of German counts and barons, Spanish grandees, and English peers, from the wormeaten instruments signed by William the Conqueror[4] down to the brand new parchment of the latest lord who has received his honors from the fair hand of Victoria.[5]

At sight of the dense volumes of smoke, mingled with vivid jets of flame, that gushed and eddied forth from this immense pile of earthly distinctions, the multitude of plebeian spectators set up a joyous shout, and clapped their hands with an emphasis that made the welkin echo. That was their moment of triumph, achieved, after long ages, over creatures of the same clay and the same spiritual infirmities, who had dared to assume the privileges due only to Heaven's better workmanship. But now there rushed towards the blazing heap a grayhaired man, of stately presence, wearing a coat, from the breast of which a star, or other badge of rank, seemed to have been forcibly wrenched away. He had not the tokens of intellectual power in his face; but still there was the demeanor, the habitual and almost native dignity, of one who had been born to the idea of his own social superiority, and had never felt it questioned till that moment.

"People," cried he, gazing at the ruin of what was dearest to his eyes with grief and wonder, but nevertheless with a degree of stateliness,— "people, what have you done? This fire is consuming all that marked your advance from barbarism, or that could have prevented your relapse thither. We, the men of the privileged orders, were those who kept alive from age to age the old chivalrous spirit; the gentle and generous thought; the higher, the purer, the more refined and delicate life. With the nobles, too, you cast off the poet, the painter, the sculptor— all the beautiful arts; for we were their patrons, and created the atmosphere in which they flourish. In abolishing the majestic distinctions of rank, society loses not only its grace, but its steadfastness——"

More he would doubtless have spoken; but here there arose an outcry, sportive, contemptuous, and indignant, that altogether drowned the appeal of the fallen nobleman, insomuch that, casting one look of despair at his own half-burned pedigree, he shrunk back into the crowd, glad to shelter himself under his new-found insignificance.

"Let him thank his stars that we have not flung him into the same fire!" shouted a rude figure, spurning the embers with his foot. "And henceforth let no man dare to show a piece of musty parchment as his warrant for lording it over his fellows. If he have strength of arm, well and good; it is one species of superiority. If he have wit, wisdom, courage, force of character, let these attributes do for him what they may; but from this day forward no mortal must hope for place and consideration by reckoning up the mouldy bones of his ancestors. That nonsense is done away."

"And in good time," remarked the grave observer by my side, in a low voice, however, "if no worse nonsense comes in its place; but, at all events, this species of nonsense has fairly lived out its life."

There was little space to muse or moralize over the embers of this time-honored rubbish; for, before it was half burned out, there came another multitude from beyond the sea, bearing the purple robes of royalty, and the crowns, globes, and sceptres of emperors and kings. All these had been condemned as useless bawbles, playthings at best, fit only for the infancy of the world or rods to govern and chastise it in its nonage, but with which universal manhood at its full-grown stature could no longer brook to be insulted. Into such contempt had these regal insignia now fallen that the gilded crown and tinselled robes of the player king from Drury Lane Theatre[6] had been thrown in among the rest, doubtless as a mockery of his brother monarchs on the great stage of the world. It was a strange sight to discern the crown jewels of England glowing and flashing in the midst of the fire. Some of them had been delivered down from the time of the Saxon princes;[7] others were purchased with vast revenues, or perchance ravished from the dead brows of the native potentates of Hindostan;[8] and the whole now blazed with a dazzling lustre, as if a star had fallen in that spot and been shattered into fragments. The splendor of the ruined monarchy had no reflection save in those inestimable precious stones. But enough on this subject. It were but tedious to describe how the Emperor of Austria's mantle was converted to tinder, and how the posts and pillars of the French throne became a heap of coals, which it was impossible to distinguish from those of any other wood. Let me add, however, that I noticed one of the exiled Poles stirring up the bonfire with the Czar of Russia's sceptre,[9] which he afterwards flung into the flames.

"The smell of singed garments is quite intolerable here," observed my new acquaintance, as the breeze enveloped us in the smoke of a royal wardrobe. "Let us get to windward and see what they are doing on the other side of the bonfire."

We accordingly passed around, and were just in time to witness the arrival of a vast procession of Washingtonians,—as the votaries of temperance call themselves nowadays,—accompanied by thousands of the Irish disciples of Father Mathew,[10] with that great apostle at their head. They brought a rich contribution to the bonfire—being nothing less than all the hogsheads and barrels of liquor in the world, which they rolled before them across the prairie.

"Now, my children," cried Father Mathew, when they reached the verge of the fire, "one shove more, and the work is done. And now let us stand off and see Satan deal with his own liquor."

Accordingly, having placed their wooden vessels within reach of the flames, the procession stood off at a safe distance, and soon beheld them burst into a blaze that reached the clouds and threatened to set the sky itself on fire. And well it might; for here was the whole world's stock of spirituous liquors, which, instead of kindling a frenzied light in the eyes of individual topers[11] as of yore, soared upwards with a bewildering gleam that startled all mankind. It was the aggregate of that fierce fire which would otherwise have scorched the hearts of millions. Meantime numberless bottles of precious wine were flung into the blaze, which lapped up the contents as if it loved them, and grew, like other drunkards, the merrier and fiercer for what it quaffed. Never again will the insatiable thirst of the fire fiend be so pampered. Here were the treasures of famous bon vivants[12]—liquors that had been tossed on ocean, and mellowed in the sun, and hoarded long in the recesses of the earth—the pale, the gold, the ruddy juice of whatever vineyards were most delicate—the entire vintage of Tokay[13]—all mingling in one stream with the vile fluids of the common pothouse, and contributing to heighten the selfsame blaze. And while it rose in a gigantic spire that seemed to wave against the arch of the firmament and combine itself with the light of stars, the multitude gave a shout as if the broad earth were exulting in its deliverance from the curse of ages.

But the joy was not universal. Many deemed that human life would be gloomier than ever when that brief illumination should sink down. While the reformers were at work I overheard muttered expostulations from several respectable gentlemen with red noses and wearing gouty shoes; and a ragged worthy, whose face looked like a hearth where the fire is burned out, now expressed his discontent more openly and boldly.

"What is this world good for," said the last toper, "now that we can never be jolly any more? What is to comfort the poor man in sorrow and perplexity? How is he to keep his heart warm against the cold winds of this cheerless earth? And what do you propose to give him in exchange for the solace that you take away? How are old friends to sit together by the fireside without a cheerful glass between them? A plague upon your reformation! It is a sad world, a cold world, a selfish world, a low world, not worth an honest fellow's living in, now that good fellowship is gone forever!"

This harangue excited great mirth among the bystanders; but, pre-posterous as was the sentiment, I could not help commiserating the forlorn condition of the last toper, whose boon companions had dwindled away from his side, leaving the poor fellow without a soul to countenance him in sipping his liquor, nor indeed any liquor to sip. Not that this was quite the true state of the case; for I had observed him at a critical moment filch a bottle of fourth-proof brandy[14] that fell beside the bonfire and hide it in his pocket.

The spirituous and fermented liquors being thus disposed of, the zeal of the reformers next induced them to replenish the fire with all the boxes of tea and bags of coffee in the world. And now came the planters of Virginia, bringing their crops of tobacco. These, being cast upon the heap of inutility, aggregated it to the size of a mountain, and incensed the atmosphere with such potent fragrance that methought we should never draw pure breath again. The present sacrifice seemed to startle the lovers of the weed more than any that they had hitherto witnessed.

"Well, they've put my pipe out," said an old gentleman, flinging it into the flames in a pet. "What is this world coming to? Every thing rich and racy—all the spice of life—is to be condemned as useless. Now that they have kindled the bonfire, if these nonsensical reformers would fling themselves into it, all would be well enough!"

"Be patient," responded a stanch conservative; "it will come to that in the end. They will first fling us in, and finally themselves."

From the general and systematic measures of reform I now turned to consider the individual contributions to this memorable bonfire. In many instances these were of a very amusing character. One poor fellow threw in his empty purse, and another a bundle of counterfeit or insolvable bank notes. Fashionable ladies threw in their last season's bonnets, together with heaps of ribbons, yellow lace, and much other half-worn milliner's ware, all of which proved even more evanescent in the fire than it had been in the fashion. A multitude of lovers of both sexes—discarded maids or bachelors and couples mutually weary of one another—tossed in bundles of perfumed letters and enamoured sonnets. A hack politician, being deprived of bread by the loss of office, threw in his teeth, which happened to be false ones. The Rev. Sidney Smith[15]—having voyaged across the Atlantic for that sole purpose— came up to the bonfire with a bitter grin and threw in certain repudi- ated bonds, fortified though they were with the broad seal of a sovereign state. A little boy of five years old, in the premature manliness of the present epoch, threw in his playthings; a college graduate his diploma; an apothecary, ruined by the spread of homœopathy, his whole stock of drugs and medicines; a physician his library; a parson his old ser- mons; and a fine gentleman of the old school his code of manners, which he had formerly written down for the benefit of the next gen- eration. A widow, resolving on a second marriage, slyly threw in her dead husband's miniature. A young man, jilted by his mistress, would willingly have flung his own desperate heart into the flames, but could find no means to wrench it out of his bosom. An American author, whose works were neglected by the public, threw his pen and paper into the bonfire and betook himself to some less discouraging occupa- tion. It somewhat startled me to overhear a number of ladies, highly respectable in appearance, proposing to fling their gowns and petti- coats into the flames, and assume the garb, together with the manners, duties, offices, and responsibilities, of the opposite sex.

What favor was accorded to this scheme I am unable to say, my at- tention being suddenly drawn to a poor, deceived, and half-delirious girl, who, exclaiming that she was the most worthless thing alive or dead, attempted to cast herself into the fire amid all that wrecked and broken trumpery of the world. A good man, however, ran to her rescue.

"Patience, my poor girl!" said he, as he drew her back from the fierce embrace of the destroying angel. "Be patient, and abide Heaven's will. So long as you possess a living soul, all may be restored to its first freshness. These things of matter and creations of human fantasy are fit for nothing but to be burned when once they have had their day; but your day is eternity!"

"Yes," said the wretched girl, whose frenzy seemed now to have sunk down into deep despondency,—"yes, and the sunshine is blotted out of it!"

It was now rumored among the spectators that all the weapons and munitions of war were to be thrown into the bonfire with the excep- tion of the world's stock of gunpowder, which, as the safest mode of disposing of it, had already been drowned in the sea. This intelligence

seemed to awaken great diversity of opinion. The hopeful philanthropist esteemed it a token that the millennium was already come;
while persons of another stamp, in whose view mankind was a breed of
bulldogs, prophesied that all the old stoutness, fervor, nobleness, generosity, and magnanimity of the race would disappear—these qualities, as they affirmed, requiring blood for their nourishment. They
comforted themselves, however, in the belief that the proposed aboli-
tion of war was impracticable for any length of time together.

Be that as it might, numberless great guns, whose thunder had long
been the voice of battle,—the artillery of the Armada,[16] the battering
trains of Marlborough,[17] and the adverse cannon of Napoleon and
Wellington[18]—were trundled into the midst of the fire. By the continual addition of dry combustibles, it had now waxed so intense that neither brass nor iron could withstand it. It was wonderful to behold how
these terrible instruments of slaughter melted away like playthings of
wax. Then the armies of the earth wheeled around the mighty furnace,
with their military music playing triumphant marches, and flung in
their muskets and swords. The standard bearers, likewise, cast one look
upward at their banners, all tattered with shot holes and inscribed with
the names of victorious fields; and, giving them a last flourish on the
breeze, they lowered them into the flame, which snatched them upward in its rush towards the clouds. This ceremony being over, the
world was left without a single weapon in its hands, except possibly a
few old king's arms and rusty swords and other trophies of the revolution in some of our state armories. And now the drums were beaten
and the trumpets brayed all together, as a prelude to the proclamation
of universal and eternal peace and the announcement that glory was
no longer to be won by blood, but that it would henceforth be the con-
tention of the human race to work out the greatest mutual good, and
that beneficence, in the future annals of the earth, would claim the
praise of valor. The blessed tidings were accordingly promulgated,
and caused infinite rejoicings among those who had stood aghast at the
horror and absurdity of war.

But I saw a grim smile pass over the seared visage of a stately old
commander,—by his warworn figure and rich military dress, he might
have been one of Napoleon's famous marshals,—who, with the rest of
the world's soldiery, had just flung away the sword that had been familiar to his right hand for half a century.

"Ay! ay!" grumbled he. "Let them proclaim what they please; but, in the end, we shall find that all this foolery has only made more work for the armorers and cannon founders."

"Why, sir," exclaimed I, in astonishment, "do you imagine that the human race will ever so far return on the steps of its past madness as to weld another sword or cast another cannon?"

"There will be no need," observed, with a sneer, one who neither felt benevolence nor had faith in it. "When Cain[19] wished to slay his brother, he was at no loss for a weapon."

"We shall see," replied the veteran commander. "If I am mistaken, so much the better; but in my opinion, without pretending to philosophize about the matter, the necessity of war lies far deeper than these honest gentlemen suppose. What! is there a field for all the petty disputes of individuals? and shall there be no great law court for the settlement of national difficulties? The battle field is the only court where such suits can be tried."

"You forget, general," rejoined I, "that, in this advanced stage of civilization, Reason and Philanthropy combined will constitute just such a tribunal as is requisite."

"Ah, I had forgotten that, indeed!" said the old warrior, as he limped away.

The fire was now to be replenished with materials that had hitherto been considered of even greater importance to the well being of society than the warlike munitions which we had already seen consumed. A body of reformers had travelled all over the earth in quest of the machinery by which the different nations were accustomed to inflict the punishment of death. A shudder passed through the multitude as these ghastly emblems were dragged forward. Even the flames seemed at first to shrink away, displaying the shape and murderous contrivance of each in a full blaze of light, which of itself was sufficient to convince mankind of the long and deadly error of human law. Those old implements of cruelty; those horrible monsters of mechanism; those inventions which it seemed to demand something worse than man's natural heart to contrive, and which had lurked in the dusky nooks of ancient prisons, the subject of terror-stricken legend,—were now brought forth to view. Headsmen's axes, with the rust of noble and royal blood upon them, and a vast collection of halters that had choked the breath of plebeian victims, were thrown in together. A shout greeted the arrival of the guillotine, which was thrust forward on the same wheels that had borne it from one to another of the bloodstained streets of Paris. But the loudest roar of applause went up, telling the distant sky of the triumph of the earth's redemption, when the gallows made its appearance. An ill-looking fellow, however, rushed forward, and, putting himself in the path of the reformers, bellowed hoarsely, and fought with brute fury to stay their progress.

It was little matter of surprise, perhaps, that the executioner should thus do his best to vindicate and uphold the machinery by which he himself had his livelihood and worthier individuals their death; but it deserved special note that men of a far different sphere—even of that consecrated class in whose guardianship the world is apt to trust its benevolence—were found to take the hangman's view of the question.

"Stay, my brethren!" cried one of them. "You are misled by a false philanthropy; you know not what you do. The gallows is a Heaven-ordained instrument. Bear it back, then, reverently, and set it up in its old place, else the world will fall to speedy ruin and desolation!"

"Onward! onward!" shouted a leader in the reform. "Into the flames with the accursed instrument of man's bloody policy! How can human law inculcate benevolence and love while it persists in setting up the gallows as its chief symbol? One heave more, good friends, and the world will be redeemed from its greatest error."

A thousand hands, that nevertheless loathed the touch, now lent their assistance, and thrust the ominous burden far, far into the centre of the raging furnace. There its fatal and abhorred image was beheld, first black, then a red coal, then ashes.

"That was well done!" exclaimed I.

"Yes, it was well done," replied, but with less enthusiasm than I expected, the thoughtful observer who was still at my side; "well done, if the world be good enough for the measure. Death, however, is an idea that cannot easily be dispensed with in any condition between the primal innocence and that other purity and perfection which perchance we are destined to attain after travelling round the full circle; but, at all events, it is well that the experiment should now be tried."

"Too cold! too cold!" impatiently exclaimed the young and ardent leader in this triumph. "Let the heart have its voice here as well as the intellect. And as for ripeness, and as for progress, let mankind always do the highest, kindest, noblest thing that, at any given period, it has attained the perception of; and surely that thing cannot be wrong nor wrongly timed."

I know not whether it were the excitement of the scene, or whether the good people around the bonfire were really growing more enlightened every instant; but they now proceeded to measures in the full length of which I was hardly prepared to keep them company. For instance, some threw their marriage certificates into the flames, and declared themselves candidates for a higher, holier, and more comprehensive union than that which had subsisted from the birth of time under the form of the connubial tie. Others hastened to the vaults of banks and to the coffers of the rich—all of which were open to the first comer on this fated occasion—and brought entire bales of paper money to enliven the blaze and tons of coin to be melted down by its intensity. Henceforth, they said, universal benevolence, uncoined and exhaustless, was to be the golden currency of the world. At this intelligence the bankers and speculators in the stocks grew pale, and a pickpocket, who had reaped a rich harvest among the crowd, fell down in a deadly fainting fit. A few men of business burned their day books and legers, the notes and obligations of their creditors, and all other evidences of debts due to themselves; while perhaps a somewhat larger number satisfied their zeal for reform with the sacrifice of any uncomfortable recollection of their own indebtment. There was then a cry that the period was arrived when the title deeds of landed property should be given to the flames, and the whole soil of the earth revert to the public, from whom it had been wrongfully abstracted and most unequally distributed among individuals. Another party demanded that all written constitutions, set forms of government, legislative acts, statute books, and every thing else on which human invention had endeavored to stamp its arbitrary laws, should at once be destroyed, leaving the consummated world as free as the man first created.

Whether any ultimate action was taken with regard to these propositions is beyond my knowledge; for, just then, some matters were in progress that concerned my sympathies more nearly.

"See! see! What heaps of books and pamphlets!" cried a fellow, who did not seem to be a lover of literature. "Now we shall have a glorious blaze!"

"That's just the thing!" said a modern philosopher. "Now we shall get rid of the weight of dead men's thought, which has hitherto pressed so heavily on the living intellect that it has been incompetent to any effectual self-exertion. Well done, my lads! Into the fire with them! Now you are enlightening the world indeed!"

"But what is to become of the trade?" cried a frantic bookseller.

"O, by all means, let them accompany their merchandise," coolly observed an author. "It will be a noble funeral pile!"

The truth was, that the human race had now reached a stage of progress so far beyond what the wisest and wittiest men of former ages had ever dreamed of that it would have been a manifest absurdity to allow the earth to be any longer encumbered with their poor achievements in the literary line. Accordingly a thorough and searching investigation had swept the booksellers' shops, hawkers' stands, public and private libraries, and even the little book shelf by the country fireside, and had brought the world's entire mass of printed paper, bound or in sheets, to swell the already mountain bulk of our illustrious bonfire. Thick, heavy folios, containing the labors of lexicographers, commentators, and encyclopedists, were flung in, and, falling among the embers with a leaden thump, smouldered away to ashes like rotten wood. The small, richly gilt French tomes of the last age, with the hundred volumes of Voltaire[20] among them, went off in a brilliant shower of sparkles and little jets of flame; while the current literature of the same nation burned red and blue, and threw an infernal light over the visages of the spectators, converting them all to the aspect of partycolored fiends. A collection of German stories emitted a scent of brimstone. The English standard authors made excellent fuel, generally exhibiting the properties of sound oak logs. Milton's works,[21] in particular, sent up a powerful blaze, gradually reddening into a coal, which promised to endure longer than almost any other material of the pile. From Shakspeare there gushed a flame of such marvellous splendor that men shaded their eyes as against the sun's meridian glory; nor even when the works of his own elucidators were flung upon him did he cease to flash forth a dazzling radiance from beneath the ponderous heap. It is my belief that he is still blazing as fervidly as ever.

"Could a poet but light a lamp at that glorious flame," remarked I, "he might then consume the midnight oil to some good purpose."

"That is the very thing which modern poets have been too apt to do, or at least to attempt," answered a critic. "The chief benefit to be expected from this conflagration of past literature undoubtedly is, that writers will henceforth be compelled to light their lamps at the sun or stars."

"If they can reach so high," said I; "but that task requires a giant, who may afterwards distribute the light among inferior men. It is not every one that can steal the fire from heaven like Prometheus;[22] but, when once he had done the deed, a thousand hearths were kindled by it."

It amazed me much to observe how indefinite was the proportion between the physical mass of any given author and the property of brilliant and long-continued combustion. For instance, there was not a quarto volume of the last century—nor, indeed, of the present—that could compete in that particular with a child's little gilt-covered book, containing Mother Goose's Melodies.[23] The Life and Death of Tom Thumb[24] outlasted the biography of Marlborough.[25] An epic, indeed a dozen of them, was converted to white ashes before the single sheet of an old ballad was half consumed. In more than one case, too, when volumes of applauded verse proved incapable of any thing better than a stifling smoke, an unregarded ditty of some nameless bard—perchance in the corner of a newspaper—soared up among the stars with a flame as brilliant as their own. Speaking of the properties of flame, methought Shelley's poetry[26] emitted a purer light than almost any other productions of his day, contrasting beautifully with the fitful and lurid gleams and gushes of black vapor that flashed and eddied from the volumes of Lord Byron.[27] As for Tom Moore,[28] some of his songs diffused an odor like a burning pastil.[29]

I felt particular interest in watching the combustion of American authors, and scrupulously noted by my watch the precise number of moments that changed most of them from shabbily-printed books to indistinguishable ashes. It would be invidious, however, if not perilous, to betray these awful secrets; so that I shall content myself with observing that it was not invariably the writer most frequent in the public mouth that made the most splendid appearance in the bonfire. I especially remember that a great deal of excellent inflammability was exhibited in a thin volume of poems by Ellery Channing;[30] although, to speak the truth, there were certain portions that hissed and spluttered in a very disagreeable fashion. A curious phenomenon occurred in reference to several writers, native as well as foreign. Their books, though of highly respectable figure, instead of bursting into a blaze or even smouldering out their substance in smoke, suddenly melted away in a manner that proved them to be ice.

If it be no lack of modesty to mention my own works, it must here be confessed that I looked for them with fatherly interest, but in vain. Too probably they were changed to vapor by the first action of the heat; at best I can only hope that, in their quiet way, they contributed a glimmering spark or two to the splendor of the evening.

"Alas! and woe is me!" thus bemoaned himself a heavy-looking gentleman in green spectacles. "The world is utterly ruined, and there is nothing to live for any longer. The business of my life is snatched from me. Not a volume to be had for love or money!"

"This," remarked the sedate observer beside me, "is a bookworm— one of those men who are born to gnaw dead thoughts. His clothes, you see, are covered with the dust of libraries. He has no inward fountain of ideas; and, in good earnest, now that the old stock is abolished, I do not see what is to become of the poor fellow. Have you no word of comfort for him?"

"My dear sir," said I to the desperate bookworm, "is not Nature better than a book? Is not the human heart deeper than any system of philosophy? Is not life replete with more instruction than past observers have found it possible to write down in maxims? Be of good cheer. The great book of Time is still spread wide open before us; and, if we read it aright, it will be to us a volume of eternal truth."

"O, my books, my books, my precious printed books!" reiterated the forlorn bookworm. "My only reality was a bound volume; and now they will not leave me even a shadowy pamphlet!"

In fact, the last remnant of the literature of all the ages was now descending upon the blazing heap in the shape of a cloud of pamphlets from the press of the New World. These likewise were consumed in the twinkling of an eye, leaving the earth, for the first time since the days of Cadmus,[31] free from the plague of letters—an enviable field for the authors of the next generation.

"Well, and does any thing remain to be done?" inquired I somewhat anxiously. "Unless we set fire to the earth itself, and then leap boldly off into infinite space, I know not that we can carry reform to any farther point."

"You are vastly mistaken, my good friend," said the observer. "Believe me, the fire will not be allowed to settle down without the addition of fuel that will startle many persons who have lent a willing hand thus far."

Nevertheless there appeared to be a relaxation of effort for a little time, during which, probably, the leaders of the movement were considering what should be done next. In the interval, a philosopher threw his theory into the flames—a sacrifice which, by those who knew how to estimate it, was pronounced the most remarkable that had yet been made. The combustion, however, was by no means brilliant. Some indefatigable people, scorning to take a moment's ease, now employed themselves in collecting all the withered leaves and fallen boughs of the forest, and thereby recruited the bonfire to a greater height than ever. But this was mere by-play.

"Here comes the fresh fuel that I spoke of," said my companion.

To my astonishment, the persons who now advanced into the vacant space around the mountain fire bore surplices and other priestly garments, mitres, crosiers, and a confusion of Popish[32] and Protestant emblems, with which it seemed their purpose to consummate the great act of faith. Crosses from the spires of old cathedrals were cast upon the heap with as little remorse as if the reverence of centuries, passing in long array beneath the lofty towers, had not looked up to them as the holiest of symbols. The font in which infants were consecrated to God, the sacramental vessels whence piety received the hallowed draught, were given to the same destruction. Perhaps it most nearly touched my heart to see among these devoted relics fragments of the humble communion tables and undecorated pulpits which I recognized as having been torn from the meeting houses of New England. Those simple edifices might have been permitted to retain all of sacred embellishment that their Puritan founders had bestowed, even though the mighty structure of St. Peter's[33] had sent its spoils to the fire of this terrible sacrifice. Yet I felt that these were but the externals of religion, and might most safely be relinquished by spirits that best knew their deep significance.

"All is well," said I, cheerfully. "The woodpaths shall be the aisles of our cathedral—the firmament itself shall be its ceiling. What needs an earthly roof between the Deity and his worshippers? Our faith can well afford to lose all the drapery that even the holiest men have thrown around it, and be only the more sublime in its simplicity."

"True," said my companion; "but will they pause here?"

The doubt implied in his question was well founded. In the general destruction of books already described, a holy volume, that stood apart from the catalogue of human literature, and yet, in one sense, was at its head, had been spared. But the Titan[34] of innovation,—angel or fiend, double in his nature, and capable of deeds befitting both characters,—at first shaking down only the old and rotten shapes of things, had now, as it appeared, laid his terrible hand upon the main pillars which supported the whole edifice of our moral and spiritual state. The inhabitants of the earth had grown too enlightened to define their faith within a form of words or to limit the spiritual by any analogy to our material existence. Truths which the heavens trembled at were now but a fable of the world's infancy. Therefore, as the final sacrifice of human error, what else remained to be thrown upon the embers of that awful pile except the book which, though a celestial revelation to past ages, was but a voice from a lower sphere as regarded the present race of man? It was done! Upon the blazing heap of falsehood and wornout truth—things that the earth had never needed, or had ceased to need, or had grown childishly weary of—fell the ponderous church Bible, the great old volume that had lain so long on the cushion of the pulpit, and whence the pastor's solemn voice had given holy utterance on so many a Sabbath day. There, likewise, fell the family Bible, which the long-buried patriarch had read to his children—in prosperity or sorrow, by the fireside and in the summer shade of trees—and had bequeathed downward as the heirloom of generations. There fell the bosom Bible, the little volume that had been the soul's friend of some sorely-tried child of dust, who thence took courage, whether his trial were for life or death, steadfastly confronting both in the strong assurance of immortality.

All these were flung into the fierce and riotous blaze; and then a mighty wind came roaring across the plain with a desolate howl, as if it were the angry lamentation of the earth for the loss of heaven's sunshine; and it shook the gigantic pyramid of flame and scattered the cinders of half-consumed abominations around upon the spectators.

"This is terrible!" said I, feeling that my cheek grew pale, and seeing a like change in the visages about me.

"Be of good courage yet," answered the man with whom I had so often spoken. He continued to gaze steadily at the spectacle with a singular calmness, as if it concerned him merely as an observer. "Be of good courage, nor yet exult too much; for there is far less both of good and evil in the effect of this bonfire than the world might be willing to believe."

"How can that be?" exclaimed I, impatiently. "Has it not consumed every thing? Has it not swallowed up or melted down every human or divine appendage of our mortal state that had substance enough to be acted on by fire? Will there be any thing left us to-morrow morning better or worse than a heap of embers and ashes?"

"Assuredly there will," said my grave friend. "Come hither to-morrow morning, or whenever the combustible portion of the pile shall be quite burned out, and you will find among the ashes every thing really valuable that you have seen cast into the flames. Trust me, the world of to-morrow will again enrich itself with the gold and diamonds which have been cast off by the world of to-day. Not a truth is destroyed nor buried so deep among the ashes but it will be raked up at last."

This was a strange assurance. Yet I felt inclined to credit it, the more especially as I beheld among the wallowing flames a copy of the Holy Scriptures, the pages of which, instead of being blackened into tinder, only assumed a more dazzling whiteness as the finger marks of human imperfection were purified away. Certain marginal notes and commentaries, it is true, yielded to the intensity of the fiery test, but without detriment to the smallest syllable that had flamed from the pen of inspiration.

"Yes; there is the proof of what you say," answered I, turning to the observer; "but if only what is evil can feel the action of the fire, then, surely, the conflagration has been of inestimable utility. Yet, if I understand aright, you intimate a doubt whether the world's expectation of benefit would be realized by it."

"Listen to the talk of these worthies," said he, pointing to a group in front of the blazing pile; "possibly they may teach you something useful without intending it."

The persons whom he indicated consisted of that brutal and most earthy figure who had stood forth so furiously in defence of the gallows,—the hangman, in short,—together with the last thief and the last murderer, all three of whom were clustered about the last toper. The latter was liberally passing the brandy bottle, which he had rescued from the general destruction of wines and spirits. This little convivial party seemed at the lowest pitch of despondency, as considering that the purified world must needs be utterly unlike the sphere that they had hitherto known, and therefore but a strange and desolate abode for gentlemen of their kidney.

"The best counsel for all of us is," remarked the hangman, "that, as soon as we have finished the last drop of liquor, I help you, my three friends, to a comfortable end upon the nearest tree, and then hang myself on the same bough. This is no world for us any longer."

"Poh, poh, my good fellows!" said a dark-complexioned personage, who now joined the group—his complexion was indeed fearfully dark, and his eyes glowed with a redder light than that of the bonfire; "be not so cast down, my dear friends; you shall see good days yet. There is one thing that these wiseacres have forgotten to throw into the fire, and without which all the rest of the conflagration is just nothing at all; yes, though they had burned the earth itself to a cinder."

"And what may that be?" eagerly demanded the last murderer.

"What but the human heart itself?" said the dark-visaged stranger, with a portentous grin. "And, unless they hit upon some method of purifying that foul cavern, forth from it will reissue all the shapes of wrong and misery—the same old shapes or worse ones—which they have taken such a vast deal of trouble to consume to ashes. I have stood by this livelong night and laughed in my sleeve at the whole business. O, take my word for it, it will be the old world yet!"

This brief conversation supplied me with a theme for lengthened thought. How sad a truth, if true it were, that man's agelong endeavor for perfection had served only to render him the mockery of the evil principle, from the fatal circumstance of an error at the very root of the matter! The heart, the heart,—there was the little yet boundless sphere wherein existed the original wrong of which the crime and misery of this outward world were merely types. Purify that inward sphere, and the many shapes of evil that haunt the outward, and which now seem almost our only realities, will turn to shadowy phantoms and vanish of their own accord; but if we go no deeper than the intellect, and strive, with merely that feeble instrument, to discern and rectify what is wrong, our whole accomplishment will be a dream, so unsubstantial that it matters little whether the bonfire, which I have so faithfully described, were what we choose to call a real event and a flame that would scorch the finger, or only a phosphoric radiance and a parable of my own brain.

PASSAGES FROM A
RELINQUISHED WORK

AT HOME

From infancy I was under the guardianship of a village parson, who made me the subject of daily prayer and the sufferer of innumerable stripes, using no distinction, as to these marks of paternal love, between myself and his own three boys. The result, it must be owned, has been very different in their cases and mine, they being all respectable men and well settled in life; the eldest as the successor to his father's pulpit, the second as a physician, and the third as a partner in a whole-sale shoe store; while I, with better prospects than either of them, have run the course which this volume will describe. Yet there is room for doubt whether I should have been any better contented with such success as theirs than with my own misfortunes—at least, till after my experience of the latter had made it too late for another trial.

My guardian had a name of considerable eminence, and fitter for the place it occupies in ecclesiastical history than for so frivolous a page as mine. In his own vicinity, among the lighter part of his hearers, he was called Parson Thumpcushion, from the very forcible gestures with which he illustrated his doctrines. Certainly, if his powers as a preacher were to be estimated by the damage done to his pulpit furniture, none of his living brethren, and but few dead ones, would have been worthy even to pronounce a benediction after him. Such pounding and expounding the moment he began to grow warm, such slapping with his open palm, thumping with his closed fist, and banging with the whole weight of the great Bible, convinced me that he held, in imagination, either the Old Nick[1] or some Unitarian infidel at bay, and belabored his unhappy cushion as proxy for those abominable adversaries. Nothing but this exercise of the body while delivering his sermons could have supported the good parson's health under the mental toil which they cost him in composition.

Though Parson Thumpcushion had an upright heart, and some called it a warm one, he was invariably stern and severe, on principle, I suppose, to me. With late justice, though early enough, even now, to be tinctured with generosity, I acknowledge him to have been a good and wise man after his own fashion. If his management failed as to myself, it succeeded with his three sons; nor, I must frankly say, could any mode of education with which it was possible for him to be acquainted have made me much better than what I was or led me to a happier fortune than the present. He could neither change the nature that God gave me nor adapt his own inflexible mind to my peculiar character. Perhaps it was my chief misfortune that I had neither father nor mother alive; for parents have an instinctive sagacity in regard to the welfare of their children, and the child feels a confidence both in the wisdom and affection of his parents which he cannot transfer to any delegate of their duties, however conscientious. An orphan's fate is hard, be he rich or poor. As for Parson Thumpcushion, whenever I see the old gentleman in my dreams he looks kindly and sorrowfully at me, holding out his hand as if each had something to forgive. With such kindness and such forgiveness, but without the sorrow, may our next meeting be!

I was a youth of gay and happy temperament, with an incorrigible levity of spirit, of no vicious propensities, sensible enough, but wayward and fanciful. What a character was this to be brought in contact with the stern old Pilgrim spirit of my guardian! We were at variance on a thousand points; but our chief and final dispute arose from the pertinacity with which he insisted on my adopting a particular profession; while I, being heir to a moderate competence, had avowed my purpose of keeping aloof from the regular business of life. This would have been a dangerous resolution any where in the world; it was fatal in New England. There is a grossness in the conceptions of my countrymen; they will not be convinced that any good thing may consist with what they call idleness; they can anticipate nothing but evil of a young man who neither studied physic, law, nor gospel, nor opens a store, nor takes to farming, but manifests an incomprehensible disposition to be satisfied with what his father left him. The principle is excellent in its general influence, but most miserable in its effect on the few that violate it. I had a quick sensitiveness to public opinion, and felt as if it ranked me with the tavern haunters and town paupers—with the drunken poet who hawked his own Fourth of July odes, and the broken soldier who had been good for nothing since last war. The consequence of all this was a piece of lighthearted desperation.

I do not over-estimate my notoriety when I take it for granted that many of my readers must have heard of me in the wild way of life which I adopted. The idea of becoming a wandering story teller had been suggested, a year or two before, by an encounter with several merry vagabonds in a showman's wagon, where they and I had sheltered ourselves during a summer shower. The project was not more extravagant than most which a young man forms. Stranger ones are executed every day; and, not to mention my prototypes in the East, and the wandering orators and poets whom my own ears have heard, I had the example of one illustrious itinerant in the other hemisphere— of Goldsmith,[2] who planned and performed his travels through France and Italy on a less promising scheme than mine. I took credit to myself for various qualifications, mental and personal, suited to the undertaking. Besides, my mind had latterly tormented me for employment, keeping up an irregular activity even in sleep, and making me conscious that I must toil, if it were but in catching butterflies. But my chief motives were, discontent with home and a bitter grudge against Parson Thumpcushion, who would rather have laid me in my father's tomb than see me either a novelist or an actor, two characters which I thus hit upon a method of uniting. After all, it was not half so foolish as if I had written romances instead of reciting them.

The following pages will contain a picture of my vagrant life, intermixed with specimens, generally brief and slight, of that great mass of fiction to which I gave existence, and which has vanished like cloud shapes. Besides the occasions when I sought a pecuniary reward, I was accustomed to exercise my narrative faculty wherever chance had collected a little audience idle enough to listen. These rehearsals were useful in testing the strong points of my stories; and, indeed, the flow of fancy soon came upon me so abundantly that its indulgence was its own reward, though the hope of praise also became a powerful incitement. Since I shall never feel the warm gush of new thought as I did then, let me beseech the reader to believe that my tales were not always so cold as he may find them now. With each specimen will be given a sketch of the circumstances in which the story was told. Thus my airdrawn pictures will be set in frames perhaps more valuable than the pictures themselves, since they will be embossed with groups of characteristic figures, amid the lake and mountain scenery, the villages and fertile fields, of our native land. But I write the book for the sake of its moral, which many a dreaming youth may profit by, though it is the experience of a wandering story teller.

A FLIGHT IN THE FOG

I set out on my rambles one morning in June about sunrise. The day promised to be fair, though at that early hour a heavy mist lay along the earth and settled in minute globules on the folds of my clothes, so that I looked precisely as if touched with a hoarfrost. The sky was quite obscured, and the trees and houses invisible till they grew out of the fog as I came close upon them. There is a hill towards the west whence the road goes abruptly down, holding a level course through the village and ascending an eminence on the other side, behind which it disappears. The whole view comprises an extent of half a mile. Here I paused; and, while gazing through the misty veil, it partially rose and swept away with so sudden an effect that a gray cloud seemed to have taken the aspect of a small white town. A thin vapor being still diffused through the atmosphere, the wreaths and pillars of fog, whether hung in air or based on earth, appeared not less substantial than the edifices, and gave their own indistinctness to the whole. It was singular that such an unromantic scene should look so visionary.

Half of the parson's dwelling was a dingy white house, and half of it was a cloud; but Squire Moody's mansion, the grandest in the village, was wholly visible, even the lattice work of the balcony under the front window; while in another place only two red chimneys were seen above the mist, appertaining to my own paternal residence, then tenanted by strangers. I could not remember those with whom I had dwelt there, not even my mother. The brick edifice of the bank was in the clouds; the foundations of what was to be a great block of buildings had vanished, ominously, as it proved; the dry goods store of Mr. Nightingale seemed a doubtful concern; and Dominicus Pike's tobacco manufactory an affair of smoke, except the splendid image of an Indian chief in front. The white spire of the meeting house ascended out of the densest heap of vapor, as if that shadowy base were its only support; or, to give a truer interpretation, the steeple was the emblem of Religion, enveloped in mystery below, yet pointing to a cloudless atmosphere, and catching the brightness of the east on its gilded vane.

As I beheld these objects, and the dewy street, with grassy intervals and a border of trees between the wheel track and the sidewalks, all so indistinct, and not to be traced without an effort, the whole seemed more like memory than reality. I would have imagined that years had already passed, and I was far away, contemplating that dim picture of my native place, which I should retain in my mind through the mist of time. No tears fell from my eyes among the dewdrops of the morning; nor does it occur to me that I heaved a sigh. In truth, I had never felt such a delicious excitement nor known what freedom was till that moment when I gave up my home and took the whole world in exchange, fluttering the wings of my spirit as if I would have flown from one star to another through the universe. I waved my hand towards the dusky village, bade it a joyous farewell, and turned away to follow any path but that which might lead me back. Never was Childe Harold's sentiment[3] adopted in a spirit more unlike his own.

Naturally enough, I thought of Don Quixote.[4] Recollecting how the knight and Sancho had watched for auguries when they took the road to Toboso, I began, between jest and earnest, to feel a similar anxiety. It was gratified, and by a more poetical phenomenon than the braying of the dappled ass or the neigh of Rosinante. The sun, then just above the horizon, shone faintly through the fog, and formed a species of rainbow in the west, bestriding my intended road like a gigantic portal. I had never known before that a bow could be generated between the sunshine and the morning mist. It had no brilliancy, no perceptible hues, but was a mere unpainted framework, as white and ghostlike as the lunar rainbow, which is deemed ominous of evil. But, with a light heart to which all omens were propitious, I advanced beneath the misty archway of futurity.

I had determined not to enter on my profession within a hundred miles of home, and then to cover myself with a fictitious name. The first precaution was reasonable enough, as otherwise Parson Thump-cushion might have put an untimely catastrophe to my story; but as nobody would be much affected by my disgrace, and all was to be suf-fered in my own person, I know not why I cared about a name. For a week or two I travelled almost at random, seeking hardly any guidance except the whirling of a leaf at some turn of the road, or the green bough that beckoned me, or the naked branch that pointed its withered finger onward. All my care was to be farther from home each night than the preceding morning.

A FELLOW-TRAVELLER

One day at noontide, when the sun had burst suddenly out of a cloud and threatened to dissolve me, I looked round for shelter, whether of tavern, cottage, barn, or shady tree. The first which offered itself was a wood—not a forest, but a trim plantation of young oaks, growing just thick enough to keep the mass of sunshine out, while they admitted a few straggling beams, and thus produced the most cheerful gloom imaginable. A brook, so small and clear, and apparently so cool, that I wanted to drink it up, ran under the road through a little arch of stone without once meeting the sun in its passage from the shade on one side to the shade on the other. As there was a stepping-place over the stone wall and a path along the rivulet, I followed it and discovered its source—a spring gushing out of an old barrel.

In this pleasant spot I saw a light pack suspended from the branch of a tree, a stick leaning against the trunk, and a person seated on the grassy verge of the spring, with his back towards me. He was a slender figure, dressed in black broadcloth, which was none of the finest nor very fashionably cut. On hearing my footsteps he started up rather ner-vously, and, turning round, showed the face of a young man about my own age, with his finger in a volume which he had been reading till my intrusion. His book was evidently a pocket Bible. Though I piqued myself at that period on my great penetration into people's characters and pursuits, I could not decide whether this young man in black were an unfledged divine from Andover,[5] a college student, or preparing for college at some academy. In either case I would quite as willingly have found a merrier companion; such, for instance, as the comedian with whom Gil Blas[6] shared his dinner beside a fountain in Spain.

After a nod, which was duly returned, I made a goblet of oak leaves, filled and emptied it two or three times, and then remarked, to hit the stranger's classical associations, that this beautiful fountain ought to flow from an urn instead of an old barrel. He did not show that he understood the allusion, and replied very briefly, with a shyness that was quite out of place between persons who met in such circumstances. Had he treated my next observation in the same way, we should have parted without another word.

"It is very singular," said I,—"though doubtless there are good reasons for it,—that Nature should provide drink so abundantly, and lavish it every where by the roadside, but so seldom any thing to eat. Why should not we find a loaf of bread on this tree as well as a barrel of good liquor at the foot of it?"

"There is a loaf of bread on the tree," replied the stranger, without even smiling at a coincidence which made me laugh. "I have something to eat in my bundle; and, if you can make a dinner with me, you shall be welcome."

"I accept your offer with pleasure," said I. "A pilgrim such as I am must not refuse a providential meal."

The young man had risen to take his bundle from the branch of the tree, but now turned round and regarded me with great earnestness, coloring deeply at the same time. However, he said nothing, and produced part of a loaf of bread and some cheese, the former being evidently home baked, though some days out of the oven. The fare was good enough, with a real welcome, such as his appeared to be. After spreading these articles on the stump of a tree, he proceeded to ask a blessing on our food, an unexpected ceremony, and quite an impressive one at our woodland table, with the fountain gushing beside us and the bright sky glimmering through the boughs; nor did his brief petition affect me less because his embarrassment made his voice tremble. At the end of the meal he returned thanks with the same tremulous fervor.

He felt a natural kindness for me after thus relieving my necessities, and showed it by becoming less reserved. On my part, I professed never to have relished a dinner better; and, in requital of the stranger's hospitality, solicited the pleasure of his company to supper.

"Where? At your home?" asked he.

"Yes," said I, smiling.

"Perhaps our roads are not the same," observed he.

"O, I can take any road but one, and yet not miss my way," answered I. "This morning I breakfasted at home; I shall sup at home to-night; and a moment ago I dined at home. To be sure, there was a certain place which I called home; but I have resolved not to see it again till I have been quite round the globe and enter the street on the east as I left it on the west. In the mean time, I have a home every where, or nowhere, just as you please to take it."

"Nowhere, then; for this transitory world is not our home," said the young man, with solemnity. "We are all pilgrims and wanderers; but it is strange that we two should meet."

I inquired the meaning of this remark, but could obtain no satisfactory reply. But we had eaten salt together, and it was right that we should form acquaintance after that ceremony as the Arabs of the desert do, especially as he had learned something about myself, and the courtesy of the country entitled me to as much information in return. I asked whither he was travelling.

"I do not know," said he; "but God knows."

"That is strange!" exclaimed I; "not that God should know it, but that you should not. And how is your road to be pointed out?"

"Perhaps by an inward conviction," he replied, looking sideways at me to discover whether I smiled; "perhaps by an outward sign."

"Then, believe me," said I, "the outward sign is already granted you, and the inward conviction ought to follow. We are told of pious men in old times who committed themselves to the care of Providence, and saw the manifestation of its will in the slightest circumstances, as in the shooting of a star, the flight of a bird, or the course taken by some brute animal. Sometimes even a stupid ass was their guide. May not I be as good a one?"

"I do not know," said the pilgrim, with perfect simplicity.

We did, however, follow the same road, and were not overtaken, as I partly apprehended, by the keepers of any lunatic asylum in pursuit of a stray patient. Perhaps the stranger felt as much doubt of my sanity as I did of his, though certainly with less justice, since I was fully aware of my own extravagances, while he acted as wildly, and deemed it heavenly wisdom. We were a singular couple, strikingly contrasted, yet curiously assimilated, each of us remarkable enough by himself, and doubly so in the other's company. Without any formal compact, we kept together day after day till our union appeared permanent. Even had I seen nothing to love and admire in him, I could never have thought of deserting one who needed me continually; for I never knew a person, not even a woman, so unfit to roam the world in solitude as he was—so painfully shy, so easily discouraged by slight obstacles, and so often depressed by a weight within himself.

I was now far from my native place, but had not yet stepped before the public. A slight tremor seized me whenever I thought of relinquishing the immunities of a private character, and giving every man, and for money too, the right, which no man yet possessed, of treating me with open scorn. But about a week after contracting the above alliance I made my bow to an audience of nine persons, seven of whom hissed me in a very disagreeable manner, and not without good cause. Indeed, the failure was so signal that it would have been mere swindling to retain the money, which had been paid on my implied contract to give its value of amusement. So I called in the doorkeeper, bade him refund the whole receipts, a mighty sum, and was gratified with a round of applause by way of offset to the hisses. This event would have looked most horrible in anticipation—a thing to make a man shoot himself, or run amuck, or hide himself in caverns where he might not see his own burning blush; but the reality was not so very hard to bear. It is a fact that I was more deeply grieved by an almost parallel misfortune which happened to my companion on the same evening. In my own behalf I was angry and excited, not depressed; my blood ran quick, my spirits rose buoyantly, and I had never felt such a confidence of future success and determination to achieve it as at that trying moment. I resolved to persevere, if it were only to wring the reluctant praise from my enemies.

Hitherto I had immensely underrated the difficulties of my idle trade; now I recognized that it demanded nothing short of my whole powers, cultivated to the utmost, and exerted with the same prodigality as if I were speaking for a great party or for the nation at large on the floor of the Capitol. No talent or attainment could come amiss; every thing, indeed, was requisite—wide observation, varied knowledge, deep thoughts, and sparkling ones; pathos and levity, and a mixture of both, like sunshine in a raindrop; lofty imagination, veiling

330 · *Mosses from an Old Manse*

itself in the garb of common life; and the practised art which alone could render these gifts, and more than these, available. Not that I ever hoped to be thus qualified. But my despair was no ignoble one; for, knowing the impossibility of satisfying myself, even should the world be satisfied, I did my best to overcome it; investigated the causes of every defect; and strove, with patient stubbornness, to remove them in the next attempt. It is one of my few sources of pride, that, ridiculous as the object was, I followed it up with the firmness and energy of a man.

I manufactured a great variety of plots and skeletons of tales, and kept them ready for use, leaving the filling up to the inspiration of the moment; though I cannot remember ever to have told a tale which did not vary considerably from my preconceived idea, and acquire a novelty of aspect as often as I repeated it. Oddly enough, my success was generally in proportion to the difference between the conception and accomplishment. I provided two or more commencements and catastrophes to many of the tales—a happy expedient, suggested by the double sets of sleeves and trimmings which diversified the suits in Sir Piercy Shafton's wardrobe.[7] But my best efforts had a unity, a wholeness, and a separate character that did not admit of this sort of mechanism.

THE VILLAGE THEATRE

About the first of September my fellow-traveller and myself arrived at a country town, where a small company of actors, on their return from a summer's campaign in the British provinces, were giving a series of dramatic exhibitions. A moderately sized hall of the tavern had been converted into a theatre. The performances that evening were, The Heir at Law, and No Song, no Supper, with the recitation of Alexander's Feast between the play and farce. The house was thin and dull. But the next day there appeared to be brighter prospects, the playbills announcing at every corner, on the town pump, and—awful sacrilege!— on the very door of the meeting house, an Unprecedented Attraction! After setting forth the ordinary entertainments of a theatre, the public were informed, in the hugest type that the printing office could supply, that the manager had been fortunate enough to accomplish an engagement with the celebrated Story Teller. He would make his first appearance that evening, and recite his famous tale of Mr. Higgin-botham's Catastrophe,[8] which had been received with rapturous ap-plause by audiences in all the principal cities. This outrageous flourish of trumpets, be it known, was wholly unauthorized by me, who had merely made an engagement for a single evening, without assuming any more celebrity than the little I possessed. As for the tale, it could hardly have been applauded by rapturous audiences, being as yet an unfilled plot; nor even when I stepped upon the stage was it decided whether Mr. Higginbotham should live or die.

In two or three places, underneath the flaming bills which an-nounced the Story Teller, was pasted a small slip of paper, giving no-tice, in tremulous characters, of a religious meeting to be held at the school house, where, with divine permission, Eliakim Abbott would address sinners on the welfare of their immortal souls.

In the evening, after the commencement of the tragedy of Doug-las,[9] I took a ramble through the town to quicken my ideas by active motion. My spirits were good, with a certain glow of mind which I had already learned to depend upon as the sure prognostic of success. Passing a small and solitary school house, where a light was burning dimly and a few people were entering the door, I went in with them, and saw my friend Eliakim at the desk. He had collected about fifteen hearers, mostly females. Just as I entered he was beginning to pray in accents so low and interrupted that he seemed to doubt the reception of his efforts both with God and man. There was room for distrust in regard to the latter. At the conclusion of the prayer several of the little audience went out, leaving him to begin his discourse under such dis-couraging circumstances, added to his natural and agonizing diffi-dence. Knowing that my presence on these occasions increased his embarrassment, I had stationed myself in a dusky place near the door, and now stole softly out.

On my return to the tavern the tragedy was already concluded; and, being a feeble one in itself and indifferently performed, it left so much the better chance for the Story Teller. The bar was thronged with cus-tomers, the toddy stick[10] keeping a continual tattoo; while in the hall there was a broad, deep, buzzing sound, with an occasional peal of im-patient thunder—all symptoms of an overflowing house and an eager audience. I drank a glass of wine and water, and stood at the side scene conversing with a young person of doubtful sex. If a gentleman, how could he have performed the singing girl the night before in No Song, no Supper? Or, if a lady, why did she enact Young Norval, and now wear a green coat and white pantaloons in the character of Little Pickle?[11] In either case the dress was pretty and the wearer bewitching; so that, at the proper moment, I stepped forward with a gay heart and a bold one; while the orchestra played a tune that had resounded at many a country ball, and the curtain, as it rose, discovered something like a country bar room. Such a scene was well enough adapted to such a tale.

The orchestra of our little theatre consisted of two fiddles and a clarinet; but, if the whole harmony of the Tremont had been there, it might have swelled in vain beneath the tumult of applause that greeted me. The good people of the town, knowing that the world contained innumerable persons of celebrity undreamed of by them, took it for granted that I was one, and that their roar of welcome was but a feeble echo of those which had thundered around me in lofty theatres. Such an enthusiastic uproar was never heard. Each person seemed a Briareus[12] clapping a hundred hands, besides keeping his feet and several cudgels in play with stamping and thumping on the floor; while the ladies flourished their white cambric handkerchiefs, intermixed with yellow and red bandanna, like the flags of different nations. After such a salutation, the celebrated Story Teller felt almost ashamed to produce so humble an affair as Mr. Higginbotham's Catastrophe.

This story was originally more dramatic than as there presented, and afforded good scope for mimicry and buffoonery, neither of which, to my shame, did I spare. I never knew the "magic of a name" till I used that of Mr. Higginbotham. Often as I repeated it, there were louder bursts of merriment than those which responded to what, in my opinion, were more legitimate strokes of humor. The success of the piece was incalculably heightened by a stiff cue[13] of horse hair, which Little Pickle, in the spirit of that mischief-loving character, had fastened to my collar, where, unknown to me, it kept making the queerest gestures of its own in correspondence with all mine. The audience, supposing that some enormous joke was appended to this long tail behind, were ineffably delighted, and gave way to such a tumult of approbation that, just as the story closed, the benches broke beneath them and left one whole row of my admirers on the floor. Even in that predicament they continued their applause. In after times, when I had grown a bitter moralizer, I took this scene for an example how much of fame is hum-

---

bug; how much the meed of what our better nature blushes at; how much an accident; how much bestowed on mistaken principles; and how small and poor the remnant. From pit and boxes there was now a universal call for the Story Teller.

That celebrated personage came not when they did call to him. As I left the stage, the landlord, being also the postmaster, had given me a letter with the postmark of my native village, and directed to my assumed name in the stiff old handwriting of Parson Thumpcushion. Doubtless he had heard of the rising renown of the Story Teller, and conjectured at once that such a nondescript luminary could be no other than his lost ward. His epistle, though I never read it, affected me most painfully. I seemed to see the Puritanic figure of my guardian standing among the fripperies of the theatre and pointing to the players,—the fantastic and effeminate men, the painted women, the giddy girl in boy's clothes, merrier than modest,—pointing to these with solemn ridicule, and eyeing me with stern rebuke. His image was a type of the austere duty, and they of the vanities of life.

I hastened with the letter to my chamber and held it unopened in my hand while the applause of my buffoonery yet sounded through the theatre. Another train of thought came over me. The stern old man appeared again, but now with the gentleness of sorrow, softening his authority with love as a father might, and even bending his venerable head, as if to say that my errors had an apology in his own mistaken discipline. I strode twice across the chamber, then held the letter in the flame of the candle, and beheld it consume unread. It is fixed in my mind, and was so at the time, that he had addressed me in a style of paternal wisdom, and love, and reconciliation which I could not have resisted had I but risked the trial. The thought still haunts me that then I made my irrevocable choice between good and evil fate.

Meanwhile, as this occurrence had disturbed my mind and indisposed me to the present exercise of my profession, I left the town, in spite of a laudatory critique in the newspaper, and untempted by the liberal offers of the manager. As we walked onward, following the same road, on two such different errands, Eliakim groaned in spirit, and labored with tears to convince me of the guilt and madness of my life.

Sketches from Memory

THE NOTCH OF THE WHITE MOUNTAINS[1]

It was now the middle of September. We had come since sunrise from Bartlett, passing up through the valley of the Saco, which extends between mountainous walls, sometimes with a steep ascent, but often as level as a church aisle. All that day and two preceding ones we had been loitering towards the heart of the White Mountains—those old crystal hills, whose mysterious brilliancy had gleamed upon our distant wanderings before we thought of visiting them. Height after height had risen and towered one above another till the clouds began to hang below the peaks. Down their slopes were the red pathways of the slides, those avalanches of earth, stones, and trees, which descend into the hollows, leaving vestiges of their track hardly to be effaced by the vegetation of ages. We had mountains behind us and mountains on each side, and a group of mightier ones ahead. Still our road went up along the Saco, right towards the centre of that group, as if to climb above the clouds in its passage to the farther region.

In old times the settlers used to be astounded by the inroads of the northern Indians, coming down upon them from this mountain rampart through some defile known only to themselves. It is, indeed, a wondrous path. A demon, it might be fancied, or one of the Titans,[2] was travelling up the valley, elbowing the heights carelessly aside as he passed, till at length a great mountain took its stand directly across his intended road. He tarries not for such an obstacle, but, rending it asunder a thousand feet from peak to base, discloses its treasures of hidden minerals, its sunless waters, all the secrets of the mountain's inmost heart, with a mighty fracture of rugged precipices on each side. This is the Notch of the White Hills. Shame on me that I have attempted to describe it by so mean an image—feeling, as I do, that it is one of those symbolic scenes which lead the mind to the sentiment, though not to the conception, of Omnipotence.

*   *   *

We had now reached a narrow passage, which showed almost the appearance of having been cut by human strength and artifice in the solid rock. There was a wall of granite on each side, high and precipitous, especially on our right, and so smooth that a few evergreens could hardly find foothold enough to grow there. This is the entrance, or, in the direction we were going, the extremity, of the romantic defile of the Notch. Before emerging from it, the rattling of wheels approached behind us, and a stage coach rumbled out of the mountain, with seats on top and trunks behind, and a smart driver, in a drab greatcoat, touching the wheel horses with the whip stock and reining in the leaders. To my mind there was a sort of poetry in such an incident, hardly inferior to what would have accompanied the painted array of an Indian war party gliding forth from the same wild chasm. All the passengers, except a very fat lady on the back seat, had alighted. One was a mineralogist, a scientific, green-spectacled figure in black, bearing a heavy hammer, with which he did great damage to the precipices, and put the fragments in his pocket. Another was a well-dressed young man, who carried an opera glass set in gold, and seemed to be making a quotation from some of Byron's rhapsodies[3] on mountain scenery. There was also a trader, returning from Portland to the upper part of Vermont; and a fair young girl, with a very faint bloom like one of those pale and delicate flowers which sometimes occur among alpine cliffs.

They disappeared, and we followed them, passing through a deep pine forest, which for some miles allowed us to see nothing but its own dismal shade. Towards nightfall we reached a level amphitheatre, surrounded by a great rampart of hills, which shut out the sunshine long before it left the external world. It was here that we obtained our first view, except at a distance, of the principal group of mountains. They are majestic, and even awful, when contemplated in a proper mood, yet, by their breadth of base and the long ridges which support them, give the idea of immense bulk rather than of towering height. Mount Washington,[4] indeed, looked near to heaven: he was white with snow a mile downward, and had caught the only cloud that was sailing through the atmosphere to veil his head. Let us forget the other names of American statesmen that have been stamped upon these hills, but still call the loftiest WASHINGTON. Mountains are Earth's undecaying monuments. They must stand while she endures, and never should be consecrated to the mere great men of their own age and country, but to the mighty ones alone, whose glory is universal, and whom all time will render illustrious.

The air, not often sultry in this elevated region, nearly two thousand feet above the sea, was now sharp and cold, like that of a clear November evening in the lowlands. By morning, probably, there would be a frost, if not a snowfall, on the grass and rye, and an icy surface over the standing water. I was glad to perceive a prospect of comfortable quarters in a house which we were approaching, and of pleasant company in the guests who were assembled at the door.

OUR EVENING PARTY AMONG THE MOUNTAINS

We stood in front of a good substantial farm house, of old date in that wild country. A sign over the door denoted it to be the White Mountain Post Office—an establishment which distributes letters and newspapers to perhaps a score of persons, comprising the population of two or three townships among the hills. The broad and weighty antlers of a deer, "a stag of ten,"[5] were fastened at the corner of the house; a fox's bushy tail was nailed beneath them; and a huge black paw lay on the ground, newly severed and still bleeding—the trophy of a bear hunt. Among several persons collected about the doorsteps, the most remarkable was a sturdy mountaineer, of six feet two and corresponding bulk, with a heavy set of features, such as might be moulded on his own blacksmith's anvil, but yet indicative of mother wit and rough humor. As we appeared, he uplifted a tin trumpet, four or five feet long, and blew a tremendous blast, either in honor of our arrival or to awaken an echo from the opposite hill.

Ethan Crawford's guests[6] were of such a motley description as to form quite a picturesque group, seldom seen together except at some place like this, at once the pleasure house of fashionable tourists and the homely inn of country travellers. Among the company at the door were the mineralogist and the owner of the gold opera glass whom we had encountered in the Notch; two Georgian gentlemen, who had chilled their southern blood that morning on the top of Mount Washington; a physician and his wife from Conway; a trader of Burlington and an old squire of the Green Mountains; and two young married couples, all the way from Massachusetts, on the matrimonial jaunt. Besides these strangers, the rugged county of Coos, in which we were, was represented by half a dozen woodcutters, who had slain a bear in the forest and smitten off his paw.

I had joined the party, and had a moment's leisure to examine them before the echo of Ethan's blast returned from the hill. Not one, but many echoes had caught up the harsh and tuneless sound, untwisted its complicated threads, and found a thousand aerial harmonies in one stern trumpet tone. It was a distinct yet distant and dreamlike symphony of melodious instruments, as if an airy band had been hidden on the hillside and made faint music at the summons. No subsequent trial produced so clear, delicate, and spiritual a concert as the first. A fieldpiece was then discharged from the top of a neighboring hill, and gave birth to one long reverberation, which ran round the circle of mountains in an unbroken chain of sound and rolled away without a separate echo. After these experiments, the cold atmosphere drove us all into the house, with the keenest appetites for supper.

It did one's heart good to see the great fires that were kindled in the parlor and bar room, especially the latter, where the fireplace was built of rough stone, and might have contained the trunk of an old tree for a backlog. A man keeps a comfortable hearth when his own forest is at his very door. In the parlor, when the evening was fairly set in, we held our hands before our eyes to shield them from the ruddy glow, and began a pleasant variety of conversation. The mineralogist and the physician talked about the invigorating qualities of the mountain air, and its excellent effect on Ethan Crawford's father, an old man of seventy-five, with the unbroken frame of middle life. The two brides and the doctor's wife held a whispered discussion, which, by their frequent titterings and a blush or two, seemed to have reference to the tri-

338 · *Mosses from an Old Manse*

als or enjoyments of the matrimonial state. The bridegrooms sat together in a corner, rigidly silent, like Quakers whom the spirit moveth
not,[7] being still in the odd predicament of bashfulness towards their
own young wives. The Green Mountain squire chose me for his companion, and described the difficulties he had met with half a century
ago in travelling from the Connecticut River through the Notch to
Conway, now a single day's journey, though it had cost him eighteen.
The Georgians held the album between them, and favored us with the
few specimens of its contents, which they considered ridiculous
enough to be worth hearing. One extract met with deserved applause.
It was a "Sonnet to the Snow on Mount Washington," and had been
contributed that very afternoon, bearing a signature of great distinction in magazines and annuals. The lines were elegant and full of
fancy, but too remote from familiar sentiment, and cold as their subject, resembling those curious specimens of crystallized vapor which I
observed next day on the mountain top. The poet was understood to
be the young gentleman of the gold opera glass, who heard our laudatory remarks with the composure of a veteran.

Such was our party, and such their ways of amusement. But on a
winter evening another set of guests assembled at the hearth where
these summer travellers were now sitting. I once had it in contemplation to spend a month hereabouts, in sleighing time, for the sake of
studying the yeomen of New England, who then elbow each other
through the Notch by hundreds, on their way to Portland. There could
be no better school for such a purpose than Ethan Crawford's inn. Let
the student go thither in December, sit down with the teamsters at
their meals, share their evening merriment, and repose with them at
night when every bed has its three occupants, and parlor, bar room,
and kitchen are strewn with slumberers around the fire. Then let him
rise before daylight, button his greatcoat, muffle up his ears, and stride
with the departing caravan a mile or two, to see how sturdily they
make head against the blast. A treasure of characteristic traits will
repay all inconveniences, even should a frozen nose be of the number.

The conversation of our party soon became more animated and
sincere, and we recounted some traditions of the Indians, who believed that the father and mother of their race were saved from a deluge by ascending the peak of Mount Washington. The children of that
pair have been overwhelmed, and found no such refuge. In the mythol-

ogy of the savage, these mountains were afterwards considered sacred and inaccessible, full of unearthly wonders, illuminated at lofty heights by the blaze of precious stones, and inhabited by deities, who sometimes shrouded themselves in the snow storm and came down on the lower world. There are few legends more poetical than that of the "Great Carbuncle" of the White Mountains.[8] The belief was communicated to the English settlers, and is hardly yet extinct, that a gem, of such immense size as to be seen shining miles away, hangs from a rock over a clear, deep lake, high up among the hills. They who had once beheld its splendor were inthralled with an unutterable yearning to possess it. But a spirit guarded that inestimable jewel, and bewildered the adventurer with a dark mist from the enchanted lake. Thus life was worn away in the vain search for an unearthly treasure, till at length the deluded one went up the mountain, still sanguine as in youth, but returned no more. On this theme methinks I could frame a tale with a deep moral.

The hearts of the palefaces would not thrill to these superstitions of the red men, though we spoke of them in the centre of their haunted region. The habits and sentiments of that departed people were too distinct from those of their successors to find much real sympathy. It has often been a matter of regret to me that I was shut out from the most peculiar field of American fiction by an inability to see any romance, or poetry, or grandeur, or beauty in the Indian character, at least till such traits were pointed out by others. I do abhor an Indian story. Yet no writer can be more secure of a permanent place in our literature than the biographer of the Indian chiefs. His subject, as referring to tribes which have mostly vanished from the earth, gives him a right to be placed on a classic shelf, apart from the merits which will sustain him there.

I made inquiries whether, in his researches about these parts, our mineralogist had found the three "Silver Hills" which an Indian sachem sold to an Englishman nearly two hundred years ago, and the treasure of which the posterity of the purchaser have been looking for ever since. But the man of science had ransacked every hill along the Saco, and knew nothing of these prodigious piles of wealth. By this time, as usual with men on the eve of great adventure, we had prolonged our session deep into the night, considering how early we were to set out on our six miles' ride to the foot of Mount Washington.

There was now a general breaking up. I scrutinized the faces of the two bridegrooms, and saw but little probability of their leaving the bosom of earthly bliss, in the first week of the honeymoon and at the frosty hour of three, to climb above the clouds; nor, when I felt how sharp the wind was as it rushed through a broken pane and eddied between the chinks of my unplastered chamber, did I anticipate much alacrity on my own part, though we were to seek for the "Great Carbuncle."

THE CANAL BOAT

I was inclined to be poetical about the Grand Canal.[9] In my imagination De Witt Clinton[10] was an enchanter, who had waved his magic wand from the Hudson to Lake Erie and united them by a watery highway, crowded with the commerce of two worlds, till then inaccessible to each other. This simple and mighty conception had conferred inestimable value on spots which Nature seemed to have thrown carelessly into the great body of the earth, without foreseeing that they could ever attain importance. I pictured the surprise of the sleepy Dutchmen[11] when the new river first glittered by their doors, bringing them hard cash or foreign commodities in exchange for their hitherto unmarketable produce. Surely the water of this canal must be the most fertilizing of all fluids; for it causes towns, with their masses of brick and stone, their churches and theatres, their business and hubbub, their luxury and refinement, their gay dames and polished citizens, to spring up, till in time the wondrous stream may flow between two continuous lines of buildings, through one thronged street, from Buffalo to Albany.[12] I embarked about thirty miles below Utica, determining to voyage along the whole extent of the canal at least twice in the course of the summer.

Behold us, then, fairly afloat, with three horses harnessed to our vessel, like the steeds of Neptune[13] to a huge scallop shell in mythological pictures. Bound to a distant port, we had neither chart nor compass, nor cared about the wind, nor felt the heaving of a billow, nor dreaded shipwreck, however fierce the tempest, in our adventurous navigation of an interminable mud puddle; for a mud puddle it seemed, and as dark and turbid as if every kennel in the land paid contribution to it. With an imperceptible current, it holds its drowsy way through all the dismal swamps and unimpressive scenery that could be found between the great lakes and the sea coast. Yet there is variety enough, both on the surface of the canal and along its banks, to amuse the traveller, if an overpowering tedium did not deaden his perceptions.

Sometimes we met a black and rusty-looking vessel, laden with lumber, salt from Syracuse, or Genesee flour, and shaped at both ends like a square-toed boot, as if it had two sterns, and were fated always to advance backward. On its deck would be a square hut, and a woman seen through the window at her household work, with a little tribe of children who perhaps had been born in this strange dwelling and knew no other home. Thus, while the husband smoked his pipe at the helm and the eldest son rode one of the horses, on went the family, travelling hundreds of miles in their own house and carrying their fireside with them. The most frequent species of craft were the "line boats," which had a cabin at each end, and a great bulk of barrels, bales, and boxes in the midst, or light packets like our own, decked all over with a row of curtained windows from stem to stern, and a drowsy face at every one. Once we encountered a boat of rude construction, painted all in gloomy black, and manned by three Indians, who gazed at us in silence and with a singular fixedness of eye. Perhaps these three alone, among the ancient possessors of the land, had attempted to derive benefit from the white man's mighty projects and float along the current of his enterprise. Not long after, in the midst of a swamp and beneath a clouded sky, we overtook a vessel that seemed full of mirth and sunshine. It contained a little colony of Swiss on their way to Michigan, clad in garments of strange fashion and gay colors, scarlet, yellow, and bright blue, singing, laughing, and making merry in odd tones and a babble of outlandish words. One pretty damsel, with a beautiful pair of naked white arms, addressed a mirthful remark to me. She spoke in her native tongue, and I retorted in good English, both of us laughing heartily at each other's unintelligible wit. I cannot describe how pleasantly this incident affected me. These honest Swiss were an itinerant community of jest and fun journeying through a gloomy land and among a dull race of money-getting drudges, meeting none to understand their mirth, and only one to sympathize with it, yet still retaining the happy lightness of their own spirit.

Had I been on my feet at the time instead of sailing slowly along in a dirty canal boat, I should often have paused to contemplate the diversified panorama along the banks of the canal. Sometimes the scene was a forest, dark, dense, and impervious, breaking away occasionally and receding from a lonely tract, covered with dismal black stumps, where, on the verge of the canal, might be seen a log cottage and a sallow-faced woman at the window. Lean and aguish,[14] she looked like poverty personified, half clothed, half fed, and dwelling in a desert, while a tide of wealth was sweeping by her door. Two or three miles farther would bring us to a lock, where the slight impediment to navigation had created a little mart of trade. Here would be found commodities of all sorts, enumerated in yellow letters on the window shutters of a small grocery store, the owner of which had set his soul to the gathering of coppers and small change, buying and selling through the week, and counting his gains on the blessed Sabbath. The next scene might be the dwelling houses and stores of a thriving village, built of wood or small gray stones, a church spire rising in the midst, and generally two taverns, bearing over their piazzas the pompous titles of "hotel," "exchange," "tontine,"[15] or "coffee house." Passing on, we glide now into the unquiet heart of an inland city,—of Utica, for instance,—and find ourselves amid piles of brick, crowded docks and quays, rich warehouses, and a busy population. We feel the eager and hurrying spirit of the place, like a stream and eddy whirling us along with it. Through the thickest of the tumult goes the canal, flowing between lofty rows of buildings and arched bridges of hewn stone. Onward, also, go we, till the hum and bustle of struggling enterprise die away behind us and we are threading an avenue of the ancient woods again.

This sounds not amiss in description, but was so tiresome in reality that we were driven to the most childish expedients for amusement. An English traveller paraded the deck, with a rifle in his walking stick, and waged war on squirrels and woodpeckers, sometimes sending an unsuccessful bullet among flocks of tame ducks and geese which abound in the dirty water of the canal. I, also, pelted these foolish birds with apples, and smiled at the ridiculous earnestness of their scrambles for the prize while the apple bobbed about like a thing of life. Several little accidents afforded us good-natured diversion. At the moment of changing horses the tow rope caught a Massachusetts farmer by the leg and threw him down in a very indescribable posture, leaving a purple mark around his sturdy limb. A new passenger fell flat on his back in attempting to step on deck as the boat emerged from under a bridge. Another, in his Sunday clothes, as good luck would have it, being told to leap aboard from the bank, forthwith plunged up to his third waistcoat button in the canal, and was fished out in a very pitiable plight not at all amended by our three rounds of applause. Anon a Virginia schoolmaster, too intent on a pocket Virgil[16] to heed the helmsman's warning, "Bridge! bridge!" was saluted by the said bridge on his knowledge box. I had prostrated myself like a pagan before his idol, but heard the dull, leaden sound of the contact, and fully expected to see the treasures of the poor man's cranium scattered about the deck. However, as there was no harm done, except a large bump on the head, and probably a corresponding dent in the bridge, the rest of us exchanged glances and laughed quietly. O, how pitiless are idle people!

*   *   *

The table being now lengthened through the cabin and spread for supper, the next twenty minutes were the pleasantest I had spent on the canal, the same space at dinner excepted. At the close of the meal it had become dusky enough for lamplight. The rain pattered unceasingly on the deck, and sometimes came with a sullen rush against the windows, driven by the wind as it stirred through an opening of the forest. The intolerable dulness of the scene engendered an evil spirit in me. Perceiving that the Englishman was taking notes in a memorandum book, with occasional glances round the cabin, I presumed that we were all to figure in a future volume of travels, and amused my ill humor by falling into the probable vein of his remarks. He would hold up an imaginary mirror, wherein our reflected faces would appear ugly and ridiculous, yet still retain an undeniable likeness to the originals. Then, with more sweeping malice, he would make these caricatures the representatives of great classes of my countrymen.

He glanced at the Virginia schoolmaster, a Yankee by birth, who, to recreate himself, was examining a freshman from Schenectady College in the conjugation of a Greek verb. Him the Englishman would portray as the scholar of America, and compare his erudition to a schoolboy's Latin theme made up of scraps ill selected and worse put together. Next the tourist looked at the Massachusetts farmer, who was delivering a dogmatic harangue on the iniquity of Sunday mails. Here was the far-famed yeoman of New England; his religion, writes the Englishman, is gloom on the Sabbath, long prayers every morning and eventide, and illiberality at all times; his boasted information is merely an abstract and compound of newspaper paragraphs, Congress debates, caucus harangues, and the argument and judge's charge in his own lawsuits. The bookmonger cast his eye at a Detroit merchant, and began scribbling faster than ever. In this sharpeyed man, this lean man, of wrinkled brow, we see daring enterprise and close-fisted avarice combined. Here is the worshipper of Mammon[17] at noonday; here is the three times bankrupt, richer after every ruin; here, in one word, (O wicked Englishman to say it!) here is the American. He lifted his eyeglass to inspect a western lady, who at once became aware of the glance, reddened, and retired deeper into the female part of the cabin. Here was the pure, modest, sensitive, and shrinking woman of America— shrinking when no evil is intended, and sensitive like diseased flesh, that thrills if you but point at it; and strangely modest, without confidence in the modesty of other people; and admirably pure, with such a quick apprehension of all impurity.

In this manner I went all through the cabin, hitting every body as hard a lash as I could, and laying the whole blame on the infernal Englishman. At length I caught the eyes of my own image in the looking glass, where a number of the party were likewise reflected, and among them the Englishman, who at that moment was intently observing myself.

*   *   *

The crimson curtain being let down between the ladies and gentlemen, the cabin became a bed chamber for twenty persons, who were laid on shelves one above another. For a long time our various incommodities kept us all awake except five or six, who were accustomed to sleep nightly amid the uproar of their own snoring, and had little to dread from any other species of disturbance. It is a curious fact that these snorers had been the most quiet people in the boat while awake, and became peacebreakers only when others cease to be so, breathing tumult out of their repose. Would it were possible to affix a wind instrument to the nose, and thus make melody of a snore, so that a sleeping lover might serenade his mistress or a congregation snore a psalm tune! Other, though fainter, sounds than these contributed to my restlessness. My head was close to the crimson curtain,—the sexual division of the boat,—behind which I continually heard whispers and stealthy footsteps; the noise of a comb laid on the table or a slipper dropped on the floor; the twang, like a broken harpstring, caused by loosening a tight belt; the rustling of a gown in its descent; and the unlacing of a pair of stays. My ear seemed to have the properties of an eye; a visible image pestered my fancy in the darkness; the curtain was withdrawn between me and the western lady, who yet disrobed herself without a blush.

Finally all was hushed in that quarter. Still I was more broad awake than through the whole preceding day, and felt a feverish impulse to toss my limbs miles apart and appease the unquietness of mind by that of matter. Forgetting that my berth was hardly so wide as a coffin, I turned suddenly over, and fell like an avalanche on the floor, to the disturbance of the whole community of sleepers. As there were no bones broken, I blessed the accident and went on deck. A lantern was burning at each end of the boat, and one of the crew was stationed at the bows, keeping watch, as mariners do on the ocean. Though the rain had ceased, the sky was all one cloud, and the darkness so intense that there seemed to be no world except the little space on which our lanterns glimmered. Yet it was an impressive scene.

We were traversing the "long level," a dead flat between Utica and Syracuse, where the canal has not rise or fall enough to require a lock for nearly seventy miles. There can hardly be a more dismal tract of country. The forest which covers it, consisting chiefly of white cedar, black ash, and other trees that live in excessive moisture, is now decayed and deathstruck by the partial draining of the swamp into the great ditch of the canal. Sometimes, indeed, our lights were reflected from pools of stagnant water which stretched far in among the trunks of the trees, beneath dense masses of dark foliage. But generally the tall stems and intermingled branches were naked, and brought into strong relief amid the surrounding gloom by the whiteness of their decay. Often we beheld the prostrate form of some old sylvan giant which had fallen and crushed down smaller trees under its immense ruin. In spots where destruction had been riotous, the lanterns showed perhaps a hundred trunks, erect, half overthrown, extended along the ground, resting on their shattered limbs or tossing them desperately into the darkness, but all of one ashy white, all naked together, in desolate confusion. Thus growing out of the night as we drew nigh, and vanishing as we glided on, based on obscurity, and overhung and

346 · *Mosses from an Old Manse*

bounded by it, the scene was ghostlike—the very land of unsubstantial things, whither dreams might betake themselves when they quit the slumberer's brain.

My fancy found another emblem. The wild nature of America had been driven to this desert-place by the encroachments of civilized man. And even here, where the savage queen was throned on the ruins of her empire, did we penetrate, a vulgar and worldly throng, intruding on her latest solitude. In other lands decay sits among fallen palaces; but here her home is in the forests.

Looking ahead, I discerned a distant light, announcing the approach of another boat, which soon passed us, and proved to be a rusty old scow—just such a craft as the "Flying Dutchman"[18] would navigate on the canal. Perhaps it was that celebrated personage himself whom I imperfectly distinguished at the helm in a glazed cap and rough greatcoat, with a pipe in his mouth, leaving the fumes of tobacco a hundred yards behind. Shortly after our boatman blew a horn, sending a long and melancholy note through the forest avenue, as a signal for some watcher in the wilderness to be ready with a change of horses. We had proceeded a mile or two with our fresh team when the tow rope got entangled in a fallen branch on the edge of the canal and caused a momentary delay, during which I went to examine the phosphoric light of an old tree a little within the forest. It was not the first delusive radiance that I had followed.

The tree lay along the ground, and was wholly converted into a mass of diseased splendor, which threw a ghastliness around. Being full of conceits that night, I called it a frigid fire, a funeral light, illumining decay and death, an emblem of fame that gleams around the dead man without warming him, or of genius when it owes its brilliancy to moral rottenness, and was thinking that such ghostlike torches were just fit to light up this dead forest or to blaze coldly in tombs, when, starting from my abstraction, I looked up the canal. I recollected myself, and discovered the lanterns glimmering far away.

"Boat ahoy!" shouted I, making a trumpet of my closed fists.

Though the cry must have rung for miles along that hollow passage of the woods, it produced no effect. These packet boats make up for their snaillike pace by never loitering day nor night, especially for those who have paid their fare. Indeed, the captain had an interest in getting rid of me; for I was his creditor for a breakfast.

"They are gone, Heaven be praised!" ejaculated I; "for I cannot possibly overtake them. Here am I, on the 'long level,' at midnight, with the comfortable prospect of a walk to Syracuse, where my baggage will be left. And now to find a house or shed wherein to pass the night." So thinking aloud, I took a flambeau[19] from the old tree, burning, but consuming not, to light my steps withal, and, like a jack-o'-the-lantern, set out on my midnight tour.

THE OLD APPLE DEALER

The lover of the moral picturesque may sometimes find what he seeks in a character which is nevertheless of too negative a description to be seized upon and represented to the imaginative vision by word painting. As an instance, I remember an old man who carries on a little trade of gingerbread and apples at the depot of one of our railroads. While awaiting the departure of the cars, my observation, flitting to and fro among the livelier characteristics of the scene, has often settled insensibly upon this almost hueless object. Thus, unconsciously to myself and unsuspected by him, I have studied the old apple dealer until he has become a naturalized citizen of my inner world. How little would he imagine—poor, neglected, friendless, unappreciated, and with little that demands appreciation—that the mental eye of an utter stranger has so often reverted to his figure! Many a noble form, many a beautiful face, has flitted before me and vanished like a shadow. It is a strange witchcraft whereby this faded and featureless old apple dealer has gained a settlement in my memory.

He is a small man, with gray hair and gray stubble beard, and is invariably clad in a shabby surtout[1] of snuff color, closely buttoned, and half concealing a pair of gray pantaloons; the whole dress, though clean and entire, being evidently flimsy with much wear. His face, thin, withered, furrowed, and with features which even age has failed to render impressive, has a frostbitten aspect. It is a moral frost which no physical warmth or comfortableness could counteract. The summer sunshine may fling its white heat upon him or the good fire of the depot room may make him the focus of its blaze on a winter's day; but all in vain; for still the old man looks as if he were in a frosty atmosphere, with scarcely warmth enough to keep life in the region about his heart. It is a patient, long-suffering, quiet, hopeless, shivering aspect. He is not desperate,—that, though its etymology implies no more, would be too positive an expression,—but merely devoid of hope. As all his past life, probably, offers no spots of brightness to his memory, so he takes his present poverty and discomfort as entirely a matter of course: he thinks it the definition of existence, so far as himself is concerned, to be poor, cold, and uncomfortable. It may be added, that time has not thrown dignity as a mantle over the old man's figure: there is nothing venerable about him: you pity him without a scruple.

He sits on a bench in the depot room; and before him, on the floor, are deposited two baskets of a capacity to contain his whole stock in trade. Across from one basket to the other extends a board, on which is displayed a plate of cakes and gingerbread, some russet and red-cheeked apples, and a box containing variegated sticks of candy, together with that delectable condiment known by children as Gibraltar rock,[2] neatly done up in white paper. There is likewise a half-peck[3] measure of cracked walnuts and two or three tin half pints or gills[4] filled with the nut kernels, ready for purchasers. Such are the small commodities with which our old friend comes daily before the world, ministering to its petty needs and little freaks of appetite, and seeking thence the solid subsistence—so far as he may subsist—of his life.

A slight observer would speak of the old man's quietude; but, on closer scrutiny, you discover that there is a continual unrest within him, which somewhat resembles the fluttering action of the nerves in a corpse from which life has recently departed. Though he never exhibits any violent action, and, indeed, might appear to be sitting quite still, yet you perceive, when his minuter peculiarities begin to be detected, that he is always making some little movement or other. He looks anxiously at his plate of cakes or pyramid of apples and slightly alters their arrangement, with an evident idea that a great deal depends on their being disposed exactly thus and so. Then for a moment he gazes out of the window; then he shivers quietly and folds his arms across his breast, as if to draw himself closer within himself, and thus keep a flicker of warmth in his lonesome heart. Now he turns again to his merchandise of cakes, apples, and candy, and discovers that this cake or that apple, or yonder stick of red and white candy, has somehow got out of its proper position. And is there not a walnut kernel too many or too few in one of those small tin measures? Again the whole arrangement appears to be settled to his mind; but, in the course of a minute or two, there will assuredly be something to set right. At times, by an indescribable shadow upon his features, too quiet, however, to be noticed until you are familiar with his ordinary aspect, the expression of frostbitten, patient despondency becomes very touching. It seems as if just at that instant the suspicion occurred to him that, in his chill decline of life, earning scanty bread by selling cakes, apples, and candy, he is a very miserable old fellow.

But, if he think so, it is a mistake. He can never suffer the extreme of misery, because the tone of his whole being is too much subdued for him to feel any thing acutely.

Occasionally one of the passengers, to while away a tedious interval, approaches the old man, inspects the articles upon his board, and even peeps curiously into the two baskets. Another, striding to and fro along the room, throws a look at the apples and gingerbread at every turn. A third, it may be of a more sensitive and delicate texture of being, glances shyly thitherward, cautious not to excite expectations of a purchaser while yet undetermined whether to buy. But there appears to be no need of such a scrupulous regard to our old friend's feelings. True, he is conscious of the remote possibility to sell a cake or an apple; but innumerable disappointments have rendered him so far a philosopher, that, even if the purchased article should be returned, he will consider it altogether in the ordinary train of events. He speaks to none, and makes no sign of offering his wares to the public: not that he is deterred by pride, but by the certain conviction that such demonstrations would not increase his custom. Besides, this activity in business would require an energy that never could have been a characteristic of his almost passive disposition even in youth. Whenever an actual customer appears the old man looks up with a patient eye: if the price and the article are approved, he is ready to make change; otherwise his eyelids droop again sadly enough, but with no heavier despondency than before. He shivers, perhaps folds his lean arms around his lean body, and resumes the lifelong, frozen patience in which consists his strength. Once in a while a schoolboy comes hastily up, places a cent or two upon the board, and takes up a cake, or stick of candy, or a measure of walnuts, or an apple as red cheeked as himself. There are no words as to price, that being as well known to the buyer as to the seller. The old apple dealer never speaks an unnecessary word: not that he is sullen and morose; but there is none of the cheeriness and briskness in him that stirs up people to talk.

Not seldom he is greeted by some old neighbor, a man well to do in the world, who makes a civil, patronizing observation about the weather; and then, by way of performing a charitable deed, begins to chaffer[5] for an apple. Our friend presumes not on any past acquaintance; he makes the briefest possible response to all general remarks, and shrinks quietly into himself again. After every diminution of his stock he takes care to produce from the basket another cake, another stick of candy, another apple, or another measure of walnuts, to supply the place of the article sold. Two or three attempts—or, perchance, half a dozen—are requisite before the board can be rearranged to his satisfaction. If he have received a silver coin, he waits till the purchaser is out of sight, then examines it closely, and tries to bend it with his finger and thumb; finally he puts it into his waistcoat pocket with seemingly a gentle sigh. This sigh, so faint as to be hardly perceptible, and not expressive of any definite emotion, is the accompaniment and conclusion of all his actions. It is the symbol of the chillness and torpid melancholy of his old age, which only make themselves felt sensibly when his repose is slightly disturbed.

Our man of gingerbread and apples is not a specimen of the "needy man who has seen better days." Doubtless there have been better and brighter days in the far-off time of his youth; but none with so much sunshine of prosperity in them that the chill, the depression, the narrowness of means, in his declining years, can have come upon him by surprise. His life has all been of a piece. His subdued and nerveless boyhood prefigured his abortive prime, which likewise contained within itself the prophecy and image of his lean and torpid age. He was perhaps a mechanic, who never came to be a master in his craft, or a petty tradesman, rubbing onward between passably to do and poverty. Possibly he may look back to some brilliant epoch of his career when there were a hundred or two of dollars to his credit in the Savings Bank. Such must have been the extent of his better fortune—his little measure of this world's triumphs—all that he has known of success. A meek, downcast, humble, uncomplaining creature, he probably has never felt himself entitled to more than so much of the gifts of Providence. Is it not still something that he has never held out his hand for charity, nor has yet been driven to that sad home and household of Earth's forlorn and broken-spirited children, the almshouse? He cherishes no quarrel, therefore, with his destiny, nor with the Author of it. All is as it should be.

If, indeed, he have been bereaved of a son, a bold, energetic, vigorous young man, on whom the father's feeble nature leaned as on a staff of strength, in that case he may have felt a bitterness that could not otherwise have been generated in his heart. But methinks the joy of possessing such a son and the agony of losing him would have developed the old man's moral and intellectual nature to a much greater degree than we now find it. Intense grief appears to be as much out of keeping with his life as fervid happiness.

To confess the truth, it is not the easiest matter in the world to define and individualize a character like this which we are now handling. The portrait must be so generally negative that the most delicate pencil is likely to spoil it by introducing some too positive tint. Every touch must be kept down, or else you destroy the subdued tone which is absolutely essential to the whole effect. Perhaps more may be done by contrast than by direct description. For this purpose I make use of another cake and candy merchant, who likewise infests the railroad depot. This latter worthy is a very smart and well-dressed boy of ten years old or thereabouts, who skips briskly hither and thither, addressing the passengers in a pert voice, yet with somewhat of good breeding in his tone and pronunciation. Now he has caught my eye, and skips across the room with a pretty pertness, which I should like to correct with a box on the ear. "Any cake, sir? any candy?"

No, none for me, my lad. I did but glance at your brisk figure in order to catch a reflected light and throw it upon your old rival yonder.

Again, in order to invest my conception of the old man with a more decided sense of reality, I look at him in the very moment of intensest bustle, on the arrival of the cars. The shriek of the engine as it rushes into the car house is the utterance of the steam fiend, whom man has subdued by magic spells and compels to serve as a beast of burden. He has skimmed rivers in his headlong rush, dashed through forests, plunged into the hearts of mountains, and glanced from the city to the desert-place, and again to a far-off city, with a meteoric progress, seen and out of sight, while his reverberating roar still fills the ear. The travellers swarm forth from the cars. All are full of the momentum which they have caught from their mode of conveyance. It seems as if the whole world, both morally and physically, were detached from its old standfasts and set in rapid motion. And, in the midst of this terrible activity, there sits the old man of gingerbread, so subdued, so hopeless, so without a stake in life, and yet not positively miserable,—there he sits, the forlorn old creature, one chill and sombre day after another, gathering scanty coppers for his cakes, apples, and candy,—there sits the old apple dealer, in his threadbare suit of snuff color and gray and his grizzly stubble beard. See! He folds his lean arms around his lean figure with that quiet sigh and that scarcely perceptible shiver which are the tokens of his inward state. I have him now. He and the steam fiend are each other's antipodes; the latter is the type of all that go ahead, and the old man the representative of that melancholy class who by some sad witchcraft are doomed never to share in the world's exulting progress. Thus the contrast between mankind and this desolate brother becomes picturesque, and even sublime.

And now farewell, old friend! Little do you suspect that a student of human life has made your character the theme of more than one solitary and thoughtful hour. Many would say that you have hardly individuality enough to be the object of your own self-love. How, then, can a stranger's eye detect any thing in your mind and heart to study and to wonder at? Yet, could I read but a tithe[6] of what is written there, it would be a volume of deeper and more comprehensive import than all that the wisest mortals have given to the world; for the soundless depths of the human soul and of eternity have an opening through your breast. God be praised, were it only for your sake, that the present shapes of human existence are not cast in iron nor hewn in everlasting adamant, but moulded of the vapors that vanish away while the essence flits upward to the infinite. There is a spiritual essence in this gray and lean old shape that shall flit upward too. Yes; doubtless there is a region where the lifelong shiver will pass away from his being, and that quiet sigh, which it has taken him so many years to breathe, will be brought to a close for good and all.

The Artist of the Beautiful

An elderly man, with his pretty daughter on his arm, was passing along the street, and emerged from the gloom of the cloudy evening into the light that fell across the pavement from the window of a small shop. It was a projecting window; and on the inside were suspended a variety of watches, pinchbeck,[1] silver, and one or two of gold, all with their faces turned from the street, as if churlishly disinclined to inform the wayfarers what o'clock it was. Seated within the shop, sidelong to the window, with his pale face bent earnestly over some delicate piece of mechanism on which was thrown the concentrated lustre of a shade lamp, appeared a young man.

"What can Owen Warland be about?" muttered old Peter Hovenden, himself a retired watchmaker and the former master of this same young man whose occupation he was now wondering at. "What can the fellow be about? These six months past I have never come by his shop without seeing him just as steadily at work as now. It would be a flight beyond his usual foolery to seek for the perpetual motion;[2] and yet I know enough of my old business to be certain that what he is now so busy with is no part of the machinery of a watch."

"Perhaps, father," said Annie, without showing much interest in the question, "Owen is inventing a new kind of timekeeper. I am sure he has ingenuity enough."

"Poh, child! He has not the sort of ingenuity to invent any thing better than a Dutch toy," answered her father, who had formerly been put to much vexation by Owen Warland's irregular genius. "A plague on such ingenuity! All the effect that ever I knew of it was, to spoil the accuracy of some of the best watches in my shop. He would turn the sun out of its orbit and derange the whole course of time, if, as I said before, his ingenuity could grasp any thing bigger than a child's toy!"

"Hush, father! He hears you!" whispered Annie, pressing the old man's arm. "His ears are as delicate as his feelings; and you know how easily disturbed they are. Do let us move on."

So Peter Hovenden and his daughter Annie plodded on without further conversation, until in a by-street of the town they found themselves passing the open door of a blacksmith's shop. Within was seen the forge, now blazing up and illuminating the high and dusky roof, and now confining its lustre to a narrow precinct of the coal-strewn floor, according as the breath of the bellows was puffed forth or again inhaled into its vast leathern lungs. In the intervals of brightness it was easy to distinguish objects in remote corners of the shop and the horseshoes that hung upon the wall; in the momentary gloom the fire seemed to be glimmering amidst the vagueness of unenclosed space. Moving about in this red glare and alternate dusk was the figure of the blacksmith, well worthy to be viewed in so picturesque an aspect of light and shade, where the bright blaze struggled with the black night, as if each would have snatched his comely strength from the other. Anon he drew a whitehot bar of iron from the coals, laid it on the anvil, uplifted his arm of might, and was soon enveloped in the myriads of sparks which the strokes of his hammer scattered into the surrounding gloom.

"Now, that is a pleasant sight," said the old watchmaker. "I know what it is to work in gold; but give me the worker in iron after all is said and done. He spends his labor upon a reality. What say you, daughter Annie?"

"Pray don't speak so loud, father," whispered Annie. "Robert Danforth will hear you."

"And what if he should hear me?" said Peter Hovenden. "I say again, it is a good and a wholesome thing to depend upon main strength and reality, and to earn one's bread with the bare and brawny arm of a blacksmith. A watchmaker gets his brain puzzled by his wheels within a wheel, or loses his health or the nicety of his eyesight, as was my case, and finds himself at middle age, or a little after, past labor at his own trade, and fit for nothing else, yet too poor to live at his ease. So I say once again, give me main strength for my money. And then, how it takes the nonsense out of a man! Did you ever hear of a blacksmith being such a fool as Owen Warland yonder?"

"Well said, uncle Hovenden!" shouted Robert Danforth from the forge, in a full, deep, merry voice, that made the roof reëcho. "And what says Miss Annie to that doctrine? She, I suppose, will think it a genteeler business to tinker up a lady's watch than to forge a horseshoe or make a gridiron."

Annie drew her father onward without giving him time for reply.

But we must return to Owen Warland's shop, and spend more meditation upon his history and character than either Peter Hovenden, or probably his daughter Annie, or Owen's old schoolfellow, Robert Danforth, would have thought due to so slight a subject. From the time that his little fingers could grasp a penknife, Owen had been remarkable for a delicate ingenuity, which sometimes produced pretty shapes in wood, principally figures of flowers and birds, and sometimes seemed to aim at the hidden mysteries of mechanism. But it was always for purposes of grace, and never with any mockery of the useful. He did not, like the crowd of schoolboy artisans, construct little windmills on the angle of a barn or watermills across the neighboring brook. Those who discovered such peculiarity in the boy as to think it worth their while to observe him closely, sometimes saw reason to suppose that he was attempting to imitate the beautiful movements of Nature as exemplified in the flight of birds or the activity of little animals. It seemed, in fact, a new development of the love of the beautiful, such as might have made him a poet, a painter, or a sculptor, and which was as completely refined from all utilitarian coarseness as it could have been in either of the fine arts. He looked with singular distaste at the stiff and regular processes of ordinary machinery. Being once carried to see a steam engine, in the expectation that his intuitive comprehension of mechanical principles would be gratified, he turned pale and grew sick, as if something monstrous and unnatural had been presented to him. This horror was partly owing to the size and terrible energy of the iron laborer; for the character of Owen's mind was microscopic, and tended naturally to the minute, in accordance with his diminutive frame and the marvellous smallness and delicate power of his fingers. Not that his sense of beauty was thereby diminished into a sense of prettiness. The beautiful idea has no relation to size, and may be as perfectly developed in a space too minute for any but microscopic investigation as within the ample verge that is measured by the arc of the rainbow. But, at all events, this characteristic minuteness in his objects and accomplishments made the world even more incapable than it might otherwise have been of appreciating Owen Warland's genius. The boy's relatives saw nothing better to be done—as perhaps there was not—than to bind him apprentice to a watchmaker, hoping that his strange ingenuity might thus be regulated and put to utilitarian purposes.

Peter Hovenden's opinion of his apprentice has already been expressed. He could make nothing of the lad. Owen's apprehension of the professional mysteries, it is true, was inconceivably quick; but he altogether forgot or despised the grand object of a watchmaker's business, and cared no more for the measurement of time than if it had been merged into eternity. So long, however, as he remained under his old master's care, Owen's lack of sturdiness made it possible, by strict injunctions and sharp oversight, to restrain his creative eccentricity within bounds; but when his apprenticeship was served out, and he had taken the little shop which Peter Hovenden's failing eyesight compelled him to relinquish, then did people recognize how unfit a person was Owen Warland to lead old blind Father Time along his daily course. One of his most rational projects was to connect a musical operation with the machinery of his watches, so that all the harsh dissonances of life might be rendered tuneful, and each flitting moment fall into the abyss of the past in golden drops of harmony. If a family clock was intrusted to him for repair,—one of those tall, ancient clocks that have grown nearly allied to human nature by measuring out the lifetime of many generations,—he would take upon himself to arrange a dance or funeral procession of figures across its venerable face, representing twelve mirthful or melancholy hours. Several freaks of this kind quite destroyed the young watchmaker's credit with that steady and matter-of-fact class of people who hold the opinion that time is not to be trifled with, whether considered as the medium of advancement and prosperity in this world or preparation for the next. His custom rapidly diminished—a misfortune, however, that was probably reckoned among his better accidents by Owen Warland, who was becoming more and more absorbed in a secret occupation which drew all his science and manual dexterity into itself, and likewise gave full employment to the characteristic tendencies of his genius. This pursuit had already consumed many months.

After the old watchmaker and his pretty daughter had gazed at him out of the obscurity of the street, Owen Warland was seized with a fluttering of the nerves, which made his hand tremble too violently to proceed with such delicate labor as he was now engaged upon.

"It was Annie herself!" murmured he. "I should have known it, by this throbbing of my heart, before I heard her father's voice. Ah, how it throbs! I shall scarcely be able to work again on this exquisite mechanism to-night. Annie! dearest Annie! thou shouldst give firmness to my heart and hand, and not shake them thus; for, if I strive to put the very spirit of beauty into form and give it motion, it is for thy sake alone. O throbbing heart, be quiet! If my labor be thus thwarted, there will come vague and unsatisfied dreams, which will leave me spiritless to-morrow."

As he was endeavoring to settle himself again to his task, the shop door opened and gave admittance to no other than the stalwart figure which Peter Hovenden had paused to admire, as seen amid the light and shadow of the blacksmith's shop. Robert Danforth had brought a little anvil of his own manufacture, and peculiarly constructed, which the young artist had recently bespoken. Owen examined the article, and pronounced it fashioned according to his wish.

"Why, yes," said Robert Danforth, his strong voice filling the shop as with the sound of a bass viol, "I consider myself equal to any thing in the way of my own trade; though I should have made but a poor figure at yours with such a fist as this," added he, laughing, as he laid his vast hand beside the delicate one of Owen. "But what then? I put more main strength into one blow of my sledge hammer than all that you have expended since you were a 'prentice. Is not that the truth?"

"Very probably," answered the low and slender voice of Owen. "Strength is an earthly monster. I make no pretensions to it. My force, whatever there may be of it, is altogether spiritual."

"Well, but, Owen, what are you about?" asked his old schoolfellow, still in such a hearty volume of tone that it made the artist shrink, especially as the question related to a subject so sacred as the absorbing dream of his imagination. "Folks do say that you are trying to discover the perpetual motion."

"The perpetual motion? Nonsense!" replied Owen Warland, with a movement of disgust; for he was full of little petulances. "It can never be discovered. It is a dream that may delude men whose brains are mystified with matter, but not me. Besides, if such a discovery were possible, it would not be worth my while to make it only to have the secret turned to such purposes as are now effected by steam and water power. I am not ambitious to be honored with the paternity of a new kind of cotton machine."

"That would be droll enough!" cried the blacksmith, breaking out into such an uproar of laughter that Owen himself and the bell glasses on his workboard quivered in unison. "No, no, Owen! No child of yours will have iron joints and sinews. Well, I won't hinder you any more. Good night, Owen, and success; and if you need any assistance, so far as a downright blow of hammer upon anvil will answer the purpose, I'm your man."

And with another laugh the man of main strength left the shop.

"How strange it is," whispered Owen Warland to himself, leaning his head upon his hand, "that all my musings, my purposes, my passion for the beautiful, my consciousness of power to create it—a finer, more ethereal power, of which this earthly giant can have no conception,— all, all, look so vain and idle whenever my path is crossed by Robert Danforth! He would drive me mad were I to meet him often. His hard, brute force darkens and confuses the spiritual element within me; but I, too, will be strong in my own way. I will not yield to him."

He took from beneath a glass a piece of minute machinery, which he set in the condensed light of his lamp, and, looking intently at it through a magnifying glass, proceeded to operate with a delicate instrument of steel. In an instant, however, he fell back in his chair and clasped his hands, with a look of horror on his face that made its small features as impressive as those of a giant would have been.

"Heaven! What have I done?" exclaimed he. "The vapor, the influence of that brute force,—it has bewildered me and obscured my perception. I have made the very stroke—the fatal stroke—that I have dreaded from the first. It is all over—the toil of months, the object of my life. I am ruined!"

And there he sat, in strange despair, until his lamp flickered in the socket and left the Artist of the Beautiful in darkness.

Thus it is that ideas, which grow up within the imagination and appear so lovely to it and of a value beyond whatever men call valuable, are exposed to be shattered and annihilated by contact with the practical. It is requisite for the ideal artist to possess a force of character that seems hardly compatible with its delicacy; he must keep his faith in himself while the incredulous world assails him with its utter disbelief; he must stand up against mankind and be his own sole disciple, both as respects his genius and the objects to which it is directed.

For a time Owen Warland succumbed to this severe but inevitable test. He spent a few sluggish weeks with his head so continually resting in his hands that the townspeople had scarcely an opportunity to see his countenance. When at last it was again uplifted to the light of day, a cold, dull, nameless change was perceptible upon it. In the opinion of Peter Hovenden, however, and that order of sagacious understandings who think that life should be regulated, like clockwork, with leaden weights, the alteration was entirely for the better. Owen now, indeed, applied himself to business with dogged industry. It was marvellous to witness the obtuse gravity with which he would inspect the wheels of a great, old silver watch; thereby delighting the owner, in whose fob it had been worn till he deemed it a portion of his own life, and was accordingly jealous of its treatment. In consequence of the good report thus acquired, Owen Warland was invited by the proper authorities to regulate the clock in the church steeple. He succeeded so admirably in this matter of public interest that the merchants gruffly acknowledged his merits on 'Change;[3] the nurse whispered his praises as she gave the potion in the sick chamber; the lover blessed him at the hour of appointed interview; and the town in general thanked Owen for the punctuality of dinner time. In a word, the heavy weight upon his spirits kept every thing in order, not merely within his own system, but wheresoever the iron accents of the church clock were audible. It was a circumstance, though minute yet characteristic of his present state, that, when employed to engrave names or initials on silver spoons, he now wrote the requisite letters in the plainest possible style, omitting a variety of fanciful flourishes that had heretofore distinguished his work in this kind.

One day, during the era of this happy transformation, old Peter Hovenden came to visit his former apprentice.

"Well, Owen," said he, "I am glad to hear such good accounts of you from all quarters, and especially from the town clock yonder, which speaks in your commendation every hour of the twenty-four. Only get rid altogether of your nonsensical trash about the beautiful, which I nor nobody else, nor yourself to boot, could ever understand,—only free yourself of that, and your success in life is as sure as daylight. Why, if you go on in this way, I should even venture to let you doctor this precious old watch of mine; though, except my daughter Annie, I have nothing else so valuable in the world."

"I should hardly dare touch it, sir," replied Owen, in a depressed tone; for he was weighed down by his old master's presence.

"In time," said the latter,—"in time, you will be capable of it."

The old watchmaker, with the freedom naturally consequent on his former authority, went on inspecting the work which Owen had in hand at the moment, together with other matters that were in progress. The artist, meanwhile, could scarcely lift his head. There was nothing so antipodal to his nature as this man's cold, unimaginative sagacity, by contact with which every thing was converted into a dream except the densest matter of the physical world. Owen groaned in spirit and prayed fervently to be delivered from him.

"But what is this?" cried Peter Hovenden abruptly, taking up a dusty bell glass, beneath which appeared a mechanical something, as delicate and minute as the system of a butterfly's anatomy. "What have we here? Owen! Owen! there is witchcraft in these little chains, and wheels, and paddles. See! with one pinch of my finger and thumb I am going to deliver you from all future peril."

"For Heaven's sake," screamed Owen Warland, springing up with wonderful energy, "as you would not drive me mad, do not touch it! The slightest pressure of your finger would ruin me forever."

"Aha, young man! And is it so?" said the old watchmaker, looking at him with just enough of penetration to torture Owen's soul with the bitterness of worldly criticism. "Well, take your own course; but I warn you again that in this small piece of mechanism lives your evil spirit. Shall I exorcise him?"

"You are my evil spirit," answered Owen, much excited,—"you and the hard, coarse world! The leaden thoughts and the despondency that you fling upon me are my clogs, else I should long ago have achieved the task that I was created for."

Peter Hovenden shook his head, with the mixture of contempt and indignation which mankind, of whom he was partly a representative, deem themselves entitled to feel towards all simpletons who seek other prizes than the dusty one along the highway. He then took his leave, with an uplifted finger and a sneer upon his face that haunted the artist's dreams for many a night afterwards. At the time of his old master's visit, Owen was probably on the point of taking up the relinquished task; but, by this sinister event, he was thrown back into the state whence he had been slowly emerging.

But the innate tendency of his soul had only been accumulating fresh vigor during its apparent sluggishness. As the summer advanced he almost totally relinquished his business, and permitted Father Time, so far as the old gentleman was represented by the clocks and watches under his control, to stray at random through human life, making infinite confusion among the train of bewildered hours. He wasted the sunshine, as people said, in wandering through the woods and fields and along the banks of streams. There, like a child, he found amusement in chasing butterflies or watching the motions of water insects. There was something truly mysterious in the intentness with which he contemplated these living playthings as they sported on the breeze or examined the structure of an imperial insect whom he had imprisoned. The chase of butterflies was an apt emblem of the ideal pursuit in which he had spent so many golden hours; but would the beautiful idea ever be yielded to his hand like the butterfly that symbolized it? Sweet, doubtless, were these days, and congenial to the artist's soul. They were full of bright conceptions, which gleamed through his intellectual world as the butterflies gleamed through the outward atmosphere, and were real to him, for the instant, without the toil, and perplexity, and many disappointments of attempting to make them visible to the sensual eye. Alas that the artist, whether in poetry or whatever other material, may not content himself with the inward enjoyment of the beautiful, but must chase the flitting mystery beyond the verge of his ethereal domain, and crush its frail being in seizing it with a material grasp. Owen Warland felt the impulse to give external reality to his ideas as irresistibly as any of the poets or painters who have arrayed the world in a dimmer and fainter beauty, imperfectly copied from the richness of their visions.

The night was now his time for the slow progress of re-creating the one idea to which all his intellectual activity referred itself. Always at the approach of dusk he stole into the town, locked himself within his shop, and wrought with patient delicacy of touch for many hours. Sometimes he was startled by the rap of the watchman, who, when all the world should be asleep, had caught the gleam of lamplight through the crevices of Owen Warland's shutters. Daylight, to the morbid sensibility of his mind, seemed to have an intrusiveness that interfered with his pursuits. On cloudy and inclement days, therefore, he sat with his head upon his hands, muffling, as it were, his sensitive brain in a mist of indefinite musings; for it was a relief to escape from the sharp distinctness with which he was compelled to shape out his thoughts during his nightly toil.

From one of these fits of torpor he was aroused by the entrance of Annie Hovenden, who came into the shop with the freedom of a customer and also with something of the familiarity of a childish friend. She had worn a hole through her silver thimble, and wanted Owen to repair it.

"But I don't know whether you will condescend to such a task," said she, laughing, "now that you are so taken up with the notion of putting spirit into machinery."

"Where did you get that idea, Annie?" said Owen, starting in surprise.

"O, out of my own head," answered she, "and from something that I heard you say, long ago, when you were but a boy and I a little child. But come; will you mend this poor thimble of mine?"

"Any thing for your sake, Annie," said Owen Warland,—"any thing, even were it to work at Robert Danforth's forge."

"And that would be a pretty sight!" retorted Annie, glancing with imperceptible slightness[4] at the artist's small and slender frame. "Well; here is the thimble."

"But that is a strange idea of yours," said Owen, "about the spiritualization of matter."

And then the thought stole into his mind that this young girl possessed the gift to comprehend him better than all the world besides. And what a help and strength would it be to him in his lonely toil if he could gain the sympathy of the only being whom he loved! To persons whose pursuits are insulated from the common business of life—who are either in advance of mankind or apart from it—there often comes a sensation of moral cold that makes the spirit shiver as if it had reached the frozen solitudes around the pole. What the prophet, the poet, the reformer, the criminal, or any other man with human yearnings, but separated from the multitude by a peculiar lot, might feel, poor Owen Warland felt.

"Annie," cried he, growing pale as death at the thought, "how gladly would I tell you the secret of my pursuit! You, methinks, would estimate it rightly. You, I know, would hear it with a reverence that I must not expect from the harsh, material world."

"Would I not? to be sure I would!" replied Annie Hovenden, lightly laughing. "Come; explain to me quickly what is the meaning of this little whirligig, so delicately wrought that it might be a plaything for Queen Mab.[5] See! I will put it in motion."

"Hold!" exclaimed Owen, "hold!"

Annie had but given the slightest possible touch, with the point of a needle, to the same minute portion of complicated machinery which has been more than once mentioned, when the artist seized her by the wrist with a force that made her scream aloud. She was affrighted at the convulsion of intense rage and anguish that writhed across his features. The next instant he let his head sink upon his hands.

"Go, Annie," murmured he; "I have deceived myself, and must suffer for it. I yearned for sympathy, and thought, and fancied, and dreamed that you might give it me; but you lack the talisman, Annie, that should admit you into my secrets. That touch has undone the toil of months and the thought of a lifetime! It was not your fault, Annie; but you have ruined me!"

Poor Owen Warland! He had indeed erred, yet pardonably; for if any human spirit could have sufficiently reverenced the processes so sacred in his eyes, it must have been a woman's. Even Annie Hovenden, possibly, might not have disappointed him had she been enlightened by the deep intelligence of love.

The artist spent the ensuing winter in a way that satisfied any persons who had hitherto retained a hopeful opinion of him that he was, in truth, irrevocably doomed to inutility as regarded the world, and to an evil destiny on his own part. The decease of a relative had put him in possession of a small inheritance. Thus freed from the necessity of toil, and having lost the steadfast influence of a great purpose,— great, at least, to him,—he abandoned himself to habits from which it might have been supposed the mere delicacy of his organization would have availed to secure him. But, when the ethereal portion of a man of genius is obscured, the earthly part assumes an influence the more un-controllable, because the character is now thrown off the balance to which Providence had so nicely adjusted it, and which, in coarser natures, is adjusted by some other method. Owen Warland made proof of whatever show of bliss may be found in riot. He looked at the world through the golden medium of wine, and contemplated the visions that bubble up so gayly around the brim of the glass, and that people the air with shapes of pleasant madness, which so soon grow ghostly and forlorn. Even when this dismal and inevitable change had taken place, the young man might still have continued to quaff the cup of enchantments, though its vapor did but shroud life in gloom and fill the gloom with spectres that mocked at him. There was a certain irksomeness of spirit, which, being real, and the deepest sensation of which the artist was now conscious, was more intolerable than any fantastic miseries and horrors that the abuse of wine could summon up. In the latter case he could remember, even out of the midst of his trouble, that all was but a delusion; in the former, the heavy anguish was his actual life.

From this perilous state he was redeemed by an incident which more than one person witnessed, but of which the shrewdest could not explain or conjecture the operation on Owen Warland's mind. It was very simple. On a warm afternoon of spring, as the artist sat among his riotous companions with a glass of wine before him, a splendid butterfly flew in at the open window and fluttered about his head.

"Ah," exclaimed Owen, who had drank freely, "are you alive again, child of the sun and playmate of the summer breeze, after your dismal winter's nap? Then it is time for me to be at work!"

And, leaving his unemptied glass upon the table, he departed, and was never known to sip another drop of wine.

And now, again, he resumed his wanderings in the woods and fields. It might be fancied that the bright butterfly, which had come so spirit-like into the window as Owen sat with the rude revellers, was indeed a spirit commissioned to recall him to the pure, ideal life that had so etherealized him among men. It might be fancied that he went forth to seek this spirit in its sunny haunts; for still, as in the summer time gone by, he was seen to steal gently up wherever a butterfly had alighted, and lose himself in contemplation of it. When it took flight his eyes followed the winged vision, as if its airy track would show the path to heaven. But what could be the purpose of the unseasonable toil, which was again resumed, as the watchman knew by the lines of lamplight through the crevices of Owen Warland's shutters? The townspeople had one comprehensive explanation of all these singularities. Owen Warland had gone mad! How universally efficacious—how satisfactory, too, and soothing to the injured sensibility of narrowness and dulness—is this easy method of accounting for whatever lies beyond the world's most ordinary scope! From St. Paul's days down to our poor little Artist of the Beautiful, the same talisman had been applied to the elucidation of all mysteries in the words or deeds of men who spoke or acted too wisely or too well. In Owen Warland's case the judgment of his townspeople may have been correct. Perhaps he was mad. The lack of sympathy—that contrast between himself and his neighbors which took away the restraint of example—was enough to make him so. Or possibly he had caught just so much of ethereal radiance as served to bewilder him, in an earthly sense, by its intermixture with the common daylight.

One evening, when the artist had returned from a customary ramble and had just thrown the lustre of his lamp on the delicate piece of work so often interrupted, but still taken up again, as if his fate were imbodied in its mechanism, he was surprised by the entrance of old Peter Hovenden. Owen never met this man without a shrinking of the heart. Of all the world he was most terrible, by reason of a keen understanding which saw so distinctly what it did see, and disbelieved so uncompromisingly in what it could not see. On this occasion the old watchmaker had merely a gracious word or two to say.

"Owen, my lad," said he, "we must see you at my house to-morrow night."

The artist began to mutter some excuse.

"O, but it must be so," quoth Peter Hovenden, "for the sake of the days when you were one of the household. What, my boy! don't you know that my daughter Annie is engaged to Robert Danforth? We are making an entertainment, in our humble way, to celebrate the event."

"Ah!" said Owen.

That little monosyllable was all he uttered; its tone seemed cold and unconcerned to an ear like Peter Hovenden's; and yet there was in it the stifled outcry of the poor artist's heart, which he compressed within him like a man holding down an evil spirit. One slight outbreak, however, imperceptible to the old watchmaker, he allowed himself.

Raising the instrument with which he was about to begin his work, he let it fall upon the little system of machinery that had, anew, cost him months of thought and toil. It was shattered by the stroke!

Owen Warland's story would have been no tolerable representation of the troubled life of those who strive to create the beautiful, if, amid all other thwarting influences, love had not interposed to steal the cunning from his hand. Outwardly he had been no ardent or enterprising lover; the career of his passion had confined its tumults and vicissitudes so entirely within the artist's imagination that Annie herself had scarcely more than a woman's intuitive perception of it; but, in Owen's view, it covered the whole field of his life. Forgetful of the time when she had shown herself incapable of any deep response, he had persisted in connecting all his dreams of artistical success with Annie's image; she was the visible shape in which the spiritual power that he worshipped, and on whose altar he hoped to lay a not unworthy offering, was made manifest to him. Of course he had deceived himself; there were no such attributes in Annie Hovenden as his imagination had endowed her with. She, in the aspect which she wore to his inward vision, was as much a creature of his own as the mysterious piece of mechanism would be were it ever realized. Had he become convinced of his mistake through the medium of successful love,—had he won Annie to his bosom, and there beheld her fade from angel into ordinary woman,—the disappointment might have driven him back, with concentrated energy, upon his sole remaining object. On the other hand, had he found Annie what he fancied, his lot would have been so rich in beauty that out of its mere redundancy he might have wrought the beautiful into many a worthier type than he had toiled for; but the guise in which his sorrow came to him, the sense that the angel of his life had been snatched away and given to a rude man of earth and iron, who could neither need nor appreciate her ministrations,—this was the very perversity of fate that makes human existence appear too absurd and contradictory to be the scene of one other hope or one other fear. There was nothing left for Owen Warland but to sit down like a man that had been stunned.

He went through a fit of illness. After his recovery his small and slender frame assumed an obtuser garniture of flesh than it had ever before worn. His thin cheeks became round; his delicate little hand, so spiritually fashioned to achieve fairy taskwork, grew plumper than the hand of a thriving infant. His aspect had a childishness such as might have induced a stranger to pat him on the head—pausing, however, in the act, to wonder what manner of child was here. It was as if the spirit had gone out of him, leaving the body to flourish in a sort of vegetable existence. Not that Owen Warland was idiotic. He could talk, and not irrationally. Somewhat of a babbler, indeed, did people begin to think him; for he was apt to discourse at wearisome length of marvels of mechanism that he had read about in books, but which he had learned to consider as absolutely fabulous. Among them he enumerated the Man of Brass, constructed by Albertus Magnus, and the Brazen Head of Friar Bacon;[6] and, coming down to later times, the automata of a little coach and horses, which it was pretended had been manufactured for the Dauphin of France;[7] together with an insect that buzzed about the ear like a living fly, and yet was but a contrivance of minute steel springs. There was a story, too, of a duck that waddled, and quacked, and ate; though, had any honest citizen purchased it for dinner, he would have found himself cheated with the mere mechanical apparition of a duck.

"But all these accounts," said Owen Warland, "I am now satisfied are mere impositions."

Then, in a mysterious way, he would confess that he once thought differently. In his idle and dreamy days he had considered it possible, in a certain sense, to spiritualize machinery, and to combine with the new species of life and motion thus produced a beauty that should attain to the ideal which Nature has proposed to herself in all her creatures, but has never taken pains to realize. He seemed, however, to retain no very distinct perception either of the process of achieving this object or of the design itself.

"I have thrown it all aside now," he would say. "It was a dream such as young men are always mystifying themselves with. Now that I have acquired a little common sense, it makes me laugh to think of it."

Poor, poor and fallen Owen Warland! These were the symptoms that he had ceased to be an inhabitant of the better sphere that lies unseen around us. He had lost his faith in the invisible, and now prided himself, as such unfortunates invariably do, in the wisdom which rejected much that even his eye could see, and trusted confidently in nothing but what his hand could touch. This is the calamity of men whose spiritual part dies out of them and leaves the grosser understanding to assimilate them more and more to the things of which alone it can take cognizance; but in Owen Warland the spirit was not dead nor passed away; it only slept.

How it awoke again is not recorded. Perhaps the torpid slumber was broken by a convulsive pain. Perhaps, as in a former instance, the butterfly came and hovered about his head and reinspired him,—as indeed this creature of the sunshine had always a mysterious mission for the artist,—reinspired him with the former purpose of his life. Whether it were pain or happiness that thrilled through his veins, his first impulse was to thank Heaven for rendering him again the being of thought, imagination, and keenest sensibility that he had long ceased to be.

"Now for my task," said he. "Never did I feel such strength for it as now."

Yet, strong as he felt himself, he was incited to toil the more diligently by an anxiety lest death should surprise him in the midst of his labors. This anxiety, perhaps, is common to all men who set their hearts upon any thing so high, in their own view of it, that life becomes of importance only as conditional to its accomplishment. So long as we love life for itself, we seldom dread the losing it. When we desire life for the attainment of an object, we recognize the frailty of its texture. But, side by side with this sense of insecurity, there is a vital faith in our invulnerability to the shaft of death while engaged in any task that seems assigned by Providence as our proper thing to do, and which the world would have cause to mourn for should we leave it unaccomplished. Can the philosopher, big with the inspiration of an idea that is to reform mankind, believe that he is to be beckoned from this sensible existence at the very instant when he is mustering his breath to speak the word of light? Should he perish so, the weary ages may pass away—the world's whole life sand may fall, drop by drop—before another intellect is prepared to develop the truth that might have been uttered then. But history affords many an example where the most precious spirit, at any particular epoch manifested in human shape, has gone hence untimely, without space allowed him, so far as mortal judgment could discern, to perform his mission on the earth. The prophet dies, and the man of torpid heart and sluggish brain lives on. The poet leaves his song half sung, or finishes it beyond the scope of mortal ears, in a celestial choir. The painter—as Allston[8] did—leaves half his conception on the canvas to sadden us with its imperfect beauty, and goes to picture forth the whole, if it be no irreverence to say so, in the hues of heaven. But rather such incomplete designs of this life will be perfected nowhere. This so frequent abortion of man's dearest projects must be taken as a proof that the deeds of earth, however etherealized by piety or genius, are without value, except as exercises and manifestations of the spirit. In heaven, all ordinary thought is higher and more melodious than Milton's song.[9] Then, would he add another verse to any strain that he had left unfinished here?

But to return to Owen Warland. It was his fortune, good or ill, to achieve the purpose of his life. Pass we over a long space of intense thought, yearning effort, minute toil, and wasting anxiety, succeeded by an instant of solitary triumph: let all this be imagined; and then behold the artist, on a winter evening, seeking admittance to Robert Danforth's fireside circle. There he found the man of iron, with his massive substance, thoroughly warmed and attempered by domestic influences. And there was Annie, too, now transformed into a matron, with much of her husband's plain and sturdy nature, but imbued, as Owen Warland still believed, with a finer grace, that might enable her to be the interpreter between strength and beauty. It happened, likewise, that old Peter Hovenden was a guest this evening at his daughter's fireside; and it was his well-remembered expression of keen, cold criticism that first encountered the artist's glance.

"My old friend Owen!" cried Robert Danforth, starting up, and compressing the artist's delicate fingers within a hand that was accustomed to gripe bars of iron. "This is kind and neighborly to come to us at last. I was afraid your perpetual motion had bewitched you out of the remembrance of old times."

"We are glad to see you," said Annie, while a blush reddened her matronly cheek. "It was not like a friend to stay from us so long."

"Well, Owen," inquired the old watchmaker, as his first greeting, "how comes on the beautiful? Have you created it at last?"

The artist did not immediately reply, being startled by the apparition of a young child of strength that was tumbling about on the carpet—a little personage who had come mysteriously out of the infinite, but with something so sturdy and real in his composition that he seemed moulded out of the densest substance which earth could supply. This hopeful infant crawled towards the new comer, and setting himself on end, as Robert Danforth expressed the posture, stared at

Owen with a look of such sagacious observation that the mother could not help exchanging a proud glance with her husband. But the artist was disturbed by the child's look, as imagining a resemblance between it and Peter Hovenden's habitual expression. He could have fancied that the old watchmaker was compressed into this baby shape, and looking out of those baby eyes, and repeating, as he now did, the malicious question:—

"The beautiful, Owen! How comes on the beautiful? Have you succeeded in creating the beautiful?"

"I have succeeded," replied the artist, with a momentary light of triumph in his eyes and a smile of sunshine, yet steeped in such depth of thought that it was almost sadness. "Yes, my friends, it is the truth. I have succeeded."

"Indeed!" cried Annie, a look of maiden mirthfulness peeping out of her face again. "And is it lawful, now, to inquire what the secret is?"

"Surely; it is to disclose it that I have come," answered Owen Warland. "You shall know, and see, and touch, and possess the secret! For, Annie,—if by that name I may still address the friend of my boyish years,—Annie, it is for your bridal gift that I have wrought this spiritualized mechanism, this harmony of motion, this mystery of beauty. It comes late indeed; but it is as we go onward in life, when objects begin to lose their freshness of hue and our souls their delicacy of perception, that the spirit of beauty is most needed. If,—forgive me, Annie,—if you know how to value this gift, it can never come too late."

He produced, as he spoke, what seemed a jewel box. It was carved richly out of ebony by his own hand, and inlaid with a fanciful tracery of pearl, representing a boy in pursuit of a butterfly, which, elsewhere, had become a winged spirit, and was flying heavenward; while the boy, or youth, had found such efficacy in his strong desire that he ascended from earth to cloud, and from cloud to celestial atmosphere, to win the beautiful. This case of ebony the artist opened, and bade Annie place her finger on its edge. She did so, but almost screamed as a butterfly fluttered forth, and, alighting on her finger's tip, sat waving the ample magnificence of its purple and gold-speckled wings, as if in prelude to a flight. It is impossible to express by words the glory, the splendor, the delicate gorgeousness which were softened into the beauty of this object. Nature's ideal butterfly was here realized in all its perfection; not in the pattern of such faded insects as flit among earthly flowers, but of those which hover across the meads of paradise for child-angels and the spirits of departed infants to disport themselves with. The rich down was visible upon its wings; the lustre of its eyes seemed instinct with spirit. The firelight glimmered around this wonder—the candles gleamed upon it; but it glistened apparently by its own radiance, and illuminated the finger and outstretched hand on which it rested with a white gleam like that of precious stones. In its perfect beauty, the consideration of size was entirely lost. Had its wings overreached the firmament, the mind could not have been more filled or satisfied.

"Beautiful! beautiful!" exclaimed Annie. "Is it alive? Is it alive?"

"Alive? To be sure it is," answered her husband. "Do you suppose any mortal has skill enough to make a butterfly, or would put himself to the trouble of making one, when any child may catch a score of them in a summer's afternoon? Alive? Certainly! But this pretty box is undoubtedly of our friend Owen's manufacture; and really it does him credit."

At this moment the butterfly waved its wings anew, with a motion so absolutely lifelike that Annie was startled, and even awestricken; for, in spite of her husband's opinion, she could not satisfy herself whether it was indeed a living creature or a piece of wondrous mechanism.

"Is it alive?" she repeated, more earnestly than before.

"Judge for yourself," said Owen Warland, who stood gazing in her face with fixed attention.

The butterfly now flung itself upon the air, fluttered round Annie's head, and soared into a distant region of the parlor, still making itself perceptible to sight by the starry gleam in which the motion of its wings enveloped it. The infant on the floor followed its course with his sagacious little eyes. After flying about the room, it returned in a spiral curve and settled again on Annie's finger.

"But is it alive?" exclaimed she again; and the finger on which the gorgeous mystery had alighted was so tremulous that the butterfly was forced to balance himself with his wings. "Tell me if it be alive, or whether you created it."

"Wherefore ask who created it, so it be beautiful?" replied Owen Warland. "Alive? Yes, Annie; it may well be said to possess life, for it has absorbed my own being into itself; and in the secret of that butterfly, and in its beauty,—which is not merely outward, but deep as its whole system,—is represented the intellect, the imagination, the sensibility, the soul of an Artist of the Beautiful! Yes; I created it. But"—and here his countenance somewhat changed—"this butterfly is not now to me what it was when I beheld it afar off in the daydreams of my youth."

"Be it what it may, it is a pretty plaything," said the blacksmith, grinning with childlike delight. "I wonder whether it would condescend to alight on such a great clumsy finger as mine? Hold it hither, Annie."

By the artist's direction, Annie touched her finger's tip to that of her husband; and, after a momentary delay, the butterfly fluttered from one to the other. It preluded a second flight by a similar, yet not precisely the same, waving of wings as in the first experiment; then, ascending from the blacksmith's stalwart finger, it rose in a gradually enlarging curve to the ceiling, made one wide sweep around the room, and returned with an undulating movement to the point whence it had started.

"Well, that does beat all nature!" cried Robert Danforth, bestowing the heartiest praise that he could find expression for; and, indeed, had he paused there, a man of finer words and nicer perception could not easily have said more. "That goes beyond me, I confess. But what then? There is more real use in one downright blow of my sledge hammer than in the whole five years' labor that our friend Owen has wasted on this butterfly."

Here the child clapped his hands and made a great babble of indistinct utterance, apparently demanding that the butterfly should be given him for a plaything.

Owen Warland, meanwhile, glanced sidelong at Annie, to discover whether she sympathized in her husband's estimate of the comparative value of the beautiful and the practical. There was, amid all her kindness towards himself, amid all the wonder and admiration with which she contemplated the marvellous work of his hands and incarnation of his idea, a secret scorn—too secret, perhaps, for her own consciousness, and perceptible only to such intuitive discernment as that of the artist. But Owen, in the latter stages of his pursuit, had risen out of the region in which such a discovery might have been torture. He knew that the world, and Annie as the representative of the world, whatever praise might be bestowed, could never say the fitting word nor feel the fitting sentiment which should be the perfect recompense of an artist who, symbolizing a lofty moral by a material trifle,—converting what was earthly to spiritual gold,—had won the beautiful into his handiwork. Not at this latest moment was he to learn that the reward of all high performance must be sought within itself, or sought in vain. There was, however, a view of the matter which Annie and her husband, and even Peter Hovenden, might fully have understood, and which would have satisfied them that the toil of years had here been worthily bestowed. Owen Warland might have told them that this butterfly, this plaything, this bridal gift of a poor watchmaker to a blacksmith's wife, was, in truth, a gem of art that a monarch would have purchased with honors and abundant wealth, and have treasured it among the jewels of his kingdom as the most unique and wondrous of them all. But the artist smiled and kept the secret to himself.

"Father," said Annie, thinking that a word of praise from the old watchmaker might gratify his former apprentice, "do come and admire this pretty butterfly."

"Let us see," said Peter Hovenden, rising from his chair, with a sneer upon his face that always made people doubt, as he himself did, in every thing but a material existence. "Here is my finger for it to alight upon. I shall understand it better when once I have touched it."

But, to the increased astonishment of Annie, when the tip of her father's finger was pressed against that of her husband, on which the butterfly still rested, the insect drooped its wings and seemed on the point of falling to the floor. Even the bright spots of gold upon its wings and body, unless her eyes deceived her, grew dim, and the glowing purple took a dusky hue, and the starry lustre that gleamed around the blacksmith's hand became faint and vanished.

"It is dying! it is dying!" cried Annie, in alarm.

"It has been delicately wrought," said the artist, calmly. "As I told you, it has imbibed a spiritual essence—call it magnetism,[10] or what you will. In an atmosphere of doubt and mockery its exquisite susceptibility suffers torture, as does the soul of him who instilled his own life into it. It has already lost its beauty; in a few moments more its mechanism would be irreparably injured."

"Take away your hand, father!" entreated Annie, turning pale. "Here is my child; let it rest on his innocent hand. There, perhaps, its life will revive and its colors grow brighter than ever."

Her father, with an acrid smile, withdrew his finger. The butterfly then appeared to recover the power of voluntary motion, while its hues assumed much of their original lustre, and the gleam of starlight, which was its most ethereal attribute, again formed a halo round about it. At first, when transferred from Robert Danforth's hand to the small finger of the child, this radiance grew so powerful that it positively threw the little fellow's shadow back against the wall. He, meanwhile, extended his plump hand as he had seen his father and mother do, and watched the waving of the insect's wings with infantine delight. Nevertheless, there was a certain odd expression of sagacity that made Owen Warland feel as if here were old Peter Hovenden, partially, and but partially, redeemed from his hard scepticism into childish faith.

"How wise the little monkey looks!" whispered Robert Danforth to his wife.

"I never saw such a look on a child's face," answered Annie, admiring her own infant, and with good reason, far more than the artistic butterfly. "The darling knows more of the mystery than we do."

As if the butterfly, like the artist, were conscious of something not entirely congenial in the child's nature, it alternately sparkled and grew dim. At length it arose from the small hand of the infant with an airy motion that seemed to bear it upward without an effort, as if the ethereal instincts with which its master's spirit had endowed it impelled this fair vision involuntarily to a higher sphere. Had there been no obstruction, it might have soared into the sky and grown immortal. But its lustre gleamed upon the ceiling; the exquisite texture of its wings brushed against that earthly medium; and a sparkle or two, as of stardust, floated downward and lay glimmering on the carpet. Then the butterfly came fluttering down, and, instead of returning to the infant, was apparently attracted towards the artist's hand.

"Not so! not so!" murmured Owen Warland, as if his handiwork could have understood him. "Thou hast gone forth out of thy master's heart. There is no return for thee."

With a wavering movement, and emitting a tremulous radiance, the butterfly struggled, as it were, towards the infant, and was about to alight upon his finger; but, while it still hovered in the air, the little child of strength, with his grandsire's sharp and shrewd expression in his face, made a snatch at the marvellous insect and compressed it in his hand. Annie screamed. Old Peter Hovenden burst into a cold and scornful laugh. The blacksmith, by main force, unclosed the infant's hand, and found within the palm a small heap of glittering fragments, whence the mystery of beauty had fled forever. And as for Owen War-land, he looked placidly at what seemed the ruin of his life's labor, and which was yet no ruin. He had caught a far other butterfly than this. When the artist rose high enough to achieve the beautiful, the symbol by which he made it perceptible to mortal senses became of little value in his eyes while his spirit possessed itself in the enjoyment of the reality.

A VIRTUOSO'S COLLECTION

The other day, having a leisure hour at my disposal, I stepped into a new museum, to which my notice was casually drawn by a small and unobtrusive sign: "TO BE SEEN HERE, A VIRTUOSO'S COLLECTION." Such was the simple yet not altogether unpromising announcement that turned my steps aside for a little while from the sunny sidewalk of our principal thoroughfare. Mounting a sombre staircase, I pushed open a door at its summit, and found myself in the presence of a person, who mentioned the moderate sum that would entitle me to admittance.

"Three shillings, Massachusetts tenor,"[1] said he. "No, I mean half a dollar, as you reckon in these days."

While searching my pocket for the coin I glanced at the doorkeeper, the marked character and individuality of whose aspect encouraged me to expect something not quite in the ordinary way. He wore an old-fashioned greatcoat, much faded, within which his meagre person was so completely enveloped that the rest of his attire was undistinguishable. But his visage was remarkably wind-flushed, sunburnt, and weather-worn, and had a most unquiet, nervous, and apprehensive expression. It seemed as if this man had some all-important object in view, some point of deepest interest to be decided, some momentous question to ask, might he but hope for a reply. As it was evident, however, that I could have nothing to do with his private affairs, I passed through an open doorway, which admitted me into the extensive hall of the museum.

Directly in front of the portal was the bronze statue of a youth with winged feet. He was represented in the act of flitting away from earth, yet wore such a look of earnest invitation that it impressed me like a summons to enter the hall.

"It is the original statue of Opportunity, by the ancient sculptor Lysippus,"[2] said a gentleman who now approached me. "I place it at the entrance of my museum, because it is not at all times that one can gain admittance to such a collection."

The speaker was a middle-aged person, of whom it was not easy to determine whether he had spent his life as a scholar or as a man of action; in truth, all outward and obvious peculiarities had been worn away by an extensive and promiscuous intercourse with the world. There was no mark about him of profession, individual habits, or scarcely of country; although his dark complexion and high features made me conjecture that he was a native of some southern clime of Europe. At all events, he was evidently the virtuoso in person.

"With your permission," said he, "as we have no descriptive catalogue, I will accompany you through the museum and point out whatever may be most worthy of attention. In the first place, here is a choice collection of stuffed animals."

Nearest the door stood the outward semblance of a wolf, exquisitely prepared, it is true, and showing a very wolfish fierceness in the large glass eyes which were inserted into its wild and crafty head. Still it was merely the skin of a wolf, with nothing to distinguish it from other individuals of that unlovely breed.

"How does this animal deserve a place in your collection?" inquired I.

"It is the wolf that devoured Little Red Riding Hood," answered the virtuoso; "and by his side—with a milder and more matronly look, as you perceive—stands the she wolf that suckled Romulus and Remus."[3]

"Ah, indeed!" exclaimed I. "And what lovely lamb is this with the snow-white fleece, which seems to be of as delicate a texture as innocence itself?"

"Methinks you have but carelessly read Spenser," replied my guide, "or you would at once recognize the 'milk-white lamb' which Una led.[4] But I set no great value upon the lamb. The next specimen is better worth our notice."

"What!" cried I, "this strange animal, with the black head of an ox upon the body of a white horse? Were it possible to suppose it, I should say that this was Alexander's steed Bucephalus."[5]

"The same," said the virtuoso. "And can you likewise give a name to the famous charger that stands beside him?"

Next to the renowned Bucephalus stood the mere skeleton of a horse, with the white bones peeping through his ill-conditioned hide; but, if my heart had not warmed towards that pitiful anatomy, I might as well have quitted the museum at once. Its rarities had not been collected with pain and toil from the four quarters of the earth, and from the depths of the sea, and from the palaces and sepulchres of ages, for those who could mistake this illustrious steed.

"It is Rosinante!"[6] exclaimed I, with enthusiasm.

And so it proved. My admiration for the noble and gallant horse caused me to glance with less interest at the other animals, although many of them might have deserved the notice of Cuvier[7] himself. There was the donkey which Peter Bell cudgelled[8] so soundly, and a brother of the same species who had suffered a similar infliction from the ancient prophet Balaam.[9] Some doubts were entertained, however, as to the authenticity of the latter beast. My guide pointed out the venerable Argus,[10] that faithful dog of Ulysses, and also another dog, (for so the skin bespoke it,) which, though imperfectly preserved, seemed once to have had three heads. It was Cerberus.[11] I was considerably amused at detecting in an obscure corner the fox that became so famous by the loss of his tail.[12] There were several stuffed cats, which, as a dear lover of that comfortable beast, attracted my affectionate regards. One was Dr. Johnson's cat Hodge;[13] and in the same row stood the favorite cats of Mahomet, Gray, and Walter Scott,[14] together with Puss in Boots,[15] and a cat of very noble aspect who had once been a deity of ancient Egypt. Byron's tame bear[16] came next. I must not forget to mention the Erymanthean boar, the skin of St. George's dragon, and that of the serpent Python;[17] and another skin with beautifully variegated hues, supposed to have been the garment of the "spirited sly snake"[18] which tempted Eve. Against the walls were suspended the horns of the stag that Shakspeare shot;[19] and on the floor lay the pon-derous shell of the tortoise which fell upon the head of Æschylus.[20] In one row, as natural as life, stood the sacred bull Apis,[21] the "cow with the crumpled horn," and a very wild-looking young heifer, which I guessed to be the cow that jumped over the moon.[22] She was probably killed by the rapidity of her descent. As I turned away, my eyes fell upon an indescribable monster, which proved to be a griffin.[23]

"I look in vain," observed I, "for the skin of an animal which might well deserve the closest study of a naturalist—the winged horse, Pegasus."[24]

"He is not yet dead," replied the virtuoso; "but he is so hard ridden by many young gentlemen of the day that I hope soon to add his skin and skeleton to my collection."

We now passed to the next alcove of the hall, in which was a multi-tude of stuffed birds. They were very prettily arranged, some upon the branches of trees, others brooding upon nests, and others suspended by wires so artificially that they seemed in the very act of flight. Among them was a white dove, with a withered branch of olive leaves in her mouth.

"Can this be the very dove," inquired I, "that brought the message of peace and hope to the tempest-beaten passengers of the ark?"[25]

"Even so," said my companion.

"And this raven, I suppose," continued I, "is the same that fed Elijah in the wilderness."[26]

"The raven? No," said the virtuoso; "it is a bird of modern date. He belonged to one Barnaby Rudge;[27] and many people fancied that the devil himself was disguised under his sable plumage. But poor Grip has drawn his last cork, and has been forced to 'say die' at last. This other raven, hardly less curious, is that in which the soul of King George I. revisited his lady love, the Duchess of Kendall."[28]

My guide next pointed out Minerva's owl[29] and the vulture that preyed upon the liver of Prometheus.[30] There was likewise the sacred ibis[31] of Egypt, and one of the Stymphalides[32] which Hercules shot in his sixth labor. Shelley's skylark, Bryant's water fowl,[33] and a pigeon from the belfry of the Old South Church, preserved by N. P. Willis,[34] were placed on the same perch. I could not but shudder on beholding Coleridge's albatross, transfixed with the Ancient Mariner's crossbow shaft.[35] Beside this bird of awful poesy stood a gray goose of very ordinary aspect.

"Stuffed goose is no such rarity," observed I. "Why do you preserve such a specimen in your museum?"

"It is one of the flock whose cackling saved the Roman Capitol,"[36] answered the virtuoso. "Many geese have cackled and hissed both before and since; but none, like those, have clamored themselves into immortality."

There seemed to be little else that demanded notice in this department of the museum, unless we except Robinson Crusoe's parrot,[37] a live phœnix,[38] a footless bird of paradise,[39] and a splendid peacock, supposed to be the same that once contained the soul of Pythagoras.[40] I therefore passed to the next alcove, the shelves of which were covered with a miscellaneous collection of curiosities such as are usually found in similar establishments. One of the first things that took my eye was a strange-looking cap, woven of some substance that appeared to be neither woollen, cotton, nor linen.

"Is this a magician's cap?" I asked.

"No," replied the virtuoso; "it is merely Dr. Franklin's cap of asbestos.[41] But here is one which, perhaps, may suit you better. It is the wishing cap of Fortunatus.[42] Will you try it on?"

"By no means," answered I, putting it aside with my hand. "The day of wild wishes is past with me. I desire nothing that may not come in the ordinary course of Providence."

"Then probably," returned the virtuoso, "you will not be tempted to rub this lamp?"

While speaking, he took from the shelf an antique brass lamp, curiously wrought with embossed figures, but so covered with verdigris that the sculpture was almost eaten away.

"It is a thousand years," said he, "since the genius of this lamp constructed Aladdin's palace[43] in a single night. But he still retains his power; and the man who rubs Aladdin's lamp has but to desire either a palace or a cottage."

"I might desire a cottage," replied I; "but I would have it founded on sure and stable truth, not on dreams and fantasies. I have learned to look for the real and the true."

My guide next showed me Prospero's magic wand,[44] broken into three fragments by the hand of its mighty master. On the same shelf lay the gold ring of ancient Gyges,[45] which enabled the wearer to walk invisible. On the other side of the alcove was a tall looking glass in a frame of ebony, but veiled with a curtain of purple silk, through the rents of which the gleam of the mirror was perceptible.

"This is Cornelius Agrippa's magic glass,"[46] observed the virtuoso. "Draw aside the curtain, and picture any human form within your mind, and it will be reflected in the mirror."

"It is enough if I can picture it within my mind," answered I. "Why should I wish it to be repeated in the mirror? But, indeed, these works of magic have grown wearisome to me. There are so many greater wonders in the world, to those who keep their eyes open and their sight undimmed by custom, that all the delusions of the old sorcerers seem flat and stale. Unless you can show me something really curious, I care not to look farther into your museum."

"Ah, well, then," said the virtuoso, composedly, "perhaps you may deem some of my antiquarian rarities deserving of a glance."

He pointed out the iron mask,[47] now corroded with rust; and my heart grew sick at the sight of this dreadful relic, which had shut out a human being from sympathy with his race. There was nothing half so terrible in the axe that beheaded King Charles, nor in the dagger that slew Henry of Navarre, nor in the arrow that pierced the heart of William Rufus[48]—all of which were shown to me. Many of the articles derived their interest, such as it was, from having been formerly in the possession of royalty. For instance, here was Charlemagne's sheepskin cloak,[49] the flowing wig of Louis Quatorze,[50] the spinning wheel of Sardanapalus,[51] and King Stephen's famous breeches[52] which cost him but a crown. The heart of the Bloody Mary, with the word "Calais"[53] worn into its diseased substance, was preserved in a bottle of spirits; and near it lay the golden case in which the queen of Gustavus Adolphus[54] treasured up that hero's heart. Among these relics and heirlooms of kings I must not forget the long, hairy ears of Midas,[55] and a piece of bread which had been changed to gold by the touch of that unlucky monarch. And as Grecian Helen[56] was a queen, it may here be mentioned that I was permitted to take into my hand a lock of her golden hair and the bowl which a sculptor modelled from the curve of her perfect breast. Here, likewise, was the robe that smothered Agamemnon,[57] Nero's fiddle,[58] the Czar Peter's brandy bottle,[59] the crown of Semiramis,[60] and Canute's sceptre[61] which he extended over the sea. That my own land may not deem itself neglected, let me add that I was favored with a sight of the skull of King Philip,[62] the famous Indian chief, whose head the Puritans smote off and exhibited upon a pole.

"Show me something else," said I to the virtuoso. "Kings are in such an artificial position that people in the ordinary walks of life cannot feel an interest in their relics. If you could show me the straw hat of sweet little Nell,[63] I would far rather see it than a king's golden crown."

"There it is," said my guide, pointing carelessly with his staff to the straw hat in question. "But, indeed, you are hard to please. Here are the seven-league boots.[64] Will you try them on?"

"Our modern railroads have superseded their use," answered I; "and as to these cowhide boots, I could show you quite as curious a pair at the Transcendental community in Roxbury."[65]

We next examined a collection of swords and other weapons, belonging to different epochs, but thrown together without much attempt at arrangement. Here was Arthur's sword Excalibar,[66] and that of the Cid Campeador,[67] and the sword of Brutus[68] rusted with Cæsar's blood and his own, and the sword of Joan of Arc,[69] and that of Horatius,[70] and that with which Virginius[71] slew his daughter, and the one which Dionysius suspended over the head of Damocles.[72] Here also was Arria's sword,[73] which she plunged into her own breast, in order to taste of death before her husband. The crooked blade of Saladin's cimeter[74] next attracted my notice. I know not by what chance, but so it happened, that the sword of one of our own militia generals was suspended between Don Quixote's lance[75] and the brown blade of Hudibras.[76] My heart throbbed high at the sight of the helmet of Miltiades[77] and the spear that was broken in the breast of Epaminondas.[78] I recognized the shield of Achilles[79] by its resemblance to the admirable cast in the possession of Professor Felton.[80] Nothing in this apartment interested me more than Major Pitcairn's pistol, the discharge of which, at Lexington,[81] began the war of the revolution, and was reverberated in thunder around the land for seven long years. The bow of Ulysses,[82] though unstrung for ages, was placed against the wall, together with a sheaf of Robin Hood's arrows[83] and the rifle of Daniel Boone.[84]

"Enough of weapons," said I, at length; "although I would gladly have seen the sacred shield which fell from heaven in the time of Numa.[85] And surely you should obtain the sword which Washington[86] unsheathed at Cambridge. But the collection does you much credit. Let us pass on."

In the next alcove we saw the golden thigh of Pythagoras,[87] which had so divine a meaning; and, by one of the queer analogies to which the virtuoso seemed to be addicted, this ancient emblem lay on the same shelf with Peter Stuyvesant's wooden leg,[88] that was fabled to be of silver. Here was a remnant of the Golden Fleece,[89] and a sprig of yellow leaves that resembled the foliage of a frostbitten elm, but was duly authenticated as a portion of the golden branch by which Æneas[90] gained admittance to the realm of Pluto. Atalanta's golden apple[91] and one of the apples of discord[92] were wrapped in the napkin of gold which Rampsinitus[93] brought from Hades; and the whole were deposited in the golden vase of Bias,[94] with its inscription: "TO THE WISEST."

"And how did you obtain this vase?" said I to the virtuoso.

"It was given me long ago," replied he, with a scornful expression in his eye, "because I had learned to despise all things."

It had not escaped me that, though the virtuoso was evidently a man of high cultivation, yet he seemed to lack sympathy with the spiritual, the sublime, and the tender. Apart from the whim that had led him to devote so much time, pains, and expense to the collection of this museum, he impressed me as one of the hardest and coldest men of the world whom I had ever met.

"To despise all things!" repeated I. "This, at best, is the wisdom of the understanding. It is the creed of a man whose soul, whose better and diviner part, has never been awakened, or has died out of him."

"I did not think that you were still so young," said the virtuoso. "Should you live to my years, you will acknowledge that the vase of Bias was not ill bestowed."

Without further discussion of the point, he directed my attention to other curiosities. I examined Cinderella's little glass slipper,[95] and compared it with one of Diana's sandals,[96] and with Fanny Elssler's shoe,[97] which bore testimony to the muscular character of her illustrious foot. On the same shelf were Thomas the Rhymer's green velvet shoes,[98] and the brazen shoe of Empedocles[99] which was thrown out of Mount Ætna. Anacreon's drinking cup[100] was placed in apt juxtaposition with one of Tom Moore's wine glasses[101] and Circe's magic bowl.[102]

These were symbols of luxury and riot; but near them stood the cup whence Socrates[103] drank his hemlock, and that which Sir Philip Sidney[104] put from his death-parched lips to bestow the draught upon a dying soldier. Next appeared a cluster of tobacco pipes, consisting of Sir Walter Raleigh's, the earliest on record, Dr. Parr's, Charles Lamb's,[105] and the first calumet[106] of peace which was ever smoked between a European and an Indian. Among other musical instruments, I noticed the lyre[107] of Orpheus and those of Homer and Sappho,[108] Dr. Franklin's famous whistle,[109] the trumpet of Anthony Van Corlear,[110] and the flute which Goldsmith[111] played on in his rambles through the French provinces. The staff of Peter the Hermit[112] stood in a corner with that of good old Bishop Jewel,[113] and one of ivory, which had belonged to Papirius,[114] the Roman senator. The ponderous club of Hercules[115] was close at hand. The virtuoso showed me the chisel of Phidias, Claude's palette, and the brush of Apelles,[116] observing that he intended to bestow the former either on Greenough, Crawford, or Powers,[117] and the two latter upon Washington Allston.[118] There was a small vase of oracular gas from Delphos,[119] which I trust will be submitted to the scientific analysis of Professor Silliman.[120] I was deeply moved on beholding a vial of the tears into which Niobe[121] was dissolved; nor less so on learning that a shapeless fragment of salt was a relic of that victim of despondency and sinful regrets—Lot's wife.[122] My companion appeared to set great value upon some Egyptian darkness[123] in a blacking jug.[124] Several of the shelves were covered by a collection of coins, among which, however, I remember none but the Splendid Shilling, celebrated by Phillips,[125] and a dollar's worth of the iron money of Lycurgus,[126] weighing about fifty pounds.

Walking carelessly onward, I had nearly fallen over a huge bundle, like a peddler's pack, done up in sackcloth, and very securely strapped and corded.

"It is Christian's burden of sin,"[127] said the virtuoso.

"O, pray let us open it!" cried I. "For many a year I have longed to know its contents."

"Look into your own consciousness and memory," replied the virtuoso. "You will there find a list of whatever it contains."

As this was an undeniable truth, I threw a melancholy look at the burden and passed on. A collection of old garments, hanging on pegs, was worthy of some attention, especially the shirt of Nessus,[128] Cæsar's mantle,[129] Joseph's coat of many colors,[130] the Vicar of Bray's cassock,[131] Goldsmith's peach-bloom suit,[132] a pair of President Jefferson's scarlet breeches,[133] John Randolph's red baize hunting shirt,[134] the drab smallclothes of the Stout Gentleman,[135] and the rags of the "man all tattered and torn."[136] George Fox's hat[137] impressed me with deep reverence as a relic of perhaps the truest apostle that has appeared on earth for these eighteen hundred years. My eye was next attracted by an old pair of shears, which I should have taken for a memorial of some famous tailor, only that the virtuoso pledged his veracity that they were the identical scissors of Atropos.[138] He also showed me a broken hourglass which had been thrown aside by Father Time, together with the old gentleman's gray forelock,[139] tastefully braided into a brooch. In the hourglass was the handful of sand, the grains of which had numbered the years of the Cumæan sibyl.[140] I think it was in this alcove that I saw the inkstand which Luther threw at the devil,[141] and the ring which Essex, while under sentence of death, sent to Queen Elizabeth.[142] And here was the blood-incrusted pen of steel with which Faust[143] signed away his salvation.

The virtuoso now opened the door of a closet and showed me a lamp burning, while three others stood unlighted by its side. One of the three was the lamp of Diogenes,[144] another that of Guy Fawkes,[145] and the third that which Hero[146] set forth to the midnight breeze in the high tower of Abydos.

"See!" said the virtuoso, blowing with all his force at the lighted lamp.

The flame quivered and shrank away from his breath, but clung to the wick, and resumed its brilliancy as soon as the blast was exhausted.

"It is an undying lamp from the tomb of Charlemagne,"[147] observed my guide. "That flame was kindled a thousand years ago."

"How ridiculous to kindle an unnatural light in tombs!" exclaimed I. "We should seek to behold the dead in the light of heaven. But what is the meaning of this chafing dish of glowing coals?"

"That," answered the virtuoso, "is the original fire which Prometheus[148] stole from heaven. Look steadfastly into it, and you will discern another curiosity."

I gazed into that fire,—which, symbolically, was the origin of all that was bright and glorious in the soul of man,—and in the midst of it, behold, a little reptile, sporting with evident enjoyment of the fervid heat! It was a salamander.[149]

"What a sacrilege!" cried I, with inexpressible disgust. "Can you find no better use for this ethereal fire than to cherish a loathsome reptile in it? Yet there are men who abuse the sacred fire of their own souls to as foul and guilty a purpose."

The virtuoso made no answer except by a dry laugh and an assurance that the salamander was the very same which Benvenuto Cellini[150] had seen in his father's household fire. He then proceeded to show me other rarities; for this closet appeared to be the receptacle of what he considered most valuable in his collection.

"There," said he, "is the Great Carbuncle of the White Mountains."[151]

I gazed with no little interest at this mighty gem, which it had been one of the wild projects of my youth to discover. Possibly it might have looked brighter to me in those days than now; at all events, it had not such brilliancy as to detain me long from the other articles of the museum. The virtuoso pointed out to me a crystalline stone which hung by a gold chain against the wall.

"That is the philosopher's stone," said he.

"And have you the elixir vitæ[152] which generally accompanies it?" inquired I.

"Even so; this urn is filled with it," he replied. "A draught would refresh you. Here is Hebe's cup;[153] will you quaff a health from it?"

My heart thrilled within me at the idea of such a reviving draught; for methought I had great need of it after travelling so far on the dusty road of life. But I know not whether it were a peculiar glance in the virtuoso's eye, or the circumstance that this most precious liquid was contained in an antique sepulchral urn, that made me pause. Then came many a thought with which, in the calmer and better hours of life, I had strengthened myself to feel that Death is the very friend whom, in his due season, even the happiest mortal should be willing to embrace.

"No; I desire not an earthly immortality," said I. "Were man to live longer on the earth, the spiritual would die out of him. The spark of ethereal fire would be choked by the material, the sensual. There is a celestial something within us that requires, after a certain time, the atmosphere of heaven to preserve it from decay and ruin. I will have none of this liquid. You do well to keep it in a sepulchral urn; for it would produce death while bestowing the shadow of life."

"All this is unintelligible to me," responded my guide, with indifference. "Life—earthly life—is the only good. But you refuse the draught? Well, it is not likely to be offered twice within one man's experience. Probably you have griefs which you seek to forget in death. I can enable you to forget them in life. Will you take a draught of Lethe?"[154]

As he spoke, the virtuoso took from the shelf a crystal vase containing a sable liquor, which caught no reflected image from the objects around.

"Not for the world!" exclaimed I, shrinking back. "I can spare none of my recollections, not even those of error or sorrow. They are all alike the food of my spirit. As well never to have lived as to lose them now."

Without further parley we passed to the next alcove, the shelves of which were burdened with ancient volumes and with those rolls of papyrus in which was treasured up the eldest wisdom of the earth. Perhaps the most valuable work in the collection, to a bibliomaniac,[155] was the Book of Hermes.[156] For my part, however, I would have given a higher price for those six of the Sibyl's books[157] which Tarquin refused to purchase, and which the virtuoso informed me he had himself found in the cave of Trophonius.[158] Doubtless these old volumes contain prophecies of the fate of Rome, both as respects the decline and fall of her temporal empire and the rise of her spiritual one. Not without value, likewise, was the work of Anaxagoras[159] on Nature, hitherto supposed to be irrecoverably lost, and the missing treatises of Longinus,[160] by which modern criticism might profit, and those books of Livy[161] for which the classic student has so long sorrowed without hope. Among these precious tomes I observed the original manuscript of the Koran,[162] and also that of the Mormon Bible in Joe Smith's authentic autograph.[163] Alexander's copy of the Iliad was also there, enclosed in the jewelled casket of Darius,[164] still fragrant of the perfumes which the Persian kept in it.

Opening an iron-clasped volume, bound in black leather, I discovered it to be Cornelius Agrippa's book of magic;[165] and it was rendered still more interesting by the fact that many flowers, ancient and modern, were pressed between its leaves. Here was a rose from Eve's bridal bower, and all those red and white roses which were plucked in the garden of the Temple by the partisans of York and Lancaster.[166] Here was Halleck's Wild Rose of Alloway.[167] Cowper had contributed a Sensitive Plant,[168] and Wordsworth an Eglantine,[169] and Burns a Mountain Daisy,[170] and Kirke White a Star of Bethlehem,[171] and Longfellow a Sprig of Fennel,[172] with its yellow flowers. James Russell Lowell had given a Pressed Flower,[173] but fragrant still, which had been shadowed in the Rhine. There was also a sprig from Southey's Holly Tree.[174] One of the most beautiful specimens was a Fringed Gentian, which had been plucked and preserved for immortality by Bryant.[175] From Jones Very, a poet whose voice is scarcely heard among us by reason of its depth, there was a Wind Flower and a Columbine.[176]

As I closed Cornelius Agrippa's magic volume, an old, mildewed letter fell upon the floor. It proved to be an autograph from the Flying Dutchman[177] to his wife. I could linger no longer among books; for the afternoon was waning, and there was yet much to see. The bare mention of a few more curiosities must suffice. The immense skull of Polyphemus[178] was recognizable by the cavernous hollow in the centre of the forehead where once had blazed the giant's single eye. The tub of Diogenes,[179] Medea's caldron,[180] and Psyche's vase of beauty[181] were placed one within another. Pandora's box,[182] without the lid, stood next, containing nothing but the girdle of Venus,[183] which had been carelessly flung into it. A bundle of birch rods which had been used by Shenstone's schoolmistress[184] were tied up with the Countess of Salisbury's garter.[185] I knew not which to value most, a roc's egg[186] as big as an ordinary hogshead, or the shell of the egg which Columbus set upon its end.[187] Perhaps the most delicate article in the whole museum was Queen Mab's chariot,[188] which, to guard it from the touch of meddlesome fingers, was placed under a glass tumbler.

Several of the shelves were occupied by specimens of entomology. Feeling but little interest in the science I noticed only Anacreon's grasshopper,[189] and a humble bee which had been presented to the virtuoso by Ralph Waldo Emerson.[190]

In the part of the hall which we had now reached I observed a curtain, that descended from the ceiling to the floor in voluminous folds, of a depth, richness, and magnificence which I had never seen equalled. It was not to be doubted that this splendid though dark and solemn veil concealed a portion of the museum even richer in wonders than that through which I had already passed; but, on my attempting to grasp the edge of the curtain and draw it aside, it proved to be an illusive picture.

"You need not blush," remarked the virtuoso; "for that same curtain deceived Zeuxis. It is the celebrated painting of Parrhasius."[191]

In a range with the curtain there were a number of other choice pictures by artists of ancient days. Here was the famous cluster of grapes by Zeuxis, so admirably depicted that it seemed as if the ripe juice were bursting forth. As to the picture of the old woman[192] by the same illustrious painter, and which was so ludicrous that he himself died with laughing at it, I cannot say that it particularly moved my risibility. Ancient humor seems to have little power over modern muscles. Here, also, was the horse painted by Apelles[193] which living horses neighed at; his first portrait of Alexander the Great, and his last unfinished picture of Venus asleep. Each of these works of art, together with others by Parrhasius, Timanthes, Polygnotus, Apollodorus, Pausias, and Pamphilus,[194] required more time and study than I could bestow for the adequate perception of their merits. I shall therefore leave them undescribed and uncriticized, nor attempt to settle the question of superiority between ancient and modern art.

For the same reason I shall pass lightly over the specimens of antique sculpture which this indefatigable and fortunate virtuoso had dug out of the dust of fallen empires. Here was Ætion's cedar statue of Æsculapius,[195] much decayed, and Alcon's iron statue of Hercules,[196] lamentably rusted. Here was the statue of Victory, six feet high, which the Jupiter Olympus of Phidias[197] had held in his hand. Here was a forefinger of the Colossus of Rhodes,[198] seven feet in length. Here was the Venus Urania of Phidias,[199] and other images of male and female beauty or grandeur, wrought by sculptors who appear never to have debased their souls by the sight of any meaner forms than those of gods or godlike mortals. But the deep simplicity of these great works was not to be comprehended by a mind excited and disturbed, as mine was, by the various objects that had recently been presented to it. I therefore turned away with merely a passing glance, resolving on some future occasion to brood over each individual statue and picture until my inmost spirit should feel their excellence. In this department, again, I noticed the tendency to whimsical combinations and ludicrous analogies which seemed to influence many of the arrangements of the museum. The wooden statue so well known as the Palladium of Troy[200] was placed in close apposition with the wooden head of General Jackson which was stolen a few years since from the bows of the frigate Constitution.[201]

We had now completed the circuit of the spacious hall, and found ourselves again near the door. Feeling somewhat wearied with the survey of so many novelties and antiquities, I sat down upon Cowper's sofa,[202] while the virtuoso threw himself carelessly into Rabelais' easy chair.[203] Casting my eyes upon the opposite wall, I was surprised to perceive the shadow of a man flickering unsteadily across the wainscot, and looking as if it were stirred by some breath of air that found its way through the door or windows. No substantial figure was visible from which this shadow might be thrown; nor, had there been such, was there any sunshine that would have caused it to darken upon the wall.

"It is Peter Schlemihl's shadow,"[204] observed the virtuoso, "and one of the most valuable articles in my collection."

"Methinks a shadow would have made a fitting doorkeeper to such a museum," said I; "although, indeed, yonder figure has something strange and fantastic about him, which suits well enough with many of the impressions which I have received here. Pray, who is he?"

While speaking, I gazed more scrutinizingly than before at the antiquated presence of the person who had admitted me, and who still sat on his bench with the same restless aspect, and dim, confused, questioning anxiety that I had noticed on my first entrance. At this moment he looked eagerly towards us, and, half starting from his seat, addressed me.

"I beseech you, kind sir," said he, in a cracked, melancholy tone, "have pity on the most unfortunate man in the world. For Heaven's sake, answer me a single question! Is this the town of Boston?"

"You have recognized him now," said the virtuoso. "It is Peter Rugg,[205] the missing man. I chanced to meet him the other day still in search of Boston, and conducted him hither; and, as he could not succeed in finding his friends, I have taken him into my service as doorkeeper. He is somewhat too apt to ramble, but otherwise a man of trust and integrity."

"And might I venture to ask," continued I, "to whom am I indebted for this afternoon's gratification?"

The virtuoso, before replying, laid his hand upon an antique dart, or javelin, the rusty steel head of which seemed to have been blunted, as if it had encountered the resistance of a tempered shield, or breast-plate.

"My name has not been without its distinction in the world for a longer period than that of any other man alive," answered he. "Yet many doubt of my existence; perhaps you will do so to-morrow. This dart which I hold in my hand was once grim Death's own weapon. It served him well for the space of four thousand years; but it fell blunted, as you see, when he directed it against my breast."

These words were spoken with the calm and cold courtesy of manner that had characterized this singular personage throughout our interview. I fancied, it is true, that there was a bitterness indefinably mingled with his tone, as of one cut off from natural sympathies and blasted with a doom that had been inflicted on no other human being, and by the results of which he had ceased to be human. Yet, withal, it seemed one of the most terrible consequences of that doom that the victim no longer regarded it as a calamity, but had finally accepted it as the greatest good that could have befallen him.

"You are the Wandering Jew!"[206] exclaimed I.

The virtuoso bowed without emotion of any kind, for, by centuries of custom, he had almost lost the sense of strangeness in his fate, and was but imperfectly conscious of the astonishment and awe with which it affected such as are capable of death.

"Your doom is indeed a fearful one!" said I, with irrepressible feeling and a frankness that afterwards startled me; "yet perhaps the ethereal spirit is not entirely extinct under all this corrupted or frozen mass of earthly life. Perhaps the immortal spark may yet be rekindled by a breath of heaven. Perhaps you may yet be permitted to die before it is too late to live eternally. You have my prayers for such a consummation. Farewell."

"Your prayers will be in vain," replied he, with a smile of cold triumph. "My destiny is linked with the realities of earth. You are welcome to your visions and shadows of a future state; but give me what I can see, and touch, and understand, and I ask no more."

"It is indeed too late," thought I. "The soul is dead within him."

Struggling between pity and horror, I extended my hand, to which the virtuoso gave his own, still with the habitual courtesy of a man of the world, but without a single heart throb of human brotherhood. The touch seemed like ice, yet I know not whether morally or physically. As I departed, he bade me observe that the inner door of the hall was constructed with the ivory leaves of the gateway through which Æneas and the Sibyl had been dismissed from Hades.[207]

NOTES

The Revised Standard Version was used for all Bible references.

VOLUME I

THE OLD MANSE

1. *The Old Manse:* After Hawthorne's marriage to Sophia Peabody in 1842, the newlyweds moved to Concord, Massachusetts, where they rented the manse built for the Reverend William Emerson, Ralph Waldo Emerson's grandfather, in 1765.

2. *venerable clergyman:* Dr. Ezra Ripley (1751–1841); Dr. Ripley married William Emerson's widow and occupied the manse for some fifty years.

3. *Bancroft:* George Bancroft (1800–1891), author of the ten-volume *History of the United States* (1834–40, 1852–74).

4. *Emerson wrote Nature:* Ralph Waldo Emerson (1803–82), philosopher and author. *Nature* (1836), his first book, set forth the primary principles of his Transcendentalist philosophy. Emerson lived at the manse for a time from 1834 to 1835.

5. *Assyrian dawn and Paphian sunset and moonrise:* Hawthorne is paraphrasing from chapter 3 of Emerson's *Nature:* "The dawn is my Assyria; the sunset and moon-rise my Paphos." Assyria was an ancient country located in modern-day Iraq. Paphos is a city on the Greek island of Cyprus and the ostensible birthplace of Aphrodite, goddess of love.

6. *one of Raphael's Madonnas:* Raphael (1483–1520), Italian Renaissance painter, surnamed Sanzio, of *St. Michael* and *Transfiguration* (plus others, including Madonnas) fame.

7. *Lake of Como:* a lake in the foothills of the Italian Alps.

8. *struggle between two nations:* the Revolutionary War (1775–83).

9. *the Concord:* a river in northeast Massachusetts. The first skirmish of the Revolutionary War occurred at the Old North Bridge, near the town of Concord, on April 19, 1775.

10. *turning a solitary spindle:* Textile mills in New England were often run on waterpower.

11. *the monument:* The monument was dedicated on July 4, 1837. Ralph Waldo Emerson's "Concord Hymn," including the famous line "the shot heard round the world," was sung at the ceremony.

12. *grave of two British soldiers . . . Zechariah Brown and Thomas Davis:* Following the battle at the Old North Bridge, the British claimed that one of the two British soldiers killed near the bridge had been scalped and his ears cut off. When questioned, Zechariah Brown and Thomas Davis asserted that they had buried the bodies of two British soldiers near the bridge, neither of which had been mutilated.

13. *Lowell:* James Russell Lowell (1819–91), poet and magazine editor.

14. *a tradition:* Though the accusation of mutilation was never proven (*see note 12 above*), accounts of the time, including testimony from Reverend William Emerson, indicate that an American did kill a wounded British soldier with a hatchet at the Old North Bridge.

15. *Thoreau:* Henry David Thoreau (1817–62), naturalist and writer. He was admired by Hawthorne for his rapport with nature and is best known for his two-year stay in a self-built cabin on Walden Pond, just outside of Concord, from 1845 to 1847.

16. *pantaloons:* tight-fitting trousers.

17. *Brook Farm:* The Brook Farm Institute of Agriculture and Education was a short-lived utopian commune in West Roxbury, Massachusetts, inspired by the philosophy of the Transcendentalists and dedicated to the principle of cooperative labor and simple agrarianism. Hawthorne joined the community in the spring of 1841, but left in less than a year, disenchanted with the combination of physical labor and communal living.

18. *Indian corn:* corn, or maize.

19. *Dutch cabbage:* a type of white cabbage.

20. *Saturn:* The Roman god of agriculture, Saturn is associated with the Greek god Cronos, leader of the Titans. Fearing a prophecy that he would be overthrown by one of his children, Cronos swallowed them all as infants until his wife Rhea tricked him into swallowing a stone and hid his youngest son, Zeus, future ruler of Olympus.

21. *umbrageous:* providing shade.

22. *aguish:* causing ague, a fit of feverish chills.

23. *lumber:* useless items stored away.

24. *oratory:* a small chapel or place of prayer.

25. *band:* a flat collar.

26. *friend of Whitefield:* George Whitefield (1714–70), English evangelist and leader of the Calvinistic Methodist Church, helped spark the Great Awakening, a period of fervent religious evangelism, during a tour of the

United States. His friend was Daniel Bliss, pastor of Concord from 1739–64.

27. *Hillard:* George Stillman Hillard (1808–79), a Boston lawyer, statesman, and editor.

28. *Papistry:* the beliefs and doctrines of the Roman Catholic Church.

29. *book of Job:* one of the books of the Old Testament. Job demonstrated his great patience when God allowed him to be sorely afflicted by Satan as a test of his faith.

30. *Liberal Preacher:* (1827–43), a monthly periodical that published sermons.

31. *Christian Examiner:* (1824–69), a bimonthly Unitarian journal.

32. *Mussulman:* Muslim.

33. *"open sesame":* the magic words that opened the thieves' treasure cave in "Ali Baba and the Forty Thieves," one of the tales from *The Thousand and One Arabian Nights.*

34. *Ellery Channing:* William Ellery Channing (1818–1901) was known as Ellery to distinguish him from his uncle and namesake, a well-known Unitarian minister and theologian. A moody and erratic poet and a follower of Transcendentalism, Channing was Hawthorne's closest friend in Concord.

35. *the Assabeth:* the Assabet River in Concord. Hawthorne enjoyed boating and fishing on it with Channing and Thoreau.

36. *couched:* lying, or reclining.

37. *Enchanted Ground . . . Celestial City:* In John Bunyan's *Pilgrim's Progress* (1678), an allegory of the Christian's journey to heaven (the Celestial City), the Enchanted Ground is a locale that hampers pilgrims by making them very drowsy.

38. *him whose career of perpetual action . . . .:* Horatio Bridge (1806–93), a college friend of Hawthorne and a U.S. naval officer.

39. *another who had thrown his ardent heart . . . :* Franklin Pierce (1804–69), a college friend of Hawthorne and president of the United States from 1853–57.

40. *her on whose feminine nature had been imposed . . . :* Margaret Fuller (1810–50), feminist writer and intellectual. As a friend of Hawthorne's and a member of the Transcendentalist Club founded by Emerson, she visited Concord frequently.

41. *Emerson:* Hawthorne was an acquaintance of Emerson's but not a follower of his Transcendental theories. (*See note 4 above.*)

42. *lapidary:* gemstone cutter.

43. *a custom house:* In 1845 Hawthorne moved back to Salem, his birthplace, to take a political appointment as surveyor of the Salem Custom House.

His experiences in that position are described in "The Custom House," the preface to *The Scarlet Letter* (1850).

44. *the African Cruiser:* Hawthorne edited the *Journal of an African Cruiser* (1845), an autobiographical account of Horatio Bridge's experiences as a U.S. naval officer. (*See note 38 above.*)

45. *some that were produced long ago: Mosses* is primarily a collection of stories written since the 1837 publication of *Twice-Told Tales;* however, it included also some earlier published tales.

THE BIRTHMARK

1. *aliment:* food.
2. *Eve of Powers: Eve Tempted,* a marble statue by American sculptor Hiram Powers (1805–73).
3. *gripe:* grip.
4. *bas-relief of ruby:* a sculpture with a slightly raised figure in red.
5. *Pygmalion:* in classical mythology, a sculptor who fell in love with the statue of a beautiful woman he had carved. In response to his prayers, the goddess Aphrodite brought the statue to life as a woman named Galatea.
6. *pastil:* pastille, a cone of perfumed paste burned to disinfect or deodorize.
7. *universal solvent:* a substance that would transmute base metals into gold.
8. *elixir vitæ:* a solution or potion believed to cure disease and prolong life.
9. *nostrum:* a medicine or panacea.
10. *Albertus Magnus:* Saint Albertus Magnus (c.1206–80), German religious philosopher and alchemist; *Cornelius Agrippa:* Heinrich Cornelius Agrippa von Nettesheim (1486–1535), German physician, philosopher, and occultist; *Paracelsus:* Philippus Aureolus Paracelsus (1493–1541), Swiss physician and alchemist; *the famous friar . . . Brazen Head:* Roger Bacon (c.1220–94), a Franciscan friar and alchemist. According to legend, Bacon constructed a brass replica of the human head that had oracular powers.
11. *Transactions of the Royal Society:* records of the British scientific organization, founded in 1660 and dedicated to scientific research, particularly in the physical sciences.

A SELECT PARTY

1. *porphyry:* a dark, purplish red stone.
2. *chrysolite:* olivine, a gray green stone.
3. *Monsieur On-Dit:* Mr. Gossip; literally, *on dit* means "they say" in French.
4. *Wandering Jew:* according to medieval legend, a man who mocked Jesus Christ on the day of the Crucifixion and, as punishment, was condemned to wander the earth until Judgment Day.

5. *Dwight, and Freneau, and Joel Barlow:* Theodore Dwight (1764–1846), American satirist; Philip Freneau (1752–1832), American poet and satirist; Joel Barlow (1754–1812), American satirist. The three were among the first authors of American literature.

6. *Davy Jones:* in folklore, the personification of the sea; best known in the phrase "Davy Jones's locker," meaning the bottom of the sea.

7. *Old Harry:* the devil.

8. *Seatsfield:* Charles Sealsfield (1793–1864), the pen name of Moravia-born writer Karl Anton Postl, whose works largely dealt with the frontier of the American Southwest. When German critic Theodor Mundt published a study in 1844 calling a writer named "Seatsfield" the greatest American author, a hunt for this unknown writer ensued. It was eventually determined that Mundt had mistaken Sealsfield's name.

9. *Chaucer's Canterbury Pilgrims: The Canterbury Tales* (composed c.1387–1400), by Geoffrey Chaucer (c.1343–1400); *the Fairy Queen: The Faerie Queene* (books 1–3, 1590; books 3–6, 1596), by Edmund Spenser (c.1552–99); *Coleridge's Cristabel: Christabel* (1816), by Samuel Taylor Coleridge (1772–1834); *Dryden's projected epic: King Arthur,* (operetta performed in 1691) by John Dryden (1631–1700). All are unfinished works.

10. *collation:* a light meal.

11. *dining with Duke Humphrey:* an Elizabethan phrase meaning "to go without dinner."

12. *syllabubs and flummery:* custardlike desserts.

13. *Nepenthe:* a drink that induces forgetfulness of sorrow and troubles.

14. *Lethe:* water from the river Lethe in Hades; those who drank of it forgot their past.

15. *Counsellor Gill:* John Gill (1732–85), American printer and newspaper publisher.

16. *Mother Carey . . . chickens:* "Mother Carey's chickens" is a traditional name for stormy petrels.

17. *Man in the Moon . . . horn lantern:* Traditionally, the figure of a man seen on the surface of the moon is said to carry a lantern and be accompanied by a dog and a bundle of sticks.

YOUNG GOODMAN BROWN

1. *Salem village:* Salem Village (now Danvers) and Salem were adjoining settlements within the township of Salem. The hysteria surrounding the 1692 witchcraft trials began in Salem Village.

2. *Old South:* the Old South Church, or Third Church, founded in 1669.

3. *King William's court:* William III, king of England from 1689 to 1702.

4. *wot'st:* knowest.

5. *the days of the martyrs:* Before the Roman emperor Constantine I (c.288–337 A.D.) converted to Christianity, early Christians were often martyred for their faith.

6. *King Philip's war:* a series of skirmishes between the American Indian chief Metacomet (King Philip) of the Wampanoags and several allied tribes and the New England colonists in 1675 and 1676.

7. *Great and General Court:* the Massachusetts legislature.

8. *lecture day:* a day midweek when scriptural lectures were given.

9. *smallage:* wild celery; *cinquefoil:* a small flowering shrub; *wolf's bane:* a poisonous plant with yellow flowers. All had supposedly occult powers.

10. *the Egyptian magi:* In Exod. 7:9–12, God commands Moses and his brother Aaron to cast down their rods before Pharaoh, where they are turned into serpents as a sign and warning. Pharaoh, however, summoned his magicians (*magi*) who turned their own rods into serpents using sorcery.

11. *Falmouth:* a town seventy miles southeast of Salem.

12. *Indian powwows:* shamans.

13. *demoniac:* one possessed by a demon or evil spirit.

14. *Martha Carrier:* one of the women accused of witchcraft at the 1692 Salem witch trials.

15. *his once angelic nature:* According to Christian belief, the devil was once a rebel angel, and cast out of heaven.

RAPPACCINI'S DAUGHTER

1. *Aubépine:* the French term for "hawthorn."

2. *Transcendentalists:* American Transcendentalism was led by a small group of Massachusetts intellectuals centered in and around Concord, so Hawthorne's perception of their universal influence is understandable. Emerson and Thoreau are the most famous of the group, which also included William Ellery Channing, Margaret Fuller, George Ripley, and Theodore Parker. The basic tenets of American Transcendentalism emphasized individual intuition and the spiritual plane of existence as apprehended through the study of nature.

3. *Eugene Sue:* Eugène Sue (1804–57), a French sensational novelist.

4. Contes deux fois racontées: *Twice-Told Tales* (1837).

5. Le Voyage Céleste à Chemin de Fer: "The Celestial Railroad"; *3 tom.:* 3 tomes, or volumes; a fabrication, as each of the stories listed was originally published in a magazine.

6. Le nouveau Père Adam et la nouvelle Mère Eve: "The New Adam and Eve."

7. Roderic; ou le Serpent à l'estomac: "Egotism; or, The Bosom Serpent."

8. Le Culte du Feu: "Fire Worship."

9. *Persian Ghebers:* followers of an ancient Persian religion, later Zoroastrianism, in which fire was especially venerated.

10. La Soirée du Chateau en Espagne: "Evening in a Castle in Spain," an imaginary title.

11. *8vo.:* octavo, referring to books approximately six by nine inches, printed on sheets folded to form eight leaves.

12. L'Artiste du Beau; ou le Papillon Mécanique: "The Artist of the Beautiful."

13. *4to.:* quarto, referring to books approximately nine by twelve inches, printed on sheets folded to form four leaves.

14. Beatrice; ou la Belle Empoisonneuse: "Rappaccini's Daughter."

15. La Revue Anti-Aristocratique: *The Democratic Review;* "Rappaccini's Daughter" was originally published in this journal in 1844.

16. *Comte de Bearhaven:* John O'Sullivan (1813–95), editor of *The Democratic Review* and Hawthorne's friend.

17. *University of Padua:* Italian university and center of scientific knowledge during the Renaissance.

18. *Dante . . . Inferno:* Dante Alighieri's *Inferno* (the first section of *The Divine Comedy* [c.1308–21]) describes the various levels and torments of hell as well as prominent sinners. Among those who sinned by squandering their possessions is an unnamed Paduan nobleman.

19. *garniture:* ornament, or embellishment.

20. *Vertumnus:* Roman god of gardens and the changing seasons. He wooed his wife, Pomona, Roman goddess of orchards, by sneaking into her locked orchard.

21. *her virgin zone:* her belt.

22. *black-letter:* a heavy, Gothic typeface.

23. *lachryma:* an Italian wine.

24. *arcana:* secrets.

25. *privity:* private or secret knowledge.

26. *Alexander the Great:* Alexander III (356–323 B.C.), Macedonian king who conquered much of Asia.

27. *Araby:* Arabia.

28. *alembic:* vessel with a beaked cap used for distilling.

29. *Benvenuto Cellini:* (1500–71), Italian sculptor and metalsmith known for his caskets, vases, medals, and other decorative objects.

30. *the Borgias:* a noble Italian family, very powerful during the fifteenth century and known for their treachery and intrigues.

31. *empiric:* charlatan.

MRS. BULLFROG

1. *calash:* a bonnet that folds back.
2. *pelisse cloth:* cloth used to make a woman's cloak or coat (pelisse).
3. *Kalydor:* a brand of skin cream.
4. *Jehu:* a hired driver, after Jehu, king of Israel (ninth century B.C.), noted for his furious chariot attacks.
5. *Old Nick:* the devil.
6. *son of Anak:* descendant of Anak; according to Biblical tradition, the Anakim were a race of giants living in Palestine and displaced by the Hebrews.
7. *Gorgon:* in Greek mythology, one of three monstrous sisters with snakes for hair whose gaze turned men into stone.
8. *amatory:* relating to love.

FIRE WORSHIP

1. *Prometheus:* According to Greek mythology, the Titan Prometheus created mankind out of earth and water and stole fire from the gods on Olympus to give to his creations.
2. *Ætna:* Aetna, an active volcano on the east coast of Sicily.
3. *the Gheber:* See "Rappaccini's Daughter," note 9.
4. *the revolution:* the American Revolutionary War (1775–83).
5. *pastoral visits:* a clergyman's visits to members of his parish.
6. *lamentable trees . . . Dante:* The *Inferno* includes a description of the Wood of Suicides, in which the souls of suicides groan out their anguish in the form of trees and bushes. (*See "Rappaccini's Daughter," note 18.*)
7. *the Norman conquerors:* William, duke of Normandy, invaded England in 1066 and established autocratic control as William I of England.
8. *bituminous:* consisting of hydrocarbons.
9. *"pro aris et focis":* for altar and hearth.

BUDS AND BIRD VOICES

1. *balm of Gilead trees:* a type of poplar tree; see Jer. 8:22.
2. *the famous "four and twenty" whom Mother Goose has immortalized:* a reference to a nursery rhyme that appeared in collections attributed to the imaginary Mother Goose. The first stanza runs, "Sing a song of sixpence / a pocket full of rye / Four and twenty blackbirds / baked in a pie."
3. *its Indian name:* the Assabet, or Assabeth, River.
4. *the receding of the Nile:* Before the construction of dams, the annual flooding of the Nile River in Egypt deposited the sediment that created rich farmland.

MONSIEUR DU MIROIR

1. *clew:* clue.

2. *Puritan:* The first Hawthorne in America emigrated with the founding members of the Puritan Massachusetts Bay colony.

3. *CABALLEROS DE LOS ESPEJOZ . . . Don Quixote:* In Miguel de Cervantes' *Don Quixote de la Mancha* (1605, 1615), Don Quixote is challenged to combat by a university student who has disguised himself as the Caballero de los Espejos, the Knight of the Mirrors. By sheer luck, Don Quixote defeats him.

4. *copperwashed:* washed or coated with copper; not of solid worth or purity.

5. *Tremont Theatre:* a popular theater in Boston.

6. *Fanny Kemble:* Frances Anne Kemble (1809–93), a successful English actress who toured in the United States for several years.

7. *Old Nick:* the devil.

8. *warming pan:* a long-handled pan filled with coals and used to warm beds.

9. *river deities, or nymphs of fountains:* According to classical mythology, every river, spring, and fountain has a minor deity that belongs to it.

10. *Lake George . . . Nature's font of sacramental water:* a lake in the foothills of the Adirondack Mountains, New York, that was originally named Lac du St. Sacrement by the French missionary who discovered it.

11. *Niagara:* Niagara Falls, two large waterfalls on the Niagara River that straddle the border between New York State and Ontario, Canada.

12. *Table Rock:* the vantage point for viewing Niagara Falls from above.

13. *Nile:* The source of the Nile River was a question of great interest in the eighteenth and nineteenth centuries, one not fully answered until 1862.

14. *Ladurlad:* the hero of Robert Southey's epic poem *The Curse of Kehama* (1810). The curse laid on Ladurlad by Kehama (a Hindu rajah with supernatural powers) reads, in part, "Earth which is mine, / Its fruits shall deny thee; / And Water shall hear me, / And know thee and fly thee . . ." (144–55). Ladurlad is thus able to travel beneath the ocean.

15. *Shaker Spring at Canterbury:* a spring at the Shaker village in Canterbury, New Hampshire.

16. *posse comitatus:* a group of citizens called upon to aid the sheriff of a county.

17. *coxcombs:* vain, conceited men.

THE HALL OF FANTASY

1. *Moorish ruins of the Alhambra:* a sprawling citadel in Granada, Spain, built by Moorish kings in the twelfth and thirteenth centuries and largely destroyed with the end of Moorish rule in 1492.

2. *the Arabian tales: The Thousand and One Arabian Nights* is a collection of

Eastern folktales dating from the tenth century that includes many stories about enchanters and sorcerers.

3. *the Bourse, the Rialto, and the Exchange:* commercial centers in France, Italy, and the United States, respectively.

4. *Homer:* ancient Greek author of the epic poems *The Iliad* and *The Odyssey*.

5. *Æsop:* Aesop, sixth-century Greek writer of fables.

6. *Dante: See "Rappaccini's Daughter," note 18.*

7. *Ariosto:* Ludovico Ariosto (1474–1533), Italian poet.

8. *Rabelais' smile:* François Rabelais (c.1493–1553), French satirist.

9. *Cervantes:* Miguel de Cervantes (1547–1616), Spanish author of *Don Quixote*.

10. *Shakspeare:* William Shakespeare (1564–1616), English playwright.

11. *Spenser:* Edmund Spenser (c.1552–99), English poet and author of *The Faerie Queene*.

12. *Milton:* John Milton (1608–74), English poet and author of *Paradise Lost*.

13. *Bunyan:* John Bunyan (1628–88), English poet, Puritan minister, and author of *The Pilgrim's Progress*.

14. *Fielding, Richardson, and Scott:* Henry Fielding (1707–54), English novelist; Samuel Richardson (1689–1761), English novelist; Sir Walter Scott (1771–1832), Scottish novelist and poet.

15. *author of Arthur Mervyn:* Charles Brockden Brown (1771–1810), first professional American novelist.

16. *Goethe:* Johann Wolfgang von Goethe (1749–1832), German writer and scientist.

17. *Emanuel Swedenborg:* (1688–1772), Swedish scientist and founder of the religious philosophy Swedenborgianism.

18. *Castalian spring:* spring near the Delphic oracle in Greece. Pilgrims purified themselves in its waters before addressing the oracle.

19. *techy:* tetchy, irritable.

20. *on 'Change:* at the stock exchange.

21. *Eldorado:* legendary city of great wealth in South America.

22. *Mammon's Cave:* the dwelling place of Mammon, god of riches, in Spenser's *Faerie Queene*.

23. *Professor Espy:* James Pollard Espy (1785–1860), American meteorologist who studied storms.

24. *gum-elastic:* rubber.

25. *shepherds of the Delectable Mountains:* In Bunyan's *Pilgrim's Progress* (1678), Christian and Hopeful are entertained in the Delectable Mountains by shepherds who show them a glimpse of the Celestial City (heaven) through a telescope.

26. *Father Miller:* William Miller (1782–1849), founder of the Second Advent-

ist sect, later the Adventist Church. From 1831 to 1844, Miller predicted that the second coming of Christ, and thus the end of the world, would occur in 1843 or 1844.

THE CELESTIAL RAILROAD

1. *City of Destruction:* The narrator's account is a parody of John Bunyan's *Pilgrim's Progress* (1678), an allegory about the Christian's tortuous journey to heaven. Bunyan's pilgrim, Christian, travels on foot from his home in the City of Destruction to the Celestial City, encountering various obstacles, dangers, and temptations along the way.

2. *kennels:* sewers. From *canel* or *cannel*, the medieval term for a "gutter" or "sewer."

3. *Slough of Despond:* a swamp into which Christian falls shortly after leaving the City of Destruction.

4. *Plato:* (c.428–347 B.C.), ancient Greek philosopher.

5. *Confucius:* (c.551–c. 479 B.C.), ancient Chinese philosopher.

6. *wicket gate:* a small gate for foot traffic, usually at the entrance to a field.

7. *Evangelist:* At the beginning of Bunyan's narrative, Evangelist (one who tries to convert others to Christianity) encourages Christian to undertake his pilgrimage by giving him a parchment roll on which is written, "Fly from the wrath to come."

8. *enormous burdens:* an individual's accumulated sins. Christian must carry his on his back.

9. *Prince Beelzebub and the keeper of the wicket gate:* The devil attempts to kill pilgrims with arrows before they can enter the gate, but Christian is pulled quickly through by the gate's keeper, Good-will.

10. *Mr. Greatheart:* Great-heart guides Christian's wife, Christiana, along the path to the Celestial City in *The Pilgrim's Progress,* part 2.

11. *Apollyon:* the angel of the bottomless pit in Rev. 9:11. Christian fights and overcomes the dragonlike fiend in the Valley of Humiliation.

12. *cockle shell and staff:* Christian pilgrims traditionally wore cockleshells on their hats and carried staffs.

13. *Interpreter's House:* Shortly after passing through the wicket gate, Christian stops at the house of the Interpreter, who offers Christian spiritual guidance.

14. *Hill Difficulty:* Unlike the railroad passengers, Christian must climb this hill before descending into the Valley of Humiliation.

15. *Palace Beautiful:* a house where pilgrims stop to rest. There, Christian is entertained and instructed by Prudence, Piety, and Charity.

16. *Valley of the Shadow of Death:* Christian passes through this dark valley, peopled with hobgoblins, after his battle with Apollyon in the Valley of

Humiliation. The path is bordered by a deep ditch and a swamp, and it runs past the mouth of hell.

17. *Tophet:* hell.

18. *mephitic:* noxious.

19. *Pope and Pagan:* At the end of the Valley of the Shadow of Death is a cave strewn about with the bones and bodies of men killed by these giants, but Pagan is dead by the time Christian passes and Pope is old and powerless.

20. *troglodytes:* primitive cave dwellers.

21. *Giant Transcendentalist:* Transcendentalism opposed the doctrinal and dogmatic aspects of traditional Christianity, substituting instead a kind of intuitive spiritualism.

22. *Vanity Fair:* Christian passes through the town of Vanity, where a fair is held all year long.

23. *persecution of Christian and the fiery martyrdom of Faithful:* In Vanity, Christian and his companion Faithful are abused, imprisoned, and put on trial because they do not take part in the fair's worldly pleasures. Though Christian escapes, Faithful is tortured and burned to death.

24. *messes of pottage:* See Gen. 25:29–37. Esau sells his birthright to Jacob for a mess of pottage (vegetable soup).

25. *ancient silver mine . . . Demas:* Demas tries to interest Christian in a silver mine in the Hill Lucre. In 2 Tim. 4:10, Demas is named as one who deserts the Apostle Paul.

26. *Lot's wife . . . pillar of salt:* Christian and Hopeful encounter a pillar of salt in the shape of a woman with "Remember Lot's Wife" inscribed on it. In Gen. 19:15–26, God decides to destroy the sinful cities of Sodom and Gomorrah but first warns Lot, his wife, and his daughters to flee Sodom and not look back. When Lot's wife does look behind her, she is transformed into a pillar of salt.

27. *giant Despair:* When Christian is tempted to leave the right path for an easier bypath, he and Hopeful stray onto the lands of the Giant Despair, who imprisons them in his Doubting Castle.

28. *Delectable Mountains . . . blind men wandered:* Christian and Hopeful traverse these mountains just before arriving at the Celestial City. There they are entertained by shepherds who show them various sights, including men wandering amongst the tombs who were captured and blinded by the Giant Despair.

29. *byway to hell:* According to the shepherds, this is the door by which hypocrites, or those who sell their birthrights, descend into hell.

30. *land of Beulah:* a beautiful land on the outskirts of the Celestial City.

31. *other side of the river:* the river of death.

THE PROCESSION OF LIFE

1. *gout:* a form of arthritis causing painful inflammation of the joints, especially in the feet.

2. *Dyspeptics:* individuals subject to indigestion.

3. *Apoplexy:* stroke.

4. *Consumption:* tuberculosis.

5. *Byron:* George Gordon Noel, Lord Byron (1788–1824), English poet. As baron, Byron lived at the family seat, Newstead Abbey.

6. *Burns:* Robert Burns (1759–96), Scottish poet and peasant farmer.

7. *factory girls from Lowell:* Lowell, Massachusetts, was a textile manufacturing center with thousands of young working-class women employed in its mills.

8. *Sapphos, and Montagues, and Nortons:* female writers from the upper classes. Sappho was an ancient Greek lyric poet from an aristocratic family; "Montagues" likely refers to either Lady Mary Wortley Montagu (1689–1762) or Elizabeth Robinson Montagu (1720–1800). Both they and Caroline Elizabeth Sarah Norton (1808–77) were English writers who moved within the highest literary and social circles.

9. *Cicero:* Marcus Tullius Cicero (106–43 B.C.), Roman politician and orator.

10. *'Change:* the Exchange, a place for the buying and selling of securities and commodities.

11. *Rogues' March:* derisive music played when driving away an undesirable individual or drumming a soldier out of the military.

12. *Quakers:* members of the Society of Friends, a Protestant sect that advocated pacifism. Male Quakers tended to wear broad-brimmed hats.

13. *Herculaneum:* Italian city buried along with Pompeii by the eruption of Mt. Vesuvius in 79 A.D. Excavation of the ruins began in 1709.

14. *lazzaroni:* idle beggars. The term refers to the homeless beggars of Naples, Italy, so called after the Hospital of St. Lazarus, which serves them.

15. *pale horse of the Revelation:* "And I saw, and behold, a pale horse, and its rider's name was Death." Rev. 6:8.

FEATHERTOP; A MORALIZED LEGEND

1. *Dickon:* probably related to "dicken," a slang term for devil.

2. *corporcity:* body.

3. *the Black Man's:* the devil's.

4. *Louisbourg:* a French fort on Cape Breton Island in Nova Scotia, a French possession from 1632 to 1763.

5. *Louis le Grand:* King Louis XIV of France (1638–1715).

6. *smallclothes:* close-fitting knee breeches or trousers.

7. *Indian powwow:* shaman.
8. *gill:* one-fourth of a pint.
9. *loadstone:* a type of magnetite that attracts iron; a magnet.
10. *tenuity:* insubstantial state.
11. *clinched:* clenched.
12. *simulacre:* effigy, or representation.
13. *trow:* believe.
14. *to the boot of them:* in addition to them.
15. *Eldorado:* legendary city of great wealth in South America.
16. *Cadiz:* port in southwestern Spain; the departure point for shipments to South America.
17. *copper farthing:* coin worth one-fourth of a penny.
18. *Gouty:* afflicted with gout. (*See "The Procession of Life," note 1.*)
19. *meerschaum:* a pipe with a bowl made of meerschaum, a white claylike mineral.
20. *peruke:* a man's wig.
21. *equipage:* a carriage, together with its horses and attendants.
22. *Grand Monarque:* Louis XIV of France (1638–1715).
23. *cession of Canada:* During the course of the eighteenth century, Britain and France vied for control over Canada as they fought each other in Europe. The final conlict, the French and Indian War (1754–63), ended with the cession of all French Canadian territory to Britain.
24. *Spanish main:* a region of South America under Spanish control in the sixteenth and seventeenth centuries, stretching from the isthmus of Panama to the mouth of the Orinoco River.
25. *cur:* mongrel dog.
26. *galvanic:* as though produced by an electric shock.
27. *Tophet:* hell.
28. *coxcombs:* vain, conceited men.

VOLUME II

THE NEW ADAM AND EVE

1. *Father Miller's interpretation. See "The Hall of Fantasy," note 26.*
2. *lazar house:* a hospital for the care of lepers.
3. *Beacon Street:* a street bordering the wealthy Beacon Hill neighborhood in Boston.
4. *Æolian harp:* a wind harp, an open box with strings stretched over it that plays when the wind blows over them.
5. *State Street:* the financial center of nineteenth-century Boston.
6. *old State House:* the meeting place of the Massachusetts legislature from

1713 to 1798, located at the corner of State and Washington streets in Boston.

7. *Exchange:* a place for the buying and selling of securities and commodities.

8. *gouty:* afflicted with gout. (*See "The Procession of Life," note 1.*)

9. *memorial . . . Bunker Hill:* The 221-foot-tall granite obelisk was finished in 1842, after some difficulty with funding, to mark the site of the Battle of Bunker Hill, the first major battle of the Revolutionary War, June 17, 1775.

10. *Harvard University:* Harvard is located in Cambridge, Massachusetts, across the Charles River from Boston.

11. *fatal apple of another Tree of Knowledge:* The biblical Adam and Eve were cast out of the Garden of Eden for eating an apple from the tree, which gave them knowledge of good and evil.

12. *cemetery of Mount Auburn:* cemetery located in Cambridge, Massachusetts, on the outskirts of Boston.

EGOTISM; OR, THE BOSOM SERPENT

1. *Dyspepsia:* indigestion.

2. *Scipio:* a Roman general and stereotypical name for African-American servants.

3. *surtout:* a close-fitting overcoat.

4. *Don Rodrigo, the Goth:* According to an anonymous Spanish ballad, Don Rodrigo, last king of the Visigoths, raped the daughter of a nobleman who then laid waste to Rodrigo's kingdom in revenge. Don Rodrigo sought penance from a hermit, who entombed him along with a giant serpent that gnawed through the source of Rodrigo's sin, his heart, and thus granted him penance and release through death.

5. *corrosive sublimate:* mercuric chloride, a poison.

6. *pilasters:* ornamental rectangular columns projecting only slightly from a wall.

7. *Jeremy Taylor:* (1613–67), Anglican bishop and author of many devotional works.

8. sui generis: unique (literally, "of its own kind").

THE CHRISTMAS BANQUET

1. *skeleton at every festive board:* a custom of the Egyptians, according to the Greek historian Plutarch (c.46–c.120 A.D.), in his *Moralia.*

2. *necromancy:* the practice of conjuring up and communicating with the dead; sorcery.

3. *apples of Sodom:* legendary apples from a tree or vine that grew on the for-

mer site of the Biblical cities Sodom and Gomorrah. The fruit looks beautiful but tastes of ashes.

4. *woful man of Uz:* the Biblical Job, a righteous man whom God allowed to be sorely afflicted by Satan as a test of his faith.

5. *cachinnatory:* consisting of loud laughter.

6. *Exchange:* a place for the buying and selling of securities and commodities.

7. *Aaron Burr's name:* Aaron Burr (1756–1836), American statesman and vice president under Thomas Jefferson. He was accused of attempting to seize U.S. territory and establish an independent nation in the American Southwest, and was tried for treason in 1807.

8. *Stephen Girard:* (1750–1831), wealthy American merchant and banker.

9. *Father Miller:* See "The Hall of Fantasy," note 26.

10. *Pandemonium:* the capital of hell in John Milton's *Paradise Lost* (1667).

11. *cur:* a mongrel dog.

DROWNE'S WOODEN IMAGE

1. *Cynosure:* literally, something that attracts attention.

2. *Fayal:* an island in the Atlantic, one of the Portuguese Azores.

3. *Admiral Vernon:* Edward Vernon (1684–1757), British admiral.

4. *Britannia:* the female personification of Great Britain.

5. *Neptune:* Roman god of the oceans.

6. *Parian or the Carrara:* types of marble from the Greek island Páros and the town of Carrara in Tuscany. Both were used extensively by sculptors.

7. *Galen or Hippocrates:* Galen (129–c.199 A.D.) and Hippocrates (c.460–c.377 B.C.) were ancient Greek physicians whose work formed the basis of European medical practice.

8. *Thames:* the primary river in England.

9. *hamadryad:* a type of nymph representing the spirit of a tree.

10. *Copley:* John Singleton Copley (1738–1815), American portrait painter.

11. *General Wolfe:* James Wolfe (1727–59), the British general responsible for the capture of the French fort of Louisburg and the city of Quebec during the French and Indian War. He was killed in the Battle of Quebec.

12. *Pygmalion:* See "The Birthmark," note 5.

13. *mechanic:* an artisan or manual laborer.

14. *hanger:* a short sword.

15. *Deacon Drowne:* The actual Deacon Shem Drowne (1684–1774) was a coppersmith, not a wood-carver, who fashioned the weather vane on the Province House and Faneuil Hall.

16. *Province House:* Built in 1679, the Province House was the residence for the colonial governor from 1718 to 1776, and then a tavern. It burned down in 1864.

THE INTELLIGENCE OFFICE

1. *Killarney:* The three Lakes of Killarney are located in southwest Ireland.
2. *Peter Schlemihl:* the hero of the novella *Peter Schlemihl's Remarkable Story* (1814), by Adelbert von Chamisso. He trades his shadow to the devil for endless wealth, but is cast out of society as a result.
3. *Pearl of Great Price:* See Matt. 13: 45–46. In a parable told by Christ, a merchant sells all he has to buy a single pearl, representing heavenly salvation.
4. *Doctor Faustus:* Johann Faust (c.1480–c.1540), German magician. According to the legends, which have given rise to numerous literary versions, Faust sold his soul to the devil in exchange for youth, power, and knowledge.
5. *man in Red . . . Bonaparte:* According to legend, Napoléon Bonaparte consulted with a supernatural being, a red man, who appeared in times of trouble.
6. *before the Flood:* prior to the Biblical flood (see Gen. 7); in ancient times.
7. *Titian's secret of coloring:* Titian (c.1490–1576), Venetian painter known for his use of color.
8. *Vanity Fair:* a symbol for the frivolous and materialistic aspects of life. (*See* "The Celestial Railroad," note 22.)

ROGER MALVIN'S BURIAL

1. *"Lovell's Fight":* In May 1725, an expedition led by Captain John Lovewell of Massachusetts moved against the Pequawket Indians of Maine, partly in retaliation for the murder of some of Lovewell's relatives but also as part of the general hostilities between Native Americans and the European colonists. Heavily outnumbered, the colonists were defeated and lost many lives. Three wounded men were left behind in the forest as they retreated. The encounter was treated in heroic terms in many later ballads and popular accounts.
2. *black-letter:* a heavy, Gothic typeface.

P.'S CORRESPONDENCE

1. *Queen Victoria:* (1819–1901); Queen Victoria of Great Britain ruled from 1837–1901.
2. *Queen Anne's time:* Queen Anne of Great Britain ruled from 1702–1714.
3. *Ben Jonson's compotators at the Mermaid:* Ben Jonson (1572–1637) and fellow English playwrights, including William Shakespeare, Francis Beaumont and John Fletcher, and Webster Ford, were accustomed to meet at the Mermaid Tavern in London; *compotators* are fellow drinkers.
4. *Lord Byron:* George Gordon Noel, Lord Byron (1788–1824), English poet.

5. *Childe Harold:* *Childe Harold's Pilgrimage* (1812–18), an epic poem detailing the moody and guilt-ridden Childe Harold's travels through Europe.

6. *gout:* See "*The Procession of Life*," note 1.

7. *deformed one:* Byron was born with a clubfoot.

8. *reconciliation with Lady Byron:* Lady Byron left her husband after the birth of their daughter in 1815. In reality, the two never reconciled, and Byron spent the remainder of his life with a string of mistresses.

9. *Puseyites:* followers of Edward Bouverie Pusey (1800–82) and his Oxford Movement, which advocated the incorporation of Catholic rites into the Anglican Church. Strict Methodism, with its emphasis on salvation through faith, and Puseyism would be near opposites, and it is highly unlikely that Byron would have joined any conventional religious sect.

10. *House of Lords:* As a peer, Byron had a hereditary seat in the House of Lords, one of the two houses of the British Parliament.

11. *Southey:* Robert Southey (1784–1843), politically conservative English poet. He and the social reformist Byron had a long-running feud over their political principles and literary styles.

12. *Moore:* Thomas Moore (1779–1852), Irish poet and friend of Byron's. One of his most popular works was the ten-part *Irish Melodies*.

13. *Childe Harold, and Manfred, and Don Juan:* the most acclaimed of Byron's works.

14. *Tophet:* hell.

15. *Thorwaldsen's statue of the poet:* Bertel Thorwaldsen (1768 or 1770–1844) completed a memorial statue of Byron in 1824, but it was refused a place in Westminster Abbey and was instead installed in the library of Trinity College at Cambridge.

16. *Abbey:* Westminster Abbey's Poets' Corner is the resting place of many of England's greatest writers.

17. *denied sepulture:* Byron's body was brought back to England but was interred in the family vault at Newstead Abbey when he was refused a place in Westminster Abbey because of his immoral lifestyle.

18. *died of fever at Missolonghi:* Byron died of a fever in Missolonghi, Greece, where he had gone to support the Greek bid for independence from the Ottoman Empire.

19. *Robert Burns:* Robert Burns (1759–96), Scottish poet.

20. *Ayrshire:* county in southwest Scotland and Burns's birthplace.

21. *Allan Cunningham:* (1784–1842), Scottish poet.

22. *song to Mary in Heaven:* "To Mary in Heaven" (1789). The song was written in memory of Mary Campbell, one of Burns's sweethearts, who died of a fever in 1786.

23. *Tam O'Shanter:* (1790), one of Burns's few narrative poems, describing the

encounter of a farmer who stayed too late drinking at the pub with a group of supernatural figures holding a dance.

24. *Sir Walter Scott:* (1771–1832), Scottish novelist and poet.

25. *Abbotsford:* the mansion Scott built with the profits from his very successful novels.

26. *amanuensis:* one who takes dictation.

27. *Dickens:* Charles Dickens (1812–70), English novelist.

28. *Pickwick Papers:* Dickens's first novel, published in installments (1836–37).

29. *Pall Mall:* a fashionable street in London and the location of many private clubs.

30. *Napoleon Bonaparte:* (1769–1821), French emperor. Defeated by a European alliance in 1814, he abdicated, but attempted to return to power in 1815 and was definitively defeated at Waterloo in Belgium.

31. *Legion of Honor:* a high French civilian and military decoration, instituted by Napoléon in 1802.

32. *St. Helena:* a British island in the south Atlantic. Napoléon was exiled there after his final defeat at Waterloo.

33. *Cæsar:* Julius Caesar (100–44 B.C.), Roman general and statesman; *Hannibal:* (247–183 B.C.), Carthaginian general.

34. *Shelley:* Percy Bysshe Shelley (1792–1822), English poet and close friend of Byron's.

35. *taken orders:* To take orders is to be ordained as an Anglican priest and accept a church office or living. As with Byron, this turn to conventional religion on Shelley's part is highly unlikely. He was expelled from Oxford his first year for the publication of a pamphlet entitled *The Necessity of Atheism.*

36. *Thirty-nine Articles:* The Thirty-Nine Articles of Religion (1571) are the doctrinal basis of the Church of England and must be assented to by every Anglican priest.

37. *Queen Mab, the Revolt of Islam, and Prometheus Unbound:* three of Shelley's most acclaimed works, published 1813, 1817, and 1820, respectively.

38. *lost in the Bay of Spezzia:* Shelley was drowned while sailing in the Gulf of Spezia in Italy, and his body washed ashore ten days later. He was cremated and buried in a Protestant cemetery in Rome.

39. *Dr. Reginald Heber:* (1783–1826), Anglican bishop of Calcutta and author of several popular hymns.

40. *see:* the jurisdiction of a bishop.

41. *Coleridge:* Samuel Taylor Coleridge (1772–1834), English poet. He, William Wordsworth, and Robert Southey were close friends, known as the Lake Poets (after their residence in England's Lake District).

42. *Christabel:* a long narrative poem never finished by Coleridge.

43. *John Murray:* (1741–1815), English founder of American Universalism, a Protestant sect very similar to Unitarianism.

44. *Wordsworth:* William Wordsworth (1770–1850), English poet.

45. *The Excursion:* (1814), a continuation of Wordsworth's acclaimed *The Prelude.*

46. *Laodamia:* (1818), a poem about the death of a Greek warrior at the start of the Trojan War.

47. *Southey:* Robert Southey (1774–1843), English poet.

48. *Old Gifford:* William Gifford (1756–1826), English satirical poet and editor of the *Quarterly Review,* known for his sour temper and attacks on young poets.

49. *Keats:* John Keats (1795–1821), English poet.

50. *Temple Bar:* a gate marking one of the entrances to the old City of London. The Temple district is home to the British legal societies or Inns of Court.

51. *porter-swollen:* porter is a dark variety of beer.

52. *bleeding at the lungs:* Keats died of tuberculosis at the age of twenty-five.

53. *Endymion:* (1818), a poem based on the Greek legend of Endymion, a young shepherd beloved by the goddess of the moon. Now considered one of Keats's best poems, it received negative reviews at the time.

54. *Quarterly Review:* a politically conservative literary review, edited by William Gifford. In April of 1818, the journal published a scathing review of *Endymion* by John Wilson Croker.

55. *Milton's days:* John Milton (1608–74), English poet.

56. *James Russell Lowell:* (1819–91), American poet and editor of the *Atlantic Monthly* and *North American Review.*

57. *Paradise Regained:* Milton's *Paradise Regained* (1671) is the sequel to his masterpiece *Paradise Lost* and tells the story of Christ's triumph over Satan's temptations, and therefore, the washing away of the original sin that lost Adam and Eve their residence in Eden.

58. *sibyl:* a prophetess, in classical mythology.

59. *House of Lords:* one of the two houses of the British Parliament in which most of the seats are held and inherited by members of the peerage.

60. *Canning:* Charles John, Earl Canning (1812–62), British statesman. He took a seat in the House of Lords in 1837 upon inheriting his mother's place in the peerage.

61. *Cobbett:* William Cobbett (c.1763–1835), British journalist and reformer concerned with parliamentary reform and the working class. He was elected to the lower house of Parliament in 1832.

62. *Drury Lane Theatre:* the oldest theater in Britain. The current building was erected in 1812 but the original was built in 1663.

63. *elder Kean:* Edmund Kean (c.1787–1833), a popular English actor known for his emotional style of acting.

64. *Mrs. Siddons:* Sarah Kemble Siddons (1755–1831), English actress and the most successful member of the twelve Kemble siblings who acted.

65. *John Kemble:* John Philip Kemble (1757–1823). He often acted alongside his sister Sarah Siddons in tragic roles.

66. *Charles Matthews:* English actor known for his U.S. performances as a blackface minstrel.

67. *Dr. Channing:* William Ellery Channing (1780–1842), Unitarian minister and theologian.

68. *John Neal:* (1793–1876), American poet and novelist.

69. *Bryant . . . Thanatopsis:* William Cullen Byrant (1794–1878), American poet. "Thanatopsis" is one of his most famous poems. The term means "a meditation upon death."

70. *Halleck . . . Fanny:* Fitz-Greene Halleck (1790–1867), American poet. *Fanny* (1819) is a long satire on local politics and is often compared to Byron's *Don Juan.*

71. *metempsychosis:* reincarnation.

72. *Whittier:* John Greenleaf Whittier (1807–92), American poet and abolitionist, known as "the Quaker Poet." The death here ascribed to Whittier, and those of Longfellow and Willis, are fanciful creations of Hawthorne's.

73. *Longfellow:* Henry Wadsworth Longfellow (1807–82), American poet and a college friend of Hawthorne's.

74. *Willis:* Nathaniel Parker Willis (1806–67), American author and editor.

75. *the Democratic:* Many of Hawthorne's stories were originally published in *The Democratic Review.*

76. *Campbell:* Thomas Campbell (1777–1844), Scottish poet and author of *Gertrude of Wyoming* (1809).

77. *Mr. Brockden Brown:* Charles Brockden Brown (1771–1810), first professional American novelist.

78. *Joel Barlow:* (1754–1812), American diplomat and satirical poet.

79. *war between Mexico and Texas:* The Texas Revolution (1835–36) resulted in the establishment of Texas as an independent republic.

EARTH'S HOLOCAUST

1. *Legion of Honor. See "P's Correspondence," note 31.*

2. *order of St. Louis:* order of knighthood established by Louis IX of France (1214–70).

3. *Society of Cincinnati:* founded by and limited to officers of the Continental Army of the Revolutionary War. Membership is passed down to the eldest sons of members.

4. *William the Conqueror:* William I of England (c.1027–87).

5. *Victoria:* Victoria I of England (1819–1901).

6. *Drury Lane Theatre: See "P's Correspondence," note 62.*

7. *Saxon princes:* the Germanic rulers of England from the fifth century until the Norman Conquest in 1066.

8. *Hindostan:* here, India.

9. *Czar of Russia's sceptre:* Nicholas I of Russia (1796–1855) brutally suppressed a Polish rebellion in 1830–31.

10. *Father Matthew:* Theobald Matthew (1790–1856), Irish priest and outspoken advocate of temperance.

11. *topers:* drunkards.

12. *bon vivants:* persons dedicated to sensuous enjoyment, especially of good food and drink.

13. *Tokay:* a sweet Hungarian wine.

14. *fourth-proof brandy:* a high-quality brandy that has been refined several times.

15. *Rev. Sidney Smith:* (1771–1845), English clergyman and writer. In 1843, having lost his money in a loan to the state of Pennsylvania, he published an attack on the state for repudiating its debts.

16. *the Armada:* the Spanish Armada, a fleet of ships launched in 1588 by Philip II of Spain to invade England. It was defeated by the British fleet and catastrophic weather.

17. *Marlborough:* John Churchill (1650–1722), duke of Marlborough and British general.

18. *Napoleon and Wellington:* Napoléon Bonaparte (1769–1821), French emperor; Arthur Wellesley, duke of Wellington (1769–1852), British general. Wellington defeated Napoléon at Waterloo in 1815.

19. *Cain:* See Gen. 4:8. Cain, son of Adam and Eve, killed his brother Abel.

20. *Voltaire:* François Marie Arouet de Voltaire (1694–1778), French philosopher and author.

21. *Milton's works:* John Milton (1608–74), English poet.

22. *fire from heaven like Prometheus: See "Fire Worship," note 1.*

23. *Mother Goose's Melodies:* a collection of nursery rhymes attributed to the imaginary Mother Goose.

24. *Life and Death of Tom Thumb:* Henry Fielding's *The Life and Death of Tom Thumb the Great* (1730), a short burlesque.

25. *biography of Marlborough:* William Coxe's *Life of Marlborough* (1818–19), a very long biography.

26. *Shelley's poetry:* Percy Bysshe Shelley (1792–1822), English poet.

27. *Lord Byron:* George Gordon Noel, Lord Byron (1788–1824), English poet.

28. *Tom Moore:* Thomas Moore (1779–1852), Irish poet.

29. *pastil:* pastille, a cone of perfumed paste burned to disinfect or deodorize.
30. *Ellery Channing:* See "The Old Manse," note 34.
31. *Cadmus:* according to Greek mythology, a Phoenician prince who founded the city of Thebes and brought the Phoenician alphabet to Greece.
32. *Popish:* a derogatory term for things Catholic.
33. *St. Peter's:* St. Peter's Basilica, in Rome.
34. *Titan:* in Greek mythology, one of a race of giant gods.

Passages from a Relinquished Work

1. *the Old Nick:* the devil.
2. *Goldsmith:* Oliver Goldsmith (c.1730–74), Anglo-Irish author. As a young man, Goldsmith traveled throughout Europe, supporting himself by playing the flute and begging.
3. *Childe Harold's sentiment:* See "P's Correspondence," note 5.
4. *Don Quixote:* In Cervantes' *Don Quixote de la Mancha* (1605, 1615), the naïve and idealistic hero, who believes himself a chivalrous knight, travels in quest of adventure with his squire, Sancho Panza, and horse, Rosinante.
5. *Andover:* Andover Theological Seminary in Andover, Massachusetts.
6. *Gil Blas: L'Histoire de Gil Blas de Santillane* (1715–35), by Alain-René Lesage (1668–1747), a picaresque romance about the adventures of a quick-witted young man.
7. *Sir Piercy Shafton's wardrobe:* Sir Piercie Shafton is an arrogant and affected English knight in Sir Walter Scott's *The Monastery* (1820).
8. *Mr. Higginbotham's Catastrophe:* one of Hawthorne's stories published in *Twice-Told Tales* (1837).
9. *tragedy of Douglas: The Tragedy of Douglas* (1756), a play by Scottish dramatist John Home (1722–1808).
10. *toddy stick:* a glass or metal spatula used to stir toddy, a punch of whisky mixed with hot water and sugar.
11. *Young Norval . . . Little Pickle:* characters in *The Tragedy of Douglas.*
12. *Briareus:* in Greek mythology, a hundred-handed giant.
13. *cue:* a roll or tail of hair.

Sketches from Memory

1. *The Notch of the White Mountains:* a gap, or pass, carved by the Saco River between the Presidential Range and Franconia Mountains of the White Mountains in New Hampshire.
2. *Titans:* in Greek mythology, a race of giant gods.
3. *Byron's rhapsodies:* George Gordon Noel, Lord Byron (1788–1824), English poet.

4. *Mount Washington:* the tallest mountain (6,288 feet) in the Presidential Range of the White Mountains.

5. *"a stag of ten":* a stag with ten points, or projections, on its antlers.

6. *Ethan Crawford's guests:* Crawford ran an inn in the Notch (*see note 1 above*). Hawthorne spent some time at Crawford's establishment in 1832.

7. *Quakers whom the spirit moveth not:* The name "Quaker" stems from the physical "quaking" that precedes moments of divine revelation. (*See "The Procession of Life," note 12.*

8. *"Great Carbuncle" of the White Mountains:* according to legend, an enormous carbuncle (a garnet or dark red gemstone cut in a rounded form without facets) hidden somewhere in the White Mountains of New Hampshire. See Hawthorne's story "The Great Carbuncle" in *Twice-Told Tales* (1837).

9. *Grand Canal:* the Erie Canal, connecting the Hudson River with Lake Erie. It was completed in 1825.

10. *De Witt Clinton:* (1769–1828), one of the canal's foremost supporters as canal commissioner and governor of New York.

11. *Dutchmen:* New York was originally a Dutch colony.

12. *Buffalo to Albany:* The canal ran from Buffalo on the banks of Lake Erie to Albany on the banks of the Hudson River.

13. *Neptune:* Roman god of water.

14. *aguish:* suffering from ague, a fit of feverish chills.

15. *"tontine":* a financial scheme in which members contribute capital and receive an annuity that increases as members die; sometimes used as a means of raising funds for hotels.

16. *Virgil:* (70–19 B.C.), Roman poet.

17. *Mammon:* the personification of greed and wealth.

18. *"Flying Dutchman":* according to legend, a Dutch captain condemned to sail against the wind until Judgment Day. The name is also commonly applied to the ship.

19. *flambeau:* a torch.

THE OLD APPLE DEALER

1. *surtout:* a close-fitting overcoat.

2. *Gilbraltar rock:* a kind of rock candy named after the British fortress located on a narrow promontory at the southern tip of Spain, which guards the narrow entrance to the Mediterranean Sea.

3. *half-peck:* a unit of dry measure equal to four quarts.

4. *gills:* a gill is one-fourth of a pint.

5. *chaffer:* bargain, or haggle.

6. *tithe:* a tenth part.

THE ARTIST OF THE BEAUTIFUL

1. *pinchbeck:* an alloy of zinc and copper; imitation gold.

2. *the perpetual motion:* a hypothetical mechanism that operates continuously and indefinitely without an external energy source.

3. *'Change:* the Exchange, a place for the buying and selling of securities and commodities.

4. *slightness:* a slighting, contempt.

5. *Queen Mab:* a miniature fairy who, in a tiny chariot, delivers dreams to men.

6. *Man of Brass, constructed by Albertus Magnus, and the Brazen Head of Friar Bacon:* See "The Birthmark," *note 10.*

7. *Dauphin of France:* the eldest son of the king of France.

8. *Allston:* Washington Allston (1779–1843), American painter. His painting *Belshazzar's Feast* was never completed.

9. *Milton's song:* John Milton (1608–74), English poet, author of *Paradise Lost.*

10. *magnetism:* an innate power or ability to exert influence over people.

A VIRTUOSO'S COLLECTION

1. *Massachusetts tenor:* in Massachusetts currency.

2. *Lysippus:* (fourth century B.C.), Greek sculptor. His sculpture of Opportunity was widely copied.

3. *the she wolf that suckled Romulus and Remus:* Romulus, the mythic founder of Rome, and his twin brother, Remus, were the sons of the war god Mars, by the daughter of Numitor, king of Alba Longa in central Italy. Set adrift as infants on the Tiber River by Numitor's usurping brother, they were rescued and suckled by a she-wolf and then raised by a shepherd.

4. *Spenser . . . 'milk-white lamb' which Una led:* Una is the allegorical representation of Truth in *The Faerie Queene,* by Edmund Spenser (c.1552–99). She is described as riding upon a white ass and leading a white lamb.

5. *Alexander's steed Bucephalus:* the warhorse of Alexander the Great (356–323 B.C.), Macedonian king who conquered much of Asia.

6. *Rosinante:* See "Passages from a Relinquished Work," *note 4.*

7. *Cuvier:* Georges Cuvier (1769–1832), French naturalist who specialized in the comparative anatomy and scientific classification of animals.

8. *donkey which Peter Bell cudgelled:* In William Wordsworth's *Peter Bell* (1819), the sinful main character beats a donkey and is surprised by a sudden rush of sympathy for the poor beast.

9. *Balaam:* Biblical prophet who beats his ass because it turns out of the path, only to discover that the ass was obeying the dictates of an angel. See Num. 22:21–29.

10. *Argus:* In Homer's *Odyssey,* Odysseus (Ulysses) returns home in disguise

and after a twenty-year absence, but is recognized and greeted by his very old dog Argus.

11. *Cerberus:* in Greek mythology, the three-headed dog that guards the entrance to Hades.

12. *the fox . . . loss of his tail:* referring to one of Aesop's fables, in which a fox who loses his tail to a trap tries to convince the other foxes to cut off their tails.

13. *Dr. Johnson's cat Hodge:* Dr. Samuel Johnson (1709–1784), English author and critic. His cat Hodge is mentioned prominently in James Boswell's *Life of Samuel Johnson* (1791).

14. *the favorite cats of Mahomet, Gray, and Walter Scott:* Muhammad (c.570–632), founder of Islam. According to legend, Muhammad cut off the sleeve of his robe to avoid disturbing his cat Muezza, who was sleeping on it; Thomas Gray (1716–71), English poet and author of "Ode on the Death of a Favourite Cat, Drowned in a Tub of Goldfishes"; Sir Walter Scott (1771–1832), Scottish novelist, poet, and doting owner of the cat Hinse.

15. *Puss in Boots:* a folktale cat who, wearing a pair of sturdy boots, helps his master find fame and fortune.

16. *Byron's tame bear:* George Gordon Noel, Lord Byron (1788–1824), English poet. Upset that Cambridge University forbade students to keep dogs, Byron adopted a tame bear as a pet instead.

17. *the Erymanthean boar, the skin of St. George's dragon, and that of the serpent Python:* All three are mythic monsters faced down by heroes. The *boar* was captured by the Greek hero Hercules. The *dragon*, a symbol for evil, was slain by St. George, the patron saint of England. The *Python* was slain by the Greek god Apollo.

18. *"spirited sly snake":* The quote is from Milton's *Paradise Lost* (9.613).

19. *stag that Shakspeare shot:* possibly a reference to the wounded stag in act 2, scene 1 of Shakespeare's *As You Like It.*

20. *tortoise which fell upon the head of Æschylus:* According to legend, the ancient Greek dramatist Aeschylus (525–456 B.C.) was killed when an eagle dropped a tortoise on his head.

21. *sacred bull Apis:* Apis was sacred to the ancient Egyptians as the earthly incarnation of the ancient Egyptian god Ptah of Memphis. After his death, the Apis bull was also associated with Osiris, Egyptian god of the underworld.

22. *the "cow with the crumpled horn," and . . . the cow that jumped over the moon:* characters in the Mother Goose rhymes "The House That Jack Built" and "The Cat and the Fiddle," respectively.

23. *griffin:* a mythical beast with the body of a lion and the head and wings of an eagle.

24. *Pegasus:* a winged horse in Greek mythology.

25. *dove...passengers of the ark:* Noah sent a dove out to test whether or not the flood waters had receded from the earth. He knew that they had when the dove returned with an olive leaf in its mouth. See Gen. 8:8–12.

26. *raven...fed Elijah in the wilderness:* The prophet Elijah was commanded by God to live hidden in the desert, where ravens brought him bread and meat. See 1 Kings 17:1–6.

27. *Barnaby Rudge:* the hero of *Barnaby Rudge* (1841), by Charles Dickens. His companion is a raven named Grip whose favorite saying is "Never say die."

28. *Duchess of Kendall:* Ehrengarde Melusina (1667–1743), daughter of the Count of Schulenburg, was the favored mistress of George I of England.

29. *Minerva's owl:* Minerva is the Roman goddess of the arts and handicrafts. She and her Greek counterpart, Athena, are particularly associated with the owl.

30. *the vulture... Prometheus:* As punishment for stealing divine fire, Zeus, the ruler of the gods, had Prometheus bound to a mountaintop rock where a vulture ate of his liver. The liver was restored each night so that the punishment might be endless. (*See* "Fire Worship," note 1.)

31. *sacred ibis:* a wading bird, native to the Nile region and sacred to the ancient Egyptians.

32. *Stymphalides:* the Stymphalian birds, large man-eating birds killed by the Greek hero Hercules as part of his Twelve Labors.

33. *Shelley's skylark, Bryant's waterfowl:* a reference to two of the poets' more famous works: Percy Bysshe Shelley's "To a Skylark" (1820) and William Cullen Bryant's "To a Waterfowl" (1815).

34. *N.P. Willis:* See "P.'s Correspondence," note 74.

35. *Coleridge's albatross... crossbow shaft:* In Samuel Taylor Coleridge's *Rime of the Ancient Mariner* (1798), the title character is doomed to wander the seas endlessly after shooting an albatross.

36. *flock whose cackling saved the Roman Capitol:* A flock of geese in a temple on the Capitoline Hill squawked and alerted the Roman Senate to an impending invasion by the Gauls in 390 B.C.

37. *Robinson Crusoe's parrot:* In Daniel Defoe's *Robinson Crusoe* (1719), the shipwrecked Crusoe has a talking parrot as a companion.

38. *a live phœnix:* according to ancient Egyptian mythology, a bird that lives five hundred years is then consumed by fire, and is reborn from the ashes.

39. *bird of paradise:* a brightly colored bird, native to New Guinea.

40. *soul of Pythagoras:* Pythagoras (c.582–c.500 B.C.), Greek philosopher who believed in the transmigration of souls, and allegedly, claimed that his soul took the form of a peacock at one time.

41. *Dr. Franklin's cap of asbestos:* Hawthorne is possibly referring to a purse

made of asbestos that Benjamin Franklin took to England as a curiosity in 1724, as mentioned in Franklin's *Autobiography*. Asbestos is a fibrous, fireproof mineral.

42. *wishing cap of Fortunatus:* According to an Italian folktale, the impoverished Fortunatus is visited by Fortune and offered health, beauty, wealth, wisdom, or strength. He chooses wealth and is given an inexhaustible purse and a wishing cap that transports him wherever he wishes to go.

43. *genius of this lamp . . . Aladdin's palace:* In one of the stories from *The Thousand and One Arabian Nights,* Aladdin is the son of a poor widow who finds a magic lamp that when rubbed releases a genie, or jinn, who overnight produces a magnificent palace for Aladdin.

44. *Prospero's magic wand:* In William Shakespeare's *The Tempest* (1611), the magician Prospero uses a staff or wand to help with his sorcery, and breaks it at the end of the play when he gives up the practice of magic.

45. *gold ring of ancient Gyges:* According to Plato's *Republic,* Gyges was a Lydian shepherd who found a gold ring with the power to make him invisible. He used the ring to kill the king of Lydia (located in modern-day Turkey) and marry the queen.

46. *Cornelius Agrippa's magic glass:* According to legend, Agrippa possessed a magic glass, or mirror, that showed him visions. (*See "The Birthmark,"* note 10.)

47. *iron mask:* An unknown man imprisoned within an iron mask died in the Bastille in 1707. Numerous versions of this story and guesses as to the man's identity have been proffered, the most famous being the novel *The Man in the Iron Mask* by Alexandre Dumas (1802–70).

48. *axe that beheaded King Charles . . . dagger that slew Henry of Navarre . . . arrow that pierced the heart of William Rufus:* Charles I of England (1600–1649) was beheaded in 1649 by the forces of Oliver Cromwell; Henry III of Navarre (1553–1610), also Henry IV of France, was stabbed to death by a religious fanatic; William II of England (1056–1100) was killed by an arrow under suspicious circumstances.

49. *Charlemagne's sheepskin cloak:* Charlemagne (c.742–814), king of the Franks and Holy Roman Emperor, usually wore a blue cloak.

50. *the flowing wig of Louis Quatorze:* Louis XIV of France (1638–1715) began wearing elaborate curled wigs to hide his baldness, and started a fashion trend that would last a century.

51. *Sardanapalus:* legendary king of ancient Assyria who dressed effeminately and would sit and comb and spin wool with his concubines.

52. *King Stephen's famous breeches:* According to a drinking song sung by Iago in Shakespeare's *Othello* (1623 First Folio edition), "King Stephen was and-a worthy Peere, / His Breeches cost him but a Crowne, / He held them Six pence all to deere, / With that he cal'd the Tailor Lowne." (2.3.1201–1204).

53. *heart of the Bloody Mary . . . "Calais":* Mary I of England (1516–58) was persuaded by her husband, Philip II of Spain, to declare war against France in 1558, and lost Calais, the sole remaining British possession on the European continent.

54. *Gustavus Adolphus:* Gustavus II (1594–1632), king of Sweden and leader of the Protestant forces in the Thirty Years' War. After his death in battle, his wife, Maria Eleonora, kept his body and then just his heart in her bedroom.

55. *Midas:* According to Greek mythology, King Midas of Phrygia voted against the god Apollo and in favor of Pan in a musical contest. As punishment, Apollo gave Midas the ears of an ass. Another story tells how, when offered one wish by the god Dionysus, he unwisely wished for everything he touched to turn to gold; when even his food turned to gold at the touch of his lips, Midas repented of his wish.

56. *Grecian Helen:* According to Greek mythology, Helen was the half-mortal daughter of Zeus, and the most beautiful woman in the world. Paris of Troy was promised her as his reward for judging Aphrodite the most beautiful of the goddesses. When he abducted her from her husband, King Menelaus of Sparta, the result was the mustering of every Greek hero and the waging of the ten-year Trojan War.

57. *the robe that smothered Agamemnon:* Upon returning from the Trojan War, Agamemnon, the leader of the Greek forces, was tangled in a robe and stabbed, not smothered, by his wife Clytemnestra as he was climbing from the bath. She was exacting revenge for his sacrifice of their daughter, Iphigenia, in an attempt to appease the gods and obtain good weather for sailing against Troy.

58. *Nero's fiddle:* The Roman emperor Nero Claudius Caesar (37–68 A.D.) allegedly was responsible for a fire in 64 A.D. that burned half of Rome, and played the fiddle (or a similar stringed instrument) while watching it burn.

59. *the Czar Peter's brandy bottle:* Peter I of Russia (1672–1725) was a heavy drinker.

60. *Semiramis:* a mythical Assyrian queen who founded the city of Babylon.

61. *Canute's sceptre:* Canute (c.995–1035), king of Denmark who successfully invaded and ruled England and the Danish provinces of Norway. To demonstrate the extent of his power, Canute reportedly used his scepter to force the sea into doing his bidding.

62. *King Philip: See "Young Goodman Brown," note 6.*

63. *little Nell:* the heroine of Charles Dickens's *The Old Curiosity Shop* (1840–41), a singularly pure and good child.

64. *seven-league boots:* boots that allow the wearer to walk seven leagues (roughly twenty-one miles) in one step; featured in various nursery and fairy tales.

424 · Notes for page 383

65. *Transcendental community in Roxbury:* Brook Farm. (*See "The Old Manse,"* note 17.)

66. *Arthur's sword Excalibar:* According to legend, Arthur, ancient king of the Britons, received the sword Exacalibur from the Lady of the Lake to help him defeat Britain's enemies.

67. *Cid Campeador:* (c.1040–1099), also known as El Cid, a Spanish warrior who fought both for and against the Moorish rulers of Spain.

68. *sword of Brutus:* Marcus Junius Brutus (c.85–42 B.C.), Roman political leader. One of the assassins of Julius Caesar, Brutus later committed suicide when his army was defeated by the forces of Marc Antony and Octavian.

69. *Joan of Arc:* (1412–31), a French peasant girl who heeded what she believed to be divine voices and led French troops to victory against the English. She was later captured by the English and burned at the stake for heresy.

70. *Horatius:* legendary sixth-century Roman hero who held off the entire Etruscan army long enough for a key bridge on the road to Rome to be destroyed.

71. *Virginius:* According to Roman legend, in the fifth century B.C., Virginius stabbed and killed his daughter Virginia to prevent her rape by Appius Claudius Crassus, a Roman statesman.

72. *Dionysius . . . Damocles:* Dionysus I of Syracuse had a sword suspended by a single hair over Damocles' head during a banquet in order to show the fawning courtier how precarious power could be.

73. *Arria's sword:* A first-century Roman noblewoman whose husband had been condemned to death for conspiracy against the emperor, Arria stabbed herself and then offered the dagger, or sword, to her doomed husband.

74. *Saladin's cimeter:* Muslim warrior and sultan of Egypt, Saladin (c.1137–93) won the city of Jerusalem back from the Christian Crusaders in 1187. A *cimeter,* or scimitar, is a saber with a curved blade.

75. *Don Quixote's lance: See "Passages from a Relinquished Work,"* note 4.

76. *Hudibras:* the hero of *Hudibras* (1663, 1664, 1678), a long satirical poem by Samuel Butler. Sir Hudibras is a stupid, greedy colonel in Oliver Cromwell's forces against Charles I of England.

77. *Miltiades:* (c.554–489 B.C.), Athenian general in charge of the victorious battle against the Persians at Marathon in 490 B.C.

78. *Epaminondas:* (c.418–362 B.C.), Theban general and brilliant tactician who was killed by a spear in a battle with Sparta.

79. *Achilles:* the greatest of the warriors in the Trojan War. His armor, includ-

ing a shield engraved with constellations, was made for him by Hephaistus, the Greek god of fire and master metalworker.

80. *Professor Felton:* Cornelius Conway Felton (1807–62), a professor of Greek literature at Harvard University.

81. *Major Pitcairn's pistol . . . Lexington:* Major John Pitcairn (1722–75) commanded the advance guard of British troops at Lexington, site of the first shots fired in the Revolutionary War. Whether he and his troops fired first or returned the fire of the colonial militiamen is uncertain.

82. *bow of Ulysses:* In Homer's *Odyssey,* Odysseus' (Ulysses') wife, Penelope, sets the suitors who have pursued her for the twenty years of her husband's absence to a final test, vowing to marry whichever of them can string the bow that Odysseus left behind and shoot an arrow through the holes in twelve axe heads.

83. *Robin Hood's arrows:* Robin Hood is a legendary medieval English hero who roamed Sherwood Forest, waylaying and robbing the rich and helping the poor.

84. *Daniel Boone:* (1734–1820), American frontiersman who explored and colonized Kentucky.

85. *Numa:* Numa Pompilius, eighth to seventh-century king of Rome. According to legend, a bronze shield fell from heaven, and it was predicted that whichever country possessed and protected the shield would have dominion over the entire earth.

86. *Washington:* George Washington (1732–99), American general and first American president. On July 3, 1774, Washington arrived in Cambridge, Massachusetts, drew his sword, and formally took command of the Continental Army.

87. *golden thigh of Pythagoras:* Pythagoras (c.580–c.500 B.C.), Greek mathematician who supposedly had a golden thigh or thigh bone.

88. *Peter Stuyvesant's wooden leg:* Peter Stuyvesant (c.1610–1672), autocratic Dutch governor of New Amsterdam (now New York), lost a leg during an attack on the Portuguese while governor of Curaçao, in the Caribbean.

89. *Golden Fleece:* According to Greek mythology, the god Hermes sent a winged golden ram to rescue Phrixus and Helle, two children ill treated by their stepmother. Helle fell off the ram but Phrixus arrived safely in Colchis, where he sacrificed the ram and hung the fleece in a sacred grove. The Greek hero Jason and a company of great heroes known as the Argonauts later stole the fleece with help from the sorceress Medea, the daughter of King Aeëtes of Colchis.

90. *Æneas:* In book 6 of Virgil's *Aeneid,* Aeneas, the founder of Rome, must visit Hades and consult with his father's shade. In order to gain entrance

to Hades, Aeneas must obtain a golden branch from a tree sacred to Proserpina, Pluto's consort.

91. *Atalanta's golden apple:* According to Greek mythology, Atalanta was a fleet huntress who refused any suitor who could not outrun her in a footrace. Hippomenes managed to beat her by dropping three of the golden apples of the Hesperides, which she stopped to retrieve.

92. *apples of discord:* According to Greek mythology, a golden apple inscribed "To the fairest" was thrown among the guests of a wedding by Eris, goddess of discord, who was angry at not having been invited. The apple was fought over by Athena, Aphrodite, and Hera.

93. *Rampsinitus:* According to legend, the Egyptian king Rhampsinitus went to Hades and played dice with the goddess Demeter, winning a golden towel, or napkin.

94. *golden vase of Bias:* According to legend, a golden cup (in some versions a golden tripod) was netted by some fishermen who disagreed about which city it belonged to. The Greek god Apollo suggested it be given to the wisest man, and it was therefore sent in turn to the seven wise men of Greece, including the sage Bias, each of whom passed it on to another, wiser man until it had gone full circle and was then dedicated to Apollo.

95. *Cinderella's little glass slipper:* In Charles Perrault's (1628–1703) version of the fairy tale, Cinderella was supplied by her fairy godmother with a magnificent dress and two glass slippers to wear to the prince's ball. In her hurry to leave by midnight, she left behind one slipper, which the prince used to locate her.

96. *Diana's sandals:* In Roman mythology, Diana is the virgin goddess of the moon.

97. *Fanny Elssler's shoe:* Fanny Elssler (1810–84) was an Austrian ballet dancer.

98. *Thomas the Rhymer's green velvet shoes:* In a seventeenth-century Scottish folk ballad, Thomas the Rhymer, or True Thomas, encounters the Queen of Elfland and agrees to serve her for seven years. She gives him "a coat of the even cloth, / And a pair of shoes of velvet green."

99. *Empedocles:* (c.495–c.435 B.C.), Greek philosopher who disappeared one night while attending a banquet held near Mount Aetna. A search later turned up one of his bronze sandals near the mountain's summit, and the stories conclude that either he threw himself into the volcano in order to find a divine death or was actually made into a deity by the gods.

100. *Anacreon's drinking-cup:* Anacreon (c.582–c.485 B.C.), Greek poet who wrote primarily about the pleasures of love and wine.

101. *Tom Moore's wine glasses:* The first book of Irish poet Thomas Moore (1779–1852) was *Odes of Anacreon* (1800).

102. *Circe's magic bowl:* According to Greek mythology, the enchantress Circe mixed drugs with wine in a bowl or cup and served the potion to men she lured to her house. The men then turned into beasts.

103. *Socrates:* (c.469–399 B.C.), Athenian philosopher tried for corrupting youth and religious heresy. He was sentenced to death and drank a cup of poison hemlock, though he had been given the opportunity to escape.

104. *Sir Philip Sidney:* (1554–86), English poet and member of Queen Elizabeth I's court. He was mortally wounded in an expedition sent to aid the Netherlands against Spain, and according to a close friend, refused a cup of water so that another dying soldier might have it.

105. *Sir Walter Raleigh's . . . Dr. Parr's, Charles Lamb's:* Sir Walter Raleigh (c.1554–1618), English explorer and author, who mounted expeditions to the New World, the source of tobacco; Dr. Samuel Parr (1747–1825), English schoolmaster known primarily as a writer of epitaphs; Charles Lamb (1775–1834), English essayist.

106. *calumet:* a ceremonial tobacco pipe used by various Native American tribes and often smoked during peace negotiations with European colonists.

107. *lyre:* a stringed instrument similar to a harp.

108. *Orpheus . . . Homer and Sappho:* In Greek mythology, Orpheus was a musician so skilled, his music enchanted men, beasts, and even trees; Homer was the ancient Greek author of the epic poems *The Iliad* and *The Odyssey;* Sappho was an ancient Greek lyric poet. In ancient Greek culture, music and poetry were inextricably intertwined.

109. *Dr. Franklin's famous whistle:* In an essay titled "The Whistle," Benjamin Franklin (1706–90) uses the figure of a whistle he naïvely purchased for an exorbitant price as a boy to represent the squandering of time, money, attention, love, etc.

110. *Anthony Van Corlear:* the town trumpeter of New Amsterdam under Peter Stuyvesant (*see note 88 above*). He allegedly drowned while rousing the countryside to the defense of the city against the British.

111. *Goldsmith: See "Passages from a Relinquished Work," note 2.*

112. *Peter the Hermit:* (c.1050–1115), French preacher and leader of a band in the First Crusade (1095).

113. *Bishop Jewel:* John Jewel (1522–1571), Anglican bishop.

114. *Papirius:* Marcus Papirius, who, according to the Roman historian Livy (59 B.C.–17 A.D.), met the Gauls' invasion of Rome (390 B.C.) seated on the portico of his mansion, bearing only an ivory staff.

115. *club of Hercules:* The mythic Greek hero Hercules is traditionally shown wielding a club.

116. *chisel of Phidias, Claude's palette, and the brush of Apelles:* Phidias (c.490–430

428 · *Notes for pages 385–386*

B.C.), Greek sculptor; Claude Lorrain (1600–1682), French landscape painter; Apelles (fourth century B.C.), Greek painter.

117. *Greenough, Crawford, or Powers:* Horatio Greenough (1805–52), Thomas Crawford (1814–57), and Hiram Powers (1805–73) were all American sculptors.

118. *Washington Allston:* Washington Allston (1779–1843), American painter.

119. *oracular gas from Delphos:* The oracle at Apollo's temple at Delphi consisted of a priestess sitting on a golden tripod over a crack in the earth that gave off certain gases, inspiring the priestess's predictions.

120. *Professor Silliman:* Benjamin Silliman (1779–1864), American chemist, geologist, and physicist.

121. *Niobe:* In Greek mythology, Niobe was a queen of Thebes who boasted of her children, holding herself above Leto, mother of the sun god Apollo and the moon goddess Artemis. All fourteen of her children were killed as punishment, and Niobe herself was transformed into an eternally weeping rock.

122. *Lot's wife: See "The Celestial Railroad," note 26.*

123. *Egyptian darkness:* utter darkness.

124. *blacking jug:* jug used to hold blacking, a shoe or stove polish.

125. *Splendid Shilling . . . Phillips: The Splendid Shilling* is a mock-heroic poem by English poet John Philips (1676–1709).

126. *Lycurgus:* seventh-century-B.C. reformer of the Spartan government. As part of an attempt to end inequality of wealth, he required that all money be made of iron, and, therefore, intrinsically worthless.

127. *Christian's burden of sin: See "The Celestial Railroad," note 8.*

128. *shirt of Nessus:* According to Greek mythology, the centaur Nessus attempted to make off with Hercules' wife Deianira and was shot by Hercules with a poisoned arrow. The dying Nessus told Deianira to save some of his blood and smear it on a shirt if she should ever need to rekindle Hercules' love for her. The shirt burned Hercules so unbearably he built himself a funeral pyre and burned away the mortal part of his being.

129. *Cæsar's mantle:* a loose coat or cloak worn by Julius Caesar (100–44 B.C.).

130. *Joseph's coat of many colors:* Jacob gave his youngest and favorite son Joseph a "coat of many colors," thereby fueling the jealousy of Joseph's brothers. See Gen. 37:3–4.

131. *Vicar of Bray's cassock:* The popular ballad "The Vicar of Bray" is about a vicar who changes loyalties and faiths as needed to hold on to his post throughout the tumultuous reigns of Charles II, James II, William III, Anne, and George I.

132. *Goldsmith's peach-bloom suit: See "Passages from a Relinquished Work," note 2.*

133. *President Jefferson's scarlet breeches:* Thomas Jefferson (1743–1826) was known to wear red breeches, as was fashionable.

134. *John Randolph's red baize hunting shirt:* John Randolph (1733–1833) was an American legislator from Virginia.

135. *Stout Gentleman:* In the short story "The Stout Gentleman," by Washington Irving (1783–1859), the narrator spends a rainy day in an inn speculating about one of the other guests known only as "the stout gentleman," but only manages to catch a glimpse of his drab-colored trousers.

136. *"man all tattered and torn":* a character in the Mother Goose rhyme "The House That Jack Built."

137. *George Fox's hat:* George Fox (1624–91) was the founder of the Society of Friends (also known as Quakers). Fox, and all Quakers, refused to use titles or to doff their hats as a mark of respect for such titles.

138. *scissors of Atropos:* one of the three Fates in Greek mythology. Clotho spun the web of life, Lachesis measured it, and Atropos cut it.

139. *Father Time . . . forelock:* a reference to the aphorism, "take time by the forelock." Father Time is traditionally represented as having a lock of hair on his forehead, so that the present time can be seized and put to use.

140. *Cumæan sibyl:* The Cumaean Sibyl is a prophetess mentioned by Virgil in *The Aeneid*. Beloved of Apollo, she was granted one wish. Holding up a handful of sand, she asked to live as many years as there were grains of sand. She forgot, however, to ask for continuing youth and gradually withered away until only her voice was left.

141. *inkstand which Luther threw at the devil:* Protestant reformer Martin Luther (1483–1546) allegedly threw an inkstand at Satan in response to Satan's temptations.

142. *Essex . . . Queen Elizabeth:* Robert Devereux, Earl of Essex (1566–1601), favorite of Queen Elizabeth I. He was executed after attempting to replace his enemies on Elizabeth's council through a coup. Earlier, Elizabeth had given Essex a ring as a token, and Essex allegedly returned the ring to her as a plea for clemency while under death sentence. Whether or not she received the ring is unknown.

143. *Faust: See "The Intelligence Office," note 4.*

144. *Diogenes:* (c.412–323 B.C.), Greek Cynic philosopher. According to legend, Diogenes walked through the streets of Athens, in broad daylight, carrying a lighted lamp and looking "for an honest man."

145. *Guy Fawkes:* (1570–1606), one of the conspirators in the Gunpowder Plot to blow up the English Parliament on November 5, 1605, as part of a protest against the severe restrictions on Catholics. Fawkes was caught entering a cellar full of gunpowder under the Parliament building.

146. *Hero:* a priestess of Aphrodite. According to Greek mythology, Hero set a lighted lamp in her window each night so that her lover, Leander, could safely swim across the Hellespont (a strait separating European Turkey from Asian Turkey) from Abydos to her (Hawthorne's placement of Hero in Abydos is erroneous). She drowned herself after she forgot the lamp one night, and Leander drowned trying to reach her.

147. *Charlemagne:* Charlemagne (c.742–814), king of the Franks and Holy Roman Emperor. He was entombed with great state in the cathedral of Aix-la-Chapelle.

148. *Prometheus: See "Fire Worship," note 1.*

149. *salamander:* Salamanders are mythical, lizardlike beings thought to be able to withstand, or live, in fire.

150. *Benvenuto Cellini:* (1500–1571), Italian sculptor and metalsmith. Cellini was reportedly shown a salamander basking in a fire by his father.

151. *Great Carbuncle of the White Mountains: See "Sketches from Memory," note 8.*

152. *philosopher's stone . . . elixir vitæ:* the two ultimate goals of the alchemist: a stone which transmutes base metals into gold, and a potion believed to cure disease and prolong life.

153. *Hebe's cup:* Hebe is the Greek goddess of youth and cupbearer to the other Olympian gods. The liquid within her cup would grant immortality to human beings.

154. *Lethe: See "A Select Party," note 14.*

155. *bibliomaniac:* an avid book collector.

156. *Book of Hermes:* a series of books, actually, attributed to Hermes Tristmegistus, the Greek name for Thoth, the Egyptian god of wisdom. They allegedly dealt with astrology, alchemy, and other metaphysical subjects.

157. *the Sibyl's books:* according to legend, the Cumaean Sibyl (*see note 140 above*) offered Tarquinius Superbus, last king of Rome nine books that described the future of Rome. He refused her high price, so she burned three of the books and offered the remaining six at the same price. Tarquinius again refused, so the sibyl burned three more, and Tarquinius purchased the remaining three books at the original price.

158. *cave of Trophonius:* Trophonius was an ancient Greek architect who helped build Apollo's temple at Delphi. He was mysteriously swallowed up by the earth at the site of what became a famous oracle.

159. *Anaxagoras:* (c.500–428 B.C.), Greek philosopher. Only fragments of his book *On Nature* still exist.

160. *Longinus:* Dionysius Cassius Longinus (c.213–c.273 A.D.), Greek rhetorician and philosopher. Only fragments of his work still exist.

161. *Livy:* Titus Livius (59 B.C.–17 A.D.), Roman historian. Of the 142 volumes of his *Annals of the Roman People,* only 35 are still intact.

162. *the Koran:* the Qur'an, the holy book of Islam.

163. *Mormon Bible in Joe Smith's authentic autograph:* Joseph Smith (1805–1844), founder of the Church of Jesus Christ of the Latter-day Saints, transcribed and translated the contents of *The Book of Mormon* (1830) from golden tablets he unearthed under the guidance of an angel.

164. *Alexander's copy of the Iliad . . . jewelled casket of Darius:* Alexander III, known as Alexander the Great (356–323 B.C.), Macedonian king who conquered much of Asia; *The Iliad,* epic poem by Homer about the Trojan War; Darius III (c.380–330 B.C.), king of ancient Persia defeated by Alexander.

165. *Cornelius Agrippa's book of magic:* His work *Of Occult Philosophy* (1533) was highly influential among occultists. Hawthorne may also be referring to a book of spells to summon the devil that various legends list as a possession of Agrippa. (*See* "The Birthmark," *note 10.*)

166. *red and white roses . . . York and Lancaster:* In the Wars of the Roses (1455–85), a series of civil conflicts between the houses of York and Lancaster over the British throne, the badge of the York faction was a white rose and that of the Lancaster faction, a red rose. The garden of the Temple was a large garden attached to the Inns of Court in the Temple district (*see* "P.'s Correspondence," *note 50*).

167. *Halleck's Wild Rose of Alloway:* a reference to the first line of the poem "Burns," by Fitz-Greene Halleck (1790–1867). The poem is a tribute to the Scottish poet Robert Burns, who was born in Alloway.

168. *Cowper . . . Sensitive Plant:* a reference to the poem "The Poet, The Oyster, and Sensitive Plant," by William Cowper (1731–1800).

169. *Wordsworth an Eglantine:* a reference to the poem "The Waterfall and the Eglantine," by William Wordsworth (1770–1850). *Eglantine* is a type of rose.

170. *Burns a Mountain Daisy:* a reference to the poem "To a Mountain Daisy," by Robert Burns (1759–96).

171. *Kirke White a Star of Bethlehem:* a reference to the hymn "Star of Bethlehem," by Henry Kirke White (1785–1806).

172. *Longfellow a Sprig of Fennel:* a reference to the poem "The Goblet of Life," by Henry Wadsworth Longfellow (1807–82), in which the goblet is wreathed with fennel.

173. *James Russell Lowell . . . Pressed Flower:* a reference to the poem, "With a Pressed Flower," by James Russell Lowell (1819–91). The flower referred to grew on the banks of the Rhine River and could once "see its shadow in the Rhine" (line 4).

174. *Southey's Holly Tree:* a reference to the poem "The Holly Tree," by Robert Southey (1774–1843).

175. *Fringed Gentian . . . Bryant:* a reference to the poem "To the Fringed Gentian," by William Cullen Bryant (1794–1878).

176. *Jones Very . . . Wind Flower and a Columbine:* a reference to the poems "The Columbine" and "The Wind-Flower," by Jones Very (1813–1880).

177. *Flying Dutchman: See "Sketches from Memory," note 18.*

178. *Polyphemus:* in Homer's *Odyssey,* the Cyclops (a mythical giant with a single eye in his forehead), who captures Odysseus (Ulysses) and his men.

179. *tub of Diogenes:* Diogenes is said to have lived in a tub as part of his belief in living a simple life. (*See note 144 above.*)

180. *Medea's caldron:* After she and Jason returned to Greece, Medea rejuvenated Jason's aged father, Aeson, by cutting him up and boiling him in a caldron with certain herbs. (*See note 89 above.*)

181. *Psyche's vase of beauty:* According to classical mythology, Psyche was a mortal woman beloved of Cupid, Venus's son. Desperately jealous of the beautiful Psyche, Venus sent her on many dangerous errands, including a trip to Hades to borrow a little beauty from Proserpina. Psyche obtained what she believed was beauty, but when she gave in to temptation and opened the container, she was overcome by the deadly sleep that the box held. Cupid later rescued her, and Psyche was made immortal and allowed to reside with Cupid in the halls of the gods.

182. *Pandora's box:* Pandora was the first mortal woman in classical mythology. To punish man for having gained the gift of fire through the wily god Prometheus, Zeus ordered Hephaistus to mold a woman out of clay. Zeus then gave Pandora a jar, or a box, full of the evils and troubles of the world. When the box was opened, the evils flew out to plague mankind, leaving only Hope behind in the container.

183. *girdle of Venus:* a magical belt that made the wearer irresistible.

184. *Shenstone's schoolmistress:* In the poem "The Schoolmistress," by William Shenstone (1714–63), the title character maintains strict order by whipping her pupils with birch rods or branches.

185. *Countess of Salisbury's garter:* Joan, Countess of Salisbury, dropped one of her garters while dancing with King Edward III (1312–77) at a ball, and the king picked up the garter and bound it around his own knee. Angry at the speculative looks this action caused, the king announced *"Honi soit qui mal y pense"* (Evil be to him who evil thinks) and made the blue garter the badge for the chivalric Order of St. George (later the Order of the Garter).

186. *roc's egg:* the roc is a mythical bird of prey of enormous size.

187. *the shell of the egg which Columbus set upon its end:* According to legend, Christopher Columbus grew angry at a group of courtiers who either doubted the possibility of sailing around the world or who denigrated the difficulty of his accomplishment, and he challenged them to stand an egg on its end. After they had tried and failed, he lightly cracked one end

of the egg and thus balanced it. The story is meant to show how obvious even difficult solutions can look once they are known.

188. *Queen Mab's chariot:* See *"The Artist of the Beautiful,"* note 5.

189. *Anacreon's grasshopper:* One of Anacreon's extant poems exalts the carefree life of the grasshopper. (*See note 100 above.*)

190. *humble bee . . . Ralph Waldo Emerson:* a reference to the poem "The Humble Bee," by Ralph Waldo Emerson (1803–82).

191. *Zeuxis . . . Parrhasius:* (fifth century B.C.), Greek painters and rivals, both known for their skill at illusionism. According to Roman encyclopedist Pliny, Zeuxis painted a bunch of grapes so lifelike that birds would peck at them. When he went to Parrhasius to boast of his accomplishment, he asked Parrhasius to draw back the curtain that covered Parrhasius's own painting, discovered that the curtain itself was a painting, and acknowledged his rival's superior art.

192. *picture of the old woman:* According to legend, Zeuxis died of laughing while painting a picture of a funny-looking old woman.

193. *Apelles:* (fourth century B.C.), Greek painter. His picture of Alexander the Great's horse was apparently so lifelike that a living horse neighed at it. He painted both Alexander himself and the goddess Venus many times. None of his works survive.

194. *Parrhasius, Timanthes, Polygnotus, Apollodorus, Pausias, and Pamphilus:* fourth- and fifth-century Greek painters. None of their works survive.

195. *Ætion's cedar statue of Æsculapius:* possibly a reference to a Spartan statue of Aesculapius, legendary Greek physician and god of medicine, carved of chaste tree wood.

196. *Alcon's iron statue of Hercules:* According to Roman encyclopedist Pliny, a Greek sculptor named Alcon, or Alkon, crafted a statue of Hercules out of cast iron, an unusual choice of material.

197. *Victory . . . Jupiter Olympus of Phidias:* The greatest work of Phidias (c.490–430 B.C.), a Greek sculptor, was the statue of Zeus (Jupiter) for the temple of Zeus at Olympia. One of the Seven Wonders of the World, it was a colossal figure seated on a throne with a scepter in its left hand and a statue of Nike (Victory) in its right.

198. *Colossus of Rhodes:* a statue of the sun god Helios that overlooked the harbor of the ancient Greek city of Rhodes. Approximately one hundred feet tall, it was one of the Seven Wonders of the World until it was destroyed by an earthquake.

199. *Venus Urania of Phidias:* Phidias created two statues of Venus, or Aphrodite, known only through later copies. (*See note 197 above.*)

200. *Palladium of Troy:* a wooden statue of the goddess Pallas Athena, given by Zeus to the founder of Troy. It was believed that the city could not be

taken so long as the Palladium was safe, and indeed the city fell after the statue was stolen by the Greek besiegers of the Trojan War.

201. *head of General Jackson . . . frigate Constitution:* In 1834, a new figurehead representing President Andrew Jackson (1767–1845) was installed on the USS *Constitution,* one of the first frigates commissioned by the new nation in 1794. The choice of Jackson was unpopular in Boston, where the president was widely disliked, and the figurehead was decapitated while the ship was in the Boston Naval Yard.

202. *Cowper's sofa:* Book 1 of William Cowper's poem *The Task* (1785) deals with the evolution of the sofa. The topic was given to him in jest by a friend.

203. *Rabelais' easy chair:* a reference to a line in Alexander Pope's poem *The Dunciad* (1728): "Whether thou choose Cervantes' serious air, / Or laugh and shake in Rabelais' easy-chair" (1.19–20).

204. *Peter Schlemihl's shadow: See "The Intelligence Office," note 2.*

205. *Peter Rugg:* According to a New England folktale, Peter Rugg was a prosperous resident of eighteenth-century Boston who had a foul temper. Caught out with his young daughter in an open carriage with a terrible storm brewing, he was told he wouldn't make it back to Boston alive. Angry, Rugg swore that he would get home that night or would never see his home again. He and his daughter disappeared during the trip back, but in after years travelers would encounter him, anxiously asking the way to Boston and always headed in the wrong direction.

206. *Wandering Jew: See "A Select Party," note 4.*

207. *Æneas and the Sibyl . . . Hades:* Aeneas asked advice of and was accompanied by the Cumaean Sibyl in his journey to the underworld. (*See note 90 above.*)

A Note on the Type

The principal text of this Modern Library edition
was set in a digitized version of Janson, a typeface that
dates from about 1690 and was cut by Nicholas Kis,
a Hungarian working in Amsterdam. The original matrices have
survived and are held by the Stempel foundry in Germany.
Hermann Zapf redesigned some of the weights and sizes for
Stempel, basing his revisions on the original design.

MODERN LIBRARY IS ONLINE AT
WWW.MODERNLIBRARY.COM

MODERN LIBRARY ONLINE IS YOUR GUIDE
TO CLASSIC LITERATURE ON THE WEB

THE MODERN LIBRARY E-NEWSLETTER

Our free e-mail newsletter is sent to subscribers, and features sample chapters, interviews with and essays by our authors, upcoming books, special promotions, announcements, and news.

To subscribe to the Modern Library e-newsletter, send a blank e-mail to: **join-modernlibrary@list.randomhouse.com** or visit **www.modernlibrary.com**

THE MODERN LIBRARY WEBSITE

Check out the Modern Library website at
www.modernlibrary.com for:

- The Modern Library e-newsletter
- A list of our current and upcoming titles and series
- Reading Group Guides and exclusive author spotlights
- Special features with information on the classics and other paperback series
- Excerpts from new releases and other titles
- A list of our e-books and information on where to buy them
- The Modern Library Editorial Board's 100 Best Novels and 100 Best Nonfiction Books of the Twentieth Century written in the English language
- News and announcements

Questions? E-mail us at **modernlibrary@randomhouse.com**
For questions about examination or desk copies, please visit
the Random House Academic Resources site at
www.randomhouse.com/academic